THE EVOLUTION GENE

The Complete Trilogy

AARON HODGES

Edited by Genevieve Lerner
Proofread by Sara Houston
Illustration by Christian Bentulan and Nikko Marie

ISBN: 978-09951365-88

ABOUT THE AUTHOR

Aaron Hodges was born in 1989 in the small town of Whakatane, New Zealand. He studied for five years at the University of Auckland, completing a Bachelors of Science in Biology and Geography, and a Masters of Environmental Engineering. After working as an environmental consultant for two years, he grew tired of office work and decided to quit his job in 2014 and see the world. One year later, he published his first novel - Stormwielder.

FOLLOW AARON HODGES...

And receive TWO FREE novels and a short story!

www.aaronhodges.co.nz/newsletter-signup/

THE EVOLUTION GENE
BOOK ONE

THE GENOME PROJECT

NEW YORK TIMES BESTSELLING AUTHOR

AARON HODGES

For the child inside us all.
Let them soar.

I
APPLICANTS

I

"Another pint, hun?"

Liz gritted her teeth as a man's voice carried to her from across the bar. Sucking in a breath, she forced a smile to her lips and looked around for the speaker. She found him sitting alone at a table in the corner, a drunken grin stretching across his unshaven cheeks. He caught her gaze and waved his empty mug.

Taking care to keep the smile plastered to her face, Liz walked across the diner to take his order.

"Just the beer, sir?" she asked, taking his mug. "It's last call."

He squinted at her as though struggling to understand her words. He was swaying slightly in his chair, and Liz was quite sure he'd already had enough. Unfortunately, her manager, Andrew, was never one to refuse a paying customer.

Finally, the man belched and waved the glass at her stomach. "What else is on the menu, love?"

He said the words with a leer that made Liz want to rip the mug from his hand and smash it over his head. Instead, all she did was smile sweetly. "Just the usual," she said, trying to keep the anger from her voice. "Kitchen is closed, though."

"Not interested in the kitchen." He leaned forward in his chair, and the stench of garlic and cigarettes wafted over Liz. "But I always wanted a taste of something rural."

Liz's stomach churned, and in a flash of anger she snatched the glass from the man's grease-stained fingers. Then, steeling herself, she took a breath, and forced a laugh. "Grass Valley Ale it is!"

Without waiting for a response, she spun on her heel and strode back through the maze of tables. Her neck prickled as she sensed his gaze on her, but she did not glance back. Retreating behind the bar, she added the dirty glass to the growing stack of dishes she had to tackle after closing, and took a fresh one from beneath the bar.

Liz paused as she turned and caught the man's beady eyes watching her from the corner. He had to be at least forty—more than twice her own seventeen years. Steadfastly ignoring his gaze, she poured out a pint of Grass Valley Ale.

"Keeping our guests happy I hope, Liz?" She jumped as Andrew appeared beside her.

At six-foot-five with a buzz cut and heavily built shoulders, Andrew towered over Liz's meagre five feet and two inches. He had served five years with the Western Allied States military before retiring from active duty and starting his own bar here in Sacramento. Or so he claimed on the memoire plastered on the back of every menu. It wasn't like there was any way to verify his story—even in the city, computers and the internet were only accessible to the rich. Where she'd grown up, they'd been lucky just to have electricity.

Crossing his tattooed arms, Andrew raised an eyebrow. She quickly flicked off the tap and placed the pint on a serving tray. "He's just drunk, Andrew," she muttered. "Nothing I can't handle."

"I didn't say handle him," Andrew replied coldly. "I said keep him happy."

Liz swallowed as he stared down at her, but she stood her ground. "That's what the beer's for." She nodded at the mug, taking advantage of the opportunity to break eye contact. "I'd better not keep him waiting."

Snatching up the metal tray, she raced back out amongst the tables. The other customers ignored her as she made her way between them. There were only a few occupied tables left now, and she was the last waitress on duty. It was a Tuesday night and her remaining patrons were mostly men in their thirties and forties—too young to have fought in the war that had claimed so many of their fathers.

"One Grass Valley Ale," Liz announced cheerfully as she placed the beer in front of the dark-eyed man. "Is that the lot for the night?"

Without answering, the man swept up the beer and gulped half of it down in a single swallow. He let out a long sigh as he placed it back on the table. "I like the taste." Before she could react, his arm shot out and wrapped around her waist. "Matter of fact, it's made me hungry for the real thing." He laughed as he dragged her forward.

Liz's heart dropped into the pit of her stomach as she felt his hand grasping her backside. The awful stench of his breath smothered her. Puckering up his lips, he tried to kiss her. She twisted away, the tray still clutched in one hand, and tried to shove him off. But even drunk, he was twice her size, and too strong to resist in such confined quarters.

"Get off," she snapped, the words grating up from the back of her throat.

"What? Think you're too good for me, ya little rural tramp?" His other hand came up, going for her breasts. "Come on, sweets, you know—"

Whatever he'd been about to say was cut off as Liz gripped her serving tray in both hands and brought it down on his head. A satisfying *clang* echoed through the room as it struck, and the hand vanished from around her waist.

The man reeled back in his chair, hands clutching at his face. Blood dribbled from a gash on his forehead, tangling with his greying hair. He lurched to his feet with a roar, sending the table and his freshly poured ale crashing to the ground. The sound of breaking glass was punctuated by his screams as Liz retreated a step, holding the tray in front of her like a shield. Her assailant swung his fists blindly in her direction, but alcohol had dimmed his senses and his blows met only empty air. Face beet red and cursing, he staggered in her direction.

"*Oy!*" Andrew's voice cut through the man's shouts like a knife.

Liz glanced back and saw him stepping out from behind the bar, the baseball bat he used to threaten rowdy customers grasped in hand.

"What's going on here?" he shouted as he marched towards them. The other patrons watched on, eyes wide, silent.

The drunkard took another step towards Liz before he seemed to catch himself. His eyes flickered uncertainly at Andrew, then back to her. "The little tramp *hit* me!"

Anger flickered in Liz's stomach. Throwing caution to the wind, she drew her lips back in a sneer. "Why don't you call me that one more time?" she growled, flourishing the tray.

Before her assailant had a chance to answer, Andrew caught Liz by the collar and hauled her back. She cried out as the tray slipped from her fingers and landed on her foot. Cursing, she staggered sideways, but before she could regain her balance, Andrew shoved her again, sending her crashing into an empty table.

"*Out!*" Andrew screamed, waving his bat above his head.

Liz scrambled back across the wooden floor, feeling the dried beer sticking to her clothes. Once out of range of his bat, she picked herself up and stood facing him. Heat rushed to her face. She struggled to keep from shaking as she clenched her fists.

"*What?*" she said through gritted teeth.

"I said *out!*" Andrew repeated, pointing the bat at her chest. "I've had enough of you. Your lot aren't worth the trouble."

Now Liz really was shaking. She opened her mouth to argue, and then snapped it closed again. Glancing around the room, she saw the eyes of everyone watching her. Ice spread through her chest as she looked back at her boss.

"What about my pay?" She tried to keep her voice as calm as possible.

"Consider it compensation for the damages." Sneering, he took a step towards her, until the bat prodded her in the chest.

Stomach twisting, Liz considered standing her ground. She needed that money—especially after the attention she had just attracted. She would have to move again now, pack her things and leave the room she'd already paid a month in advance for. With only the measly tips she'd made earlier in the night, she wouldn't have the cash for another room.

But she could see this was not a fight she was going to win. Letting out a long breath, she flicked a strand of curly black hair from her eyes and snorted. "Good riddance," she spat.

Spinning on her heel, she headed for the door. Her face burned as half a dozen eyes followed her. As she passed the last table, she paused, then lurched sideways, upending its contents onto the floor. The two men sitting there shouted and jumped to their feet as beer splattered them. By the time they turned their attention on her, Liz was already gone.

Outside, Liz blinked, struggling with the sudden darkness. The bar had no windows facing the road, and with the streetlight out front broken, it took a moment for her eyes to adjust. Not knowing if anyone was going to come after her, she quickly started off along the street, her hands still trembling with pent-up rage.

"Hope you enjoy cleaning up," she muttered under her breath.

Internally though, she cursed herself, even as she tried to contrive a plan that didn't involve sleeping on the streets for the rest of winter. Staying in this suburb was no longer an option—not after the commotion she'd just caused. Even though Andrew had been paying her under the table, it wouldn't take long for rumors to spread about the ferocious rural girl he'd employed. Then it would only be a matter of time before someone came asking questions.

Taking the next street on her right, Liz disappeared into the shadows between the buildings. She was on the outskirts of Sacramento, California, where the streets were still relatively quiet, free of the traffic clogging the center. Even so, she could never quite feel comfortable in a city. The countryside was her home—as everyone here was quick to remind her—but there was no work for her there. And while she could get by on what she trapped and scavenged in the summer, she couldn't stand the thought of another winter exposed to the icy elements.

So at the first whiff of cold, Liz had packed up her rucksack and headed for Sacramento. It was a long way from her hometown, but she was terrified anywhere closer might raise suspicions, make it easier for them to find her.

Until now, she had thought she'd made the right choice. From the tips she'd scraped together at the bar, she'd managed to rent what amounted to a closet in the basement of an apartment building. It was cold and damp, containing nothing more than a moldy mattress, but it was better than being woken up by falling snow. And it was off the books, too—safe.

But winter was barely a month old, and she'd already blown it. Her teeth chattered as a cold wind whirled down the street, and Liz cursed herself for leaving her hole-ridden coat back in the bar. There would be no going back for it now. Scowling, she shoved her hands into the tiny pockets of her jeans and did her best to ignore the cold.

Liz glanced around again as she passed beneath a flickering streetlight. The urbanites could say whatever they liked about their shining condos—she still felt safer wandering the streets of any rural village than she did here. While she hadn't been troubled yet, she now kept a knife in her boot at all times. It paid to be prepared.

Unseen clouds blacked out the moon and stars, and the next streetlamp was a good two hundred yards away. Liz's heart started to race as the darkness pressed in around her. She picked up the pace, berating herself for her paranoia.

Reaching the next corner, Liz let out a long breath as she realized it was her street. Preoccupied, she'd lost track of the turns, but somehow had still ended up in the right place. Pulling her hands from her pockets, she power-walked towards the cul-de-sac at the end of the lane. Her apartment building was dark, and the only illumination was a flickering streetlight hovering above the turnabout.

Halfway down her street, Liz caught the faintest whisper of

something behind her. Goosebumps shot down her neck, and she looked back slowly, expecting to see a stray dog wandering across the road…

…and screamed as a shadow rushed towards her.

Adrenaline kicked in as the man lunged, and she lurched back, hearing the *whoosh* as a fist shot past her head. A curse followed, then the weight of his body crashed into her. But she was ready now, already pivoting on her heel, allowing his bulk to slide by her. The man staggered past, and she leapt, driving her foot into the small of his back to send him toppling to the ground.

Then she was sprinting away, eyes fixed on the light at the end of the lane, and the iron door to her apartment building. If she could just make it inside…

Liz barely managed five steps before two men emerged from the shadows ahead, cutting off her escape. She staggered to a stop as they started towards her. Neither spoke, but they moved with a deliberate calm, as though they had all the time in the world to catch her.

Ice spread through Liz's veins as she turned to flee back down the lane, and found her first attacker on his feet, barring the way. For an instant she froze, her insides turning to liquid, panic taking hold. But it only lasted a second—there was no time for hesitation out on the streets.

Dropping to one knee, she inconspicuously slipped the knife from her boot, and then leapt at the first man. A low growl rumbled from her throat as her anger took light. It had already been a bad night—she wasn't about to let these thugs make it worse.

The man hadn't seen her knife. His teeth gleamed in the light of the distant lamp as he smiled and opened his arms to catch her. The next second, he was staggering backwards, eyes blinking rapidly as he reached for the blade embedded in his chest.

Sneering at his surprise, Liz tried to yank back her weapon, but he sagged to the ground before she could dislodge it. She cursed, wasting half a second considering going after it, and then leapt free—only for his thrashing arms to take her legs out from under her. She crashed into the asphalt, her bones jarring at the impact. Fabric tore around her knees as she scrambled back to her feet.

She tried to run again, but the other two were on her now. A hand caught Liz's hair and pulled her backwards. Screaming, she twisted and swung at her assailant. Her fist went wide as the man leaned back, but her second blow caught him square in the throat. He staggered, but his grip didn't falter, and Liz shrieked as she was dragged down with him.

Tears sprang to her eyes as she yanked back her head and felt a clump of hair tear free. Something wet and sticky trickled down her skull, but she ignored it and tried to regain her feet.

A cry tore from her lips as the last assailant tacked her from behind. The breath rushed from her chest as his weight drove her face first into the ground. Choking, she thrashed beneath him, trying to break free, to gulp in a mouthful of air, but his weight pinned her down. Stars streaked her vision as she gasped, and finally managed to suck in a breath.

"Doctor," came the man's voice from right above her head, followed by the crackle of a radio. "We have her."

"On my way, Commander," a woman's tinny voice replied.

Liz's blood chilled at the voice. This was no drunken attack, no crime of opportunity. They had been waiting for *her*. Sucking in another half breath, she managed to croak out a pathetic cry for help. Iron fingers dug into the base of her neck and ground her face into the asphalt.

"Quiet," her captor growled.

Liz stilled, even as her mind went into overdrive, seeking a way out. Her ears twitched as a distant *tap-tapping* echoed along the street. Her heart soared as she recognized the sound of footsteps. She cried out again, louder now, and received a blow to her head for the effort. Stars swirled in her vision again as the strength fled her limbs.

"Enough of that," a woman's voice came from overhead.

For a second, Liz thought someone had heard her calls.

"Yes, Doctor," her captor replied.

Liz's hope crumbled to dust as she realized the footsteps belonged to the woman from the radio.

"You're sure she's the one?" the woman asked.

"Matches the photograph," came the reply.

"Excellent."

The sound of leather scuffing against concrete followed. Cracking open her eyes, Liz saw a sleek black pair of women's shoes beside her face. Presumably they belonged to the doctor, but Liz could see nothing more of the woman.

"Please," Liz managed to croak, "you've got to help me. You've got the wrong girl."

Neither of her captives deigned to reply. In her heart, Liz knew her words were a lie, that her past had finally caught up with her. She'd thought she'd covered her tracks so well, moving around, shifting from town to town, using a fake name, keeping off the records. On her brightest days, she'd thought they might have finally stopped looking, that they'd given up.

How naive she'd been.

She flinched as something cold pressed against her neck. Gas hissed and she felt a sharp pinch, then the pressure was gone. But now a strange warmth was spreading slowly down her spine, numbing as it went, and she realized they'd injected her with something.

Liz knew it was hopeless, that it was already too late and the drug would soon render her unconscious, but she thrashed all the same. The man holding her swore and his grip on her neck tightened, hurting her. She cursed him, calling them every filthy word she could remember, but it was no use. He had her pinned on her stomach and there was nothing she could do to free herself.

Then suddenly, the iron fingers were gone, the weight on her back vanished. Hope swelled in Liz's chest, and she struggled to sit up, to scramble to her feet and race down the lane—back to the bar, to the cold, to the countryside, anywhere but these men and the doctor.

Instead, she found her limbs twitching uselessly, her body unresponsive, her mind falling away into a swirling darkness.

Too late, she opened her mouth to scream.

2

Chris let out a long sigh as he settled into the worn-out sofa, then cursed as a broken spring stabbed him in the backside. Wriggling sideways to avoid it, he reached for the remote, only to realize it had been left beside the television. Muttering under his breath, he climbed back to his feet, retrieved the remote, flicked on the television, and finally collapsed back into the sofa. This time he was careful to avoid the broken spring.

He closed his eyes as the blue glow of the television lit the living room. The shriek of commercials followed, but he barely had the energy to be annoyed. He was still at school, but he'd had to take on an afternoon job at the construction site down the road to help his mother make ends meet. Even with the extra income, they were struggling. His only hope was passing the entrance exams for the California State University and winning a scholarship. Otherwise, he would have to beg his supervisor for an apprenticeship.

"Another attack was reported today from the rural town of Julian." A reporter's voice broke through the stream of adverts, announcing the start of the six o'clock news.

Chris's ears perked up and he looked quickly at the television. Images flashed across the screen of an old mining town, its dusty dirt roads and rundown buildings looking unchanged since the

1900's. A row of horse-drawn carriages lined the street, their owners standing alongside them.

It was a common sight in the rural counties of the Western Allied States. The divide between rural and urban communities had grown in the thirty years since California, Oregon and Washington had declared their independence from the United States. Today, there were few citizens in the countryside able to afford luxuries such as cars and televisions.

"We're just receiving word that the police have arrived on the scene," the reporter continued.

On the television, a black van with the letters SWAT painted on the side had just pulled up. The rear doors swung open, and a squad of black-garbed riot police leapt out. They gathered around the van and then strode on past the carriages. Dust swirled around them, but they moved without hesitation, the camera following them at a distance.

The image changed as the police moved around a corner into an empty street. The new camera angle looked down at the police from the rooftop of a nearby building. It followed the SWAT unit as they split into two groups and spread out along the street, rifles at the ready.

Then the camera panned down the street and refocused on the broken window of a grocery store. The camera zoomed, revealing the nightmare inside the store.

Chris swallowed as images straight from a horror film flashed across the television. The remnants of the store lay scattered across the linoleum floor, the contents of broken cans and wine bottles staining the ground red. Pieces of humanity were scattered amongst the wreckage, torn arms and shattered legs lying apart from their motionless owners. Chris's stomach twisted as he looked into the eyes of the dead and saw the terror of their final moments reflected back at him.

Finally the camera tilted and panned to the sole survivor of the carnage. The man stood amidst the wreckage of the store, blood streaking his face and arms, staining his shirt red. His head was bowed, and the only sign of life was the rhythmic rise and fall of his shoulders. The camera zoomed in on his face, revealing cold grey eyes. They stared at the ground, blank and lifeless.

Struggling to contain the meagre contents of his stomach, Chris looked away.

"The *Chead* is thought to have awakened at around sixteen hundred hours," the reporter was saying now, drawing Chris back to the screen. "Special forces have cleared the immediate area and are now preparing to engage with the creature."

"Two hours." Chris jumped up as a woman's voice came from behind him.

He spun on his heel, then relaxed as his mother walked in from the kitchen. "I thought you had a night class!" he gasped.

His mother shook her head, a slight smile touching her face. "We finished early." She shrugged, then waved at the television. "They've been standing around for two hours. Watching that thing. Some of those people were still alive when it all started. They might have been saved. Would have, if they'd been somebody important."

Chris pulled himself off the couch and embraced his mother. He kissed her cheek and she returned the gesture, before they both turned to watch the SWAT team approach the grocery store. The men in black moved with military precision, jogging down the dirt road, sticking close to the buildings. If the *Chead* came out of its trance, no one wanted to be caught in the open. While the creatures looked human, they possessed a terrifying speed, and had the strength to tear full-grown men limb from limb.

As the scene inside the grocery store demonstrated.

Absently, Chris clutched his mother's arm tighter. The *Chead* were a curse throughout the Western Allied States, or WAS as many called them, a dark shadow left over from the days of the American War. The first whispers of the creatures had started in 2030, not long after the fall of the United States. They had been dismissed then as a rumor, the new country eager to move on from the decade-long conflict. Attacks had been blamed on resistance fighters in rural communities, who had never fully supported the severance from the United States.

In response, the government had imposed curfews in the affected counties, and sent in the military to quell the unrest. But their measures had done nothing to stem the attacks, and eventually, accounts by survivors had filtered through to the media. Claims surfaced that it was not soldiers behind the butchery, but members of the community. The perpetrators were always different, but the story was the same. One day the assailants were ordinary neighbors or colleagues – the next, monsters capable of tearing their loved ones to pieces.

By the time the first creature was captured, rural communities had suffered almost a decade of terror at the hands of the monstrosities. The government and their media agencies had pointed the blame in every direction, from poor rural police-reporting, to secret operations by the Texans to destabilize the Western Allied States.

On the television, the SWAT team had reached the grocery store and were now gathering outside, their rifles trained on the entrance. One lowered his rifle and stepped towards it, the others covering him from behind. Reaching the door, he stretched out an arm to pull it open.

The *Chead* didn't make a sound as it tore through the store windows and barreled into the man. A screech came through the old television speakers as the men scattered before the creature's ferocity. With one hand, the creature grabbed its victim by the throat and hurled him across the street. The *thud* as he bounced off a concrete wall was audible over the reporter's microphone.

The sight of their companion's untimely demise seemed to snap the other members of the squadron into action. The first pops of gunfire followed, but the *Chead* was already on the move. It tore across the dirt road, bullets raising dust-clouds around it, and smashed into another squad member. A scream echoed up from the street as man and *Chead* went down, disappearing into a cloud of dust.

Despite the risk of hitting their comrade, the other members of the SWAT team did not stop firing. The chance of survival once a *Chead* had its hands on you was zero to none, and no one wanted to risk the creature escaping.

Roaring, the *Chead* reared up from the dust, then spun as a bullet struck it in the shoulder. Blood blossomed from the wound as it staggered back, its grey eyes wide, flickering with surprise. It reached up and touched a finger to the hole left by the bullet, its brow creasing with confusion.

Then the rest of the men opened fire, and the creature fell.

3

Doctor Angela Fallow squinted through the rain-streaked windshield, struggling to catch a glimpse of her subject in the lengthening gloom. A few minutes ago the streetlights had flickered into life, but despite their yellowed glow, shadows still clung to the house across the street. Tall hedges marked the boundary with the neighboring properties, while a white picket fence stood between her car and the old cottage.

Leaning closer to the window, Angela held her breath to keep the glass from fogging, and willed her eyes to pierce the twilight. But beyond the brightly-lit sidewalk, she could see nothing but darkness. Letting out a long sigh, she sat back in her seat. There was no sign of anyone outside the house, no silent shadows slipping closer to the warm light beckoning from the windows.

At least, no sign that could be seen.

Berating her nerves, Angela turned her attention to the touchscreen on her dashboard. She had no wish to see a repeat of the casualties her team had suffered in Sacramento. She cursed as the soft glow of the screen lit the car, before she remembered the tinted windows made it impossible for anyone to see inside.

Angela pursed her lips, studying the charts on the screen one last time. It showed a woman in her early forties. Auburn hair hung around her shoulders and she wore the faintest hint of a smile on her red lips. The smile spread to her cheeks, crinkling the skin around her olive-green eyes.

Margaret Sanders.

Beneath the picture was a description of the woman: height, weight, license number, last known address, school and work history, her current occupation as a college professor, and marital status. The last was listed as widowed with a single child. Her husband had succumbed to cancer almost a decade previously.

Shaking her head, Angela looked again at the woman's eyes, wondering what could have driven her to this end. She had a house, a son, solid employment as a teacher. Why would she throw it all away when she had so much to lose?

Idly, she wondered whether Mrs. Sanders would have done things differently if given another chance. The smile lines around her eyes were those of a kind soul, and her alleged support of the resistance seemed out of character. It was a shame the government did not give second chances—especially not for traitors of the state.

Now both mother and son would suffer for her actions.

Tapping the screen, Angela pulled up the son's file. Christopher Sanders, at eighteen, was the reason she had come tonight. The assault team would handle the mother and any of her associates who might be on the property, but Angela had other plans for the son. Like the rest of her subjects, he would need to be taken alive—and unharmed.

His profile described him as five-foot-eleven, with a weight of 150 pounds—not large by any measure. Her only concern was the black belt listed in his credentials, though such accomplishments were rarely relevant when it came to a real fight. Particularly when the target was unarmed, unsuspecting, and outnumbered.

Then again, the girl had given them more trouble than anyone had expected.

Forcing her mind back to the present, Angela tapped the screen again, and a picture of her target popped up. A flicker of discomfort spread through her stomach. His brunette hair showed traces of his mother's auburn locks, while the hazel eyes must have descended from a dominant *bey2* allele in his father's chromosome. A hint of light-brown facial hair traced the edges of his jaw, covering the last of his teenage acne. Despite his small size, he had the broad, muscular shoulders of an athlete, and there was little sign of fat on his youthful face.

After a long moment, Angela flicked off the console. She hoped this would be her final assignment. For months now, she had overseen the collection of subjects for the new trials, and the task had not gotten any easier with time. The children she'd taken haunted her at night, their accusing stares waiting whenever she closed her eyes. Her only consolation was that without her, these children would have suffered the same fate as their parents. At least the research facility gave them a fighting chance.

And looking into the boy's eyes, she knew he was a fighter.

Angela closed her eyes, and shoving aside her doubt, she pressed another button on the car's console.

"Are you in position?" she spoke into the empty car.

"Ready when you are, Fallow," a man replied.

Nodding to herself, Fallow reached beneath her seat and retrieved a steel briefcase. Unclipping its restraints, she lifted out a jet injector and held it up to the light. The stainless-steel instrument appeared more like a gun than a piece of medical equipment, but it served its purpose well. Once her team had Chris restrained, it would be a simple matter to use the jet injector to anesthetize the young man for transport.

Removing a vial of etorphine from the case, she screwed it into place and pressed a button on the side. A short *hiss* confirmed it was pressurized. She eyed the clear liquid, hoping the details in the boy's file were correct. She had prepared the dosage of etorphine for Chris's age and weight, but a miscalculation could prove fatal.

"Fallow, still waiting on your signal?" the voice came again.

Fallow bit her lip and closed her eyes. She shivered in the cold of the car.

If not you, then someone else.

She opened her eyes. "Go."

❧ 4 ☙

The screen of the old CRT television flickered to black as Chris's mother switched it off. Her face was pale when she turned towards him, and a shiver ran through her.

"Your grandfather would be ashamed, Chris," she said, shaking her head. "He went to war against the United States because he believed in this country, because thought we could be the light to the madness that had overcome the old union. He fought to keep us free, not to spend decades haunted by the ghosts of our past."

Chris shuddered. He'd never met his grandfather, but his mother and grandmother talked of him enough that Chris felt he knew him. When the United States had refused to accept the independence of the Western Allied States, his grandfather had answered the call to defend their young nation. Enlisting with the WAS Marines, he'd marched off to a conflict that had quickly expanded to engulf the whole of North America. Only the aid of Canada and Mexico had given the WAS the strength to survive, and eventually prevail against the aggression of the United States. Unfortunately, Chris's grandfather had not.

"Things will change soon," Chris said. "Surely?"

His mother crinkled her nose. "I've been saying that for ten years," she said as she moved towards the kitchen, ruffling Chris's hair as she passed him, "but things only ever seem to get worse."

Chris followed her and pulled out a chair at the wooden table. The kitchen was small, barely big enough for the two of them, but it was all they needed. His mother was already standing at the stove, stirring a pot of stew he recognized as leftovers from the beef shanks of the night before.

"Most don't seem to care, as long as the attacks are confined to the countryside," Chris commented.

"Exactly." His mother turned, emphatically waving the wooden spoon. "They think it doesn't matter, that their shining cities will protect them. Well, it won't stay that way forever."

"No." Chris shook his head. "That one in Seattle…" He shuddered. Over fifty people had been killed when a *Chead* woke in a shopping mall. Police had arrived in less than ten minutes, but that was all the time it had needed.

Impulsively, he reached for the pocket watch he wore around his neck. His mother had given it to him ten years ago, at his father's funeral. It held a picture of Chris's parents, smiling on the shores of Lake Washington in Seattle, where they'd first met. His heart gave a painful throb as he thought of the terror engulfing the city.

Noticing the gesture, his mother abandoned the pot and pulled him into a hug. "It's okay, Chris. We'll survive this. We're a strong people. They'll come up with a solution, even if we have to march up to the gates of congress and demand it."

Chris nodded, and was about to speak when a crash came from somewhere in the house. They pushed apart and spun towards the kitchen doorway. Though they lived in the city, they barely had the money to survive week to week, and their house was not in the safest neighborhood.

It was well past the eight o'clock curfew now. Whoever—or whatever—had made the noise was not likely to be friendly.

Sucking in a breath, Chris moved into the doorway and risked a glance across the lounge. The single incandescent bulb cast shadows across the room, leaving dark patches behind the couch and television. He stared hard into the darkness, searching for signs of movement, and then retreated to the kitchen.

Silently, his mother handed him a kitchen knife. He took it after only a second's hesitation. She held a second blade in a practiced grip. Looking at his mother's face, Chris swallowed. Her eyes were hard, her brow creased in a scowl, but he did not miss the fear there. Together they faced the door—and waited.

The squeak of the loose floorboard in the hallway seemed as loud as a gunshot in the silent house. Chris glanced at his mother, and she nodded back. There was no doubt now. Someone was inside.

A crash came from the lounge, then the thud of heavy boots as the intruder gave up all pretense of stealth. Chris tensed, his knuckles turning white as he gripped the knife handle. He spread his feet into a forward stance, readying himself.

The sound of breaking glass came from their right as the kitchen window exploded inwards, and a black-suited figure leapt into the room. The man bowled into his mother, sending her tumbling to the ground before she could swing the knife. Chris sprang to the side as another man charged from the lounge, then drew back and hurled his knife.

Without pausing to see whether the blade struck home, Chris twisted and leapt, driving his heel into the midriff of the intruder standing over his mother. But the man was ready for him, and with his greater bulk, he brushed off the blow. Stumbling sideways, Chris clenched his fists and charged again.

The man grinned, raising his hands to catch Chris. With his attention diverted, Chris's mother rose behind him, knife still in hand, and drove the blade deep into their attacker's hamstring.

Their black-garbed attacker barely had time to scream before Chris's fist slammed into his windpipe. The intruder's face paled and his hands went to his throat. He staggered backwards, strangled noises gurgling from his mouth, and toppled over the kitchen table.

Chris offered his mother a hand. Before she could take it, a creak came from the floorboards behind him. The man from the lounge loomed up, grabbing Chris by the shoulder. Still on the ground, his mother rolled away as Chris twisted around, fighting to break the man's hold. Cursing, he aimed an elbow at the man's gut, but his arm struck solid body armor and bounced off.

The body armor explained what had happened to the knife Chris had thrown, but before he could process what the information meant, another crash came from the window.

His mother surged to her feet as a third man leapt inside. Still holding the bloodied knife, she screamed and charged. Straining his arms, Chris bucked against his captor's grip, but there was no breaking the man's iron hold. Stomach clenched, he watched his mother attack the heavily-armed assailant.

The new intruder carried a steel baton in one hand, and as she swung her knife it flashed out and caught her wrist. His mother screamed, and the blade tumbled from her hand. She retreated across the room, cradling her arm. A fourth man appeared in the doorway to the lounge. Before Chris could shout a warning, he grabbed her from behind.

His mother shrieked and threw back her head, trying to catch the man in the chin, but her blows bounced off his body armor. Her eyes widened as his arm went around her neck, cutting off her breath. Heart hammering in his chest, Chris twisted and kicked at his opponent's shins, desperate to aid his mother, but the man showed no sign of relenting.

"*Mom!*" he screamed as her eyes drooped closed.

"Doctor Fallow, situation under control. You're up," the man from the window spoke into his cuff. He approached his wounded comrade, whose face was turning purple. "Hold on, man. Medical's on its way."

"Who are you?" Chris gasped.

The man ignored him. Instead, he went to work on the fallen man, removing his belt and binding it around the man's leg. The injured man groaned as the speaker worked, his eyes squeezed closed and his teeth clenched. A pang of guilt touched Chris, but he crushed it down.

"What the hell happened?" a woman exclaimed as she entered the kitchen.

The woman was dark-skinned, but the color was rapidly

fleeing her face as she looked around the kitchen. She raised a hand to her mouth, her eyes lingering on the blood, then flicking between the men and their captives. Shock showed in their amber depths, but already it was fading as she reasserted control. Lowering her hand to her side, she pursed her red lips. Her gaze settled on Chris.

A chill went through him as he noticed the red-emblazoned bear on the front of her black jacket. The symbol marked her as a government employee. These were not random thugs in the night. They were the police, and they were here for Chris and his mother.

Nodding to herself, the woman reached into her jacket and drew something into the light. The breath caught in Chris's throat as he glimpsed the contraption in her hand. For a second he thought it was a pistol, but as she drew closer he realized his mistake. It was some sort of hypodermic gun, some device he'd only thought existed in old movies. In real life though, it was far more terrifying than anything Hollywood had ever produced.

"Who are you?" Chris croaked as she paused in front of him.

Her eyes drifted to Chris's face, but she only shook her head. She studied the liquid in the vial attached to the gun's barrel, then looked back at Chris, as though weighing him up.

"Hold him," she said at last.

"What?" Chris gasped as his captor pulled his arms behind his back. "What are you doing? Please, you're making a mistake, we haven't done anything wrong!"

The woman didn't answer. Chris struggled to escape as she raised the gun to his neck, but the man only pulled his arms harder, sending a bolt of pain through his shoulders. Biting back a scream, Chris looked up at the woman. Their eyes met, and he thought he saw a flicker of regret in her eyes.

Then the cold of the hypodermic gun touched his neck, followed by a hiss of gas as she pressed the trigger. Metal pinched Chris's neck, and then the woman stepped back. Holding his breath, Chris stared at the woman, his eyes never leaving hers.

Within seconds, the first touch of weariness started to seep through Chris's body. He blinked as shadows spread around the edges of his vision. Idly, he struggled to free his arms, so he might chase the shadows away. But the man still held him fast. Sucking in a mouthful of air, Chris fought against the exhaustion. Blinking hard, he willed himself to resist the pull of sleep.

But there was no stopping the warmth spreading through his limbs. His head bobbed and his arms went limp, until the only thing keeping him upright was the strength of his captor.

The woman's face was the last thing Chris saw before he slipped into the darkness.

5

Liz shivered as the air conditioner hummed, sending a blast of icy air in her direction. Wrapping her arms around herself, she closed her eyes and waited for it to pass. The scent of chlorine drifted on the air, its chemical reek setting her head to pounding. Her teeth chattered and she shuddered as the whir of fans died away. Groaning, Liz opened her eyes and returned to studying her surroundings.

She had woken ten minutes ago in this thirty-foot-wide concrete room. A single door stood closed on the opposite wall, a small glass panel revealing a bright hallway beyond. It appeared to be the only exit, but it might as well have been half a world away. Between Liz and the door stood the wire mesh of her five-foot by five-foot steel cage.

Trembling, Liz gripped the wire tight between her fingers and leaned her head against it. She tried to search the vaults of her memory, to recall how she had come to be there, but her last recollection was of serving beer to a drunken customer in Andrew's pub.

A curse slipped from her lips as the blast of the air conditioner returned. Without her jacket, her clothes were no match for whatever freezing temperature the climate control had been set to. To make matters worse, her boots were gone, and the concrete was like ice beneath her feet.

At least I'm not alone, she thought wryly, looking through the wire into the cage beside her.

A young man somewhere around her own eighteen years lay there, still dozing on the concrete floor. His clothes were better kept than her own, though there was a bloodstain on one sleeve. From the quality of his shirt, she guessed he was from the city. Pale skin, untouched by the scorching heat of the countryside, only served to confirm her suspicions.

Groaning, the young man began to stir. Idly, Liz wondered what he'd make of the nightmare into which he was about to awaken.

She shivered, not from the cold now, but dread. Casting her eyes around the room, she sought one last time for something, *anything*, that might offer escape. Long ago, her parents had warned her of the fate destined for those who drew the government's ire. Though never reported, disappearances had been common in her community. Adults, children, even entire families were known to simply disappear overnight. Few were brave enough to voice their suspicions out loud, but everyone knew who'd taken them.

It seemed after two years on the run, those same people had finally caught up with Liz.

The clang of the door as it opened tore Liz from her thoughts. She watched as two men pushed their way past the heavy steel door and stepped into the room. They wore matching uniforms of black pants and green shirts, and the gold- and red-embossed badges of bears on their chests confirmed Liz's suspicions—she'd been taken by government soldiers. The men were armed with rifles and moved with the casual ease of professional killers.

Liz straightened as their eyes alighted on her, refusing to show her fear. She suppressed a shudder as broad grins split their faces. Fixing a scowl to her lips, she crossed her arms and stared them down.

"Feisty one, ain't she?" the first said in a strong Californian accent. Shaking his head, he walked past the twin cages to a panel in the wall.

"Looks like the boy's still asleep," the second commented. "Gonna be a nasty wake-up."

Together, the men opened the panel and retrieved a hose. Thick nylon strings encased the outer layer of the hose, and a large steel nozzle was fitted to its end. Dragging it across the room, they pointed it at the sleeping boy and flipped a lever on the nozzle.

Water gushed from the hose and through the wire of the cage, engulfing the unconscious young man. A bloodcurdling scream echoed off the walls, and he seemed to levitate off the floor. Another cry followed as he thrashed against the torrent.

Liz bit back laughter as his scream turned into a gurgle. The men with the hose showed no such restraint, and their laughter echoed loudly in the confined space. Ignoring the young man's strangled cries, they held the water steady until it seemed he could not help but drown in the rushing water.

When they finally shut off the nozzle, the boy collapsed to the floor of his cage, gasping for breath. He shuddered, spitting up water, but the men were already moving towards Liz, and she had no more time to consider his predicament.

She raised her hands as the men stopped in front of her cage. "No need for that, boys. I'm already clean, see?" She did a little turn, her cheeks warming as she sensed their eyes on her again.

The men chuckled, but shook their heads. "Sorry girl, boss's orders."

They pulled the lever before Liz could muster up any other arguments.

Liz shrieked as the ice-cold water drove her back against the rear of the cage. She lifted her hands in front of her face, fighting to breathe, but it made little difference against the rush. Gasping, she choked as water flooded down her throat, and fell to her knees. An icy hand seemed to grip her chest as she inhaled again, turning away to protect her face. The power of the water forced her up against the wire, and she gripped it hard, struggling to hold herself upright.

When the torrent finally ceased, Liz found herself crouched on the ground with her back to the men. She did not turn as a coughing fit shook her body. An awful cold seeped into her bones as she struggled for breath. Water filled her ears and nose, muffling the words of the men, until she shook her head to clear it.

Tightening her hold on the wire, Liz used it to pull herself to her feet. Head down, she gave a final cough and faced the room.

The men were already returning the hose to its panel in the wall. They spoke quietly amongst themselves, but fell silent as the hinges squeaked again. A group of men and women entered the room. There were five in total, three men and two women. Each wore a white lab coat with black pants, and golden bears pinned to their collars. Four carried electronic tablets, their attention on the little screens, while the fifth approached the guards. They straightened as he stopped up in front of them, their grins turning to staunch grimaces.

"Are our latest subjects ready for processing?" the man asked, his voice cool.

One of the guards nodded. "Yes, Doctor Halt. We just finished hosing them down."

Halt smiled. "Very good." He dismissed the men with a flick of his hand and turned to face the cages.

Pursing thin lips, Halt paced around Liz's cage in a slow circle. His grey eyes never left her as he completed the circuit, and eventually she was forced to look away. He watched her like a predator studying its prey, eyeing up which piece of flesh to taste first. Wrapping her arms around herself, Liz fixed her eyes to the concrete and tried to ignore him.

When she looked up again, Halt had moved on to the young man in the other cage. But her fellow captive was ignoring the doctor, and was instead staring at the group of people in lab coats. His brow creased, as though struggling to recall a distant memory.

"*You!*" the boy shouted suddenly, slamming his hands against the wire. "You were at my house! What am I doing here? *What have you done with my mother?*"

Halt frowned, glancing back at the group of doctors. "Doctor Fallow, would you care to explain why the subject knows your face?"

The woman at the head of the group turned beet-red. "There were complications during his extraction, Halt." She spoke softly, but there was a challenge beneath her words. Goose-bumps spread down Liz's spine as she recognized the voice, though she could not recall from where. "I had to enter before the subject was fully secured, or we risked further casualties amongst the extraction team."

Halt eyed her for a moment, apparently weighing up her words, before nodding. "Very well." He turned back to the cages. "No matter. Elizabeth Flores, Christopher Sanders, welcome to your new home."

Icy fear gripped Liz by the throat, silencing her voice. They knew her last name. That meant they knew who she was, where she came from. The last trickle of hope evaporated from her heart.

Christopher was not so easily quelled. "What am I doing here? You can't hold us like his, I know my rights—"

Halt raised a hand, and Liz's neighbor fell silent. Standing outside Christopher's cage, Halt stared through the wire. "Your mother has been charged with treason."

Color fled the boy's face, turning his skin a sickly yellow. He swallowed and opened his mouth, but no words came out. Tears crystallized at the corner of his eyes, but he blinked them back before they could fall.

Biting her tongue, Liz watched the two face off against one another. She was impressed by Christopher's resilience. He might speak with the accent of someone from the city, but he seemed to possess more courage than any of the boys she'd once known at her boarding school. If his mother had been accused of treason, it meant death for her and her family. The elderly would be afforded an exception, but her children…

Liz turned her attention to the group still lingering behind Halt. If that was the reason Christopher was here, she didn't like her chances. She had feared the authorities would come for her, and had done her best to avoid detection. But with government agents hiding behind every shadow, she had always known it was only a matter of when, not if, they found her. It seemed her time was finally up.

And yet, she needed to know: how much did these people truly know about her?

6

"What about me?" Liz croaked. "My parents are dead. I've done nothing wrong."

Halt's scowl deepened. "Elizabeth Flores." He paused, looking her up and down with a sneer. "Vagrant, beggar, fugitive. You have escaped justice for long enough. After what your parents did, did you really think we would not come for you? That we would not hunt you to the ends of the earth?"

White-hot fire lit in Liz's chest, but she forced herself to take a deep breath and swallow the scream building in her throat. She wanted to deny the accusations, to curse him and the others, but she knew there was no point. She had tried that once before, when they had first come for her. But one look at her ragged clothes, at the curly black hair and olive skin, and they had dismissed her words as lies.

Her shoulders slumped as Halt looked away. Wrapping her arms around herself, she staggered to the back of the cage and sank to the floor. She wasn't giving up, not yet, but she knew when silence was the better course of action.

Unlike her fellow prisoner.

"What is this place?" Christopher's voice was soft, as though if he whispered, Halt's answer might offer some sort of mercy.

Liz glanced at him, watching as he lost the battle with his

tears. Despite herself, sympathy swelled in her chest. She knew what it was like, to lose one's parents. She would not wish it on anyone.

"This is your redemption." Halt spread his arms, including them both in the gesture. "This is your chance to redress the crimes of your parents, to contribute to the betterment of our nation. The government has seen fit to offer you both a reprieve."

"How generous of them," Liz muttered from the floor.

She shivered as Halt's eyes found hers. They flashed with anger, offering a silent warning against further interruptions. Pursing her lips, she gripped the wire tighter. It cut into her fingers as she willed herself to remain silent.

"My mother was not a traitor," came Christopher's response. "How dare you—"

Halt waved a hand and the guards who still waited at the back of the room came to life. They marched past the silent group of doctors and approached Chris's cage. One produced a key, and a second later they had the door open. They moved inside, and a brief scuffle followed as they tried to get their hands on the boy. One staggered back from a blow to the face before the other managed to use his bulk to pin Christopher to the wire.

When both guards had a firm grip on him, they hauled Christopher out and forced him to his knees in front of Halt. The doctor loomed over the boy, arms folded. He contemplated Chris with empty eyes, like a spider studying a fly trapped in its web. Liz watched on in silence, hardly daring to breathe as Halt nodded to the guards.

The one on the left drew back his boot and slammed it into Christopher's stomach. He collapsed without a sound, mouth wide, gasping like a fish out of water. A low wheeze came from his throat as he rolled onto his back and strained for breath. It came with a sudden groan, before another boot crashed into his side, almost lifting him off the ground.

A scream tore from the young man's throat as he tried to roll into a ball. But the other guard only grabbed him by the scruff of his neck and hauled him back to his knees. The two of them looked at Halt then, waiting for further instruction.

Halt approached, one finger tapping idly against his elbow. Softly, he continued as though nothing had happened. "As I was saying, you have been given a reprieve. But the crimes of your parents still stand, as does the sentence on your lives. You no longer exist in the eyes of the state. You are no one, nothing but what we permit you to be. If you're lucky, we might find you worthy of our work here." Liz shivered. She had no idea what work Halt was talking about, but she had a feeling she wouldn't like it. "More likely though," Halt continued, "you will die. But know at least that your deaths will have advanced the interests of our fine nation."

Chris was still kneeling on the ground between the guards, his breath coming in ragged gasps. Halt eyed him, as though weighing whether his words had sunk in.

"In the meantime, you will respect and obey your betters," Halt murmured. "Soon, you will be shown to your new accommodation, but first, I want to be sure you understand the gravity of your situation. Christopher Sanders, why are you here?"

On the ground, Chris looked up at the doctor. His eyes shone, but no tears fell. Turning his head, he spat on the concrete. "She's a terrible cook." He coughed, then continued, "but that hardly makes her a traitor—"

The guard's fist caught him in the side of the head and sent him crashing to the floor. A kick followed, and for the next thirty seconds the thud of hard leather boots on flesh echoed through the room. When the guards finally retreated, the young man lay still, his soft moans the only sign of life.

"Get him up," Halt commanded.

Together, the guards hauled the boy back to his knees. This time Halt leaned down, until the two of them were face-to-face. "Well?"

Christopher's shoulders sagged. A sob came from him, and for a second Liz thought he would not speak. Then he nodded, a whisper following. "Okay," he croaked, "okay...my mother...is a traitor." He looked up as he finished, a spark of flame still burning in his eyes. "*Are you happy?*"

The doctor studied him for a long while, as though weighing up the admission alongside his show of defiance. Finally he nodded, and the guards grabbed Christopher by the shoulders and muscled him back into the cage.

The clang as the door closed sent a sliver of ice down Liz's spine. She stared at the floor, sensing the eyes of the room on her, and waited for Halt's words.

"Elizabeth Flores." His voice snaked its way around her, raising the hackles on her neck. "You have been on the run for a long time. Surely you, at least, must admit to your parents' crimes?"

Looking up, Liz found the cold grey eyes of the doctor watching her. She suppressed a shudder and quickly looked away. Taking slow, measured breaths, she beat down the rage burning in her chest. She took one step, then another, until she reached the front of her cage. Leaning against the wire, she looked at the doctor and raised an eyebrow.

"What would you like me to admit to?" she whispered.

Halt took a step back from the cage, but she did not miss the way his eyes lingered on her. She gave a little smirk as he growled. "Disgusting girl," he spat. "Admit that your parents were monsters—that you aided them, that for years you have run from the law, hiding from justice."

A tremor shook Liz and she bit her lip to keep from screaming at him. Closing her eyes, she sent out a silent prayer for the souls of her parents. Their faces drifted through her mind—smiling, happy, at peace. They had been kind and sweet, only ever wanting her to be happy, to have a better life than the one they'd lived. For years they had scraped and saved to send her to boarding school in the city. The day Liz had been accepted, she'd never seen them so happy. And for three years, she had suffered the taunts of her peers in that school to keep them that way.

But they were long gone; they didn't care what she said about them. There was no need for Liz to suffer, to bleed for their memory. Not now, when there was no hope of escape. But silently she made a vow: to bide her time and conserve her strength, until an opportunity showed itself.

When she opened her eyes again, she found the cold grey eyes of Halt looking back, and smirked.

"Fine, I admit it. My parents were monsters. What of it?"

She almost laughed as the doctor's face darkened, an angry red flushing his cheeks. He clenched his fists and made to approach the cage before stopping himself. Flashing a glance over his shoulder at their audience, he shook his head and smiled.

"Very good," he said, eyeing the two of them. "So, we understand one another."

7

Chris gripped the wire of his cage as Doctor Halt eyed his two prisoners. Clamping his mouth shut, he ignored the voice in his head that was screaming for answers. His whole body ached where the guards had struck him, and he was not eager to repeat the experience. The ugly thugs were grinning at him now, as though daring him to give them another chance. Instead, he bit his tongue and waited to see what came next.

His mind was still reeling, struggling to put together the pieces of his scattered memories. Images from the night flashed through his mind—the *Chead* on the television, the men in his house, his mother falling.

His throat contracted as Halt's words twisted in his mind.

Traitor.

A tremor shook him and he suppressed a sob. The sentence for treason was death. Often just an accusation was enough to doom someone. Now his mother had been taken, stolen away by the woman in the white coat.

Holding his breath, Chris struggled with his fear, his terror that she might already be gone. That he might now be alone, an orphan in a harsh, unforgiving world.

He took a great, shuddering breath. That was the least of his problems now. Whatever his mother's fate, Chris could do nothing for her, not so long as he remained trapped in this cage.

Halt's voice drew Chris's attention back to him. "Now that we have an understanding, it is time to prepare you for your time here." A thin smile spread across his lips. "Take off your clothes."

An icy hand gripped Chris's chest as Halt folded his arms. Behind the doctor, the guards edged closer, broad grins splitting their faces. A sharp intake of breath came from the other cage, but otherwise the young woman did not move.

Chris shrank away from the wire. "Why?"

Halt took a step forward. "Now, Christopher, I thought we'd moved past this. The dog does not question his master."

Clenching his fists, Chris shook his head. His eyes travelled past Halt, to the audience of doctors, lingering on the face of the woman, the doctor called Fallow. "This isn't right," he breathed.

Halt let out a long sigh and waved the guards forward. They moved towards Chris's cage with a cold proficiency. Chris hesitated, but they were already reaching the door and fumbling with the latch. Quickly, he began to unbutton his shirt, his cheeks flushing with embarrassment.

Outside, the guards paused, looking back at Halt in question. The doctor nodded curtly, and they retreated a step.

In the cage, Chris stripped off his clothing piece by piece, shivering as the icy breath of the air conditioner brushed his skin. The hairs stood up on the back of his neck as he pulled off his underwear and tossed them to the floor. Turning sideways, he bowed his head, struggling to cover himself.

Then he reached up and unclipped the chain hanging around his neck. It came away easily, the little pocket watch falling into his hand. Trembling, he flicked open the metal catch and looked at the faces of his mother and father, at their kind smiles, the life in their eyes.

Struggling to hold back tears, he closed the watch again and placed it gently, reverently, on his pile of clothes.

Standing, he felt the eyes of the gathered doctors roaming over his naked flesh, examining him, seeking out his every secret. A deep sense of helplessness rose in his chest, threatening to overwhelm him. Cheeks flushed, he stared hard at the ground, fighting to ignore the world.

"Very good, Christopher." Halt's voice was patronizing, and Chris almost choked on the shame that rose in his throat. "And you, Elizabeth?"

From the corner of his eyes, Chris caught movement in the other cage. He watched as Elizabeth approached the front of her cage. She wore a smirk on her lips, but her blue eyes flashed with unconcealed rage. She pressed herself against the wire and stared at Halt.

"Come and get me," she hissed.

Chris's eyes widened. After her earlier acquiescence, he had not expected her to resist.

Halt only gave a slow shake of his head. "Bring her," he said, gesturing to the guards.

The guards marched past him and yanked open the door to Elizabeth's cage. She retreated quickly, waiting as the first guard pushed his way inside. Then with a wild shriek, she attacked. At maybe one hundred and twenty-five pounds, she was dwarfed by the guard. But her sudden violence caught him by surprise, and he stumbled backwards into his comrade.

As the two of them went down in a heap, Elizabeth leapt for the door. She made it across the threshold before the first guard managed to stagger upright. His arm swung out, catching her by the foot, and she slammed into the concrete outside the cage. With a screech, she kicked out with her free leg, slamming her heel into the guard's face. He gave a muffled curse, but held on.

In seconds, the other guard was on his feet. He strode across to where Elizabeth still fought to free herself, reached down, and grabbed her hair in one meaty hand. The girl let out a pained cry as he lifted her up and held her off the ground. Tears streamed down her cheeks as she kicked feebly at empty air, her hands batting at his chest.

With a contemptuous flick of his arm, the guard tossed her aside. Elizabeth crashed hard into the concrete. She struggled to her knees, but a heavy boot drove down onto her back, sending her face first into the floor.

Halt walked across and knelt beside the girl, a cold smile on his snakelike lips.

"Elizabeth." Halt's voice was laced now with honey. "Be a good girl, now. You cannot begin your time here with those reminders of your old life. Remove your clothes."

Chris shuddered as Halt stood and watched the girl lift herself to her hands and knees. One trembling hand reached for the buttons of her shirt and began to pluck them open. Chris looked away, unwilling to participate in her shaming.

He glanced up a minute later as the sound of metal striking concrete rang through the room. His eyes were drawn to the object now lying on the ground between Halt and the shivering girl. The thick steel links of a chain lay between them like a snake, the silver metal shining in the fluorescent lights. For an instant, Chris wondered where it had come from, but his thoughts quickly turned to what it was.

A collar.

8

"Put it on." Halt's voice slivered through the room, cold, commanding.

Elizabeth flinched away from him, but the guard's hand flashed out and caught the girl by the hair again. He shoved her back to her knees in front of the collar. A growl came from her throat as she glared up at Halt. For a second, Chris thought she would fight, but she only reached out with one trembling hand and picked up the collar.

The young woman's mouth twisted into a grimace as she held the steel linked chain in front of her. She closed her eyes, her nostrils flaring as she sucked in a breath. Chris waited, his own breath held, aware his turn would soon come.

"This is what you want, you disgusting—" Elizabeth broke off as a guard's fist sent her reeling across the floor.

Naked, she straightened on the ground, the collar still in hand. She looked at Halt, and then away again. With trembling hands, she lifted the collar to her throat. The *click* it made as it locked around her neck echoed loudly in the concrete room.

Halt smiled and clapped his hands. The guards grabbed Elizabeth by each arm and hauled her up. With a few shoves, they had her back in the cage. A pile of orange clothes was tossed in with her before the steel door swung shut. Then Halt turned on Chris, waiting naked inside his own cage.

"I suppose it's my turn then?" he asked with false bravado.

Halt stared Chris down, the grey eyes piercing him. Horror curled its way up Chris's throat as he felt his cheeks warming. His eyes drifted towards the other doctors, who still stood in silence. The guards approached his cage, one carrying a bundle of orange clothing, the other a steel linked collar identical to the one Elizabeth now wore.

"Move to the back of the cage," one of the guards ordered.

Clenching his fists, Chris stumbled back from the door as the guard flicked the latch and pushed it open. His body ached from his beating, and in the narrow space he didn't like his chances of besting the two men. He had already watched the girl attempt that approach, and fail. He would have to wait, bide his time until an opportunity arose.

Inside the cage, one guard collected his clothes, replacing them with the orange bundle. The collar was placed on top of the pile, and then the two men retreated, swinging the door shut behind them.

Chris looked at Halt, waiting for an order. When none was forthcoming, he crossed to the pile and picked up the collar. Raising an eyebrow, he tried and failed to suppress his sarcasm. "What are we, your pets?"

Halt smirked. "Would you like another lesson, Christopher?"

Letting out a long breath, Chris shook his head. He squeezed his fist, letting the cold metal of the collar dig into his flesh. His heart pounded hard in his chest, screaming a warning. Somehow, he knew if he obeyed, if he put on this collar, there would be no going back.

Dimly, he remembered a story his father had told him when he was younger. It had been almost ten years since the cancer had taken him, but he could still recall his father's voice with crystal clarity. His rough baritone drifted up from Chris's memories, as he described how the *Mahouts* in Thailand had once tamed their elephants.

The *Mahouts* placed chains around the legs of young elephants and attached them to heavy pegs in the ground. Whenever the young elephants tried to escape, the chain would contract, cutting into the elephant's leg, making it bleed. Eventually, the captive elephant would realize the futility of trying to escape.

As adults, the same chain and peg were used to restrain the giant creatures. And though by then they possessed the strength to escape the peg and chain, they never made the attempt again.

Silently, Chris wondered if that was to be his fate, if the collar in his hands would become the chain that bound him to a lifetime of servitude.

But looking at Halt, Chris knew he had no choice but to obey.

He raised the collar to his neck with deliberate slowness, as though he were approaching some great precipice. A tingle ran through him as the metal touched his skin, and a terrifying dread closed around his throat. A voice screamed for him to run, to hurl the collar away from him.

Instead, he closed his eyes and pulled the collar closed. The steel links slid across his flesh, icy to the touch, and came together with a loud *click*.

Struggling to breathe, Chris sank to his knees and fumbled for the pile of clothes. A sudden, desperate shame at his nakedness took him. He felt exposed, as though his nudity highlighted his new bondage, relegating him to nothing but an animal.

Quickly he scrambled into the bright orange uniform, and then sat with his knees pulled up to his chest. A tide of despair rose in his throat, but he pushed it down, struggling to keep a flicker of hope burning. The collar's icy grip seemed to tighten, stealing away his breath. A claustrophobic scream grew in his throat as he gasped for air.

Halt only gave a satisfied nod and stepped back from the cage.

Glancing at the other cage, Chris saw that Elizabeth had managed to pull on her own orange jumpsuit. The heavy fabric clung to her frame, and Chris couldn't help but think of what he'd glimpsed of her while naked. A bruise showed on her forehead when her clear blue eyes flickered in his direction. His cheeks warmed as she raised an eyebrow. Her wild black curls hung around her shoulders, the ends jagged and split, as though they'd been cut by a knife.

Taking a breath, the young woman pulled herself to her feet. The collar flashed around her neck, an all too vivid reminder of their new position. Her fists clenched and her lips drew back in a snarl, but otherwise she remained quiet.

Halt gave a satisfied smirk. "Very good. I'm pleased to see you're fast learners. Perhaps you will surprise me yet." Chris flinched as Halt clapped his hands again. "Now, before you are taken to your new quarters, I must warn you: I have little patience for agitators. Dissent will not be tolerated. Those collars are more than they appear. Do not attempt to remove them. Any effort to tamper with them without the correct key will have… unpleasant results."

Chris swallowed hard. A trickle of sweat ran down his neck and he tasted bile in his throat. He clenched his teeth and fought to keep himself from throwing up whatever remained in his stomach. In the opposite cage, Elizabeth showed no sign she'd heard Halt's words. She stood with her eyes closed, one arm pressed against the chain-link wall, as though that was the only thing keeping her upright.

When neither of them spoke, Halt continued: "The collars are a disciplinary tool, to rein in unruly subjects when they step out of line."

Leaning against the wall of his cage, Chris stifled a yawn, unwilling to show his fear. "And how exactly do they 'punish us'?"

The doctor glared at him, then gave a slow shake of his head. "Perhaps you are not as quick to learn as I thought."

He pulled down his sleeve, revealing a sleek black watch on his wrist, all shining metal and glass. As he tapped its surface, the screen glowed bright blue. Another tap, and a loud beep came from Chris's collar. The hairs stood up on his neck as Halt looked at him.

"Your collars are capable of delivering an electric shock of five hundred volts, at up to one hundred milliamps. They are activated remotely by these watches, which you will find all personnel within the facility are equipped with." A slow grin spread across Halt's face. "A single swipe of the screen, by any doctor or guard, and all collars within a twenty-foot radius are activated. Or an individual subject's collar may be chosen at our discretion. Perhaps you need a demonstration?"

Silently, Chris shook his head. From the corner of his eye, he saw the girl make the same gesture.

Halt watched them, his eyes aglow with a strange light. "You don't seem too enthusiastic," he laughed. "Too bad." Before anyone could move, he pressed a thumb to his watch.

Chris's collar gave a loud beep. He opened his mouth, but before any sound could escape, fingers of fire wrapped around his throat, cutting off his cry. His jaw locked as electricity surged through his body. His back arched and the strength went from his legs, sending him toppling to the concrete. A burning cramp tore into his muscles as he thrashed against the ground. The water that still pooled beneath him soaked through his clothes, but he barely noticed.

A buzzing filled his ears, but through it, he could hear Halt's voice. "This is twenty milliamps. Enough to deliver a painful shock, even freeze your motor functions. Not enough to kill—at least not when delivered for short periods of time."

Another beep sounded, and the flow of electricity ceased. Chris slumped to the ground, eyes closed, a low moan rattling in his chest. The sudden absence of pain was a sweet relief. He sucked in an eager breath, the cold air burning his throat.

As the last twitch in his muscles ceased, he cracked open his eyes and looked through the wire. He had fallen on his side and now found himself looking across at Elizabeth. She was on the ground as well, her tangled hair covering her face, her limbs splayed out across the concrete. Her forehead sported a nasty cut where she must have struck the ground.

Halt stood between the cages, the same dark grin twisting his face. His eyes found Chris's, and the smile spread.

"Welcome, Christopher and Elizabeth, to the Genome Project."

9

Angela Fallow waited until the door closed behind her before allowing the mask to crack. A sharp sob cut the air as she stumbled across the room and collapsed onto the bed. The feather-down duvet cushioned her fall, but it did nothing for the burden weighing on her soul. Burying her head in a pillow, she finally allowed the tears to flow.

What have I done?

For years she had worked in government laboratories, studying the creatures that had come to be known as the *Chead*, examining their genetic composition and identifying chromosomal alterations within their DNA. While the more superstitious citizens of the Western Allied States regarded the *Chead* as some paranormal phenomenon, she had dedicated her life to actually dissecting the mysteries of the creatures.

She had been the first to discover the link between the *Chead* awakenings across the country. A short sequence of nucleic acids in one of her samples had put her on the trail, and within days she had confirmed her suspicions. Whether the *Chead* had woken in rural California or downtown Seattle, the same virus was present in the genome of every known *Chead*.

Porcine Endogenous Retrovirus, or PERV, was a well-known retrovirus amongst the scientific community. Since the turn of the twentieth century, the virus had been used to exchange DNA between pig and human cells. PERV was a provirus—meaning upon contraction it fully integrated into the host genome. This led to its initial use in the modification of genes within the organs of pigs, to increase their receptivity when transplanted into human subjects.

But Angela had checked the records of every *Chead,* and none had ever been a candidate for xenotransplantation.

Normally, the virus alone would have meant little. There was not a person alive whose chromosomes did not contain some viral elements. In fact, many scientists speculated that proviruses played a significant role in evolution, altering genes and alleles at a rate far faster than ordinary mutation.

However, once the link was discovered, it had not taken Angela long to piece out other discrepancies in the *Chead* chromosomes. Alongside the PERV recombinations, she identified genome markers with foundations in everything from primates to canines, eagles to rabbits. Even genes from rare animals such as the Philippine Tarsier and Cnidaria had featured in the genetic puzzle.

In the end, the evidence all pointed to a single, undeniable conclusion.

The *Chead* were no accident. Someone had created them, had designed a virus and released it into the world.

The question of *who* remained unanswered, though the government had quickly pointed the blame on that old enemy—the United States. Or at least the scattered states that remained of the once-great nation.

But the *who* was not Angela's concern. Now knowing the cause, she had applied herself to countering its spread. Fortunately, the virus did not appear to be contagious. No cases had been reported of friends or family contracting the virus from awakened *Chead*, though the government still rounded them up as a precaution.

That left the question of how the victims were infected. She suspected an external source was at work there, though if true, it was up to others to solve that puzzle.

As for those already infected, Angela had failed time and time again in the search for a cure. Ordinary viruses incorporated themselves into the host DNA, much as the *Chead* virus had done. However, the similarities ended there. Symptoms of an ordinary viral infection arose when a virus began self-replication, eventually leading to cell rupture and the spread of virons to other cells. Sickness showed as human cells were hijacked by the virons and used for further self-replication.

Instead of following this route, the *Chead* virus remained latent within its host's DNA. In fact, it was almost perfectly incorporated into the human chromosome. The symptoms exhibited by the *Chead* were the result of gene expression in the cells themselves—only appearing once those genes activated. Similar to how many babies had blue eyes at birth, until their genes for brown eyes began to express.

In other words, the virus was a part of the *Chead* now, and no matter how Angela tried to approach the problem, she could find no possibility for a cure.

Upon learning of her discovery, the government had made the call to take Angela's research in a new direction. They had transferred her here to work with other doctors on the Genome Project – their own answer to the spread of the *Chead.*

A new virus was being shaped, one of such complexity and ingenious, Angela could not help but wonder how long it had been in development. Once perfected, it would change the world forever. Now, with Angela's help, they were close to a breakthrough. Initial trials on bovine subjects had proven successful, but Halt and his government overseers wanted more. They were desperate for an answer, for a beacon of hope to hold up to the people. Even the usually ice-cold Halt had appeared flustered in recent weeks, and she sensed that far more than her career rested on what happened over the next few weeks and months.

Shivering, Angela wrapped her arms tightly around herself. Not for the first time, she wondered what her life would have been like had she taken a different path. Deep in her soul, she still longed for the wild open space of the countryside, the endless stars and unmarked horizons. Her family's ranch had been remote, far from the bustling hives of the cities—though of course, it had not really been *theirs*. They worked the land, harvested the crops, while the landowner in the city took the profits.

As a young girl, she had resented that fact, and the limitations of rural life. So she had studied and schemed, and won a place in a scholarship program in Los Angeles. She had grasped the opportunity with both hands, and run off to find her place in the big wide world.

Funny how things changed, with thirty-five years' worth of wisdom.

The world was a wild place, but in the city, life was far less forgiving than in the country.

Angela shuddered as she heard again the awful screams, watched as the girl writhed on the floor of the cage. In the silence of her mind, Angela imagined the girl's crystal blue eyes seeking her out, begging for help.

Another sob tore from Angela's throat. Those eyes, that face; they were so like her own. In those youthful features, she saw her past, saw the girl she had once been reflected back.

What have I done?

The question came again, persistent. She had never thought it would come to this. When Halt had told her their plan to gather candidates for human trials, it had seemed simple. Family members convicted of treason were destined to suffer the same fate as the accused. So why not make use of those lives?

Young, healthy candidates were needed for the trials to maximize the chances of success. The children of traitors seemed the perfect answer to their needs.

Only now that she faced the reality of that decision, it was more awful than she could ever have imagined. Halt might see the children as a means to an end, but Angela could not look past their humanity. Halt was a monster, seeming to delight in the breaking of each new candidate, but for Angela, the guilt ate at her soul.

She heard again the *thud* of fists on flesh. Her stomach swirled and it was all she could do not to throw up.

"What have I done?" she whispered.

The plain walls of her private quarters offered no answers, only their silent judgement. This was her life, this little white room, the empty double bed, the white dresser and coatrack beside the door. Her woolen fleece hung on the rack, untouched for weeks now.

Staring at it, Angela was taken by an impulse to escape, to leave this place and walk out into the wilderness beyond the facility's walls. She stood and tore the coat from its rack. Swinging it around her shoulders, she fastened the buttons and pushed open the door.

The corridor outside ran left and right. Left led deeper into the facility, where her laboratory and the prison cells waited. She turned right, moving past the closed doors of the staff living quarters. It was well past midnight, and everyone else would have retired long ago. Only the night guards would be awake.

It only took a few minutes to reach the outer door—a fire exit, but from past excursions she knew there was no alarm attached. The heavy steel door watched her approach, unmoved by her sorrow. Placing her shoulder to it, she gave a hard shove and pulled at the latch.

The sharp screech of unoiled hinges echoed down the corridor, followed by a blast of cold wind.

Clenching her teeth, Angela pushed it wider and slipped out into the darkness. She pulled her coat tighter as a tendril of ice slid down her back, and listened as the door clicked shut behind her. She wasn't concerned—there were no locks on the outer doors. Out here, break-ins were the least of their worries.

Beyond the light streaming from the facility, night beckoned. Angela sucked in a long breath of mountain air and looked up at the sky. A thousand pinpricks of light dotted the darkness, the full scope of the Milky Way laid bare before her. The pale sliver of a crescent moon cast dim shadows across the rocky ground, where a thin layer of snow dotted the stones.

Shivering, Angela watched her breath mist in the freezing air. It was eerie, staring out into the absolute black. Other than the stars, no light showed beyond the facility. They were far from civilization here, miles into the mountains, as remote as one could be within the Western Allied States.

Staring at the stars, Angela could almost imagine herself a child again. A desperate yearning rose within her, to return to the simplicity of that life, to the warmth of her family ranch.

She sucked in another breath, watching the darkness, imagining the long curves of the hidden mountains. The first snow had arrived a few days ago, heralding the onset of winter. Climatologists were predicting a strong *El Niño* though, meaning a mild winter.

Standing there in the darkness, with the icy wind biting at her skin, Angela could not help but disagree. This winter would be long and savage, and few at the facility would survive it. Only the strongest would endure.

She hoped the candidates would prove up to the challenge. They had only one chance, one opportunity. Fail now, and the government would end it all.

Bowing her head, Angela turned back to the fire door. She pushed it open and returned to the warm light of the corridor. Once inside, she leaned against the door and slid to the floor.

Just a little longer. She clung desperately to the thought.

Just a little longer, and she could rest, could put this all behind her.

Just a little longer, and she would save the world.

10

Clang.

Liz flinched as the cell door slammed shut behind her, the harsh sound slashing through her self-control. She clenched her fists, fighting to stop the trembling in her body. Every fiber of her being screamed for her to run, to hide, but she sucked in a breath instead, calming her nerves. Cold steel pressed against her throat, a constant reminder of her captivity.

A sharp pain came from her palms as her nails dug into flesh. With a great effort, she unclenched her fists. The breath caught in her throat, but she swallowed and sucked in another, refusing to give in to her panic. The thick threads of the orange uniform rubbed her skin uncomfortably, though in truth its quality was better than anything she'd scavenged in the past two years.

Liz cast her eyes over her new home. The plain concrete walls matched what she'd glimpsed of the rest of the facility on the short trip from cage to prison cell. The journey had taken less than five minutes, a quick march down long corridors, past open doors and strange rooms filled with glass tubes and steel contraptions. Some she recognized from her boarding school: beakers and test tubes and other things she'd forgotten the names of. But most were beyond her understanding—plastic boxes that hummed and whirred, steel cubes of unknown purpose, containers filled with a strange, gel-like substance.

The guards had ushered them past each room with quick efficiency, leaving no time for questions. Only once had Liz paused, when they'd passed a room apparently used as a canteen. The smell of coffee and burnt toast wafted out, and she'd seen a dozen people sitting around a table, talking quietly. Before Liz could speak, a guard had jabbed the butt of his rifle into the small of her back.

A little gasp had burst from her lips, and several people inside had glanced her way. Several had raised their eyebrows at the sight of her, but a moment later they returned to their conversations. Seeing their indifference, Liz had felt the last of her courage curdle.

From there they'd been led through a thick iron door, into the grim corridor of a prison block. Faces lined the cells to either side of them as they marched past. Wide eyes stared out, their owners no more than children, ranging from around thirteen to twenty years of age.

Now Liz stood in a tiny concrete cell, the iron bars at her back locking her in, sealing her off from the outside world. Two sets of bunk beds had been pushed against the walls on her left and right, while at the rear a toilet and sink were bolted into the floor. Curtains dangled down beside the toilet, presumably to offer some small semblance of privacy.

And between the bunks stood her new roommates.

The boy and girl stared back at Liz and Christopher. The boy stood well over six feet, his muscled shoulders and arms dwarfing the girl beside him. His skin was the dark hue of a Native American, except where a scar stretched down his right arm. Black hair hung around his razor-sharp face, and hawkish brown eyes studied her with detached curiosity.

The girl beside him could not have been a starker contrast. Her pale skin practically shone in the overhead lights, unmarked by so much as a freckle, and at around five foot three, she barely came up to the boy's chest. She stood with arms folded, her posture defensive, though with her thin frame Liz doubted she could fend off a toddler. Long hair hung down to her waist, the scarlet locks well-trimmed but unwashed. Had it not been for that, Liz might have thought she'd just finished a photoshoot.

But on closer inspection, Liz noticed the faint marks of bruises on her arms, the traces of purple on her cheeks, and dark circles beneath her tawny yellow eyes. Cuts and old scars marked her knuckles, and several of her once-long nails were broken.

Maybe not so harmless after all, Liz mused.

The boy from the cages, Christopher, stood beside her, completing their party of four. Although it wasn't much of a party. So far they'd gone a full minute without speaking.

Outside, the last thud of boots ceased, and the crash of the outer doors closing heralded the departure of their escort.

Between the bunks, the boy came to life. "Welcome to hell." He spoke with a northern accent as he offered a hand. "I'm Sam, I'll be your captain today. Ashley here will be your hostess."

Beside him, Ashley rolled her eyes but did not speak.

Liz winced as she recognized the urban twang. With her pale skin, it was obvious the girl had never spent any time in the sun tending to crops or livestock, but Liz had at least hoped she might share a kinship with the boy. A lonely sorrow rose within her as she wrapped her arms around herself. It seemed not only was she to be locked away, but her roommates were going to be a bunch of kids straight out of prep school.

"Ah..." Christopher sounded confused by their new roommate's banter. "My name's Chris, and ah...this is Elizabeth, I guess."

Liz heard the shuffling of feet, no doubt the sound of the two shaking hands. Shivering, she blinked back the sudden tears that sprang to her eyes, determined to keep her weakness to herself. Her head throbbed where the guards had struck her, and a dull ache came from the small of her back.

The tremor came again, the cold air of the room eating at her resistance. She looked up to find three sets of eyes studying her. A frown creased Sam's forehead and his mouth opened, as though to ask a question, but she turned away before he could speak. A sudden yearning to be alone took her, a need for the peaceful quiet of open fields and forests. The concrete walls seemed to be closing on her, the still air suffocating.

Her eyes found the beds, taking in the unmade sheets on the bottom two. The sheets of the top bunks were pulled tight, untouched by sleep.

Without a word, she stumbled past Sam and Ashley and grasped at the ladder. Arms shaking, she pulled herself up and rolled onto the hard mattress of her new bed.

"She's a friendly one," Sam's voice carried up to her, but Liz only closed her eyes, and willed away the sounds. Her breath came in ragged gasps as she tried to still her racing heart.

"She's just scared," was Chris's uncertain reply.

You're wrong, she thought.

She was angry, horrified, frustrated, and more than anything in the world she just wanted to curl up in a corner and cry. But instead, she found herself trapped in a tiny cell with three teenagers from the city—two young men and a woman who would never understand her, her past.

"She should be," said Sam, his voice taking on a bitter tone, "you two haven't even seen the worst of it yet."

Sam's voice put Liz on edge, dragging her back from the peace she sought, but she kept her mouth shut. Scuffling came from below as the three moved, then her bunk shifted as someone sat on the bed underneath her. Cracking open one eye, Liz saw the two boys still standing, and guessed Ashley had retreated to her bed.

"I don't plan on sticking around to find out," Chris spoke in a hoarse whisper. "I have to get out of here."

Laughter followed his statement. "Don't we all, kid," Sam replied jokingly, "but it's kind of a one-way ticket."

"I don't care." Chris's voice was sharp with anger. "Fallow… that woman, she took my mother. I can't, I can't let anything happen to her."

"Tough luck, kid. Wherever she is, she's going to have to cope without you. The only way out of here is in a body bag. Just be glad it wasn't our pal Doctor Halt who grabbed her—although I'm sure he could arrange a reunion if you asked him nicely."

Below, Chris swore. "How can you joke?" he snarled, his voice rising. "Don't you understand? There's been some mistake. My mother hasn't done anything wrong. Her father died in the American War; she would never betray the WAS—"

"And you think we're any different?" the larger boy snapped, the humor falling from his voice. "You think we all conspired against the government? Don't be a fool. There's no going back, no changing things now. Not for any of us."

Silence fell over the cell. A grin tugged at Liz's lips as she embraced the quiet, taking the opportunity to calm her roiling thoughts. The lights were bright overhead, burning through her eyelids, but at least the assault on her ears had ceased. Thinking of the other three, she felt a pang of empathy, a sadness for their loss. They were orphans now too, same as her.

Perhaps she was not so alone, after all.

"It doesn't matter." Chris's voice came as a whisper now. "I'll find a way."

Sam chuckled. "You and what army? Even if you could remove that collar, if you could break out of this cell, where would you go? Who would help you, Chris? You're the son of a traitor, a fugitive without rights."

A rustling came from below, followed by a yelp. Liz's eyes widened as Chris pushed Sam up against the wall.

"She's not a traitor," Chris retorted, "and like I said, it doesn't matter. I'm not going to sit here and give up. I'm not going to let them win."

Sam's eyes hardened and he reached up with deliberate slowness to remove Chris's hands from his shirt.

"Listen, *kid*." His voice was threatening now. "You still don't get it, do you? We mean *nothing* to these people. You'll find that out tomorrow, how *little* your life means. They'll kill you the second you cross them."

"Let them try," Chris snapped.

Sam's face darkened, and then it was his turn to grab Chris by the shirt. Without apparent effort, he lifted Chris off the ground, leaving the smaller boy kicking feebly at empty air.

"Believe me, I couldn't care less if you get yourself killed,"

Sam snapped, "but since we're trapped in here together, chances are, your stupidity will get us *all* executed—"

Sam broke off as Chris twisted in his grasp and drove a foot into the larger boy's stomach. Air exploded between Sam's teeth as he staggered backwards, dropping Chris unceremoniously. Chris landed lightly on his feet and straightened, eyeing Sam from across the cell.

Liz raised an eyebrow as the two faced off against each other.

"*Enough*!" A girl's sharp voice cut the air.

The two boys jumped as Ashley strode forward with a catlike grace to stand between them. She turned to Sam and placed a hand on his chest. Her eyes flickered from him to Chris, a gentle smile warming her face.

"Enough," she said again, softly this time. Even so, there was strength to her words.

Liz watched with surprise as Sam's shoulders slumped, his tension fleeing at Ashley's touch. Chris stared, his eyes hesitant, before lowering his fists. The smile still on her lips, Ashley gave a quick nod.

"We can't fight amongst ourselves," she chided, like a teacher reprimanding her students. "Sam, you know that better than anyone. We need each other."

She turned towards Chris then, her eyes soft. "Chris, I know you're afraid, that you're terrified for your mother. I know it's awful, that you're confused. But you must calm yourself. Your mother would not want you to throw your life away."

Liz blinked, shocked by the calm manner with which Ashley had taken control of the situation. Despite her reservations, she found herself warming to the girl.

Below, Ashley turned back to Sam. "Sam, you can't hide behind that charade. Not from me." She paused, her tawny eyes watching him. "Not after everything we've been through."

Sam bowed his head. "You caught me, as usual," he said with a shrug, before throwing himself down on his bed. "I still don't want him getting us all killed, though!"

Ashley nodded. Her eyes swept the room, lingering for a

second as they caught Liz watching her, before turning to Chris. She approached him and placed a hand on his shoulder.

"You are not alone, Chris," she whispered. "Wherever you came from before, we are in this together now. We're family, you and I. All of us." Ashley's voice shook as she spoke. "And you're right. We can't just give up. We *will* find a way out of here, together. Whoever these people are, they are only human. They're not perfect. Eventually they'll make a mistake, leave some hole in their defenses. And when they do, we'll be ready for them; we'll take our chance."

Liz's heart lurched as the yellow eyes flickered back to her. "That goes for you too, Elizabeth."

Warmth spread to Liz's cheeks as the other girl watched her. She nodded slowly, struggling to cover her embarrassment. Listening to Ashley's words, she could almost feel a flicker of hope stir inside her. Maybe she wasn't alone after all. Whatever their differences, Ashley was right. They were in this together now.

Sitting up, Liz placed her hands on the bed and propelled herself off the side. She landed lightly, her bare feet slapping against the concrete, and straightened in front of Ashley. A smile, genuine now, tugged at her lips, but she tried to maintain a stoic expression. She didn't want to get too far ahead of herself—they were still from the city, after all.

Liz took a deep breath and offered Ashley her hand.

"You can call me Liz."

II

TRYOUTS

11

Chris exhaled hard as he rounded the final bend in the track, his lungs burning with the exertion. Pain tore through his calves and his stomach gave a sickening lurch, but he pressed on. The dusty track gripped easily beneath his bare feet, propelling him on towards the finish line. From behind came the ragged breathing of the others, some hot on his heels, others a long way back.

Allowing himself a smile, Chris glanced to the side, and almost tripped when he saw Liz draw alongside him. The black-haired girl had her head down, eyes fixed to the track, and was picking up the pace. Panting hard, Chris followed suit, and side by side, they raced down the final straight.

Over the last few yards, Chris's feet barely touched the ground. Shadows swirled at the edges of his vision, exhaustion threatening. Through the darkness, he glimpsed Liz pulling ahead, saw her wild grin as she crossed the line a millisecond before him.

Drawing to a stop beside her, Chris shook his head, his mouth unable to form words. Bending in two, he sucked in a mouthful of air. He felt lightheaded, his lungs aflame. It took him a full minute to catch his breath. By then the others had finished up the race.

Lowering himself to the ground, Chris blinked sweat from his eyes. Using one large orange sleeve, he wiped his forehead clear and shook his head at Liz.

"You're fast," he croaked.

It was the second day since their awakening, and the two of them had still barely spoken. Despite her reluctant greeting in the cell, Liz remained withdrawn.

The young woman only shrugged. Two blue eyes glanced down, then away. "It's the air," she breathed. "We're in the mountains—I can taste it. You're probably not used to the altitude."

Chris nodded, stars still dancing across his vision. A groan built in his throat as he saw Liz straighten, but he pushed it down and lifted himself to his feet. Ignoring the ache in his muscles, they joined the others.

Sam and Ashley stood with their hands on their hips, looking like they'd barely broken a sweat. Chris cursed himself for exerting so much energy. Who knew what else the day had in store for them?

Yesterday, he and Liz had been taken into a laboratory and put through a series of tests. The doctors had worked with a cool efficiency, asking questions, giving instructions, taking measurements, all the while steadfastly refusing to engage with their captives. Behind the doctors, the guards had been colder still, their hard eyes following the prisoners' every movement.

The tests had been simple enough, little more than a thorough examination by the local GP. But now, it seemed, the easy part was over. That morning they had been roused in the early hours by a shrieking alarm and the sudden brilliance of overhead lights. For a few seconds Chris had tried to resist, exhausted after a long night spent tossing and turning, unable to sleep. But Sam and Ashley had been insistent, dragging them from their beds to stand for inspection.

Within minutes, the guards had marched past. A doctor had accompanied them, pausing outside each cell to make notes on his electronic tablet. Chris had shivered as the man's eyes fell on him. There was a mindless, mechanical way in which he took the roster, as though this was no more than an inventory check at the grocery store.

When the doctor had departed, the guards returned with a trolley. The hallway had rung with the sound of bowls sliding through metal grates. Chris had stared for a long while at the oatmeal congealing in his bowl before the rumbling of his stomach won him over. Resigning himself, he'd taken up his spoon and eaten all he could.

Then their escort of doctors and guards had arrived, taking them from the quiet of their cell and marching them through the facility to this field—if it could be called that. The open space was the size of a football field, but there was not a blade of grass in sight.

Instead, a fine dust covered the ground, spreading out across the oval like snow. A running track ran around its circumference, edged by tall, imposing walls that hemmed them in on all sides. The cold grey concrete stretched up almost thirty feet, interspersed with the metal railings of observation decks. A dozen guards looked down on them, rifles held in ready arms. The only building was a stone tower that rose some forty feet from the center of the field.

Overhead, the sun beat down from a cloudless blue sky. The world outside was hidden by the walls, and whether Liz's mountains existed beyond remained a mystery.

Other than the doctors and their escort of guards, the field was empty. The doctors had made quick notes on their ever-present tablets, before nodding to the guards. Orders had been barked, and the four of them had set off running.

Now they stood together in a little circle, panting softly as they waited for the next command. The doctors hovered nearby, their attention fixed on their tablets, talking quietly amongst themselves. The guards stood nearby, their dark eyes fixed on the prisoners.

Beyond the little group of overseers, a red light started to flash above the door they'd entered through. A buzzer sounded, short and sharp. The guards straightened, turning to face the entrance as the door gave a loud *click* and swung inwards.

Another group of doctors entered, followed by four prisoners in matching orange uniforms. Chris scanned the faces of the doctors, searching for Fallow, but there was no sign of her. His shoulders slumped and he clenched his fists, struggling to contain his disappointment. The woman was his only remaining link to his mother, but Fallow had been conspicuously absent since their initiation.

As the group walked towards them, Chris sensed movement beside him. Glancing at the others, he was surprised to see Sam's face harden, the easy smile slipping from his lips. The older boy grasped Ashley by the wrist, nodding in the direction of the newcomers. Ashley's face paled and she stumbled sideways before Sam caught her.

"What?" Chris hissed.

The two glanced at one another and then shook their heads. "Nothing," Sam muttered.

The new group of inmates reached them before Chris could ask anything more. They hovered a few paces away, three boys and a girl, studying Chris and the others with suspicion. Chris stared back, wondering at the reaction of Sam and Ashley.

Clearing his throat, one of the doctors stepped between the two groups. He glanced at his tablet, then left and right. "Ashley and Samuel. Richard and Jasmine. You have already qualified for the next round of trials. You're here to ensure your health does not deteriorate."

Chris watched a flicker of discomfort cross the faces of a boy and girl in the opposite group, and guessed they were the ones the man was addressing. Richard sported short blond hair and angry green eyes that did not waver from Ashley and Sam. He was almost a foot shorter than Sam, but more than matched the larger boy for muscle. He kept his arms crossed tight, his stocky shoulders hunched, and a scowl fixed on his face.

The girl, who he guessed was Jasmine, stood head to head with Richard, a matching glare on her lips. Her hair floated in the breeze, the black locks brushing across her face. The skin around her brown eyes pinched as she turned towards Chris and caught him staring. Air hissed between her teeth as she raised one eyebrow.

Chris quickly looked away, his heart beginning to race. The doctor standing between them had turned his attention back to them.

"Elizabeth, Christopher, today we will test your fitness and athleticism, to assess your suitability for the next stage of the program. William and Joshua will be joining you. I suggest you get acquainted."

Chris's gaze drifted to the other two boys, and found them staring back. Their eyes did not hold the same animosity as Jasmine's and Richard's, just a wary distrust. The one on the left was a scrawny stickman of a figure, his long arms and legs little more than bone. Sharp cheekbones stood out on his face, and his jade-green eyes held more than a hint of fear. The other was larger, his arms well-muscled, but he did not match Richard or Sam for sheer bulk. He stood several inches above Chris's five-foot-eleven, and had long blond hair that hung down around his shoulders.

Seeing neither of the two were about to introduce themselves, Chris made to step towards them, but Sam's hand flashed out, catching him by the shoulder. Chris glanced at the larger boy and raised an eyebrow, but Sam only shook his head. Settling back into line, Chris glanced at Liz and saw his own confusion reflected in her eyes. Ashley's hand was clenched around Liz's wrist, holding her back.

The doctor glanced between the two groups, and with a shrug, pressed on. "Very well." He cleared his throat. "All of you, line up." He paused as the eight of them moved hesitantly to stand in one line, and then nodded. "Today—"

The doctor broke off as the buzzer by the entrance sounded again. As one, the group turned towards the door. Chris shuddered as he saw Doctor Halt striding towards them.

12

Doctor Halt's arms swung casually at his sides, as though this were no more than a Sunday stroll for him. A smile played across his thin lips. He drew to a stop alongside the doctor that had been addressing them.

"Doctor Radly," he said, his voice like honey. "How goes training day?"

"...Good," Radly answered with hesitation. He was obviously surprised to see Halt. "How can I help you, sir?"

Soft laughter whispered from Halt's lips. "I thought I might assist." His eyes slid over the group of prisoners. "We need to advance our schedule—the Director is demanding results."

Radly bit his lips, eyeing Chris and the others uncertainly. "We have four candidates ready in this unit. We still need time to assess the remaining four. Most of the other units are on a similar progression."

Shaking his head, Halt strode down the line of prisoners. When Halt had passed, Chris risked a glance at the others. Sam and Ashley stared straight ahead, steadfastly ignoring the presence of Richard and Jasmine beside them. On Chris's other side, Liz stood with her arms folded, while beyond the two newcomers wore uncertain frowns.

The crunch of gravel warned Chris of Halt's return, and he

quickly faced straight ahead again. The man stared hard at Chris as he passed, then moved on to Liz. The thud of his boots continued down the line as he went on to examine Joshua and William, before returning once again.

Scowling, Halt returned to Doctor Radly. He pointed at Liz, then to the lanky boy from the other group. "Those two." He scowled. "Pitiful creatures if ever I saw them. They won't last long."

Radly opened his mouth, then closed it. Glancing at his e-tablet, he shook his head and looked back at Halt. "Sir, we have a framework in place…" He trailed off beneath Halt's withering stare.

Silence fell across the group of doctors. Chris glanced sideways at Liz, his heart beating hard against his chest. The girl stood staring straight ahead, her brow creased, fists clenched at her side. Though she did not move an inch, Chris could sense the tension building in her tiny frame, like a cat preparing to spring.

"Well, let's see," came Halt's voice again. A second later he strode past Chris and stopped in front of Liz. "Elizabeth Flores." He looked her up and down, but Liz did nothing to acknowledge his presence. Nodding, Halt moved onto his next victim. "William Beth." He smirked. "A sorry excuse for a man."

A tremor went through the boy as he stepped back and raised his hands. "Please, sir, please, I'll do whatever you say."

Halt advanced, and the boy stumbled backwards. His feet slipped in the dust and he crashed to the ground. Towering over him, Halt sneered. "Pathetic," he spat. "Get up."

William nodded. He scrambled to his feet, eyes wide with terror. "Please—"

His plea was cut short as Halt's hand flashed out and caught him by the throat. Without apparent effort, the doctor hoisted the boy into the air. William gave a half-choked scream, his face paling. His hands batted at Halt's arm, his legs kicking feebly in the air, but Halt did not waver. He watched with cold grey eyes as the boy's struggles slowly grew weaker.

Chris watched in horror, his mouth open in a silent scream. A voice in his head shouted for him to help the boy, but as he shifted, an iron hand caught him by the wrist. He glanced back, opening his mouth to argue, but the words died on his lips. There was a cold despair in Sam's eyes, a haggard look to his face. Slowly, he shook his head.

Turning back, Chris watched as Halt tossed William aside. A low groan came from the boy as he landed, his legs collapsing beneath him. Dust billowed as he fell. Gasping for breath, he struggled to his hands and knees and tried to crawl away.

Halt followed at a casual stroll. Without taking his eyes from the boy, he spoke. "You are all here by my will. But I have no use for the weak." Apparently losing patience with his victim, he drove his boot into the small of the boy's back. William collapsed face-first into the ground.

Lifting his foot, Halt stared down at the boy. "Get up."

Arms shaking, William managed to lift himself to his hands and knees. His face beet-red, he looked up at Halt. Swaying where he crouched, a tremor shook him, but he made no move to stand.

"Wretched specimen," Halt growled. "Well, if won't get off your hands and knees, it'll have to be pushups."

A confused look came over the boy's face. "Push…pushups?"

"Yes." Halt took a step closer, his face darkening. "This is your last chance to prove yourself."

William shook his head. "I…what?"

"*Now!*" Halt glanced at the other doctors, who stood unmoving, their eyes on the trembling prisoner. "Radly, you can call the count."

At Halt's feet, a sharp sob came from William. Slowly, he placed his hands on the ground and spread his legs. As Radly shouted out each number, William lowered himself to within an inch of the ground and then straightened his arms again.

Chris and the others watched on as Radly continued to count. Beside him, Liz's expression was unreadable, though there was a slight sheen to her eyes.

As Radly reached fifteen, William's arms began to tremble. His breath came in ragged gasps and his face flushed red. A shudder ran through his bony body, and with a sob he collapsed to the ground. A triumphant grin spread across Halt's face.

"Sixteen," Radly repeated the call.

"Please," William coughed, lying with limbs splayed across the ground, "please, please I can't!"

"Keep going," Halt snarled.

He tried, no one could take that from him. Veins bulging in his forehead, teeth clenched, arms shaking with the effort, the boy managed half a pushup before he collapsed again. This time he didn't bother to beg, but just lay staring up at Halt, a haunted look in his eyes.

Halt glanced at Chris and the others. "In case you were wondering, this is what 'weakness' looks like." His cold eyes still on them, Halt reached down and tapped the sleek black glass of his watch.

Chris flinched as an awful scream came from the boy. He stumbled backwards as William started to thrash, half-gasped screams clawing their way up from his throat. Eyes wide and staring, William's head slammed back against the ground. His fingers bent, scrambling at the steel collar around his neck, even as another convulsion tore through him.

Panic gripped Chris and he stepped towards the boy. Sam's iron grasp stopped him again, pulling him back. Chris swore, struggling to break free, unable to stand by and watch the torture any longer. But Sam stood unyielding, though his eyes never left the convulsing boy. Ashley stood as still as a statue, her eyes fixed on William, her face expressionless. Her scarlet hair blew across her face, but she did not so much as raise a hand to brush it away.

The fight went from Chris in a rush.

"Such a shame, to see our people come to this," Halt said, his words slithering through the air. "Once upon a time we were proud, strong. Our forefathers marched to war with joy in their hearts and sent the cowards of the United States scurrying. Even then they did not stop. They followed the enemy back to their holes, and left a smoking crater in the heart of their so-called democracy."

Chris gritted his teeth. William's struggles were weakening, his eyes sliding closed. Agony contorted his features, twisting his face into an awful scowl.

And still Halt spoke. "How your ancestors would turn in their graves to know of your treachery, of your betrayal of the nation they fought to create."

Chris forced his eyes closed. The hand on his shoulder gave a gentle squeeze, but Sam stayed silent. Through the strangled screams, Halt's words dug their way into Chris's consciousness. The wrinkled, smiling face of his grandmother drifted through his mind. He remembered her telling him how her husband, Chris's grandfather, had fought and died in the American War.

In 2020, horrified at the chaos engulfing their nation, a conglomerate of Washington, Oregon and California had unilaterally ceded from the United States. Arizona and New Mexico had quickly joined them, as support poured in from Canada and Mexico.

War was quick to follow, and a decade of conflict had brought both sides to their knees. Only one last, desperate gamble by the Western Allied States had assured their victory. In one decisive nuclear strike, Washington, DC was left in ruins, the leadership of the United States decimated in a single day. The union had crumbled then, leaving a scattering of independent states who either sued for peace, or were overrun.

Many argued the values of both nations had been lost the day Washington DC fell. The Western Allied States had been left tainted, their ideals corrupted by that one act of nuclear evil. Watching Halt torture the helpless boy, Chris could not help but agree.

"Perhaps some of you will prove worthy, might one day live up to the memories of your ancestors."

Arms folded, Halt stared down at the boy. The light on William's collar still flashed red, though his twitching had slowed to little jerks of his arms and legs. He let out a long sigh. "I will give the boy this, he does not die easily." He reached for his watch.

"*Halt.*" Halt froze as a woman's voice carried across the dirt field.

The group turned as one, staring as Doctor Fallow strode through the doorway. Chris blinked. So engrossed had he been in William and Halt, he had not heard the buzz of her entrance. Now, as she marched across the dusty ground, Fallow tapped the watch on her wrist. Beside Halt, William's convulsions came to a sudden stop.

For a moment, Chris thought the boy had finally succumbed to the collar. Then a low groan came from his twisted body, and Chris let out a sigh of relief.

Fallow drew to a stop in front of Halt, her eyes flashing with anger. "What the *hell* do you think you're doing?" she growled.

13

"What the *hell* do you think you're doing?" Angela Fallow growled, her heart pounding as Halt turned to face her.

"My job." Halt's eyes flashed, and Angela took an involuntary step backwards.

Silently cursing her weakness, Angela drew herself up. "Your job is to oversee this facility, Halt. Mine is to ensure we have the right candidates for the project." Her eyes flickered to the boy at Halt's feet, and her stomach swirled.

He lay unconscious on the ground, an angry red rash spreading out from beneath the collar at his throat. He gave the odd twitch as his muscles spasmed, but otherwise he was still, the only sign of life the dull rattling of his breath. It looked like she had arrived just in time. One of the doctors had alerted her to Halt's interference with their e-tablet, but she had been on the other side of the facility.

Halt took a step towards her, his fists clenched. "Need I remind you, Fallow, you answer to me."

This time Angela did not back down. She lifted her head, facing the taller doctor. "Not in this, Halt. The trials are *mine* to oversee. The framework was designed by all of us; we *all* agreed to follow it while vetting the candidates." She twisted her lips. "However distasteful some of us may consider the methods."

Taking another step, Halt towered over her. His eyes burned, and for a long moment, he did not speak. She stared him down, unwilling to break, to give in. Halt had gone too far, stepped a mile past the lines of human decency. Whoever their prisoners were, they did not deserve to be treated like this.

The breath went from Halt in a rush. He waved a hand and turned away. "Very well, Fallow." He said the words lightly, but she did not miss the warning beneath them. He glanced at the watching doctors. "We shall do things your way. But we cannot wait. I want the next round of trials started tomorrow. The final batch of candidates are needed by the week's end."

Swallowing, Angela glanced at her coworkers. They hovered in a group, a mixture of fear and disdain in their eyes. She knew some would support her, eager to do things by the book. But others she was not so sure about. They were more willing to take risks, to press on without concern for the candidates brought to the facility. Or they were just plain terrified of Halt.

Angela could not blame them for their fear. She had once regarded the man with respect, but since his elevation to head doctor, he had revealed a darker side. Doctors who crossed him were terminated without cause, safety procedures had been cut, and with the subjects, there were no limits to his cruelty.

She eyed him now, silently calculating the population of subjects still to be vetted. There were two hundred prisoners in the facility, with roughly half of them already processed. That left a hundred candidates still to vet—of which fifty would hopefully survive to begin the experiment. It would take a mammoth effort to have them ready by the end of the week.

And that wasn't even accounting for the final touches she needed to make on the virus.

"A week's not enough time," she said.

Halt shrugged. "I'm sorry, Fallow, that's out of my hands. The Director wants results. The population is growing restless. They want answers, protection, and if the government doesn't provide them..." He trailed off.

Angela eyes travelled over the prisoners in their orange jumpsuits. She shivered as she caught the boy from San Francisco watching at her. She quickly looked away again, seeing the accusation written across his face, hearing again the screams of his mother as they took her.

Biting her lip, Angela faced Halt. "We'll have to skip the resting period. It may result in a sub-optimal outcome."

Halt waved a hand. He was already moving towards the doorway, leaving his victim lying facedown in the dust. "You will find a solution, Fallow." Their eyes met. "I know you will."

Angela's breath caught in her throat, but she held his gaze until he turned away. She shuddered as he disappeared through the iron doors, the fight falling from her like water. A muffled groan slipped from her lips, but she bit it back and turned towards the gathered doctors.

They stared back at her, awaiting instruction.

Angela straightened. "Okay, you heard Halt. We need to get these candidates classified. You know the drill." She clapped her hands and smiled as the other doctors broke from their silent reverie.

One by one, they moved away, each taking one of the orange-garbed candidates with them. Doctor Radly took the boy, Christopher, by the arm, but the boy's eyes were fixed in her direction. Looking away, Angela studied a cloud overhead. Her mind drifted, remembering again the way Margaret Sanders had fought. The woman had downed a highly-trained Marine—had almost killed him, in fact.

A mother's love.

Idly, she remembered her own mother, the way she had fussed over their little family. Despite the wide expanse of the property on which they'd lived, they had always struggled, making do with what rations the landowner left for them. But her mother had suffered their poverty with good grace, stewing rabbit bones and baking hard bread in the coal oven.

She imagined that Margaret Sanders possessed a similar resolve, a determination to do whatever it took to protect her family.

So why, then, had she been so foolish? Her treason had doomed herself and her son. Only by the grace of the government had Chris not been tossed into an interrogation cell alongside her. She shuddered, thinking of those dark places, imagining the woman's pretty face bruised and beaten.

Out on the field, Chris was running as he had been instructed, while Doctor Radly studied readings on his tablet. The collars transmitted a constant stream of data: heartbeat, blood pressure, oxygen levels, and a range of other readings. That information would be used to rank them later.

Watching the candidates, Angela turned her thoughts to what lay ahead. She shuddered as a darkness settled on her soul. Again, she reminded herself what was at stake, of the necessity of these trials. Again, she could not quite convince herself.

14

Chris drew in a long breath as he studied the wall before him, and tried to quell the trembling in his knees. The sound of the other candidates training echoed from all around him, but where he stood, Chris was alone. The stone tower in the center of the field stretched some forty feet above him, its surface smooth but for a series of climbing holds leading to the top.

"What are you waiting for?" The doctor assigned to Chris interrupted his thoughts. "Get on with it. Climb."

Swallowing, Chris flicked the man a glance. The collar seemed to tighten around his throat as he glimpsed the watch on his captors wrist, and shuddering Chris returned his gaze to the wall. There was little Chris had encountered in his short life that scared him, little except the unique terror that gripped him at the thought of falling from such a height.

The wall had no ropes or harness, just the ugly grey holds jutting from the smooth stone. One mistake, and he would tumble back to the hard ground. If he was lucky, the fall might only wind him, but from the full forty feet…

He shuddered again as the trembling spread to his whole body. It wasn't even the thought of injury that had him frozen – he'd been hurt countless times sparring at his Taekwondo Dojang

– it was the thought of those few moments falling, of tumbling through the air, helpless to save himself.

"Chris!" He swung around as a voice shouted from the across the field. Sam had stopped in the middle of the running track and stood watching him. Their eyes met, and Chris saw the urgency there as he called again. "Climb!"

Before Chris could reply, Sam set off once more, leaving him alone with the doctor and the tower.

Except Chris no longer felt quite so alone. Another glance around the field, and he saw Ashley give a little wave, even caught what might have been the slightest of nods from Liz. He swallowed, their encouragement swelling in his chest. For a second, the terror seemed to recede, and he stepped up to the wall and took a firm grip of the first hold.

Hand over hand, Chris hauled himself up as the doctor watched on from below. The first ten feet were relatively easy, but as he went higher, Chris's terror came creeping back. Nearing halfway, he made the mistake of glancing down. Twenty feet of open air opened up beneath him, and he gripped his holds tighter, pulling himself tight against the wall.

He stayed frozen there for a long while, eyes squeezed shut, listening to the sounds of movement coming from around the field. He imagined Sam and Ashley and Liz watching him, heard their silent encouragement, but so far off the ground, the thought no longer held the same power. With each passing moment his terror grew, fed by the gulf beneath him, his imagination already playing out the fall that would see him tumble helplessly to the earth.

"Are you done, candidate?" the doctor called from below.

Candidate.

The word rung in Chris's mind, reminding him of what these people thought of him. He and the other prisoners were just numbers to these doctors, failed examples of humanity that served no purpose but to die in whatever horrible experiments they had in mind. Anger flared in Chris's chest, burning at the terror, and gritting his teeth, Chris started upwards once more.

Towards the top, the handholds became smaller and more

sparse, forcing Chris to study his path carefully. His arms were burning from the exertion, but his rage gave him strength, and he continued up, clinging to the tiny holds like his life depended on it.

By the last ten feet, the holds were barely large enough for two fingers to hold. His whole body trembling and his breath coming in raged gasps, Chris forced himself onwards. He refused to look down, knowing it would only serve to feed the terror still nibbling at his insides, though eventually would need to if he was to climb back down.

Straining his leg to reach a better foothold, a sudden cramp tore through his calf. Crying out, Chris almost lost his holds from the shock of the pain. His leg spasmed and he stretched it out, struggling to keep his grip with just three points of contact for support. Slowly the pain dwindled, and taking a breath, Chris found a new foothold and continued.

When he finally reached the top, Chris experienced a moment of panic as his hand reached up and found only empty air. It took him several seconds of fumbling blinding around above his head before he caught the lip of the wall. A wave of relief swept over him, and using both hands, he pulled himself up and levered himself onto the top of the tower.

His heart pounding in his ears, Chris sucked in a breath and looked around. The tower rose above the walls of the facility, and from his vantage point he could see beyond the training field to the lands beyond their prison.

A heavy fog had swept in with the afternoon, obscuring much of his view, but Chris could still see enough to feel the harsh fingers of despair clawing at his throat. Above the white clinging to the barren earth, towering mountains rose around the facility, their jagged peaks capped with snow.

Wherever they had been brought, it was a long way from civilization. Even if they managed to escape their prison, where would they go? In such a remote landscape, it would not take long for the elements to claim them. Even if they somehow survived the cold, they would soon starve in the barren land.

"Excellent work," the doctor's voice carried up to Chris, slicing through his despair.

He felt a strong urge to hurl himself from the tower and crash down on the man. From the such a height, the impact would probably kill them both. It might have been worth it, but just the thought had Chris gripping the stone beneath him tighter.

"Down you come then," his overseer continued, returning his attention to the e-tablet the doctors seemed to carry everywhere with them.

Chris swallowed. The way down was going to be even worse. He would have to be continuously looking down in search of the next hold. There would be no ignoring the open air beneath him. Feeling the fear returning, he looked around the field. The eyes of his friends were turned in his direction, and he recalled Ashley's words from back in their cell.

We are in this together now. We're family, you and I. All of us.

Nodding to each of them, Chris tightened his grip on the wall and levered himself over the edge. The climb down seemed to take an age, and even in last ten feet Chris dared not release the wall for fear of his body crumpling on impact with the ground.

When he finally stepped down onto the field, his legs were shaking so badly they almost gave way beneath him. He stumbled a step before recovering, then straightened and faced the doctor.

"So, doc, what's next?"

15

Liz lay in the darkness, eyes open, staring into empty space. Somewhere above was the concrete ceiling, but in the pitch-black she imagined it was the sky that stretched overhead, infinite in its expanse. Only there were no stars, no moon or drifting satellites, and in her heart, she could not convince herself of the illusion.

In her heart, she remained trapped, locked away within the soulless walls of the facility.

She could still feel the boy watching her, begging for help, for an end to the torture. A shudder ran through her as she remembered the way Halt had looked at her, the piercing grey of his eyes as he weighed her worth. It had been so close, a different toss of the coin, and he might have chosen her…

Biting back a sob, Liz closed her eyes, though it made no difference in the dark. She had wanted to go to him; only Ashley had stopped her. Instead, she had stood in silence, hand in hand with the girl from the city, as William slid towards death.

Liz shivered, a scream building in her throat. She bit it back, and drew the thin blanket closer around her. Goosebumps pricked her skin as she rolled onto her side. Her body ached and a constant thudding came from her temples. The doctors had subjected them to eight hours of relentless exercise, until the sun had finally dipped below the towering walls. By then, her body had been little more than a series of bruises. A measly meal of broiled stew in their cell had followed, though in truth it was better than most of what she'd scavenged in Sacramento. Then the lights had clanked off, plunging them into the darkness.

"You okay, Liz?" Ashley whispered from below.

Liz suppressed a shudder.

Am I okay? She turned the question over in her mind, wondering whether she would ever be okay again. At the thought, a yearning rose within her, a need for companionship, for comfort.

"I'm alive," she replied, then: "What about you?"

Out on the field, Ashley had barely moved while William lay writhing in the dirt. Her face had remained impassive; the only sign anything was amiss her iron-like grip around Liz's hand. Afterwards, Ashley had moved through the drills and tasks set by the doctors with an eerie calm, as though her mind were far away, detached from the horror of her situation.

There was a long pause before Ashley answered. "I'm alive too." Her breath quickened. "That's saying a lot."

"How long…how long have you and Sam been here?"

Another pause. "Weeks, a month. I've lost count of the days."

"And…and you've seen things like that, like today with William?"

Below, Ashley gave a sharp snort. "That, and more." She shifted in the bed, causing the bunk to rock.

Liz shivered, thinking of the icy glances that had passed between Ashley and Sam, as well as the others. "What about the two in the other group, Richard and Jasmine?"

"What about them?" Ashley's response was abrupt, her voice sharp.

"You know them," Liz whispered, aware she was treading on dangerous ground. "Who are they?"

"You'll find out soon enough, Liz. Best you not worry about it."

Liz swallowed. Ashley's reply brooked no argument, and an uneasy silence fell between them. For a while, Liz lay still, staring into space, wondering at Ashley's words. Below, Sam gave a snort and rolled in his bed. Liz stifled a groan as a rumble came from the boy's chest and he started to snore.

"The boys don't seem to be having any trouble sleeping," she muttered, hoping Ashley was still awake.

"You know what boys are like," came Ashley's reply. Liz could almost hear the girl smiling. "Emotional capacity of a brick and all…" Her voice faded for a moment. "Sam…he closes it off I think, buries it deep. It comes out in other ways though, like how he reacted to Chris when you arrived."

"And you?" Liz couldn't help but dig deeper. Through the heat and torture, the agonizing exercises and the hard-faced stares of the doctors, Ashley had not missed a beat. She had smiled through each new challenge, as though privy to some secret joke, moving with that same fluid grace Liz had noted when she'd first seen her.

When Ashley did not answer, Liz pressed on. "You looked so calm, even when…" She trailed off as William's agonized face reappeared in her mind.

"I was?" Ashley sounded surprised. Sheets rustled in the darkness. "I wasn't. Inside I was screaming, but I've learned when to keep things to myself, when not to draw attention. Even before this place, it was a skill I'd mastered."

Liz sat up at that. "What do you mean?"

Quiet laughter came from below. "I've had a lot of practice, Liz. My parents worked for the government."

An icy hand slid its way down Liz's throat and wrapped its fingers around her heart. Her breath stuttered, the cold steel pressing against her throat. She grasped at the covers, tearing at the cheap fabric.

Below, Ashley was still talking. "They worked in media relations, of all things. No one important, nothing to do with the President and his people. Just a couple of analysts in a tiny department of our fine administration." Her last sentence rang with sarcasm. "But even two lowly analysts quickly discovered there's no such thing as free speech these days. *Especially* for those close to power. They had to learn to wear masks, to hide their true beliefs about the goings-on of the government. By the time my older sister and I came along, they had become masters at it. So I guess you could say, I learned from the best."

"Why would they stay?" Liz tried to keep the emotion from her voice, but the question came out harsh, accusing.

"Why?" Ashley paused, as though considering the question. "For my sister and me, I guess. To give us a better life. They may not have agreed with everything the government did, but they knew leaving was not really an option. Their careers would have been destroyed. They didn't want to raise their daughters on the streets."

"Yes, it's not much of a life," Liz all but growled.

Ashley fell silent, and for a long while it seemed she would not reply. Guilt welled in Liz's chest, but she pushed it down.

"Didn't really matter in the end, did it? They sacrificed their beliefs, their integrity, so we could live, but it didn't make any difference. They were found out for doing something wrong, I guess. Must have been, because here I am."

Liz's anger dwindled with Ashley's words. It was not the girl's fault she'd been born into wealth, while Liz had been condemned to the poverty-stricken countryside. Even so, she could not quite set aside the emotion, could not quite let it go.

"Sorry," she offered at last, her tone still harsh. "It's just, for as long as I can remember, the government has been the enemy. Even as a child, they were the people who came and took our food, the landowners who held our lives in the palm of their hands. Then, when I was older, after my parents…after they passed…" She shook her head, angry images flashing through her mind.

"I understand," Ashley's whisper came from below. "But none of that matters now, does it? Whoever our parents were, whatever we've been through, we've arrived in the same place. We're both trapped in the same nightmare. You'll learn that, soon enough."

"It gets worse?" Liz spoke the words without emotion. Her energy was spent, and she could hardly bring herself to care about whatever fresh trials the morning might bring.

"Only if you're human," Ashley replied.

The words rang with finality and Liz sensed the conversation had come to an end. Shivering, she hugged the covers tight around her. Suddenly she longed to be wrapped in another's arms, to be touched by another human. An image of her mother drifted into her thoughts, a warm smile on her lips, eyes dancing with humor.

Biting back a cry, Liz buried her head in the pillow, anxious to hide her sorrow. As she cried, another thought rose, a question that demanded an answer. One she should have asked. Silently, she cursed her selfish grief.

"Ashley," she breathed. "What happened to your sister?"

Silence clung to the darkness, and long minutes passed, until Liz was sure the girl had already fallen asleep.

"She's dead." The answer came just as Liz was preparing to give up.

Sobs came from below, carrying with them the pain of loss.

"I'm sorry," Liz whispered, the words hollow, even to her.

Ashley did not reply, and Liz lay back on her bed, listening as Ashley's crying faded away.

It was a long time before sleep found Liz.

16

Liz stumbled as she entered the room, the sudden, brilliant light blinding her. Stars danced across her vision as behind her, the door slammed closed. She jumped at the sound, and almost tripped, before managing to right herself. Straightening, she blinked again and finally took in her surroundings.

Overhead, fluorescent bulbs lined the ceiling, filling the room with their distant whine. Otherwise, the room was unlike anything she'd seen so far. Three walls were covered by white padding, while the third shone with silver glass, its surface reflecting her tangled hair. She shivered, seeing the exhaustion in her eyes, the bruises marking her cheeks.

For three days, the doctors had taken them to the outdoor field and driven them through an endless series of tests and exercises. Unused to the strain, Liz had quickly learned that failure meant pain. She had been forced to dig deep within herself, to stores of strength she hadn't known she possessed, in order to survive. But now things had changed again.

She took another step into the room, the soft floor yielding beneath her feet. Turning from what she guessed was a one-way mirror, she faced the boy standing in the center of the room. His long blond hair hung in dirty clumps around his face, where purple bruises matched Liz's own. He bit his lip, his eyes flickering around the room, uncertainty writ in his every gesture. Behind him was another door, its surface padded like the one through which she had entered.

Joshua, she thought, recalling his name from their first day on the training field.

He looked at her as she thought his name. "What's going on?" he croaked.

Liz shrugged and shook her head. "I don't know, Joshua."

They had not spoken since that first day. Ashley and Sam had been insistent, refusing to even acknowledge the other group of inmates. Somehow, Liz did not think their rule applied now.

Before either of them could speak further, a loud squeal interrupted them. Liz winced, the hairs on her neck standing up as a crackling voice followed.

"Welcome," the voice began, coming from somewhere in the ceiling. "Congratulations on surviving this far. As you know, only the strongest are needed for the final stages of our experiment."

Liz crossed her arms and turned to face the mirror. Raising an eyebrow, she rolled her eyes so those behind could see. She was sick of listening to these people, sick of them acting like they owned her. Collar or no, she refused to be treated like an animal any longer, to bend to their will.

The voice ignored her display of insolence and continued: "Unfortunately, time constraints require us to press on. This phase of the project must be completed by week's end. That means omitting the standard rest period for new subjects such as yourselves."

"Hardly seems fair," Liz muttered under her breath, flashing a quick grin at Joshua.

Joshua shrugged and cast another uncertain look at the glass. They stood in silence, waiting for the voice to continue. "Regretfully, we must cull our population of candidates for our next phase. Only the strongest would survive the final process regardless, and we do not have the resources to waste on failed specimens. Thus, only the best will survive today."

Liz shuddered at the casual way the voice described ending their lives. She recalled the faces lining the corridor outside their cell. Some of them might have been as young as thirteen. Their whole lives were ahead of them. And these people wished to snuff them out, to slaughter them like they were no more than field mice beneath their boots.

Joshua seemed a little younger than her, maybe seventeen years old. He was a little taller too, and bulkier, with the broad shoulders of a swimmer. His amber eyes were watching her now, his fear shining out like a beacon.

"Only one of you will leave that room alive. You must decide for yourselves whether you possess the will to live. To the victor, goes life."

Liz glanced from the mirror to Joshua and back. She sought out some sign of the watchers beyond, but the glass showed only the horror on her face. And the boy's wide eyes, the hardening of his brow, his fists clenching as he faced her.

Whatever her own thoughts, Joshua had clearly already made up his mind.

Only if you're human. Ashley's words from their midnight conversation returned to her.

They weighed on Liz's soul as she watched Joshua, saw his muscles tensing. In that moment, she knew in her heart that she too would do whatever was necessary to survive.

The fear had already fallen from Joshua's face. His eyes weighed her up. A smile spread across his lips as he realized his chances of victory were high. There was no question who the doctors expected to survive.

He stepped towards her, and Liz quickly retreated. She studied him as they circled one another, searching for a weakness. It was easy to see she could not match his strength, but she was light on her feet and hoped he might prove overconfident. After two years on the streets, wandering between towns and cities, Liz was no stranger to a fight.

Yet with the padded walls ringing her in, there would be no room to run if she made a mistake. If he caught her in his long arms, it would all be over. Though his capacity for murder was yet to be tested, she had no desire be at his mercy.

She certainly would not be giving him any second chances.

Joshua gave a shout and leapt towards her, eating up the space between them in a single stride. Liz twisted as he came for her, jumping backwards to avoid his flailing arms, and smiled as he staggered past. Despite his greater size, the boy was no fighter.

Maybe she had a chance after all.

Joshua came to a stop near the wall and spun to face her. A wicked scowl crossed his face. Liz swallowed hard and braced herself.

Raising her fists, she nodded. "Let's get this over with then."

A low growl came from Joshua as he started forward again, his footsteps controlled now, each movement carefully measured. Liz spread her feet wide and slid one foot backwards, readying herself. She had no intention of letting him get close enough to grab her, but he needed to be a *little* closer yet.

As Joshua took another step, she screamed and hurled herself forward. His eyes widened, but close as they were, he had no time to react. Liz slammed her fist into the center of his chest, aiming for the solar plexus.

Air exploded between the boy's teeth and he staggered backwards, a half-choked groan rattling from his throat. The color fled his face as he clutched his chest, mouth wide and gasping.

Watching his distress, Liz hesitated, guilt welling within her. Joshua hadn't been expecting her to fight back, certainly not with such sudden violence. But as he bent in two, wheezing in the cold air, she knew she could not spare him. If he recovered, he would not fall for the same trick twice.

Doubled over, Joshua's head provided the perfect target. Liz clasped her hands together and brought them down on the back of his head.

Joshua's legs buckled and he slammed into the ground without a sound. His arms splayed out on either side of him and a muffled groan came from his mouth. Relief swept through Liz at the sound—at least she hadn't killed him. Maybe they would allow him to live. After all, they couldn't have expected her to win this matchup.

Turning to the one-way mirror, she raised an eyebrow in

question. As she did, Joshua's hand shot out and grabbed her by the leg.

Liz screamed as fingers like steel closed around her ankle and yanked, sending her crashing to the ground. The shock of the fall drove the breath from her lungs, and she gasped, struggling to breathe. Pain shot through her ankle as the fingers squeezed. Cursing, she kicked out with her foot, but Joshua surged forward and caught it in his other hand.

Panic clutched Liz's stomach as she fought to break his grip. Sucking in a lungful of air, she tried to roll away, but his hands held her like iron shackles. However hard she strained, they refused to give. Joshua's teeth flashed as his lips drew back in a grin.

In a sudden rush, he dragged her across the floor, pulling himself up as he did so. He released her, but before she could squirm free, Joshua's weight crashed down on her chest, pinning her down.

Hands fumbled at her throat, fingernails tearing at her skin.

Liz lashed out with a fist, catching Joshua in the side of the head. He reeled sideways, but his weight did not shift and she failed to break free.

Recovering his balance, Joshua snarled and raised a fist. Liz raised her arm in time to deflect the blow, but a scream tore from her lips as it glanced from her shoulder. She swung at him again, but there was no strength in the blow this time and it bounced weakly off his chin.

Liz was not so lucky.

Stars exploded across her vision as Joshua's fist connected with her forehead. Her head thudded back into the soft ground. Distantly, she thought how considerate it was for the doctors to have provided a padded floor while their prisoners beat each other to death. Then another blow slammed into her jaw, and the fight went from her in a sudden rush. Darkness spun at the edges of Liz's vision.

Cold fear spread through her stomach as a tentative hand wrapped around her neck. She sucked in a breath as the pressure closed around her throat. Panicked, she stared up at Joshua, silently pleading for mercy.

Joshua stared back, his eyes hard, lips drawn back in a snarl, teeth clenched in rage. Whoever he'd been before entering this room, that Joshua was long gone. He'd been burned away, the innocence of the boy replaced by anger, by bitter hatred, by the desperation to live.

Fire grew in Liz's chest, willing her to action. She kicked feebly, trying to maneuver herself into a position to attack. But his weight was far beyond her strength to lift. Before she could struggle further, he lifted her head and slammed it back into the ground. Despite the spongy surface, Liz's vision spun.

She opened her mouth, gasping in desperation, but the pressure did not relent and she managed only a whisper of a breath. Darkness filled the edges of her vision as every muscle in her body began to scream. Bit by bit her strength slipped away, replaced by the endless burning of suffocation.

On top of her, Joshua leaned closer, eyes wide with vicious intent.

In that moment, Liz saw her opening.

He was so close, just inches away. She could not miss. With the last of her strength, she clenched her fist and drove it up into Joshua's throat. The steel rim of the collar bit into her knuckles, but behind it, she felt something give, something fracture with the force of her blow.

The pressure around her throat vanished as Joshua toppled backwards. A low gurgling echoed off the walls as he gasped, his hands going to his own neck, his legs thrashing against the soft floor.

Liz sucked in glorious breath, her throat aching from the icy air. She struggled to her hands and knees, still coughing and wheezing. Her head swirled and the room spun, but she dug her nails into the spongy floor and willed herself to remain conscious.

Get up, Liz!

Slowly, Liz pulled herself to her feet and stood swaying in the center of the room. The white lights burned her eyes, blinding her, but she clenched her fists, and by sheer will stayed upright.

She looked down at Joshua, bracing herself to continue the fight. Her stomach lurched when she saw him.

Joshua no longer moved, no longer thrashed, no longer breathed. His mouth hung open, and his eyes were wide and staring, but the boy within was gone. His face was a mottled white and purple, the veins of his neck bulging, and a black bruise was already spreading from beneath his collar.

Joshua lay dead at her feet.

Tears ran from Liz's eyes as she sank to the ground.

The darkness came rushing up to meet her.

17

Chris watched as William staggered upright, his heart sinking at the thought of fighting another round with the sickly boy. To his relief, William's strength failed him, and he toppled forward, landing with an undignified *thud* on the padded floor.

Closing his eyes, Chris let out a long sigh.

It's over.

The thought was scant comfort. In the end, it hadn't been much of a fight. William was tall and had long arms, but there was not a scrap of muscle on him. And he had never quite recovered from that first day on the field. Young and inexperienced, he had attacked Chris first, but his heart had never been in it, and Chris had easily deflected his clumsy blows.

Crossing his arms, Chris had looked at the glass, and shaken his head in defiance.

A harsh beep had come from his collar, followed by a bolt of electricity that sent Chris to his knees. Gasping, he reached for his throat, but the shock had already ceased.

The voice had come again as Chris regained his feet.

"That was your only warning. Engage with your opponent, or forfeit your life."

Out of options, Chris had obeyed. Despite their captor's

command, Chris had held back, pulling his blows where he could. But as the fight progressed, William had grown desperate, fighting harder, and Chris had been forced to act.

A kick to William's head had sent him reeling, and he'd never recovered.

Now Chris waited, guilt eating at his stomach, curdling the measly remnants of his breakfast. He stared into the mirrored glass, struggling to pierce the reflection, to find the faces of their tormentors. Whoever they were, Chris hated them with a violence he had not thought himself capable of.

The door behind William opened with the whisper of oiled hinges. Two guards entered, followed by a woman in a white lab coat. His heart lurched—but then he realized the woman was not Fallow. One of the guards checked on William, while the other approached Chris, gesturing him back against the wall.

Once the doctor was satisfied both prisoners were secure, she strode across the room to the fallen boy. A wireless headset was wrapped around her left ear, half hidden by the curls of her auburn hair. She spoke as she moved, transmitting observations to whoever was on the other end. In one hand, she carried a sleek steel instrument.

Chris shivered as he recognized the jet injector, identical to the one Fallow had used on him the night he'd been taken.

The doctor crouched beside William, still talking into her headset. The boy was on his hands and knees, struggling to find his balance. The woman laid a hand on his shoulder.

"Subject is still conscious. He appears to be suffering from a concussion. Assessment?"

A low groan came from William as he turned towards the woman. "Wha…what happened?"

Chris closed his eyes, guilt welling within him. He had seen these same symptoms in his Taekwondo Dojang, when younger fighters got carried away sparring without wearing their head guards. Still, he didn't think he'd hit William that hard, just enough to take the fight out of him.

The doctor was nodding to the voice in her ear. "Affirmative.

There would be no purpose in resuming the fight. Administering the injection."

Before Chris could react, the woman leaned down and pressed the jet injector to William's neck. The hiss of gas followed as the vial attached to the gun emptied. Quickly, she withdrew the gun, stood, and retreated across the room.

Still on the ground, William raised a hand to his neck in bewilderment.

The woman watched on, her face impassive, arms crossed and fingers tapping against her elbow.

Whatever had been in the injection did not take long to work. Chris stood frozen in place as William started to cough. Then, without warning, his eyes rolled back in his skull. A violent shudder went through him as he took a desperate gasp, as though he were sucking air through a straw. He bent over, groaning, his mouth moving as though he were trying to speak. Wild eyes flickered around the room, pleading for help.

The spell broke as Chris's gaze met William's. He started forward, but the outstretched arm of a guard barred his way. Before Chris could slip past, the man grasped him by the shirt and tossed him back against the wall. The pads broke the impact, but Chris staggered as he landed and barely kept his feet.

He looked up in time to see William pitch face-first into the ground, a low moan marking his final exhalation of breath. His feet kicked for a second longer, then stilled. Silence fell across the room as the guard stepped back from Chris and faced the doctor.

The woman crouched again beside William. She touched a finger to his neck, then gave a curt nod.

"Subject has expired. Subject Christopher Sanders is cleared for advancement." The words were spoken without emotion, as though she were discussing the weather.

"*Why?*" Chris screamed.

The woman looked up quickly, her eyes widening. The guards edged forwards, placing themselves between Chris and the doctor.

"Why?" Chris said again, taking another step.

The woman's surprise faded, though her eyes flickered to the guards before she addressed him. "He was weak. He would not have survived Phase Two. This was the humane option."

"*Humane?*" Chris clenched his fists. "He was helpless!"

"Because of his concussion, he passed without knowing what was happening," The doctor spoke with a calm efficiency, as though explaining something to a child.

A wild anger took Chris then, an impossible rage that swept away all caution. He leapt without thinking, fingers reaching for the woman's throat. The guards raced to intercept him, but Chris never made it that far.

Agony tore through his neck, spreading instantly to his every muscle, taking his feet out from under him. He screamed as he struck the ground, and felt the pain of a thousand needles stabbing him. His head thumped against something solid as a convulsion rippled through him. The reek of burning flesh reached his nostrils and his back arched.

When the agony finally ceased, he found himself staring up at the ceiling. The bright light sliced through his skull, and he quickly closed his eyes again.

Movement came from nearby, followed by a voice. "Try that again, and we will find someone else to take your place."

Chris opened his eyes to find the woman standing over him. She held a finger over her watch, a ready smile twisting her lips.

He nodded, swallowing hard as the collar pressed against his throat.

"This is for the greater good, Christopher," the doctor continued. "Without us, you would already be dead. At least here, we have given you a fighting chance. Trust me when I say the government interrogators are not nearly as humane."

She stood then, waving a hand at the guards. "Get him up."

Rough hands grasped Chris beneath his shoulders and hauled him to his feet. He stumbled as they held him, struggling to control his legs. They jerked and twitched, refusing to obey, but eventually he got them firmly on the ground. Even so, the guards did not release him, perhaps knowing from experience how unstable he was.

"Bring him," the woman said as she turned and opened the door.

Chris's gaze lingered on the dead boy as the guards dragged him from the room. William still lay where he had fallen, still and silent, eyes wide and staring from the lifeless husk of his body.

Then they were outside, marching back down long white corridors. Distantly, Chris thought they were heading for the cells, but he paid no attention to his surroundings. His mind was elsewhere, locked away in the room with William, the dead eyes still staring at him.

It's your fault. The thought ate at him.

William had never stood a chance. The minute they'd entered the room, the boy's life had been forfeit. These people had known it, had wanted it to happen.

Doors slammed as they moved deeper into the facility. He knew where they were heading now, that he would soon find himself back in the tiny cell. The others would be waiting for him. And they would know, would see the truth in his eyes.

That he was a killer.

18

The steel door to the prison block appeared ahead, the guards outside already opening it. In a blink, Chris and his captors were through, and they were marching him down the rows of cells. Only a few faces remained now to watch Chris's return.

On first glimpse, Chris thought his cell was empty. He felt a second's relief, that he might not yet have to face the accusations of his cellmates, but as the guard drew the door open, he glimpsed movement from Liz's bed. Her haggard face poked into view, and she watched in grim silence as the guards propelled Chris inside.

Steel screeched behind him, followed by the *clang* of the locking mechanism. Footsteps retreated down the corridor, fading until another *clang* announced the guards' departure from the prison block.

Standing there, Chris's legs began to shake. Gasping, he gripped the metal bar of his bunk, struggling to stay upright. He closed his eyes, waiting for Liz to speak, to hurl her accusations.

You killed him.

The words screamed in his mind, but Liz remained silent. Only the distant whisper of other prisoners could be heard. He took a deep breath, tasting the bleach in the air, the blood from a cut on his lip.

"Are you okay?" He jumped as Liz finally spoke.

He looked up then, finding Liz's big eyes watching him, and saw his own pain reflected in their sapphire depths. She sat on her bunk, knuckles white as she gripped the metal sidebar. Her eyes shone, and a single tear streaked her cheek.

"No." Chris's shoulders slumped. "You?"

She shook her head, looked away, but he had seen the guilt in her eyes. The truth hung over the room like a blanket, smothering them.

They were alive. And that could only mean one thing.

Chris took a better grip of his bunk and hauled himself up. Crawling across the sagging mattress, he collapsed into his pillow. Then he turned and saw Liz still watching him. Her lips trembled. There was no sign of the proud, defiant girl he'd first seen in the cages. The last few days, last few hours, had broken her.

Broken us both, a voice reminded him.

Chris pushed himself up and twisted to face Liz. "Did you…?" His voice trailed off. He couldn't finish the question.

Her crystal eyes found his. "Yes," she whispered.

A chill went through Chris at her words. He stared at her, noticing now the purple bruise on her cheek, the dried blood on her lip. His eyes travelled lower and found the swollen black skin beneath her collar. He shuddered. Her struggle had been far more real than his. He remembered the boy Joshua, guessed he was the one…

"What happened?" he asked.

Liz closed her eyes. "I didn't mean…" She sucked in a breath, and her eyes flashed open. "I didn't *want* to," she growled.

Chris nodded, leaning back against the concrete wall. "You did what you had to."

"He would have killed me," she continued as though he had not spoken. "I had to do it. He left me no choice…"

Chris felt a sudden urge to wrap his arms around the young woman, to hold her until the pain left her. This was a side of Liz he had not seen, a vulnerability beneath the armor she'd worn from the first moment he'd laid eyes on her. Gone was the hardness, the distant air of superiority. The foulness of this place had consumed everything else, had reduced them both to shadows of their former selves.

He could almost feel his humanity fading away, slipping through his fingers like grains of rice. With each fresh atrocity he witnessed, with every awful thing they forced him to do, he lost another part of himself, took one step closer to becoming the animal they thought him to be. One way or another, soon he would cease to exist. Nothing would remain of the boy his mother had raised.

"It doesn't matter," Chris said. Liz looked up at his words, and he continued, his voice breaking. "Whether you killed him or not, only one of you was ever walking out of that room. After my…after William fell, he couldn't stand, couldn't defend himself. A doctor came. She executed him."

A sharp hiss of breath came from Liz, but it was a long time before she replied. "Who are these people?"

Monsters, Chris thought, but did not speak the word.

Across from him, Liz started to cough. A long, drawn-out series of wheezes and gasps rattled from her chest, going on and on, until her face was flushed red and her brow creased with pain. Finally, she leaned back against the wall, panting for breath.

"Are you okay?" Chris whispered.

Liz opened her eyes and stared at him. "Of course, city boy. I can take a beating."

Chris winced. His own anger rose but he bit back a curt reply. There was no point taking offense. He could see her pain, knew where the anger came from. He had not missed the coldness with which she addressed himself and their cellmates at times, her hesitation to join their conversations.

Another rattle came from her chest as she laid her head back against the wall.

"We're not all bad, you know," he said at last. "Not all rich, either. There are a lot of people who disagree with the government now, even in the cities. There have been protests…"

"Protests?" Liz coughed, her voice wry. "Well, nice to hear you're getting out."

Chris sighed. "I understand—"

"You don't," Liz said, cutting him off. "You think you do, but you don't. You can't. Because while you lived your cozy life in the city, I was forced onto the streets. Not because I wanted to, not because I had a choice, but because everyone I knew was dead. Slaughtered."

Shivering, Chris opened his mouth to reply, then thought better of it.

Liz eyed him for a moment before continuing: "I had nowhere to go, no one left to turn to. I thought the police would help, that they would protect me. But when they came, they looked at me like I was nothing, like I was an inconvenience to them. They would have arrested me, thrown me in some place like this if I hadn't run."

Chris looked away from the pain in Liz's eyes. He stared at his hands, the bruises on his knuckles. His stomach clenched with guilt.

"I'm sorry," he whispered at last. "You shouldn't have been treated that way. It's not right." He paused. "Was it a *Chead*?"

Liz flinched at the word. When she did not reply, Chris went on. "Mom always said something needed to be done, that her father would have been ashamed with what's happened since the war. We should never have let things get so bad." He took a breath. "But that doesn't change what I said. We're not all evil, Liz. Some of us want to fix things, want the government to be held accountable."

"So I should just give all of you the benefit of the doubt? For decades you ignored the *Chead*, let them terrorize the countryside. You only cared when they came for you." Liz snapped.

"No," Chris replied softly. "You should judge us by our own actions, not those of others." He breathed out. "A long time ago, I might have hated you too, Liz. Feared you for being different, for speaking with a rural accent."

"But not now?"

He shook his head. "No…" He trailed off, remembering a

time long ago. "When I was younger, I was running late getting home from school. It was getting dark, and we don't live in a good neighborhood. When I was nearly home, a man stepped out of an alleyway. He had a knife."

"Let me guess, he was from the country too?"

Chris laughed softly. "No, he spoke like a normal person." He couldn't help but tease her for the assumption. "But I think he was an addict of some sort—his eyes were wild and his hands were shaking. Before I had a chance to reach for my bag, he swung the knife at me, caught me in the shoulder. I still have the scar…"

Liz nodded. "I saw."

Chris glanced across at her, his cheeks warming. He remembered his embarrassment when they'd been forced to remove their clothes. Apparently, Liz had allowed her eyes to roam more than he had.

"What does this have to do with anything, Chris?"

Chris shrugged. "I think he would have killed me if someone else hadn't come along." He paused, looking across at Liz. "I don't know where he came from, but suddenly there was a man standing between us. *He* spoke with a rural accent, told the mugger to leave. When the man didn't listen, my rescuer took his knife away and sent him running."

"And this suddenly changed your mind about us?"

Chris shrugged. "Not overnight, no. But the man walked me home, right to my front door. He even helped mom with my wound. He didn't have to help me, could have left me to die, dismissed me as some spoiled brat who deserved it. But he chose to help me instead. Since then, I've tried to do the same. To give people a chance, whoever they are."

Liz let out a long sigh. "And you want the same from me now?" she asked. "Because some man from the country saved you from a mugger?"

Chris chuckled. "It would be nice to start with a clean slate."

"After today, I'm not sure that's possible for us, Chris. Joshua's blood is on my hands…"

"No," Chris replied firmly. "It's on theirs."

Liz nodded, but they both knew the words meant little. They might not have had a choice, but that did little to lessen the burden.

"We're all in this together now, aren't we?" Liz repeated Ashley's words from all those days ago, on the day they had arrived.

Chris's gut clenched as he realized that she and Sam still had not returned.

On the other bed, Liz continued, her voice hesitant. "Okay, Chris," she whispered. "I'll give you a chance."

"Thank you," he said after a while.

Silence settled around them then. Chris stared up at the ceiling, struggling to resolve the emotions battling within him. William's face drifted through his thoughts, his eyes wide and staring, but the guilt felt a little less now. Liz had faced the same question, given the same answer.

Somehow, that made things just a little easier to bear.

Long hours ticked past and the others did not return. Chris and Liz waited in the hushed stillness of the cell, listening to the thump of the guard's boots outside, the whisper of voices from the other cells. Liz's breath grew more ragged.

Finally, the bang of the outer door announced the arrival of newcomers. The soft tread of footsteps followed, moving down the corridor. Metal screeched as cell doors opened, and the footsteps continued on towards them.

Chris sat up as shadows fell across the bars of their cell. Relief swelled in his chest when he saw Ashley and Sam standing outside. Hinges squeaked as the door opened and they stumbled inside. Sad smiles touched their faces as they saw Chris and Liz.

"So," Sam breathed. "You're alive."

19

Angela shoved the door to Halt's office open without pausing to knock and strode inside. She glimpsed surprise on the harsh lines of her supervisor's face as he looked up, though it vanished by the time the door slammed shut behind her. Anger took its place as Halt half-rose from his chair, fists clenched hard on his desk.

"What—?"

"You have no right!" Angela yelled, cutting him off.

Halt straightened. "I have every right," he said, his voice low, dangerous.

Hands trembling, Angela approached his desk. "It's not ready, Halt," she hissed. "You can't start those trials tomorrow. I need more time."

Rising, Halt walked around his desk, until he stood towering over her. Angela stared back, defiant, anger feeding her strength. She had just learned Halt planned to initiate the next phase of the project tomorrow. The same project she had dedicated the last five years of her life to.

"The Director wants results, Doctor Fallow," Halt said between clenched teeth, "and you've been stalling."

Angela refused to back down. "I've been doing my job," she snapped, "and I'm telling you, *the virus is not ready!*"

Halt smiled. "I've looked over your work, Fallow." Angela shivered at his tone. "And I say it's ready. After all, fortune favors the bold."

The words of the old Latin proverb curled around Angela's mind as she stepped back. They reminded her of Halt during her early days. The government had sent him to her after she'd discovered the truth about the *Chead*, bringing her their new virus.

Angela drew in a breath to steady herself. "There are still problems with the uptake," she said. "You could kill them all with your recklessness."

"The alterations will work—"

"Of course they will," Angela interrupted. "Animal trials have shown us as much. It's their immune response that concerns me. Their bodies will tear themselves apart fighting the virus."

Halt waved a hand as he moved back behind his desk. "Should that eventuate, we will administer immunosuppressants until the chromosomal changes have set." He sat back at his desk, one eyebrow raised. "Is that all?"

"Immunosuppressants?" Angela pressed her palms against the desk and leaned in. "We'll have to move them to an isolation room, watch them around the clock. They wouldn't last a day in the cells."

"Whatever it takes, Fallow." Halt stared her down. "We can't wait any longer. The President himself wants answers. We'll be shut down if we don't provide them soon. The attacks are growing worse. The authorities are desperate."

"What?"

Halt leaned back in his chair. "We have underestimated the *Chead* for too long. The Director should have given us the funding we needed for this years ago. There was an attack in San Francisco yesterday. They've reached the capital, Fallow."

Doubt gnawed at Angela's chest at his words. "You really think this is the answer?"

"Of course." Halt regarded her with a detached curiosity. "Do not lose focus now, Doctor Fallow. Not when we're so close. This project will change everything. When we succeed, the

Western Allied States will herald in a new era of human evolution. The *Chead* will be hunted down and eradicated, our enemies at home and abroad consigned to the pages of history."

Staring into her superior's eyes, Angela shuddered. Naked greed lurked in their grey depths. For the first time, she allowed herself to look around, to take in the grisly display lining the walls of Halt's office. The sight she had been doing her best to ignore.

Halt's office was lined with shelves, each holding dozens of jars filled with clear fluids. Suspended in the liquid within them were animals of every shape and size. Birds and lizards, cats and snakes and what looked like a platypus stared down at her, their eyes blank and dead. An opossum curled around its ringed tail on the shelf behind Halt's head, while beside it a baby chimpanzee hugged its chest. With its eyes closed, it might have been sleeping.

Angela looked away, struggling to hide her disgust from Halt.

"Soon they will all be obsolete," Halt commented, noticing her discomfort.

"Yes." She almost choked on the word.

But at what cost? she added silently.

Halt eyed her closely. "Was there anything else, Doctor Fallow?"

Angela shook her head. She knew when she was defeated. Turning, she all but ran from the room. She closed the door carefully behind her, her anger spent. Once outside, she placed a hand against the wall, shivering with sudden fear. Events were accelerating now, slipping beyond her control, and it was all she could do to keep up.

In her mind, she saw images of San Francisco, the steep roads teeming with life. She imagined the devastation a *Chead* would cause in such a place, the mindless slaughter. Bodies would pile up as police struggled to reach the scene through the traffic-clogged streets. How long might the *Chead* have run rampant?

Straightening, Angela turned from Halt's door and started down the corridor. Tomorrow, if they succeeded, the world would change. Humanity's evolution would take one giant leap forward, and one way or another, there would be no going back.

A sudden doubt rose within her, a fear for what was to come. What if they were wrong? What if they failed, and it was all for naught?

And what if they succeeded? What then?

Her skin tingled as she recalled Halt's words, heard again his triumphant declaration.

Our enemies, at home and abroad, will be consigned to the pages of history.

20

A cold breeze blew across Liz's neck, rustling the branches above her head. She picked up the pace, eyeing the lengthening shadows. She was close to home now, the path familiar beneath her feet, but it was a steep climb and she had no wish to attempt it in the dark.

The forest was eerily silent, the usual evening chorus of birds and insects mute. It put her on edge, and her eyes scanned the scraggly trees neighboring the path, seeking danger. Their dense branches shifted with the wind, but otherwise there was no sign of movement.

She moved on.

Behind her, the path wound down through the forest. The mountain on which their homestead perched stood alone amidst the Californian floodplains, looking out across their broad expanse. All around the rock were the lands of the Flores family—or at least the lands they managed. Once they'd been theirs, but no longer.

Liz smiled as she approached the final bend in the track. The house was only a thirty-minute walk up the mountain, but she was glad to see the end of it. It had been a long journey from San Francisco.

The trees opened out, revealing the homestead sitting at the trail's end. Liz listened for the first shouts of welcome. Her family employed a dozen laborers on the property, and most were like family to her.

Silence.

Liz shivered as she closed on the homestead. Her eyes flickered around the collection of buildings, searching for movement, for signs of life.

It was only then she saw the bodies.

They lay strewn across the ground, torn and broken, their faces grey and dead. Blood splattered the walls nearby, streaked across the peeling paint. She looked over the bodies, lingering on their faces. There was Nancy, the old woman who had helped raise her, who had cooked meals while her mother helped in the fields. And there, Henry, the man her father thought of as a brother.

Standing amidst the carnage, Liz turned to the building she called home. Without thinking, she started towards it. Her movements were jerky, her breath coming in desperate sobs. Reaching the old wooden door, she pushed it open.

It swung inwards without resistance, revealing the wreckage within. Swallowing a scream, Liz staggered inside, taking in the shattered plaster walls, the torn-up floorboards. Dust and rubble lay strewn across the floor, mingling with the blood pooling at the end of the corridor.

Barely daring to breathe, Liz stepped inside the house. With cautious footsteps, she slid down the corridor, her eyes fixed on the blood. She winced at each soft thump of her boots, the sound impossibly loud in the silent house.

The corner neared. In a sudden rush, Liz darted forward, desperate to see…

Liz screamed and threw up her arms, tearing herself from the nightmare. Her eyes snapped open, but absolute darkness blanketed her, and she screamed again, thrashing against the tangle of covers wrapped around her. She rolled, slamming into the safety bar. It groaned and gave way, and suddenly Liz was falling, a final scream tearing from her throat…

Thud.

Agony lanced through her arms as she struck the concrete. The last tendrils of the dream fell away, plunging her back into reality—and the pain that went with it. She groaned, her throat burning as it pressed against the cold steel of her collar.

"What?" a voice shouted, somewhere in the darkness.

"Who's there?" someone else yelled.

"Liz?" She recognized Chris's voice.

Above her, Chris's bunk rattled. Then hands were reaching for her, grasping her shoulder, pulling her up.

"Are you alright?" Chris's voice came again.

Half in shock, Liz couldn't manage more than a nod. Distantly, she was surprised at the tenderness in his words, his sudden concern. A second later, she realized he could not see her nod. Opening her mouth, she managed a croak: "Yes."

As sanity slowly returned, embarrassment swept through Liz. She closed her eyes, silently berating herself for her panic. It had been so long since she'd had the dream—months, maybe even a year. Why had it returned now, after all this time?

"What happened?" Sam's voice was heavy with sleep.

"Sorry," Liz murmured, her heart still racing. "Just a bad dream."

"Some bad dream." Ashley's hand settled on her shoulder. "Go back to bed, Sam. You need your beauty sleep."

A string of inaudible mumbles came from Sam's bed, but was quickly followed by snoring.

Arms shaking, Liz pulled herself up, helped by Chris on one side, Ashley on the other.

"It's okay," she murmured and then suppressed a groan.

Her throat was aflame, throbbing with each beat of her heart. She tried to swallow, but it only made the pain worse. The steel collar dug into her swollen throat. Gasping, she fought for breath.

"What's wrong?" Chris asked in the darkness.

"My throat," Liz gasped.

"Water." Somehow, Chris understood. "Ashley, help me get her to the sink."

Sharp pain sliced Liz's shin where she'd landed as she tried to take her weight. With a silent moan, she collapsed against her friends. To her right, Ashley swore as the shift in weight sent her stumbling into the bed. Then she straightened, getting her body beneath Liz's shoulder, and helped her the few steps to the sink.

Liz slumped to the ground as Ashley released her. The sound of running water followed, while Chris helped her to sit comfortably.

"Here," Ashley whispered. "Open your mouth, Liz. The water will help."

Liz obeyed as Ashley fumbled at her face in the pitch-black. She almost lost an eye before Ashley finally found her lips. Cool water dribbled into her mouth, trickling from the palm of the girl's hands. Swallowing slowly, Liz sighed as the cold spread down her throat.

Ashley repeated the procedure three more times before Liz's breathing eased. At last she croaked for them to stop, and they settled together on Ashley's bed.

"How are you feeling now?" Ashley whispered.

In the other bed, Sam was still snoring. Listening in the darkness, Liz found herself jealous of the boy's ability to sleep through anything. She desperately needed the release of sleep, to escape the pain of her beaten body. But she knew it would not come now, not after the dream.

"I'm okay," she breathed. "You should go back to sleep."

A soft chuckle came from the girl. "My bed's a little crowded now. It's okay, I think the lights will turn on soon."

Her words were met by a distant clang, followed by a low buzzing in the ceiling. Liz blinked as white light flooded the room. She raised an eyebrow at Ashley, sitting beside her, yellow eyes ringed by shadow, scarlet locks tangled with sleep. A smile tugged at her lips.

A groan came from the opposite bed as Sam rolled over and pulled the pillow over his head.

"God," came Chris's voice from her other side.

Liz turned to face him. "What?"

He blinked and shook his head. "Your neck—no wonder you couldn't breathe. It's a rather attractive shade of purple."

Liz touched a finger to her throat, but flinched as the muscles spasmed. She bit her lip, swallowing the pain. "I've had worse."

She felt Chris shudder, but he said nothing.

For the next few minutes they sat in silence, listening to the growing crescendo of Sam's snores. Finally, Ashley stood and crossed to his bed. Taking a hold of his blanket, she tore it away, exposing his half-naked body to the cold. His curses echoed from the walls as Ashley retreated to her bed, bringing Sam's cover with her.

Liz chuckled as Ashley spread the cover over them, trying to ignore the burning from her throat. "Thanks, I was getting cold," she said, grinning at the other girl.

"Hey!" Sam was sitting up now, blinking hard in the fluorescent light. He tossed his pillow across the room. Chris caught it easily and placed it behind his head.

Liz smiled as a little of the weight lifted from her heart. Wriggling her backside, she snuggled in beneath the blanket, basking in the warm bodies to either side of her. They grinned as Sam found his shirt from the night before and pulled it over his broad shoulders. Liz watched with a tinge of disappointment as he covered himself.

"Hey, my eyes are up here, ladies," Sam laughed.

Liz snorted. "Like I'd be interested in a city slugger like you, Sam."

Ashley and Chris chuckled while Sam rolled his eyes. Then the clang of the outer door echoed down the corridor, plunging the room into silence. The smiles fell from their faces as they shared sad glances, the weight of yesterday's guilt returning.

"What happens next?" Chris murmured.

Sam's eyes flickered towards Ashley. "After we…survived, you two showed up," Sam replied with a shrug. "You know the rest."

Beside her, Ashley shifted on the bed. "Yesterday, on the training field, the doctors were talking," she said in a low voice. "I overheard a bit. They were talking about things moving ahead. So who knows what comes next?"

The bed shifted again as Chris pulled himself up. A pang of sadness touched Liz as his warmth left her side. He moved to the bars and glanced down the corridor. "Well, whatever comes next, at least breakfast is on its way." He spoke the words with a false lightness, failing to hide the strain beneath, but Liz appreciated his attempt to brighten the gloomy discussion.

Sam groaned. "Don't suppose it's something other than that gruel they call oatmeal?"

"Sure, what's your order? I'll give them a shout." Chris laughed.

"I'll take some eggs with a side of bacon. Maybe some hash browns. Oh, and a burger. You got all that?"

"How about a television while you're at it, Chris?" Ashley added.

Shaking his head, Chris returned to the bed and slid in beside Liz. "Ah, bacon. I can't even remember the last time we had that at home."

As his warmth returned Liz found herself sliding closer, until her side pressed up against him. A tingle ran up her arm at the touch, and she held her breath, waiting for him to pull away. When he didn't move, she smiled, only then recalling his comment about the bacon. Her grin spread. While the food on the ranch had not technically been theirs to eat, her family had made an art of pilfering extra supplies whenever they were available. Bacon had been just one of the many luxury food items she'd enjoyed.

"Oh, I don't know, back on the farm we had bacon and eggs for breakfast most days. It gets a little old."

She laughed as the three of them turned to stare at her. Unfortunately, her mirth was too much for her throat, and she broke into a coughing fit. It was a few minutes before she found her voice again.

"Country secret," she croaked at last, and the others groaned.

The screeching wheels of the breakfast cart came to a halt outside their cell. The guard banged his rifle against the bars while the other opened the grate through which they passed the food.

"Come and get it." The guard with the gun laughed. "Big day for you, I hear."

Chris retrieved the four bowls of oatmeal, much to Sam's chagrin, and they sat down to their meal.

Afterwards, the four of them lay back and waited, listening for the sound of the outer door. Closing her eyes, Liz did her best to ignore the agony that was her neck. Her good mood quickly fell away as the pain beat down on her. Silently, she cursed the doctors, the guards and their guns, even poor, dead Joshua for his vicious attack.

"What do you think that guard meant?" Sam asked after an hour, addressing what they had all been wondering at.

"Nothing good," Chris offered unhelpfully.

"Well, they need us alive for something," Ashley put in. She had joined Sam on the other bed now, surrendering her bed to Liz and Chris. "Whatever this place is, it's top secret. My parents weren't the most connected of individuals in the government, but most things reached the rumor mill at some point. I don't think this place was ever mentioned. As far as the media are concerned, the children of traitors were..." Her voice trailed off, and Liz felt a pang of sadness for the girl.

Without speaking, Sam reached up and placed an arm around Ashley, drawing her into a hug. Watching them, Liz's sadness grew, rising from some lonely chasm inside her. The last two years had been long and hard, and more than once she had found herself craving the touch of another human being. Licking her lips, she glanced at Chris, then gave herself a silent shake. Drawing up her knees, she hugged them to her chest.

Movement came from beside her, but it was just Chris rearranging himself on the bed. He spoke into the uncomfortable silence. "Maybe it's the same with our families then. Maybe they've been taken someplace else." There was no mistaking the tremor of hope in his voice.

As the others nodded, Liz closed her eyes. The others might still cling to the thought their families lived, but there was no such hope for hers.

"Wouldn't that be nice?" Sam replied with false cheer. "We can all have a reunion someday, share torture stories around the campfire—"

"Shut up, Sam." Ashley pushed him away and looked at Chris. "We can only hope, Chris. Although my sister..." She bowed her head, eyes shining. "She got in the way. They never gave her a chance."

Before any of them could respond, a loud clang echoed down the corridor.

The four of them exchanged a long glance.

"Showtime," Sam whispered.

21

The screech of iron rollers carried down the corridor as a cell door slid open. Liz and the others jumped from their beds and pressed themselves up against the bars. Head hard against the cold steel, Liz strained for a glimpse of what was happening. The faces of their fellow inmates appeared behind the bars of the other cells.

At the very limits of her view, Liz could just make out a group of doctors talking quietly around the cell at the end of the corridor. Beside them, guards were shouting at the occupants. They carried steel batons now, instead of the familiar rifles of the past few days.

The guards disappeared into the cell. The raised voices of the prisoners echoed down to them, followed by the muffled thud of steel on flesh.

Retreating from the bars, Liz looked at the others. Sam and Chris stared back, their eyes wide, uncertainty written across their faces. Ashley only pursed her lips, her gaze roaming the cell.

Liz returned to the bars as a girl's cry echoed down the corridor. She watched the doctors gathering around a steel trolley. One was leaning over an open drawer on the side of the cart. Reaching inside, he drew out a packet of syringes. Vials of a clear liquid followed, which he handed out to the other doctors. Together, they turned and followed the guards into the cell. Another shriek echoed down the corridor, a boy's this time.

"What's going on?" Chris asked from behind her.

Liz glanced at the others. "It's some sort of injection. They've got syringes and a trolley loaded with God only knows what else."

As she finished speaking, a long, drawn-out scream erupted from the cell at the end of the corridor. Liz flinched, pressing her face hard against the bars. Distantly she remembered the faces of the two captives in that cell: a young girl with blonde hair, a boy with dreadlocks.

The girl's scream slowly faded, but before it ceased the boy's voice joined in, carrying the awful notes of agony to their little cell. Liz shuddered, fighting the urge to cover her ears. The shrieks rose and fell, twisting and cracking, almost inhuman in their anguish.

Turning, she saw the blood draining from the other's faces, felt her own cheeks grow cold with a terrible fear.

Finally the screams died away, leaving only silence.

The screech of trolley wheels on concrete followed as the doctors made their way to the next cell.

"What do we do?" Chris asked again.

"We fight," came Ashley's reply.

Liz turned and stared at the girl, her heart thudding hard in her chest. "*What?*" From down the corridor came the rattle of another cell opening. "What about the collars—?" She broke off as a cough tore at her throat.

Staggering past the others, she fumbled at the sink and turned the faucet. As she drank, Ashley continued: "Those batons, why do they need them?" Her voice was calm now. "They haven't needed them until now."

"It's like you said before," Sam mused. "They don't want us dead. They've been saving us for something. For *this*."

"Really?" Chris snapped. "Because I'm pretty sure they just killed those two."

"They're not using the collars," Liz croaked as she re-joined them. The realization had come as she pressed her mouth to the faucet, making the collar dig into her neck. "No guns *or* collars."

Sam grinned and cracked his knuckles. "In that case, I agree with Ashley."

Liz leaned against the pole of her bunk bed, drawing reassurance from its solidity. She looked at the others, her stomach fluttering. Sam looked more alive than she'd ever seen him, his eyes alight with a frightening rage. Chris stood beside him, tense and ready, one eye on the door to the cell.

And Ashley…just looked like Ashley—cool, calm, collected. She pushed past the boys as another scream rattled from the walls. As Liz and the others took up station near the door, Ashley crouched between the beds and lifted a piece of railing which lay wedged against the wall. Liz blinked, realizing it was the broken safety railing for her bed.

Ashley offered Sam the bar. Teeth flashing in a grin, he took it and held it up to the light. The three parts of the rail formed a distorted U-shape, with two short pieces of steel jutting from the longer center piece.

"Work at the joints, see if you can break them apart," Ashley said.

As Sam set to work trying to separate the bars, Ashley moved to the front of the cell and resumed her watch. Liz joined her, and together they followed their captors' slow progress through the prison.

"They're done with us," Chris whispered behind them.

Outside, the screams continued, at times fading, only to resume after the doctors entered the next cell.

"No," Ashley whispered. Her eyes took on a haunted look. "I think they're only just getting started."

"Here." Liz turned and Sam offered her one of the smaller bars. He grinned. "Just pretend they're city sluggers like me."

Liz smiled grimly. Silently, she reached out and squeezed his arm. He nodded and moved to Ashley and Chris, offering them the other two bars. Ashley took one, but Chris shook his head. His eyes did not leave the corridor, but he spoke from the side of his mouth.

"I'd prefer to keep my hands free, thanks."

Outside, the doctors had reached the cell directly across from them. Its only occupant stood at the bars, watching as the doctors drew to a halt outside. His eyes were bloodshot and tears streamed down his face.

"Please, I never did anything wrong." His voice was feeble, barely a whisper.

He retreated into his cell as the guards slid open the door. Before he could so much as raise his fists, they were on him, batons flashing in the fluorescent lights. A few seconds later they had him pinned to the bed. Without preamble, the doctors entered the cell. One pulled down the inmate's pants, while another prepared the needle. They gave him an injection into his buttocks, then the doctors and guards retreated from the cell, slamming the door closed behind them.

Liz flinched as the boy screamed and began to writhe. Then the guards stepped between them and the other cell, and there was no more time to consider their neighbor's plight.

Clenching her hand hard around her improvised weapon, Liz watched as the guards gathered near the door. The pain in her throat had strangely faded, leaving only a dull ache. Blood pounded in her ears as she tensed, readying herself.

"Stand back, drop those," one of the guards ordered, eyeing their makeshift batons.

When they didn't move, he turned to look at the doctors.

"What are you waiting for?" Doctor Radly's voice carried into the cell. "Get in there and take those off them. You know we can't use the collars. We can't have any interference with their nervous system."

The guard nodded and reached out to unlock the door. The others gathered behind him, seven in total, their batons held ready.

A strange calm settled over Liz as the door slid open, the terror of the past few days falling away. This was it. This was their only chance. If they failed, she knew in her heart they were lost.

As the first of the guards moved into the cell, movement flickered beside Liz. She turned in time to see Chris lunge forward. The guard grinned and raised his baton, but Chris was faster still. Leaping lightly from the concrete floor, he twisted in the air to avoid the guard's blow, and then drove his boot into the side of the man's head.

Liz gaped as the man's eyes rolled up in his skull and he collapsed to the ground.

Chris landed lightly in the doorway and retreated to re-join them.

"Six to go." He grinned, his smile infectious.

Shaking her head, Liz gripped the metal bar tighter and tried to hide her shock.

Outside, the remaining guards grabbed their fallen comrade by the feet and dragged his unconscious body out into the corridor. One of the doctors crouched beside him and placed a stethoscope to his chest. Radly glanced down at the man, then back at the guards. Each of them dwarfed even Sam's large frame, but still they stood, hesitating in the hallway.

"Well?" Radly snapped. "What are we paying you for? Get in there!"

The guards shared a glance, then approached together. Pushing the sliding door wide open, they entered as a group this time. They paused for a second in the entryway, hefting their batons, then rushed forward.

Liz tensed as a guard came at her, his baton flashing for her face. She ducked, and the hackles on her neck tingled as it whistled over her head. Then she lifted her own weapon and drove it into the man's midriff.

The blow caught him as he was moving forward, and his own weight drove the air from his lungs. Liz lifted her bar to strike him again, then threw herself to the side as another guard swung at her. The clang of steel rang out as the baton left a dent in the bunk bed behind her.

Recovering, she turned and found the first guard already straightening. The two of them bore down on her, forcing her away from the others.

Liz gripped her makeshift weapon tight, knowing she was

hopelessly outmatched. Snarling, she threw herself forward anyway. They grinned, raised their batons. Then another guard staggered into them, sending them stumbling forward. Seeing her chance, Liz swung her pole into the face of the nearest guard.

There was a satisfying *crunch* as her baton struck home, and he dropped without a sound. She leapt for the gap he'd left, trying to re-join the others, but the second guard had already recovered. He stepped in to block her, his baton already in motion. The blow caught her in the stomach, knocking the breath from her lungs and sending her backwards into the wall.

Groaning, she tried to recover, but a fist caught her in the side of the face. Her feet crumpled beneath the force of the blow, and she slid sideways into the crook between the wall and the bunk. Tasting blood in her mouth, she tried to get her hands and knees beneath her, but a heavy boot crashed into her back, pinning her down.

Her ears ringing, Liz twisted, desperate for a glimpse of the others. But the fight was already over. In the narrow confines, the guards' weight and numbers had made short work of the four prisoners. Sam lay immobilized on his own bed, one arm twisted behind his back and a guard's knee pressed between his shoulder blades. Ashley was similarly restrained on the floor nearby, while Chris still stood, his arms held by a man on either side of him. The last guard was just getting to his feet, a nasty bruise on his forehead.

"About time," Radly's sarcastic voice came from somewhere out of view. "Would you like something easier next time? Maybe some toddlers?"

The guards were silent as the doctors filed in, carrying an assortment of vials and syringes. As the doctors prepared themselves, Radly looked around the room. His eyes settled on Liz. "Get her up."

Tears stung Liz's eyes as a rough hand grasped a handful of her hair and pulled. Screaming, she drove a fist into the man's side, but the blow hardly seemed to faze him. A sharp pain came from her scalp as he pulled again. Kicking and screaming, Liz was hauled to her feet.

"This one's feisty," the guard commented as he tossed her onto Ashley's bed.

Before Liz could free herself, a guard landed on her back. An awful helplessness welled in her as she tried and failed to shift his weight. Pain lanced from her scalp again as the guard yanked her head back, forcing her to look at them.

"Stay still," he growled in her ear.

"Please don't do this," Ashley pleaded from the floor.

The thud of a boot striking flesh silenced her desperate words. A low groan followed. Liz twisted again, trying to get a glimpse of her friend, but the white coat of a doctor moved to block her view. Doctor Radly stared down at her.

"Enough," Radly said, his tone brooking no argument.

Unlike Halt, Radly did not appear to take any joy in their pain. Rather, he didn't seem to care about their comfort one way or another. He moved around the cell with a cold efficiency, retrieving a stoppered vial from the hands of another doctor. Lifting a nasty-looking syringe, he eyed the thick needle for a second before driving it through the vial's rubber stopper. Then he drew back the plunger and the liquid disappeared into the syringe.

"Doctor Faulks," Radly said, addressing someone standing just outside of Liz's view, "this is the PERV-A strain?"

"Yes," a woman's reply came quickly. "We've already finished with the B strain. The rest are marked down for PERV-A."

Nodding, Radly turned back to Liz. "Hold her." Liz shuddered as the guard shifted, taking a firmer grip of her shoulders.

From the corner of her eye, she watched Radly approach, his gloved hands cradling the syringe. He disappeared from her line of vision. Seconds later, firm hands tugged at her pants, and a cold breeze blew across her backside. She tensed, pushing back against her assailant's relentless strength.

A sigh came from behind her. "This will go easier for you if you relax, Ms. Flores."

Hearing her last name sent a bolt of shock through Liz. For a second she hesitated, then bit off a string a profanity that would have made even her father blush.

Another sigh, then a cold cloth pressed against her butt-cheek. A shiver raced up her spine, more shock from the violation than from the cold. A low, guttural growl built in her throat, and the guard's knee pressed harder into the small of her back. She no longer cared. A desperate horror was growing within her, an awful fear, a need to break free.

She screamed again, writhing and bucking beneath the guard, straining to shift his weight.

A sudden pinch came from her naked backside, followed by a strange pressure that spread quickly across her cheek. It was gentle at first, a cold numbness that tingled as it went. But it warmed quickly, like a fire gathering heat, until her muscles were aflame from its touch. The tingling raced outwards, spreading to her legs and back.

Liz gasped, fighting the pain, desperate to fend it off. She gritted her teeth, tensing against its relentless spread. The pressure on her back vanished as the guard released her, but by then she barely noticed. Her attention was elsewhere, her focus fixed on the sensations rippling through her body.

Then, as though a switch had been flicked, the muscles down the length of her back locked in a sudden cramp. Pain unlike any Liz had experienced closed around her, walling her off from the world, trapping her in the fiery arms of its cage. Her eyes snapped open, but all she saw were stars, whirling across her vision, blinding in their brilliance. In the distance she heard a scream, a girl's voice tearing at the blackness of her mind, but she could do nothing to help her now.

Agony engulfed her body, her mind, her very soul.

III

REBIRTH

22

C*old.*

The thought filtered through the thick sludge of Chris's mind, parting the darkness like a curtain. Then it was all around him, wrapping his body in an icy blanket, turning his breath to ragged gasps. A shiver caught him, rippling down his body, throwing off the last dregs of sleep.

Frozen air burned his nostrils as he inhaled, bringing with it the familiar tang of bleach. But there was more to the scent now, an underlying stench of rot and decay that made his stomach swirl. Opening his mouth, he tasted the metallic reek of blood and vomit.

Sound was the next sense to return. His ears tingled, catching the murmur of a breath, the creak of metal joints moving beneath restless bodies, the hiss of an air conditioner. From somewhere in the room came the whisper of machines, the familiar whine of overhead lights.

I'm alive. The words whispered in Chris's mind, though he couldn't quite recall why that surprised him.

Keeping his eyes closed, he sucked in another breath, struggling to restore the shattered pieces of his consciousness. Dimly he remembered the fire burning up his spine, spreading to his chest, filling his lungs. But there was no pain now, only the dull ache of his muscles, as though they had lain unused for countless days.

How long? His brow creased.

How long had he lain here, unconscious, in the clutches of whatever drug the doctors had given him?

Sounds came from all around him, growing louder, echoing as though from a wide expanse. Chains rattled as he moved his arms, and he felt the cold touch of steel restraining his wrists. Without opening his eyes, Chris knew he'd been handcuffed to the bed.

Apparently, the doctors weren't taking any chances with their patients.

Memories drifted through the darkness of his thoughts, rising as though from a fog. Images of the fight flashed by, the *crack* as Sam fell to a baton, the *thud* of Ashley hitting the floor. He had not seen what happened to Liz, not until the guards had overwhelmed him, and he'd found her curled up in the corner.

Helpless, he had watched as they'd lifted Liz onto the bed and injected her with something. Her screams had been instant and horrifying, so deafening that even the guards had retreated from her. Her agony tore at his soul, begged for him to save her from the monsters. But he had been powerless against the raw strength of the men on either side of him.

His heart beat harder at the memory. A sense of urgency took him, and he shifted his arms, testing the movement allowed by the handcuffs. The links rattled as he ran a hand along the chain and found where they attached to the bed's guardrail.

Other sounds came to him now: the beeping of a nearby machine, the whir of a pump, the hiss of air escaping tubes. His breath quickened, and he heard the beeping accelerate, matching the racing of his heart.

Somewhere in the room, a door banged. Chris froze, his fingers still clenched around the metal bar. The soft tread of footsteps crossed the room, followed by voices.

"Has the danger passed?" Halt's voice came from Chris's right.

"We think so." Chris recognized Fallow, though her voice was strained, exhausted. "It was a close thing though. I *told* you it wasn't ready."

"Perhaps," Halt replied, "but we expected losses. Despite our best efforts, some of the candidates were simply too weak to withstand the morphological alterations."

"We lost forty percent!" Chris winced as Fallow's voice cracked. He heard a sharp exhalation of breath, before she continued in a calmer voice. "I expected mortality to be less than fifteen. As it is, we barely have a viable population. If we'd had more time…"

"More time?" Halt laughed. "That is the cry of a coward, Fallow! More time, more money, always more *something!*" He took a breath. "As Archimedes once said: 'Give me a lever and a place to stand, and I will move the earth.' But us mere mortals only have the time and resources the government has provided us. And our time is up."

"The *government* will not be satisfied with a forty percent mortality rate, Halt," Fallow growled.

"No," came the head doctor's swift reply, "but if the survivors show promise, you will have won the time you need to find perfection, Fallow."

Silence followed. Slowly their footsteps came closer. Listening to the beep of the machine beside him, Chris held his breath, struggling to slow his racing heart.

"And have we succeeded, Fallow?" Halt's voice was eager.

It was a while before the woman replied. "The results are mixed. Tissue samples taken over the last few weeks show a steady integration between the host chromosomes and the viral DNA. Candidates who received the PERV-A strain have advanced more rapidly than PERV-B, and now show complete integration. However, we have yet to determine whether the altered genomes are expressing correctly."

"Excellent." There was unmasked glee in Halt's voice. "When do you expect they'll be ready to test genome expression?"

"We've taken them off the immunosuppressants. So far they've shown no adverse reactions. We expect them to wake from their comas over the next few days. Once they're conscious, we can begin testing their basic motor skills and cognitive function, to determine whether the virus had any degenerative effects..." Fallow trailed off as Halt snorted.

"We don't have time to waste on your procedures, Fallow. We need to move onto the second phase. For that we need *results*."

"I don't see how—" Fallow began.

"Don't give me that, Fallow," Halt snapped. "You know very well there is no need for your tests. As far as the Director is concerned, there is only one test the candidates need to pass."

There was a long pause before Fallow replied. "Halt..." Her voice was entreating now. "That's simply not possible. They've been unconscious for weeks. The recovery time alone...they're in no condition—"

"If the experiment succeeded, recovery time should not be an issue." Halt's voice sounded like he was just a few feet away now. "Look, this one appears to be conscious."

A tingle raced up Chris's spine at the man's words. Silently he fought the instinct to leap from the bed and flee. His arms prickled as goosebumps spread along his skin.

"You're right." Fallow's murmur seemed to come from directly overhead. "Her heartbeat has recovered to normal levels."

A girl's cry came from nearby, followed by the angry rattle of chains. Chris cracked his eyes open a fraction, desperate to see what was happening. Pain shot through his skull as white light streamed between his eyelids, momentary blinding him. Then the light faded and the room clicked into focus. Rows of beds stretched across a wide room, each occupied by an unconscious patients dressed in green gowns. A tangle of tubes and wires covered each body like a spiderweb spun around a fly. From the brief glimpse he caught, Chris guessed there were some seventy beds, though many were empty.

The girl Halt and Fallow were discussing was sitting up in the hospital bed directly across from Chris. Her back was turned to him, and both her arms were chained to the railings. Curly black hair tumbled around her shoulders, and with a shiver of recognition, Chris realized it was Liz.

She's alive!

Chris struggled to muffle his sharp intake of breath. Beside him, the beeping of the machine started to race. He clenched the sidebar of his bed until his palms hurt. Through the shadows of his eyelashes, he watched Halt move to stand over Liz.

"Incredible." Halt was studying the machine beside Liz's bed. Lines and numbers flashed across the screen, Chris guessed providing readings from the tubes and wires that covered Liz. "Look at her vitals."

Fallow stood in silence beside him, shadows ringing her eyes, her lips pursed tight.

Halt shook his head. "I would say she is fully recovered, wouldn't you, Doctor Fallow?"

Reluctantly Fallow nodded, a look of resignation coming over her face.

"Excellent, then I see no reason to delay. Get her ready."

Blood pounded in Chris's head, drowning out all reason. He didn't know what Halt had planned for Liz, what fresh horrors awaited her, but he refused to lie quietly while she faced it alone. Whatever happened, they were still in this together. For all he knew, Sam and Ashley might already be gone, but Liz still lived. He would not lose her now.

"Leave her alone," he growled, sitting up in the bed.

Liz turned towards him, her eyes widening with shock. Behind her, Fallow's face seemed to crumple, while a grin spread slowly across Halt's face. In that instant, Chris felt a pit open in his stomach; a sudden realization he had made a terrible mistake.

Still, it was worth it to see the relief sweep across Liz's face.

"Excellent." Halt clapped his hands. "Bring him, too. It may even the odds."

23

Liz shivered as Fallow unlocked the cuffs around her wrists. Blinking, she looked at the woman's face. Her features faded in and out of focus. A wave of nausea swept through Liz's stomach, and she had to clench the sidebar to steady herself.

"Are you okay?" Fallow asked.

Liz flinched as a hand touched her shoulder. "*Don't!*" she growled, leaning back.

Closing her eyes, Liz willed her stomach to settle, then opened them again. To her relief, the features of Fallow's face finally snapped into place. She blinked again, surprised to see the dark rings beneath the woman's eyes, the patchwork of tiny cracks across the skin of her cheeks, the thin red capillaries threading her eyes. Her head swam; she had never noticed so much detail in a person's face before.

"I'm sorry." Liz's ears twitched at the sound, before a harsh shriek cut through the words.

She recoiled, slapping her hands over her ears. Distantly she heard the doctor's voice over the ringing. A hand reached for her, but she twisted, falling sideways on the bed. Fallow paused, staring down at her, and then retreated a step.

Slowly the ringing died away, and Liz finally removed her hands from her ears.

"I'm sorry." Fallow's voice was a whisper now, but Liz heard it with perfect clarity. "How do you feel?"

Gritting her teeth, Liz glanced across at Chris. As their eyes met her heart lurched, and she felt again the relief that had swept through her when he'd sat up.

He's alive!

Despite the apparent odds against them, the two of them had survived whatever demented experiment the doctors had performed on them. Beside her, Fallow was removing the various tubes and wires that linked Liz to the machine.

"Why are you doing this?" Liz tried and failed to keep the loathing from her voice.

Fallow sighed, her eyes flickering away. "You'll find out soon enough, Elizabeth."

Liz stared at the grief shining from Fallow's eyes. Despite herself, she found herself pitying the woman, though she could not say why. Even so, the doctor's words triggered a sense of foreboding, and Liz pressed on, desperate to exploit the woman's weakness.

"You don't have to do this," she whispered. "Halt's gone. You could let us go, unlock our collars."

A faint smile twitched on Fallow's lips. "A tempting proposition." She shook her head. "They'd kill you both before you reached the front door. And then they'd come for me." Their eyes locked, but after a moment Fallow only smiled and continued with false humor. "Besides, you are the culmination of my life's work."

"What about *our* lives?" Chris's snarl came from behind Liz. "What right—?"

He broke off as Fallow raised a hand, her smile fading. "You know the law, Christopher. Your mother was found guilty of treason. In due time, she will answer for those crimes. As her son, you would have faced the same fate."

To Liz, Fallow's words sounded hollow, as though they left a bad taste in her mouth. Even so, after that the woman ignored their pleas. Moving to Chris, she removed the cuffs and wires. Within a few minutes she had them on their feet, dressed in fresh orange jumpsuits, and staggering around the room like senior citizens.

Liz's legs trembled with each step, refusing to obey the simplest of instructions. A dull ache was quickly spreading up her hamstrings, and several times she had to grab at neighboring beds to steady herself. Chris was no better; he managed to knock over a series of machines within two steps of leaving his bed, after which he promptly crashed to the linoleum floor.

From the corner of her eyes, Liz caught movement from several of the beds, but the doctor was too preoccupied with Chris to notice. Steadying herself, she took a moment to search the room for Ashley and Sam. But the fluorescent light caught in her eyes, and she found her vision shimmering, the room becoming a blur. By the time it cleared, Fallow was already shepherding them towards the doorway.

Outside, Liz's legs finally started to obey, though they remained stiff and sore. Chris was steadily improving too, but he still needed Liz's shoulder for support. Two guards stood on either side of exit, but neither made any move to follow them. Fallow kept pace several feet behind them though, no doubt ready to use the collars should they place a foot out of line.

Step by faltering step, they made their way through the facility, obeying Fallow's direction whenever they came to an intersection. Within a few turns, Chris had recovered enough to walk unaided, though it was a while before he managed more than a slow shuffling. Fortunately, the doctor did not seem to be in any hurry.

Despite their slow pace, the journey could not last forever, and all too soon they found themselves outside a familiar white door. Liz shivered as she looked on it, memories of her fight with Joshua spiraling through her mind.

She turned as Fallow spoke from behind them. "Go in."

Wordlessly, Liz shook her head. Dread wrapped around her stomach as she reached out and took Chris's hand. Together they faced the doctor, standing straight now, the strength slowly returning to their limbs.

"We won't." Liz drew herself up and stepped towards Fallow. "I won't."

Fallow retreated. She lifted her arm, the watch on her wrist flashing in warning. "Won't what?" Fallow asked.

"I won't fight her," Chris coughed. "I'd rather die."

Fallow's shoulders slumped and she gave a little shake of her head. "That's not…no." She gestured with a hand. "Just go."

Liz and Chris shared a glance, still hesitating. Despite Fallow's strange reassurance, fear gnawed at Liz's stomach, a dread she could not shake. The last time she'd entered this room, an innocent boy had lost his life. She had almost lost her own. Her hand drifted to her throat, but there was no pain now, only the cold reminder of the collar nestled beneath her chin.

How long were we asleep?

"Don't make me use the collars." Fallow lifted her finger to her watch.

They went.

As the door clicked shut behind them, Liz found herself standing again in the padded room, blinking in the brilliant light. An awful smell wafted through the air, a sickly sweetness that clung to her nostrils. As her vision cleared and the room came into focus, she realized with a sharp inhalation that they were not alone.

A boy stood in the center of the room. He wore an orange jumpsuit that matched their own, though she had never seen him before in the cells. His head was bowed, and his breath came in ragged gasps, his shoulders trembling with each violent exhalation. He held his hands clenched at his side, and though his eyes were open, he did not seem to have noticed them. Black hair dangled in front of his face, obscuring the rest of his features.

Liz edged towards him, her heart beating hard in her chest. Behind her, Chris gasped, and she felt his hand on her shoulder. But she twisted free, her panic growing. Gripped by a desperate need to see, to know for sure, she slid closer.

Leaning down, she peered into the boy's eyes.

Hard grey irises stared back, their surfaces glazed, unseeing.

But as she watched, they blinked, the life behind them stirring.

Liz screamed.

24

Chris recognized what the boy was the instant they stepped into the room. Though there was no outward difference to his appearance, there was a strangeness to his hunched stance, something about how he stood that gave it away. The stench of him was strong in the room, a cloying sweetness that clung to the air.

He didn't need to see the grey eyes to know what the boy was.

Chead.

He had tried to stop Liz, but she'd only shaken herself free and crept closer. Clenching his fists, he tested his strength, surprised by how quickly it was returning. His attention was drawn back to Liz as she bent down to peer into the boy's face.

Then she was staggering backwards, her scream reverberating around the room. The *Chead's* features contorted, the ripple of awakening sweeping across its face, and then Chris was retreating too, fumbling at the door, shouting for help, knowing it would not come.

Beside him, Liz screamed again and staggered sideways. Chris's hand flashed out, catching her sleeve and dragging her back to him. She started to thrash, and her panic swept through him, waking him from his stupor. He shoved Liz behind him and faced the *Chead.*

He froze as he found the iron-grey eyes watching him. A smile spread across the creature's face, sending pure terror sizzling through every fiber of Chris's being. Another shriek came from behind him as Liz pounded on the padded door.

Taking a breath, Chris stepped towards the *Chead*, an eerie calm coming over him. He placed himself squarely between Liz and the creature, ignoring the urge to turn and shake her, to pull her back from the edge. Liz's words were still fresh in his mind, and he heard again the agony in her voice as she'd told him of her parents' death at the hands of a *Chead*.

He couldn't blame her for panicking.

Chris stared into the eyes of the *Chead*, searching for a sign of sanity, for a hint of the human it had once been.

The *Chead* raised an eyebrow. "Welcome," it whispered, the word sounding strange from its mouth, robotic, as though speech did not come easily to it.

For a second all Chris could do was stand and gape. He blinked, moving his mouth, struggling to find the words. "Wha… what?" he finally managed.

Grey eyes flickered from Chris to Liz. With deliberate slowness, the *Chead* turned and began to pace. It walked first towards the mirror, pausing as its reflection rose up before it, a snarl twisting its lips. Then it spun, moving back past Chris and Liz until it reached the far wall. A growl rumbled from its chest as it turned and repeated the maneuver, its jerky movements like those of a caged animal. Metal shone around its neck, and for the first time Chris realized it too was wearing a collar.

"What. Am. I?" The creature ground out the words. It paused and looked straight at Chris. "You already know that…"

Chris did not reply. His mind was still reeling, struggling to comprehend one irresolvable revelation: it could speak—not just that, it understood him. No newspaper, no television channel had ever mentioned a *Chead* speaking, never mind being self-aware. As far as the public were concerned, the things were monsters—uncontrollable, terrible, killing machines.

They did not think.

They certainly did not talk.

"How?" Chris croaked.

He could sense Liz behind him regaining her composure. The thuds on the door had ceased, her screams dying to soft gasps. On trembling legs, Liz stumbled forward to join him. Out of the corner of his eye, he watched a shiver run through her and reached out an arm. Their hands touched, their fingers entwining. He gave her hand a squeeze and turned back to the *Chead*.

It had stopped its pacing and stood again in the center of the room, watching them. Its nostrils flared as it inhaled.

"You smell…different," it said, then: "How do I speak?" It spoke Chris's question aloud.

Chris nodded his confirmation.

A smile spread across the *Chead's* face. "I learned." It nodded towards the mirror. "From them…"

Liz's hand shook in Chris's grip, but when he looked at her, Liz's eyes remained fixed straight ahead, her lips pressed tightly together.

The *Chead's* head bent to the side, as though in curiosity. "You are different," it said again, its smile spreading, though there was no humor in its eyes. "Like me."

Chris's stomach clenched at its words. "What do you mean? We're…we're not like you…" he croaked.

An awful laughter crackled up from the thing's throat. "They succeeded…these jailers of ours." The boy's face twisted horribly, until it seemed some demon now possessed the boy. Speech seemed to come easier to it now. "But I wonder, is it enough?"

It stepped towards them then, the grin fading.

As one, Chris and Liz retreated across the padded floor, until their backs were pressed against the door.

Chris raised his hands in surrender. "Please, wait, you don't have to do this."

The *Chead* paused, the hard glint in its eyes wavering. It shook its head. "But I do. It is my nature…isn't it?" It took another step, its eyes flickering to the one-way glass. "Besides, it's what *they* want."

Snarling, the *Chead* leapt towards them.

Without pausing to think, Chris pushed Liz from him and stepped in to meet the creature's charge. From the corner of his eye he saw Liz stagger sideways. Then the *Chead* was on him, its fist flashing for his chest. Acting on instinct drilled into him by years of Taekwondo, he threw up an arm, and the blow glanced from his forearm.

Chris gasped as pain jolted his wrist. Then the weight of the creature crashed into him, flinging him backwards into the wall. The *Chead* was on Chris before he could recover, catching him by the shoulders. His stomach twisted as the long arms lifted him. Panicked, he kicked out, driving a desperate blow into the boy's head.

To his surprise, the *Chead* reeled back. A savage growl came from its throat as it tossed him aside. Chris bent his head and braced his arms as the ground raced towards him. He struck with a thud and rolled, spinning to come to his feet in one fluid movement. Straightening, he faced the *Chead.*

The creature stared back, watching him like a predator stalking its prey. Slowly it lifted an arm and wiped a trickle of blood from its lip.

Chris's gaze flickered as he caught sight of Liz. She moved to join him, her eyes flashing. "Don't do that again," she growled.

Nodding, Chris turned his attention back to the *Chead*. It seemed hesitant now. Chris was glad for its caution. On the television, he'd watched a *Chead* tear men apart, seen throats ripped out and skulls shattered by a single blow. Tasers did little to slow them, and bullets only seemed to anger them unless they struck something vital.

Unarmed and trapped in the tiny room, Chris did not like their odds.

Yet somehow, his blow had rattled it.

Pushing down his fear, Chris edged away from Liz. Whatever their chances, they had to try. At least they outnumbered the *Chead*. They needed to make the most of that advantage.

The *Chead* snarled as he moved, its head turning to follow him. Chris watched as Liz edged sideways in the opposite direction. The *Chead* ignored her though, clearly seeing Chris as the greater threat.

Chris just hoped Liz had the strength to prove it wrong.

The *Chead's* grin returned as Chris came to a stop. A low rumble quivered in its chest. It stepped towards him, legs tensing to spring. Chris raised his fists in reply. Sliding one leg backwards, he twisted sideways, planting himself in a defensive stance. Flashing a grin he did not feel, he gestured the creature forward.

As Chris hoped, his impudence ignited a flash of anger in the *Chead*. Adrenaline pounded in his ears as it charged, and he reacted without thought, years of training taking over. One hand swept up to deflect a blow flashing for his face. The force of the attack sent him reeling, but stepping back he managed to keep his balance, already watching for the next attack.

Another fist came at his face and he ducked. His surprise grew as the attack flew past. He'd seen a *Chead* shatter bones with a single blow. By all rights, Chris's arm should have been crushed. Yet somehow he was holding his own.

The *Chead* seemed to have realized this too. Snarling, it hurled itself at Chris with renewed fury. A fist flashed beneath his guard and struck him in the stomach. The breath hissed between Chris's teeth as his lungs emptied. Wheezing, he tried to retreat, but the Chead was too close.

With a shriek, Liz leapt into the fray. Bent in two and gasping, Chris caught a glimpse of her tangled hair and flashing blue eyes as she drove her foot down into the back of the *Chead's* knee.

Screaming, it collapsed.

25

The second Liz had seen the stone-grey eyes of the *Chead*, the memories came flooding back, and she'd found herself back in her parents' house, in the home she'd been raised in. Once, it had been a safe place, a sanctuary amidst the harsh world outside.

Now though, in her memories, a perpetual shadow hung over its wooden hallways, sucking away the light, the life it had once born.

In her mind, she saw again the rubble-strewn corridor, the broken floorboards and pooling blood. She saw herself turn the corner, saw the body lying in the corridor, strangely whole, while those outside had lain in pieces.

And her mother, standing over the body, her grey eyes staring.

With a scream, Liz tore herself from the memory, returning to the present, to the room, and to Chris.

And to the *Chead.*

Still reeling, caught in the clutches of remembered horror, she'd barely heard the conversation between Chris and the *Chead*. She had only woken when Chris had pushed her from the path of *Chead's* charge. Anger had lit in her stomach, waking her from the fear, restoring her to life.

Now, as she edged sideways around the *Chead*, she let that anger grow, fed it with every injustice she'd ever suffered. It was her only weapon now, her only strength against the sheer ferocity of the creature standing between them. Opposite her, Chris faced the creature, drawing it away, until its back was turned to her. But before she could strike, the *Chead* leapt for Chris.

Fear chilled her stomach as blows crashed against flesh. To her surprise, Chris did not go down. Edging closer, she saw him deflect another blow, his arms moving faster than thought, the *crack* of fists connecting with bone ringing from the walls.

Liz stared, her mouth wide with disbelief. What she was watching was not possible. Chris was keeping pace with the violent speed of the *Chead*, matching it blow for blow, punch for punch. Her eyes could barely keep up with their frenzied movements. The air itself seemed to shake with the strength of each clash, and still Chris stood, holding his own.

What have they done to us?

Her skin tingled as the question whispered in her mind. But there was no time to contemplate the answers, no time to consider the implications. Instead, she gathered herself and slid closer, searching for an opening.

Then, an attack slipped beneath Chris's guard. It slammed into his stomach, driving him to his knees. The color fled his face as the *Chead* stepped in, raising a fist to deliver the final blow.

Seeing her chance, Liz sprang forward and drove her heel into the back of the *Chead's* knee. Idly, she hoped whatever changes had been wrought on the *Chead* had not removed the cluster of nerve endings located behind the kneecap.

The boy's bloodcurdling shriek answered her question. The *Chead's* leg crumbled beneath the force of the blow, sending it crashing to the ground. Clenching her teeth, Liz stepped towards it as Chris rolled away.

She swung a kick at its head, but the *Chead* was already recovering. Quick as a cobra it twisted, a hand flashing out to catch her by the leg. Before she could free herself, it stood, grey eyes glittering. A growl came from its throat as it lifted her by the leg and held her upside-down. Gasping, she fought to break its hold, but its fingers were like iron. Knowing it was useless, Liz lashed out with a fist, catching it in the cheek.

Shock reverberated up her arm as the blow connected. The fingers around her leg loosened, and suddenly she was falling. She landed awkwardly and looked up to see the *Chead* stumbling backwards, one hand raised to its face. It straightened with a roar, its gaze sweeping down to find her on the floor.

Liz's courage crumbled as she looked into its awful eyes. All semblance of humanity had fled the creature now, melting in the red-hot flames of its rage. Hardly daring to breathe, she backed towards Chris, any thoughts of attacking falling away.

Snarling, it stepped after her.

"Now you've done it," Chris panted, his hand reaching for hers.

She clenched her hand around his, drawing strength from his presence, then released him. Together they watched the *Chead* approach.

With a roar, it leapt.

Chris sprang forward to meet it, screaming his defiance. He deflected the first swing of the creature's fist, but this time the force of the blow sent him reeling, and Liz had to step aside to avoid him. Then the *Chead* was on her, fists flying, lips drawn back in a snarl, its half-mad screams echoing from the mirrored glass.

A fist caught Liz in the cheek, staggering her, then the *Chead's* shoulder crashed into her chest. The breath rushed from her lungs as she was thrown backwards into the wall. Her head whipped back, striking the padding, and despite the soft surface, her vision spun. Groaning, she slid down the wall, struggling to catch her breath.

Across the room, Chris fought on, but he was no longer a match for the *Chead's* strength. And it was faster now, its speed and ferocity far beyond human capabilities. With contempt, it knocked aside his blows. A fist crashed into his face, sending him stumbling backwards, but he refused to yield. Straightening, he launched himself back into the fray.

Desperately, Liz struggled back to her feet.

A shout drew her attention back to the fight. The *Chead* had caught Chris's fist in one hand. Chris screamed again, though this time neither of them moved. An awful *crack* came from Chris's fist as he sank to his knees. The color fled his face and he gave an awful groan. One-handed, he struggled to get his feet back under him—until the *Chead's* other hand smashed into the side of his head. Chris went limp at the blow, his breathing ragged, one hand still caught in the creature's grip.

Silently, Liz stood. The *Chead's* back was turned to her, its attention focused on tearing Chris limb from limb. She flinched as another blow thudded into Chris's head. This time he made no effort to avoid it. A low gurgle came from his throat as the *Chead* lifted him by the arm, dragging him back to his feet.

Liz moved quickly, knowing she only had seconds to act. The soft floor made no noise beneath her bare feet. Without pausing to think, she hurled herself at the creature's back. This time she aimed high, sweeping her forearm over its shoulder. Before it could react, she pulled her arm tight against its throat and leaned back. Her feet caught the ground and she pulled harder, dragging it backwards off-balance.

The *Chead* gave a strangled cry. Releasing Chris, it turned its attention on her. Knowing she could not match its strength or weight, Liz allowed herself to fall backwards, dragging the *Chead* down with her. It landed on her chest, driving the breath from her lungs, but still she held on, forearm tight across its collared throat.

Sensing its plight, the *Chead* thrashed against her. Its legs kicked out, catching Liz in the shins. Pain lanced from her leg as something went *crack*, but no force on earth would make her let go now.

Not even death.

Long seconds passed, and the creature's struggles weakened. Its legs no longer beat against the floor, and its relentless strength no longer pressed so hard against her.

Movement came from beyond the *Chead*. Chris staggered to his feet, his face already turning purple from bruises, one eye so swollen she could barely see it. Even so, he stumbled forward and fell to his knees beside her. Raising his fist, he drove it into the *Chead's* face.

Liz felt the power of Chris's blow through the *Chead.* Its body went limp in her arms, but still she did not relent.

Only when she was satisfied it was no longer moving did Liz loosen her grip. With Chris's help, they heaved the dead weight from her chest.

Then she was embracing Chris, pulling him to her, clinging desperately at his back. An awful sob built in her chest and escaped in a rush. Chris's arms tightened around her, and then he was sobbing too, his hot wet tears falling on her shoulder.

They clung to each other in silence, and let the horror wash over them.

26

Chris looked up as a click came from the doorway. Halt stood there, a triumphant grin stretching across his thin lips. His eyes feasted on the two of them, shining with a wild exaltation.

"It worked," he said, his voice raw. He stepped into the room, two guards following him before the door swung shut. "The genomes are expressing—a few at least. Muscle density factor, reaction time, agility, it's all there..."

As the man rambled, Chris struggled to pull his mind back to the present. He wrapped his arm around Liz, pulling her tight against him. She shivered and they shared a glance.

Then she turned, facing Halt. "What have you done to us?" she croaked.

Halt drew to a stop. He blinked, looking almost surprised, as though he had forgotten they could speak. His smile faded as he crossed his arms. "We have enhanced you, my dear. Made you better...made you *useful.*" He almost spat the last word.

Chris met the man's iron gaze. "*Why?*" He gestured to the *Chead.* "Why would you do this? Send us in here to die?"

Halt stepped towards the unconscious *Chead.* "To see if you would live," he answered, looking back over his shoulder. "To see if we had succeeded in creating a weapon that could match the *Chead.*"

Rage constricted Chris's chest at the doctor's words. He stared up at the man, struggling to breathe. Pain shot from his knuckles—where the *Chead* had held him—as he clenched his fists. Glancing at his hand, he saw it had already swollen to twice its usual size.

He shuddered.

It would have killed me.

"You changed us." Liz was speaking again, her voice barely audible. "Did something to us...while we slept. *How...why?*" Her voice cracked. She was shaking in his arms, though whether from rage or some other emotion, Chris could not tell.

Chuckling, Halt walked towards them. "It was a simple matter, in the end. A little retrovirus, some genetic mapping of various species—chimpanzees, wolves, felines, eagles, and so on. Isolating the desirable genes took time, as did altering their repetition sequences to be accepted by human cells." He shrugged. "But, well, the results were worth the effort. And the best is yet to come." An awful grin spread across his face.

With Halt's words, Chris mind finally caught up with events. Revulsion struck him as he realized the truth—that the *Chead* had not been weaker than those on the television. It was he and Liz who had changed. They were stronger.

And it was Fallow and Halt who had changed them.

A scream built in Chris's chest as he looked at the doctor. An awful sense of violation wrapped around his throat. He clenched his fist again, felt the pain, its sharpness anchoring him to reality. He felt defiled, like something had been taken from him, stolen. The pain built in his hand, but it was nothing to the desecration of his body. He drew back his lips in a snarl.

Halt watched them, his expression unchanged, but his hand drifted towards his watch. Tension hung in the air as Chris's rage gathered strength.

Then a groan came from across the room. Halt's eyes flickered towards the *Chead.* Chris followed his gaze and saw the creature had rolled onto its side. It moaned again, then started to cough. Its eyes fluttered but did not open.

"It's still alive." Halt sounded surprised. He turned back to Chris. "Kill it."

"What?" Chris blinked, staring at the doctor in disbelief.

"Kill it," Halt repeated. "That monstrosity is not worthy of this earth. Kill it, Christopher. Prove you are its superior."

"No." Chris was surprised by his own resolve. Releasing Liz, he faced Halt, determined to defy him. "I won't."

Halt shook his head and held up his arm. The watch flashed on his wrist. "Do not waste my time, Christopher. Kill the *Chead*, and we can move on from this unpleasant business."

A peal of laughter came from beside Chris, then Liz spoke. "No, Halt. We won't. We're not your creatures, your slaves to do with as you please. Whatever you've done to us, we're still human."

Halt did not move. His eyes flickered for a second to Liz, then back to Chris. "I will give you one last chance, Christopher. Kill the *Chead*. *Now!*"

"You're the monstrosity, Halt," Chris replied.

"Very well." Halt looked at Liz again. "If that is your decision..."

He pressed his finger to the watch.

Chris closed his eyes and braced himself for the pain. Sucking in a breath, he waited for the familiar fire to encircle his throat, to sap the strength from his legs, to lock his muscles in knots of agony.

It never came.

A high-pitched scream erupted from his right. Chris spun, his eyes snapping open to see Liz crumpling to the ground. The color fled her face as she clutched desperately at her throat. Her feet drummed against the soft floor and a strangled scream escaped her.

Then she fell silent, her last gasps of air stolen away.

Chris threw himself forward, desperate to reach her, but strong arms grasped him around the waist and hauled him back. He lashed out with his elbow, catching the guard in the face, and the hands released him. He glimpsed the man falling backwards, the other stepping towards him, but he was already at Liz's side, reaching out, grabbing her by the wrist…

A jolt of electricity flashed between them, and Chris was hurled across the room.

Coming to rest a few feet away, Chris shook his head and struggled to sit up. Liz still writhed against the soft floor, her back arching, her mouth wide and gasping. Her fingers clawed at her throat, tearing at the collar's metal chain. But there was no dislodging the steel links.

Halt stepped between them, a grim smile on his serpent lips. "Seventy-five milliamps," he said, shaking his head. "Enough to cause severe muscle contractions, respiratory failure, death."

Behind him, Liz was as pale as a ghost, her throws of agony already growing weaker. Her mouth opened, gasping like a fish out of water. Yet somehow, her crystal eyes found his. Shining with tears, they pierced him, conveying her silent command.

Don't give in!

A sob rattled up from Chris's chest as he closed his eyes, unable to watch any longer. Bowing his head, he cradled his shattered fist. Despair rose within him, overwhelming.

"*Please!*" His cry echoed from the one-way mirror.

A sudden stillness came over the room. Lying on the ground, Chris did not move, unable to look, to witness the consequence of his defiance. So long as he did not look, he could deny the truth.

Liz couldn't be gone, couldn't be dead.

But in his heart, Chris knew he had to face the truth. Blinking back tears, he sucked in a breath and lifted his head.

Liz lay where she had fallen, her limbs splayed out at random angles, the tangles of her hair caught on her face. The collar shone from her neck, the red light finally gone out.

Staring at her broken body, a pit opened in Chris, a gulf of despair that threatened to swallow him whole. A desperate sob tore from his throat, a cry of anguish, a plea for life. Lifting himself, he crawled towards her. He could feel his strength failing, the last drops of energy leaving him, but with a final lunge he reached out and grasped her wrist.

At his touch, Liz's chest moved. A soft cough came from the fallen girl as her eyelids fluttered.

"*What?*" Halt snarled.

The door clicked again, and Doctor Fallow stepped into the room.

27

"Enough, Halt," Angela said, so angry she was almost tripping over the words.

Halt turned to stare at her, eyes wide, his surprise already turning to rage. She knew she'd crossed a line by defying him now. This time, there were no other doctors to back her up—the others were still tending to the survivors of the PERV-B strain.

"Excuse me?" Halt sounded almost bemused.

"I said, that's enough," Angela repeated, mustering her courage.

A few moments ago, she had been driven to act. Watching Halt's cruelty, his determination to bend the candidates to his will at any cost, had pushed her over the edge. Whatever good she'd hoped might come from her work, it was not worth this. Halt's actions were brutal and pointless and wasteful, a display that did nothing more than serve the man's ego.

And Angela could not bear to watch the girl die. She could not shake that feeling of kinship, could not help but see her own youthful self in the girl's eyes.

So she had acted. She had superseded Halt's controller from within the observation room, disabling the collars of the two subjects. As supervisor of the project, her watch had precedence over every other controller in the building—even Halt's.

This isn't right. The words whispered in her mind as she looked at the boy and girl. *They're just kids.*

Biting her lip, she straightened, preparing herself for Halt's rage. "There's no justifying this, Halt. They passed the test. The project is a success. But this…" She waved a hand to indicate the girl. "This display is pointless. I won't allow it."

Halt shifted on his feet. A strange calm seemed to have come over him. "You won't allow it?"

Angela found herself retreating a step, though the doctor had not moved. "No," she said, shaking her head. "I've disabled their collars."

"You forget yourself, doctor." Halt still spoke in a soft voice. "These displays of insolence…are becoming problematic."

"They are *my* candidates, Halt."

For a moment, he did not reply. His eyes studied her, sweeping over her body, cold and calculating. Angela lifted her chin, facing him down.

At last, Halt nodded. He waved to the guards. "Get them up. Return them to their cell."

As the guards started toward Christopher and Elizabeth, Halt turned back to Fallow. He stood deathly still, poised in the center of the room as the guards shepherded the two teenagers from the testing room. His eyes did not blink, never left Angela's face. Only when the door clicked shut did he step towards her.

"Just because their parents were traitors–"

"*How dare you?*" Halt interrupted, almost shouting now.

Fallow found herself retreating from the man's rage, but in just two steps she found herself pressed up against the mirror, the cold glass at her back, with nowhere left to look but the doctor.

Halt came at her in a rush, his hand flashing out to catch her by the throat. His fingers clenched tight as she opened her mouth to scream, stealing away her voice. His lips drew back in a scowl as he leaned in.

With a sudden, violent shove, Halt slammed her head back into the glass. Stars spun across Angela's vision and her knees went weak. Pain lanced through her skull as Halt pulled her towards him, until their faces were less than an inch apart.

"If you *ever* defy me again, I will see you in a cage with your precious candidates," he ground out through clenched teeth.

Red exploded across Angela's vision as he slammed her into the mirror again. Then the fingers released her, and with a muffled sob she slumped to the ground.

Halt looked down at her, open contempt in his eyes. "The experiment will continue," he said. "I will see that the final doses are administered to the candidates. Those still unconscious will remain in their comas until our research has been completed."

Darkness swept across Angela's vision, rising up to claim her. She fought to hold it off as Halt crouched beside her.

"Tell me doctor, you aren't really so naïve, are you?" he asked, his voice taken on an amused tone. "Did you truly buy the company line?"

"What?" Fallow croaked, her mind swamped, unable to piece together the meaning behind Halt's words.

The man chuckled. "Their parents were never traitors, Fallow," he said.

"Then who?" Fallow whispered, her heart pounding in her ears.

Halt shrugged as he stood. "People who wouldn't be missed, or those who might have stood in our way at the wrong time." His grin spread. "Anyone we could find, really."

"No..."

"Yes," Halt cut her off, "and if you don't want to be the next on the executioner's block, I suggest you return to your laboratory. If our new virus succeeds, I might just let you live."

28

Clang.

Chris slumped to the ground as the cell door slid closed behind them. Liz staggered past him and toppled onto Ashley's bed. The guards had practically carried her this far. Despite faring slightly better than Chris in the fight, her collar had left its mark. The damage ran deep, each inhalation bringing an awful coughing and gurgling from her chest.

Unfortunately, Chris wasn't in much better shape.

Whatever Halt had said about success, Chris still lacked the relentless strength of the *Chead*. When it had caught him, no amount of skill, training or mutated muscle had been enough to save him from its grasp.

Thank God for Liz, he thought.

She lay sprawled across the bed, her face half-buried in the pillow, her back rising with each labored breath. Every few seconds she would groan, but otherwise she lay still.

Getting to his hands and knees, Chris crawled across the cell to Sam's bed and pulled himself up. Under the circumstances, he didn't think the others would mind if they borrowed them. Both beds were neatly made up, the covers pulled tight, the presence of their two friends wiped clean.

Minutes slipped by as he lay there, his face throbbing where the *Chead* had struck him. After a time, the clang of the outer door carried down the corridor. Idly, Chris wondered if someone had come to finish the job the *Chead* had started. There was no one else inside the prison block now. The other cells were empty, the faces that had once lined the corridor either dead or gone.

No, whoever it was had come for them.

Unable to summon the energy to move, Chris lifted an eyelid and looked out into the corridor. A woman stood outside the bars, her hands fiddling nervously with the hem of her lab coat. For a second he thought it was Fallow, before he realized she was too young, her hair blonde instead of brown. A guard stood beside the woman, looking bored.

"I'm…I'm to give you a round of antibiotics," she squeaked.

On the opposite bed, Liz did not so much as stir. Stifling a groan, Chris rolled onto his side. "Really?" he coughed. "You people are all of a sudden concerned for our wellbeing?"

The woman gave a nervous nod. "Could you, could you get to the back of the cell, please?"

Chris blinked. If he hadn't been in so much pain, he would have laughed. Instead he looked at Liz, then back at the doctor. "Sorry, lady. But I don't think we're going anywhere."

"But…but you're meant to…"

Closing his eyes, Chris lay back on the bed. "Just get it over with. Have the guard ready to press his little button, if it makes you feel better."

The woman hesitated another second, and then nodded. A buzzer sounded and the cell door slid open. The little doctor hopped into the cell, a packet of syringes held in one hand, a vial of clear liquid in the other.

Briefly, Chris contemplated resisting. After everything they'd been through, he distrusted even this harmless-looking woman. Who knew what new horror might wait in the vial? But a hollow feeling sat in his stomach, an awful, helpless weakness that sapped him of the will to fight.

After all, what was the point in fighting now? It was too late—they'd already lost, had already been damaged beyond repair.

Chris slumped into his pillow and watched as the woman stopped beside Liz.

"She's unconscious," she said, sounding surprised. "I thought…I thought the experiment was a success."

"You'll have to ask your boss about that." Chris paused, his thoughts drifting. "Where are our friends? What's happening to them?"

The woman was busy preparing her syringe, and it was a moment before she answered. It wasn't until she leaned over Liz that he heard her whisper. "The others are being kept in their comas," she breathed. "To make the change easier."

Chris watched as the woman inserted the needle into the middle of Liz's back and depressed the plunger. Then she moved over to him, the needle disappearing into a bag marked *Biological Waste*. Another appeared as she raised the vial.

Turning away, Chris winced as the needle pinched his back. The cold tingle of the injection spread between his shoulder blades as the woman stepped back. To his relief, there was no pain, and the cold sensation quickly faded.

"Are we done, Doctor Faulks?" came the guard's voice from outside the cell.

"Yes." Chris glanced up at the sound of retreating footsteps. He watched the woman reach the door and turn back, her eyes catching in his. "I'm sorry."

Then she was gone.

Chris frowned, already resigning himself to whatever fresh torment had been in the injection. He was certain now it had not been antibiotics. Something in the doctor's face as she looked back, in her final words, had warned him.

At least this time there was no pain.

A gurgling sound came from Liz's bed, drawing Chris's attention back to his friend. She had rolled onto her back now, her mouth wide and gasping. Her eyes were closed, her brow creased as though she were struggling to wake. Fingers clenched at the sheets and the veins stood up against her neck.

Chris's heart lurched and a sense of urgency gripped him. Careful to protect his injured hand, he rolled from the bed and crawled across to the other set of bunks. Pulling himself up beside Liz, he reached for her as she started to thrash. A wild arm swung out, catching him in the face, and her foot struck a pole, making the bunk shake. Another awful gurgle came from her chest.

"Liz, Liz, *stop*," Chris shouted, struggling to calm her.

With growing fear, he realized what was happening to her. She was choking, drowning in the fluid filling her lungs.

Ignoring the agony in his hand now, Chris caught Liz by the shoulder as another convulsion took her. He pulled her close, fighting to hold her, to turn her on her side. Desperate fists beat against him, and fire ripped up his arm as she struck his broken hand. Gasping, he twisted, and narrowly avoided a wild thrust of her knee.

Chris heaved, pulling Liz onto her side. As she rolled, he saw her eyes were wide open and staring, though it was clear she remained unconscious. Bloodshot veins threaded the whites of her eyes, and a trickle of blood ran from her nose, staining the white of her pillow.

As she settled onto her side, a ragged gasp tore from her lips. Her chest rose, the gurgling fading to a whispered cough. She gulped again, wheezing in the cool air, as though still struggling to take in enough oxygen. Chris tilted her head forward slightly, memories of a high school first aid class guiding him.

Moving her upper arm, he placed the hand beneath her head, then pulled her knee up towards her chest. Liz's breathing eased as she settled into the Recover Position, the gurgling fading as her airways cleared.

Finally, Chris let out a long sigh, satisfied that for the moment she was safe. Holding her in place, he sent out a silent thanks that Liz was so small.

Only then did his own weariness return. His head sank onto the pillow as he watched Liz, a smile pulling at his lips. Her eyes had closed again, her lips parted just a fraction. A wisp of hair fluttered against her nose with each exhalation.

As the adrenaline faded, the sharp throb of Chris's hand

returned. He stifled a groan of his own, eager not to disturb Liz now that she had settled.

Closing his eyes, he saw her again in the padded room, thrashing on the floor, and felt again the awful helplessness. He shuddered and pushed the image away.

Only Fallow's intervention had saved her, saved them both.

Fallow.

The woman's face drifted through his mind. She had been a part of this from the start, had admitted her role in this whole project while helping them prepare for their fight.

You are the culmination of my life's work.

Was that why she had saved them, why she'd stopped Halt from killing Liz? Or was there more to it? Had the woman's conscience gotten to her?

Chris struggled to concentrate, but cobwebs tangled with his thoughts, and he could find no answers to his questions. His body throbbed, the ache of a dozen bruises dulling his mind. Heat radiated from Liz, banishing the cold of the cell. Distantly, he felt the pull of sleep.

His eyes fluttered open, catching a glimpse of Liz. The pained twist of her lips had faded, revealing a softness in her face, the kindness of the girl hidden within. Her breathing had quieted now, and her eyes quivered beneath her eyelids, lost in some dream.

The weight of exhaustion slowly dragged Chris's eyes shut again. He knew he should move, should return to his own bed, but he could not find willpower. His last ounce of energy had fled.

Within seconds, the soft wrappings of sleep had claimed him.

29

Light burned at Liz's eyelids, dragging her from her dreams, back to the pain. It washed over her like rain, a tingle that burned in her every muscle. Gritting her teeth, she willed the agony to fade, to release her from its fiery grip. Slowly it slipped away, until only embers remained.

Liz took a breath, suppressing a groan as the ache returned, now an icy frost that filled her lungs. Then she paused as movement came from beside her. Cracking open an eye, she found Chris asleep beside her. She frowned, the beginnings of anger curling in her stomach. Then a dim memory surfaced, of water all around her, of drowning in a bottomless ocean, of fire in her chest as she breathed the salty liquid. Then…Chris's hands on her shoulders, pulling her up, dragging her to the surface. The relief of fresh air, filling her lungs, of oxygen flooding her body.

Her anger vanished, replaced by a warmth that swept away the pain. She looked at Chris, watching the soft rise and fall of his chest, the flickering of his eyelids. She remembered her fear as the *Chead* beat him to the ground, the terror that had risen within her. Yet instead of panic, it had filled her with purpose, with the need to act, to save him.

A moan came from Chris and he wriggled beneath the thin blanket, drawing closer. Slowly his eyes cracked open.

"You know, when I said I'd give you a chance, I didn't mean it as an invite..." she teased, a playful smile tugging at her lips.

She caught him as he flinched away. Gently taking up his good hand, she pulled him back, drawing him closer, until only an inch separated them.

"Don't," she murmured, basking in the heat of his body. "Don't."

His hazel eyes stared back at her, bloodshot but clear, and filled with...something. She leaned in, trying to make out what, and her mouth brushed against his. A jolt of energy passed between them, and then she was kissing him.

She felt Chris grow tense, and for a second thought he would pull away.

Then his hand was in her hair, and he was kissing her back, his lips hard against hers. A prickling came from her hip as he gripped her. Blood pounded in her ears, spreading outwards until her entire body was tingling. She wrapped her arms around Chris, holding him tight, leaving no escape. Goosebumps prickled her skin as fingers slid to the small of her back.

The scent of him filling her nostrils, Liz parted her lips, her tongue flicking out to taste him. His tongue found hers, and they danced to a rhythm all of their own. Her mind fell away, drowned by the rush of blood to her head. Her pain was forgotten, replaced by threads of pleasure winding through her body. Her skin was aflame, burning wherever he touched.

She slid her fingers through his hair, pulling him deeper into the kiss. Hunger filled her then, a need that grew with every heartbeat. A moan slipped from her lips and she gripped him hard, desperate now.

Chris flinched in her arms and she paused, remembering his broken hand. For a moment they slowed, but their lips did not part, their tongues still dancing, tasting. Liz wriggled in under his arm, her chest pounding like a drum as he held her.

Liz drew back then, sucking in a breath. Opening her eyes, she looked at him, saw the smile tugging at his lips. She shivered, a memory rising of the horror from the day before. A sour taste filled her mouth, the pain returning. She blinked, and a tear streaked her cheek.

"What are we doing, Chris?" she whispered.

Chris pulled back, his eyes sad. Reaching out, he wiped away her tear, then kissed her on the forehead. "What do you mean?"

"What's the point?" she choked, closing her eyes, the darkness welling within. "They could kill us tomorrow, mutate us beyond recognition, burn the last traces of humanity from us, like that thing—"

She broke off as Chris kissed her again, fast and hard. He pulled back, looking her in the eye. "We can't let them win, Liz," he whispered. "They've taken so much from us already, used us, stolen our humanity. But they can't take our spirit, our hope. It's all we have left. And I won't let them take it."

"Haven't they already?"

Chris only smiled. "Not yet. It's like Ashley said—they're only human. They'll make mistakes." The fingers of his good hand found hers, and squeezed. "When they do, we'll be ready."

Staring into his eyes, Liz could almost bring herself to believe.

Almost.

Still, he was right. They couldn't let their captors win. For the moment, they still had each other. She would not let them take that from her too. Leaning in, Liz gave herself to the fire burning within. Their mouths locked and she pressed herself hard against him, her hands sliding beneath his shirt. A wild hunger filled her, her kisses becoming ravenous. His arm went around her again, gripping her with a new fierceness. His lips left hers as he pulled away—then they were at her neck, stoking the flames within.

She groaned, arching backwards, her fingers tight in his hair.

His hands slid beneath her shirt, trailing down her back, tingling wherever they touched. The warmth inside her spread, and she started to tremble. Lost in her passion, she leaned in and nipped at his neck.

Liz smiled as Chris gave a little yelp. His hands continued to roam, though they had not yet gone far enough for her liking. She slid her fingers through the buttons of his shirt and began to undo them. A fine layer of hair covered his chest, which was surprising muscular. His skin was hot beneath her fingers.

She groaned as Chris's mouth found its way to the small of her throat. With a rush of impatience she helped him with her own buttons, knowing his good hand was already occupied. His lips slid lower, his tongue darting out, tasting her, even as his hand etched invisible trails across the soft skin of her back.

Then he paused, his fingers stilling on her back. Liz stifled a moan as she opened her eyes. She found him staring up at her from between the folds of her breasts, fear sparkling in his eyes. Her stomach twisted as ice slid down her spine.

"What?" she whispered.

"There's…there's something wrong. There are…lumps," Chris replied softly.

Liz's cheeks burned, but her fear fell away. Laughing softly, she shook her head. Her hands slid through his hair, drawing him to her, until his lips brushed across her nipples. She arched her back as Chris groaned. Barely able to catch her breath, Liz slid her hands lower, sliding them beneath his waistband, reaching for him…

But he pulled away again, shaking his head. "No," he said, his cheeks reddening, "not…not those."

The hackles rose on Liz's neck at the look on his face. Her lust went from her in a rush. "What?"

"On your back," Chris said, barely breathing. "There's… something on your back."

Again, fear flooded Liz. Sitting upright, she craned her neck, straining to see. Her movements grew frantic as she fumbled at her shirt, tugging at the collar, desperate to rid herself of it. Chris reached out, trying to calm her, but she pushed him away. Fabric tore and the shirt came loose. Throwing it aside, she twisted her neck again and looked.

Beside her, Chris's face was flushed, a flicker of desire still lurking in his eyes. But in that moment she no longer cared. Her naked back shone in the fluorescent lights, the lumps unmistakable. They bulged in the center of her back, on either side of her spine, midway between her arms and hips.

Pressure grew in Liz's chest, escaping as a low whine, a muffled scream. Horror swept through her, a raging anger at the doctors, at their violation of her body. Another shriek built, but she swallowed it down, blinking back tears.

Her eyes burned as she looked at Chris, saw the fresh tears in his eyes.

"Where does it stop?" she whispered.

☙ 30 ❧

Within hours, Chris discovered the same growths on his own back. Though there was no pain or discomfort, they ignited a terror that threatened to overwhelm him. Whatever the doctors had done to them, it seemed they'd failed after all.

They made a mistake. The words whispered in his thoughts, along with something else, a familiar word, a horror from his childhood.

Cancer.

The memory of his father's illness still lay heavy on his mind—the wasting sickness, the slow loss of strength, of life. Despite its ferocity, his father had fought back, had even won, for a time. But cancer was like a weed, always there, waiting to return. It wore you down, drew the life from you one drop at a time.

And his father, once larger than life, had been laid low.

As the hours ticked past, Chris could think of no other explanation for the lumps. Vicious and unrelenting, the cancers would spread through their bodies, poisoning their blood, feeding on their strength, until there was nothing left but empty husks.

Lying on the bed, he held Liz in his arms, each alone in their own thoughts.

The next day, they woke to the first beginnings of pain. It began as a soft twitch in the center of his back, radiating outwards from the strange protrusions. The ache pulsed, flickering with the beat of his heart, but growing sharper with each intake of breath. Hour by hour it spread, threaded its way into his chest, until it hurt just to breathe.

For Liz, it was worse. When she woke she could barely speak. Her skin had lost its color; even the angry red marks beneath her collar had paled to white. By lunch she could no longer lie on her back, and when he touched her forehead, he found her skin burning with fever.

Each hour the lumps grew. Their skin stretched and hardened around the protrusions, darkening to purple bruises. Each bulge was unyielding to their scrutinizing prods, and soon tiny black spots appeared on their surfaces.

When the lights woke them on the third day, Chris could hardly move from the pain. Agony wove its way through his torso, spreading out like the roots of a tree, engulfing his lungs, reducing each breath to a battle, a desperate fight for life.

The next time a guard arrived with food, Chris could no longer tell whether it was breakfast or dinner. He blinked hard into the light, pain lancing his skull. The room spun and then settled into a double image. His stomach churned as two Liz's appeared to stand over him, offering a bowl of dark-colored stew. He saw her waver on her feet, and blindly took the bowl before she fell.

Sitting back, he raised a shaking spoonful of broth to his mouth, but there was no taste when he swallowed. His stomach swirled again, then he began to heave. He barely made it to the toilet. A moment later, Liz was beside him at the sink.

Afterwards, Chris slid to the ground, his head throbbing in the blinding light. Liz sat with him, her head settling on his shoulder. For a moment the pain faded, giving in to a wave of warmth. He closed his eyes, savoring Liz's closeness, but the relief did not last long. His stomach lurched again, and he released Liz and crawled back to the toilet.

The *clang* of the lights going out was a welcome relief.

Stomach clenched, lungs burning, head thumping, Chris returned to the beds. Stars danced across his vision, but he hauled himself up, no longer caring whose bed it was. The room stank of vomit and spilled food, of unwashed bodies and blood. The scent of chlorine had long since been overwhelmed.

Caught in the clutches of fever, Chris lost all track of time. At some point he felt Liz's body beside him. He drew comfort from the heat of her presence, in the closeness of her face. Then her face warped, and it felt as though his own body was distorting, and he forced his eyes closed.

Wild colors spun through his mind as time passed. At one point he remembered calling out, begging the guards to come, to bring the doctors, to bring anyone. But no one came, no one responded, and he soon gave up asking for help. He started asking for death instead.

In his dreams, he saw his body slowly decaying, watched his veins turn black, his arms begin to rot. Then he would find himself whole, riding in the passenger seat of his father's '68 Camaro, his dad driving, an infectious grin on his youthful face. A moment later he was in a hospital, the smell of bleach and the beeping of machinery all around. And his father, lying in a bed, his arms withered, his face lined with age. Only the smile was unchanged.

The image faded, and Chris was back in the cell, back with the pain. Looking at his arms, he wondered what was real, what was not. One instant it was night, the next the blinding light of day, then back to black. At times he would wake, gasping for air, shivering beneath the blanket, and know in his heart he was dying.

Once, he dreamed that he was flying, soaring through mountains, far from the nightmares of their prison cell.

Then he woke.

31

It was a long time before Chris realized he was no longer dreaming. He shivered as the cold air wrapped around him, but otherwise there was no discomfort. The pain had vanished, and for a second he considered the possibility that he was dead. Then a groan came from someone nearby, and he knew he was not alone.

Forcing open his eyes, he peered out from the shadow of his bunk bed, searching for Liz.

The first thing he realized was that they hadn't been alone in their fever dreams. Someone had entered the cell while they slept, and cleaned the vomit and blood from the room. Liz lay in the opposite bed, covered by a strange-looking blanket of black feathers. She shifted beneath it, then blinked across at him, raising a hand to shield her face. Her lips parted as she licked her cracked lips.

"Chris?" she croaked.

"I'm here," he replied, his throat raw. A desperate thirst clutched him, and he looked to the sink, wondering if he had the strength to reach it.

In the other bed, Liz slowly sat up, the blanket still clinging to her. Dimly, Chris made to do the same, but a weight on his back pressed him down. Reaching back, he felt soft feathers brush his hand. He shrugged, trying to dislodge the blanket as he lifted himself to his hands and knees.

Chris paused, a distant thought tugging at his memories, but it faded again before he could catch it. He cast a questioning look at Liz, but she said nothing. He clenched his fists, feeling a wrongness about himself, but unable to trace the source.

Shaking his head, Chris pushed the last of the fever dreams away and rolled out of the bed onto his feet. To his surprise, the weight came with him, pushing him forward. Off-balance, he crashed to the floor in a tangle of limbs and feathers.

"Chris?" Liz's voice shook.

Confused, Chris frowned at her from the floor. He pulled himself up, but the weight still clung to his back. Only sheer determination kept him from toppling over backwards. He froze when he saw the look on Liz's face.

Eyes wide, she sat half-crouched on the bed. Her mouth opened and closed, but no sound came out. Her arm shook as she raised it and pointed. Shivering, Chris looked behind him, fear of the unknown rippling down his spine. But his bed was empty, the feather blanket trailing out behind him.

Chris started to turn back to Liz, then paused. He blinked, staring at the tawny brown feathers of his blanket. There was something wrong about the way they hung between himself and the bed, something not quite right.

Stretching out a hand, Chris tried to dislodge the blanket from his shoulders. He flinched as his hand brushed against something unexpected, something hard beneath the blanket. Withdrawing his hand, he looked at Liz, but she still sat in silence, her mouth agape.

With a rush of courage, Chris reached behind his neck and ran a hand down his spine.

He found the growths where they had been before, midway down his back. They had changed—becoming long shafts that stretched far beyond his reach. A soft down of feathers covered their length, sprouting from his flesh as though they had every right to be there.

Wings.

His mind spun. He shook his head, refusing to face the truth, though they lay stretched out before his eyes. He trembled, and watched the shiver run down the wings, the tawny brown feathers quivering in the cool air.

A muffled sob came from the other bed. Liz had struggled to her feet, revealing the long black wings hanging from her own back. They stretched out to either side of her, each at least ten feet long, the large black feathers tangling with the sheets on the bed. Where the feathers bent, Chris glimpsed soft white down beneath, small feathers curled in upon themselves, clinging close to her flesh. They shone in the overhead lights, seeming almost aflame, as though Liz was some avenging angel descended from heaven.

Wings.

Warmth spread through Chris's chest, mingling with the horror. A profound confusion gripped him: a disgust at this fresh violation, the further loss of his humanity—but also wonder, an awe for the trembling new limbs on his back.

Wings.

He looked at Liz. Her eyes were wide, glistening with tears. Her lips trembled, a shudder running through her body. Through her wings.

For the first time, Chris realized they were both naked. Strangely, it no longer seemed to matter. After all they had suffered, all that had been done to them, Chris's body hardly felt like his own. He felt apart from it now, separated from his nakedness.

A tear spilled down Liz's cheek, and he knew the same thought had occurred to her. He stepped across the room, struggling for balance, and pulled her to him. He shivered as her arms went around his waist and her head lifted, drawing him in.

A fire ignited in Chris's chest as their lips met. His hands slid up into her hair as her tongue darted out, sliding between his lips. The taste of her filled him, the intoxicating scent of her hair toying with his nostrils.

After a long minute, Liz pulled back. Raising a hand to her face, she wiped away her tears. She looked at her wings then, her lips twisting as though in thought. They hung limply from her back, feathers quivering, and he knew what she was thinking.

Liz closed her eyes, her face tightening, the lines of her jaw deepening. Her brow creased, and behind her the black-feathered wings twitched. They began to shake, then lifted slightly and half-opened. There they paused, as though lacking the strength to go any further.

Eyes still closed, Liz bit her lip, and persisted.

Bit by bit, her wings spread, until they seemed to fill the cell. They stretched more than twenty feet, twice the length of their beds, so that their tips poked out through the bars into the corridor.

Twenty feet of jet-black feathers, of curly white down, of a majestic, undefinable magic.

When Liz opened her eyes again, Chris saw the wonder there, the fear falling away before it.

At a nod from her, he shut his own eyes and sought to do the same. Reaching down into the depths of his consciousness, he followed the tingle that came from his back, the newfound sensations originating from the limbs. As he concentrated, the tingle spread along his spine. The hairs stood up on his neck as new connections formed within his mind. His neurons flared into life, recognizing the presence of new muscles and bone and flesh.

A tremor shook the weight on his back. There was a wrongness to that weight, an awkward presence to it, like clothes that did not quite fit. But opening his mind, he tried to accept it, to embrace it.

At last, Chris opened his eyes. A sharp *crack* sounded as his wings snapped open, unfurling to fill the room. Feathers as long as his forearm brushed against the far wall, touched the bars of the cell, and he *felt it*, sensed the pressure against his feathers.

He grinned at Liz, unable to keep the wonder from his face. She grinned, laughed, opened her arms to embrace him.

With a deafening shriek, an alarm began to sound.

32

Angela strode around the corner and started towards the wide iron door at the end of the corridor. Heavy locking bars stretched across the dull metal, and a guard stood to either side, watching her approach. Each held a heavy rifle and wore the familiar trigger watch on his wrist. With a flick of a finger, the watches could activate all collars in their immediate vicinity, incapacitating any threat the prisoners within might pose.

Or at least, that was the idea.

Today, the watches had been reduced to worthless pieces of steel and glass. Just minutes before, Angela had entered her code to deactivate all the collars inside the facility. Halt, in his arrogance, had thought her cowed by his violence, that her fear would prevent her fighting back after his proclamation.

Instead, his revolution had given Angela the resolve to act.

Left alone in the padded room, fading in and out of consciousness, Angela had finally seen the true futility of her research. It had never been about a cure, or a weapon to fight the *Chead*. It had always been about *this*, this need for power, for a weapon to use against their enemies.

Whatever the cost.

And Angela knew, threats or no, she could not allow the project to continue.

Climbing to her feet, the weight of regret heavy on her shoulders, Angela had settled on a new path.

Now the time to act had come, and she could not hesitate.

Ahead, the guards pulled back the bolts, and the iron door swung open with a *screech*. Angela walked past the guards without breaking stride, nodding as she went.

A hushed silence hung over the narrow corridor within, as faces turned towards her. Another *screech* and the door swung shut, sealing her inside. Sucking in a shuddering breath, Angela started forward, careful to keep to the center of the hall, beyond the reach of grasping arms.

Stone-grey eyes followed her down the passage.

Tension hung like a blanket on the air as she made her way past the cells. Hate radiated from the dark creatures pressing up against the prison bars. There were meant to be ten in all: five boys, five girls.

Ten vicious killing machines, hungry for blood, for freedom.

The *Chead* watched her as she reached the corridor's end and turned back. There she paused, a frown crossing her face as she looked into one of the cells. It was empty, one of the girls was missing.

It made no sense, but there was no time to adjust her plan. She had to act. Each of the creatures had been captured in the wilderness, or suffered the change in other experiments. Each was destined to die here, never again to feel the heat of the sun on their skin. Their eyes would never see the beauty of the mountains beyond the walls, their ears would never hear the roar of ocean waves.

Or at least, that had been Halt's intention.

The *Chead* wore the familiar steel collars on their neck, but because of Angela's interference, those collars were now little more than decorative necklaces.

Standing at the end of the corridor, Angela faced the exit. Cells stretched out on either side of her, the males to her left, females to her right. Something about the *change* accelerated the development and reproductive drive of the *Chead*. Left to their own devices, they bred like rabbits. And while most of the occupants appeared almost fully mature, the oldest was just thirteen years old.

Angela steeled herself and started back towards the exit. The grey eyes followed her, alive with intelligence, searching for an opportunity. One second, one slip; that was all they needed. Several men had already lost their lives by wandering too close to the bars. Angela would not make that mistake.

But she needed them to see her, to be awake.

To be ready.

As she approached the entrance to the prison block, the guard by the door reached out to open it. She glanced at his face as she passed, a flicker of guilt touching her. But it was too late for regrets now. It was time.

As the door reached its apex, Angela looked at her watch. It was more advanced than the others, controlling more than just the candidate's collars. As head geneticist and supervisor of the project, she had control over many of the security protocols in the facility. Halt had not thought it necessary to override them.

Angela pressed her finger to the touchscreen.

Behind her, a buzzer screeched, followed by the rattling of cell doors opening. Angela leapt forward as the guards looked up, confusion turning quickly to open terror as the *Chead* emerged from their cages. The men stood frozen as Angela darted past them and began to run.

The screams of the dying chased her down the corridor.

ANGELA'S BREATH CAME IN RAGGED GASPS AS SHE TOOK A CORNER. From behind her came the roar of gunfire and the howls of the *Chead*. Overhead, lights flashed, and somewhere in the building a siren screeched. Muffled voices erupted from speakers along the corridors, a robotic voice asking her not to panic.

The thump of approaching boots came from ahead. She tensed as two guards raced into view, then relaxed as they sprinted past her, guns held at the ready. Their eyes barely registered her, but she saw their fear. Just as well. With a nine

Chead loose in the building, they would be hard-pressed to survive.

A minute later she drew up outside the other prison block. She had hesitated before detouring here—only two of the seven survivors from the PERV-A strain were locked within. But Elizabeth was here, with her haunting blue eyes, and Angela could not bring herself to abandon the girl.

Fortunately, the guards had already abandoned their posts—though whether to face the *Chead* or run, she wasn't sure. The door to the cell block had been left open, and she stepped inside, shivering as her eyes swept over the rows of empty cells.

So much loss.

Angela closed her eyes, regret welling within her. How had she been so blind? She had allowed her ambition to surpass caution, to blind her to the atrocities within the facility. Her morals, her integrity, all had been lost because of her drive to succeed.

And these children had paid the price.

Moving down the corridor, Angela searched for the two she had come for. She froze when she found them, her breath catching in her throat.

She had seen them in their fever-induced sleep, had seen the others in their comas. She already knew the experiment had succeeded; that the homeotic genes had taken. Stimulated by the final injection, they acted like a master switch, triggering the cluster of genes embedded in the candidates' genomes. The genes corresponding to wing growth.

Angela had watched the wings grow, watched the feathers sprout like seedlings from their skin. Even so, she was not prepared for the sight that greeted her.

Elizabeth and Christopher stood in all their glory, wings spread wide, stretching out to fill the cell. They had found the ragged clothes she'd left by their beds, with the clumsy holes she'd torn in the backs. The girl's black feathers pressed against the brown of the boy's, their wings entwining in the tiny space.

Angela's heart ached with the wonder of it.

"What's happening?" Christopher demanded.

Blinking, Angela tore herself from her stupor. She shook her head, then looked down at her watch and pressed a button. The cell door slid open with a dull rattle.

The two of them stood within, looks of wary surprise appearing on their faces.

"Come on," Angela said. "We're getting out of here. Hurry, the others should be awake by now."

Christopher's hand drifted to his collar. Angela shook her head and reached into her pocket. "They're deactivated." Finding the little key, she tossed it to the girl. "Here, that'll unlock them. But *hurry*."

Within seconds, their collars lay discarded on the ground. Angela watched them embrace, saw the tears shining in their eyes, but she could not pause to celebrate their freedom. Apprehension nibbled at her stomach, an awful fear that they would be caught.

"*Come on*," she urged again, waving them towards the door. "We need to find the others."

Their eyes widened then, their mouths opening in question, but she was already moving away. Sirens still sounded and red lights flashed in the ceiling, but there was no sign of movement as they re-entered the corridors. The guards remained preoccupied at the other end of the facility, and she hoped the other civilians would have already retreated to the safe room by now.

Silently, she led them through the maze of the facility, to the isolation room where the other survivors of the PERV-A strain had remained in their drug induced comas. She had swapped out their medication that morning, replacing them with saline. They would be awake by now, and she prayed they had not wandered from the room while she detoured.

Unfortunately, the surviving PERV-B candidates were lost to her. They still lay in their comas, their bodies wracked with fever, struggling to accept the chromosomal alterations of the virus. There was nothing she could do for them now.

Ahead, the door to the isolation room lay unguarded. She smiled, glad her distraction had proven so effective. With luck, they'd be long gone before anyone noticed their absence. If the guards even managed to regain control of the facility. She had seen a single *Chead* tear a man to pieces. With nine…she didn't like to think what nine *Chead* might be capable of.

But there was no more time to think of that. Angela pushed open the door and led the way inside.

IV
ESCAPE

33

Liz stumbled through the door after Chris. Every step was a struggle to keep upright. The new weight on her back threw her whole coordination out of sync, leaving her feeling strangely out of proportion. Even the simple act of closing her wings had taken several attempts, but she and Chris had finally managed to pull them tight against their backs. Even so, they niggled at her consciousness, an alien presence that would not go away.

The thought of freedom drove her on, and the knowledge that each step carried her closer to a possible reunion with Ashley and Sam. She sucked in a breath, savoring the feel of her naked neck. The collar was gone, her throat free of its steel encasing. It felt like a lifetime ago since she'd put on the awful contraption. Perhaps it was.

Blinking, Liz returned her mind to the present. Looking around, she recognized the room they had awoken in after their first injection. Beds still lined its length, but they were empty now. The whir of machines filled the air, their tubes and wires dangling free. Her chest contracted as her eyes swept the room, searching for her friends.

A thud came from their right, and she spun, raising her fists to defend herself.

Then she lowered them. Beside her, Chris chuckled. Together they watched the figure sprawled on the ground struggling to sit up.

It took a few seconds for Sam to get his tangle of arms, legs and copper wings under control, and several more before he managed to stand. A string of curses echoed from the walls as he finally pulled himself up, red in the face, puffing like he'd run a marathon. Then Liz's eyes drifted past Sam, and she gave a wild yelp.

Ashley strode forward, her lips twitching with suppressed humor. She moved with the same casual grace as before, her long legs easily finding their balance as she weaved between the empty beds. Trailing out behind her, a pair of snow-white wings shone in the overhead lights. They quivered as she moved, slowly lifting from the ground, expanding across the room.

Liz laughed again as the two of them came together in a hug. She clung to her friend for a moment, Ashley's grip just as tight. When they finally broke apart, Ashley looked past Liz and raised an eyebrow at the doctor.

When Fallow did not speak, Ashley nodded and turned back to Liz. "I guess we found their weakness."

Chris shrugged. "She found us."

The distant wail of sirens prickled at Liz's ears, reminding her they weren't out of danger yet. Before she could speak, though, another movement came from the far side of the room. Beyond Sam, she found the remaining survivors of the project.

Her heart sank as she looked at Richard and Jasmine. Their attitude towards the four of them didn't seem to have changed in the untold weeks they'd lain unconscious. They stood on the far side of the room, arms crossed and eyes hard with suspicion. But it was not their faces that drew her attention. Their wings lay half-furled behind them, each sporting dark emerald feathers, like those of some tropical parrot. Their eyes caught hers and Liz quickly looked away, unable to face their unspoken accusations, their anger that she was alive, while Joshua was gone.

Of course, she thought. *Of everyone else who could have survived, it would be Richard and Jasmine…*

Well, Richard and Jasmine, and the girl.

Standing beside them was a young girl of maybe thirteen years. Locks of grey hair tumbled around her face, and her eyes were wide with fear. A button nose and freckled cheeks only served to make her look younger. How she could have survived this far, Liz could not begin to guess. She shivered as the girl's eyes, one blue, the other green, found her from across the room.

Looking away, Liz cast her gaze around the room one last time, searching for the others. There had still been dozens of candidates left the last time she had been there. But now there was only the seven of them, each sporting the plain grey uniforms they'd found at the ends of their beds.

"Where are the others?" she whispered, turning to face Fallow.

The doctor bowed her head. When she did not respond, Chris repeated Liz's question. "Doctor Fallow, where are the rest of them?"

Fallow looked back up, her eyes flashing. "Don't call me that. I don't deserve to be called 'doctor' after what I've done. My name is Angela." Her voice shook. "And the others did not survive. The physiological changes…their bodies could not support them. Even unconscious, the accelerated wing growth was too much. Their hearts gave out from the strain."

An awful anger spread through Liz as she stepped in close to the doctor. Fallow flinched, but this time she did not look away. "How many did you kill?" Liz hissed.

Angela Fallow closed her eyes. "I've lost count." Her eyes snapped back open. "But it ends here. I won't let them take you too."

Liz might have struck her if Chris hadn't placed a hand on her shoulder. Looking at him, she saw the sadness in his eyes, the same sorrow from which her own rage spawned. She stepped away from Angela and hugged Chris to her. She smiled as Ashley joined them, then Sam.

"Ahem." Liz looked up at a new voice. Richard raised an eyebrow and tapped a finger to his collar. "Someone care to share the key?"

Chris nodded. Reaching into his pocket he pulled out the little key Angela had given them and handed it over. The clink of the thick steel collars striking the concrete followed as the five of them freed themselves.

"Are you okay there, Sam?" Chris asked, as Sam finally managed to unlock the clasp of his collar.

Sam cursed beneath his breath and tossed the collar aside. "Almost," he said, a shiver running through his copper feathers. Slowly his wings contracted. "Don't know what the idiots were thinking, putting these clunky things on our backs." He paused, eyeing Angela uncertainly. "Err, no offense, Doc—I mean, Angela?"

Angela shook her head, a sad smile touching her lips. "It's alright. You have every right to complain. I would have…I would have stopped them before they gave you the injection, but I was unconscious. Then I had to wait…until you were stable again."

"It's okay." Of all of them, Ashley seemed the best adapted to her new appendages. She looked over her shoulder, smiling. "I kind of like them."

"Yeah." Sam's voice was gruff, but he continued with his usual humor. "But yours are tiny. Did you have to make mine so *big?*"

Angela raised a hand to her mouth, trying to hide her smile. "It took some research of various avian species to get our specifications right. We looked at genome variation between Andean Condors and the Wandering Albatross to identify the genes relating to wing size in fragmented DNA from *Argentavis magnificens*."

"Argentavis what?" Richard growled from nearby.

"The largest known bird to have flown," Jasmine said, surprising Liz.

Angela nodded. "It could weigh up to two-hundred fifty pounds. Once we'd identified all the genes related to wing surface area, we linked them with those controlling your own height and weight. Thus, why yours are so…big, Samuel."

Sam glanced at Ashley. "I think she's calling me fat…"

Smiling, Liz looked around their little group, a strange elation rising within her. Even with the open animosity of Jasmine and Richard, there was a connection between the seven of them now, a shared experience which could not be denied. Of all the desperate souls who had passed through this place, they alone had survived.

They alone had evolved.

"But why?" she asked suddenly, swinging on the doctor. "Why do any of this?"

"To stop the *Chead*," Angela whispered, "or at least, that's what we were told. The creatures are spreading, and humanity is hopelessly outmatched. We needed something more, soldiers able to match them for speed and power, who could detect their presence, whether in a crowd or a field of corn. Your strength, your senses, your wings, they were all meant for the sole purpose of hunting down the *Chead*."

"Were?" Ashley asked.

Angela shook her head. "I am afraid Halt and his superiors have ulterior motives."

"Not if I can help it," Sam growled and started towards the exit. "I don't know about you lot, but I'm about ready to leave."

"Wait!" Chris called him back. He looked at Angela. "What about our parents?"

"They're…not here," Angela replied shortly. "I'm sorry, Christopher, but we can do nothing for them here. Your friend is right, it's time we left."

There was a strange pitch to Angela's voice, and Liz sensed there was more she wasn't telling them. But before she could question the doctor further, Angela started towards the door. The others exchanged glances, still processing the barrage of information. Feathers rustled as wings were furled, and then Chris started after her, Liz close behind.

Ahead of them, Angela was reaching out to open the door, when it suddenly swung inwards to meet her.

And Halt stepped into the room.

34

Liz froze at the sight of Halt, her heart dropping into the pit of her stomach. His eyes swept the room, widening, his brow wrinkling with rage. Before any of them could react, his gaze settled on Angela. Clutching a pistol in one hand, he sprang.

Angela managed a scream before he was on her, his arm wrapping around her waist, spinning her against him. Pressing the gun to her head, he drew back his lips.

"What do we have here, doctor?" Halt snarled. Angela flinched as he jabbed the gun into her ribs. "Have you betrayed me? Have you betrayed us all?"

Clenching her fists, Liz inhaled, scenting gunpowder in the air. Halt's gun had already been fired recently; this was no idle threat. A cold grin twisted his lips as Angela struggled in his grasp.

"*That's enough!*" he growled.

Halt swung the gun, catching Angela in the forehead. She slumped in his arms and he turned his attention on Liz and the others. "Don't come any closer."

Liz suppressed a moan. Angela had gone limp, but her eyes were still wide and staring. Her hands swiped feebly at Halt, but he was twice her size. Biting her lip, Liz glanced at the others.

Her arms shook, the sensation spreading through her body, down her spine, to the foreignness of her wings. A phantom ache started in her throat, a distant reminder of the collar pressing against her flesh.

I won't go back.

She flinched as her fingernails dug into her palms. Drawing in a deep breath, she unclenched her hands, trying to calm herself, to find a way out of the trap. Her eyes travelled across the space between herself and Halt.

Too far.

But Chris was closer. From the corner of her eyes, Liz saw him slide another step towards the doctors. If he could reach Angela…

No, they were still too far away.

She looked back at Angela, seeing the emotion washing over the doctor's face—fear, anger, regret. The woman's head sagged as her eyes slid closed, her whole body trembling. Then her head snapped up, a new resolve now shining from her face. The fear had vanished, replaced by…

Liz opened her mouth to shout, but she was already too late. She wasn't sure what she would have said anyway. Would she have begged Angela not to act? Or had she only wanted to thank her, for finally freeing them?

Either way, Liz never got the chance. Angela jerked in Halt's arms, hurling her weight backwards. Small as she was, it was still enough to throw Halt off-balance. He cursed, struggling to recover.

In that instant, Chris charged. His wings snapped out to beat the air as he leapt, closing the gap in seconds. Arms wide, he reached for the doctor…

Boom.

The roar of the gun was so sudden, so deafening in the sealed room, that Liz found herself stumbling back in shock.

Then Chris barreled into Halt, his fist catching the man in the face, hurtling him through the air. He struck the floor with a dull thud, bounced once, before the concrete wall brought him to an abrupt stop. A low groan whispered from his lips as he slumped down and lay still. The gun slid across the floor, coming to rest in a nook between the floor and the wall.

Chris landed lightly on his feet, wings still outstretched, eyes locked on their tormentor. But Liz was already sprinting forward, falling to her knees beside Angela. A dark pool was spreading around the woman, the overhead lights glimmering on its scarlet surface. Her eyes were open, staring at the ceiling, her mouth wide in a silent scream. One hand still clutched at her chest, where a small red mark stained her lab coat.

Liz knelt beside her, tears misting her vision. A low moan came from her throat as she reached out and shook the woman. The soft pad of footsteps came from behind her, but she took no notice.

Disbelief threaded through her mind. Whatever her crimes, Angela Fallow had been the only one in this place to show the prisoners any compassion. Twice she had stopped Halt's torture, and in the end, she had followed her conscience, had freed them from their cells.

Now she was dead.

A terrible rage rose in Liz's chest, driving her to her feet. She leapt at Halt, crossing the room in a single bound. She reached down and grasped him by his lab coat, hauling him to his feet. Almost without effort she lifted him up and slammed him into the wall. He groaned, his eyelids flickering as she pinned him there, but he did not wake. Gritting her teeth, Liz drew back a fist.

Ashley caught her arm before the blow could fall. Liz half-turned, straining against the other girl, a snarl rumbling up from her chest. Frustration built inside her and she spun. Dropping Halt, she swung at Ashley instead.

Ashley leaned back and Liz's blow found only open air. Her other hand shot out, catching Liz in the chest, pushing her back. Stumbling, Liz straightened and leapt at her. A terrible rage burned within her, filling Liz with a need to rend, to tear the flesh from her enemies.

"*Liz!*" Ashley yelled, raising an arm to protect herself.

The scream gave Liz pause. Blood pounding in her head, she

drew back, even as a voice in her head shouted for her to attack. She sucked in a breath and the red haze faded, revealing the fear dancing in the eyes of her friends. Taking in another mouthful of air, she faced Ashley.

"*Why?*" she asked, her voice breaking. "Why did you stop me?"

"He's not worth it," Ashley breathed. "He's not, Liz. Don't let this place turn you into them. Don't let it make you a cold-blooded killer."

Liz clenched her fists, trembling with the effort to suppress her rage. Red light flickered across her vision as she looked down at Halt, and she fought the impulse to snap his neck.

She bowed her head. "He'll come for us," she whispered.

"They'll come for us anyway," Chris replied, placing a hand on her shoulder. "Besides, I doubt he'll be…*anything* after this. They were always talking about needing results." He waved a hand. "And this seems just about the opposite of that."

Slowly, Liz allowed her body to relax. Looking at Chris, she nodded.

He stepped forward then, arms opening, drawing her to him. They stood there in silence, holding each other, the others forgotten, the nightmare around them a distant memory.

When they finally parted, they turned to face the others. Ashley and Sam, Richard and Jasmine, and the strange little girl stared back. Their eyes shone with emotion: hope mixed with anger, love with hate. Shivering, Liz looked at Chris.

"Let's go."

35

The tired hinges of the door screeched as Chris threw himself against it. His shoulder throbbed, and his wings gave a little flap, but on the next blow the door caved. He stumbled after it, his momentum carrying him outside, where a blast of icy air caught in his wings and hurled him backwards. Pain shot through his bare feet as he stumbled on stones. Dropping to his knees, he braced himself against the howling wind, and glanced back at the others.

They filed out after him, one by one, their eyes alight with wonder. Turning, Chris looked out over a world blanketed in white. Flakes of snow swirled around them, drifting ever downwards, their intricate patterns catching in the light shining overhead. Clouds covered the sky, but after so long inside, it still seemed impossibly bright. Blinking back tears, Chris drank in the world around him.

Rocky mountains stretched high above them, sprouting like enormous trees from the slope on which they stood. Sheer escarpments of rock raced upwards, disappearing into the clouds, their surfaces white with ice. Farther down the valley the snow and ice gave way to barren rock.

Around the facility there were no trees or vegetation, only jagged gravel that promised to make walking difficult. They hadn't stopped to search for better equipment, and now Chris shivered as the icy air tore through his thin clothing. A dull ache began at the base of his skull, though despite their now undoubted height above sea level, his breath came easily.

Chris stared up the valley, his eyes trailing over the snow-covered boulders, up to where the slope disappeared into a narrow gorge. Glancing back down, he studied the valley as it fell away from the facility. There was not a sliver of cover in sight. Even so, down was tempting. Down would bring them to warmer air, out of the mountains, towards civilization. Perhaps they could find someone there to help them, to protect them from the monsters that would hunt them.

Steeling himself, Chris dismissed the temptation. It was the route their jailers would expect them to take, and without cover, the chase would be over before it began.

No, they needed to do the unexpected. They needed to go higher.

The others gathered, huddling close, wings wrapped tightly around their bodies to fend off the frigid air. His body trembling violently, Chris did the same, his wings curving around to encase him. The relief was instant, and the cold creeping through his chest vanished.

The others were watching him, wonder and fear mingling on their faces. They knew the next few hours would decide whether they lived or died. Whatever Angela had done to distract the guards, it wouldn't keep them busy forever. Before long, men with guns would come for them. Chris wanted to be far away by then.

Quickly he explained his plan, watching as Liz, Sam and Ashley nodded. Richard and Jasmine only stood in sullen silence, their faces expressionless, while the young girl hovered on the edge of the circle. So far they hadn't gotten a word from her. She huddled in close to Jasmine, a nameless, unknown quantity. Not for the first time, Chris wondered how she had survived Halt's trials.

When Chris finished speaking, he eyed Jasmine and Richard, expecting them to argue, but they only nodded. "Let's go then," Richard said abruptly.

Relieved, Chris turned and began the long trek up towards the canyon. He moved as fast as the jagged gravel allowed him, wincing with each step. Silently he cursed their haste. Boots would have saved them time and possible frostbite out in the mountains, but there was no going back now. He made sure the others were following and pressed on.

Half an hour passed as they made their slow way up. The wind howled, threatening to hurl them from the rocky slope, but they continued, wings pulled tight around them. Briefly, Chris considered trying to use them, but dropped the thought just as quickly. Conditions were not ideal for a first attempt at flight.

When they finally reached the canyon mouth, Chris paused, glancing back as the other filed up behind him. One by one they joined him in the shadow beneath the cliffs. Within, the canyon twisted deeper into the mountains. A river flowed along its far side, and the roar of water echoed around them.

The hairs on Chris's neck tingled as he looked down the valley and saw black-garbed figures spilling from the facility. They gathered near the high walls, concentrating around several figures in white. Chris blinked, and the scene below came into sudden focus. It was as though a film had been removed from his eyes, and now the whole world was revealed to him in more detail than he could ever have imagined.

There was fear on the faces of the guards as they huddled close together, their rifles clutched tight. Blood and tears marked their clothing, and Chris wondered what exactly Angela had done to distract them.

His attention was drawn to the doctors standing with them. There was no sign of Halt, but he recognized Doctor Radly and Faulks. They didn't seem to have noticed Chris and the others yet, but it would only take one glance change that.

Silently, Chris waved for the others to get into cover, not trusting his voice, in case it carried down to those below. He scrambled up the last few feet of the gravel slope and dropped down into the canyon.

The others were quick to join him, coming over the lip one

by one. They retreated behind the boulders lodged in the mouth of the pass, their eyes on Chris, waiting for him to speak.

Heart pounding in his chest, Chris slipped back out from behind the boulders. Crouching low, he half-crawled back up to the gravel lip. At the entrance to the pass, he dropped to his stomach and crawled the last few inches. There, he lifted his head and peered at the facility.

And immediately dropped back down.

36

Chris slammed his fist into the gravel, cursing their luck.

A few more seconds, and we would have been clear.

He slid down the slope to the others. Biting back his frustration, he only shook his head at their questioning looks. Below, a line of black figures were streaming up towards the canyon. They had been spotted. Now all they could do was flee, and hope to outrun their pursuers.

"They've seen us," he hissed. He began to thread his way through the boulders strewn across the canyon floor. "Let's go."

Gritting his teeth against the howling wind, Chris picked his way over the rocky ground, taking care to avoid patches of ice. The stones were slick, worn smooth by the passage of floodwaters, but at least they were gentler on his feet. Above them the canyon walls closed in, stretching up two, almost three hundred feet.

Rocks ground against one another as the others followed, shifting beneath their weight. To their right the river tumbled over its stony bed, roaring as it rushed down a series of cascades, making its slow journey through the twisting canyon. In the spring it would rise with the melting snow, filling the gorge, but still in the grips of winter, it remained thankfully low.

Chris's gaze carried up the valley, following the sheer walls as they twisted out of sight. He scanned the ground ahead, picking out a trail amidst the rock-strewn ground. He was quickly adapting to the weight of his wings. His muscles surged with a newfound energy, with the joy of freedom. Behind them the mouth of the canyon remained empty, but even so he picked up the pace, springing from stone to stone with hardly a pause between. Fear of the guards and their guns drove him on. Though they were moving at a good pace, their pursuers did not have to catch them—only set them in their rifle's sights.

Redoubling his efforts, Chris felt the granite cliffs press in around him. From somewhere ahead, the roar of water grew louder. Like distant thunder it drew him on, calling him deeper into the mountains. Sucking in great mouthfuls of damp air, Chris raced for the first bend in the canyon.

Boulders the size of cars littered the ground. Where the canyon narrowed they clustered in groups, almost blocking their passage. They scrambled over them one by one, slipping on the wet surfaces while the others watched, awaiting their turn.

Chris's ears tingled as a voice carried up the canyon. Acting on instinct, he grabbed Liz and pulled her behind a boulder, waving for the others to get down. An instant later the shriek of bullets tore the air, followed by the sharp *crack* of rock shattering. Cowering behind shelter, they watched as the boulder on which they'd just been standing disintegrated. Hot lead tore great chunks from the rock, turning smooth stone to pockmarks.

For a moment, Chris stood frozen, terrified by the sheer display of power. In his mind he saw himself caught by the bullets, saw his flesh tear and his bones shatter. Then Liz grasped him by the shoulder and shook him. He blinked, returning to the present to find her crystal eyes staring at him, just a few feet away.

On impulse he grabbed her by the waist and pulled her close. They kissed, hard and fast, the moment filled with a desperate passion, with the thrill of a chase. A second later they broke apart and turned to face the others. Richard raised an eyebrow, but Chris ignored him. The first bend in the canyon was close now, just a few more yards away. But in the open space they would be exposed to the guards and their unforgiving bullets.

Yet they had to move. No doubt men were already climbing towards them, growing closer with every passing second.

"We run for it," was all Chris said, before he turned and leapt from cover, unwilling to wait and see whether the others followed.

The buzz of bullets turned to a roar as he appeared from behind the boulder. Then he was racing across the open ground, stones slipping beneath his bare feet, faster than thought. With each step the shriek of bullets grew louder, as the guards far below adjusted their aim. Stone chips tore his flesh as the impact of bullets shook the ground beneath him. He ducked low, the hackles on his neck rising in anticipation of pain.

His wings snapped open, beating hard, driving him faster. He stumbled as he miscalculated his next jump, almost falling before recovering with a wild wave of arms. Liz bounded past, flashing him a sideways glance. But he was already up and beside her, pushing hard, his lungs burning not with exhaustion, but fear. Around him he heard the gasps of the others, their desperate, unintelligible cries.

And over it all, the screech of bullets.

Suddenly the air was clear, the cliff rising up to shield them from view. Together they drew to a stop, sucking in long mouthfuls of air, their eyes wild as they looked at each other, shocked and elated, thrilled by their survival.

They did not pause for long. They had won a respite, but they were still far from free. Ahead the canyon narrowed, the twists and turns coming closer together, and for the next thirty minutes they did not see their pursuers again. The rocks grew larger, until only boulders remained. They blocked the gorge, the creek threading its way between them, over and under, plunging ever down towards the hidden guards. The roar of water continued to grow, and the taste of the air changed, filling with moisture. In his mind, Chris pictured the stream cascading down into the canyon, and prayed it would offer them an escape.

He pressed on, drawing the others with him. The canyon

floor grew steeper, winding up towards the clifftops high overhead. Their progress slowed, the going becoming more difficult. In places they were forced to backtrack where the way grew too steep, too treacherous to pass.

Finally, Chris bounded around the final bend in the canyon. The roar of water turned to a deafening thunder. His stride slowed as he took in the sight above. Beside him, Liz continued her upward march, her head down, eyes fixed on the ground. It was only when he reached out and grabbed her shoulder that she looked up, that she saw where he had led them.

37

Chris had not been wrong about the waterfall. Three hundred feet above their heads, a river rushed over the edge of the cliff and out into the void. Water filled the air, whirling as it was caught by the wind, turning it to a fine mist, to a light rain that fell all around them. At the base of the falls, the remains of the river crashed down onto a jagged pile of rocks. From there, the stream wound its way through the canyon to where the seven of them stood.

Beyond the waterfall, the canyon twisted back on itself, ending in a wall of sheer rock. A pile of rubble had accumulated against the cliff opposite the waterfall, stretching up almost two hundred feet. Straggly patches of vegetation sprouted from the rubble, fed by the ready source of water.

Chris closed his eyes, feeling the spray of water on his cheeks, even where they stood several hundred feet away. It settled in his hair and trickled down his face, until he gave an angry shake of his head and wiped it away. He clenched his fists, shivering with cold and frustration.

There was no way they could climb those cliffs, no way they could reach the top before the bullets of the guards found them. He had led them to a dead end, into a trap. With the guards closing in, there was nowhere left to go.

Looking at the others, he saw his despair reflected in their faces. Only Ashley seemed undaunted. She walked up beside him, her eyes traveling up the canyon, to the pile of rubble. He turned, following her gaze, straining to see through the mist. Jagged boulders clustered around the top of the rubble, and the cliffs above them were cracked and broken. At some point, part of the cliff must have given way. There was no telling for sure, but from a distance it looked as though there was a crack they might be able to climb.

"Let's go," Ashley said, flashing him a smile as she took the lead.

Chris was glad to relinquish the position. The weight of failure hung heavy on his shoulders. The others did not speak, but he could feel the eyes of Jasmine and Richard on his back. Ahead, Ashley seemed to glide across the rocks, moving with a grace Chris wished he could match. She reached the rubble mound well before the rest of them and started up.

Following her, Chris only managed a few steps before the loose gravel slipped beneath his feet. He threw out an arm, grasping the branches of a disheveled bush, then screamed as thorns tore into his palm. Cursing, he regained his balance and released the bush, only then daring to look at his hand.

Dark marks spotted his palm, the broken thorn tips embedded deep in his flesh. Blood seeped from a dozen cuts and the skin was already turning red around the marks. He swore again, but there was little he could do about it now. Cradling his arm, he moved after Ashley.

The mist closed around them as they climbed, soaking them to the skin. Chris shivered as a drop of water ran down his back and caught in his feathers. A tingle ran up his spine as a thought came to him. The feathered appendages trembled in response.

Fly!

Chris shook his head, casting the idea back out into the void. With the winds roaring through the canyon, and the cliffs pressing close, it would be suicide.

As they neared the top of the mound, the wind picked up speed. It howled down over the cliffs to pummel at them, tearing at their wings and threatening to send them plummeting to the rocks far below. Above, the river continued its eternal plunge over the granite cliffs, filling the air with swirling clouds of water vapor.

A cry came from above. Chris looked up in time to see Ashley slip, then threw himself to the side as a rock bounced down towards him. He shouted a warning to the others, but thankfully they had spread out, and it tumbled harmlessly past them.

Recovering, Ashley continued her ascent, though Chris noticed she was favoring her left hand now. But she was already drawing level with the ring of boulders crowning the slope. Picking up his pace, Chris soon joined her at the base of the great rocks. Together they waited for the others to join them.

Once the seven had gathered on the narrow ledge, they turned to face the boulders. Here, Ashley took the lead again, squeezing in between two of the boulders. The way was narrow, and the extra bulk of their wings didn't help, but with a little difficulty, Chris managed to follow her. Ahead, the crevice ended at another boulder, but Ashley was already making short work of scrambling up, using the rocks on either side of her to climb.

Chris waited for her to reach the top before starting his ascent. The sharp pitch of the boulders and his injured hand made it difficult to find purchase. Cursing to himself, he pressed his back against one of the rocks to wedge himself in place, then levered himself up bit by bit using his arms and legs.

When he reached the top, Ashley was already gone. Following her wet footprints through the boulders, his optimism began to return. If they could wedge themselves into the crack in the cliff, they might be able to scramble up in the same way he had just managed. It would be a long and difficult haul—at least a hundred feet remained to be climbed—but it was better than waiting for the guards to catch them.

Chris stumbled as he emerged onto open ground. Realizing he was in the center of the ring of boulders, he looked around and found Ashley with her head pressed against the cliff, her fists clenched against the sheer stone. She turned as he approached, her eyes finding his.

His stomach twisted as Ashley slid down the wall until she sat, and covered her face with her hands. Her shoulders heaved as silent sobs shook her, tears spilling between her fingers.

Behind her the cliff stretched up another hundred feet, smooth and unmarked, the shadow they had thought was a crack no more than a change in the rock, a darker shade of granite.

They were trapped.

38

Liz paused as she emerged from the boulders and found Chris and Ashley slumped against the cliff. Their faces were ashen, their eyes despondent. In that instant, she knew they were finished. Her shoulders sagged, but she moved across to Chris and placed a hand on his head. He did not look up, just sat staring at the barren gravel.

Crouching, Liz pulled him to her chest. Stones rattled as Sam appeared beside her. He squatted by Ashley, whispering softly to her, pulling her up, getting her moving again. Trapped or not, there was no time to pause, to sit and wait for death to come for them.

"I'm sorry," Chris murmured.

Liz slid her fingers through his hair and down to his chin, turning his head to face her. "This isn't your fault, Chris. You were right, this was our best chance. If we'd gone the other way, they would have already shot us dead. Now get up. We have to decide what to do next."

It took several tugs on Chris's arm before he gathered himself and stood. By then, Sam had Ashley looking more herself, though Liz suspected she was only wearing a brave face. But then, that's all any of them had left now.

"So, what now?" Jasmine crossed her arms, her eyes flashing as she looked around the circle. "I'm not going back."

Richard nodded his agreement.

Liz shivered, thinking of the guards creeping up the canyon towards them, of their black rifles shining in the afternoon light, promising death.

No, we can't go back.

To go back now would be worse than if they'd never escaped. They had tasted freedom, had rid themselves of the awful collars and breathed the fresh mountain air. And freezing though they were, with their wings drawn tight around their torsos, they were alive.

"There's nowhere left to go," Chris said, his voice cracking.

"Then we fight," Sam put in, his brow creased. Liz had never seen him so serious.

Around the circle, the others nodded, but Liz found herself shaking her head. Stepping past them, she climbed the nearest boulder, until she was perched atop it. She stared out over the gorge, peering through the swirling mist, seeking out their pursuers. The wind tore at her, sending her black hair flying across her face, but she ignored it.

She heard scuffling from behind her as the others climbed up, but did not turn. "What do you think?" she shouted over the wind.

Chris and the others gathered around her and looked out over the edge.

Chris swallowed and retreated a step, his eyes widening. The others stood in varying states of fear, though none were as close to the edge as Liz. To her right was the slope they'd just climbed, but directly beneath the boulder, the gravel fell away in a sheer drop, all the way to the canyon floor two hundred feet below.

Standing there, Liz felt no fear, only a silent resolve.

She would not go quietly back to her chains, to the cold cruelty of the doctors, to their needles and torture. She would not surrender to their bullets, to their harsh violence.

No, she would fight, she would resist, she would rage.

"You know," Ashley mused beside her, "they say birds just

know. That their parents push them from the nest, and before they hit the ground, it comes to them."

"Care to go first?" Sam muttered.

Silence fell then as they each stared out over the canyon, watching as the tiny specks of the guards came into view. They crawled towards them like deadly ants, eyes searching the boulders strewn around them. Their gaze did not lift to where the seven of them stood, not yet.

Shivering, Liz looked at the others.

They looked back, waiting.

Turning to the edge, Liz took a deep breath. Movement came from beside her as Chris stepped forward, his fingers reaching out to entwine with hers. He glanced at her, his face drained of color. Naked fear looked out from his eyes, and she remembered his haunting climb up the training tower. Even so, he smiled.

"Just like baby birds, right?" He tried to laugh, but it came out more as a shriek.

Liz nodded, her stomach swirling. She closed her eyes, focusing on the foreign appendages on her back, feeling their presence, embracing them. They were still alien to her, a violation of her body…but she needed them now, needed to embrace them as a part of her.

Concentrating, Liz willed them to life.

With a *crack* of unfurling feathers, the great black expanse of her wings snapped open. The others gasped, but beside her Liz sensed movement. She smiled as Chris's tawny brown wings stretched out towards her own. A tremor shook her as their wingtips met, their feathers brushing together.

Liz flashed one last look back at the others. They wore wide grins on their face now, and their eyes were alive with excitement. She grinned back, and with Chris beside her, turned to face open air.

Together, they leapt out into the void.

39

Chris's stomach lurched into his chest as he plunged from the edge. The ground raced towards him at a terrifying speed, the jagged rocks looming large in his vision. His fear of falling realized, he opened his mouth and screamed.

Then his wings gave a sharp *crack* as they caught the air, and he was soaring, the wild wind catching in his twenty-four-foot wingspan, driving him up, up, up. His stomach twisted again, dropping sharply as the ground fell away. Chris let out another scream as he shot past the pale faces of his friends still standing atop the boulders.

The fear slid like Chris like water, and concentrating, he focused on turning, beating his wings to counter the powerful drafts swirling around him, and risked a wave to those below. The others waved back, then with only a moment's hesitation, they followed Chris and Liz off the cliff.

Chris swirled, his wings turning by what seemed to be a will of their own, and watched his friends plummet from the cluster of boulders. They dropped a dozen feet before their wings caught, halting their freefall and sending them hurtling back up into the sky. Broad grins split their faces, their eyes wild, their laughter echoing off the cliffs. In those briefest of moments, their hunters, their fears, all were forgotten. There was only the joy of flight.

But it could not last. An ache began in the center of Chris's back, and already he could feel the strain in his chest and abdomen, the muscles pulling tight to keep his wings moving. With their broad expanse, there seemed to be no need for giant wingbeats, but even the incremental adjustments of feathers and muscle was draining him. Looking at the others, he could see the strain beginning to affect them as well.

The mist swirled, providing them some cover from the guards below, or at least he hoped.

Sucking in a breath, he shouted across to the others, his words barely audible over the *thump* of wingbeats. "We have to fly over the cliffs!"

He had been studying the cliffs as the others gathered around him. They still towered overhead, their peaks tantalizingly out of reach. With the swirling winds hindering them, it would take a massive effort to climb those last hundred feet. He looked again for the guards and found them near the base of the rubble. They were looking up the slope, but they still had not spotted their winged prey.

After all, who would have guessed they could fly?

Returning his attention to the cliffs, Chris willed himself upwards. Muscles strained across his back and chest, his feathers shifted, and with a surge of elation he rose several feet. The others followed him, their faces creased with concentration, their eyes fixed on the ledge above. It wasn't far and still growing closer, but the winds were shifting, fighting against them. And as they neared the top, the raging waters grew closer, soaking them through, stealing away the last of their warmth.

Still they pressed on, their wings beating hard in the thin air. Water accumulated on their feathers, weighing them down. Chris's stomach tightened as muscles he'd never used stretched and twisted, driving his wings forward, sending him upwards.

Bit by bit, the top of the cliffs drew closer.

When they were still thirty feet away, Chris risked a glance down, and swore.

The guards were looking up at them, hands pointing, their eyes wide and mouths hanging open. Already one was dropping to his knee; others quickly followed suit. Rifles lifted to shoulders and a gun barrel flashed. In the open air, the seven of them presented an easy target.

By a will of their own, Chris's wings twisted, sending him whirling sideways, even as he screamed at the others.

"Look out!"

Suddenly the air was alive with the screech of bullets. The others scattered like a flock of doves, flying outwards in all directions, though they strained to keep rising, to reach the clifftops, and safety.

Every inch of his body screaming, Chris drove himself on. Threads of terror wrapped their way around him, but somehow he found the strength to hold on. His wings worked by instinct now, alive with desperation, driven by the need to escape.

Abruptly he found himself in clear air. One instant the whiz of bullets and howling wind was all around him, then it was gone. Looking down, he realized he had made it, that he had crossed the threshold of the cliffs. The canyon had disappeared from view, dropping away as he shot over the icy ground a few feet below, still tracking the stream upwards.

Glancing back, he watched Sam shoot up over the lip of the cliff and then dive towards the ground, quickly followed by Jasmine and Richard. They evened out about thirty feet from the ground and raced towards where Chris was coming to a stop. They wore broad grins on their faces, though their cheeks were red and their breath billowed in clouds of vapor.

Chris looked past them, holding his breath, waiting for Ashley and Liz and the girl.

They appeared one by one, Liz first, then the girl, and finally, rising laboriously into sight, Ashley. Liz and the girl swept down towards them, but Ashley was struggling to maintain her height. Her wings were barely moving now, and her face was turning purple. She hovered over the lip of the cliff, drifting slowly towards them, driven by sheer determination.

Her eyes closed with sudden relief as she reached the clear

air. Straightening out, her wings spread wide to catch the gentler breeze. A smile warmed her face as she looked across at them.

Then her smile faltered, her eyes widening as a shot echoed up from below. A red stain flowered on her chest and blood sprayed the air. Without a sound, Ashley's wings folded, and she plummeted to the icy ground.

40

Ashley lay in a tangled mess of limbs and feathers and wings, her flesh torn and broken, her face buried in snow. The only signs she lived came from the slow rise and fall of her back, the low gurgling from her chest. She coughed, half-rolling to reveal her battered face. Blood seeped from between her lips in a slow trickle, staining the snow beneath her.

She didn't move as they raced to her side. Her eyes were closed, and there was little chance she could be conscious after the fall. Chris was shocked she was even alive—though he wasn't sure if that was a blessing for her, or a curse. Her wings lay at awkward angles around her, and when he glanced at her legs he had to look away.

The bullet had taken her in the back and passed straight through her. Somehow it had missed her heart, but with the blood bubbling from her mouth, it appeared to have found a lung.

Another groan rattled from Ashley's chest, tearing at Chris's heart. He crossed the last few feet between them and crouched beside her. Tears built in his eyes, but angrily he wiped them away. He grasped Ashley's hand and gave it a gentle squeeze.

"Ashley," he whispered as the others gathered around them. "Ashley, it's okay, we're here."

Ashley. Brave, bold, elegant. When he'd first laid eyes on her, he'd thought her fragile, a sheltered city girl incapable of standing up for herself. She had put those misconceptions to rest with her first words. And time and time again since. She had proven herself stronger than any of them, her will unquenchable.

And now she lay here on the side of a mountain, her blood staining the frozen earth, and there was nothing any of them could do to help her.

She was dying.

Stones crunched as Sam crouched beside him, tears streaming down his face. Stretching out a tentative hand, he wiped the blood from Ashley's lips, as though that simple act might wake her, might bring her back to them. A sob tore from his throat as a fresh bubble of blood rose between her lips and burst.

He reached for her, as though to draw her into his arms, and then stopped. He knelt there with one arm outstretched, torn between his desperation to help her, and the fear he would only hurt her further.

The others stood around in silence, each lost in their own thoughts.

Long minutes dragged by as they watched her struggle, her every breath a desperate battle. They had time to spare now, though in truth all thought of escape had vanished. On the snowy plateau, they sat by their friend and watched her life slipping away.

As minutes ticked towards an hour, Ashley still clung to life. Her body was torn and broken, her lifeblood staining the snow red, but still she breathed, still she fought on.

Finally, Chris knew they could wait no longer. Sucking in a breath, he stood. Tears stung his eyes as Liz joined him, sliding an arm beneath his shoulder. He looked at the others, saw the indecision in even Jasmine and Richard's eyes. They could not stand here waiting for Ashley to die. And yet, they could not abandon her, could not let her last moments on this earth pass alone on this harsh mountainside.

He looked at the others, hating the question in their eyes.

They wanted him to make a decision, though he was not sure when he'd become their leader. It felt strange, especially given Richard and Jasmine's animosity. But there was no time to debate it now.

"We can carry her," Chris whispered at last.

"No," Sam croaked, surprising him. The young man looked up at Chris, his eyes red with tears, and shook his head. "No, you can't bring her with you. She'll only slow you down."

"We can't leave her," Liz said.

Sam closed his eyes, a shudder going through him. "I know," he breathed.

Chris stared at him, a tightness growing in his stomach. "What are you saying, Sam?"

"Go, Chris." Resolve shone in Sam's eyes now. "Go. Take the others with you. Leave, fly away from here, be free. I'll look after her." His voice broke as he finished, but there was steel in his words.

Looking at Sam, Chris wondered at the young man's courage. He opened his mouth to argue, to convince his friend to come with them, that they could carry Ashley, could keep her comfortable until…

"Maybe they can save her…" Sam finished.

With those five words, Chris realized they would never change Sam's mind. He meant to sacrifice himself for Ashley. He would give away his freedom, his life even, if there was the slightest chance she might live. Looking at her, Chris tried and failed to summon the same hope. Between the bullet and the fall, there was little left of the graceful girl he had known.

Yet still Ashley fought on, her iron will unyielding. Thinking of the miracles the facility had performed on them, he wondered if Sam might be right.

At last he nodded. In his arms, Liz began to tremble, but he pulled her tight before she could try to argue. She glanced at him, anger burning in her eyes, but he only shook his head.

This was Sam's decision to make. His alone.

Jasmine and Richard shared a glance. Whatever their history with Ashley and Sam, Chris doubted they had ever wished for this. Perhaps they would even miss his light-hearted presence.

"Good luck, Sam," Chris said, swallowing hard.

Sam nodded and then turned back to Ashley. With the utmost care, he slid his hands beneath her back and lifted her into his arms. She gave a tiny groan as she left the ground, seeming to shrink into Sam's massive frame. Her head lifted, her eyelids fluttering, before she nestled into the crook of Sam's arm and still once more.

Gently, Jasmine and Richard helped tuck the shattered mess of Ashley's wings into Sam's arms. Then they stood in silence as Sam moved back towards the cliffs. His copper wings slowly spread as he walked, his back straight, his gaze fixed straight ahead. He did not look back as he reached the edge. Without hesitating, stepped out into open air.

They stood for a moment after he had disappeared, waiting for the gunfire, praying he would reach the ground safely. But they did not go to the edge. They did not watch.

Chris didn't know about the others, but he could not bear to see Sam return to his chains.

Finally, Chris wiped away his tears and faced the others. They stood shivering in the cold mountain air, their eyes red, their faces pale. He could see the questions on their lips, but there was only one thing left for them to do now.

Fly.

41

The *Chead* paused in the doorway, momentarily blinded by the light streaming down from the infinite expanse stretching up above its head. Scraping noises came from behind it as the survivors of its pack shuffled forward, eager to take their first steps out into the world beyond.

They had fought hard, the *Chead* and its brethren. The men who'd stood against them had been feeble, weak creatures that broke easily. The first had died screaming as the *Chead* had rushed from their cages to tear them limb from limb. More death had followed as the nine *Chead* rampaged through the facility, eager for retribution against their tormentors.

Yet few of the hated white coats had fallen into their clutches, and eventually the humans had organized themselves, pinning the *Chead* and its brethren down with their foul weapons. The first of them had died, then another. Finally they had been forced to retreat, though the humans had not yet gathered the courage to follow.

The *Chead* smiled at the thought, its heart beginning to race. Its gaze swept the jagged earth rising up around the facility, the boulders and crevices offering them concealment. If the humans came after them, if they tried to hunt them down…

It paused as it caught the scent of humanity in the air. Turning, it stared up at the jagged slope above them. The grey and white of snow and rock appeared empty. There was no movement, no sign of life, and yet the *Chead* knew the humans were there, hidden somewhere in the twisting cliffs. It licked its lips, laughter building in its chest.

The other *Chead* gathered nearby, their grey eyes intent on the cliffs, their ears twitching at the distant *clacking* of stones shifting beneath human feet. Smiles crossed their lips as they looked to their leader, awaiting his decision.

The *Chead* was about to lift its hand, when it scented something else. It paused, breathing it in, tasting the strange sweetness to it, familiar, and yet unmistakably different from the feeble humans. The others stirred, impatient for the hunt, for the kill.

Still, their leader hesitated. Memories stirred as it recalled the strange creatures it had fought so many weeks ago. It frowned, seeing again the battle, the desperation of its foes as they sought to fight back. Their defiance had driven the *Chead* into a familiar fury, one which no enemy could hope to survive.

Yet the strange creatures had lived. They had not been *Chead*, but together the boy and girl had possessed a strength far beyond their human captors. Together, they had defeated it.

The *Chead* shivered, just the memory threatening to ignite its fury. It drew in a long breath of the icy air, seeking calm. The jagged earth up around them promised freedom, if only they kept their minds. It could not afford to surrender to the rage now, not when they were so close.

Distantly, the *Chead* recalled what had come next. The traitor in the white coat had demanded the *Chead's* death, had tortured the strange creatures to force them to its will.

And they had refused.

The *Chead's* ears twitched as a gunshot rang from the cliffs. More followed, echoing down the valley to where the *Chead* stood.

The hunt begins, the *Chead* thought as it watched the mountains.

The humans no longer seemed interested in the escaped *Chead.* They had found new prey. Glancing down the valley, the *Chead* contemplated the empty ground, the freedom it offered.

Another *boom* drew its gaze back to the mountains. A distant scream whispered in its mind, as it saw again the boy standing in defiance of the traitor, and the girl writhing on the ground.

Letting out a long breath, the *Chead* started up the slope.

With a crunch of gravel, the others followed.

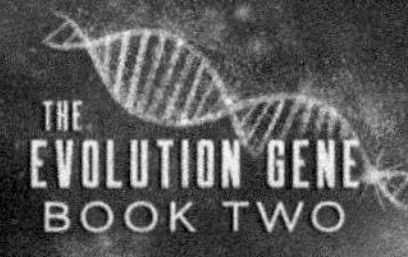

THE PURSUIT OF TRUTH

NEW YORK TIMES BESTSELLING AUTHOR

AARON HODGES

Wander.
Until you find a place to call home.

I

FLIGHT

✣ I ✣

ONE WEEK LATER

Chris grabbed at the lip of the cliff and hauled himself over the edge. Rolling clear of the hundred-foot drop, he shivered as the icy air cut through the rips in his shirt. He grimaced at the angry red grazes on his bare hands and feet. The frozen rock had been merciless, unforgiving of the slightest mistake. But with the wind howling around the mountain peak, he'd had little choice but to make the climb.

A dull ache started in the base of his skull as he settled down on the rocky escarpment and looked back over the valley he and his friends had just traversed. Beyond his desolate perch, the mountains stretched up around him, their ice-capped peaks vanishing into the swirling clouds. Cliffs peeked out from the snowy blanket, their rocky faces pockmarked and broken, while in the valley below, shattered rock lay embedded in the barren earth. A frozen stream carved its way through the valley, its crystal surface as clear as day from Chris's vantage point far above. The wind screeched as it raced between the peaks, and the mountains echoed with the distant rumble of falling snow. Every so often he would hear a sharp *crack* and flinch, expecting bullets to follow—but it was only the sound of breaking rock or ice.

Chris sat for a long time watching the valley, checking for

signs of their pursuers. Amidst the broken rocks of the peak, he would be all but invisible to anyone below, but even so he felt exposed on the escarpment. He suppressed a shudder, imagining a black-garbed huntsman staring down the barrel of a rifle, lining him up, pulling the trigger.

Closing his eyes, Chris took a breath and shoved his fear aside. He couldn't afford the luxury of panic now—none of them could. Somewhere out in these mountains, Doctor Halt and his people were hunting them. And Halt had already shown he would do whatever it took to stop them.

Tears burned Chris's eyes as he remembered Ashley falling, saw again her blood spraying the air and her broken body crumpling to the rocks. And Sam, lifting her into his arms, carrying her back to the torment they had just escaped—on the impossible hope she might be saved.

Angrily, Chris reached up and wiped away the tears before they turned to ice. Allowing his vision to clear, he cast one last look out over the valley. But there was no sign of movement, no hint of life amidst the desolate mountains, and nodding to himself, he slid backwards out of the wind.

Retreating to the cliff he had just climbed, he lowered himself over the edge and began his descent. A hundred feet below, the others would be watching him from their ledge, but he did not look down. After the week-long flight through the mountains, his chest and abdomen ached constantly. A sharp pain prickled the small of his back when he inhaled; it was almost a relief to use his arms and legs for a change.

His strength was flagging, starved away by the sparse meals of moss and thistles they'd resorted to eating in their desperation. Only once in the last week had they eaten well—when Richard had spotted a fish trapped in a frozen pool. The ice had been difficult to break, and they had eaten it raw, but at least it had given them the strength to continue another day.

Since escaping the facility, Chris and his friends had travelled west—as far as they could tell. They had been climbing higher into the mountains, up long gorges and narrow passes, until now, finally, they seemed to have reached the peak. Below, a new valley sloped down to the west, its floor falling gently as it wound its way through the mountains. Beyond waited civilization, the wide expanses of the Western Allied States.

Not that any of them knew what they'd do once they got there.

For Chris at least, one objective drove him on more than any other—to find his mother, and save her. He had not seen her since that night in San Francisco, so many countless weeks and months ago now. Accused of treason, she would face the death sentence. But that didn't mean she was gone.

It couldn't.

Chris forced his thoughts back to the climb. The rock was slick with ice and the weight of his injuries would have slowed anyone else. But after all they'd been through, after the depraved experiments, the torture and imprisonment, Chris was beyond pain now. He moved down the cliff without effort, his fingers gripping to the smallest of cracks, his toes finding the tiniest footholds. Holding his own weight no longer bothered him; the exertion of the climb was no more than a brief inconvenience. The doctors in the facility had succeeded beyond their wildest dreams.

If only it had been worth the cost.

Unbidden, William's face appeared in Chris's thoughts, his features distorted, his limbs flailing as he thrashed on the floor of the padded room. A woman stood over him, a grimace on her lips, the metallic jet-injector clenched in one hand.

The image faded, only for a fresh memory to take its place. He saw again Angela Fallow's body, sprawled on the laboratory floor, blood oozing from the bullet wound in her chest. And Halt, standing over her, the gun still clutched in his fist. A well of hatred opened within Chris, fueled by the vile, despicable things the man had done to bend them to his will.

If not for Angela, they would still be his, trapped in their cages, helpless to defend themselves against his depravity. She had freed them, opened the cells, unlocked the collars, given them back their lives.

And she had died for it.

Chris's stomach lurched suddenly as he missed his next foothold. Cursing, he scrambled for purchase, his weight falling onto his only handhold. The sharp rocks sliced into his fingers, and instinctively they loosened. With a shout, he fell backwards into empty space.

In that instant, time seemed to slow. His heart beat hard in his chest as he scanned the rock, spying out a fresh set of holds. Twisting in the air, his hands flashed out to catch them, and his feet settled back into a groove in the rock. He pulled himself close to the rock face and let out a long breath.

Nice moves. Chris could almost hear Sam's voice, rich with his familiar humor. Swallowing, he fought back tears and continued his climb down.

When he was still a dozen feet above the ledge, he released the cliff and fell the rest of the way. He dropped to his knees as he landed, and then straightened.

The others gathered around him, their faces pale with cold and exhaustion, their eyes ringed by shadows. They looked at him expectantly. For close to a week they had travelled in near silence, their conversation dimmed by what they had lost, by their own private torments, and the buzz of far-off helicopters. He had expected it from Jasmine and Richard—the two had been nothing but antagonistic since the day he'd met them—but even Liz had been distant, as though the weight of everyone they'd left behind hung between them.

He looked at her now, finding her blue eyes behind the tangles of black hair. They showed the same faraway look of the past few days, and he forced himself to look away as a thousand doubts rose inside him.

Jasmine stood beside Liz with her arms crossed, her brown eyes hard and her straight black hair billowing in the wind. Her tanned skin matched Liz's, but at five foot five she was the taller of the two. Jasmine stood shoulder-to-shoulder with Richard, a stark contrast to his short blond hair and pale skin. Both wore their trademark grimace, their brows creased by scowls.

Ignoring their animosity, Chris searched for the fifth member of their little party. His stomach twisted as he found the young girl sitting on the ledge. They were not even halfway down the cliff here, and her legs dangled out over a five-hundred-foot drop. Her grey hair swirled in the breeze and while he could not see her face, it was easy to picture her strange multicolored eyes.

A shudder went through him as he turned back to the others. The girl couldn't be older than thirteen. How had she survived the facility? They were no closer to getting those answers. For the whole week, she had remained stubbornly mute. They didn't even know her name.

"There's no sign of anyone behind us," Chris said finally, as the wind howled, trying to steal away his voice. Here in the mountains it never ceased, and not for the first time he wished for more than the thin rags Angela had provided them. "It looks like we've reached the top. If we keep heading west, I think we'll eventually find our way back to the Western Allied States."

"Good," Jasmine said. "I'm sick of the cold."

Chris caught a flicker of irritation in Liz's eyes, but she only nodded. "Should we push on more today, or find a place to camp for the night?"

Beyond their precarious ledge, the sun still hung between the towering peaks. Chris grimaced, the ache in his back giving a sharp throb. Pain radiated out into his chest like the threads of a spiderweb. His muscles were stiff, and his stomach rumbled with hunger. Silently he wondered how much longer they could last before their altered bodies finally reached the limits of their endurance. But there were still several hours of daylight left. They could not afford to waste them.

"Let's push on," he said, moving past them.

He paused at the edge of the cliff and glanced across at the young girl. She sat in silence, her strange eyes watching him. Shaking his head, he turned away, trying not to show his discomfort. The new valley stretched away below, twisting past the sharp escarpment on which they were perched. The rocky spire made for the perfect viewpoint, though for an ordinary human it would have taken long hours to climb. And when they finally reached the top, they would still have to face the long, treacherous climb down.

The five of them had no such problem.

Staring into the distance, Chris's keen eyes picked over the faint patches of tussock grass and broken boulders scattering the slopes. Low clouds drifted here and there, but for the most part the air was clear, his view unobstructed. The valley stretched away for miles, finally ending in a distant wall of rock.

Turning his mind inwards, Chris focused on the ache in his back. A twitch ran through him, radiating outwards, waking his body for action. Bones and muscles stretched as he readied himself.

Looking at the five-hundred-foot drop, Chris struggled to suppress the old fear that gripped his stomach. Heights held no sway over him now; it was just that his mind had yet to adjust to that fact. Clenching his fists, he drew in another breath.

Movement came from Chris's left as Liz stepped up beside him. Her eyes caught his, and she flashed him a grin. No more than a brief twist of her lips, shy and uncertain, but it was more emotion than she'd shown him in days. He smiled, feeling warmth seeping back into his heart, pushing back the terrors of the last week.

Returning his attention to the edge, Chris closed his eyes, and stepped out into empty space.

His stomach lurched into his chest as he started to fall. Icy air roared past his ears, and opening his eyes, he saw the barren earth rushing up towards him. He glanced sideways as a wild scream came from beside him, and found Liz falling as well, a mad joy dancing in her crystal blue eyes.

Together, they plummeted towards the rocky ground.

Grinning, Chris returned his attention to the ache in his back. His whole body burned now, the rush of adrenaline lighting up every fiber of his being. He could feel the ache spreading, tingling outwards into the foreign flesh and bone that sprouted from his back. With an eager laugh, he willed them to life.

With a sharp *crack*, his wings snapped open. His stomach lurched again as twenty-four feet of feathers caught the air and sent him soaring into the sky. The earth fell away as the wind rustled his tawny brown wings.

A surge of joy filled Chris's chest as he looked out over the valley floor. Boulders and cliffs flashed past, as from his right came the thump of another set of wings. Liz fell into formation beside him, her jet-black feathers stretching out towards his own. A sense of contentment settled over him as they touched.

From behind came the familiar crack of unfurling wings as the others followed.

2

Darkness pressed in all around, encasing Liz, locking her away from the light. She struggled against it, flailing at unseen tendrils, but her hands found only empty air. When she opened her mouth to scream, darkness poured down her throat, suffocating her cries.

The scene changed. A dull black surface formed beneath her feet, though the darkness still pressed in all around. A long, beastly howl echoed from somewhere in the pitch-black. The sound sent tingles racing down her spine. She started to run—then sprint—through the darkness, as scrambling footsteps came from somewhere behind her.

The howl came again, conjuring up specters of the unseen beast. A cry tore from Liz's lips as she slipped. Scrambling on the smooth surface, she raced on, her mind spinning out of control.

But however hard she ran, the footsteps behind still grew nearer, the howling louder.

Heart pounding, Liz gasped for air. She could feel the beast approaching, could sense its very presence. Fear flooded her, robbing her of strength. Her chest burned, her lungs screamed. Step by step, her pace slowed.

At last she could go no further. Panting, Liz drew to a stop, great sobs tearing from her throat. She turned to face the swirling darkness and waited for the beast to appear.

The black boiled, spreading like a cloud, reaching out to touch her. She flinched and scrambled back. With the movement, the fog parted, giving way to the approaching footsteps.

Liz moaned as a woman stepped into view. Her skin was a pale white, the scarlet locks of her hair stained black. Her lips twisted with rage, and her tawny yellow eyes glowed in the pitch-black. Great white wings beat hard on her back, sending the darkness swirling out towards Liz.

Liz stood frozen in place as Ashley's fingers bent into claws and reached for Liz's throat. In one movement, she lifted Liz into the air. A snarl hissed from Ashley's lips as she raised a fist.

"You left me!"

With a muffled scream, Liz tore herself from the dream and sat bolt upright. For a moment the darkness clung to her, choking her, filling her with panic. Then her gaze found the jeweled stars stretching across the night sky, and the bright glow of the half-moon, and she let out a long breath.

Liz clutched her chest and willed her heart to slow. She shivered, recalling Ashley's face in the dream and the pallid grey of her skin. Silently, she wondered whether it was an omen, whether her friend had truly passed from the light.

Was your sacrifice for nothing, Sam?

Wrapping her arms around her chest, Liz banished the thought. Her wings rustled and tightened around her, sealing in the warmth. She smiled then. The strangeness of their presence faded more each day. Flight was becoming easier, her muscles slowly learning to cope with the strain, though her chest and abdomen still ached at the end of each day.

Hunger was their most pressing concern now. They had hardly eaten since escaping the facility, and the pangs of her empty stomach were quickly sapping her strength. A frozen fish Richard had found had saved them, but Liz wasn't sure whether she could last until they got lucky again.

Realizing all thought of sleep had left her, Liz pulled herself up and moved away from the others. Her stomach gave another growl, and she placed a hand over it, willing it to silence. Tomorrow she hoped they would reach the mountain forests. She knew how to forage there, where to find berries and grubs and edible roots. In the harsh alpine tussock she was out of her depth, but the forest she knew well.

Striding across the rubble-strewn slope, Liz was drawn towards the distant chatter of the stream. Even in the darkness she could easily make out rocks and boulders in her path. She had spent enough time walking dark country roads to know it was not natural, but she had long since given up questioning her newfound abilities.

She pictured the stream ahead, its white waters cascading between the boulders. Until today, the rivers they'd passed had been frozen solid. But it seemed they had finally descended low enough to escape the ice.

Her thoughts turned to Chris as she continued across the barren ground. They'd hardly spoken since the day Ashley had fallen. Almost unconsciously, Liz had found herself raising old walls around her heart, distancing herself from the boy. Now, a lonely gulf stretched between them, and sadness touched her. She mourned for Ashley and Sam, but she did not want to lose Chris too.

Finally, Liz drew to a stop beside the creek. Her feet ached from the cold, though they had slowly toughened over the last few days. Shivering, she looked down at the stream. Here the bank was only a few feet high, with piles of smooth gravel pushed up around its base. The opposite bank was maybe twenty feet away, though the waters themselves were just a couple of yards wide.

Lit by the moonlight, the stream swirled over its rocky bed, the current fast and uninviting. But further upstream, Liz caught a glimpse of calm water, a pool where the creek widened. When she'd left the others, she'd had a vague idea of splashing water on her face. Now Liz felt an urge to submerge herself, to allow the icy waters to wash away her nightmares.

Slipping off her shirt, she clenched her teeth against the mountain breeze, then quickly kicked off her pants. She walked to the edge of the pool and slid one toe into the water, then gasped as it immediately went numb. Already regretting the idea, she folded her wings tight against her back and pressed on. She moaned as the water reached her knees, then waist, then chest. Finally, when Liz could barely breathe for the cold, she ducked beneath the surface.

Two minutes later Liz returned to the bank, her teeth chattering, panting for breath, the oxygen sucked from her lungs by the icy waters. Goosebumps stood up along her arms and legs, and her waterlogged wings weighed heavily on her back. A shiver spread down their length, and her feathers stood on end to shake the water free. Liz rushed to her clothes, desperate for their scant warmth. Another tremor went through her wings, spraying water everywhere.

Smiling, Liz pulled her wings tight against her back again and slipped on her shirt. As it settled into place, she allowed her wings to relax again, and they extended through the holes cut into the back of her top. Then she scrambled into her underwear and pants, eager for their warmth. Though her skin was still damp, they at least offered some protection from the wind.

As she turned to face the water again, a rattle of stones came from overhead. She froze at the sound, and a voice called down from overhead.

"How's the water?"

3

Liz turned slowly and found Richard perched on the bank above her. Warmth spread to her cheeks, before her brow knitted into a furious scowl. Unsure how much he'd seen, Liz crossed her arms and raised an eyebrow, trying to hide her embarrassment.

"Enjoy the show?" she growled.

Richard jumped from the rock and landed lightly beside her. "Sorry, I didn't look," he murmured, taking a seat on a boulder beside the river and looking up at the sky. "I was just…walking."

Grinding her teeth, Liz struggled to control her anger. A red glow flashed across her vision as she clenched her fists. She fought the urge to pick Richard up and hurl him into the water. But he only sat with his back to her, seemingly ignorant to her rage, and after a long moment Liz let out her breath. Even through her anger, she sensed a difference about Richard tonight, a change in him.

"What happened to him?" Richard finally asked, still staring at the half-moon. "To Joshua?"

The tide of Liz's anger retreated, cold fingers of guilt rising to take its place. She bit her lip, the horror of her fight with the boy Joshua rushing back. She saw him again atop her, felt his fingers wrapping around her throat, the burning in her lungs.

Glancing away from Richard, she reached down and picked up a stone, then tossed it across the pool. It skipped twice before landing on the other bank.

"I killed him," she replied finally. "Not the doctors, or the guards. I did it."

From the corner of her eye, she saw Richard nod. "I thought so." From his tone, Liz thought that would be the end of the conversation, but he continued: "I saw the marks on your neck, when you walked past our cell. What happened?"

Blood pounding in her ears, Liz seated herself next to the boy. They sat in silence for a while, watching the glistening waters, as she turned the memories over in her mind. Then slowly, reluctantly, she recounted the fight. How she had struck Joshua down in the first minutes, and thought him beaten. How he had taken her by surprise, caught her and overpowered her before she could scramble free. And how she had killed him with one final, desperate blow.

Richard said nothing as Liz told her story. When she finally finished, the silence resumed, marked only by the whisper of the river as it tumbled over its stony bed. Strangely, Liz felt a weight lifting from her chest with the confession. She had not spoken to anyone but Chris about Joshua, and even then, she had not told him the full story.

She had expected Richard to rage at her when she finished, to scream and shout, to accuse her of murder. Joshua had been his cellmate, presumably his friend. But he said nothing, just sat quietly beside her, watching the water as it made its long journey through the mountains towards the distant coast.

"I'm sorry," she said at last.

Richard shrugged. "We weren't close." He glanced in her direction. "After what happened last time, Jasmine and I weren't keen to bond with the newbies."

Liz swallowed at the despair in Richard's eyes. She wanted to ask more, to discover the truth behind their feud with Sam and Ashley, but the words stuck in her throat.

"We were all close in the beginning, the eight of us," Richard said, seeming to pluck the questions from her mind. "Jasmine and I were in separate cells from Ashley and Sam and the... others, but we spent time on the training field together. That was before things got bad, before people started to die."

"How long were you there for?" Liz managed to croak.

"Eight weeks before you lot showed up," he replied. "For the first three weeks, there were no deaths. Then things changed, the doctors became more urgent, pushed us harder. They started taking us away in twos..." He trailed off, swallowing. "Faces began to go missing."

"And then they came for you?"

Richard nodded. "It wasn't until I ended up in that padded room with Jeremy...it wasn't until then that I realized how evil the doctors were, how perverse. We refused at first, when the voice told us to fight. But they made us..." His voice broke as he started to sob.

"You killed him," Liz murmured.

Richard didn't look up. "He was my friend," he said, his voice filled with self-loathing. "I told them I'd rather die. But those damn collars...and then Jeremy..."

Tears streamed down Richard's face. Liz reached out a hand and squeezed his shoulder. A shiver went through him, spreading to the dark green wings hanging limply from his back.

After a long pause, Richard sucked in a breath and continued. "Jeremy refused to play their games. I'll never forget his face, when he looked at me that last time. He had a sad smile on his lips, but his eyes...there was no give in them. He shook his head, then turned and walked across to the one-way mirror. Before anyone could react, he slammed his head into the glass," Richard swallowed, his voice trembling. "He did it three times before the guards reached him. They tackled him to the ground, but by then he barely had the strength to stand. The mirror was covered in his blood. It didn't take long for the doctors to make their decision."

Liz closed her eyes, imagining the scene. Chris had told her what had happened when William could no longer fight. A doctor had entered and given the boy a lethal injection. He had died writhing in agony.

"You didn't kill him, Richard," she whispered. "His blood is on their hands."

Richard's green eyes were watching her. They glinted in the moonlight, and she quickly looked away, unable to face the despair lurking in their depths. "You and Chris, you have no idea what it's like. You didn't know Joshua and William, when you fought them. It was different for us. We had faced the horrors of the facility together, suffered hand in hand against whatever those monsters threw at us. And then to stand there, to make that choice. No, I didn't kill him." Richard let out a long, shuddering breath. "But I would have. I think he knew that."

Silence met his words. Liz stared at the sky, unable to find an answer, to comprehend the guilt and sorrow warring within the boy beside her. Richard was right. Joshua had been a stranger to her. It shouldn't have mattered, but it did. When it had come down to his life, or her own, the answer had been simple.

Finally, she spoke again: "It was the same for Ashley and Sam. You must know that. So why do you hate them?"

"Hate them?" Richard shook his head. "I don't hate them. They did what they had to in order to survive, just like the rest of us. But…every time I see them, I see Jeremy again, standing there, sacrificing his life for mine. I can't face them, because all they do is remind me what happened, of what I would have done to save myself."

"But when Ashley fell…"

He shivered then. "We were dead to each other a long time ago, Liz," he said, his voice breaking, "but, in truth, I didn't have the courage to say goodbye."

On an impulse, Liz reached out and wrapped an arm around Richard. The boy crumpled at her touch, his strength failing him. She pulled him tight against her, feeling his sorrow, his silent sobs as he buried his head in her shoulder.

When Richard finally drew back, he could not meet her eyes. "Thank you," he whispered. Slowly, he recovered his composure. "I guess, in the end, it won't matter. We're all going to end up like Ashley, one way or another."

Liz flinched at the bitterness in Richard's voice. Icy fingers wrapped around her throat, like the ghost of the collar she had once worn. Ashley's face from the dream appeared in Liz's mind, the accusing eyes, the pallid grey fingers reaching for her. Pushing down against the rock, she stood.

"No," Liz said, drawing in a mouthful of the mountain air. She concentrated on her wings, felt them lift and stretch, her black feathers tingling in the breeze. Looking down at Richard, she shook her head. "They won't catch me. They won't take me back. I'd rather die."

Richard gave a sad smile. "Brave words, but how long will they last? How long will any of us last against them? They're after us now—Halt, the guards, the government, *everyone.* They'll come for us with everything they have. We've kept ahead of them in the mountains, but out there—" he waved a hand down the valley "—in the lowlands, in the cities, that's *their* territory."

"The cities might belong to them, but the countryside is *mine*," Liz growled. "Out here, the government is not the power it pretends to be in the cities. The Western Allied States are huge—they cannot be everywhere, see everything. The people in the countryside tolerate them, because they don't have the power to resist, but there is no love lost for the government here. That's how I avoided them for so long."

Richard shrugged. "We're a little more conspicuous now. You know, with the wings and all."

Liz laughed softly. "There is that." She smiled. "But we can hide our wings. We'll find jackets or something. We can avoid the hunters, at least until the chase dies down."

"They'll hunt us to the ends of the earth, Liz. We're a dark secret they want buried. Even our wondrous Electors are bound to ask a few questions of the President if the truth comes out." Richard paused. "And besides, a life on the run doesn't sound like much of a life to me."

Liz shivered, remembering the long days and nights alone in the wild, the uncertainty, the fear of being caught. She had spent two years living that life, not knowing when the day would finally come that they found her. "No..." she whispered, "it's not. We need to fight back."

It was Richard's turn to chuckle. "Sure, let me know how that works out."

"We'll find a way," Liz replied, recalling Ashley's words from so long ago. "They're only human, Richard."

Richard's emerald eyes found her in the darkness. "After all they've done, do you truly believe that?" he asked. "The ways they've changed us, they're not possible, Liz. These people, they lost their humanity long ago."

Shivering, Liz look away, the wings suddenly heavy on her back. Everything they had become, every extra ounce of strength, of agility they now possessed, was thanks to Halt and Angela and the other doctors. All seemed far beyond the realms of possibility. Liz's stomach clenched as she realized she had no response to Richard's words.

Silence fell then, as each drifted into the chaos of their own thoughts. Returning to the boulder, Liz resumed her seat. Together, they sat looking out over the mountains, watching as the glow of the new day slowly appeared over the distant peaks.

As the sun's warmth found her, Liz closed her eyes. Whatever had come before, today was a new day, and she was determined to make the most of it.

After all, who knew how many they had left?

4

Chris sucked in a breath, reveling in the icy air filling his lungs. A gale howled around him, tugging at his lengthening hair and rustling his feathers. His wings stretched out on either side of him, their concave surface catching in the wind, sending him higher and higher, until the treetops were little more than specks far below.

A mile above the rugged ground, Chris watched the giant redwoods drift by. They stood in groves amongst their smaller relatives, towering above the rest of the forest, striving for glory. But their height was nothing to what Chris and Liz and the others had achieved. Their only rivals were the snow-capped mountains at their backs. A cloudless sky extended all around, seeming to stretch away to infinity.

For a while, Chris allowed the others their wonder, savoring in the freedom of the open air. Just a short week ago, heights had been a terror to him, the thought of plummeting helplessly to his death his greatest nightmare. Now he was the master of the sky, his fears caged, vanquished by the power of his wings.

Sadly, they could not remain in the open for long. Beyond the jagged peaks, they were exposed in the empty sky. Though there had been little sign of pursuit in the mountains, they had heard the helicopters in the distance. There was no doubt the government would be coming for them.

Folding his wings, Chris pulled into a dive and shot towards the distant trees. The air whistled in his ears and tore at his clothing as he gave a wild scream. Slowly, he eased his wings out a few inches, lifting his body slowly from the dive. As the trees closed, he unfurled them to their full length, leveling out just above the canopy.

The others joined him, and together they drifted over the treetops. Chris noticed even Jasmine wore a wild grin, her eyes alive with exhilaration. Chris allowed himself to glide lower, scanning the dense branches, searching for a way through. His chest burned and pain threaded its way down his back. He desperately needed to rest, and he doubted the others were any better off.

Spotting a gap, he made for it, struggling to retract his wings enough to fit through without going into freefall. Even so, he felt his descent accelerating. As he lurched in the air, a branch caught his arm, throwing him off-balance. Then he was through, dropping into the open space beneath the canopy.

Finding himself still thirty feet above the ground, Chris quickly spread his wings. His descent slowed, but he was still falling too quickly when he struck the ground. The shock of the impact took his feet out from underneath him, and he rolled to break his fall.

Coming to a rest on his back, Chris picked himself up and brushed off the pine needles, hoping the others had not seen his uninspiring landing. His cheeks warmed as he found them standing nearby, broad grins on their faces.

He flashed his best scowl. "And that, children, is how *not* to land."

Liz laughed. "Who are you calling 'children'? Pretty sure half of us are older than you."

Chris shrugged and rolled his shoulders, trying to remove the knot that had collected in the muscles between his shoulder blades. His wings seemed to connect in some way to just about every muscle of his back, as well as those in his chest and abdomen. The collective strength of those muscles, along with their increased muscle density, provided them the power they needed for flight.

Unfortunately, it also meant every inch of his torso burned at the end of each day.

"How do we get back up?" Jasmine was looking at the canopy.

Where they stood on the forest floor, the hole they'd passed through was invisible. An army of trees surrounded them, their red trunks straight and smooth as they reached for the hidden sky. Brown pine needles smothered the ground, and there was no trace of any undergrowth. Distantly, Chris recalled from biology class that redwood species leeched chemicals into the topsoil, removing nutrients and preventing other plant species from colonizing.

"I think we should go on foot for a while," he said at last. Their progress would be slow, but at least they would be hidden from prying eyes. "I don't think I can fly much farther without food, and it feels too exposed up there, out of the mountains."

"Well, what are we waiting for then?" Richard made a face, then turned and walked off through the trees. Jasmine followed him, the young nameless girl shadowing her, leaving Liz and Chris staring after them.

Rolling his eyes, Chris flashed Liz a halfhearted grin and started after them. In truth, he was glad to relinquish the lead. He still wasn't quite sure how he'd ended up with the unofficial title, but the weight of responsibility had quickly grown exhausting, and he could use the rest.

His heart warmed as Liz fell in beside him and reached out to take his hand. She grinned, her eyes shining with some hidden emotion. He found himself smiling back, the gesture genuine now.

"How are you feeling?" he asked.

Jasmine, Richard and the girl were pulling ahead, picking their way easily over the tree roots. But with Liz's warm fingers clutched around his hand, Chris felt no rush to catch up. Liz's sudden show of affection had stirred him from his melancholy, and he found himself thinking again of the night in the cell, when he had first fallen asleep beside her.

Liz shrugged. "I'm okay." She bit her lip and looked away. "I'm sorry I've been…distant."

Chris squeezed her hand and pulled her towards him. Sliding his arm around her waist, he held her close. He kissed the top of her head, breathing in the rich scent of her hair. She shifted closer, nestling her head beneath his chin. They walked like that for a while, until it became too awkward to manage while avoiding the roots and spiderwebs crisscrossing the path.

"How are your wings feeling?" he asked eventually.

At their mention, Liz's wings lifted slightly, shivering in the air before settling back against her clothing. "Not too bad." Liz turned and winked at him. "I'm a bit lighter than you. Less work."

Laughing, Chris bent himself to the task of keeping up with Richard. He had to admit, the boy set a cracking pace, and he was soon puffing hard in the morning air. The scent of the pine trees brought back distant memories, and Chris found his thoughts drifting to more pleasant times, to cold mornings spent beneath Christmas trees, opening presents with his mother and father.

Each lost in their thoughts, they steadily made their way down through the foothills. Signs of life were everywhere now. Deep scars in nearby tree trunks showed where bears had marked their territory, some more than twice Chris's height. Dry pine needles crunched beneath their feet, warning the forest creatures of their approach, but Chris still caught flickers of movement from the corners of his eyes, as squirrels and mice ducked out of sight. The soft chirp of cicadas marked the end of winter. Silently, Chris wondered whether the world had changed during their long months of imprisonment.

By sunset, the air beneath the trees was filled with the buzz of insects. The first chirps of the evening chorus soon followed, as birds flitted between the tree trunks, chasing their prey.

Without the sun or mountains for guidance, it was difficult to judge their progress, but Chris guessed from the burning in his thighs they'd walked several miles. It was a frustrating pace after their rapid flight through the mountains, but there was little they could do about it.

Liz at least helped to fill their empty stomachs. As they walked, she collected berries and nuts from various trees and plants. At one point, she even gathered a few fat white grubs from beneath the bark of a tree. Hungry as he was, Chris wolfed it all down without question, though he hesitated maybe half a second longer with the grubs.

They finally came to a stop as darkness fell beneath the trees, settling down in a shallow indentation in the earth. It offered little in the way of protection, but it was the best they could find in the shadows. As they had done every night since their escape, they set a watch. Richard drew the short straw for first watch, and one by one the rest of them drifted off to sleep.

An hour later, Chris woke to a hand on his shoulder. Blinking in the darkness, he found Liz sitting beside him, a sly smile on her face. Before he could question her, she leaned down and pressed her lips to his. Still groggy, he struggled to wake as her fingers twisted in his hair. Then he was kissing her back, hard and fast.

When she finally pulled away, Chris took the chance to catch his breath. He reached out and pulled her close, his heart beating hard in his chest.

"Who's on watch?" he breathed.

"Richard still." She smiled in the darkness. "He's over there. Come on." She stood, tugging at his hand.

Chris obeyed, staggering to his feet as Liz pulled him in the opposite direction from where Richard sat. With the thick canopy overhead, the darkness was complete, and even with their heightened senses they struggled to find a path. Still half-asleep, Chris stumbled along after Liz, barely able to keep up. But each time he slowed, she would look back, her eyes flashing, her eager smile drawing him on.

They managed maybe a dozen yards before Chris tripped over a tree root. Toppling forwards, he dragged Liz with him, and together they tumbled to the ground. They rolled across the soft bed of pine needles, their wings pulled tight against their backs, their whispered laughter echoing through the trees.

When they finally came to a stop, Chris found himself lying atop Liz. He stared down at her, wondering at the brightness of her sapphire eyes, and found himself smiling again.

"Hey there." He smiled at her.

Giggling, Liz tried to wriggle free, but he refused to move, pinning her to the ground. Leaning down, he kissed her. She stilled as their lips met, her hands no longer pushing him away, but wrapping around him, pulling him closer.

She let out a long breath when they parted, and laughed again. Then her wings beat suddenly against the ground, and she rolled, sending Chris toppling sideways. Before he could recover she leapt on his chest and straddled him.

"Gotcha," she laughed.

Chris gently brushed a pine needle from her hair. Her eyes closed at his touch and her breath quickened. Silently, she reached up and pressed his hand to her cheek.

"Chris," she breathed.

Then she was leaning down, her lips pressing against his, and their hands were fumbling at each other's clothing. White-hot fire swept through Chris, stealing away thought and reason, leaving only the burning of desire. Blood pounded in his ears as the buttons of his shirt gave way, and he felt the heat of Liz's hands on his chest. He fumbled with Liz's top as need rose within him. With an awkward, desperate wriggle, she pulled it over her head, leaving it tangled in the black feathers of her wings.

Chris sucked in a breath, his eyes devouring every inch of her naked body. Her breasts shone in the darkness. He cupped them in his hands and felt a tremor go through her. Her eyes narrowed to slits and groaning, she leaned down, pressing herself against him. Chris jumped as her teeth nipped lightly at his neck, a moan escaping him. Together they rolled across the soft pine needles, bodies and wings entwined.

The heat spread to Chris's stomach as Liz's hands continued to explore, making their way down his back, sliding beneath his pants. She grinned, pinching his backside, and Chris quickly followed suit, enjoying the smooth feel of her skin beneath his fingers.

He could see the lust in Liz's eyes, a mirror of his own. Their lips came together again. Chris's pants were unceremoniously tossed aside, then Liz's. They pressed against one another, hip to hip, chest to chest, mouth to mouth. Their wings rustled and spread, wrapping them both in a blanket of feathers.

Panting, they separated for a second, taking the moment to regain their breath, to recover their sanity. Liz's eyes were huge as she watched him, her pupils narrowed to tiny points. Her fingers trailed their way down his stomach, as his own hand drew circles on her hip. They kissed again, softly now, all their concentration on the exploring hands.

Chris heard Liz's breath quicken as his hand drifted lower, finding the softness of her pubic hair. Then it was all he could do to breathe himself, as her hand found its way to him. A moan rumbled from his chest she grabbed him, and he pushed his own fingers further, felt her wetness.

He could feel Liz trembling, her body moving in concert with his own, encouraging him to greater heights. His other hand slid up her body, brushing across her nipples. Her breasts were soft, yielding beneath his touch. As he grasped them Liz gave another groan, her eyes turning feral.

"Oh, Chris…" she whispered, her breath hot in his ear.

Then she was atop him, her hand drawing him to her. Chris gasped as they came together, the last of his breath stolen away. But it didn't matter, because Liz was moving against him, every thrust of her hips drawing him deeper. Sitting up, he kissed her breasts, his tongue circling, his teeth nibbling.

Amidst their passion, he realized their wings had spread, their movement sending quivers down their length. As quickly as it came, the thought was gone, consumed by a tide of ecstasy.

Growling, he grasped Liz by the waist and lifted her, flipping her to her back. Her arms wrapped tightly around him, her fingers curling in his hair, his feathers. A moan tore from Liz as he pressed down, their pursuers, their torments, their danger all forgotten now. Black hair hung across her face, but gently Chris brushed it aside, his lips finding hers again, stealing her breath.

A pressure built within Chris, growing with every thrust, with every gasp of the girl beneath him. Liz groaned again, her legs wrapping around him as she begged him to go faster. Pain shot from his shoulder as she bit him, hard now, but he no longer cared. With a cry she threw back her head and started to convulse, her hips still locked tight around him. Her movements shattered the dam within Chris, and he found himself gasping atop her, their cries echoing through the trees.

Finally, they both collapsed to the ground. Bodies entwined, arms wrapped around one another, they panted in the darkness. The shudders rippling through their bodies slowed, their breath returning. Opening his eyes, Chris found Liz watching him. A smile tugged at her lips as her arms tightened around him.

"Well, I'd say that was living."

5

Darkness hung over the forest like a blanket, turning the pale trees to ghostly specters. The dense canopy stretched overhead, the thick leaves and branches hiding even the brilliance of the half-moon. Not a breath of wind stirred, and only the far-off hoot of an owl broke the heavy quiet.

Through the darkness came the soldiers—one, two, a dozen. They moved with measured steps, each taken with painstaking care, every man striving for silence. One misstep, one twig broken beneath a careless boot, and they would be exposed. But these men were professionals, and they did not make mistakes.

Captain Scott's eyes scanned the shadows ahead, seeking out the first sign of their quarry. Through the green glow of his night-vision goggles, he watched his men fan out around him, rifles held at the ready. In the darkness they were indistinguishable from one another, but all were his brothers. Each was a veteran of a dozen campaigns, with tours in foreign states as far afield as Texas and Spain.

Earlier they had watched from their vantage point as their prey emerged from the mountains and entered the woods. With long-range infrared sensors, they had tracked the group's progress through the trees, unwilling to act until the party stopped for the night and slept.

It had been a long wait, but ultimately their patience had been rewarded. Maps of the Sierra Nevada had suggested this was one of three valleys the group could have emerged from. Teams were stationed at the other two, but Scott had never doubted theirs would be the one. After all, God was on his side.

Aware of the enhanced nature of their prey, he had waited until well after midnight to order the final approach. His dossier suggested their prey's heightened sense of smell and hearing might warn them of an enemy's presence, but with the group asleep, he hoped that advantage would be neutralized.

Shouldering his rifle, the captain paused as the first glow of a sleeping body came into view. He raised a hand, signaling to his men. All movement ceased. Scott waved to his two lieutenants, and together the three of them continued forward. He kept the barrel of his gun trained on the sleeping figure as two more came into view. Each of his men were armed with M16 rifles loaded with 5.56mm caliber rounds. Their orders were to take the group captive—but lethal force had been authorized if necessary. Their orders came from the very top, and Scott had no intention of allowing embarrassment to fall on his superiors.

A few feet from the campsite, he hesitated, his eyes flickering around the clearing. Through the ghostly tree trunks, he studied the three sleeping figures, and silently cursed.

Where were the other two?

One of the bodies moved, shifting silently on a bed of pine needles. The glowing green blob was slightly apart from the other two, and sat slumped sideways against a tree. Scott smirked as he realized the boy had fallen asleep on watch. No soldier in his team would dare commit such a dereliction of duty.

Suddenly the figure straightened, sitting bolt upright against the tree. His head lifted, and Scott cursed as the boy looked at him.

"*Go!*" he screamed through his earpiece.

6

Chris jerked awake as a scream shattered the night's silence. Struggling up, he bit back a cry as he found himself trapped in a tangle of feathers and limbs. Liz cursed as he tripped over her wing and almost landed on her, before finally getting his extended limbs under control.

Movement came from nearby as Liz joined him, her eyes wide. He reached out and caught her arm, and for a moment she stilled. The two of them peered through the darkness, searching for the source the commotion.

Bang.

They jumped as the gunshot sounded in the trees. Together, they spun towards the sound. Chris had lost all sense of direction, but he had no doubt if they followed the noise, they would find the others. He glanced at Liz. She nodded back, and they began to run.

Another *boom* came from ahead and Chris cursed under his breath. How had the hunters found them? There was no time to ponder the answer. Ahead, silhouettes slid between the trees, closing on their campsite.

Leaping over a fallen tree, Chris gritted his teeth and picked up the pace. Liz landed softly beside him, her wings partly extended, her lips drawn back in a snarl. Branches cracked beneath their feet, but Chris took no notice. The woods were alive with sound now, as bodies crashed through the undergrowth, converging ahead of them.

Chris saw a ring of men standing between the trees. Without thinking, he leapt towards them, but Liz's hand flashed out and caught him by the wrist, pulling him back. He cursed, but she silently grasped him by the waist and dragged him down behind a fallen tree. She raised a finger to his lips as Chris opened his mouth to argue, and the words died on his tongue.

Silence fell as they crouched in their hiding place. Chris struggled to control his breathing, to slow the wild beating of his heart. Slowly the stupidity of their mad rush trickled into his consciousness. From his brief glimpse, there were at least a dozen men in the forest. If the government had sent them, they weren't messing around. Only the chaos of men closing on the campsite had kept them from being noticed.

He glanced at Liz and nodded his thanks, but her attention was on the campsite. Silently, Chris lifted his head and peered out from behind the fallen tree.

The circle of men stood twenty feet away. As he watched, several more moved from the trees to join them. In the darkness, Chris couldn't tell whether they were soldiers, but the rifles they carried were all he needed to see. The men held them with a professional ease, several pointed out at the surrounding trees, while the others were kept trained on the prisoners crouched in the center of the circle.

Richard, Jasmine, and the girl knelt between soldiers, their hands held behind their heads, eyes fixed on the ground.

Chris cursed silently, wondering how the three had been taken unawares. Studying the soldiers, he bit his lip, his heart sinking. He realized now they wore goggles over their eyes, no doubt some form of night vision technology. There would be no taking them by surprise.

"What do we do?" he whispered to Liz.

"We have to save them," she replied.

Chris glanced at her. "You think they'd do the same for us?"

Her eyes found him in the darkness, clear and resolute. "It

doesn't matter. Whether we like it or not, they're all we've got now. We can't leave them."

Chris let out a long sigh and looked away. He clenched his fingers in the dirt, trying and failing to find an argument against Liz's words. But he knew in his heart she was right. Friend or foe, the five of them were all that remained now of the hundreds who had suffered the horrors of the facility. For better or worse, they were bound by that experience.

"Please." Chris looked up as Richard's voice carried through the trees. "Please, don't do this. Don't make us go back."

Most of the men ignored the desperate plea, but one stepped in close and slammed the butt of his rifle into Richard's face. Richard reeled backwards from the blow, his arms windmilling as he crashed to the dirt. He recovered quickly, and roaring, leapt to his feet.

"Don't." The soldier's tone was calm, as though he were disciplining a toddler. "Unless you want your friends' lives on your conscience."

Richard froze, his body taut, fists clenched at his side. A long moment passed, and the shadowy men edged closer to the prisoners, their guns raised. Finally Richard's shoulders slumped, and he bowed his head in defeat.

"Excellent," the man said, then waved at the circle of soldiers. "Pack 'em up, boys. The other two are still out there somewhere. There's a good chance they'll be back. I want these subjects secured before then."

Several of the soldiers lowered their weapons and leapt to do the man's bidding. Pulling flexicuffs from their belts, they stepped towards the captives, while the remaining soldiers covered them with their rifles.

"Now's our chance," Liz whispered.

Chris nodded, eyeing the space between them and the soldiers. Preoccupied with their prisoners, the men had taken their eyes from the surrounding trees. If Chris and Liz were quick, they could take them by surprise. Even with their goggles, the soldiers would be at a disadvantage in the darkness. In the confusion, Richard and the others might have a chance to slip free.

Silently, Chris gathered himself to attack.

Before either of them could move, a whisper of movement came from behind them, and a voice growled from the darkness.

"Don't move."

7

Captain Scott crossed his arms and watched as his men secured the prisoners. Covered by their comrades, two slung their rifles over their backs and stepped towards the boy. They grabbed him by both arms and forced them behind his back. The half-folded wings sprouting from the small of his back made the task difficult, and the boy himself wasn't making things any easier.

"Please," he begged as a third soldier stepped forward with the cuffs. "You don't know what you're doing, what they'll do to us."

Scott stared down at the boy, reading the terror in his eyes. The prisoner tried to flinch away as he approached, but his men held him tight. Smiling, he drove a fist into the prisoner's face. The boy reeled back, and only the men holding his arms kept him from falling.

"*Silence*," Scott growled. "By the law of our land, you should be dead already. You were offered mercy, offered a chance at redemption. But you threw it all away." He raised his fist again, his anger catching light.

Before the blow could fall, a bloodcurdling howl echoed through the forest. Scott froze. He stared at the prisoner for another second, and then whirled to face the trees. The darkness remained absolute, but with their goggles, any approaching enemies would be easily detected.

There was nothing.

His men shifted nervously around him as they scanned their surroundings, weapons at the ready. Scott took a step towards the trees, unslinging his rifle as he moved. Beyond his circle of men, the forest was empty.

Shaking his head, he cast one last glance at the pitch-black trees, and then started to bark fresh orders to his men. Before he could finish, an audible *thud* came from behind him.

Then someone began to scream.

Scott spun, raising his rifle to fire, already cursing his decision not to execute the prisoners. Whatever their orders, he should have trusted his instincts. He had seen *Chead* in action, had glimpsed the aftermath of their slaughter inside the facility. However pathetic the three teenagers seemed, they were far too dangerous to hold captive.

But as he turned, he found the prisoners still on their knees. He hesitated, then making up his mind, he lifted his rifle and aimed it at the boy. Before he could fire, one of his men staggered into his line of sight. The soldier reached out a hand, fumbling at Scott's vest, and then collapsed soundlessly to the ground.

As the man went down, another figure moved within the circle. Even in the strange glow of his night vision goggles, Scott knew it was not one of his men. It wasn't even human.

He stumbled back as the *Chead* leapt, its feral growl rumbling through the darkness. Movement came from overhead, and then ethereal green figures were falling from the trees, landing amongst his men with catlike grace.

Chaos engulfed the night.

Gunfire roared to Scott's right, snapping him from his shock. He lifted his rifle and fired a round at the silhouette stalking towards him, but it dove into the glowing mess of men and *Chead*, and his bullets found only dirt. Cursing, Scott spun, barking fresh orders as he searched for another target.

"Men, form up on me! They're in the trees!"

His orders fell on deaf ears as his men descended into panic. Disordered, they stumbled away from the onslaught of superhuman creatures. The *Chead* darted amongst them like wolves in a henhouse, rending and tearing as they went. To his left, a soldier reeled back, a fountain of green sprouting from his chest, his high-pitched scream dying to a whisper.

Scott fired as the *Chead* leapt from the soldier's lifeless body. The bullets shrieked, tearing through a nearby tree trunk, but the creature was already gone, its powerful legs sending it soaring. It landed on another of his men, its weight driving him to the ground. A sharp *crack* followed as the creature slammed the man's skull into the earth.

A flash of gunfire lit Scott's night vision, momentarily blinding him. Turning away, he shouted again over clamor, his fear rising.

"Men, on me, *goddammit*!" He hurled himself to the side as a body flew past where he'd been standing. It crashed to the ground a few feet away and did not move.

Rolling across the pine needles, Scott regained his feet. All around him, green figures blundered between the trees, all semblance of order lost. In the chaos, the prisoners had vanished, either killed or fled, but he no longer cared. Survival was his only goal now.

Scott realized he'd drifted from his circle of men. He now found himself away amongst the trees, standing on the edge of the desperate battle between his men and the *Chead*.

Heart pounding, the captain gripped his rifle tight and weighed his options. Though the chatter of gunfire still sounded, from where he stood it was clear the battle was lost. The *Chead* were too fast, too powerful in close quarters, especially in the darkness. The second it took his men to distinguish between friend and foe was all the creatures needed.

No, this was a lost cause. His men were as good as dead.

Scott forced himself to turn away. Shame rose in his throat as he started to run, fleeing the chaos. The screams of dying men chased after him, rising up through the howls of the *Chead*, piercing him to his soul. A voice inside screamed for him to turn back, to stand alongside his men, to die a soldier's death.

But his terror was greater still, and he raced through the darkness, desperate to escape the slaughter.

Scott paused as silence fell over the forest. He glanced back in the direction of the battle, suddenly uncertain. Had they succeeded after all? Had his men done the impossible, and fought off the *Chead?* But he heard no triumphant cries, no wild shouts. No sound at all, in fact.

Swallowing, he looked around. The forest was deathly still now. Not so much as the chirp of a cricket broke the silence. He shuddered, and then he was running again, a pure, unadulterated horror gripping him.

He ran for what felt like hours, stumbling over roots and crashing into the pale shadows of tree trunks. He ran without thought of where he was going, only of what came behind, of the death that stalked him through the ill-fated woods.

Finally, lungs burning, body aching, Scott could run no more. He staggered to a stop, shoulders heaving, one arm clutching at a tree trunk for support. Bending in two, he gasped in great lungfuls of air. He had lost all track of time, all sense of direction, but he was sure he'd traversed several miles.

Straightening, he let out a long breath and looked around. Somehow in his terrified flight, he'd managed to keep hold of his rifle and night vision goggles. He studied his backtrail, searching for movement, for the telltale glow of warm bodies. But the forest remained empty, and nodding to himself, he turned away.

...And froze as an ethereal green figure stepped from the trees ahead.

Soft laughter whispered through the forest as the *Chead* approached. Through the glow of his goggles, Scott watched a vicious grin twist its features. Out of sheer instinct, he raised his rifle, but the *Chead* was faster still. With brutal ease, it tore the weapon from his grasp and hurled it away.

Iron fingers gripped Scott by the throat and lifted him into the air. The *Chead* stared up at him, its eyes bright in the glow of his goggles.

"*Human*," the creature spoke in a guttural growl.

Scott gasped feebly in its grip, mouth wide, struggling for breath. He kicked out at the creature, slammed his fists into its arms, anything to break its hold. Fire burned his lungs and darkness swirled at the edges of his vision, but nothing he did seemed to have any impact.

As his sight began to fade, Scott remembered, finally, the EPIRB on his vest. It would bring help, send the helicopter straight to his location. With the last of his strength, he slammed his fist into the button on his shoulder. The EPIRB gave a low beep, then fell silent.

A smile tugged at his lips as he looked down at the creature. His lungs screamed for air and a dull pounding drummed on the back of his skull, but help was on its way.

"*You will not own us.*" The *Chead's* teeth flashed.

Scott opened his mouth to scream as the grip around his throat tightened. Stars flashed across his vision as the creature struck him in the face. Darkness loomed, threatening to swallow him.

No! he screamed in the silence of his thoughts as the *Chead* raised its fist again.

And then everything went black.

8

"*Go, go, go!*" Chris shouted over the gunfire.

He darted under the flailing arm of a soldier and leapt towards Richard and Jasmine. The young girl was already on her feet, but the other two were slower. They still knelt on the ground, mouths wide, staring at the horror unfolding around them.

But there was no time to contemplate the fate of the soldiers. Chris grabbed Richard by the collar and hauled him to his feet. Liz did the same with Jasmine, and then they were moving again, sprinting through the dying men and howling *Chead.*

A second later they were amongst the trees, the chatter of bullets and awful screams behind them. Chris raced on, catching glimpses of the others as they stumbled through the dark. None of the five made an effort to mask their passage. If the *Chead* had wanted them dead, they would already be in the ground.

Instead, the creatures had saved them.

Chris swallowed as he ran, remembering the *Chead's* sudden appearance. The creature had frozen them with a whisper, its cold grey eyes stealing away their voices. Silently, it had lifted a finger to its lips and shook its head. Then it was gone.

A few seconds later, the screaming had started.

Now as Chris fled, questions raced through his mind, one

after another. Who were these *Chead?* Where had they come from? Why were the creatures helping them?

There was no time to stop and wait for answers. Despite the *Chead* having the element of surprise, the soldiers were well-trained and well-armed. There was no guarantee the *Chead* would be victorious. If the soldiers prevailed, Chris doubted they'd still be in the mood to take prisoners—only bodies.

Leaping a fallen log, Chris ran on, silently cursing their sluggish pace. The time for stealth was over—they needed to be airborne, to take to the skies and leave the soldiers and *Chead* far behind. He searched the canopy for a hole, for any gap in the branches that might allow them to escape. But the trees stretched out overhead, unbroken.

They ran for over an hour before finally reaching a clearing. By then, the sounds of battle had fallen silent, and the first rays of the morning sun were streaming through the canopy. The clearing appeared out of nowhere—one moment they were racing through the trees, the next there was light all around, and they were stumbling to a stop.

Long grass stretched out for a hundred feet from where they stood, sloping gently down towards the west. The others drew up around Chris, their shoulders heaving as they caught their breath, their wings already stretching to embrace the light. They stood on the edge of the tree line, but as Chris looked across the clearing, he realized they were not alone.

A herd of goats stood amongst the long grass, their white coats shining in the sun. Their heads were raised, their beady eyes turning to stare at the intruders. Sleek black horns twisted from their heads and blades of grass hung absently from their mouths. A kid danced amongst the adults, ignorant to the danger posed by humans.

Before either group could react, an angry roar erupted through the clearing. The goats scattered in all directions. Screaming, several bolted towards Chris and the others. A swirling wind raced after them, bending the grass beneath it, tearing leaves and branches from the trees.

"Get down!" Chris heard someone shout as a shadow flickered at the edge of his vision.

Chris obeyed without thinking, hurling himself down amidst the long grass. He glimpsed the others following suit, then a terror-stricken goat leapt past, obscuring his vision. The dark silhouette of a helicopter followed, blades whirling, sun glinting from its metallic body.

Then it was gone, disappearing in the direction of their camp. Chris waited in the long grass, listening as the angry buzz of its blades faded, waiting for the pilot to realize their mistake, to turn back. It took a long time to convince himself it was truly gone. If the helicopter had had infrared sensors like the soldiers, the goats must have camouflaged their presence.

Finally he stood, fists clenched, heart still pounding hard in his chest. The stench of gasoline now stained the air, and Chris could feel his panic rising. He closed his eyes, struggling to hold back the terror of the night. His legs shook as he realized how close they had come to disaster.

"Chris…"

He turned to find Liz standing beside him. Their eyes met, then they were embracing, and Chris could feel her shuddering with the same horror. They clung together for a long minute before breaking apart.

Taking a breath, Chris finally managed to push past his fear. "Are you okay?" he asked, looking at the others.

Richard and Jasmine stared back, their hair frazzled, their faces marked by dirt. Otherwise, they looked no worse for their brief period in captivity. The young girl sat in the grass between them, her grey wings hanging limply from her back. Richard kept his expression carefully blank as he nodded, but Chris could see the fear behind his eyes.

Jasmine's brow creased in anger. "We're fine," she snapped, stepping towards him, "but where the hell were the two of you?"

Chris blinked, almost retreating from the force of her fury. "What?"

"Where were you?" Jasmine hissed, jabbing her finger at them like a knife. "When the soldiers came, when we woke with guns in our faces. *Where were you?*" She all but screeched the last words.

She broke off as Richard placed a hand on her shoulder. "Jas, don't," he breathed, looking across at Chris. "I saw them go off. I was on watch." He bowed his head. "It was my fault. I was so tired, I must have fallen asleep."

Chris's stomach wrenched at Richard's words. A hiss came from Jasmine as she twisted away from Richard. She pushed him in the chest, sending him stumbling back. "*You fell asleep?*"

Holding up his hands, Richard tried to retreat, but Jasmine shoved him again. The boy made no move to defend himself, only bowed his head before her rage. With a shriek, Jasmine swung a fist at his face. The blow caught him in the cheek and sent him reeling. Tripping over his own feet, Richard crashed to the ground.

Before Jasmine could land another blow, Liz caught her by the arm. "Jasmine, *stop!*"

Growling, Jasmine turned on Liz. Quick as a cat, Liz caught her by the other wrist. "Don't," she snapped, looking Jasmine in the eye. "It's not his fault. We should have come back earlier, taken over the watch. We were careless, foolish. We should have guessed they'd be waiting for us to leave the mountains. We could spend all day debating whose fault this is, but there's no time. That helicopter will be back any minute."

Chris swallowed. Liz was right—there was no way of knowing whether those in the helicopter already knew what had happened to the soldiers, but it wouldn't take them long to find out.

"We have to risk it," Liz continued, "we have to fly. If we stay low to the trees, it'll be difficult to spot us. But we need to get clear of this forest, and fast. The whole place is going to be flooded by soldiers when they see what the *Chead* did."

"How?" Richard asked as he picked himself up. Ignoring the glare Jasmine shot him, he gestured at the sky. "There's no cliffs to jump off around here, in case you hadn't noticed."

Chris looked across the clearing, studying the gently sloping ground, and the trees on the far side. "I think we can do it," he answered. "If we run hard across the clearing, I think we'll be able to generate enough lift to take off. Just like a kite."

He flashed the others a grim smile, and then started to run. Darting across the damp grass, he spread his wings and picked up the pace. The air cracked as twenty-four feet of tawny brown feathers beat down. Muscles tensed along his torso as the wind caught in their expanse.

Gritting his teeth, Chris watched as the trees on the far side raced towards him. When there were only a few feet remaining, he sucked in a breath and sprang. His auburn wings beat down, and his stomach lurched as he lifted higher. He grinned as the earth fell away, then he banked quickly to skirt the trees on the other side of the clearing. Circling back, he watched as the others followed after him.

When the five of them were airborne, Chris shot above the treetops. He cast a glance back in the direction the helicopter had taken, but the sky was empty. It could not have gone far though, and shifting his wings, he raced down the valley towards the distant Californian plains. Wings cracked as Liz settled in beside him, her eyes fixed straight ahead.

A broad valley opened around them, the redwoods covering its floor like a carpet. To either side, low cliffs hemmed them in, stretching down to the mouth of the valley, where the last of the hills gave way to floodplains.

Chris scanned the cliffs as they flew, searching for the shadow of a cave in which they might hide, but there was nothing. He could still see no sign of the helicopter, but over the roar of the wind, he heard the whine of an engine again, drawing closer.

Ahead, the cliffs bent away to the right as the valley altered course. Straining his wings, Chris shot for the cliff-face to their right, where the curve in the rock would hide them from the helicopter farther up the valley. Beside him, Liz's black wings were a blur, beating hard to keep her above the treetops. They were so close that Chris could have reached out and touched the pine needles.

He allowed himself a grim smile as they passed around the curve in the cliff and out of view. But the respite would not last long. Ahead, the cliffs ended abruptly, while below the forest spilled out onto the Californian plains and gave way to the prairies. Beyond, brown fields stretched as far as the eye could see. Sheep and cattle dotted the land, but the open space offered nothing to hide them from the prowling eyes of the chopper.

Beside him, Liz shouted and suddenly banked to the right. He cried after her, but her hand rose, waving them to follow. Then she was racing away, leaving Chris and the others no choice but to give chase. His eyes roamed over the land beyond, finding a small mountain rising amidst the endless flat. Liz was making straight for it.

Realizing her plan, Chris picked up the pace, his wings beating hard to catch her. Below, the forest turned to dry grass. Their shadows flashed across the fields, their wings stretched wide. The mountain grew larger, extending five hundred feet above the prairies. Scraggly trees covered its steep slopes, though they would offer little cover. He hoped Liz knew what she was doing.

The mountain stood at least two miles from where the valley ended. Flying hard, they raced to close the gap, ever aware of the growing buzz of the helicopter.

When they were still a few hundred feet away, the thud of whirling blades turned suddenly to a roar. Ahead, Liz folded her wings and plummeted from the sky. Chris dived after her, pulling his wings tight against his back, spiraling down towards the plains below. Less than a hundred feet from the ground, Liz snapped her wings back open. The air cracked as they caught, halting her fall. She shot towards the mountain.

Leveling out, Chris gave in to his fear and glanced back. The chopper had emerged from the mouth of the valley and was hovering above the last stretch of trees, a dark shadow staining the sky. So far it did not seem to have spotted them. Filling his lungs, Chris pressed on.

The mountain rose before them, a dark blemish on the endless grasslands. Liz banked as she reached its rocky edge, flying horizontal to its slopes until she disappeared around the far side of the mountain.

One by one, they followed her.

The mountain's shadow fell across Chris's wings, hiding him from view. He let out a breath he hadn't realized he'd been holding and started to slow, expecting Liz to pull up, and then realized she was still flying hard around the mountainside. His chest burned and a sharp cramp had begun in the small of his back, but Liz wasn't giving them any time to argue. Feeling the ache of their weeklong flight through the mountains in every inch of his body, Chris continued after her. Mutated physiology or not, he desperately needed food and rest.

Liz drifted closer to the mountainside, the beat of her wings slowing as she neared its rocky slopes. The scraggly trees were taller on this side of the mountain, offering at least a little cover from prying eyes. Ahead, Chris noticed a sharp split in the mountainside, as though some giant had carved a piece of rock from the steep slopes.

Chris frowned as he realized Liz was making straight for the crease, as though she had known it was there all along. He blinked as shapes took form within the shadows. A cluster of buildings clung to the mountainside, all but invisible in the gloom of the valley. Thick vines and creepers clung to the aluminum roofs and wooden walls, and it was clear the settlement had long been abandoned. Even so, the sight sent a tingle of renewed energy through Chris, and he raced to catch up with Liz.

A few minutes later, he touched down in the broken courtyard between the buildings. His wings shook with the effort, and he stumbled slightly as his legs took his weight. Folding his wings, he groaned at the ache spreading up his back. He kneaded the side of his head, feeling the first tingles of a migraine.

Liz had landed a full minute before him and was already moving towards the largest building. Before he could call out, she pushed through the broken door and disappeared inside. Exhausted, Chris shook his head and chased after her, leaving the others to catch their breath outside.

Pausing on the threshold of the house, he looked down the empty corridor. Dust covered the floor, untouched except where Liz's footprints led down the hall. A dark stain marked the floorboards at the end, and an untouched silence clung to the shadows. Taking a step inside, Chris found himself wondering why the occupants had left this place.

His ears twitched as he sensed movement from deeper inside the building.

"Liz?" he called.

When she did not answer, Chris swore softly under his breath, and started along the corridor. Apprehension grew in his chest as he followed Liz's footprints through the dusty rooms.

He found her in what must have been the lounge. She stood in the empty room, back turned and head bowed, wings half-spread behind her. Her body shook with silent tears.

Chris quickly crossed the wooden floor and placed a hand on her shoulder. She shivered at his touch, and a single sob tore from her throat. The first prickles of fear touched Chris as she turned, her blue eyes finding his.

"Liz, what is this place?" he whispered.

Tears streaked her cheeks as she looked up at him. "Home."

ENJOYED THIS BOOK?

Then follow Aaron Hodges and receive a free short story:
www.aaronhodges.co.nz/newsletter-signup/

Phase One: Complete.
The Evolution Gene continues in...

II
HOME

PROLOGUE

Sam groaned as the first tingle of consciousness tugged at his mind. He fought against it, clinging to the dark cloud of oblivion, desperate for its cold, numbing comfort. But slowly the light trickled in, casting out the black, dragging him back to the agony of his body.

He winced as fire boiled through his muscles. Another groan tore from his lips. A low gurgle started in his chest and made its way up his throat, until the metallic taste of blood filled his mouth. Rolling onto his side, he spat on the concrete. He swallowed, and felt the steel collar press against his Adam's apple.

Lying there with his eyes closed, his memories slowly returned. He saw again Ashley's fall, her wondrous white wings folding in on themselves, her plummet to the snowy ground. He remembered lifting her broken body, his whispers as he begged her to fight, to live. Then the short flight from the cliffs, his wings straining hard to keep them both aloft, the ground rising up to meet them.

And the guards waiting, their rifles held at the ready, watching their approach.

They had taken Ashley from him the moment he'd landed. Sam had made no effort to resist—the doctors in the facility were the only ones who could save her. After securing Ashley, the guards had turned their attention on him. The hulking captain had stepped forward and slammed his rifle into Sam's stomach, driving the air from his lungs. As he crumpled, something hard had struck him in the back of his head, toppling him to the ground. Steel-capped boots had descended on him then, smashing him in the face and ribs, slamming into his back, crushing the fragile feathers of his wings.

Unable to defend himself, Sam had curled into a ball and waited for death. Finally, a blow had caught him in the side of the head, and he'd gladly given himself over to the darkness.

Hours later he'd woken in this room, to a group of hard-faced men in suits standing over him. At his first sign of movement, two guards had sprung forward and pulled him to his knees. His head still spinning, Sam had met their questions with stony silence.

Who was Angela Fallow working with?

How did she free you?

Where are they going?

He'd been rewarded another beating when he refused to answer. A blow had caught him in the forehead and sent him reeling sideways. As he tried to roll free of the guards, the collar around his neck had pulled him up short. Only then had he noticed the short length of chain connecting it to a bolt in the ground. Helpless, he had looked up in time to catch a boot to his face.

For days now, his captors had tortured him. He no longer knew whether it was day or night. Time had lost all meaning. Only the presence of his tormentors mattered now. Sometimes they would leave him alone for long hours—other times, they seemed to reappear within minutes. Drifting in and out of consciousness, Sam found his senses crumbling, his sanity falling away.

Images flashed through his mind, some faster than thought, others lingering. He saw Ashley standing in their cell, the familiar smile on her face, her movements lithe and graceful. Then the image changed, and he would see her lying still, her face a pallid grey, her eyes empty.

Other visions followed, filling his mind, reminding him of past horrors. He watched again the boy convulsing on the training field as Halt stood over him, smelled the stench of death and decay in the medical room, saw the blood staining the padded walls.

Saw the blood on his hands, and his friend, lying still on the ground.

Saw the accusing stares of Jasmine and Richard.

Gritting his teeth, Sam pushed away the memories and pulled himself to his knees. He winced as the chain went taut, the collar cutting into his flesh. The chain was so short he could not stand—only crouch on his hands and knees. His muscles ached from disuse and constant pain ran down his spine. A sharp twinge came from his ribs with each intake of breath. Air whistled through his broken nose, and his stomach cramped with a ravenous hunger.

Sam's heart started to race as he heard the faint click of the door handle. His left eye was so swollen he could barely see through it, but he forced his right to open. The harsh light burned, but slowly the room came into focus. Other than a plain steel chair that sat just out of reach, the room was unadorned, the white walls and concrete marked only by his blood.

Beyond the chair, the door unlocked and two guards pushed their way into the room. Sam watched as they took up stations on either side of the chair, then returned his attention to the doorway.

His stomach lurched as Doctor Halt stepped into the light. He shrank back as the doctor's cold grey eyes found him on the floor. Days without food or sleep had stolen Sam's strength, and now even the brief task of sitting up left him gasping.

"Samuel," Halt's voice slithered through the air, "you disappoint me."

Stalking across the room, Halt lowered himself onto the chair and crossed one leg over the other. His long black pants and white lab coat were immaculate—a stark contrast to the filthy rags Sam wore. The doctor's brow creased as he pursed his thin lips.

Sam looked into the doctor's eyes and suppressed a shudder. There was no hint of compassion there, not a spark of pity.

Halt leaned back in his chair and tapped one finger against his elbow. "Fallow has caused us a considerable setback, Samuel." He looked around the room, shaking his head. "The President wants answers—-answers we do not currently possess."

Sam bit his lip and looked away. An image flickered into his mind—of Angela Fallow sprawled on the laboratory floor, her lifeblood pooling around her. He tasted bile in his throat and swallowed hard.

"Samuel, you must see the folly of protecting her," Halt whispered, his voice cutting through Sam's thoughts. "The woman is dead. Just tell us who aided her, and this torment will cease. You will be moved to more comfortable facilities, provided with regular meals. Just give us what we want."

Closing his eyes, Sam almost wished he had the answers Halt demanded. But in the scant minutes they had spent in the medical room, he had never thought to ask how Angela had freed them all, or why. He'd been too preoccupied with other things, like why wings had suddenly sprouted from his back.

Sam forced a smile. "Look." He coughed out the word, then turned his head and spat a gob of bloody saliva on the concrete. "I wish I could help you, Halt. The woman called me fat. Believe me, I'd sell her out in an instant, if I could."

A weary look passed across Halt's face. "So you say." He looked at the grey walls, as though there was more to its plain surface than met the eye. There wasn't—Sam had spent enough time staring at them himself to know that. Shaking his head, Halt went on, talking almost to himself. "The survivors of the B-strain will have to suffice. They're all we have—for now."

Sam's heart lurched. "Ashley," he wheezed, his fingers clawing at the concrete. "She's not…"

Halt's lips twitched. "How quaint, the two of you formed a bond." He waved a hand, as though dismissing Sam's concerns. "The girl lives."

Tears stung Sam's eyes as a sob tore from him. Ashley lived.

His sacrifice had not been in vain. The weight of the chain around his neck grew the slightest bit lighter.

His vision blurring, Sam looked up at Halt. "Thank you."

Halt only shook his head. "I did what was necessary," he said, his voice cold. "Thanks to the damage caused by Doctor Fallow, we have no candidates to spare. The President is demanding a demonstration of our success. We will need as many healthy specimens as possible to ensure the project's survival."

Something in Halt's words made the sudden hope in Sam's chest die. He clenched his fists, summoning his last reserves of defiance. "I won't help you, Halt."

Doctor Halt stared at him a moment, then pulled himself to his feet. "A shame." A harsh smile spread across his face. "You don't really think they can escape, do you, Samuel?"

Halt moved to the door. Pulling it open, he glanced back. "If so, you are mistaken. Our hunters will have them soon. Then they will join you in here," Halt growled, before turning to the guards who still stood on either side of his chair. "For now, I will entrust your care to these gentlemen. When you're ready to cooperate, do let me know."

With a swirl of his lab coat, Halt was gone. The hulking guards stepped forward as the door slammed shut behind him. Grim smiles spread across their faces as they drew steel batons from their belts.

Sam's defiance withered as the two men closed on him. He shrank away, but the chain brought him up short, leaving him crouched helpless on the ground. A whimper rose in his chest, and he fought the urge to beg, knowing that would only make it worse.

One raised his baton.

Sam closed his eyes, and waited for the pain.

9

Liz closed her eyes and listened to the silence of the house. Or what might have once been silence, before the awful experiments that had changed them all forever. Now, she could hear the whisper of a mouse in the ceiling, the soft creak of wooden boards cooling in the night breeze, could smell the dried blood in the hallway and the reek of mildew and dust. And beneath that, the familiar smells of home. Gone were the voices, the life she had once lived, but the shell endured, and with it, the memories.

Darkness concealed the empty rooms and wall she knew so well. Somewhere outside, a cricket chirped, and she could hear the soft breathing of the others as they slept nearby. Richard and Jasmine lay on opposite sides of the lounge. Jasmine had hardly spoken since almost being captured back in the forest, but she and the young girl seemed to have bonded. The enigmatic thirteen-year-old lay curled up next to Jasmine, her eyelids flickering gently with some dream. Chris was somewhere outside, keeping watch while the others rested. They were taking no chances now, not after what had happened the night before, when the soldiers had almost caught them.

They'd spent the day huddled inside the house, listening for the telltale buzz of the chopper, praying its search would not reach their lonely mountain. The shadow of the valley and wooden walls would not shield them from a persistent search, but at least they were hidden from casual observers. The dark contraption would have to come close to find them; they would hear its approach long before then.

The long hours had been spent exploring the house. Liz had helped retrieve what remained of her parents' clothing. Most of the items were moth eaten and covered in mildew, but they were still far better than the rags they'd escaped in. There were also several pairs of shoes, and heavy jackets they could wear to cover their wings.

When the shadows of nightfall fell across the plains beyond the mountain, the group had finally relaxed. Richard, showing a practicality Liz would never have guessed at back in the facility, had ventured into the forest, returning an hour later with a turkey, its neck broken and dangling from his bloody hand. In the meantime, Liz and the others had gorged themselves on oranges and half-green apples hanging from the nearby trees.

In the pitch black, Richard had set about lighting a fire in the long-dead woodstove. He, too, had hardly spoken since the incident in the forest, and Liz could sense the weight he carried on his shoulders. Whether it was remembered terror or guilt at having fallen asleep on watch, Liz could not tell. But she could do nothing to help him. The burden of her own memories hung over her now, rising from a past she'd thought long buried.

She had thanked him for the meat, though. The turkey had been old and tough, probably one of the birds her father had once kept, but to her half-starved stomach it had seemed a banquet. With her hunger sated, she'd felt her strength returning.

Now, in the darkness of night, Liz finally found the courage to face her past. Memories drifted through her mind—of her parents sitting around the kitchen woodstove, of the taste of her mother's rabbit stew, of long days spent manning the fields surrounding their solitary mountain peak.

Her parents and the other workers had tended to the great herds of cattle and sheep which grazed on the prairies, often spending cold nights sleeping beneath the stars when the beasts took them to the furthest pastures. Though little of the profits went to her family, it was an honest living, and they had been happy here.

Now the ranch had been abandoned, the land left untended, the buildings allowed to succumb to nature's encroachment. She wasn't surprised. It would have been hard to convince even the bravest of workers to return here after what had…happened.

Letting out a breath, Liz climbed to her feet. She felt a desperate need for company, to escape the lonely whispers of this place. Her cheeks flushed as she recalled the night before—Chris's hands around her, his lips on her neck, his flesh pressed hard against hers. She shivered and moved through the darkness. Following the old, familiar hallways, Liz made her way outside.

It took a long time to find him. Only when a stray root sent her sprawling to the ground did Liz hear a voice call from overhead. Looking up, she realized he was sitting on the tin roof. He smiled and waved for her to join him.

Taking hold of a steel drainpipe, Liz clambered up in the same manner she had done so many times before. She strode across the roof, taking care to follow the nails that marked the support beam, and lowered herself down next to Chris.

"Couldn't sleep?" he asked. He wrapped his arm around her waist and pulled her close.

Liz nodded and looked out into the darkness. The clouds had gathered late in the afternoon, and now the sky was a solid black, the moon and stars hidden away. Even so, her altered eyes could still make out the distant fields, still glimpse the telltale movement of the grass as the wind blew across the plains. Branches rustled around them, raising goosebumps on her arms. Shivering, she wriggled in closer to Chris, hoping to steal some of his warmth.

He smiled and his wings lifted, enfolding them both in his auburn feathers. Liz settled beneath his arm and closed her eyes. They were silent for a while, content to share the quiet of the night, and the comfort of each other's presence.

"What happened here, Liz?" Chris whispered at last. "Where did everyone go?"

Liz shuddered, and Chris tightened his grip around her, his

fingers giving her arm a reassuring squeeze. It took a long time to gather her thoughts, to face the terror, but Chris waited patiently, his mouth shut, silent.

"They're dead," she said finally.

Chris nodded. "The *Chead*?"

Swallowing, Liz recounted her story. "It seems so long ago now. I had just gotten back for the summer, had caught the bus all the way from San Francisco. My parents lived here, along with the farmhands who helped them in the fields. They managed the land all around this rock."

"Your family owned it all?" Chris asked

Liz snorted. "Of course not. Before the American War, it was Flores land. But after…" She shrugged. "Like most rural families, my grandfather fell into debt after the war. He had to sell off his holdings to settle his obligations. We were lucky the landholder allowed our family to stay on as managers."

She waited for Chris to comment, but he said nothing, and she turned her thoughts back to the night that everything had changed. "I got in late that day. It was almost dark, but I was excited to see my parents and friends. The workers were practically family. I was daydreaming as I walked up. At first, I didn't notice the silence..."

Chris's arms tightened around her. She found his eyes watching her, soft in the darkness. Biting her lip, Liz summoned her courage. "The farmhands were…scattered around the courtyard—some whole, others in pieces. But there was no sign of my parents."

She broke off again as tears brimmed in her eyes. Angrily, she wiped them away. Her fists clenched, but she forced herself to relax, to breathe. "I didn't think. I ran into the house, screaming their names. Inside, everything was torn and broken. At the end of the corridor, I could see blood on the floor. It was only then that I stopped, that reason caught up to me. But by then it was too late. I couldn't stop myself, I had to see, had to know…" A sob tore from her chest.

Strong arms held her close as she struggled to control her grief.

"Your parents?" Chris whispered.

Liz shuddered again. She bit her lip, determined to continue, to speak the words she had never dared voice aloud. "My father," she croaked. "He lay in the hallway, it was his blood..." She shook her head. "But my mom...my mom was standing over him, her head down, her shoulders shaking. And her eyes...her eyes were *grey*, Chris." She choked on the last words. "She had changed into one of *them*."

Burying her head in Chris's shoulder, she waited for him to reply, unsure how he would respond. But he said nothing, only held her tightly. When she finally looked up, there were tears in his eyes. Leaning down, he kissed her gently on the forehead.

"I'm sorry," he whispered.

They said nothing for a long time then, just sat together, staring out into the night. The wind began to pick up strength, shaking the branches hanging over the roof. Liz shivered, pulling her own wings tighter as she nestled in next to Chris. Her head lay on his chest, and she could hear the steady thud of his heart. Reaching out a hand, she entwined her fingers with his.

"What happened next, Liz?"

She sucked in a breath, her thoughts drifting back, remembering the cold grey eyes staring from her mother's face. There had been nothing left of her crystal blue gaze, of the gentle kindness she offered to all she met—only the *Chead* had remained. But as they'd found Liz, there had been a flicker of recognition, of *something* other than animalistic hunger.

"She left," Liz whispered. "I never understood why. I stood in that corridor for a full minute, too scared to move a muscle. But she just stood there, staring. Then, she seemed to come alive. She walked past me like I wasn't even there. I never saw her again."

She didn't add that it had been three days before anyone showed up, because the landowner finally reported a missing shipment of goods from the farm. Those three days were little more than a haze for Liz. Her mind had receded, succumbing to shock. She had spent hours crumpled on the hallway floor. Some form of awareness had eventually returned, and she'd woken covered in blood, her father's dead eyes watching her. Screaming, she'd fled into the forest.

After that, Liz could remember only flashes. Standing in a shower, the blood streaming down the drain. Then looking into a shallow grave, her father lying amidst the dirt. The taste of vomit in her mouth, the reek of death.

It wasn't until the police arrived that her sanity had finally returned. She had told them what had happened, watched as the SWAT team entered the forest, listened to their reassurances. But later, as she sat shivering in the back of a wagon, she had heard the policemen talking. They did not believe her story, that the *Chead* had spared her.

Liz's senses had come crashing back when they started to discuss where to take her. Her parents' warnings had returned, about the police and the disappearances, so common in the countryside. Silently, she'd slipped away into the woods, and never looked back.

Now, on the roof with Chris, Liz could hardly believe she had returned. An awful loneliness rose within her, a desperate grief for her parents and the life she had once lived. Sobbing, she clung to Chris, lost in the terror of her past, in the madness that had swallowed her existence.

☙ 10 ❧

Chris watched as the first light of the morning sun touched the horizon. It began as a soft glow far in the distance, still hidden by the curve of the earth, but it quickly rose into view. Light shone across the plains, turning the fields of grass to gold, revealing the black and white dots of sheep and cattle. He closed his eyes as the rays reached him on the rooftop, basking in their warmth.

Turning on his side, he watched Liz where she lay curled up beside him. One of his wings was draped across her like a blanket, and she clutched it in her fingers, a soft smile touching her lips. Her own wings had relaxed with sleep, and now hung limply behind her.

His mind drifted, recalling again the story she had told him. He shivered, unable to comprehend the shock, the horror she must have felt, witnessing her mother…change. He bit back a sob as he thought of his own mother, and wondered at her fate.

Where are you, Mom?

He still clung to the hope that she lived, that the government had spared her from execution, or had delayed her sentence. He couldn't bring himself to face the alternative, that she might be gone, that he might be alone.

If she was gone, he didn't know how he would go on.

Grimacing, Chris forced his thoughts to more practical matters. They were a long way from safety yet. They'd found a temporary asylum on Liz's ranch, but it was only a matter of time before the search reached the lonely mountain. Today, tomorrow maybe, but no longer than that. Once the helicopter found the dead soldiers and realized the escapees had breached their cordon, the hunters would come for them. They had to be far away by then.

But with wide plains stretching to the west, they would be spotted in minutes if they flew.

Chris stifled a yawn and rose to his feet, struggling to free his wings from Liz's unconscious grip before tucking them against his back. Liz stirred with the movement, her eyelids flickering briefly, before settling back into sleep. Crouching down, he gently lifted her into his arms.

Letting her great black wings trail out beneath her, Chris crossed to the edge of the roof and jumped. His own wings snapped out as they fell, catching him and slowing his descent. He landed with the soft thump of bare feet on dirt and retracted his wings. Idly, he wondered again at the strange new appendages, at how quickly his friends had all adapted to their presence. Though he occasionally still tripped over their bulk, each day his wings became more a part of him.

He found Jasmine and Richard in the living area. Richard stood by the window, looking out over the plains. He glanced up as Chris entered, then resumed his silent vigil. Jasmine was in the adjoining kitchen, silently licking her fingers. A guilty look crossed her face when she saw him, and she quickly looked away. Glancing at the countertop, Chris saw the remains of the turkey had been picked clean. His stomach gave a sharp rumble at the sight.

Shaking his head, Chris crossed the room. The young girl lay asleep beside the long-dead fireplace, her grey wings pulled tight around her. He laid Liz beside her. To his surprise, the younger girl gave a soft murmur, and her arms stretched out to embrace Liz.

Chris smiled at the sight, warmth spreading through his

chest. Whatever pain Liz still felt from her parents'...death, she was no longer alone. She had a new family now—even this strange little girl, it seemed.

He looked back at Jasmine and Richard, sensing the tension hanging over the room. They had said little yesterday of the ambush in the forest. They had all been too exhausted, still in shock after what had happened, what they'd witnessed. Jasmine hid it well, but he could see her fear, concealed beneath the anger. The encounter with the soldiers had frightened her to the core.

"Good morning," he offered softly.

Richard turned from the window. "You didn't wake us, for the watch?"

Chris shook his head. "I couldn't sleep anyway. I thought you could all use the rest."

Jasmine snorted as she walked out of the kitchen. "Yeah, right. Not because you were worried *he* might fall asleep again."

Richard bowed his head and looked away, but she advanced on him, fire burning in her eyes.

Quickly stepping into her path, Chris raised his hands. "It's not his fault, Jasmine."

"No?" Her brown eyes bored into him, emerald wings trembling on her back. "What about you and Liz then? Wandering off into the forest, leaving us all alone. I guess we know how things stand between us, don't we?"

"How things stand?" Chris stepped towards her, until only an inch separated them. "How things stand is the two of you have never been anything but antagonistic to us. And why? Because we were forced to fight your friends? Because we were jailed with Ashley and Sam?"

Jasmine refused to back down. Her eyes were like daggers as she looked up at Chris. "They killed our *friends*," she snapped.

"And you didn't?" Richard interrupted their exchange. His face was hard now. "You made the same choice, Jasmine. Or else Chelsea would be here instead of you, wouldn't she?"

Air hissed between Jasmine's teeth as she paled. "Don't you *dare* bring her into this!"

"*Stop!*" Chris shouted over the two of them. He glanced at Liz and was relieved to see she still slept. He went on in a softer tone, "Stop this, both of you. We've all been forced to do things we regret. We went through that hell together, in case you'd forgotten. But we're all that's left now. We're all any of us has. We have to find a way to work together."

Jasmine drew in a long breath as she looked at Chris. She opened her mouth to speak, but her voice cracked, and suddenly she seemed to shrink. Hugging herself, she turned away. "You don't understand," she whispered. "When they caught us…when we were kneeling there on the ground…I've never been so afraid, knowing they were taking us back, that there was nothing I could do to stop it from happening."

"Jasmine…" Richard's voice was soft as he stepped towards her.

"*Don't!*" Jasmine shrank away. "Just…don't, Richard."

"It wasn't his fault, Jasmine," Chris said again. "You saw how many there were, the weapons they had. They would have killed us if we'd tried to run. I don't think it would have mattered in the end, whether Richard was awake or not."

A strained silence fell across the room. Chris shivered as a cold breeze drifted in from the front door. He moved into the kitchen and attempted to scavenge a scrap of meat from the turkey carcass.

"What *did* happen back in the forest, Chris?" It was Richard who spoke, but when Chris looked up, he saw Jasmine shifting closer too.

Giving up on the turkey, he picked up a stray apple they'd picked earlier and took a bite. The memory of the *Chead* falling from the trees returned, and with it the screams of the soldiers. His stomach churned and he tossed the apple back onto the bench.

"The truth? I don't know. We were watching you from the trees, talking about how to rescue you." He eyed Jasmine pointedly at that. "But before we could act, the *Chead* appeared. I didn't even hear them approach. One stepped between us and the soldiers and told us to stay. The others melted into the trees and attacked the men holding you."

Jasmine shuddered. "Why would they help us?"

Chris shrugged. He had been asking himself the same question. That, and where they had come from, what they'd been doing in the forest in the first place. He started to speak, when a voice came from the doorway behind them.

"Well, what do we have here?"

❧ 11 ❧

"Well, what do we have here?"

For a moment, time seemed to slow. Chris spun and glimpsed the figure in the shadows of the entrance. Stepping forward, he placed himself between the intruder and the sleeping girls. His lips drew back in a snarl as he raised his fists, but within, a desperate fear wrapped around his chest, draining his strength.

The *Chead* reclined in the doorway, arms crossed, its features twisted with dark amusement. Long black hair hung around its face, but there was no mistaking the grey eyes that marked its kind. The orange jumpsuit it wore was torn and stained, the sleeves ripped clean off at the shoulders. Sleek, powerful muscles rippled along its arms as it stepped into the room. It appeared to be around Chris's own eighteen years, though there was no telling with the *Chead*. A sickly-sweet scent reached Chris's nostrils as the creature looked around, its very presence a threat.

Chris's stomach lurched as he realized he knew the creature. It was the same *Chead* from the facility, the same one he and Liz had fought—and spared. He swallowed as its eyes fixated on him. He tensed, preparing himself.

The *Chead* smiled. "Come now." The words were spoken hesitantly, but there was no mistaking their power. "If we wished you dead…we would have left you to…the humans."

"Stay where you are," Chris hissed, his wings snapping open. "Don't come any closer."

The *Chead's* eyes lingered on Chris's wings as it took another step. "Curious..." Its voice grated in his ears. Lifting a hand, it reached out to touch his wing. Chris took an involuntary step back, and the *Chead* chuckled.

Swallowing his fear, Chris growled, "Get out."

The *Chead's* cold eyes drilled into him. Chris shuddered, but he refused to give any more ground. He could sense the others behind him, hovering close, and drew strength from their presence.

"You're outnumbered," he breathed. "Leave, *now!*"

A sly grin spread across the *Chead's* lips as it cackled. Movement came from around them, as the other creatures Chris had glimpsed in the forest filed in from the hallway. Unable to control his fear, Chris retreated until he collided with Richard. The *Chead* spread out around the room, forcing the three of them back towards the fireplace. Chris counted seven pairs of grey eyes watching them.

The first of the *Chead* moved forward, until it stood face-to-face with Chris. He flinched as it reached out and stroked his feathers, but there was nowhere left to go now.

"Curious," it repeated, its words smoother now. It looked at him. "So...I was not wrong."

Chris took a long breath, struggling to control his panic. "What do you want, *Chead?*"

"So... impolite." A broad grin split its face as its gaze travelled past him, to where Liz still lay asleep. Absently, Chris wondered whether she would sleep through a hurricane. "We are not yet...all present."

It started to step past him. Anger lit in Chris's chest and he moved to intercept it. Whatever these creatures wanted, he wasn't about to let them harm Liz. Not without a fight.

Before he could take a step, two *Chead* leapt from the circle and caught him by the arms. Grunting with the effort, they hauled him back. A smile on its lips, the first *Chead* strode past him to where Liz and the young girl lay by the fireplace.

"The other...one." It turned and grinned at Chris, its stilted voice touched by humor. "My...champions."

Chris was about to reply when movement came from the *Chead's* feet. Quick as a cat, Liz leapt from the ground and tackled the creature from behind. The suddenness of her attack sent it stumbling forward. Before it could recover, she wrapped an arm around its throat.

The *Chead* fought to regain control, but Liz spread her wings and beat them hard. Still off-balance, the *Chead* lost its footing and was dragged backwards as Liz took flight. Landing in the corner, the *Chead* now locked tightly in her grasp, she faced the remaining *Chead.*

"*Back!*" she snarled.

The other *Chead* exchanged uneasy glances. Then the creature in Liz's grip twisted, its elbow flashing back into her face. A harsh *crack* echoed through the room as the blow staggered her. With a violent jerk, the *Chead* tore itself from her arms and sprang free.

Chris tensed against the two *Chead* holding him, preparing to fight, but the first *Chead* only laughed. Shaking its head, it turned its back on Liz and stalked to Chris.

"The girl is...spirited." Teeth showed as its lips curled back into a grin. "She is...yours?"

Shrieking, Liz launched herself across the room. The *Chead* spun and parried a wild attack from Liz. It caught her by the wrist. A low rumble sounded in Liz's chest as she swung again with her free hand, but the *Chead* easily caught the blow in its other hand. Grinning, it stared down at her. Liz glared back helplessly, both hands now trapped in its iron grasp.

Then her knee flashed up, straight into the *Chead's* crotch. The *thump* as it struck made even Chris wince, and the *Chead* folded like grass before the wind.

"My name is Liz," she growled down at the creature, "and I belong to *no one.*"

The *Chead* chuckled as it straightened. "Such fire..." it said, bowing its head, "my...apologies."

"*Hecate!*" Chris jumped as a new voice shrieked from the corner.

Everyone in the room turned as a ball of grey hair and feathers barreled past. The first *Chead* stumbled back, surprise showing on its face as the young girl tackled it. Her laughter echoed through the room as they went down in a heap.

Chris could only stand and stare open-mouthed as the girl sat up and grinned down at the *Chead*. The *Chead* frowned at her.

"What the hell is going on?" Jasmine yelled. She took a half step towards the girl, lifting an arm as though to reach for her, before dropping it back down.

From the frown wrinkling its forehead, Chris could tell that the *Chead* was just as confused. Carefully, it disentangled itself and regained its feet. It cast a quick glance around at its fellow *Chead* as the young girl stood and frowned at it.

"What's the matter, Hecate?"

The *Chead* shook its head. "How...do you know my name...child?"

Chris watched the joy slip from the young girl's face. She took a quick step back. "You don't remember," she whispered. Tears beaded her eyes. A sob tore from the girl, and turning, she hurled herself at Jasmine.

Jasmine staggered as the tiny girl hugged her leg. Righting herself, Jasmine looked around the room, as confused as anyone else. When no one spoke, she crouched and drew the trembling girl into her arms.

The first *Chead* stood staring at the girl, his brow still creased in a frown, its eyes hesitant. Finally, it turned to Chris and raised an eyebrow. "Strange..." it murmured, its nostrils flaring. "Strange company...you keep."

Still shaking somewhat, Chris moved between Jasmine and the *Chead*. "How does she know you?"

"I do not...remember," the *Chead* whispered, shaking its head.

A feral anger rose in Chris's chest, born of frustration, of the secrets the doctors had kept from them, of their powerlessness even now they were free. He advanced, until he stood face-to-face with the *Chead.*

"What are you doing here, Hecate?" he snapped. "Why did you save us from the soldiers?"

Chris clenched his fists, bracing himself. He knew where the *Chead* had come from, that the creatures had been prisoners like them. But that still did not explain their appearance in the woods.

The smile fell from the *Chead's* lips at Chris's words. "A debt…was owed," it murmured, shifting on its feet. "You spared…my life. You suffered…for me."

Its eyes flickered towards Liz as it spoke, and Chris saw again the scene in the padded room, saw Liz writhing in agony, the shock collar flashing around her neck. Halt had tortured her when Chris refused to kill the *Chead* they had defeated. He shuddered and his hand drifted unconsciously to his throat. But the cruel collars were long gone, and angrily he pushed the memory away.

"She called you Hecate," he said, his anger fading as quickly as it had come. "That is your name?"

The *Chead* smiled. "So it would seem." A dull laughter rattled in its throat.

Chris shivered. Despite its appearance, despite the young girl giving it a name, an inhuman quality remained to the creature, a terrifying *otherness* that made him want to turn tail and flee. Silently he forced himself to swallow the sensation.

"Thank you, Hecate." He paused, unsure how to continue. "How…how are you here? How did you escape?"

"The woman…released us." Hecate's eyes flashed, the grin turning feral. "Oh, the fun we had…before we left."

Chris blanked. Finally, they knew how Angela Fallow had created the distraction that had allowed her to free them. She had unleashed the captive *Chead* on her unsuspecting colleagues. He shuddered at the slaughter that must have followed. It was a wonder anyone had survived to come after them. But then, a well-placed bullet could still stop a *Chead* in its tracks. In the long corridors of the facility, the guards would have eventually overwhelmed the creatures.

"How did you find us?" Liz asked.

"After...my brother and sister...fell, we left." The *Chead* eyed them with a grin. "You fly slowly...sleep too much. Your stench...was not hard to track."

Chris wrinkled his nose, trying to ignore the cloying sweetness the *Chead* carried with them. It was overpowering, though he had never heard it mentioned on the news. He guessed that an enhanced sense of smell was yet another alteration they could chalk up to Halt and Fallow's meddling.

Sense of smell aside, Chris guessed there was more to the *Chead's* actions than Hecate was letting on. "I don't think you followed us all this way, and saved us from those soldiers, just to say thank you."

The *Chead* smiled again. "You are...correct." Teeth flashed as his grin widened. "We came to see...if you would join us."

"Join you in what?" Liz asked softly.

Hecate turned to look at her. "In the war...to come."

Chris blinked. "The war to come?"

"For all our existence...we have suffered," Hecate said, eyes flashing. "We have been beaten. Tortured. Murdered. Our only memories...are of captivity. But now that we are free...we will make our tormentors pay."

"You want to fight the government?" Liz breathed.

"Government?" The *Chead*'s head bent to the side. "What is government? It is humanity...that made us suffer. It is humanity...that must pay."

Chris blinked. Behind him, Richard snorted. "All of humanity?" he asked, his voice rich with sarcasm. "There are millions of people in the Western Allied States. The government alone has thousands of soldiers. Against what, the seven of you?"

Hecate turned to face the taller boy. "Their soldiers are *nothing*," he growled. "The *Chead* are *legion*."

Though Hecate's words made no sense, Chris felt himself grow cold. Ice trickled down his back as he studied the unyielding figure of the *Chead*, imagining an army of such creatures. Then he shook his head and dismissed the image. The facility did not contain an army, just these seven. Hecate was clearly deranged, driven mad by his imprisonment.

Beside Chris, Richard laughed. Before any of them could react, Hecate sprang forward and caught him by the shirt. Growling, the *Chead* hauled Richard into the air. Richard swore as his feet left the ground, and he lashed out with his fist. The blow caught Hecate square in the face and sent him staggering backwards.

Richard stumbled as Hecate released him, his wings flaring out to steady him.

"Some legion," Richard spat. He looked around the room, defiant, a wild anger in his eyes. "You're not even a match for us, are you?"

Hecate straightened, but he made no move towards Richard. Instead, he turned to Chris. "Consider my offer," the *Chead* grated. "Are you with us…or with *them*?"

Chris shook his head. Pity swelled inside him, a sadness for the hate and torment that had shaped these creatures. Despite their brutality, despite the slaughter and destruction that followed their awakening, he sensed a depth to the *Chead*. There was more to them than the feral creatures he had seen on the television.

They were more human than anyone realized.

Yet Hecate and these others, held captive in the cold walls of the facility, had never had a chance to discover that humanity. The cruelty of Doctor Halt had shaped them, molding them with hate and fear, allowing nothing else to grow.

"I'm sorry, Hecate," he said to the *Chead*, "we cannot help you. Doctor Halt and the ones who supported him are our enemy. Not humanity. After all, we are human ourselves."

Now it was the *Chead's* turn to laugh. "So you think…but will *they?*"

12

Liz let out the breath she'd been holding as the last *Chead* departed. Heart still pounding, she moved to the window and watched as their shadows slid from the house into the surrounding trees. For a long time she stood watching the woods, waiting to see if they would return. But the only movement came from the wiry branches swaying in the morning breeze, and finally she returned to the others.

Richard and Jasmine still stood in the middle of the room, their faces pale. The young girl clung to Jasmine's leg, the occasional tremor of her wings betraying her fear. As Liz moved away from the window, Chris stepped from the hallway and looked at her.

"They're gone?"

She nodded, and he crossed the room and pulled her into his arms. Holding him tight, Liz struggled to relax, to cast aside her fear. But even with the heat of the moment gone, the fear clung to her, spreading until her whole body was trembling. The breath rattled in her chest as she closed her eyes, and saw again the boy's grey eyes staring down at her.

After a few moments, the terror passed, and she loosened her grip on Chris. Their eyes met as they parted, and she nodded at Chris's unspoken question.

"I'm okay." She looked at the others. "What about you, Richard, Jasmine?"

"I'm fine." Richard shook his head. "They're not so terrifying in person, right Jas?"

Jasmine stepped away from him, taking the girl with her. A hurt look crossed Richard's face and his shoulders slumped, but Liz ignored him. Jasmine would get over what had happened in the forest, eventually. They all would.

Chris chuckled. "They're terrifying enough for me." Shaking his head, he settled his gaze on the young girl still clutching at Jasmine's trousers. He crossed the room and knelt beside her. "Hey there."

The girl whimpered and shrank away as Chris offered his hand. Her wings rose to hide her face, her feathers trembling. Chris sighed and raised his eyebrows at the others.

"Any ideas?" he asked. "This is getting a little ridiculous."

Liz rolled her eyes and looked at Jasmine. "How about you boys go out back and pick some fruit? Give us girls some time to talk."

Richard and Chris shared an awkward look, but in the end they did as she said. Liz watched them go, then turned to face the two girls. Jasmine stared straight back, her eyes hard and arms folded defensively.

Ignoring Jasmine's frosty glare, Liz strode across the room and lowered herself onto the wooden floor. She crossed her legs and nodded at Jasmine, indicating for her to do the same. The taller girl hesitated, then snorted and joined Liz on the ground. Sitting cross-legged, Liz watched in bemusement as the younger girl crawled into Jasmine's lap and hid her face beneath her wings again.

Liz smiled, and even the corner of Jasmine's lips tugged upwards. Scooting forward, Liz rested a gentle hand on the young girl's wings. She could feel them trembling. It was obvious the girl was terrified. Silently, Liz stroked her feathers, waiting for the shaking to stop.

When the girl finally seemed to be calming down, Liz spoke in her friendliest voice. "Hello again!" She paused, struggling to find the words she needed. "I thought it was about time us girls had some alone time. Richard and Chris have gone to find us some breakfast, and those creatures aren't coming back. You're safe, you can talk to us."

Somewhat to Liz's surprise, the girl's wings retracted, revealing her pale, tear-streaked face. She blinked up at Liz, then turned to look around the room. Liz withdrew her hand and sat up straighter, waiting to see what the girl would do. The mismatched blue and green eyes swept the room once, then again, before she was apparently satisfied they were alone. In a quick burst of movement, she scrambled from Jasmine's lap to sit between them, crossing her legs to mimic the older girls.

Jasmine and Liz shared a glance before turning back to the girl.

"My name is Liz," Liz said, "and this is Jasmine."

The girl nodded silently, her eyes flickering between the two of them.

"Can you tell us your name?" Jasmine asked, leaning in, a friendly smile on her lips.

The girl swallowed. She looked around the room again, then nodded. "My name is…Mira," she whispered.

Grinning at their success, Liz carefully held out her hand. "It's nice to meet you, Mira."

Mira stared at her hand, her eyes wide, as though unsure what to do with it. After a minute Liz gave up and withdrew her hand. Ignoring the awkward moment, she pressed on. "Where do you come from, Mira?"

The girl blinked. "Come…from?" She looked from Liz to Jasmine. "I don't know…"

Mira's lips quivered and tears gathered in her eyes. Jasmine let out an impatient sigh.

Seeing Jasmine's frustration, Liz spoke quickly, before the other girl did something to drive Mira back into her shell. "It's okay, Mira. Maybe we can help you." Smiling, she put an arm around the young girl.

Mira shuddered. With a violent shove, she pushed Liz away from her. Liz gasped at the girl's strength and fell backwards onto the wooden floor. Eyes flashing with grief and anger, Mira leapt to her feet.

"*It's not okay!*" Mira screeched, the words tumbling from her now. "He doesn't remember. The bad doctor made me remember, but not Hecate, and now *he's gone!*"

Liz and Jasmine stared up at the girl. Her wings had spread with the angry words, and her shoulders shook with every harsh intake of breath. Slowly, Liz drew herself to her feet, Jasmine rising beside her. Movement came from the hallway, but Liz raised a hand, signaling for the boys to stay put.

"Mira," Liz said softly. "Who is Hecate?"

Mira shuddered as she looked from Liz to Jasmine. Her lips trembled and for a second, Liz thought she would not answer.

"Hecate…he's…Hecate is my brother."

13

Sam winced as the steel door clicked open. A sob tore from him, and he scrambled backwards. The collar snapped tight around his throat, halting his retreat. A desperate scream built in his chest.

Every muscle, every bone in his body ached. Even the sleek copper feathers of his wings were twisted and broken. They lay scattered around the room like fallen leaves, torn from his flesh when his captors grew tired of beating his body. There was no escaping the pain now. It was always there, even in his dreams.

And now his tormentors had returned for more.

Clenching his fists against the concrete, Sam clung to the last traces of his sanity. The soft pad of footsteps drew closer. He waited for the telltale creak of the chair as someone sat, but it did not come. Another tremor went through him, and he squeezed his eyes shut.

"Good morning, Samuel." Sam jumped as Halt's voice broke the silence.

Tears stung his eyes as he looked up. Halt stood over him, arms folded, his cold eyes staring. Sam no longer knew how long it had been since he'd last seen the doctor. His torture had been left to others.

A flutter of anger rose in Sam, little more than a spark of the rage that had once fueled him. Looking into Halt's remorseless eyes, even that fell away, leaving Sam alone with his terror. His shoulders slumped and tears spilled down his cheeks. Another sob tore from his throat.

"Please," he choked, all trace of defiance stripped away. "Please, no more, I can't…"

Sam flinched as Halt shifted, but the doctor only crouched beside him, a grim smile on his pale face. Halt patted him on the shoulder.

"My dear Samuel," he whispered, almost pleasantly. "It pains me to see you suffer so. You are one of our chosen, one of the few deemed worthy of this gift. Do you not wish to be free again?"

Huddled on the floor, with Halt's warm hand on his shoulder, Sam barely registered the doctor's words. But the last few syllables clung to him, piercing the fog of his shattered body, pulling him up from the darkness.

Free again…

Standing, Halt retreated to the iron chair. Entwining his fingers, he looked down at Sam. "I have an offer for you, Samuel."

Deep within, Sam could hear a voice shouting, telling him to fight, to resist the man's words. He knew anything Halt offered had to be a trick, a ploy to lure him into some fresh torment. And yet, Sam could not help but cling to his words like a drowning man, desperate for a lifeline.

"Please," he croaked. "I'll do anything. Just, no more, *please!*"

Halt chuckled and climbed to his feet. "That's good to hear, Samuel." The door clicked open, admitting two guards. Halt waved to Samuel. "Unlock the chain."

Sam shrank against the concrete as the men approached. Both had rifles slung over their shoulders and batons clipped to their belts. But for once they did not use them. Instead, one produced a key and unlocked the bolt that fixed his chain to the ground. Lifting the end, the guard offered it to Halt.

Trembling, Sam did not move as Halt took the chain and gave it a tug.

"Stand, Samuel," Halt ordered softly. "Join me. There is someone who would like to see you."

Goosebumps ran down Sam's spine at the words. Pulling himself to his feet, he allowed Halt to lead him from the concrete room into the long corridors of the facility. His bones creaked with each step, his muscles aching from the long days spent huddling on the ground. He stumbled after Halt, the weight of his half-folded wings heavy on his back. From behind him came the thud of boots as the guards followed, their rifles at the ready now.

The trip did not take long. A few quick turns down the brightly lit corridors, and Halt drew to a stop again. He released the chain to Sam's collar and nodded at the door. "I'll give you some time to get reacquainted."

Sam shuddered, his sluggish mind struggling to comprehend what game Halt was playing. He couldn't believe this was truly happening. Surely it was a trap, some cruel trick to shatter the last traces of his sanity.

But there was no turning back. His heart thudding hard in his chest, Sam reached out and turned the door handle. He stepped inside as the door swung open, leaving the doctor and guards behind. His eyes swept the room, taking in the white-washed walls and grey linoleum floor. It was empty except for a single hospital bed.

Ashley lay with her eyes closed, the sweaty tangles of her scarlet hair swirling out across the pillows. She wore plain green hospital scrubs, the short sleeves and low collar revealing the full extent of her injuries. Purple bruises marked her face and arms, and red abrasions streaked her chest, bound now by stitches. Needle marks dotted her arms, and tubes and wires encased her elegant body, stretching back to the host of machines sitting at the head of the bed. Her pale white wings hung limply beneath her, tangled with the thin sheets that covered half her body. A familiar steel collar shone around Ashley's throat, and handcuffs bound her arms to the metal rails running horizontally along the hospital bed.

A wave of relief swept through Sam as he saw her chest

move. His heart lurched, his breath catching in his throat. In an instant he had crossed the room.

"*Ashley*," he breathed.

Ashley's eyelids fluttered at the sound. A crease marked her forehead as her eyes opened, her tawny yellow irises shining in the bright light. They widened when she found him standing over her.

"Oh, *Sam*," she whispered. "What have they done to you?"

Sam only shook his head. Carefully taking a seat on the side of the bed, he reached out and took one of her hands.

"It was worth it," he said softly. "You're alive, Ashley. *You're alive*."

He could hardly believe what he was seeing. In the countless days of torment, in his darkest hours, he had long since convinced himself she was gone, that he had sacrificed himself for nothing. But now here she was, alive and breathing, staring at him with those haunting amber eyes, and it was all he could do not to crumble with the joy in his heart.

Alive.

"What did you do, Sam?" Ashley asked, her voice barely audible over the beeping machines.

Sam attempted a laugh, but a sharp pain pierced his chest, and it turned into a groan. He shook his head. "What I had to. What needed to be done, to save you."

Ashley closed her eyes a moment, pain flickering across her face. She squeezed his hand, then released him. "You shouldn't have done this, Sam," she murmured, and he saw tears glistening in her eyes. "I wanted you to be free."

Sam wiped away the tear that streaked her cheek. "Sorry, Ash," he said, smiling, "but you know I make poor decisions when you're not around."

Color warmed Ashley's cheeks. "Sam…"

Sam leaned forward and pressed his lips to hers, cutting off whatever she had been about to say. He felt her tense for a second, then she was returning the kiss, tilting back her head, drawing him in. A warm tingle spread through Sam as their tongues met, the taste of her filling him. He ran a hand through her hair, drawing her deeper. The pain of his body melted, giving way to his passion.

A click came from the door, and they pulled quickly apart, turning to see who had entered.

Halt's thin lips twisted into a smile as he crossed the room. He ignored them as he drew up on the other side of Ashely's bed. Standing in silence, he studied the screens of the machines connected to Ashley, nodding to himself.

"It looks like she will recover," he said at last. "With the proper care, of course."

"What do you want, Halt?" Ashley croaked.

"From you, my dear?" His lips hardened into a frown. "Nothing. For now, it is Samuel we need."

The agony of Sam's tortured body returned in a rush, and he felt again the awful helplessness of his tiny prison. Ashley's fingers tightened around his hand, and there was a glimmer of fear in her eyes.

"Thanks to the unfortunate actions of Doctor Fallow, we have found ourselves short of successful candidates from the project," Halt continued. "The PERV-A viral strain your group received has proven far less…lethal than our alternative strains." He pursed his lips. "Of those who received the PERV-B strain, only two remain…intact."

Sam clenched a fist around the sidebar of Ashley's bed. "How many have you killed, Halt?"

Ignoring the question, Halt lowered himself into the chair on the opposite side of the bed. "Due to our shortage of viable candidates, I have decided to forgive your past…transgressions." His lips twisted into a scowl. "We cannot afford to terminate successful candidates, however vexing their actions."

Sam took a long, shuddering breath, silently cursing the man's cruelty. *Now* they could not afford to terminate candidates? For long weeks and months, he had watched children marched from the prison block, never to return. He had stood in a padded room and been forced to choose his own survival over his friend's. He could still see Jake's face, his eyes staring up at him, pleading for his life…

The breath caught in his throat and he quickly pushed away the memory. "What do you want, Halt?" he said, echoing Ashley's earlier question. He summoned as much defiance as he could muster, but even to his own ears, his words lacked conviction.

"If the President and his Director are to continue funding for this project, we must provide them with results. Our successful candidates must be presented to the public."

Shivering, Sam thought back to the prisoner block, to the lines of staring faces. All gone now, all dead but for the seven of them, and the two candidates who had survived the other strain. His stomach twisted at the horror, at the specter of death hanging over their lives.

And now Halt wanted Sam's help to continue his monstrous project?

"No." Sam gritted his teeth. "I'd rather die."

Halt let out a long breath and shook his head. His smile faded as he turned to look at Ashley. "Such a disappointment." He spoke the words in barely a whisper.

Before Sam could react, Halt's hand flashed out and caught Ashley by the wrist.

Sam rose from the bed, his lips curling into a snarl. He clenched his fists, ready to put an end to the monstrous doctor once and for all. He was so furious that even in his weakened state, he was sure he could snap the man's neck before the guards arrived.

"Stop." Halt's command echoed through the room, freezing Sam in place. He nodded to the watch on his wrist, reminding Sam of the collar around his neck. "That's quite enough. Sit down, Samuel."

Sam knew he was beaten. Slowly, he lowered himself back into place on the bed.

Halt nodded and returned his attention to Ashley. A cold smile lit his face as he lifted her hand. Her forehead wrinkled with pain at the movement.

"She is still weak," Halt whispered. "With the drugs and antibiotics in her system, any ordinary human would be in a coma. As it is, they have rendered her no stronger than a child."

At that, Halt grasped Ashley's hand. With deliberate slowness, he bent back one of her fingers. Groaning, Ashley tried to pull away, but the handcuffs held her in place. In a rage, Sam started to stand, but Halt lifted his arm, flashing the controller on his wrist.

"Fallow's commands have been overridden, so I suggest you sit, Samuel. I doubt your friend is strong enough to survive the shock from her collar."

His words ignited a terrible fear in Sam. Ashley lay in the bed, her eyes shining with the pain, but she did not speak. Halt still held her finger, bending it backwards to the limit of ordinary movement. Sam and Ashley's eyes met, and she slowly shook her head.

Sam let out a long, rattling breath and settled back on the bed.

"Very good," Halt whispered, "but it is too little, too late. You are a slow learner, Samuel, and so another lesson must be given." He punctuated his words with a sharp lurch of his wrist, and something went *crack.*

Beside Sam, Ashley threw back her head and screamed. She thrashed in the bed, the movements weak and restrained by the handcuffs, her face contorted in agony. Her feet kicked out, as though fighting off some unseen enemy. Sam reached for her, but her cuffed hand threw him back.

On the other side of the bed, Halt still held Ashley's other hand in an iron grasp. Sam's eyes trailed down her arm, to where one finger was now bent at an awful angle.

"You bast—"

Without taking his eyes from Sam, Halt jerked his hand. Another *crack* followed and Ashley shrieked again, her free hand clawing at the metal bar, powerless to escape. Her screams faded and her eyes rolled back in her skull. Before she could lose consciousness, Halt tugged at her broken finger, and the focus returned to her eyes. A low whimper came from her throat as her eyes found Sam, begging him to save her.

"Move an inch, Samuel, and I'll break another," Halt growled.

Ashley lay taut as a wire, her hair a tangled mess around her face, her good hand clenched tight around Sam's wrist now.

"Please," Sam whispered, biting back tears. This was worse than the cells, worse than the collars, worse than his silent beatings in the whitewashed room. "Please, stop. I'll do whatever you want."

Halt's smile spread. "Very good, Samuel," he whispered. "I always had faith you would come around to our way of thinking." He released her hand.

Tears streaked Ashley's face as she stifled a sob. Sam's heart warmed at the defiance in her eyes, but they both knew there was no resisting this man. He had proven time and again that his cruelty knew no bounds, that no one was beyond his power.

"Tomorrow, we will move you both to our complex in San Francisco," Halt continued. "You, Samuel, will join the survivors of the B-strain. They are still uncomfortable with their abilities. You will show them what they are capable of. In a week, the three of you will be presented to the public. You will be the new face of our fight against the *Chead*, the shining light of hope. Do you understand?"

Sam nodded, not trusting himself to speak.

"Good." Halt's gaze flickered to Ashley. "So long as you cooperate, Ashley will receive the best of care. One day soon, I hope she will join you. For now, though, her wellbeing is in your hands, Samuel. Fail us, and I will make you watch as I break every bone in her little body."

At that, Halt caught another of Ashley's fingers in his slender hand. He gave a sharp twist, shattering the bone in one swift, violent movement.

14

"Your brother? That's not possible…" Liz muttered, before she realized what she'd said.

She tried to take her words back, but it was already too late. Silently she cursed as Mira retreated across the room. Finding herself in the corner, the girl crumpled to the ground and curled into a ball. Harsh sobs followed as the grey wings rose to cover her again.

To Liz's surprise, Jasmine strode past her and crouched beside Mira. Wrapping the girl in her arms, she glared up at Liz. "Well done," Jasmine hissed, "and I thought I was the blunt one."

Guilt welled in Liz's chest, but as she started towards the others, the girl growled. Liz froze, her heart inexplicably beginning to race, and she took a quick step back again. She had felt the girl's potency just a moment earlier, and despite Liz's own strength, one look into the girl's mismatched eyes was enough to give her second thoughts about grabbing her.

Movement came from the entrance as the boys returned. They had found an old potato sack somewhere and filled it with fruit from the trees behind the house. Her stomach growled at the sight.

"You did well," Chris said softly, offering her an apple. He grinned. "Well, better than me anyway."

Liz took the apple with a smile and pulled him to her. Her fear faded as his arms went around her, and for a second she closed her eyes, letting the worries of the world recede. But even in Chris's strong embrace, Liz could not quite banish her dread.

She knew it was not just the girl. It was everything that had happened since their escape. The soldiers, the helicopter, the *Chead*. Things were spinning out of control, and she felt as though they were all racing towards some terrible, awful fate.

When they finally separated, Liz kissed Chris lightly on the cheek before facing the room. Mira had somewhat recovered, but her lips remained clamped shut, and no amount of prodding would get her talking again.

Liz moved to the window and looked out through the dust-streaked glass. Her stomach clenched with the realization that the boys were back inside—there was no one keeping watch. Cursing under her breath, she peered outside, her heart suddenly racing.

The midday sun beat down on the iron-roofed buildings, harsh and unforgiving despite the cold winds blowing down from the mountains. Relentless heat was a grim reality of life on the prairies. Her parents and their farmhands had worked the early mornings and late evenings to avoid the scorching sun, taking siestas from midday into the afternoon. But even with those precautions, heatstroke and dehydration were common.

Liz stood for a long time at the window, her eyes searching the shadows. Her stomach twisted with unease, refusing to be quelled by the silence outside. It swirled and shrank, and a wave of nausea rose in her throat. Prickles of fear spread down her spine as she finally turned back to the others.

"We should go," she announced, surprising herself.

The others stared back. Richard frowned and Jasmine snorted. Even Mira took a moment to look up. Only Chris seemed to take her seriously.

"What?" he asked.

Liz looked around their little group, her urgency growing. "I think we should get out of here, right now."

Jasmine pulled herself to her feet, one hand still resting in Mira's grey hair. "It's got to be a hundred and twenty outside," she argued. "I don't know about you, but I'd like to keep my skin intact."

"What's wrong, Liz?" Chris ignored the others, his eyes on hers.

She shook her head. "I'm not sure. It just doesn't feel right, staying here. Not after the *Chead*…"

"They were pretty quick to take off, Liz," Richard replied. "I don't think they're coming back."

"I know," Liz murmured. She bit her lip. "I still don't like it. If they could find us so easily, how long before the soldiers do the same? And what if the *Chead* were followed here?"

As she spoke the words, Liz's sense of urgency exploded, like sparks catching in leaf litter. In her mind, she pictured soldiers creeping through the woods around the house, rifles held at the ready. Suppressing a shriek, she reached out and grabbed Chris by the wrist.

"The *Chead* could have led them right to us," she hissed.

Chris stared back, his hazel eyes dark in the shadows of the room. Then he was nodding, spinning to face the others, words tumbling from his mouth. "Liz is right," he said, already moving.

Sweeping up the heavy jacket he'd claimed as his own, Chris looked around the room. Liz's fear was spreading as the others realized the sense in her words. Richard moved into the kitchen and collected the sack of fruit, while Jasmine grabbed up the bundle of jackets they'd piled in the corner. She tossed one to Richard as he emerged from the kitchen, before offering one to Liz.

Richard took the lead, sack slung over one shoulder, jacket bundled under arm. Jasmine came after him, leading Mira by the hand, while Liz and Chris brought up the rear.

Liz paused in the doorway, turning to cast a final glance over the living room. Grief rose in her throat. Even empty, without furniture or family, this was still her home. Her two years on the run had not changed that. This was where she had taken her first steps, where her father had taught her to tie a lasso. It was where she had been loved, where she had been safe. It was the last connection to her past, to her mother and father and friends.

She turned away as tears blurred her vision. Something tore inside her as she moved down the corridor after the others, as though something precious and fragile had been shattered. She held her breath, struggling to keep back the tears, and rushed out her front door.

"Where do we go?" Richard asked as she emerged into the sunlight.

"Into the forest," Liz croaked, "up the mountain to the tree line. We can't risk flying, not if they're watching. We'll make better time moving at the forest edge, but we'll still be under cover."

Richard nodded and started into the woods. Together, they worked their way into the scrub and up the steep slope, using the low-lying trees as cover. Thick branches twisted overhead, pressing in on them and making movement difficult.

Liz had made the climb many times as a child, but she was older now, no longer small enough to slip easily between the dense branches. Small, sharp stones covered the hillside, and she was grateful for the boots they'd scavenged from her house. She grasped at tree trunks each time her feet slipped, always clambering upwards, her fear driving her on.

Within minutes they were all panting, even their newfound strength and endurance struggling with the steep mountainside. The unstable slope required time and patience, but their frantic rush to clear the ranch left no room for caution.

It took them an hour to reach the tree line.

They were just in time.

Gasping for breath, Liz lowered herself onto the rocky scree as the others collapsed around her. The mountain stretched up another hundred feet to the summit, but from here on the slopes were barren. She looked back at the trees, past the scraggly branches, searching the valley for a last glimpse of her home.

For a second, everything was quiet. Below, the brown fields stretched out from the mountain, the tiny specks of cows and sheep moving slowly over the flat surface. The grey lines of empty rivers wound their way across the plains. Amidst the trees below, she glimpsed the dull gleam of a metal roof, but otherwise the ranch was hidden from view.

Then movement on the horizon drew her gaze. An ugly dot marred the endless blue sky, still a long way off, but as she watched, it grew. Soon, a low rumbling reached them on the mountain. Within a minute, the speck had doubled, then tripled in size. A dark, menacing presence, it raced towards their little mountain sanctuary.

Sunlight glinted off metal as the jetfighter banked, its speed slowing as two dark shapes disconnected from its underbelly. The missiles shot across the sky, leaving long white streaks of cloud behind them. The shriek of the engine rose to a roar, its angry voice echoing from the slopes, deafening.

Liz rose quickly to her feet, but there was no time to run, to take flight. Only to stare as death raced towards them. Beside her, Jasmine screamed and tripped on the loose gravel. Richard caught her before she fell, and she clung to him, their eyes fixed on the approaching missiles, their animosity momentarily forgotten.

The ground shook as the missiles struck, slamming into the slope far beneath them. A scream built in Liz's throat as she watched the fiery blossom rise from the mountainside. She glimpsed an iron roof lift into the air, and wooden boards disintegrating, then Chris was there. He pulled her to him, wrapping her in his arms, drawing her away from the sight. But even turned away, she could still see the image in her mind, of the flames consuming everything she'd ever known. She could feel the heat on her back, even from where they stood high above, and hear the wild howls of the flames.

Sobbing, she buried her head in Chris's shoulder. For a long while, they stood together like that, unable to move. Eventually she heard the others stirring, and felt Chris preparing to release her. She hugged him harder for a second, and then released him. Turning to stare down the slope, she watched the flames licking the hillside, spreading through the forest, consuming all they touched.

Silently, she turned away.

III

RENEGADES

15

Chris sighed as he lowered himself into the plastic chair. His legs ached from the long march around the mountain, and his arms and face throbbed where sunburn had started to set in. His pale skin had darkened over the days since their escape, but it was still no match for the scorching rays of the midday sun.

Closing his eyes, he rested his head against the cold brick wall behind him. Not for the first time in the last few hours, he sent up silent thanks for Liz. If not for her quick thinking, they would have been caught in the inferno that had swallowed the ranch. Whether the missiles had been meant for the *Chead* or themselves, they would probably never know.

Afterwards, Liz had led them around the mountain in silence. Her movements had been stiff, almost robotic, and his attempts to reach her had fallen on deaf ears. Admittedly, Chris and the others had been little better. Chris was still struggling to comprehend the display of power they had witnessed, how close to death they had come. So they followed Liz across the mountain slopes without complaint.

An hour later, Liz had finally started down the side of the mountain. Chris and the others breathed sighs of relief as they re-entered the trees. As the wiry branches closed over them,

Chris caught a brief glance of the plains below. The brown fields still stretched out in all directions, but here the thin line of a road cut away from the mountain. It led west, where a cluster of buildings hovered beneath a shimmering haze.

They descended rapidly through the trees, chasing after Liz. She leapt between patches of bare earth, landing on roots and grabbing branches, barely pausing to recover her balance. Chris and the others followed as best they could, even their newfound agility struggling to keep pace with the silent girl.

When they reached the bottom, Liz glanced briefly at the sky, and then stepped into the open. She moved without hesitation, striding determinedly out into the long brown grass. As she walked, she pulled on the jacket she had taken from the house, hiding her wings beneath the denim fabric. Folded tightly against her back, they still left a bulge beneath the jacket, but Chris hoped the casual observer would be fooled. He and the others quickly followed suit.

They'd already weighed the risks of flight and dismissed the idea. It would be suicide during daylight. A bunch of flying teenagers would not go unnoticed, even in the sparsely populated countryside. At least on the ground they might pass as ordinary people. And while the long grass offered little cover, it was better than nothing.

They walked for an hour through the open paddocks, keeping parallel to the road, before Liz suddenly looked back. She squinted, her eyes traveling past Chris, down the road to where it twisted around the mountain. Chris followed her gaze and saw a cloud of dust approaching. The clatter of iron hooves and the hard thuds of wheels reached them a second later.

He shared a glance with the others, and then ducked down into the long grass. Waiting in the meagre cover, Chris watched the dust cloud approach. It quickly grew larger, though he knew from the sound it was not a car. A few minutes later, horses took shape amidst the dust, followed by a cart on steel-rimmed wheels. A man sat on the bench up front, reins held in one hand as he urged the horses onwards.

Chris let out a sigh and settled down in the grass to watch the wagon pass, but as it neared, Liz lifted herself up and started towards the road. He swore as she walked out onto the dirt track and waved at the man with the reins.

A shout came from the road and the clatter of hooves slowed. Chris glanced around for the others, but the long grass hid them from view. He swore again, then pulled himself up and started after Liz.

"Woah!" The driver's voice carried across the field as the wagon drew to a stop.

Liz was already moving towards the wagon, a grin on her face. Chris stumbled after her, Jasmine, Richard and Mira emerging from the grass around him.

"Hey there, little missy." Chris noted a southern twang to the man's accent. "Whatcha doing all the way out here?"

"We've come down from the Huerta property," Liz replied easily. "The landowner's kids are visiting. My sister and I wanted to show them the town while they're here."

The wagon driver looked up and noticed the rest of them for the first time. His eyes slid over Jasmine without concern, but his brow hardened as his gaze settled on Chris, Richard and Mira, taking in their pale skin and cropped hair. Chris stared back, surprised at the sudden hostility in the man's eyes.

"The Huerta's a long way off," he said, his tone gruff. "Don't see ya folks around here a lot. Ya walk the whole way?"

Liz nodded, displaying her best smile. "Camped under the stars last night. Shoulda seen the city slicker's eyes when they saw them."

The man laughed at that, and after another moment's hesitation, he nodded. "Righto. Let it not be said old Ronaldo forgot his manners. Jump in the back, folks. You can ride up here with me, missy."

Liz joined him with a laugh, while the others climbed warily into the hay stacked high in the back of the wagon.

A few hours later, after a bumpy ride that left Chris's backside aching, the wagon finally rumbled into town. The driver pulled over in the main street to let them out and wave goodbye. He was heading to a property further along the highway, but he gave them directions to the only motel in town.

After he'd driven off, Liz promptly ignored his instructions and led them down a side street. As they wound their way through the town, Chris could not help but stare at the world in which he now found himself. It was as though they had stepped backwards in time. There was the occasional old car or truck parked in the streets, rust-speckled and broken, but it seemed most made do with wagons and horses. They lined the streets, waiting outside the old buildings as their owners came and went.

Chris half-expected men in cowboy hats to stumble from the local pub and start a gunfight. But with the sun creeping towards the distant horizon, the roads were quiet, and most people avoided the strangers passing through their midst.

Only when Liz drew up outside the bus station did Chris finally guess her intentions. Before he had a chance to stop her, she walked up to the lady standing behind the only ticket booth. Pulling a thin black wallet from her pocket, she handed over a wad of bills. She returned soon after, clutching a bundle of tickets.

"Where did you get that?" Richard asked, nodding at the wallet.

She shrugged in response, her eyes expressionless. "We needed it more than him."

Chris swallowed. Ignoring the others, he stepped in close to her. She flinched, but he grabbed her before she could move, and wrapped her in a hug. She resisted for just a second, stiffening and trying to pull away, but he refused to release her, and she crumpled in his arms.

"It's okay," he whispered. He drew her quietly past the ticket booth, where the woman still stood watching them.

Liz was shaking in his arms. Hot tears soaked into his shoulder as harsh sobs tore from her throat. Unable to find the words to comfort her, to make everything okay, Chris did the only thing he could. He held her in silence and waited for her grief to pass.

Slowly the tears faded and her shaking subsided. When she

finally pulled away, her eyes were wet, but with a gentle smile she leaned forward and kissed him on the cheek.

"Thank you," she whispered.

Chris smiled. "For what?"

She only shook her head. Taking a breath, she looked at the others, who still waited nearby. Richard and Jasmine stood apart from one another, the wounds not quite healed between them. Mira wandered off amongst the rows of plastic chairs, her hands in her pockets as she eyed the tiny food stand opposite the ticket booth.

Looking back at Liz, Chris reached up and wiped the remaining tears from her cheek. "So, where are we going, Liz?"

Liz's lips tightened. "San Francisco." She cast a defiant look around, as though daring them to object. "I'm tired of running, of hiding. Sooner or later, they're going to kill us. Or worse, catch us and take us back. We have to find a way to fight back, to put an end to this once and for all."

"And going to the capital is how we do that?" Richard scowled. "That sounds like suicide to me. You can count me out."

Chris's stomach twisted. "Are you sure about this, Liz?"

Pursing her lips, she nodded. Her eyes locked with Richard's. "You were right, that night in the mountains, Richard. Living on the run, never knowing when the hunters will finally catch up, it's not a life at all. Trust me, I've lived it. We have to find a better way."

Jasmine had been unusually silent, but she stepped forward then. "There's hundreds of street cameras, police, informants. How do we avoid them?"

Liz shrugged. "We keep our heads down, stick to the crowds. San Francisco is a city of millions. However hard they try, they can't keep them all in line." She paused, her eyes sweeping over them. "Besides, they've got your families. If they're still alive, we can't turn our backs on them."

That last point had marked the end of any further argument. The discussion carried on for a few more minutes, but the thought of finding their parents, of possibly rescuing them, had taken the fight from Richard and Jasmine.

Now, as Chris settled back in the bus station chair, he smiled at the thought of the five of them taking the bus. It was genius of Liz, really. With the wide-open plains, they could not fly during the day, and at night they would have no way of telling which direction they were heading in. The bus would have no such problems. And better yet—it was the last thing Halt and his hunters would expect. After all, who would take the bus, when they could fly?

The only problem was the wait. For the last two hours, the five of them had tried lying in various positions on the plastic seats, struggling to get comfortable steal a bit of rest. The bus was already an hour late, and there was still no sign of its arrival.

He hoped it would be in better condition than the other vehicles they'd seen in town, but from the state of the bus station, that was a faint hope. A corrugated iron roof stretched overhead, still radiating the heat of the day, but there were no walls to keep out the wind. The ticket booth was even smaller than their prison cells in the facility. The lady behind the glass had her feet up on the bench, and was reading from a book entitled *Wild.*

Opposite the booth stood the food cart. From the pictures on its side, Chris could see that it offered an array of burgers and hotdogs. None looked particularly appetizing, but the faint scent of food still made Chris's stomach rumble. Unfortunately, there was not enough cash left in the stolen wallet for food, and they were forced to make do with the fruit in their sack.

A television flickered on the wall of the ticket booth, facing the row of seats in which they sat. Glancing at the screen, Chris frowned as the image went black, before a new image appeared on the screen. A man stood on a steel podium, facing a crowd of journalists. He wore a dark red tie and his short grey hair was slicked flat against his skull. Holding his shoulders straight, he looked out over the crowd. Prominent cheekbones gave his face a harsh look in the glow of the overhead lights. His hazel eyes fixed on the camera as he waited for the reporters to settle.

Chris stared at the screen, his heart pounding. A sense of

premonition tingled in the back of his mind. Swallowing, he looked at the others. The man's face was one they all knew. In fact, it was impossible to forget.

The man standing on the podium was the President of the Western Allied States.

16

"Ladies and gentlemen," the President began, his voice smooth, tone somber. "I am here today with news on our recent troubles."

As he spoke, the President stared straight into the camera, his eyes seeming to reach through the television. Chris shivered, glancing around to see if the others were watching. The volume was low, but he had no trouble picking out the words.

"As you are aware, we have recently stepped up our domestic counter insurgency efforts. Acting on intelligence provided by the Director of Domestic Affairs, numerous rebel groups and their foreign benefactors have been apprehended in recent months."

"Mr. President!" A woman's voice carried through the speakers as a reporter stepped forward. Two men in suits moved to intercept her, but the President waved them down and nodded for the woman to continue. "Could you give some indication of how these groups were identified?"

"I'm afraid that's classified," the President said, staring down his nose at the woman, "but I assure you, both myself and your Electors have scrutinized the source and can testify to its legitimacy. There can be no doubt, these are dangerous persons—both to our individual security, and the safety of our nation."

The President paused then, waiting to see whether the

woman would interrupt again, before continuing: "Let me assure you, the full force of the law has been brought down on these individuals. Enhanced interrogation methods have allowed us to identify ringleaders and collapse networks of foreign spies who have been working to undermine our sovereignty. Those found guilty of treason have been executed, while their families and close associates have been detained and sentenced to follow in their steps."

The others were all staring at the television by now. This was the first news they'd heard about their abductions, about how their disappearances had been presented to the public. It seemed Doctor Halt had been telling the truth when he'd said their families had been accused of treason.

Chris's stomach twisted at the mention of execution. He felt a hand on his arm and glanced up to see Liz watching him. He attempted a smile, but the effort was a miserable failure. Silently, he turned back to the television.

On the screen, the President was still speaking. "While we are confident our actions have discouraged further resistance by these groups, there has been an unfortunate setback." He paused, and Chris's heart lurched as he realized what was coming. "Several associates of these traitors recently escaped from a secure facility in the Californian mountains. While we had hoped to quickly reacquire these individuals, to date they have evaded our best efforts to bring them to justice. Our soldiers have suffered several casualties due to their actions. Unfortunately, we believe they may have now reached civilian populations."

The President broke off as the mob of reporters started to shout questions. Across the bottom of the screen, four faces flashed into view. Chris swallowed as he saw his own face staring back at him, alongside mugshots of Liz, Richard and Jasmine. Strangely, Mira's face was missing, and again he wondered about the girl's strange past.

He glanced at the woman in the ticket booth, and the man working the food stand, but neither were paying any attention to the broadcast.

The reporters had quieted now, allowing the President to

continue: "As I said, these four individuals are considered armed and highly dangerous. They should not be approached under any circumstances. The parents of each were apprehended for their involvement with rebel activities, and were sentenced to death for high crimes against the state. Their sentences were scheduled for the December executions, and were carried out as part of the New Year's Eve celebrations. Unfortunately, this only makes these individuals more dangerous—they have nothing left to lose..."

The President's mouth continued to move, but Chris no longer heard the words. Blood pounded in his ears, drowning out all other sound. An awful pain lanced through his chest, as though someone had just driven a knife into his heart. He gasped, struggling suddenly for breath, as the pain swept out to consume him. Inside, he could feel something breaking, something shattering into a thousand pieces. A low moan built in his throat, as from some great distance he heard Liz's voice, calling his name.

In a trance, Chris turned to stare at her. Liz spoke again, her lips moving, her eyes watering with unspilt tears, but no sound reached Chris's ears. She leaned forward, her arms wrapping around his chest, pulling him to her, but still Chris felt nothing. An empty void had opened inside him, stretching out to swallow him whole.

His stomach swirled and a sick nausea rose in his throat. Pushing Liz away, he staggered to his feet. He felt a desperate need to scream, to shout and shriek and rage, to lash out until the entire world felt his pain.

Then an image of his mother rose in his mind, her eyes warm and lips curled in a smile, and despair swept away his fury.

Chris sank back onto the plastic seat, and buried his head in his hands.

❧ 17 ❧

Liz winced as the bus lurched over another pothole, sending her bouncing towards the roof. The engine roared as they raced down the gravel road, its maintenance long forgotten by a government intent on expanding its own wealth. A massive network of railroads crisscrossed the prairies, carrying harvests from distant properties to the cities and their shipping ports, but for the locals, the bus was their only choice for transportation. No one Liz knew could afford the passenger train, let alone a car.

Now, some eight hours into the bus ride, Liz was still struggling to sleep. When they'd first boarded, the bus had already been packed with passengers, and they had been forced to stand. The bus stopped constantly to pick up and drop off passengers though, and slowly they edged further down the aisle in the hope of finding seats.

Even without the boiling sunlight, the heat in the bus was suffocating. The breeze from the open windows barely reached them in the aisles, and by the time a seat opened beside Liz, her head was swimming.

Unfortunately, Liz knew from experience that the seats were little better than standing. The old benches were meant to fit two passengers, but the cramped conditions meant three people squeezed onto each. This left Liz perched half in the aisle, still far from the cool breeze coming through the windows. To make matters worse, she could feel the muscles of her wings beginning to ache beneath her jacket, and when she leaned against them, a sharp ache quickly developed in her back.

Finally, the two large women in the seats beside her rose and shuffled their way off the bus. Liz quickly moved across to take the window seat, allowing the others to figure out who would take the two remaining spaces. Mira and Jasmine soon slid in beside her, while Richard and Chris stayed standing.

Liz's heart twisted as she looked up at Chris. He had not spoken since the broadcast. His eyes had taken on a haunted look, and his skin was a pallid grey beneath the red of his sunburn. She desperately wanted to pull him into her arms, to hold him and love him until he was whole again, but when she'd tried earlier, Chris had been as stiff as a board, his eyes blank, void of emotion. When the bus had arrived, he'd pushed her away and boarded without a look back.

Now, closing her eyes, Liz prayed he would be okay. They had to stick together, had to be strong if they were to survive. They were alone now—truly alone, the five of them against the world.

Mira seemed to be the only one of them capable of sleeping through the hellish bus ride. She was nestled between Liz and Jasmine, curled up on the seat with her knees tucked beneath her chin. Glimpsing a tangle of feathers hanging out from beneath Mira's purple jacket, Liz carefully tucked them back out of sight. She smiled, realizing it had been one of her mother's favorites. She had often worn it when the winter storms rolled in, bringing with them the howling wind and drenching rains.

But the memory brought back the image of her home disintegrating in the flames. She turned away, struggling to banish the sight, lest she fall back into an abyss of her own.

"They didn't have her picture up," Jasmine's voice whispered from the darkness.

Liz looked across at her. The bus was full, but most of those sitting appeared to have nodded off. Even the people standing looked asleep on their feet, their eyes closed, heads leaning against arms clenched around steel poles. Only Chris and Richard remained awake.

"It's strange, isn't it?" Liz replied finally. She eyed Jasmine carefully. Since the incident in the forest, something had changed in her. She seemed to be less antagonistic, less distant, though it was difficult to tell for sure. "And she thinks the *Chead* is her brother."

"It doesn't make any sense," Jasmine murmured.

Liz bit her lip, recalling what they knew about Mira, but the puzzle pieces refused to fit. They fell silent as the bus pulled to a stop in front of a tiny shack, allowing a new passenger to stumble aboard. The man leaned against a pole and closed his eyes, apparently well used to the torture of the night bus.

As the engine roared once more, Liz changed the subject. "Do you really think…do you believe what the President said?"

"He had no reason to lie," Jasmine replied quietly.

After a moment's hesitation, Liz reached out and squeezed Jasmine's shoulder. She could hear the grief in the girl's voice, the unspoken sorrow. They had all been so focused on staying alive, on surviving the horrors of the past weeks and months, that the fate of their parents had become a distant worry. But that distance had crumbled, exposing them to harsh reality.

Liz looked away and stared into the darkness outside the bus. Clouds had rolled in with the evening, and now the sky was dark, the open plains hidden beneath the blanket of night. In the faint light of the bus's headlights, Liz saw her reflection in the clouded glass. Her hair was a wild tangle, her eyes hard, her brow creased.

She stared at the face, so different from the girl she had once been. Even before she'd been taken, her life after the loss of her parents had been harsh. It had taken its toll. She had become hard, unforgiving in her desire to survive. It was a fate she would not wish on anyone.

"I hope it was quick." She turned back as Jasmine spoke. Tears streamed down the other girl's face as she continued, "I hope they didn't suffer."

Liz looked at the girl, surprised by her strength. She remembered then how Jasmine had reacted in the forest, when the soldiers had captured them. While Richard had begged, Jasmine had been silent, offering only a frosty glare to the circle of soldiers. And after hearing the fate of her parents, it seemed she was coping better than anyone.

"What did they do, your parents?" Liz asked suddenly, sensing a need in Jasmine to talk, to remember.

The other girl fell silent, and Liz thought for a second she'd misread Jasmine's mood. She was starting to turn away, preparing herself for another attempt at sleep, when Jasmine finally spoke.

"They were managers in a rural meat packing plant." Jasmine's voice barely rose above a whisper. "They didn't even put up a fight. We were sitting around the table, just starting dinner, when the SWAT team kicked down the door. They told us we were under arrest, cuffed our hands behind our backs before we could even think of resisting. Then they led Mom and Dad out of the room, and pulled a hood over my head. A few minutes later, I heard a woman's voice, then something cold pinched my neck. That's the last thing I remember before I woke up in the facility."

Liz shivered at the simplicity of Jasmine's story. The passiveness with which her parents had surrendered only served to highlight the absurdity of their charges. Surely traitors would fight, would resist capture to their dying breath.

"I'm sorry," she breathed.

"Don't," Jasmine cut in. She looked away, her eyes turning distant. "I don't need your false pity, Liz. We both know we've only stuck together this long because it's our best chance of survival."

Liz blinked at the harsh tone to Jasmine's voice. She fell silent, turning over the other girl's words, wondering whether they were true. She was right, in a way. There had been little love lost between them in the past, though she had thought that might be changing.

"You're wrong," she said at last. When Jasmine didn't turn around, she continued, "We're in this together because, whatever you may think, we're family now. The five of us are all we have left."

"Yeah, right," Jasmine hissed, struggling to keep her voice under control. She looked at Liz then, her eyes hard. "In the forest, if the *Chead* hadn't come, you would have left us for dead—"

"No," Liz said, cutting her off, "if the *Chead* hadn't come, we would have found a way to save you."

Jasmine only snorted. Liz sighed as the silence stretched out between them. She looked down at Mira sleeping, thinking idly that at least one of them was enjoying the ride. She reached out and stroked the girl's soft grey hair, wondering again at the mystery surrounding her.

"Whatever you think, we *are* family, Jasmine," she said at last. "Maybe this is just about survival for you, our little group. But it's not for me, and it's not for Chris."

"I guess we'll see," Jasmine replied.

Liz nodded. Her gaze turned back to the aisle, where Chris stood with his head leaning against a steel pole. His eyes were closed, though she doubted he was sleeping.

"I'm worried about him," she said suddenly, not caring whether Jasmine listened or not. "I don't know what's going to happen when we reach San Francisco, what he'll do."

"Probably something stupid," Jasmine said wryly.

"I'm serious," Liz growled. "I'm afraid he'll do something reckless, something that will get him killed. I'm afraid I'm going to lose him."

"Maybe," Jasmine murmured, "and maybe he'd be right to do it. I mean, what's our alternative? Our parents are dead. We're wanted fugitives. And you haven't exactly been forthcoming with ideas to bring down the government. Maybe reckless is what we need." She paused. "Besides, I'd rather go down fighting than go back to being a slave."

Jasmine's hand drifted to her throat, to the soft flesh where her collar had once rested. Liz found herself shivering as she remembered the awful devices, the agony as electricity burned through every nerve in her body. Even so, she shook her head.

"It doesn't have to come to that," Liz argued. "Not if we're smart, if we lay low. Our parents wouldn't have wanted us to throw away our lives."

Laughter came from the darkness. "Lay low? We're heading into the very heart of the government's power." Jasmine's eyes flashed as she looked at Liz. "No, Liz. If we did what our parents wanted, we would have never left those mountains."

Liz fell silent at that, unable to argue with Jasmine's words. Closing her eyes, she turned them over in her mind, wondering if they were true, what her parents would have thought of her now. What would they want her to do?

She smiled as she recalled a time when she was young, when bandits had come to their lands and stolen their livestock. Her mother and father had gathered up the farmhands and started handing out rifles. They had ridden off at dawn, and returned by dusk, the missing livestock in tow.

"You're wrong, Jasmine," she said at last. "They would want us to fight back."

18

Sam sucked in a breath as he walked across the open hall, the wooden boards creaking beneath his boots. His body felt fresh, all but recovered from the relentless beatings. Even after everything he'd witnessed over the past few months, it still shocked him how quickly he'd healed. Within a day, the bruises and swelling around his eye had started to fade. Yet another boon of their genetic manipulation, he guessed.

The thought did nothing to lift his spirits. He had not seen Ashley since that fateful day in the facility. He'd hoped to see her when they shifted him to San Francisco, but he had been alone in the prison van. His collar chained to the floor, he had spent the long journey with nothing but the roar of the engine and the stench of gasoline for company. The road had been old and rutted, bouncing him around like a sack of old potatoes. Within hours the air had become blistering, the steel walls burning with the heat of the sun.

Sam had suffered the journey without complaint though, thankful to at least be free of his empty prison cell, of the relentless torture.

Now as he strode across the hall, his body healed and fresh clothes on his back, he could almost imagine himself free. Almost

—if not for the unrelenting pressure of the collar around his neck.

He kept his wings pressed tightly against his back as he moved. Like the rest of his injuries, they were healing nicely, and he now felt at ease with the strange appendages. Distantly, he recalled the difficulty he'd had even standing when they'd first appeared. It would have been embarrassing, if he'd not been so preoccupied with escape.

Armed with the memory, he knew he should have viewed the spectacle taking place in the center of the hall with more compassion. But he could not help but grin as he watched the antics of the boy and girl he had come to meet.

They clung desperately to one another as they staggered across the wooden floor, their long black wings hanging behind them like dead weights. Their mouths were open and panting as they struggled to remain upright. Every so often one would shriek and topple to the ground. They seemed to lack any control over their wings, which would shift position almost spontaneously, throwing them off-balance just when they seemed to find their feet.

The girl sported long blonde hair and had plain brown eyes, and stood at least a foot shorter than Sam's own six foot five. Her features were sharply pronounced, and he noticed several bruises spotting her pale skin. Of the two, she seemed to have the better control over her faculties, though that was not saying much.

The boy's dark skin and athletic build stood out in stark contrast to his partner. Even stooped by the weight of his wings, the boy was as tall as Sam. The only feature the two shared were their brown eyes and black wings—and those differed vastly in size.

Neither had noticed Sam's approach. When he finally drew to a stop beside them, he was forced to clap his hands to get their attention. Their eyes widened when they found him standing beside them, and they promptly toppled onto their backsides.

Sam laughed, then quickly masked it with a cough. He raised an eyebrow. "That was graceful."

The boy scowled up at him. "I'd like to see you do any better."

Sam smiled. With a sharp *crack*, his wings snapped open, the copper feathers spreading out to shade the two teenagers from the overhead lights. Their mouths dropped to the floor and the color fled their faces.

As Sam slowly contracted his wings, the girl stuttered. "How…how did you do that?"

Sam laughed as he offered her a hand. Pulling the girl to her feet, he held her steady and smiled. "What's your name?"

The girl hesitated. "Francesca," she mumbled finally, then waved at the boy who was still finding his feet. "This is Paul. You look familiar. Who are you?"

"My name is Sam. We were probably neighbors in the facility. It seems we belong to the rather exclusive group of unfortunate souls lucky enough to have survived that nightmare." He paused. "But the two of you look like you just woke up."

The two shared a glance. "The last thing we remember was the injections in our cell, and passing out from the pain," Francesca said. She took a breath. "Next thing we know, we're in some prison van. And there was just the two of us. Well, us two, and the girl."

Sam's heart skipped a beat. "What girl?"

"Didn't get a name." Paul had finally found his feet. "She looked pretty beaten up. Big bandages around her chest and things."

Sucking in a lungful of air, Sam struggled to contain his excitement. "Describe her."

"Ahhh," Francesca bit her lip. "Skinny girl, pale skin, red hair?"

Sam closed his eyes, a smile tugging at his lips.

Ashley.

"You know her?" he heard Paul ask.

Sam nodded. "Did she say anything?"

"Not much," Francesca offered. "Like we said, she was pretty beaten up. She just warned us about…well, these." She gestured to her wings with a shrug.

"Yes, you do seem to be having some problems," Sam said, smirking. "You looked like newborn foals, stumbling around like that."

Paul scowled. He crossed his arms defiantly, but the effect was somewhat diminished as his wings shifted, throwing him back off-balance.

Sam chuckled as the boy stumbled sideways into Francesca. "Halt wasn't kidding when he said you might need some help."

The two exchanged glances as they steadied themselves. "Halt sent you?" Francesca asked.

The smile fell from Sam's lips as he nodded. He eyed them both, weighing them up. They were vaguely familiar, though he could not recall any particular time he had seen them in the facility. Both looked fit and well-toned, in good shape considering the time they had spent in the coma. The girl looked like she could have been a cheerleader in her former life—her long blonde hair and pale skin certainly matched the stereotype. In contrast, the boy could have been a linebacker.

But who were they really? And could he trust them?"

"I'm here to teach you how to use those," Sam said at last, deciding to withhold judgement for the moment, "to show you what you're capable of."

"What we're capable of?" Paul frowned.

"Yes." Without warning, Sam sprang forward and grabbed the boy by the shirt. With one hand, he lifted him from the ground.

Paul gasped, his eyes bulging as he stared down at Sam. "What—?"

He broke off as Sam released him. He landed easily on his feet, but the weight of his wings pulled him off-balance again, and he crashed back to the wooden floor. He stared up at Sam, eyes wide, mouth hanging open.

"How did you do that?" Francesca whispered. "He must weigh 250 pounds, at least."

Sam offered Paul a hand. When the boy was back on his feet, he grinned at the two of them. "Oh, that's just the tip of the iceberg, kiddos."

19

Chris staggered as he stepped off the bus, his legs almost giving way. The trip had passed by in a blur of anger and grief, the long hours trickling away with every lurching mile. The journey had extended through the night and most of the next day. Now, almost twenty-four hours after they'd first stepped aboard the steel contraption, they had finally reached San Francisco.

Blinking in the fading light, Chris struggled to take in his surroundings. They were on the edge of downtown San Francisco, somewhere amidst the cramped jumble of buildings that was the National Bus Station. People crowded the sidewalks and asphalt, racing between the lumbering buses, struggling to find their way through the packed space.

Since the end of the American War, the population of San Francisco had exploded. Land downtown had quickly dried up, forcing the National Bus Service to cram the last twenty years of growth into the eighty-year-old station. Now the facility was bursting at the seams. Their bus had taken an hour just to maneuver its way through the lines of buses waiting outside.

Chris sucked in a breath of cool air, unable to summon the energy to care about the bodies pressing in around him. Without checking to see whether the others followed, he moved off through the station. A dull emptiness swelled within him, a lonely gulf that sucked away all emotion, leaving him alone, stranded amidst his sorrow.

Threading his way through the garbage littering the sidewalk, Chris scanned the crowds, searching for an exit. Concrete walls surrounded the boarding area in a U shape, with a narrow entranceway for the buses on the opposite side of the station. But there were numerous doorways through which passengers could enter and exit. Spotting one nearby, Chris made for it, wrinkling his nose as he stepped over a puddle that smelled distinctly of urine.

The doorway led him indoors, where the press of people became even denser. Without fans or air conditioning, the heat inside was stifling, despite the fresh breeze outside. His frustration growing, Chris shoved his way through the crowd and made his way towards a glowing blue sign that read 'exit'.

Outside, the crowds thinned a little, though the sidewalks were still a mess of human refuse. Before he could go any further, someone grabbed him by the arm, and a voice called his name.

"Chris…" He found Liz staring up at him as he turned, pain shining from her crystal eyes.

Looking down at the girl, Chris searched for the emotions she'd only recently ignited within him. The pit in his chest twisted, and something flickered inside him. Then it was gone. He shuddered as the sense of loss spread. In its place was a desire to run, to escape.

He tore his hand from her grip and spun away. She called after him, but on the noisy street he didn't hear her words. His feet carried him quickly down the sidewalk, away from the others, away from his grief.

A host of makeshift market stalls had been erected on the sidewalks nearest the station, though many were beginning to pack away their wares for the night. Steel braziers burned on the street corners, hotdogs and hamburger patties charring on the blackened grills. Beggars sat beneath their piles of rags, squeezing in amongst the host of humanity. Some held out hands in silent beseechment, but most just sat staring into space, their eyes devoid of hope, of life.

Chris moved on in silence, head down, refusing to meet the eyes of those he encountered. A woman tried to step into his path, pushing some jeweled necklaces at him, but he shoved his way past. The woman staggered backwards into an overflowing garbage can. Screams of abuse carried after him, but Chris was too consumed to hear her anger.

His own rage was far greater.

As he made his way through the tangled streets, darkness continued its descent over the city. He left behind the bustling marketplace, moving onto quieter sidewalks, to silent streets. The only pedestrians now went quickly about their business, eager to be home. Chris knew the neighborhood's reputation, knew it wasn't safe. At nightfall, only the boldest would dare to be outside.

Footsteps came from behind Chris as the others struggled to keep pace with him. Soft voices called after him, but still he did not turn back. Overhead, the streetlights flickered on, but half of their bulbs were broken and they did little to illuminate the darkness.

"*Chris!*" Liz's voice was insistent now. "Chris stop! We need to get off the streets, before—"

Liz broke off as a scream came from ahead. Chris paused mid-stride, the high-pitched shriek cutting through his thoughts, lifting him momentarily from the spiral of despair. He looked up as it came again, recognizably female now.

A need rose in Chris's chest—to act, to fight, to do *something.* His mother was dead, publicly executed as part of some sick New Year's celebration, and he had been powerless to stop it.

But he was powerless no longer.

Fists clenched, Chris began to run.

He leapt over a pile of garbage, his keen eyes scanning the sidewalk, picking a path through the refuse. Ahead, he glimpsed an alleyway. The scream came again, echoing from the shadows of the alley.

As he turned the corner, Chris took in the scene without

breaking stride. In the shadows, a young girl lay sprawled on the ground, her eyes wide with terror, two men standing over her. A gash marked her forehead, and her long brown hair lay in tangles across her face. Her coat was torn, its copper buttons lying scattered on the concrete.

She looked up as Chris appeared, her mouth opening to scream again. Before she could, one of the men slammed a boot into her stomach. She crumpled beneath the blow, gasping against the filthy ground.

A low growl rose from Chris's chest. His boot brushed against a can as he moved, sending it rattling down the alleyway. The men spun at the sound, their eyes finding Chris in the shadows.

Chris hesitated as he saw the police badges shining on their chests, the blue uniforms stretched over their muscular frames. One held a baton casually in his hand, and both wore guns holstered on their belts.

The one who had kicked the girl rested a hand on his gun and shouted: "You'd best head back to wherever you came from, kid."

The other moved towards the girl as the speaker stared Chris down. Chris bit his lip, measuring the distance between himself and the attackers. Only ten feet separated them—he could cross that distance in a second. He smiled.

The policeman's eyes widened as Chris leapt. His hand tensed, hesitating a second before pulling the weapon from its holster. To Chris, he might as well have been moving in slow motion. By the time the gun slid free, Chris had already closed the distance. His hand flashed out, catching the man by the wrist.

The gunman cursed, struggling to break Chris's hold. He quickly discovered he was no match for Chris's mutated strength. Grinning, Chris squeezed. A satisfying *crack* came from his foe's wrist. The gun dropped uselessly to the ground as the man screamed.

Chris caught a flicker of movement from the corner of his eye. Turning, he saw the other policeman draw his gun. Chris grasped the first man by the collar and hurled him at the other officer. The man flew through the air, his arms windmilling, and landed on his colleague with an audible *thud*.

Wearing a smile on his lips, Chris strode towards them. The two tripped over themselves trying to get back to their feet. He laughed at the terror he saw in their eyes. Gone were his days of running away, of hiding and sulking while his tormentors enjoyed their privileged lives. The President was right about one thing—he had nothing left to lose. He would act, would watch the government and all its members burn if he could.

The second man still had his gun, and he pointed it at Chris from the ground. Chris sprang sideways as the barrel flashed, heard the *crack* as lead struck the brick wall. He kept moving as the man fired again, then he dove forward and kicked out at the gun. It went off one last time before his boot sent it flying sideways into the wall.

A sharp pain sliced through Chris's arm and he reeled back. Anger took light in his chest, boiling up from within, and the pain faded. Red stained his vision as he looked at his enemies. The man whose wrist he'd broken was on his feet again. With a cry, he swung his baton at Chris's face.

Snarling, Chris caught the baton mid-swing. The man paled, but Chris gave him no time to retreat. Grabbing his arm in an iron grip, Chris dragged him forward into a crunching headbutt. The blow staggered him, but Chris wasn't finished. Catching the man, he swung him around, hurling him headfirst into the wall.

A sickening crunch came from the man's skull as he struck. He slid down the wall and lay unmoving on the ground, a dark stain spreading out around him.

Ecstasy swept through Chris as he turned on the remaining attacker. Rage boiled through his veins, numbing him to everything else. He stepped forward, watching with satisfaction his victim's terror. Then he leapt.

The policeman raised his hands in a desperate effort to defend himself, but he crumbled beneath Chris's first blow. Chris landed on the man's chest, his weight driving the breath from his opponent's lungs. Mouth wide, the man gasped for air. Chris threw back his head and laughed.

A wild joy swept through Chris as he punched the man in the face. The policeman's head snapped back, bouncing from the concrete. His eyes rolled into his skull and a low groan rattled from his chest, but Chris no longer cared. He lashed out again, his knuckles cracking as they slammed into flesh, the sound of blows echoing down the alleyway.

By the time Liz and Richard pulled Chris away, he was covered in blood. Rage drowned his thoughts, and he hissed as they grabbed him, struggling to break free. Twisting, he tried to lash out, but Richard and Liz held him tight, their strength more than a match for his own, and finally the fight began to drain from him. The red faded from his vision as his heartbeat slowed.

Chris slumped in their arms, gasping as the pain returned. Pain shot through his arm, and fiery needles radiated down to his hand.

But it was nothing to the ache in his heart, the agony of his loss.

A sob built in his chest, persistent, undeniable. It tore from his lips as the first tears spilled. He cried out as Liz pulled him to her, burying his head in her shoulder, holding her tight, as though his very life depended on it. Fear rose inside him, that if she let him go, he would slip away, would lose himself forever in the depths of his despair.

"What are we doing, Liz?" The words rose from somewhere inside of him. "It's all out of control."

She shivered and hugged him closer. But she did not answer, and they stood together in silence, amidst the long shadows of the alleyway.

Closing his eyes, Chris surrendered to his grief. He let it wash over him, to ebb and flow with the pain of his body. He embraced it, accepted it. Slowly, the tension went from him, the mad chaos that had taken hold falling away. Through it, he sent up an offering, a thought, a final farewell to the woman who had raised him.

Mom, I love you.

20

Liz shifted nervously on her feet as Daniella, the girl Chris had rescued in the alleyway, stuttered through her story. She had been speaking for ten minutes already, the words tumbling from her in a rush as she told her mother about her rescue. The older woman stood beside the girl, eyes wide and face pale as she stared at the five intruders on her doorstep.

It hadn't been until after the confrontation in the alley that Liz had realized Chris had been shot. Though the wound was hardly bleeding, Chris himself had gone into shock. As he'd started to shake, Liz had lowered him to the ground and emptied the last apples from their sack. She'd used the sack to bind his arm, but with the filthy conditions, she knew it would need further attention, and soon.

It was then that the girl Chris had rescued had reminded them of her existence. Staggering to her feet, she'd introduced herself in a quivering voice as Daniella. She looked to be around twenty years of age, and while obviously terrified, she had managed to stammer her thanks, before noticing Chris's bullet wound.

To Liz's surprise, the sight of Chris's injury had galvanized Daniella. She'd insisted they come with her to her mother's apartment. That was where she'd been heading when the policemen offered to escort her home.

Liz and the others had reluctantly agreed. While some of the color had returned to Chris's face, the risk of his wound becoming infected was too great out in the street. It needed to be cleaned at the very least, and there was no way they could take him to a hospital.

Now Daniella was finally wrapping up her story, finishing with how Chris had been shot and needed help. She fell silent, and her mother turned back to the group.

Liz's cheeks warmed as the woman's gaze fixed on her, suddenly and uncomfortably aware of the filthy state of her clothes. It had been a long time since her dip in the mountain river. The five of them were well used to their own stench, but she winced at what the woman must think. Gritting her teeth, Liz readied herself for the woman's dismissal.

All of a sudden, Daniella's mother clapped her hands. "Thank you, children," she all but shrieked. Her words trailed off, her eyes drifting to Chris, who Liz supported over her shoulder. She blinked, seeming to take in the bloodstained bandage. "You're injured."

"Yes, Mom, I told you!" Daniella said.

The mother frowned, flicking an irritated glance at her daughter, before drawing Chris and Liz into a gentle hug. "Oh, thank you, thank you so much," she said, her voice warm now. She looked at Chris. "We'd better take a look at that, hadn't we?"

Chris nodded, his lips drawn tight. The tension fled Liz as Daniella's mother moved to a cupboard in the wall. She closed her eyes, relieved to let an adult take control. Since their escape, she'd hardly had time to breathe, let alone rest. Now she wanted nothing more than to sleep for a week and let someone else worry about their future.

"Take a seat," Daniella's mother said, gesturing to the couch as she rifled around the closet. "Don't worry about the mess. I can't *believe* this. Now where is that first-aid kit? It's not much, you should really see a doctor, go to the hospital or something...but I suppose you can't really do that, can you? What is this city coming to, policemen assaulting citizens, it's like we're out on the *farms* or something. My name is Danny, by the way. Short for Daniella, but went and gave that name to my daughter, didn't I?"

Liz clenched her teeth at the woman's casual insult about her heritage, but she shoved down her anger with an inward shake of her head. The police who patrolled the village near her family's farm might have worked for the government, but they had been valued members of the community. They had certainly never gone around trying to rape young girls.

Leading Chris to the couch, Liz let out a sigh of relief as they sank onto the soft cushions, though she winced at the dirt they left on the white fabric.

"Ah-ha!" Danny emerged from the closet holding a red pouch marked by a white cross. She stepped around the coffee table and took a seat on the other side of Chris.

The woman had regained her composure now, and quickly threw herself into the task of patching up Chris. Idly, Liz wondered how much good the little first aid kit could do for a bullet wound, but at that moment it was the best they were going to get.

Beside her, Chris winced as the woman unwrapped their makeshift bandage. Liz smiled, reaching out to take his good hand. Their fingers entwined and she flashed him her best smile. "Don't be a baby."

"It's okay!" Daniella interrupted. She took a seat on the coffee table in front of them. "Mom will patch you up."

Chris nodded his thanks and returned her smile. Liz suppressed a growl, reminding herself of the trauma the girl had just experienced. She was only trying to show her thanks, though Liz couldn't help but feel a twinge of jealously at the way Chris smiled back at her.

Danny hissed as the last layer of bandage came away, revealing the jagged tear the bullet had left in Chris's arm. Blood had congealed around the wound, along with a fair sprinkling of dirt and grime. Muttering to herself, Danny started rummaging in her first-aid kit.

She came up a second later with a bottle of rubbing alcohol.

Chris's eyes widened, and Liz gave his hand a squeeze. She flashed a look at Richard, hoping he caught its meaning. If the pain became too great, they might have to hold Chris down.

"Hey, I saw that," Chris grumbled. "Don't get any ideas, you two. I'll be good." With that he leaned back into the couch and offered his arm to Danny.

He flinched as Danny brushed an alcohol-soaked cloth across the wound, but Liz held his hand tight and he steadied. A low whimper came from his throat as the woman cleaned out the dirt.

"You big wuss," Liz whispered in Chris's ear, then smiled as he turned to look at her.

Ignoring Daniella on the coffee table, Liz kissed him hard on the lips. He melted beneath her, relaxing into the couch as she pressed herself against him. A snort of indignation was followed by a thud as Daniella stood and stamped away. Liz felt a twinge of guilt—the girl had only been trying to be supportive—but at least she'd distracted Chris from the pain.

"That help?" she asked, pulling back a fraction.

Chris gave a wry grin and nodded. Liz stroked his cheek, feeling the soft hairs of his unshaven chin. He closed his eyes, seemingly relaxed, though Liz knew well the agony of rubbing alcohol on open wounds.

A few minutes later, Danny finally announced she was done. "I think the bullet passed straight through," the woman chattered as she started to apply antiseptic cream. "Definitely should be seen by a doctor, though. I hate to think what might happen if it became infected. You could lose your arm! Oh, I don't know, such a mess, I wish we could do more for you. You look like such nice kids. Where are you from?" She looked around the room, taking in the state of their clothes and their filthy faces. "It looks like you've come a long way?"

Liz nodded, thinking quickly. "We came down from Seattle. Just finished school and heard there might be work here. Our bus broke down on the way though—took days to get here, by the time they sent a replacement and all that."

The woman nodded. "Oh dear. Well, I'm not sure about the

work—I'm just a lowly office lady—but why don't you help yourselves to the bathroom? Clean yourselves up and spend the night. Really, it's the least we can do!"

"Yes, stay," Daniella said, seeming to have recovered from her earlier dismay. She stood in the doorway to what looked like the kitchen, arms crossed.

Glancing at the others, Liz hesitated. She knew they should leave, that there were soldiers out hunting for them, and a price on their heads. Staying meant risking the lives of Danny and Daniella, or the possibility of the two realizing they were fugitives. But at the thought of refusing, the aching of her body returned. She looked around the room, seeing the exhaustion on the faces of her friends. Just the idea of returning to the streets, to the darkness and the danger, was unthinkable.

And the thought of a hot shower was all but irresistible.

21

Liz closed her eyes as the hot water rained down over her face. Heat engulfed her head, muffling the distant sounds she could hear from the neighboring apartments. The water filled her nose as well, washing away the stench of her body. The loss of sensation came as a relief, and she realized then the strain the constant barrage to her senses had become.

She shivered, wondering how long she could stand it, whether the human mind was designed for so much input. Or would the sensory overload one day become too much, the barrage of sights and smells and sounds overwhelming? What would become of her then?

Sucking in a breath through the running water, Liz pushed the thought away.

Live in the moment, she thought to herself.

She smiled, savoring the sensation of hot water on her skin. It ran down her head and through her long hair, dripped from her shoulders, down to her matted feathers. How long had it been since her last hot shower? Certainly not in the facility, where they had been lucky if the guards remembered to feed them, let alone take them to be hosed down. Nor while she'd been on the run. There'd been no chance of that, not while she'd been moving from village to village, never knowing when her next meal might come, let alone a bath.

No, it had been at the boarding school her parents had sent her to. Much as she'd hated the place, hated being the only rural girl amidst the ranks of rich city kids, she could not deny the place had its luxuries. Though her parents' ranch had had hot water, it was heated by the fireplace, so was only available in the winter. And then only if you were one of the first to rise in the mornings.

Which as a teenager, meant there'd been as much of a chance of Liz getting a hot shower as there was of her winning the lottery.

Rubbing her hands over her arms, Liz watched the dead skin flake away. Blood and dirt dripped to the tiled floor and swirled in the gathering water, before finally disappearing down the drain. Liz watched it go, strangely entranced. She found herself wishing she could wash away the darkness inside her the same way, that she could turn back the clock to before all this happened.

She jumped as someone knocked on the door and a voice called out. "Liz?"

Liz smiled as she recognized Chris's hesitant tone. Silently she slipped from the shower and moved across the bathroom, her wings clenched tightly against her back to keep them from dripping. Standing behind the door, she pulled it open, reached out into the corridor, and pulled Chris inside.

His eyes widened as he saw her standing there naked, her hair and skin wet from the shower, her wings slowly spreading out behind her. She laughed as his cheeks reddened, secretly pleased at the effect she had on him. Though he still wore his filthy clothes, she stepped in close, until their faces were just an inch apart. Wrapping her arms around his waist, she pulled him into a kiss, taking care not to bump his injured arm.

Their lips met and she felt him stiffen against her. Then he was kissing her back, his tongue slipping between her lips. She moaned as his good hand slid up to her breast. Biting his lip, she began to undress him, tugging him towards the shower as she did so. Before they went any further, she wanted him *clean.*

Dragging Chris beneath the hot water, she wrapped her arms around his waist, her heart racing as his chest slid against her. Her skin tingled as his good hand slid up her back, to where her wings stretched out behind her. They brushed against her feathers, sending ripples of pleasure down the length of the alien limbs. His fingers continued up, tangling in her hair, pulling her lips to his, and then he was kissing her hard, pushing her back against the wall of the shower.

Giggling, Liz slid sideways away from him. She snatched up the soap and tossed it to Chris. "Clean first. Before you get that wound dirty again. We'll bandage it up afterwards."

Chris laughed, his eyes burning, but with a wry smile he obeyed. She watched the dirt and blood run from him with the same curiosity she'd felt before. Even now, amidst the heat of their passion, she could sense the pain radiating from Chris. He had been so reckless since the news report, as though he no longer cared whether he lived or died. Boarding the bus, walking through the dangerous neighborhoods of San Francisco…it was all so different from the Chris she knew. The Chris she knew would fight to the death for the ones he loved, but he would never think of putting them in danger.

Thankfully, he seemed more himself now, more like the Chris that had survived and escaped the facility alongside her. The pain still shone from his eyes, a sharp, more recent reflection of her own, but it seemed contained now, under control. Silently, Liz prayed that was true.

Chris gave a low growl as he scrubbed the last patch of dirt from his skin and tossed the soap aside. He looked at her, his eyes feral as he drank her in. Liz smiled, basking in his gaze as she crossed her arms and raised an eyebrow.

"Well, what are you waiting for?" She put her arms on her hips. "I'm all yours…"

Eyes dancing, Chris pulled her to him. She gasped as he pushed her up against the shower wall, his muscular body hot against hers. Their wings spread, and a tremor shook Liz as their feathers entwined. Then Chris's lips were on her neck, biting and licking, and the breath went from her in a rush.

Heat flushed through her abdomen as he moved lower, his tongue circling her breast, drawing closer to her nipple with each pass. Growling in frustration, Liz entwined her fingers in Chris's hair and pulled him to her. She gasped as his teeth nibbled at her nipple, his tongue flicking out to taste her. Her desire took light as Chris's attention moved to her other breast, but it was no longer enough.

Tightening her grip in his hair, she pushed him down, betraying her eagerness with a moan. The soft whisper of Chris's laughter came from below, but he obeyed. He kissed his way down her abdomen, his every movement adding fuel to the flame burning within her.

Liz was trembling by the time his tongue found her. Her mouth opened, but no sound came out. Breath hissed from her throat as she struggled to breathe, her back arching with each stroke of his tongue. Her fingers were so tight in Chris's hair now, she was surprised he did not cry out. Instead, his good hand found its way to her ass, pulling her tight against him, leaving no escape.

Not that she would want to.

Slowly the pressure within her built, the flames of her ecstasy fed with every kiss. Her wings spread behind her, her feathers shaking along with every tremor that swept through her body. Water rained down around them and the air was heavy with steam, but Liz hardly noticed. Her every sense, every thought was focused on Chris, on the roughness of his tongue, the feel of his hand around her.

She came in a sudden rush, the pressure inside suddenly crashing through the gates of her self-control, her body giving way to the throes of ecstasy. Unable to help herself, Liz cried out, her whole body aflame as she gripped desperately at the shower walls.

Then Chris was standing again. Her lips found his as she drew him into a kiss, their tongues dancing, though she was still struggling to breathe. His body leaned in against her, pressing her back against the wall, and she realized his hand was still around her waist. A gasp escaped her as his grip tightened, his one hand lifting her slightly.

Their lips broke apart, and she found herself looking into his hazel eyes. Amongst the pain and hurt, she saw the desire lurking there, the need. She reached up to stroke his hair, a smile on her lips, then lowered her hands to his hips, drawing him to her.

Liz gasped as he entered her. Quickly, she wrapped her legs around his waist. The last tingles of her orgasm were still fading, but her need had not lessened, and she wrapped her arms around him, holding him tight as he began to move inside her.

The fire within reignited as Liz moved her hips with his body, her lips on his neck, her fingers like claws in his back. She cried out again, no longer unable to resist, to control her body's reactions. Every inch of her was aflame, joined as one with the man she held in her arms.

Chris was groaning too, his eyes wild, his breath hot in her ear. Pressed against the wall, wet hair fell across Liz's face as she tried to breathe, to regain some of her senses. But with Chris within her, with his arms around her, his body pressed against her, it was all she could do to keep her head above the surface.

Finally, Chris began to slow, his breath coming in hard, ragged gasps. Liz grinned as he brushed the hair from her face. His eyes danced as he cupped her cheek, and her heart swelled as he leaned in to kiss her.

He'd grown still now, but the flames still burned in Liz, and she began to rock her hips again. Chris groaned, his body stiffening around her, but it was her turn now, and she would show him no mercy. Her hips moved faster, her fingers digging harder into his back as she felt the pressure building within once more. A sharp cry tore from her, but beneath her Chris was silent, hardly breathing, as though he had suddenly turned to glass and might shatter at any moment.

With a cry, he broke. His hips thrust forward to meet hers, and Liz felt her own well breaking, the heat sweeping outwards, sending her body into convulsions. Their arms locked around one another and between gasps their lips met.

Finally, as the tremors slowed, Liz unwrapped her legs from around Chris's waist and lowered herself to the floor. Her knees shook as they took her weight, and she would have fallen if she hadn't thrown out a hand against the wall for support. Panting hard, she stepped from the shower. Warmth spread through her stomach, seeping outwards to fill her, lighting every nerve in her body afire.

She smiled as Chris followed her out, his fingers sketching a trail through her waterlogged feathers. Closing her eyes, Liz trembled at his touch, still surprised by the sensitivity of their new limbs. Idly she wondered if Daniella or Danny had noticed the lumps beneath their jackets. She supposed they hadn't—otherwise who knew what they would have done?

Pulling two towels from the rack, she handed one to Chris before drying herself. Watching Chris from the corner of her eye, she smiled as he struggled to dry himself with one hand. She was surprised how little his injury had slowed him. In fact, the bleeding already seemed to have stopped. Even so, she knew from working with animals on the farm that it should be stitched. Unfortunately, hospital grade stitching did not come in your standard first-aid kit. Still, at least his wound was now clean and dry, and they could bandage it when they returned to the living room.

While drying themselves, they spread out their wings, basking them in the overhead heating lamp. Their feathers stood on end, and every so often a tremor would go through them, spraying water across the room.

Afterwards, they pulled on the clean clothes Danny had given them. Her husband was apparently away on business—he was a translator of some sort—and she'd suggested it was a good opportunity to get rid of his old clothes. Looking at the fine shirts, Liz lamented the need to tear holes in the back to fit their wings.

Once dressed, Liz eyed her old jacket with distaste. Her wings were enjoying their freedom—they quickly grew cramped under the jacket. And now that she was clean, she could smell the reek of sweat and mildew coming from the heavy denim. But unless they wanted to terrify their friendly hosts, there was little choice. Reluctantly, they pulled on the jackets and slid out the door.

Warmth touched Liz's cheeks as she found Jasmine, Richard and Mira waiting in the hallway. Her mouth dropped open and she glared at Chris. "You didn't mention they were outside!"

Chris's cheeks were beet-red, but Jasmine cut in before he could respond. "It got a little awkward in the living room," she said, her face deadpan. She glanced at the others and shrugged. "Guess I'm next."

She disappeared into the bathroom before Richard or Mira could argue.

22

Her cheeks still flushed, Liz watched Jasmine disappear into the bathroom and then turned to the others. Richard bowed his head and tucked his hands into his pockets, a frown on his lips.

In a rush of empathy for his situation, Liz reached out and squeezed his arm. Richard looked up at her, his eyes shimmering in the glow of the single lightbulb. No words passed between them, but after a moment he nodded and looked away.

Liz took Chris's hand and led him back into the living room. She frowned at Jasmine and the others' lack of courtesy—and foresight. Someone should have stayed with Daniella and her mother, if only to keep them safe. As they moved down the corridor, she heard raised voices, and recognized the faint whine of a television. The floorboards squeaked beneath their feet, announcing their approach, and the voices suddenly broke off.

The door clicked as Liz pushed it open and stepped into the living room. She'd been too exhausted to take in the space earlier, but now her eyes passed slowly over the room. The apartment was plain and in places the paint was flaking from the walls, but it still contained far more wealth than her parents could ever have hoped for. Steel bolts held the front door closed, while to their left another door opened into the kitchen. On their right was a dining table, and beyond, the white couch and television. Behind the television, a broad window looked out over the city, at the distant skyscrapers and steep hills of San Francisco.

To Liz's surprise, the television screen was black, though she was sure she'd heard it a moment earlier. Daniella sat on the couch, but her mother was standing, already starting towards them.

"How was your shower?" Danny smiled.

Liz's ears twitched at her tone. Was her voice slightly higher than before? She closed her eyes, weariness settling around her shoulders like a cloak. Forcing a smile, she nodded at Danny, dismissing her worries.

"Wonderful, thank you," Chris said. He was smiling, apparently at ease. "Just what we needed after that bus ride."

Danny nodded absently as Daniella lifted herself from the couch. Reaching out, she tugged at the sleeve of Chris's jacket. "You're still wearing your jacket. Wasn't what I picked for you… more comfortable?"

"Leave him alone, Daniella," Danny said sharply. Liz's head jerked up as the woman strode across and pulled Daniella away. "They can wear what they want."

Daniella scowled, pulling herself free of her mother's grip. "They don't *have* to."

Danny folded her arms and stared down at her daughter. The girl held her ground, until with a grunt, she turned and pushed past Liz, disappearing down the hallway. Shaking her head, Danny offered them a weary smile. "Would you like some coffee, dears?"

Exhausted as she was, Liz wanted nothing more than to sleep. Coffee was the last thing she needed. But the woman was already moving away, muttering about brewing a pot as she disappeared into the kitchen. Liz glanced at Chris, but he only shook his head. She noticed his face was pale, and taking his arm, she sat with him on the couch.

Liz picked up the first aid kit. She carefully rolled up Chris's sleeve and applied a fresh layer of antibacterial cream to his wound. She was surprised by how healed it was already looking.

She'd been right earlier—the bleeding had stopped, and was it her imagination, or did it look smaller? She dismissed the thought as absurd and started applying a bandage.

Jasmine reappeared as Liz was finishing up. Her skin was red from scrubbing and her black hair hung damp around her face, but she looked cleaner than Liz had ever seen her. She still wore the old jacket from earlier. Liz wriggled on the couch, reminded of the water slowly dripping from her feathers down her back.

She smiled as Jasmine approached. "Good shower?"

Jasmine smiled back, her face relaxed. "I could barely bring myself to get out. Where's Daniella and her mother?"

"Daniella's down the hall somewhere," Liz replied. "Her mother is making coffee."

Jasmine wrinkled her nose. "I hope it's decaf. Who's taking first watch?"

"I think Richard still owes us one there," Liz replied softly.

She watched Jasmine's face darken, but Liz had decided the feud between the two had gone on long enough. Richard had made a mistake; he would have to live with it. But if they were to survive, the five of them needed to get along.

"You have to forgive him eventually, you know," she whispered.

Jasmine looked up at that. Her eyes softened for a second, before her jaw clamped tight. "Do I?" she growled. "And why is that?"

Liz didn't back down. "Because he's family."

"I..." Jasmine closed her eyes suddenly, her shoulders slumping. She dropped to the couch beside them and drew her knees up to her chest. "They almost caught us. Because of him."

"I know," Liz said, shrugging, "but in the end, we're just kids, Jasmine. We're not soldiers, we're not trained for this, whatever mutations they managed to cram into our DNA."

Jasmine lowered her gaze but did not respond. Liz smiled, hoping she might have at least made a crack in the girl's defenses. Leaning into the crook of Chris's good arm, she closed her eyes. It felt good, basking in his warmth, and she could feel sleep beckoning as they waited for Richard and Mira to return.

Mira appeared from the shower next. She moved silently across the room and quickly climbed onto Jasmine's lap. Liz smiled inwardly as Jasmine rolled her eyes. She was beginning to suspect that Jasmine enjoyed Mira's affections more than she let on. Eventually Richard emerged too, still drying his hair with a towel.

He paused beside the couch, a frown creasing his forehead. "Where's Daniella and her mother?"

Liz blinked, struggling to look around, her mind foggy with sleep. She shook her head, suddenly realizing Richard was right. Daniella's mother still had not returned with the coffee. What was taking the woman so long?

She sat up, but before she could stand, Danny finally reappeared. She paused in the doorway, a steaming mug in each hand. Striding across the room, she placed the cups on the coffee table.

"Everyone clean? Good, good, I'm so glad, must be a relief after that trip. Where did you say you came from again? Seattle, right? Such a long, long way." She paused, looking at Jasmine and Richard. "More coffee?"

Before either could answer, she raced back into the kitchen.

Watching the woman depart, Liz struggled to muster her thoughts, and decided the coffee might not be a bad idea after all. Much as she'd like to leave their worries for the morning, they needed to figure out a plan. She lifted the nearest mug and took a long gulp.

Beside her, Chris groaned and sat up, blinking sleep from his eyes. He spotted the second coffee and swept it up before anyone else could claim it.

Liz sighed as the hot liquid warmed her chest. Though winter was behind them, the nights were still icy, and the house felt cold after the heat of the shower. The others remained where they were, Richard standing, Jasmine and Mira curled up on the couch beside her.

"That was…strange," Richard remarked, his eyes on the kitchen doorway.

Taking another sip of her coffee, Liz's mind finally began to work again. She frowned, thinking of the voices she'd heard earlier, how she'd been sure the television had been on.

"Danny turned off the television, before we came in…" Liz mumbled her thoughts out loud.

Richard looked around. "What?"

"They were watching the television while we were in the shower. I heard it. But they switched it off when they heard us coming."

Frowning, Richard picked up the remote and flicked on the television. The speakers blared, but Richard quickly hit the mute button. The five of them stared as a man appeared on the screen, pointing to a map of the Western Allied States, and the rainclouds approaching San Francisco.

But that was not what drew their attention.

A banner ran along the bottom of the screen, bright red with white text that spelled out "WANTED FOR TREASON." Beneath, four faces stared from the screen. Liz's stomach twisted as she recognized her own picture, an awful fear clamping around her chest.

Richard turned off the television. "We have to get out of here."

The lights went out.

23

Sam ducked as Paul's fist flashed for his face, then backpedaled as the boy chased after him, giving Francesca time to regain her feet. Paul stumbled, then recovered quickly, but the second was all Sam needed to leap clear, his copper wings beating slightly to carry him across the hall.

Paul and Francesca gathered themselves and came after him. They moved with more confidence now, finally growing used to the alien weight of their wings, though they were still far from perfect. Unlike Sam and the others, they were taking a long time to adjust. Their wing movements were still stiff and robotic, their responses delayed, as though the connection between their minds and the new limbs was not quite complete.

They stalked towards Sam now, faces grim as they watched for a hint of his next attack. Sam grinned and let them come. It had been days since their first meeting, but the two had proven to be slow learners. He had been wondering whether the lack of immediate danger might be slowing their progress. After all, it had been the rush of adrenaline, the desperate need to escape, that had driven Sam and the others to leap from the cliff and fly.

So Sam had decided a change of tack was needed.

As Paul stepped forward, Sam tensed and sprang at the younger boy. Paul's eyes widened, but Sam was already on him, his wingtip swinging out to catch the boy in the face. He felt a satisfying thud and grinned as Paul stumbled back, clutching his nose.

Growling, Francesca took Paul's place. Her sudden charge caught Sam by surprise, and he staggered sideways as her fist crashed into his ribs. Wincing, he retreated a step, silently admiring her strength. Whatever problems they might have with their wings, there was nothing wrong with their other enhancements.

The girl came at Sam again. He twisted sideways to avoid her attack, then caught her by the wrist. Francesca gasped as he used her momentum to fling her over his shoulder. The girl hurtled through the air, arms raised to break her fall. At the last second, her wings snapped open, slowing her descent. Francesca yelped in surprise, then dropped lightly to the ground. Blinking, her wings still half-spread, she turned to stare at Sam.

"Very good," he grunted. "Now show me what you've got."

Ignoring her still gaping face, Sam leapt high, his wings snapping out to catch the air. With one powerful stroke he crossed the hall and drove his booted foot into the girl's midriff. The blow sent her bouncing across the wooden floor, until she came to rest near the far wall. Wheezing, she struggled to right herself.

An angry growl came from behind Sam, and he spun in time to block a savage attack from Paul. A fist crashed into Sam's wrist, sending a shock juddering down his arm. Grimacing, Sam retreated, twisting to avoid another wild swing. Then his knee flashed up, catching Paul in the stomach and stopping him in his tracks.

They drew back a step then, pausing to weigh each other up. Sam had to admit, the two were good fighters, but that was no surprise. They had to be, to have survived this long. If not for his greater experience with his altered body, Sam doubted he could have taken them both. As it was, he was enjoying the chance to vent his frustration.

Sam tensed as Paul came at him in a rush of fists and elbows. He blocked each calmly, before leaping forward to grasp Paul by the shirt. Pivoting on his hip, Sam hurled the boy across the room in the same manner he had Francesca.

Unfortunately, Paul's wings did not come to his rescue. He rose in an arc and then crashed down into the wooden floor with a thud. Shaking his head, Sam watched the boy stagger to his feet, his lips drawn back with rage.

"You need to stop thinking, and *act*," Sam hissed. He leapt forward and slammed a fist into Paul's stomach, sending him reeling.

Pale-faced and gasping, the younger boy struggled to recover. He raised his fists and deflected another blow from Sam. Then he was charging forward, his arms grasping Sam around the midriff and tackling him to the ground. The breath exploded from Sam's lungs as he landed on his back.

Rolling, Sam sent Paul stumbling backwards with a sweep of his wings. They beat again as he leapt into the air, carrying him to safety.

Landing lightly, Sam fought to regain his breath as he berated himself for lowering his guard. Across the room, Francesca had re-joined Paul. They stood together, waiting for him to make the next move. Grinding his teeth, Sam flashed an unconvincing grin and stepped towards them.

It was their turn to watch him come. Both suddenly looked confident in their abilities now. It seemed he might have been right, that adrenaline was what they needed to help their minds gel with the alterations to their bodies.

They attacked together as he stepped into range, Paul half a step ahead of Francesca. Working in concert, they forced Sam back a step, then another. Sam reeled as a blow struck him in the face, followed immediately by a kick to the hip. His anger flared, and growling, he allowed it free rein. It swept out to engulf him, pouring fresh energy into his limbs.

Sam's head spun, his vision flashing red. Heart thudding in his chest, he twisted as Paul came at him again. Faster than thought, he caught the boy by the throat and hauled him into the air. Blood throbbed in Sam's ears as he watched the boy kick feebly in his grasp, hardly feeling the blows as Paul struggled to free himself.

Dimly, Sam heard a scream. Turning, he raised an arm to fend off a blow from Francesca. She stumbled sideways as he struck her, but quickly righted herself and came at him again. Sam snarled and hurled Paul aside, all his rage focused now on the girl.

Fear flashed in Francesca's eyes and he grinned. She stumbled back, but it was too late now. Sam charged, reaching out to catch the arm she'd raised to defend herself. In one fluid movement, he hoisted Francesca above his head and hurled her at the wall.

Her wings flared open in a desperate attempt to stop herself, but this time her momentum was too great. She struck the wooden wall hard and fell to the ground in a tangle of limbs and feathers. A low moan came from her throat as she struggled to rise.

Sam clenched his fists, reveling in his power. Smiling, he stepped towards the girl. She was still straining to right herself. He hauled her up. Her brown eyes flickered, staring at him in helpless terror.

Sam paused, a whisper of doubt cutting through the scarlet of his rage. An image passed across his vision, superimposing itself over the girl's face—of a boy, his face bloodied and bruised, on the ground, gasping for breath. He watched the boy struggling to stand, to regain his feet and continue to fight.

And he saw the blood covering his hands, the bruises on his knuckles.

Jake.

Releasing Francesca, Sam staggered backwards at the memory of his friend. Guilt welled inside him, sweeping away the rage, and the red faded from his vision. A low whine came from his throat as he sank to the ground.

Sam glanced around, his heart racing as he found Paul on his knees. The boy was gasping, clutching at his bruised throat. Beside him, Francesca stumbled to her feet, her legs unsteady beneath her. Fury lit her eyes.

"What the *hell* was that?" Francesca gasped.

Before Sam could answer, a slow clapping carried across the open hall. They turned as one and stared as Halt walked slowly towards them, a smile on his thin lips.

"Well done, Samuel," he breathed, his eyes shining. "It looks like we're almost ready."

24

Chris threw himself to the floor as the door to the apartment shattered inwards. Something went skittering across the floor, then a blinding flash of light and deafening sound exploded through the room. A scream came from his right as red lines streaked his vision. He shouted at the others, but over the ringing in his ears, Chris couldn't even hear his own voice.

Blinking in the darkness, Chris struggled to regain his night vision. Pain came from his arm, but he pushed it aside. Scrambling on his hands and knees, he looked up as the thud of boots on tiles came from the doorway. Little white suns danced across his sight, but between them he glimpsed the silhouette of a man.

They're here!

"Get away from the door!" he called, rolling behind the couch.

Another *thud* came from the doorway. He crawled towards the window, praying the others would have the same thought. The apartment was on the fifth floor—if they could break the glass and fly away, the hunters would not be able to follow them.

Chris's heart leapt as he heard glass shatter. Straining his eyes, he tried to see who had made it to the window first. Red streaks still flashed across his vision, but they were starting to fade, giving way to darkness. The room slowly came into focus.

He smiled at their hunters' error. With their altered senses, darkness was no hindrance to them. Now, even with night vision goggles, the soldiers were at a disadvantage. Crawling out from the cover of the couch, he looked at the window, expecting to see Liz or one of the others there.

Instead, two hulking figures stepped through the broken window. Sleek night vision goggles covered their eyes and each gripped a rifle to his chest. Glass cracked beneath their boots as they fanned out.

How? They were five stories up, how could soldiers have gotten in through the window?

Chris backpedaled behind the couch, but this time he was too late. As he ducked out of sight, the men turned towards him and raised their weapons. Gunfire crackled, and Chris hurled himself to the ground, bracing himself for the bite of their bullets. He knew the flimsy sofa would provide little defense.

To his surprise, the pain did not come. A series of heavy *thunks* came from the sofa, as muzzle flashes lit the room. Chris glanced over the cushions, and then dropped back down with a curse. Half a dozen darts had embedded themselves in the fabric. The hunters weren't here for blood—their guns were loaded with tranquilizers to knock them out. They wanted to take the five of them alive.

Over my dead body, Chris thought grimly.

He tore off his jacket and flexed his wings. Gathering himself, Chris listened for the telltale crunch of heavy boots on broken glass. Before he could act, Liz scrambled around the edge of the couch to join him. Her wings were already out, her sleek black feathers blending in with the shadows.

The tread of a boot carried to their ears. He smiled, pleased by the caution their hunters were showing. These men were clearly wary of their prey. Chris just hoped that he and his friends lived up to their reputation.

A roar sounded from the other end of the room. Glancing around the corner of the couch, Chris saw Richard and Jasmine charge the soldiers by the window. Wings out, lips drawn back in wild snarls, they attacked like avenging angels descended from heaven. The soldiers moved with painful slowness, unable to match the speed of their winged prey. In a second Richard was on them, Jasmine just one step behind.

The first of the two soldiers cried out as Richard tore the rifle from his grasp and hurled it at his face. Chris stood to join them, but movement from the door drew his attention. Silhouettes strode through the darkness, fanning out across the room, already raising their weapons to take aim.

Knowing Richard and Jasmine were in their sights, Chris didn't hesitate. He dived at the nearest figure, catching the man off-guard and hurling him backwards. The others turned towards the commotion, momentarily distracted, and Liz launched herself into their midst.

Five silhouettes staggered back from her fury. One went down in a pile of feathers and fists. A second later Liz sprang back up, already after a fresh target. The soldier she'd struck lay unmoving behind her.

One of the men pointed his weapon at Liz, but Chris was on him before he could fire. Chris only had one good arm to work with, but in close quarters, that was all he needed. Balling his fist, he punched the soldier in the chest. Even through body armor, Chris heard the satisfying *crack* of breaking ribs. As the man gasped and sank to his knees, Chris spun on his heel and drove his boot into the side of the man's head.

The man dropped like a sack of potatoes, and Chris moved on, his keen eyes searching for another victim. Panic had caught amongst the soldiers, the fury of Liz's attack scattering them. Muffled thuds came from the window as Richard and Jasmine finished off the hunters there. Only two soldiers were left standing on Chris's side of the room. Grinning, he stalked towards them.

Before he could catch them, more men swept in through the open door. Chris swore as rifles were pointed in their direction, and he dove towards the dining table. Liz was already there. She hurled it on its side, and they dropped behind it, the *crack* of steel darts on wood following an instant later.

Heart racing, Chris crouched behind the table and waited for the firing to stop. He prayed Richard and Jasmine had not been caught in the crossfire. He hadn't seen what happened to Mira, but he hoped the girl had found cover somewhere.

Silence fell as the gunfire ceased. Chris glanced around the table in time to see Jasmine and Richard make a break for the window. The path was clear now, the men that had crashed through lying unconscious on the ground. Jasmine was in the lead, her long legs carrying her across the room before the soldiers in the entranceway could take aim. Her wings spread as she neared the window.

Movement came from beyond the curtains as a soldier landed in the room, his rifle already raised. Caught midstride, Jasmine had no time to react as the barrel flashed. But beside her, Richard was already moving, shoving her aside. He cried out as half a dozen darts sprouted from his chest.

Richard's eyes widened as he stumbled, then with a roar he threw himself at the man in the window. The soldier staggered sideways as a blow from Richard caught him in the temple, but two more men had already appeared to take his place.

And Richard was slowing now. Another dart struck him in the chest. He staggered back, still shielding Jasmine with his body as they retreated behind the sofa.

The squeak of a floorboard reminded Chris of the soldiers near the door. He glanced at Liz and found her crystal eyes watching him in the darkness. He swallowed and gave a smile that did not reach his eyes.

"I'll take the ones on the right. You get the left," he whispered.

Liz nodded and gripping the edge of the wooden table, she hurled it across the room. The intruders had spread out to encircle their hiding place, but several near the door were still standing close together. They lifted their guns at the movement, before the dark shadow of the table slammed into them, crushing them against the wall.

Chris charged the remained soldiers, taking advantage of their momentary shock to close with them. But they were ready this time. Two already had their rifles at their shoulders. The barrels flared as Chris reached his target. He felt a sharp pinch in his side as he leapt and drove his boot into the man's face.

The force of his kick sent the soldier flying back into his comrades. Cursing, Chris reached down and tore the dart from his side. Balling his hand into a fist, he tested his strength, but he could feel no difference. A dull ache came from his wounded arm, but otherwise his bullet wound from the alleyway had not slowed him. He chalked that up to some increased resilience, and then hurled himself at his next victim.

In the cramped quarters of the apartment, the men struggled to bring their bulky rifles to bear on the winged teenagers. Guns flashed, but with Chris and Liz amidst their ranks, they were just as likely to hit each other as their prey.

Wings flaring, Chris leapt at another man, driving both feet into his sternum and hurling him across the room. Beside him, Liz slammed her shoulder into a soldier's chest. The force of the impact sent the man staggering into the soldier alongside him, and the two went down in a pile of limbs.

But even as the soldiers fell, more poured in through the door and window. Beyond the broken glass, Chris glimpsed a zipline running to a neighboring building and realized there was no escape in that direction.

Jasmine was still laying into the men around her, but Richard sat crouched at her feet, his head bent, wings limp. The beginnings of despair clutched at Chris's throat. Outnumbered and surrounded, there was no escape now.

A sharp pain stabbed at his back. Chris spun and wrenched the weapon from the soldier's arms. Clubbing his attacker over the head with the heavy rifle, he turned again and hurled it at another invader. The force behind the projectile knocked the man out cold.

A scream came from Liz, and Chris turned in time to see her go down beneath a pile of soldiers. A second later she was up again, hurling the soldiers from her, scattering them like leaves before the wind. Chris started towards her but staggered as his leg suddenly went numb. His vision whirled and his stomach wrenched as nausea swept through him.

Another soldier ran at him, gun raised to finish him off. Straightening, Chris twisted as the gun went off, but the tranquilizer had dulled his reactions, and another dart caught him in the shoulder. Growling, he grasped the barrel of the gun and tried to wrench it from the soldier's grip. To his surprise, the man held on. The barrel boomed again, sending a dart straight into Chris's chest.

The strength fled Chris's legs and suddenly he found himself on his knees. An eerie calm settled over him as he looked up at the soldier, watching as the rifle fired a third time. He didn't feel the third dart strike. A great weariness settled over him as he swayed on his knees.

"Liz," he breathed, watching her across the room.

He looked down at his chest, at the darts protruding from his flesh. He fought to reach up, to tear them out, but his arms refused to obey. They hung limp at his side, dead weights as the soldier drove a boot into his stomach.

"*Chris!*" He heard Liz's voice from a distance.

He struggled to keep his eyes open, to find her in the growing shadows. But the darkness rose up to swallow him, and he fell away into oblivion.

25

"*Chris!*" Liz screamed as she saw him go down.

Hurling aside a soldier, she leapt over the bodies scattered across the floor and charged the man standing over Chris. He looked up as she closed on him, even managed to lift his rifle, before her fist caught him in the face. The force of her blow sent his head whiplashing backwards and he crumpled without a sound.

But she had turned her back on the other soldiers now, and two raised their guns and opened fire. Her wings cracked open, the long black feathers brushing aside the darts. Even so, she felt a pinch in her shoulder as one found her flesh. Gritting her teeth, Liz crouched and hauled Chris up, then stumbled away from the door.

Liz heard the click of guns being reloaded, and ahead she saw Jasmine stumble. The girl still stood over Richard, half a dozen bodies scattered around her. Liz felt a surge of hope, that maybe they could carry the boys to the window, that they might still escape. Then she saw the darts protruding from Jasmine's shoulder and arms, saw the girl's wings beginning to slump, and the hope withered in her chest.

Lowering Chris to the floor beside Richard, Liz drew back her lips and snarled. More men were pouring in through the window. Beyond the shattered glass, a steel cable led across to a neighboring building, where a dozen men still waited to join the fight.

Hissing, Jasmine gathered herself and leapt at a cluster of men, scattering them with her fury. Teeth clenched, Liz followed after her. But it was clear the darts were beginning to take effect. She could see Jasmine slowing, her blows now lacking power. Jasmine tore a rifle from a soldier and slammed it into his stomach. The man staggered, but seconds later he straightened and drew a steel baton from his belt.

Jasmine stumbled as the baton caught her in the side of the head. She retreated a step as Liz sprang past and sent the soldier reeling with a blow to the face. This time he did not get back up. Side by side, they retreated to where Richard and Chris lay.

"Go, Liz," Jasmine panted. "Get out of here, before they get you, too."

Liz shook her head and reached out to steady Jasmine as she stumbled. "I told you, we're family." Liz forced a smile. "And we're not finished yet."

Baring her teeth, Liz tore into another intruder as Jasmine slumped to her knees. Her fist crashed into his face, but as she recovered, Liz felt a sharp pinch in her backside. Swearing, Liz caught the soldier by the shoulder and spun towards the hunters creeping towards them from the doorway. In one fluid movement, she hurled the man into their midst.

She grinned as the soldiers scattered, then swore as her leg suddenly went numb. She clenched her fists, fighting back the weakness, as soldiers closed in around her. They must have been running short of ammunition, because they hesitated before firing, waiting to see whether she would fall.

Liz swayed on her feet. She glanced at Jasmine. Her heart clenched as she saw her friend collapsed over Richard. Swallowing, Liz faced the circle of soldiers, alone now against a dozen men. She sucked in a breath, and then stepped towards the nearest man.

Crack.

A gun roared, and another dart tore into Liz's side. She staggered, the numbness spreading, but she took another step. Gunshots sounded again, and she felt two more stabs of pain from her back. By then she'd reached the man. Stretching out an arm, Liz clawed at his weapon, but he only retreated a step. Then he slammed the butt of his rifle into her face.

Light flashed across Liz's vision as the blow struck, driving her to her knees. Swaying, she cursed her weakness and fought to regain her feet. But the tranquilizer pumping through her veins was too much for her now. With agonizing slowness, she toppled backwards to the ground.

The soldier smiled down at her. Reaching for a radio strapped to his shoulder, he spoke into the microphone. "Targets neutralized. We're ready for you, Doctor."

Liz's stomach clenched and tears stung her eyes as she looked up at the man. Despair wrapped around her throat and she found herself begging, "Please, just kill us. Don't let him take us back."

Grinning, the soldier drew back his boot and drove it into her face. The blow slammed her head back into the floor. Liz tasted blood in her mouth as the man lifted his foot again and hammered the steel-capped boot into her side. The force of the kick lifted Liz and sent her sprawling across the ground.

Lying on her side, she listened as the man's footsteps retreated. She lay staring at the open door, struggling to sit up. But her limbs refused to obey. To her horror, Liz found she could no longer even close her eyes.

Around the room, the soldiers were pulling the night vision goggles from their faces. The lights flickered back on, filling the room with blinding white. Pain stabbed at Liz's eyes. She willed them to close, without success.

Moments later, footsteps came from the hallway outside. A man appeared in the doorway, wearing a familiar white lab coat. Liz's stomach clenched as she looked at his face. The last traces of her courage crumbled away.

Halt looked strangely older, his face lined and his grey hair streaked by white. Only the icy smile was unchanged. Arms folded, he crossed the room until he came to a stop beside Liz. "Well done, Commander. They are all present?"

Before the soldiers could respond, a wild shriek erupted from the kitchen, and Mira leapt into view.

Her grey wings flashed as she emerged from her hiding place and shot straight at Halt. He staggered as the girl crashed into his chest, her unnatural strength knocking him back.

Liz's heart fluttered as Mira tore at Halt's face, her lips drawn back in an animalistic snarl. Taken by surprise, the soldiers retreated before her fury. Sensation tingled in Liz's chest as she found herself hoping Mira would tear Halt's head from his shoulders.

Cursing, Halt straightened. His arm shot out, catching Mira by the throat. Liz's heart lurched in sudden fear, before she reminded herself Mira's augmented strength was more than a match for an ordinary human. She would snap Halt's arm like a twig.

Mira squirmed in Halt's grasp, then lifted her hands and brought them down on Halt's wrist. Liz watched, waiting for the sharp crack of breaking bone, for Halt's scream and Mira to slip free.

Halt smiled. He lifted Mira higher, even as she kicked and tore at him, and with casual ease hurled her into the wall. Mira shrieked as she struck, and then slumped unmoving to the floor.

Turning to the commander, Halt shook his head. "I suggest you secure the subjects properly, *Commander*. We wouldn't want any more…incidents." He looked around, his eyes sweeping the shattered remnants of the apartment. "When you're done, take care of the woman and her daughter. They did a great service to this country, reporting the fugitives. But we can't have any witnesses of this…unfortunate episode."

Then Halt turned and looked down at Liz, the smile still frozen on his thin lips.

And his cold grey eyes pierced her.

IV

CHEAD

26

Agony pulled Chris back from the darkness, dragging him slowly towards wakefulness. He made to sit up, but instead flopped sideways as he found his arms fastened behind his back with steel cuffs. A sharp ache came from his wound and he bit back a cry. Rolling onto his side, he clenched his teeth, swallowing the pain and forcing his eyes to open.

His heart sank as the room shifted into focus. The first thing he saw was a wall of thick wire mesh. A quick glance around confirmed his suspicions—he was in a cage. Apparently, someone had decided handcuffs were not enough to hold them.

He allowed his eyes to roam the rest of the room and breathed a sigh of relief as he found the others nearby. They had each been given a cage of their own. He spotted Liz lying unconscious, her wings sprawled limply around her. Richard, Jasmine and Mira were in the cages beyond her.

Struggling to sit up again, Chris cursed the cuffs holding his hands fastened behind his back. His wings shifted, stretching out to help steady him. In the narrow confines of the cage he had little room to maneuver, but he finally managed to get to his knees.

A moan came from Liz's cage, and he scooted across to the wire and peered through. A purple bruise darkened her forehead, but otherwise she seemed unharmed. He let out a breath as her eyes fluttered open.

"Chris," she murmured.

Before he could warn her, Liz tried to sit up, and promptly fell on her face. A string of curses rolled off the concrete walls as Chris suppressed his laughter. Movement came from the other cages as the rest of their party woke.

Trying to rise a second time, Liz managed to rock back on her haunches. Her eyes narrowed and she shot him a look. "You didn't see that," she muttered, then looked around, taking in the row of cages and plain concrete walls. "Where are we? Trying to recreate our first date, Chris?" Her tone was light, but he could hear the fear beneath her attempt at humor.

Chris looked away, blinking back sudden tears. He strained his wrists against the cuffs, but pain shot from his wound, and he quickly gave up. With his arms locked behind his back, he couldn't leverage his full strength against them anyway.

"I don't know, Liz," he said finally. He bowed his head. "I'm sorry, this is all my fault."

His voice cracked as guilt swept over him. What had he been thinking, rushing off the way he had? They'd had no business being in that alleyway. If not for his stupidity, he would never have been injured, and they would never have found themselves in Daniella's apartment.

"Don't be an idiot, Chris." Liz leaned her head against the wire and closed her eyes. "You couldn't have known Daniella and her mother would betray us. Besides, do you really think I would have stood there while those policemen attacked her? You were just a step ahead of the rest of us."

"I was reckless," Chris argued. "I rushed in without thinking, without caring what happened. If I'd been more careful, if I'd listened to you, none of this would have happened."

"Maybe." Liz shrugged. "They had guns though, Chris. If you hadn't acted so quickly, we would never have gotten close to them, and we might not have saved Daniella. How's your arm?"

"Sore. Not as bad as last night, though," he replied.

Liz smiled, but before she could respond, the door on the

opposite wall clicked and swung open. Three men stepped through, wearing the familiar blue uniforms of the guards at the facility. Chris's heart sank.

No, we can't be back.

His worst suspicions were confirmed as Doctor Halt followed the guards inside. He wore the same white lab coat and sleek black pants as the last time Chris had seen him, though his face was lined by stress, and he seemed older. A thin smile on his lips, Halt strode forward, letting the door slam shut behind him.

"Awake at last, I see." His voice was cold as he walked down the row of cages, surveying each of them in turn. Chris noticed Jasmine, Mira and Richard were sitting up now, their eyes plastered to the ground, unwilling to meet Halt's gaze.

Halt reached the end of the row and turned back, stopping finally in front of the guards.

"All still in one piece, it seems," he said, arms clenched behind his back. "Fallow's little escapade did not prove so disastrous after all. We'll call it as an unplanned test run, I suppose. The President and his Director will certainly be pleased with the results. It's lucky this facility was never fully decommissioned, after our move into the mountains."

Chris stared up at the man, struggling to shake off the clutches of despair. But crouched on the ground, his arms bound behind his back and the wire mesh hemming him in, he could not summon the energy to offer resistance.

"This isn't the end, Halt," Liz growled from her cage. She struggled to sit up straight, her wings flailing against the wire.

Halt stepped up to her cage, the smile falling from his lips. "You're wrong, Ms. Flores. This is very much the end. The President will soon approve the extra funding I need to continue with my project. Once I've finalized matters here in San Francisco, I will have you all shipped back to our primary facility. There, I will watch you get torn apart, piece by delicate piece, and I will use what we find to perfect our recombinant DNA. You and your little friends will be consigned to the pages of history, remembered as nothing more than stepping stones on our path to the perfect soldier."

Chris shuddered. There was an almost fanatical rage in Halt's eyes as he glared down at Liz.

But shaking her head, Liz laughed in the face of Halt's fury. "I know what you are, Halt," she replied. "I saw what you did to Mira, before I passed out. You're not human; you're *Chead!*"

Chris gaped at Liz's accusation. He stared at Halt, watching for some reaction. The doctor's grey eyes hardened, and his posture seemed to stiffen. He glanced at the guards. "*Out!*" he snapped. The men obeyed without question, and Halt turned back to Liz. "You had best keep such notions to yourself, Ms. Flores. Or I may decide to dissect you right here in San Francisco."

Liz snorted. "Go ahead. I'd rather die than go back to that place."

"And what about your friends?" Halt said dangerously. He glanced at the others, a sneer twisting his face. "Such a sordid bunch. It sickens me to see such precious gifts go wasted on the progeny of traitors."

"Our parents weren't traitors!" Chris snapped.

Halt waved a hand. "They were traitors to our principles, with their talk of change and reform. Such beliefs can only lead to our downfall."

In the cage beside her, Chris's mouth hung open. A tremor rippled through him. "You mean you killed my mom because she wanted to make things better," he grated.

"Did Fallow never tell you? No matter, no one would believe you anyway." Halt laughed. "Now, as invigorating as this conversation is, I am needed elsewhere. On my return, you'll each be introduced to a fresh set of collars—and a lesson in etiquette to go with them. For now, you'll have to make do with the company of the guards." He shouted out, and the guard stepped back into the room. "They haven't had much excitement all the years this facility has been out of action, so I'm afraid their conversation skills may be lacking. But they'll ensure you don't have any mishaps."

With that, Halt turned and walked from the room. The three guards edged forward to take his place, their rifles held loosely against their chests. Their eyes flickered over the rows of cages, lingering on Liz and her outstretched wings.

All the fight seemed to leave Liz with Halt's dismissal. She sat with her head bowed and shoulders slumped, unaware of the guard's attention, until one of them spoke. "You think they're real?"

Another of the men laughed. "You heard the doctor—they're experiments." He stepped closer to the cage and raising his rifle, slammed it into the mesh.

The wire of Liz's cage rattled, and she glanced up, her eyes widening. The guard laughed again as her wings lifted slightly from the ground. He turned to the others. "Look pretty real to me!"

The guards stepped closer, peering through the wires at the dark feathers filling the cage. The cages were only ten feet wide, but Liz's wingspan spread more than twenty, and they pressed up against the wire. Chris could hardly blame the men for their curiosity, though it made him sick to his stomach, seeing Liz treated like a caged animal.

"You think she can actually fly?" another of the guards muttered.

"Of course she can fly," the first replied. "You think these people are *stupid* or something? Why would they give her wings if she couldn't use 'em?"

"Piss off," Liz snapped. Still crouched on the ground, she retreated to the back of the cage.

Outside, the guards looked at each other and then burst into laughter.

"Feisty, isn't she?" The first guard grinned, leaning against the wire. "What's your name again, pretty girl? Elizabeth, wasn't it?"

Liz pursed her lips and looked away.

"Leave her alone," Chris growled from his cage, but the men ignored him.

"Let's take a closer look, shall we, boys?" the man who appeared to be the ringleader suggested.

The others paused, sharing a glance. "Don't think that's a

good idea, Franco. The doctor seemed pretty keen on keeping them where they are."

Franco only laughed. "Who's going to know? Look at her, she's tiny! And her hands are cuffed. You think we can't take her?"

The second guard fell silent, still shaking his head, but the third shrugged. "Can't hurt. You heard the doctor. They're going to put her down when he gets back anyway. May as well grab a few feathers to show the boys at the pub."

That was enough for Franco. Removing a set of keys from his belt, he turned back to Liz's cage. Heart thudding in his chest, Chris scrambled to get his legs beneath him, and finally managed to haul himself up. Stumbling forward, he threw himself against the wire to catch the men's attention. His wings stretched out, slamming against the steel.

The men paused and turned to stare at him.

"Leave her alone," Chris growled. "If you touch her, I swear I'll kill you all."

The men glanced at one another, momentarily taken aback by Chris's ferocity. Then the man called Franco grinned, glancing down the row of cages. "What do you know, they've all got wings, boys." Turning his back on Chris, he stepped up to the door of Liz's cage. "This one's still the prettiest though."

Chris swore and threw himself against the wire again, but the men ignored him again. Inside her cage, Liz crouched on the ground, still struggling to find her feet. Gritting his teeth, Chris strained against his cuffs, fighting the agony that lanced down his arm. The cold steel sliced into his skin but did not give.

He watched on, helpless, as Franco unlocked Liz's cage. The other two stood back as the door swung open, their rifles trained on Liz. Rage flashed in her eyes as she prepared to launch herself at the men, guns or no.

Franco paused in the doorway, studying her closely. Smiling, he raised his hand and pointed at Chris. "I wouldn't, my dear. Randell, Oliver, shoot the boy if she tries anything."

Liz's shoulders slumped. Franco laughed again and stepped into the cage, despite the string of curses Chris hurled in his direction. Grabbing a fistful of Liz's hair, he dragged her to her feet. Her screams echoed through the room as he hauled her from the cage. Her wings flapped, slamming into the wire mesh, but with her hands pinned behind her back, she had no means to defend herself.

Chris stared, helpless, as the guard shoved Liz into the middle of the room. She stumbled forward, a gasp tearing from her throat as he released her. Eyes wide, she spun, her wings fanning out to fill the room. Her skin had paled, the dark bruise on her forehead standing out in stark relief. Rage shone from her eyes as she faced the ring of men.

A low growl rattled from her throat as one of the men grabbed at her feathers. She spun at him as he tore a fistful loose. He held them up in triumph. "They're real, boys!" He laughed as he looked at Liz. "You don't mind if I take a souvenir? Don't think you'll be needing them, where the doctor is taking you."

Liz stalked towards him, but Franco stepped in behind her. Before Liz could turn, he slammed the butt of his rifle into the back of her head. She staggered at the blow, losing her balance and crashing to the floor in a tangle of feathers. Without her arms, she could do nothing to break her fall. Before she could recover, Franco drove his boot into the small of her back, pinning her to the concrete.

Grinning, he looked at the others. "What should we do with the birdie now?"

27

Sam stood in the wings of the stage and looked out over the crowd that had gathered beyond the podium. They stood in silence, staring up at the figures on the stage, waiting for the announcement. The national press stood at the front, their cameras pointed up at them, red lights flashing as they prepared to broadcast to the country.

Swallowing, Sam glanced at Paul and Francesca. They stood to either side of him, their faces tight with fear, their eyes lingering on the man standing beside Halt. A dozen black-suited bodyguards ringed the two men, their hard eyes scanning the crowd. They were clearly taking no chances.

Not with the life of the President of the Western Allied States.

Whispers spread through the crowd as the President squared his shoulders and stepped into view. Striding across to the podium, he looked out over the gathered faces. He moved with a regal grace, carrying about him the air of a man used to power. Not surprising, after the long decades he had served as President.

Placing one hand on the smooth mahogany podium, he waved to the crowd. The whispers dimmed to sudden silence, as everyone present looked up in expectation. Even the sharp clicking of cameras died away. It had been a long time since the

President had spoken in such a public setting. Usually he broadcast announcements from his office, or in private press conferences. Now, the whole nation waited with bated breath to hear what he had to say.

"My fellow citizens of the Western Allied States," he began, his smooth voice carrying over the crowd. "Thank you for joining me here today. I know times have been hard. I appreciate your courage today, to stand with me here in defiance of those who seek to terrorize us."

He fell silent, his eyes sweeping the crowd, as though he were speaking to each and every soul present. "But I have come here today to tell you the dark days are numbered, that a solution is at hand."

Whispers spread as heads turned to one another in question. The President opened his hands, and the silence resumed. Halt stepped from the shadows and approached the podium.

"My people have been working on a solution to combat the menace of the *Chead*," the President continued. "Though our enemies abroad would see us fall to the chaos they have seeded, their attacks will only make us stronger. The terror they seek to spread will only unite us in our efforts to defeat them. And now we have an answer to their monstrosities, a beacon of hope to light our way."

He paused, letting his words sink in, the anticipation to build. Then he continued: "Our scientists have taken inspiration from the evil of the *Chead*. They have studied their physiology, identified their weaknesses, and developed an answer."

Sam let out a long breath. That was their cue. He glanced at the others, hesitating on the brink. It was not too late to turn back, to flee the stage and deny Halt and the President their victory. But even as he tensed, an image of Ashley flashed into his mind, of her strapped to the bed, and Halt standing over her.

The fight fled him, and he hesitated no longer.

The crowd stilled as Sam stepped into the light. He could sense Paul and Francesca at his shoulders, but he kept his eyes fixed on Halt, on the triumphant grin on the doctor's face. His heart sank, but he strode to the front of the stage and looked out over the mass of humanity gathered for their presentation.

They were on Fisherman's Wharf, on a makeshift stage set up at Pier 39. The crowd stretched out along the waterfront in either direction, as far as the eye could see. A stillness came over them as they looked up at the three teenagers standing alongside the President, their foreheads creasing in confusion.

The President raised a hand. "Ladies and gentlemen, I give you the future."

At the President's words, Sam closed his eyes.

Forgive me.

With a sharp *whoosh*, his wings snapped open, the great expanse of his copper feathers spreading to fill the stage. Behind him, he heard the others following suit. Opening his eyes, he looked out again at the crowd.

A thousand faces stared up at him. Mouths hung open and eyes bulged at the impossibility of what they were witnessing. Not a soul moved. Not a voice spoke. The silence was absolute, stretching over the crowded streets like a blanket.

Then the whispers began, quietly at first, but growing to a rush, as though a dam had broken. As one, the reporters began to shout questions. Cameras flashed and the crowd jostled forward, desperate for a closer look.

Sam lowered his head, struggling to hold back tears. The collar pressed tighter around his throat, and shivering, he silently retracted his wings. Glancing at Halt, he saw the exaltation on the doctor's face and closed his eyes again, unable to face the shame welling up within him.

What have I done?

28

"*Liz!*" Chris cried.

His chest constricted as he heard the others screaming from the neighboring cages. He threw himself at the wire mesh, felt the cold steel cutting into his face, and stumbled sideways. His wings beat the air, keeping him upright, tearing at his steel confines, desperate to escape. But nothing he did made a difference. Heart racing in his chest, he watched the nightmare unfolding outside his cage.

Liz lay pinned beneath the guard's boot, her hands still cuffed behind her back, her wings beating weakly against the cold concrete. She kicked out with her feet, but the other guards stood out of range and only laughed. Then one drew back his boot and kicked her in the side. The blow drove the breath from Liz's lungs, folding her in two.

In his cage, Chris cursed the men, threatening bloody murder, but intent on their victim, they ignored him. Liz shrieked as Franco crouched over her and grabbed a handful of her hair. Jerking back her head, he forced her to look at him.

"You be good now, Elizabeth." He sat back on his haunches and nodded at the cages. "Or an accident's going to happen to one of your buddies there."

Liz only growled and strained against her cuffs. Her wings

swung out, catching Franco in the ribs and toppling him to the floor. He cursed as he landed on his backside. Another of the guards stepped forward and stamped on Liz's wing. She arched her back as he ground her feathers into the concrete, a silent scream tearing from her throat.

Regaining his feet, Franco dusted himself off and scowled down at Liz. He kicked Liz again, and laughed as she strained to draw breath.

"Please," Liz managed to croak. "*Just leave us alone!*"

The grin on Franco's face spread as he crouched beside her again, but Chris felt a touch of premonition at Liz's words. He frowned, leaning against the wire, peering out at the tangle of bodies. Liz lay stiff against the floor, her wings retracted protectively against her back now. She did not move as Franco reached out and stroked the black feathers, speaking softly. "Just be a good girl, and I'll put you back in one piece."

The hackles stood on Chris's neck as the guard brushed the hair from Liz's face. A scream built in his throat, a desperate cry of anger, of untold rage. He strained against the cuffs, the steel cutting into his wrists. Pain streaked from his bullet wound, but he didn't care, hardly noticed.

Liz had gone deathly still. Smiling, Franco bent down, reaching for her…

As his hands brushed her skin, a bloodcurdling scream filled the room, so loud Chris thought his ears might burst. Unable to cover them, he sank to his knees, and watched through watering eyes as the guards reeled back.

The scream died as quickly as it had begun. The guards blinked. Franco cursed and stepped towards Liz, but before he could reach her, a sound like nails on a chalkboard rent the air. It was followed by the soft tinkle of steel chains striking concrete.

A feral growl rose from where Liz lay huddled on the ground. A shudder went through her feathers, her wings snapping open. Then Liz was crouched on all fours, her hands suddenly free, her black hair pasted across her face. Her eyes flashed in the glow of the overhead lights, falling on the three guards.

Chris staggered back from the wire of his cage. The breath

caught in his throat and he struggled to breathe, to comprehend what he was seeing. His stomach twisted and he shook his head, clenching his eyes closed.

When he opened them again, nothing had changed.

Liz still crouched on the ground, her lips drawn back in a snarl, her wings tensed behind her. And her eyes…her eyes had changed. Gone was the crystal blue he knew so well.

In their place were the cold grey of the *Chead*.

The guards stumbled backwards, their mouths falling open as they fumbled for their weapons. Before they could so much as scream, Liz sprang.

The first guard collapsed as she collided with his chest, bearing him to the ground. He managed half a shriek before Liz tore out his throat. Blood sprayed the air, cutting off his screams, as a low gurgling started in his chest. He gasped, eyes wide as blood filled his lungs. Laughing, Liz turned on her next victim.

The second guard almost managed to raise his rifle before Liz was on him. She tore the weapon from his terrified hands and hurled it aside, then caught him by the neck. His mouth opened, but he couldn't even scream as she slammed him into the wall. A sickening *crunch* came from his skull, and his eyes rolled up into the back of his head.

Tossing the man aside, Liz stepped over the lifeless body, her grey eyes tracking Franco as he stumbled back from her. He screamed, fumbling for his rifle, but she was too fast. He retreated as she stripped it from his hands, until his back pressed up against Chris's cage.

"No, please, no, *don't!*" He shrieked the last word as Liz charged.

He raised his arms to protect himself, but Liz caught him by both wrists. With a sickening wrench, she tore his arms apart.

Chris blanched and forced himself to look away. But he could not block out the sounds of rending flesh and breaking bones. His stomach churned as Franco screamed and began to beg. Another *thud* came, then another scream. Wild laughter filled the room.

When the guard finally fell silent, Chris could hardly bring himself to look.

Liz stood outside his cage, her clothes covered with blood, even the feathers of her outstretched wings stained by it. Her shoulders rose and fell in a rhythmic fashion, her grey eyes watching him. Her lips drew back in a snarl as he moved, and slowly she reached out a hand to the wire. Gripping it between her fingers, she began to squeeze.

Chris swallowed as the steel bent before her strength. He retreated until his back was pressed against the rear of the cage. Fear wrapped its way around his stomach as he stared at Liz, searching for the girl he loved, begging for this all to be a nightmare.

But there was no sign of blue in Liz's eyes, and snarling, she threw herself at the wire. The steel rattled and bent beneath the impact but did not give. Chris strained against his handcuffs, as the others screamed in their cages. Blood pounded in his ears, muffling their words, but it didn't matter. The handcuffs refused to give.

He looked up at Liz as she attacked the wire again. He recognized the madness in her eyes. It was more than just the grey of the *Chead*. In the facility, Chris had proven he could match the *Chead's* strength. But he could still recall the rage that had overcome Hecate at the end of their fight. With that fury had come a renewed strength, a fresh power that had left Chris begging for mercy.

He saw that rage in Liz's eyes now. She would tear him limb from limb.

Unless he could reach her.

"Liz," he shouted. Summoning his courage, he stepped up to the wire. "Liz, please, it's me, Chris. Please, come back to me."

He flinched as Liz roared and threw herself at the wall of the cage again. His heart pounded hard against his ribs as the poles supporting the corners bent beneath the impact.

"Liz, *stop!*" Chris screamed as she attacked again.

His words fell on deaf ears, and he retreated to the corner, watching as the poles continued to bend inwards. The others stood in the nearby cages, watching now in terrified silence, desperate not to draw Liz's attention.

Despair rising in his chest, Chris slumped to the floor. He couldn't stand to lose Liz, not like this, not now. She alone had drawn him back from the brink, from the gulf of despair into which he had fallen. If he lost Liz too, he didn't know how he would go on.

Not that that would matter, if she got his hands on him.

He looked into her eyes, watching her throw herself mindlessly against the wire, still not quite believing what he was seeing.

How could this happen?

Finally, he had to look away, to close his eyes and wait for the end to come. To his surprise, a sudden silence fell over the room. Looking up, he found Liz still standing outside his cage. She blinked, and her chest swelled as she sucked in a great, shuddering breath.

For a long while, she stood still, fists clenched at her sides. Chris stared into her eyes, searching for a trace of the crystal blue, hardly daring to breathe. Time stretched out, long seconds uncounted.

Then Liz shook her head and retreated a step. Her head twisted, her gaze sweeping the room, seeming to take in the devastation for the first time. A shiver went through her as she lifted her head, her nostrils flaring.

A low growl came from her throat as she turned towards the door. Her shoulders rose as she drew in another breath. She shook her head, snarling at the bodies lying scattered around her.

"Liz," Chris whispered, desperate to reach her.

She whirled at his voice, eyes wide, flashing with sudden fear.

Then she spun back to the door, and fled.

29

The *Chead* roared as a bullet grazed her shoulder. Then she was amongst the humans and their puny weapons, tearing and rending. They fell back before her fury. Their screams sent a thrill through her veins, but they quickly fell silent. She stood amidst their bodies, the scent of blood strong in her nostrils, and searched for fresh victims.

Alone.

Growling, the *Chead* moved on. Turning a corner, she found the woman she'd missed, staggering away down the corridor. Rage filled her as she leapt, bearing the woman to the floor. Her screams fell silent as the *Chead* tore out her throat.

The *Chead* straightened and scanned the corridor, searching for movement. Blood stained the walls, and no human had escaped her vengeance. Lifting her head, she tasted the air, seeking out the strange smell. It called to her, alien but familiar. Desire tingled in her veins as she breathed it in. Turning, she followed it.

The *Chead* moved down the long corridors on silent feet, her senses reaching out, searching for signs of life. But there were no more sounds now. The stark white corridors were empty, the group she had slaughtered perhaps the only occupants.

Turn back.

The *Chead* hesitated as a voice whispered in her mind. Snarling, she pushed it aside and continued after the scent. It grew stronger with every step, rich and sweet and irresistible. Her pace quickened, desire mingling with rage, muting the need to rend and tear.

Long minutes later, the *Chead* found her way barred by a steel door. She paused. Lifting her head, she breathed deeply, tasting the scent she tracked. It hung heavy around the door. There could be no doubt. The source was beyond.

Clenching her fists, the *Chead* charged. Again and again she hurled herself at the door, feeling it bend and shift with each blow, rattled by her power. She sensed movement, and redoubled her efforts, determined not to let the source of the scent escape.

Stop, said the voice again, but she ignored it.

Roaring, the *Chead* drove herself against the door a final time. Hinges shrieked, and with a crash it buckled inwards, collapsing to the ground beyond. Triumph quickened the *Chead's* racing heart, and teeth bared, she stepped inside.

30

Chris sagged against the wall of his cage as Liz fled through the door. His shoulders slumped and he slid to the concrete. Closing his eyes, he sucked in a deep, shuddering breath.

What the hell is going on?

His mind was still reeling, struggling to comprehend what he'd just witnessed. But there was no denying it—Liz had changed, had succumbed to the relentless rage of the *Chead*. The vile guards had never stood a chance. And neither had he.

"Chris?" Richard's voice came from nearby.

Chris opened his eyes and looked through the wire at the others. They huddled in their cages, wide eyed and pale with shock. Richard had found his feet, but Jasmine and Mira still sat on the floors of their cages, their faces lined with exhaustion. He could feel the same fatigue throbbing in his temple, and found his mind drifting.

What did they use in those tranquilizers?

"What did you say, Richard?" he asked, fighting against the weariness.

Richard eyes were lingering on the slaughter Liz had left behind. Blood and body parts lay scattered across the floor, barely recognizable as the three men who had stood there a few minutes earlier.

"We have to go," Richard said grimly. "Can you get out?"

Chris quickly assessed the damage Liz had inflicted on his cage. The poles had bent, but not broken, and the thick wire still hemmed him in on all sides. Grimly, he shook his head. Then he saw a glimmer of metal amidst the bloody mess on the floor outside his cage.

He scrambled forward eagerly. "The keys!"

Twisting, he tried to reach them through the mesh. But cuffed together, his hands didn't fit between the wire. He looked at Richard and Jasmine, despair welling in his chest.

"I can't reach them," he said.

Jasmine snorted. "You clearly haven't watched enough crime shows."

So saying, Jasmine lay down on her back and bent her knees. With her arms still cuffed behind her, she lowered her hands until they rested under her backside. Then she lifted her stomach, stretched her arms down and passed them beneath her feet. Hands now in front of her, she climbed to her feet and grinned.

"Now you," she said.

Chris, Richard and Mira quickly repeated the procedure. When Chris looked back up, Jasmine was staring down at her hands, her forehead creased. Veins stood out along her arms as she strained. With her hands in front, she could now bring the full force of her enhanced strength to bear. Slowly, the chains of her handcuffs buckled, until with a violent jerk, they snapped apart.

Jasmine grimaced. "These people have underestimated us for the last time. Come on, Chris, get the keys."

Chris nodded. Tensing his arms, he pulled them apart. Pain streaked from his bullet wound, but he resisted it, determined not to let the others down, and a few seconds later the steel gave way with a shriek. Dropping to his knees, he reached a hand through the wire links and retrieved the keys from the bloody floor.

Within minutes, the four of them stood outside the cages amidst the carnage their friend had left behind. The keys had also unlocked the broken remains of the handcuffs, although it had taken precious time to find the right key amidst the bulging chain.

Looking at the slaughter, Chris forced himself to avert his eyes. He saw the questions in the others' expressions, mirroring those spinning through his own mind. Why had Liz changed? And were they destined to follow her? Would they all turn into monsters, one by one?

Shuddering, he pushed away the thought. "We'd better get out of here. Liz can't have gone far."

Richard frowned. "Chris…" He lowered his head and looked away. "Chris, Liz is gone. You saw her eyes. Whatever that was, I don't think she's coming back from it. We can't waste our time looking for her. Halt could be back any minute."

Chris stared at Richard, the first embers of rage catching in his chest. "How can you say that?" he snapped. "After everything we've been through, how can you even think about leaving her?"

"I don't like it any better than you do." Richard met Chris's eyes for just a moment, long enough for him to see the sorrow there. "But we have to be realistic. She turned, Chris. She's *Chead* now. She's gone."

"No." Chris stepped in close and grabbed Richard by the arm. "She's not. She's still in there. You saw her, she had the chance to kill me, but she didn't. I'm not leaving her."

Richard pulled his arm free and turned to Jasmine. "Jasmine…" he started, then stopped, still unsure of himself with her. "Jas, tell him we have to go."

Chris looked at Jasmine, pleading silently for her help. He was so tired, his strength at its end. He couldn't do this without them.

Jasmine's eyes flickered from Chris and back to Richard, a frown twisting her lips. Finally, she let out a long breath, and stepped up beside them. Her eyes fixed on Richard as she drew him into her arms.

Richard's eyes widened at her sudden show of affection, but a second later his arms went around her, hugging her back. They stood for a second in silence. Finally, Jasmine pulled away again and looked up at Richard.

"Thank you, Rich," she said, smiling. "You took a bullet for me, back in the apartment."

"Well, they were darts..." Richard trailed off as Jasmine placed a hand on his chest.

She turned back to Chris, her eyes resolute. "And so did Liz. I told her to run, to leave us behind. She could have gotten free, but she chose to stay and fight for us." She looked at Richard. "If our positions were reversed now, she wouldn't leave, Rich. We're family, we have to help her."

The two of them stood staring at each other for a long moment, before Richard closed his eyes and nodded.

Just then, a low whimper came from Mira. Chris stumbled back as she sprang at him. Her wings beat down, carrying her past as Chris leapt from her path. But she was not attacking him. With another strike of her wings, she disappeared through the open door.

Chris swore and raced after her. He heard footsteps and muttered curses as the others followed, but outside Mira was already fleeing down the long corridor. Sucking in a breath, Chris followed, desperate to catch the girl before she got them all killed.

At the end of the corridor, Mira took a sharp turn to the right. Chris picked up the pace, afraid of losing her. A trail of bloody footprints led in the direction they were heading, and silently he prayed Mira did not encounter Liz.

Turning the corner, his stride faltered as he found a fresh scene of slaughter. Bodies lay scattered down the length of the corridor, but Mira was already pulling away, her wings beating sporadically to hurry her along. Panting, Chris leapt the bodies of two men. A twisted rifle lay on the floor nearby, while another had been embedded in the wall.

Ahead, Mira vaulted around another bend. Chris barreled around the corner, his wings outstretched to keep his balance. She was still fifty feet ahead, but he was closing in fast. The hushed voices of the others chased after him as he glanced around, expecting guards or doctors to appear. But the hallways remained empty, and he guessed Liz had killed her victims before they'd had a chance to sound the alarms.

Slowly he closed the gap with Mira, until only a few feet separated them. As he reached out to catch her, Mira's wings beat down, sending her soaring out of reach. Swearing, Chris tried to do the same, but he crashed to the ground as his wings struck the walls on either side. The narrow corridors fit Mira's smaller wingspan perfectly, but rendered his useless. Climbing to his feet, he continued the chase.

The game of cat and mouse ended abruptly as Mira drew to a stop. Chris's arms windmilled, and he staggered sideway into the wall to avoid knocking the girl off her feet. He quickly reached out and grabbed Mira by the arm.

As the others drew up behind him, he straightened, finally noticing where Mira had led them. The first thing he saw was the bloody footprints. They were fainter now, but there was no doubt in his mind they belonged to Liz. His eyes travelled further down the corridor, to where a steel door lay crumpled on the ground.

His stomach twisted and he glanced at Mira. She stood beside him, staring through the broken doorway, her shoulders rising and falling with each shallow breath. Her wings shuddered on her back, and her whole body was coiled tight as a spring.

"Where have you brought us, Mira?" Chris whispered.

31

Liz rose slowly from the darkness, following the soft whispers of a familiar voice. Tendrils of madness trapped her, threatening to pull her back down, but the voice was urgent, insistent. It lifted her from the haze, pulling her into the light, returning her to reality.

She shuddered as sensation returned. A scream built in her throat, but she swallowed it down. Blinking, she bit back a sob as her memories clicked into place. Trapped in her own body, she had been helpless to stop the creature's slaughter.

A wild fury had taken her when the guards had grabbed her. Lying there, she had felt a pressure building in her chest. As they reached for her, that pressure had snapped, and rage had swept her away. Powerless against it, Liz had closed her eyes and succumbed.

When they opened again, it had been the *Chead* who looked out.

The steel handcuffs had given way like paper before her power, and her tormentors quickly followed. She could still remember the ecstasy, her wild joy at the slaughter, the pleasure she'd taken ripping her enemies limb from limb.

Tasting bile in her throat, Liz rolled onto her side and threw up.

Her arms shook as she finally sat up. A memory flickered into her mind, and she recalled the voice that had called her back. Blinking, she was surprised to find herself on a narrow hospital bed in some kind of infirmary. Liz's gaze swept her surroundings, settling on the occupant of the neighboring bed. Her heart froze in her chest as time seemed to slow, all sound falling away.

Ashley smiled back, red hair spilling across the pillow, white wings hanging half-folded to either side of her. Her face was ghostly pale, still marked by faint traces of bruising, and a steel collar shone around her throat. Both of her hands had been handcuffed to the railing of the bed, and she wore a silk gown with long sleeves that covered her arms. An IV bag hung from the wall beside her bed, a thin tube delivering its contents through a stent in her arm.

"You back with us, then?" Ashley murmured, her voice faint.

"*Ashley!*" The word tore from Liz's lips as she leapt from the bed and hurled herself at her friend. "You're alive!"

She could hardly believe her eyes, hardly trust that Ashley was really there. Last Liz had seen her, Ashley had been a broken mess, her chest torn open by a bullet, her wings shattered by the fall. Yet here she was, still sporting bandages around her chest, but whole, alive.

Ashley chuckled. "No thanks to you," she croaked. "Thought you were going to kill me."

Liz shuddered, the horror of her change returning. "I don't know what happened…"

With the words, a dam shattered within Liz, and she felt all the horror, all the terror and anger, the devastation of the past weeks come crashing down on her. Sobbing, she hugged Ashley again, overwhelmed. Then Ashley was crying as well, as they shared in one another's grief.

Time passed. Holding tight to Ashely, Liz could almost imagine herself a child again, safe in her mother's embrace. She breathed in Ashley's scent, hardly able to believe the girl was really there, that she had survived. And if that was true, then Sam…

Liz sat up straight as movement came from the shattered

doorway. The breath caught in her throat as Chris appeared. His mouth dropped opened as he found the two of them sitting on the hospital bed. Liz closed her eyes, unable to face his horror at what she'd done. Blood matted her wings and hair, covering her in a grotesque paste Liz feared she could never wash away. Silently, she waited for Chris's judgement.

A hand brushed her cheek, lifting her chin. Her eyes fluttered open and she found Chris beside her, his arms open to embrace her.

"Liz," he breathed, his voice filled with wonder. "Your eyes, they're blue."

With a half-choked cry, Liz threw herself into Chris's arms. His hands went around her, stroking her wings as she hugged him with all her strength. His shirt slid up, and she felt the warmth of his flesh beneath her fingers. Desire flickered within her…

Suddenly Chris was screaming. Shoving her away, he stumbled back from her, his face twisted in pain. He crashed into another hospital bed and crumpled to the floor. Mouth open, Liz went to help him, but froze when she saw his back.

As though kissed by fire, an angry red rash had appeared on his skin where her fingers had touched him. She looked down at her hands as Chris writhed on the ground, clawing at his back. His wings slammed into the spare hospital bed, sending it crashing to the floor. A sound came from the doorway, and Liz saw Mira, Richard and Jasmine staring back at her. She swallowed a shriek of her own.

What have they done to me?

On the floor, Chris's thrashing began to slow. He panted in the quiet, his eyes clenched shut as he fought some unknown battle, some unspeakable pain.

Finally, he stilled. Blinking, he looked around. Liz groaned as she saw his bloodshot eyes, desperate to go to him, but fear held her back. With a moan, Chris climbed to his knees, his limbs trembling with the effort.

"What…" he croaked, his voice trailing off. Grimacing, he tried again. "What is going on, Liz?"

"I don't know," Liz whispered, tears in her eyes. She shook her head. "I don't know. I'm so sorry."

The others edged forward. Liz did not miss the nervous glances they cast her way. She hung back as they helped Chris up off the floor. There was no missing the pain in Chris's eyes as he looked at her. He opened his mouth to speak, but instead, a voice came from behind them.

"If you lot don't mind…" Ashley interrupted, a sharpness to her voice. "Halt could be back any second."

There was no missing the terror in Ashley's voice at the mention of Halt's name. Liz returned quickly to her side. Taking care not to touch her skin, she carefully pulled the stent from Ashley's arm. She was about to try breaking the handcuffs when Richard appeared at her side.

"Here, try these," he said, offering her a ring of keys.

Liz nodded her thanks and quickly set about finding the right key. The cuffs gave an audible *click* as they came free. Liz stepped back to make room for Ashley to stand. She managed to swing her legs out over the side, but there she paused, swaying where she sat.

"Are you okay, Ashley?" Liz asked, concerned.

Ashley nodded and gestured at the IV. "They've been keeping me drugged," she murmured. "So…weak."

She began to topple backwards, but Richard stepped forward quickly and caught her by the waist.

"Easy there," he said. He flicked a glance at Liz. "Let's save the reunion for later, shall we?"

Liz nodded, but Chris spoke from beside her. "What about her collar?"

"The keys," Richard hissed, gesturing for them. Liz passed them over and he began to flick through the chain, searching for the familiar shape of the key that had freed them back in the facility.

"I'm sorry, guys," Ashley whispered, her eyelids fluttering. "I don't know if I can…"

"It's okay, Ash," Chris said. "We can carry you."

"So long as we do it quickly," Jasmine added. "It's been a

while since…Sooner or later, someone is going to stumble on those bodies."

Liz's stomach twisted at her words and she quickly looked away, unable to meet the others' gazes.

"What about Sam?" Chris asked. "Do you know where he is?"

A pained looked crossed Ashley's face as she shook her head. "Halt…using him for something."

Swearing, Liz clenched her fists, feeling the rage building within her again. She took a breath, trying to calm herself. What would Halt do to Sam, when he discovered Ashley was gone? But they could not leave her here, to suffer whatever fresh torments Halt might have in store.

A *click* came from Ashley's collar as it opened, and they slid it free. Chris stepped up beside Richard.

"Here, let me take her."

He slid his hands under Ashley's back and gently lifted her into his arms. He staggered slightly and she whimpered, but her eyes were barely open now. Whatever they'd been drugging her with had stolen her mutated strength.

"*Chris*, your wound!" Liz gasped as she saw a trickle of blood running down his arm. Heart in her throat, she stepped towards him.

"I'm fine," Chris grunted through clenched teeth. "It's okay, I can do it. It'll be slow, but I don't want to hurt her anyway."

"Don't be stupid, Chris," Richard argued. "Let me take her."

Chris shook his head. "No, she's our friend, I'll take her. And you're uninjured. You should go ahead with Jasmine, make sure the path is clear for us. We'll follow."

Richard hesitated, glancing at Jasmine. "She's our friend too, Chris. I won't leave her, not again." He drew himself up. "We're in this together, all of us."

Chris smiled. "I know. But we don't even know the way out. You need to find it for us." He hesitated, glancing at Liz. "Don't worry if you get too far ahead, we'll find you."

After a long pause, Richard nodded. "Okay," he whispered.

Looking around the room, he met each of their gazes, and

then turned away. Jasmine joined him, casting one last glance over her shoulder before heading for the door.

"Wait!" Chris called, and the two paused in the doorway. "If anything goes wrong, meet us at Daniella's apartment. It's the last place they'd expect us to go."

With a final nod, the others moved off, and Liz turned to look at Chris. The silence stretched out between them as she struggled to find the words. "I'm sorry," she whispered finally. "Sorry I hurt you."

He shook his head. "It's not your fault."

Yet she could see pain in the tightness of his face, the fear that lurked behind his eyes. A terror rose in her chest, that things might never be the same between them again. But there was no time to linger on the thought.

She nodded. "Let's go."

32

"I want to see her, Halt," Sam growled as he settled into the back of the limousine.

Halt sat in the opposite seat, his grey eyes hardening. Beside Sam, Paul and Francesca shifted nervously, their mouths clenched shut. There was a sickly sweetness in the air, and swallowing, Sam felt the cold metal of his collar press against his throat. But he would not back down, not this time.

"Is that so?" Halt whispered.

"I did what you asked," Sam replied. "I taught them to use their wings. I've shown myself to the public, gotten you your funding." His shoulders slumped and nausea swirled in his stomach. "Please, Halt. I just want to see her, to know she's okay."

Sam was begging now, but he no longer cared. He had to know it had been worth it, that he had not betrayed everything he believed for nothing.

Halt stared out at the passing crowds. His face was impassive, his eyes unreadable. Only his voice betrayed his excitement. "The President is impressed." A smile warmed his lips. "I will have all the funding I could ever need. You have done well, Samuel. Let it not be said that I do not reward good behavior. I will grant you an hour with the girl."

"Thank you, Halt," Sam croaked, bowing his head. He

closed his eyes, picturing Ashley, already imagining her in his arms again. She was alive. He would see her soon. It had all been worth it.

Or had it?

His joy curdled at the thought of the countless lives he'd doomed to the horrors of the facility, of the sons and daughters who would now vanish into the Californian mountains, never to return. How many more would die now, because of him?

And what would happen once Halt succeeded? Once he perfected his virus, and turned his enhanced soldiers loose on the world?

The drive back through San Francisco seemed to take an age. The four of them sat in silence for the rest of the journey, Halt in his triumph, Sam and the others lost in their own personal nightmares. When the limo finally pulled to a stop, Sam could hardly wait to escape the stifling compartment. But he sat patiently with the others, waiting for Halt's command. Like mutts on a leash, they knew the consequences of disobedience.

Once outside, Halt called for them to follow, and they filed out of the limousine one by one. To Sam's surprise, they were not in the grim underground parking lot where they'd been picked up earlier, but on the sidewalk outside a massive marble courthouse. They stood at the bottom of the steps leading up to the building, where a revolving door waited between thick stone pillars.

Sam glanced at Halt. "I thought we were going back to your facility."

Halt smiled. "We are."

Without waiting for a response, he started up the staircase, gesturing for them to follow. Sam glanced at the others, but they kept their lips shut tight. There had been no love lost between them since the incident in the training hall.

Clenching his fists, Sam started after Halt. He still didn't know what had happened that day, what had made him so violent. One second he'd been enjoying the test of his strength and abilities, the next he'd found himself pounding the two teenagers into the ground. He shuddered at the memory, and the nightmares it conjured.

Halt paused at the top of the stairs and waited for them to catch up, before continuing through the revolving door. Within, a tall-ceilinged entrance hall greeted them. Marble pillars lined the walls and the domed ceiling had been painted with a mural showing the story of the American War. Along the length of the hall, brave WAS soldiers were fighting off the villainous forces of the United States. Above the doorway, a mushroom cloud sprouted from the ruins of the once-famous White House.

The hall was mostly open space, but around its edges, wooden benches had been placed between the pillars. There, men and women in expensive suits lounged in silence, their rigid postures and gold-embossed wristwatches conveying their wealth. At the far end, several reception desks stood in front of a row of elevator doors.

Straightening his shoulders, Halt strode down the center of the hall, waving the teenagers after him. Sam scowled as whispers echoed around the chamber, as the men and women on the benches noticed them. His wings shifted uncomfortably—he had pulled them tight against his back, but they were still obvious to anyone who looked. And just a few hours earlier, his face had been plastered across national television. In seconds, every eye in the hall was transfixed on the three of them.

"Is that? It can't be! It's them...look at those feathers!" The voices chased after them, growing louder with their every footstep.

His cheeks warming, Sam tried to close his ears to the watchers and stared straight ahead. He knew what Halt was doing. He wore an arrogant smile as he walked, basking in the attention. This was his moment, his victory, and he was making sure everybody knew it. With his white lab coat, he could hardly have stood out in greater contrast to the suits who surrounded them—but there was no mistaking who held the power here.

The woman behind the reception desk stood as they approached, her eyes flicking nervously between Halt and his slaves. "Welcome...Doctor Halt." She faltered, then smiled. "Congratulations on your announcement."

Halt nodded. "Thank you, Janet. We'll be needing the elevator to the subterranean department."

"Of course, Doctor."

The receptionist turned to her computer, and a whirring sound came from one of the elevators. The numbers above the door flashed, but Halt had already turned away and was now languishing against the desk, the smug grin still on his lips.

Sam's eyes widened as the elevator doors slid open and a familiar girl stepped out. Two more familiar faces followed, then froze as they looked around. For a second, they hesitated, but no one else seemed to have noticed them, and silently they crept away from the elevators.

Sam could only stare as Richard, Jasmine and the young girl slid around the far end of the receptionist's desk, his heart pounding hard in his chest. He glanced at Halt, wondering how the doctor had not noticed them. Breath held, he clenched his fists against the desk, and silently screamed for them to go faster.

They made it another two steps before Halt looked up.

33

"*You!*" Halt hissed. "What are you doing out of your cages?"

A hushed silence fell over the hall as all eyes turned to look at the group huddled around the far side of the receptionist's desk. Richard and Jasmine stood frozen in terror, their wings half-spread, staring at Halt and Sam.

Halt brushed past Sam and strode towards them, a scowl darkening his face. "You thought you'd just walk out the front door, did you?" he growled.

The others straightened as he approached. Richard stepped between them. "You can't stop us," he snapped. "And I'd rather die than go back to your cages."

Behind him, Jasmine was struggling with the young girl from the first facility. A shriek echoed through the hall as her wings flapped at Jasmine's face, but the older girl's grip did not falter. Anger shone from the young girl's multicolored eyes as she bared her teeth at Halt.

"I will happily oblige," Halt growled. Leaping forward, he flicked out his hand to catch Richard by the throat.

Richard gasped as he was hauled into the air. "*What?*" he gaped, clawing at the doctor's fingers. His wings flailed wildly behind him, but nothing he did seemed to have any impact on Halt.

Smiling, Halt tossed Richard aside. He crashed into the heavy metal desk with a *thud.*

"An unfortunate accident," he said as he started towards the boy. "I thought I'd finally deciphered the *Chead's* compatibility issues." Richard had regained his feet, but a blow from Halt staggered him. Beyond, Jasmine and the young girl had stilled, and were now watching Halt with wide eyes. "Unfortunately, I was wrong."

"Bastard," Richard snapped. He threw himself at Halt, but the doctor spun and his elbow caught Richard full in the face, knocking him on his back.

"I lost myself for a while there," Halt continued conversationally as he drove his boot into Richard's stomach. The boy crumpled at the blow and tried to roll away. Halt stepped after him. "When my mind finally returned, I knew I had failed, that I had become *Chead*, and what that meant."

Richard crawled to his knees and looked up at Halt. "That you turned into a right bastard?" He spat blood on the marble floor. "Hate to tell you this, but you always—"

He broke off as Halt kicked him again. The blow sent him sliding across the floor to where the others stood. Jasmine released the young girl and crouched quickly beside him, helping him up.

"It means I will grow old before my time!" Halt shrieked. "That I will be dead within the decade."

He advanced, but before he could reach them, the young girl shrieked and threw herself at him. He spun, brushing off her attack and catching her by the wrist. The anger faded from his eyes as he looked down at her, his smile returning.

"But you, my sweet Mira, you are my answer, my salvation!" His voice was exultant now. He looked down at Jasmine and Richard. "Tell me, children, did you know she was *Chead?*"

Their eyes widened and Halt laughed. "All these weeks, and you never realized the truth?" He let out a long breath. "Thank God for Fallow—her virus worked, better than she could ever have imagined."

"Let her go," Richard snarled, climbing to his feet.

Halt ignored him. "If only she was still alive to see it." His tone was regretful, as though he'd forgotten he had been the one who'd killed her. "Not only did she help me to perfect humanity, she created a virus capable of superseding the *Chead*."

"Only the lucky ones," Jasmine snapped. "Or have you already forgotten all the kids who died because of your experiments?"

"Yes, yes, yes." Halt waved a hand, as though washing himself of the crime. "But thanks to Samuel here, I have all the funding I need to perfect it." A bemused smile played across Halt's lips as he looked at Sam and his companions. "And save myself from the corruption of the *Chead*." His face twisted, as though he were disgusted at what he had become.

"What did you do?" Richard whispered, his eyes finding Sam's across the hall.

Sam quickly looked away, but Halt answered for him. "He showed the world what you're capable of," he said, "and proved that I don't need the two of you." He clapped his hands. "Now, if you don't mind, my patience grows thin. Samuel, Paul, Francesca—take care of them."

"*What?*" Sam gasped.

Spinning, Halt raised his wrist. Light reflected from his watch as he spoke. "Do it."

Despair rose in Sam's throat as he bowed his head, but there was no choice. Paul and Francesca stepped forward reluctantly, their eyes wary. The collar seemed to constrict around Sam's throat as he swallowed. There was no need for Halt to explain the threat.

He looked again at Jasmine and Richard. There was no love among the three of them, not now, not since they'd faced the final test in the facility. That day had left blood on all their hands, a shared guilt, a common hatred.

Even so, he had no wish to fight them.

Gritting his teeth, Sam stepped up beside Paul and Francesca to square off against the two intruders. Jasmine and Richard shared a glance, their emerald wings stretching wide.

"Give up," Sam called across to them. "You're outnumbered. We don't want to hurt you."

Richard didn't try to hide the contempt in his eyes. "Give up?" he asked. "What have they done to you, Sam? How can you stand there and ask us to go back? You know what they'll do to us."

Sam ran a hand through his long hair, struggling to keep the pain from his face. He knew Richard was right, but he could not turn back now. He had come too far.

"So be it," he breathed.

To either side of him, Paul and Francesca started forward. Growling, Sam leapt. His wings beat down, launching himself at Richard. But snarling, Jasmine bounded between them. Her fist slammed into Sam's ribs and sent him reeling, the fury of her onslaught catching him unawares. On his other side, Richard charged, but Paul and Francesca threw themselves into the fray, driving Richard back. The three of them went down in a rush of flailing limbs and feathers.

Sam swore as Jasmine's wingtip flashed out and caught him in the face. Lurching back, he raised his fists and gathered himself, narrowing his eyes as she came at him again. He tensed as she stepped close, but before he could attack, she leapt, and her foot flashed out to catch him in the collarbone.

"*Traitor!*" Jasmine shrieked and attacked again.

Sam finally managed to duck a blow, and then dove forward. Catching Jasmine around the midriff, he hurled her backwards. She spun, her wings beating hard to break her fall. Smiling, she rose into the air. Adrenaline pounding in his skull, Sam stretched his wings and took flight.

Above, Jasmine rose to the ceiling, her emerald wings shining in the fluorescent lights. Without warning, she dropped like a stone towards him. The move caught Sam by surprise. Her boot crunched into his face and he went crashing back to the floor. The impact drove the breath from his lungs, and gasping, he struggled to sit up.

A scream came from overhead, and by sheer instinct Sam

rolled to the side. Jasmine struck the ground where he had lain with a harsh *crack*. Marble chips sliced the air as the tiles shattered beneath her.

Recovering, Sam climbed to his feet as she straightened. Spinning, his wings extended, catching Jasmine square in the face. Taken unawares, she staggered, and he saw his opening.

Sam lunged forward, slamming a fist into Jasmine's shoulder. His arm shook with the force of the blow, but he felt no sense of satisfaction when the smaller girl stumbled back. Straightening, Jasmine growled and came at him again, but Sam was ready for her this time.

His boot flashed out, catching her in the stomach. Breath hissed between her teeth as the blow connected, and she slumped to her knees. Reluctantly, Sam clasped his hands together, and as Jasmine tried to regain her feet, he brought them down.

She looked up at the last second, but there was no time to avoid his attack. The force of the blow drove her into the tiles. Her wings thrashed, forcing Sam to leap clear. When he looked back, Jasmine was struggling to stand, but the blow to her head had rattled her. Her eyes rolled back in her skull, and she toppled face-first to the ground.

Panting, Sam stood over her. An awful guilt ate at his stomach as her eyes flickered open. A moan came from her throat as she looked up at him, her brown eyes glazed.

"Please, Sam," she coughed. "Don't make me go back. Kill me, but don't make me go back.

Sam shivered, his heart clenched in a vice. The breath caught in his throat, and images rose from his memory. Looking down at Jasmine, listening to her beg, he saw again the padded room, saw the pain in Jake's eyes as Sam chose his own life over his friend's.

And he knew he could not do it again.

Letting out a long breath, he shook his head. "I can't do this."

He turned away from Jasmine then, closing his ears to her pleas. Looking across the hall, he saw Richard pinned against the far wall, desperately trying to hold off Paul and Francesca. The young girl had crumbled at Halt's feet, the fight gone from her. His face dark, he reached down to drag her away.

"Halt!" Sam screamed. "Leave her alone."

34

Chris stumbled as Ashley's weight shifted in his arms. Pain flared from his bullet wound and he gritted his teeth, but it wasn't half as bad as the night before. It was clear now that the virus had changed more than just their muscles, had given them more than just wings. It was the only explanation for Ashley's miraculous recovery. Before they'd left the infirmary, they had checked the wound beneath her bandages—it was almost healed.

A whimper came from Ashley, and Chris slowed his pace. He took the opportunity to catch his breath and glanced ahead at Liz.

She strode down the long corridor, following the faint scent of Richard and Jasmine, her shoulders rigid. Chris swallowed, fighting the need to go to her, to spin her around and tell her everything would be okay. Remembered agony rippled down his back he turned his eyes to the floor.

In his arms, Ashley moved again. He glanced down as her eyes fluttered open, a frown creasing her brow. "Chris?"

His heart lifted at her words. A smile spread across his face as he drew to a stop. Ashley wriggled in his arms, lifting her head to look around. "Liz?"

Liz grinned as she turned back. "Welcome back." She started forward, then paused, her shoulder falling.

Ashley closed her eyes with a groan. "Feels like I've been hit in the head with a brick."

"Chris probably bumped it on the way out of the infirmary," Liz commented wryly.

Chris found himself laughing. "Hey, I was careful. Besides, I've been shot, so join the club, Ash."

Ashley raised an eyebrow. "Pretty sure I joined that club first," she said with a grin, "but put me down if you're that much of a baby. I think I can walk now."

Carefully putting Ashley on her feet, Chris made sure she was steady before releasing her. "Take it easy," he said, offering his arm.

Nodding, Ashley panted as she straightened. Her snowy wings hung behind her, flexing slightly with each breath. She gave Chris's arm a squeeze and he nodded back.

Her eyes flickered between Chris and Liz. "No answers to your little problem yet?"

The smile fell from Liz's face. She quickly looked away, but Chris had caught the shimmer of tears in her eyes. "Come on," she said shortly, "before Richard and Jasmine get too far ahead."

They started off again, still moving slowly to allow Ashley time to recover. She was uneasy on her feet, no doubt due to the drugs lingering in her bloodstream. But that she was standing at all, just a few weeks after being shot from the sky, was a miracle in itself.

"What are you guys doing here?" Ashley asked as they walked. "What madness made you come back?"

In the lead, Liz snorted. "Blame Chris," she replied, apparently having recovered some of her humor. She looked back. "He was distracted by a pretty girl. Got us all caught."

"Sounds about right," Ashley laughed.

"It wasn't *that* bad," Chris said in halfhearted defense, shifting Ashley's weight on his shoulder.

"Hmm, let's see. You got shot…" Liz counted off his failings. "Got us caught and locked away. Is there something I'm forgetting?"

"Hey, we found Ashley, didn't we?"

Liz snorted again and Ashley laughed. They drifted into silence as they made their way down the long corridors. No one appeared to stop them, and Chris found himself pondering what had happened to everyone. Other than the dozen or so Liz had…killed, they had not seen another living soul.

Idly, he wondered where they were now, where such a place could be hidden amongst the packed skyscrapers of San Francisco. The facility was massive, but he hadn't glimpsed a single window so far. The weight of the concrete walls and ceilings pressed in around him. His wings twitched, and a longing for the escape of open skies rose inside him.

Soon.

Chris let out a long breath as they turned another corner and found a set of elevator doors waiting for them. The scent of the others lingered strongly in the corridor, and he hoped they had found the right way out.

Liz strode into the elevator as Chris and Ashley staggered after her. Ashley was taking more of her own weight now. She disengaged herself from Chris as they stepped inside and leaned against the wall. Liz pressed the button for the lobby.

"Hope there's no one home," she murmured.

The elevated shuddered and started moving upwards.

We're underground, Chris realized.

Within seconds, the lift shuddered to a halt again. They shared glances as the doors slid open, readying themselves for whatever waited. But nothing could have prepared them for what they stepped into.

A massive hall opened out before them. A row of reception desks stood in front of the elevators, behind which three terrified women were huddling. Beyond, pure chaos had engulfed the gallery. Men and women stumbled across the tiled floor, rushing for the revolving door at the far end of the hall, while in the middle of the open space, five winged figures fought in a blur of sound and movement.

A flash of green and copper feathers came from overhead as Sam soared upwards to clash with Jasmine, but a sharp kick of her boot to send him crashing back to the ground. A shriek drew their attention to where Richard stood wrestling with two newcomers. Chris stared as Richard leapt into the air, his wings beating hard, only for the boy to jump on his back. Black wings tore the air as he dragged Richard back down. They smashed into the tiles and rolled. Richard was up first, but the girl was on him before he could recover, sending him staggering back towards the far wall.

And in the center of it all, Halt.

The doctor stood with his arms folded, a calm smile twisting his lips. His grey eyes watched the scene with detached interest, as though this was no more than a game to him. Mira lay slumped at his feet, but as Chris watched, Halt reached down and grabbed her by the arm.

Halt hauled Mira up and held her in front of his face. "Ah, my little miracle." He laughed as she struggled, but even her enhanced strength could not break the doctor's grip.

Liz was right: Halt was Chead.

The thought sent a chill through Chris's stomach as he stepped from the elevator. He had barely had time to consider her accusation back in the cages, but the scene before him left no doubt.

Silently, they slid towards the reception desks, seeking cover as they struggled to figure out what was happening. Ashley moved without aid now, and some of her old sharpness had returned to her eyes. They crouched behind the desks as the women fled into the elevator.

"Halt!" A familiar voice echoed through the hall. "Leave her alone."

Chris's heart soared when he saw Sam striding across the hall, his copper wings spread, his face filled with rage.

Halt stared at the boy for a second, seemingly taken aback by Sam's pronouncement. His surprise did not last long, however, and scowling, he tossed Mira aside and pressed a finger to his watch.

A collective scream carried across the hall as Sam and the two winged strangers crumpled, their hands clutching desperately at their necks. His face dark with rage, Halt strode across the hall to Sam and drove his boot into their friend's stomach.

"How dare you defy me!" Halt screamed, his rage echoing from the ceiling as Sam clawed at the tiles. Caught in the clutches of the shock collar, he could do nothing to defend himself.

On the other side of the hall, Richard stood over the boy and girl he'd been fighting, his eyebrows raised in surprise. A smile tugged at his lips as his gaze found Chris and the others.

Ignoring him, Chris started towards Halt. He leapt past Mira as she staggered to her feet, gesturing for her to stay back. This had gone on long enough. It was time they rid themselves of the vile doctor. And this time, there would be no mercy.

Chris was still a few feet away when Halt looked up and saw him coming. The doctor drove a final kick into Sam's side before turning to face the new threat. A wild grin spread across his lips as Chris leapt.

At the last second, Halt twisted away, leaving Chris clawing at empty air. A fist caught him in the stomach. The breath exploded between Chris's teeth as he staggered back. Straightening quickly, he went for the doctor again.

Halt moved to meet him. Chris's instincts kicked in and he turned, shifting himself from the doctor's path. As Halt barreled past, Chris lifted his leg and drove his knee into the doctor's stomach. Halt crumpled beneath the blow, and grinning, Chris stepped in to finish him.

An awful growl rattled up from Halt's throat. He straightened suddenly, and before Chris could jump back, a fist caught him in the side of the head. Stars spun across his vision as he staggered, the strength fleeing his limbs. Before he could recover, a second blow caught him in the chin, lifting him from his feet.

Chris gasped as he crashed onto the hard tiles. Bones creaking, he struggled to sit up, but a heavy boot landed on his chest. Ears ringing, breath straining, he collapsed back to the ground.

And then, with a bloodcurdling scream, Liz appeared from nowhere and slammed into Halt. Her wings extended, the force of Liz's attack lifted Halt off his feet and hurtled him through the air. Heart pounding, Chris struggled to sit up, to find the strength to help Liz.

But she didn't need it.

Halt was cursing, clutching his arm where Liz had grabbed him. He staggered back, his grey eyes wild as he looked at her.

"*You!*" he snarled.

Baring her teeth, Liz advanced on him. "What did you do to me?" she shrieked, eyes wild.

His face pained, Halt stood staring at his wrist where she'd touched him. "The nematocysts are functioning," he murmured, almost to himself. "Incredible."

"Nematocysts?" Liz hissed, closing in on him.

Halt shook his head. By the tightness to his face, Chris could tell he was still struggling to cope with the pain of Liz's touch. Chris did not envy him.

"Stinger cells, from marine jellyfish," Halt explained, wonder and pain mingling in the lines of his face. "The virus has incorporated them into your skin cells. But we thought the gene had remained dormant. Something must have triggered them. Fascinating."

"Glad you think so," Liz snapped.

Distracted, Halt did not realize his danger until it was too late. Lips drawn back in a snarl, wings extended, Liz sprang. Catching Halt by the throat, she lifted him into the air.

Halt growled, struggling in her grasp. Then his eyes bulged, and a short, sharp shriek rattled up from his throat. Liz's eyes flashed, speckles of grey appearing amidst the blue as she lifted him higher. The doctor's feet kicked helplessly at empty air as his face paled. The veins on his forehead bulged, and his skin turned an awful red where Liz held him.

Chris shuddered as Halt moaned, the low, pitiful sound of a dying animal. He couldn't imagine the pain, the pure agony that must be sweeping through the doctor's body. He had only felt Liz's touch for an instant, and that had been enough to take his feet out from under him. This…this was infinitely worse.

Purple lines ran up Halt's neck, radiating out from Liz's fingers. His struggles weakened, the whites of his eyes now stained red. A low whine came from his mouth. Chris could see the life fleeing his body, suffocated by Liz's touch.

Then he was still.

With a casual shrug of her shoulders, Liz tossed Halt's lifeless body aside.

Chris swallowed as she turned towards him. Her grey-speckled eyes watched him, and for a moment he wondered who was looking out from them—Liz, or the *Chead*. Then she blinked and the grey faded, the blue swelling to replace it.

She shuddered, her shoulders sagging. Finding his feet, Chris started towards her, then froze at the memory of her touch.

Hurt flashed across Liz's face as she saw him hesitate.

Without speaking, she turned away.

35

A red-hot poker twisted in Liz's chest as she saw the fear flash across Chris's face. She sucked in a breath, fighting back the sting of tears, and turned her back on him. Across the hall, she saw Ashley and Sam embracing. Sam's collar lay on the ground beside them, the key they had used on Ashley's earlier still in the lock. Beside them, Jasmine had staggered to her feet. Mira huddled under her arm, her cheeks streaked by tears.

Pushing aside her pain, Liz moved to join them. She heard Chris's footsteps behind her but did not look back. In that moment, she didn't have the strength face him, though all she wanted was to bury her head in his shoulder. Glancing at her hands, despair rose in her throat as Halt's words echoed in her mind, threatening to drown her.

Would anyone ever hold her again?

Halt was dead, but what did it matter, now that he had forever altered them, after he had taken their families and stolen their lives?

She looked up, seeing again Ashley and Sam, and her pain receded slightly. She had never expected to see them again, but despite the odds, they were alive. All that was left to do now was walk through the front door, and they were free. The last of the occupants had fled through the revolving door, leaving them alone in the hall.

Her eyes drifted beyond their little group, to where Richard still stood near the elevators. He was crouched over the strangers he'd been fighting, trying to remove their collars. Sam and Ashley were too preoccupied to have noticed his plight. Wearily, Liz moved towards them to retrieve the key.

As she moved, a bell dinged from the direction of the elevators. She turned to see the metal doors slide open. A woman stepped into view. Her cool gaze swept the hall, taking in the scene in an instant. Lifting an arm, she pointed at them. Soldiers stepped from the elevator behind her, rifles at the ready.

Then there was no more time for thought.

On the far side of the hall, Richard saw the men approaching. He looked at Liz, terror flashing across his face. Their eyes met, and he stilled, the fear falling from him. He nodded at her and turned away.

"*No!*" Liz screamed.

But too late. Richard was too far away, cut off from the exit by the men and their guns. Straightening, he spread his wings and roared. The guards swung around at the sound, and Richard charged.

The others turned as the first gunshot rang through the hall. They weren't using darts now, and still several feet from his foes, Richard lurched as a bullet took him in the shoulder, but he did not slow. He plowed into the first man, bearing him to the ground and tearing the weapon from his grasp.

He was up again a second later, already charging the next soldier. A gun roared again, and blood blossomed from Richard's chest. He stumbled, almost went down, before steadying and smashing the man into the ground.

Spinning, Richard met Liz's gaze from across the hall. "*Go!*"

Tears shimmered in Liz's eyes, but suddenly she was sprinting for the door, and the others were beside her. Chris was half-dragging Jasmine, even as she pleaded for them to go back, to leave her behind.

Boom. Boom. Boom.

Liz winced with each gunshot, but she did not look back. With every step, she expected hot lead to tear through her, for a hail of bullets to bring them all down. They raced towards the exit, wings spread and beating hard, half-sprinting, half-flying.

Chris shoved Jasmine through the revolving door first, Ashley and Mira cramming in behind her. Chris followed, then Sam, as Liz cast one final look behind them.

Richard swayed on his feet, looking around at the ring of guards. His wings slumped to either side of him, torn and broken by bullets, and blood stained his shirt. He staggered for a second and then straightened, his green eyes looking up to catch Liz's gaze. A smile tugged at his lips as he lifted his arm, as though in farewell.

Liz turned away as the roar of gunfire filled the hall.

36

Hecate drew to a stop at the edge of the empty stream and looked back, checking that the others were close. They trickled in one by one, picking their slow way across the plains. The harsh sun beat down from overhead, burning their pale skin, even as the orange globe dropped towards the distant peaks. Their shadows cast long silhouettes across the grass.

As the *Chead* drew up around him, Hecate's thoughts drifted back to the strangers they'd left behind. In his mind's eye, he saw again the explosion on the mountainside, the inferno engulfing the buildings. Out on the plains, Hecate had watched the flames, waiting to see whether anything had survived.

But no winged creatures had emerged, and as dusk fell, he had finally turned away.

Now, days later, Hecate still felt the pang of regret.

Such a waste.

The boy and girl had been talented, strong. The *Chead* could have used their strength. Still, it mattered little now.

For days they had raced across the grasslands, their powerful legs carrying them easily over the flat ground, following the distant scent. They rarely stopped for rest, and hunted on the move, slaughtering chickens and other livestock when their hunger demanded it. They reveled in their freedom, in the touch of the breeze on their skin, the sun on their faces.

Though none could recall a time before the facility, each of the *Chead* possessed a rugged endurance, an ability to run for endless days and nights. Imprisonment had not lessened them—the doctors had been sure to keep them fit and healthy, the better for their experiments.

Now, Hecate could sense the wind changing, carrying with it fresh traces of the scent they followed. A delicious sweetness filled the air, somehow both familiar and alien. It was close now, its source at hand.

The others smelled it, too. They shifted around him, lifting their faces to breathe it in. They growled, and Hecate nodded. He leapt down onto the stream bed.

Starting upriver, Hecate listened to the crunch of gravel as the others followed. His eyes scanned the riverbed ahead, searching for the source of the scent, but finding only grey stones. There was no water here, only the empty husk of the once great river. Perhaps as spring set in, the snow on the distant peaks would melt, and return the waters to the dried-out river. But for today, the river remained dead.

Ahead, Hecate's keen eyes alighted on a shadow amidst the stones. Drawing to a stop, he allowed the others to gather once more. His lips twitched as he looked at the cave. The worn bedrock around the entrance suggested the river had once plunged underground here, falling into depths unknown. Now though, with the waters gone, the entrance to the cave stood open.

The sweet scent of the *Chead* hung thick in the air.

Grinning, Hecate dropped into the darkness.

V
AFTERMATH

37

Maria Sanders sighed as her alarm sounded in the darkness. Stretching out an arm, she pressed the snooze button, silencing the shrill buzzing. Somewhere outside a cricket chirped, and beyond her windows the world remained dark. Maria stared up at the ceiling, struggling to summon the will to move.

She had barely slept all night—but that was hardly unusual. These days she was lucky if she got a few hours. Silently, she tried to recall how long it had been since the insomnia began, but she'd long since lost count of the days. All through winter she had struggled on, but even the promise of summer's return did nothing to ease her suffering.

Nothing would; not now.

Her daughter was dead, and she had given up hope of ever seeing her grandson again.

Cursing, Maria pushed back the despair and willed herself into action. Climbing from the bed, she lugged herself across the room to her dresser. Her joints popped as she moved, stiff with cold and old age, and she sighed. In all her long life, her body had never let her down. Yet now, when she needed it the most, she found herself trapped in the body of an old woman. If only she were still young, then maybe she could have done something, could have saved them…

Maria shivered. Pushing the thought aside, she struggled into the old uniform she had left folded on the dresser. It was a poor fit—the pants were too baggy, and the shoulders dwarfed her shrunken frame. But then, it had never been meant for her.

Closing her eyes, Maria pictured her late husband's face, forever frozen in his youth. He had always been smiling, his hazel eyes alight with a love of life. How he would rage now, to know what had happened, to hear how they'd treated his daughter. Margaret had been the light of his life, his special girl, his legacy to the world.

Now she was dead, executed by the very nation Charles had given his life to defend.

Maria picked up the last piece of the uniform. Holding the medal in her hand, she recalled the day they had presented it to her. Her heart full, she had stood with the other widows of the American War and received her husband's honors. Now, her hands shook as she pinned the silver cross to her chest.

My shield.

She closed her eyes and sent out silent thanks for her husband's courage. His sacrifice had saved them all—his wife, his child, his nation. He and a thousand others like him had stood together against the wrath of the United States, and emerged victorious. Now, Charles protected her still, granting her respect and admiration in a society desperately short on both.

Moving into the kitchen, Maria prepared herself a pot of oatmeal. Her appetite had gone the same way as her sleep, and food no longer held any pleasure for her. Still, she needed the sustenance. It would be a long day.

The sun was starting to shine between the curtains as she sat down for her breakfast. Her thoughts drifted as she ate, and she found herself wondering how everything had gone so wrong. They had started with such noble ideals, this young nation of hers, but somewhere, they had lost their way.

That was the nature of war, she guessed. The conflict between the Western Allied States and the United States had been long and bloody, only ending when the WAS ignited a nuclear fuse in Washington, DC. Millions of innocent lives had been lost, but with their leadership shattered, the USA had finally crumbled.

After almost a decade of war, peace had returned to the American continent. Yet even then, there had been those who questioned if the cost had been worth the victory.

Twenty years later, Maria knew the truth. In the end, the WAS had become the very evil it had sought to escape. And that evil had come for her family.

She had been the first to discover the break-in. As she often did, Maria had dropped by her daughter's house for breakfast. But instead of the usual warm greeting, she had found the front door hanging from its hinges, a house in darkness, and nothing but a pool of blood in the kitchen. Struggling to control her panic, Maria had stumbled to the phone and dialed the police.

The operator assured her that help was on its way, but it was two hours before a single police officer appeared. By then, Maria's breath was coming in panicked gasps and a sharp pain was beginning in her chest. She followed the officer through the house, watching as he made a cursory inspection of the kitchen. She was desperate to hear reassurance they would find her daughter and grandson, but the officer only shrugged, and told her they would follow up with the appropriate departments.

Afterwards, Maria returned home in a state of shock, terrified for her family, unable to understand why the police had treated her so coldly. The next day she called the station again, then when that failed, her local Elector. She even tried a private investigator, but after listening politely to her story, they all gave her the same answer: there was nothing they could do.

A week later, she had finally received her answer. A letter had arrived, addressed to 'The parent(s) of Margaret Sanders'. She'd torn open the envelope and read the fateful words she had been dreading.

Guilty of treason.

Even now, those words still rang in her ears. She had tried to petition the government, to convince them of her daughter's innocence, anything that might clear her name. Their response had been a stony silence. In desperation, she'd begged them to at least spare her grandson Chris's life, to grant him a pardon as they had done for her. Why should she be spared for her age, she had argued, when Chris had barely had a chance to live?

When even that failed, Maria had begged just to be able to see them, to have one last chance to hold her daughter and grandson in her arms.

But the next time Maria had seen her daughter was during the New Year's celebrations. Sitting alone in her living room, Maria had watched, listless, as the President gave his State of the Union Address. At the end, he had read out a string of names. She'd known it was coming, but Maria still winced when she heard her daughter's name.

Margaret Sanders.

Tears spilled down Maria's cheeks as her daughter walked out onto the stage. Margaret was bound hand and foot, chained to her fellow prisoners. Her arms and legs were as thin as bone, her face shrunken to a shadow of itself. Her eyes were distant as she stared into the camera, and her hair hung in greasy tufts, doing little to conceal the purple bruises that marked her face.

Maria sank to the floor as the prisoners stopped in front of a line of soldiers. In desperation, she clung to the television, as though by will alone she might reach through and pull her daughter to safety. The President was still talking, his voice ringing with passion, but Maria didn't hear a word of what he said. All she could do was watch as her daughter fell to her knees, as the soldiers lifted their rifles, as the roar of gunfire filled her living room.

Groaning, Maria tore herself away from the memory. Wiping her eyes, she stood and placed the half-eaten bowl of oatmeal in the sink. As she scrubbed the dish clean, she forced her mind to other thoughts—to the one hope she still had left.

Chris had escaped. It was all over the news. Men had even come to question her, but she had gleefully told them to go to hell. Even under the threat of arrest she'd refused to speak.

They'd torn the house apart searching for him, but in the end they had left with nothing.

No doubt they were watching her now, but she knew Chris wouldn't be foolish enough to return. It just meant she had to be more careful with her own objectionable activities.

Rage had consumed Maria after her daughter's death. She had fed it, directed it, and discovered new purpose. Rather than wallow in her grief, she'd gone looking for others like her, for the relatives of dissidents, the families of those taken by the government. It had been a difficult search. Government policy was to arrest the immediate family of traitors, and it had been weeks before she heard the first whispers of a resistance group.

The Madwomen.

Even now, the name made Maria smile. She didn't know who had coined it, but it couldn't have been more appropriate. Out of respect for the generation who had fought in the American War, those over sixty-five were pardoned for the crimes of their relatives—even in the case of treason. In its arrogance, the government no longer saw Maria and her aging generation as a threat.

One day soon, Maria hoped to prove them wrong.

For now, their numbers were small, and they could not risk outright defiance. But they could remind the people of their past, of the war they had fought for their freedom. They could wear the uniforms and commendations of their fallen heroes, and stand in protest against oppression.

They could march.

38

"*We are still gathering information, but it is with profound regret that I can now confirm twelve civilians have been killed in the worst terrorist attack our nation has seen in decades.*"

Chris stared at the television, watching the scenes around the courthouse unfold. He barely heard the woman's words, until the camera flickered back to an image of her. She stood alone on the podium, her face somber as her hazel eyes stared into the camera. Blonde hair hung around her ears, untouched by grey. A splash of makeup added color to her prominent cheekbones, and mascara around her eyes gave her a predatory look. Chris shivered as he realized that they were now her prey.

She wore a neatly tailored blue suit and an expensive pearl necklace, but there was nothing else to suggest this was the most powerful woman in the Western Allied States. But then, the Director of Domestic Affairs did not need elaborate decorations to remind people of her authority.

"We can now reveal that, an hour ago, the four renegades we have been hunting launched a treasonous attack against the Supreme Court in San Francisco. Using black-market rifles, they attempted to execute the judges and attorneys they believe responsible for their convictions. Fortunately, the timely arrival of special forces brought an end to their attack. Through the bravery

of our soldiers, one of the fugitives was killed. Unfortunately, the remaining three again escaped custody."

"Richard," Jasmine groaned.

"As a precaution, the President and I have decided to implement martial law across the city while we seek to apprehend these criminals. The army is being brought in to patrol the streets of San Francisco and aid in our search for these fugitives—"

The old television gave an audible *clunk* as Chris flicked it off and tossed the remote down on the coffee table. It was the only thing in the room left intact. The rest of the apartment had been torn to shreds by the SWAT team that had ambushed them there just a day ago. The front door had been smashed off its hinges, the kitchen table was missing several legs, and broken glass from the shattered window covered the floor. They had done their best to prop the front door up in its frame, but there was nothing they could do about the icy breeze blowing through the window.

"What now?" Sam asked in a hollow voice.

He was seated on the floor beside the coffee table, his long legs stretched out in front of him. He looked at Chris with haggard eyes, his expression partially concealed by his long hair. The broad expanse of his copper wings hung limply behind him. His muscular frame radiated exhaustion. Of all of them, Chris had expected Sam to be the most optimistic after escaping the clutches of Halt and his guards. But then, Chris could only imagine the horrors his friend must have suffered during his prolonged captivity.

"We go back," Jasmine replied as she paced the length of the room. "We find him, save him, like we did with you."

Her voice trembled, and Chris could sense her rage, lingering just beneath the surface. Her fists clenched, Jasmine reached the window and spun to face them, her emerald wings stretching out to either side of her. Her black hair fluttered in the breeze as her eyes travelled over each of them, daring them to defy her.

"Jasmine…" Chris trailed off as she took a step towards him.

"He's alive." She grated out her words between clenched teeth.

Chris flinched from the fury in her eyes, but another voice rose to meet Jasmine's challenge.

"He's dead, Jasmine," Ashley said, her voice sucked dry of emotion. "After what Liz saw...he couldn't have survived."

Ashley lay with her head in Sam's lap, her amber eyes staring up at the ceiling. Her scarlet hair hung around her face in a disheveled mess, but her white feathered wings were tucked tightly against her back. She had always been thin, but now she was almost skeletal, her cheekbones standing out in stark relief against her pale skin. In the weeks they'd been separated, she seemed to have shrunk—not just in body, but in spirit. The fire in her eyes, that had given them all courage on their darkest days at the facility, was gone.

Jasmine strode across the room until she stood over Ashley. "*You* survived."

Ashley didn't move. "Barely." Her voice was little more than a whisper. "And sometimes I wished I hadn't."

"There were too many, Jasmine." Liz moved between the girl and Ashley, forcing her back. After what had happened in the courthouse, no one wanted to get too close to Liz. "I saw him, at the end. They all opened fire. It was too much, even for one of us."

Chris nodded his agreement. It had only taken one bullet to knock Ashley from the sky. Despite their enhanced strength and accelerated healing, she had been incapacitated for weeks. She still sported a red mark, where the wound had almost healed. But from what Liz said, Richard had taken a dozen bullets or more in his final stand. There was no coming back from that.

Liz and Jasmine stood off against each another, their eyes locked in a silent battle of wills. Liz's curly black hair matched Jasmine's, but her eyes were a crystal blue instead of brown. Staring into those eyes, Chris felt a yearning to go to her, to pull her into his arms and run his hands down her black feathers, to lift his fingers to her chin and kiss her. He imagined those big blue eyes staring up at him, alight with passion.

Then he saw them changing, hardening to grey, and he felt

again the pain of her touch. Shivering, Chris forced himself to look away before she saw his terror.

"I don't care," Jasmine snarled. "He's one of us, remember? We're family—that's what you said. We have to go back for him."

"Jasmine…" Liz's voice dropped to a whisper, and Chris could see her pain.

Jasmine snorted, her eyes flashing. "So that's how it is." She shook her head. "I guess he was right. We should have never gone looking for you. Maybe then *he* would be here instead of you."

With that, Jasmine spun on her heel and fled up the corridor. Chris watched her go—flinching as a door slammed—and then turned to the others. They had taken to the sky after fleeing the courthouse, disappearing into the winding hills and skyscrapers of San Francisco. Unprepared, their pursuers had never stood a chance of keeping up with them. They had taken refuge here, in Daniella's apartment, in the hope it was the last place their hunters would look for them.

When they'd finally reached the apartment, the six of them had entered cautiously, taking care not to make any noise in case Daniella or her mother were still home. But the house was silent, and it was only when Chris and Sam entered Daniella's bedroom that they'd discovered what had become of the two women.

Daniella had lain facedown beside her bed, her mother just a foot away. A trail of blood marked the path the woman had taken to try and reach her daughter. Both were long dead, murdered by the same government they had sought to protect, for the crime of seeing what Chris and the others truly were.

Looking at them, Chris had struggled to find some emotion for their deaths. It seemed like he *should* feel something, that their deaths should mean something to him. But after watching the vile guards attack Liz, after witnessing Halt's cruelty, after seeing Richard die, it felt as though he had nothing left to give.

Now, Chris wondered how much time they had before someone noticed the women were missing and came looking for them. The apartment had been staged as a home invasion gone wrong—only a giant crack in the television had spared it from disappearing with the rest of the apartment's valuables. Sooner rather than later, they would have to leave this place, though where they would go, he didn't know.

After the news broadcast they'd just seen, nowhere would be safe. They were terrorists now, the instigators of a terrible attack on innocent civilians. Before, a few people might have recognized them from the fugitive reports, but now their faces would be known to everyone in the country.

"What about…my brother?" a small voice croaked.

Chris looked across to where Mira sat on the couch, her grey wings wrapped around her tiny body. She had hardly spoken since fleeing the courthouse, but now she sat up and wiped a tear from her cheek.

"I'm sorry, Mira," Liz whispered as she sat beside the girl. She rubbed her back over her shirt, taking care not to touch skin. "We don't know where he went."

The girl's lip trembled, but she nodded. "They took him from me," she whispered. "I want to make them hurt."

On the floor, Sam chuckled. "Where did you find this girl, Chris?"

Chris smiled. "Don't worry, Mira," he said, "we will. But first, we need to rest."

Mira nodded. She stood and jumped down from the couch and disappeared up the corridor without another word. Chris watched her go, recalling what Sam had told them after the courthouse.

Did you know she was Chead?

It explained everything: how she had known the *Chead* that had escaped the facility, that Hecate was her brother, though he did not remember her. Halt must have separated them, used her to test whether Doctor Fallow's virus could supersede the *Chead* virus. It appeared they had succeeded—for the most part.

Chris shivered, recalling Liz's transformation, how she had almost been lost to the *Chead* rage. Somehow, Ashley had managed to call her back, though Chris feared…

"Does she give anyone else the creeps?" Sam murmured. He

was still staring down the hallway after Mira. "Like, maybe we shouldn't close our eyes around her…"

"Afraid of a little girl, Sam?" A wry smile twisted Liz's lips.

"Little girl or no, she used to be *Chead*," Sam argued.

"Not anymore," Chris said, a little too sharply.

The others looked at him with eyebrows raised, but he only shook his head. His legs suddenly weary, Chris crossed to the sofa and sat carefully next to Liz. His heart sank as she edged away from him, but he suppressed the urge to pull her back.

"Halt cured her," he added finally.

"What about her brother?" Liz murmured. "And the rest of them? If there's a cure…"

"There's not much we can do about it," Chris replied. "Not with the army after us."

"At least it's not Halt." Sam almost spat the words. He glanced at Liz. "Thanks for putting an end to him, Liz."

Liz shrugged, and her eyes remained fixed on the floor. "It was Richard who got us out," she whispered.

They fell silent at that. Guilt swelled in Chris's throat as Richard's face flickered into his thoughts. The boy's emerald eyes shone in the darkness, angry, accusing. They had left him behind, left him to be overwhelmed by the soldiers, to fall to their bullets. In his heart, Chris knew there had been nothing they could have done, that Richard had chosen to sacrifice himself to save them all. But even so…

He shook his head, and his mind drifted again, returning to the cold words of the Director.

Terrorists.

He shivered. The word had terrible connotations. Every man and woman in the Western Allied States would be hunting them now. There would be nowhere to run, nowhere to hide. It was only a matter of time before they were caught. And this time, there would be no cages, no steel collars, no injections. Just a line of soldiers on a stage, a camera in their faces, and the flash of gunfire ushering them into the darkness.

39

Liz let out a long breath as she moved into the corridor. The silence in the living room had become suffocating, and she was glad to escape. Coming to a stop, she leaned her head against the wall. A scream built in her chest, and she clenched her fists, struggling to contain it. Images of the courthouse ran through her mind, over and over, an endless loop she couldn't seem to break.

Halt thrashing in her hands, his face turning red, then purple, his strength slowly trickling away.

The look on Chris's face, the terror in his eyes.

And Richard—brave, stupid Richard—telling her to run, while he turned to face the soldiers.

She shivered, fighting back tears. It was all too much. How could she go on after what had happened, after what she'd done?

Looking at her hands, Liz searched for some hint of a change, some indication of the new power at her fingertips.

Nematocysts.

That was what Halt had called them, the tiny stinger cells that now lined her skin. But even to her enhanced vision, her hands looked as they always had. There was no sign of their deadly nature, of the agony they could unleash with just a touch. She clenched her fists again, feeling a sharp pain as her fingernails dug into her flesh. But that was nothing compared to what Chris had felt when she'd touched him.

Nothing compared to the agony in Halt's face as he died.

Shivering, Liz cast the image aside. She sensed movement from behind her and heard distant voices as the others whispered about setting a watch. After her fight in the courthouse, Liz figured she'd earned a respite from first watch, and quickly moved deeper into the corridor. The door on the right led to Daniella's room, and Liz had no desire to face the horror there. Steeling herself, she moved to the second door through which Jasmine and Mira had escaped, and slipped inside.

Liz paused as the door clicked closed behind her, waiting for Jasmine's anger. When there was no response, she shrugged and looked around. Danny's bedroom was sparsely decorated—the white walls were empty, and the dressing table was bare except for a couple of family portraits. Jasmine lay tucked beneath the blankets of the queen bed, while Mira's smaller figure was curled up at the foot of the bed.

Shaking her head at Mira's strange sleeping preferences, Liz crept across the room and lay down on the other side of the bed from Jasmine. As Liz stared vacantly at the ceiling, she guessed from Jasmine's rigid stillness the other girl was not actually asleep.

Listening to the soft whisper of her friend's breath, Liz searched for something to say, for some words of comfort. Jasmine had been closer to Richard than anyone; the two had been cellmates, had faced the Halt's trials together.

A dull ache began in Liz's back where her wings extended from her spine. Rolling onto her side to face Jasmine, she was surprised to find the other girl staring back at her.

"I can't do it, Liz," Jasmine murmured.

"Can't do what?" Liz whispered back.

Jasmine's eyes were stained red and wet from crying. Sniffing, she used her sleeve to wipe away her tears.

"Go on. Keep running. Keep fighting." She took a breath. "I'm not strong enough. I feel like I'm teetering on a cliff, and without Richard there to hold me, I'll fall."

The image of Richard screaming for them to run flickered into Liz's mind. She shuddered and pushed it away. "But you have to," she replied. "We all do. Otherwise, he died for nothing."

"I never asked him to!" Jasmine sat up suddenly, throwing off the covers. Along her back, her emerald feathers stood on end. "I never wanted him to."

To her surprise, Liz found herself smiling as she thought of the blond boy. They hadn't gotten off to the best start, with herself and Chris getting caught up in the feud between the older prisoners. But since their escape, Liz had come to respect Richard's quiet strength.

"Sometimes we don't get to choose what people do for us," Liz murmured, remembering the sacrifices her parents had made to send her to the private school she'd hated, "but you still have to accept it."

"*I can't!*" Jasmine was standing now, her wings extended, her face a mask of rage. She shook her head. "Don't you get it? He died because of me! Because of everything I said after he fell asleep on watch, because of what I said about family and going back for *you*."

Jasmine slumped to the floor, where she knelt in a pile of ragged clothes and feathers. Liz crouched on the bed beside her, thinking again about the time in the woods, when the soldiers had almost captured them. Only the intervention of the *Chead* had saved them. The incident had left Jasmine shaken, and she'd lashed out at Richard.

"I don't think it was you, Jasmine," she whispered, remembering a conversation she'd had with Richard high in the Californian mountains. It seemed like a lifetime ago now. "I think it was for Jeremy…to repay his sacrifice."

On the floor, Jasmine stilled. She looked up at Liz, her eyes wide. "He told you about Jeremy?"

Liz smiled and nodded. "When we were still in the mountains. He told me what Jeremy did, how he chose to sacrifice himself rather than let Richard fight him."

A sob tore from Jasmine's throat and she tugged at her own

hair. Liz longed to go to her, to pull her grieving friend into her arms, and offer whatever comfort she could. But she hesitated, knowing her touch no longer brought relief, but agony.

"He's really gone, isn't he?" Jasmine said at last.

Liz nodded, her own eyes wet with tears. Jasmine sucked in a breath to steady herself, and then stood. She sat on the edge of the bed, staring into the darkness. A wave of weariness washed over Liz, and closing her eyes, she lay back down.

"He wanted to leave you, you know." Liz's spine tingled as Jasmine spoke. "He said you were gone, that you'd turned, and we should leave. *I* convinced him to stay."

"Jasmine..." Liz whispered.

The girl lay down beside her, her eyes closed. "So it's still my fault. And yours, and Chris's for getting us caught in the first place. And Ashley's for slowing us down, and Sam's for attacking us." Jasmine shivered, and her eyes found Liz's in the darkness. "So why do we all get to live, when he had to die?"

Liz opened her mouth, but her throat was dry, and she couldn't find the words. She managed to croak something unintelligible, then shook her head. There were no answers to Jasmine's question, no reason in this cruel world of theirs. A longing rose inside her, to feel another's embrace, to be held in strong arms and comforted.

Suddenly it was Liz who was crying. The tears came hot and fast, streaming down her cheeks to soak her pillow. She wrapped her arms around herself, but there was no comfort there, no reassurance. Her gut churned and Liz felt an empty hole in the bottom of her stomach as she realized she might never feel the warmth of human touch again.

Then Jasmine's hands were taking her by the shoulders, drawing her close, though she was careful not to touch Liz's skin.

"Liz...I'm so sorry," she heard the other girl whisper.

Liz fought to swallow her sobs, and slowly, slowly, they died away. Finally, she drew in a long breath and looked at Jasmine. Her friend stared back, her tear-streaked face no doubt a mirror of Liz's own. Unexpectedly, she found herself smiling.

"What a mess the pair of us are." She laughed.

Jasmine grinned back, though Liz could still see the emotion welling just beneath the surface. "He'd be pretty pleased if he could see us." Liz shook her head. "A couple of pretty girls crying over him."

The silence resumed then, though it was no longer strained, and Liz found herself drifting off towards sleep. The images returned, flickering in the darkness behind her eyelids—Halt, Chris, Richard.

"What now?" It took a long time for Liz to realize she hadn't dreamed the question.

She struggled to make her mind work. "We stick together."

"How do we stop them?" Jasmine pressed.

An image appear in Liz's mind, of a blond boy soaring through the mountains, a grin on his youthful face. Richard had never believed they could win, that there could be anything for them but a life on the run. Yet in the end, he had sacrificed himself to save them all. She would never forget it.

"We'll find a way." Liz smiled. "Somehow."

40

Sam startled awake as a voice shouted in the darkness. Someone started to thrash beside him, and something hard struck him in the chin. Gasping, he rolled away and tried to sit up, but a feathered limb struck him again, flinging him back.

"*Ashley!*" he shouted. "Ashley, stop, it's okay, it's me, Sam."

A sudden stillness came over the room and Sam let out a long breath. Struggling to his hands and knees, he crawled across to where he'd been lying with Ashley. She sat on her haunches, her amber eyes wide, almost glowing in the darkness. Her white wings caught the light of the distant moon, and Sam could almost believe this was not Ashley at all, but some angel come to take him away.

He shivered and blinked, and she was just Ashley again.

Poor, terrified, Ashley.

He reached out and drew her to him. She crumpled at his touch and he pulled her close, feeling the bones beneath her flesh. Her wings drooped, seeming dull and lifeless now, lacking the spark of a moment before.

"Ash, it's okay, you're safe."

She trembled in his arms. Burying her head in his shoulder, Ashley started to whimper. Gently, he stroked her hair, whispering to her in the darkness, promising her it would be okay, that Halt was gone.

"You guys good?" Chris's voice came from near the door, but Sam waved him back.

"He's coming," Ashley said, pulling away.

Sam shivered. Ashley's eyes were wide open, but they did not seem to see him. She stared into the distance, unblinking, as though still deep in sleep. He lifted a hand and cupped her cheek.

"Who's coming?" he whispered.

"Halt." Her voice was hollow, despairing.

"Oh, Ash." Sam hugged her again, as though his embrace alone could heal her. "He's gone, Ash. He's dead."

At his words, Ashley went limp in his arms. He looked at her face and saw that her eyes were closed now. Holding her carefully, he lowered her back to their makeshift bed of blankets and pulled them tight around her. Then he brushed the hair from her face and kissed her lightly on the forehead.

"Is she okay?" Chris's voice came again.

Nodding, Sam stood. He wouldn't sleep now, not after the abrupt awakening, and he crossed the room and took a seat on the floor across from Chris. The other boy didn't speak for a while, just sat staring at the door, as though there was something fascinating about the way it had been torn free of its hinges.

"It's my fault, you know," Chris said finally. His eyes never left the door.

Sam shook his head. "What do you mean, Chris?"

Chris sighed. "That we were ever here. I…there was a news report, about my mom being executed." His voice cracked at that, but he swallowed and went on. "I lost it. I heard a girl screaming and I didn't even think. I killed the policemen that were attacking her, and she brought us here. But her mom betrayed us, and now…" He waved a hand. "They're dead. Richard is dead."

Sam sat in silence for a while, staring at Chris, watching the dim light of the moon playing across his friend's face. His eyes were harder than the last time Sam had seen them, when he'd bid them all farewell in the mountains. He hadn't expected to see any of them again. He'd given himself up for dead when he'd taken Ashley back to the facility.

Despite everything, Sam found himself smiling. "If you want to think of it that way, Chris, then it's also your fault that we're free. And that Halt's dead." He paused, and guilt touched his chest as he remembered Paul and Francesca. He'd left them behind. "We all have our regrets, Chris. You can't blame every bad thing that happens on your own mistakes."

"But I should have been better," Chris said, bowing his head. "Somehow, somewhere out in those mountains, I became their leader. They trusted me to keep them safe. Instead, I got us all caught, got Richard killed."

Sam sighed, thinking of the headstrong boy he'd first met back in their prison cell. Chris had come a long way since then. "You did the best you could, Chris. But we were never trained for this; at the end of the day, we're just a bunch of teenagers. We're going to make mistakes. But we can't let them stop us. We have to keep moving, keep fighting. Otherwise, they've already won."

Chris nodded. Finally he turned to meet Sam's eyes. "It's good to have you back, Sam." He grinned. "Although I'm sure the President will miss having you as his poster boy."

Sam groaned. "How did you find out about that?"

"I got bored. I figured the TV wouldn't wake you guys up if I put it on mute. The only news bigger than you was us." His smile faded. "Why did you do it? Surely you know…"

"I know," Sam said, cutting him off. His heart twisted and he struggled to keep his voice steady. "Believe me, I know."

"Then why?"

Sam shook his head. "Halt saved her, Chris," he whispered. "Halt saved Ashley—and then threatened to kill her if I didn't help him. He broke her fingers in front of me, and there was nothing either of us could do to stop him. I…I didn't have a choice."

His voice cracked at the end, and he hung his head. Guilt welled in his chest, threatening to drown him. Whatever he said, Sam had known it was wrong—that by helping Halt he was condemning countless others to torture and death. How many other children would they take for their sick experiments, now they'd won the public's support? How many more would die in agony?

"I understand." He looked up as Chris spoke. A frown creased the boy's face. "Is that why Ashley seems so…different?"

"I don't know what he did to her…afterwards," he said. "Halt wouldn't let me see her. Just sent me to teach those two kids what they could do."

"Who were they?"

"The only ones who survived the second strain of the virus," Sam replied, "Paul and Francesca. We weren't…close. But…I shouldn't have left them there, not like that…"

He shivered as he recalled his last glimpse of Paul and Francesca. Ashley had managed to unlock Sam's collar, but the soldiers had appeared before anyone could free the others. They'd left them writhing on the courthouse floor, with however many volts of electricity surging through their bodies.

"There wasn't any time," Chris offered. "We barely made it out of there as it was."

"I know." Sam shook his head. "But I still left them."

Silence fell between them, but as Sam's thoughts began to drift, Chris spoke again. "Do you think she'll be alright?"

Sam looked at the bundle of blankets where Ashley slept, turning the question over and over in his head. In the heat of their escape, Ashley had seemed almost herself. But as the cocktail of drugs and adrenaline in her system faded, she'd grown quiet. By the time they reached this apartment, the lighthearted girl they all knew so well had become withdrawn, her manner silent and jumpy.

"I don't know," he whispered finally. "I hope so. Halt's dead, we all saw him die. He can't haunt her forever."

For a while Chris didn't reply, just sat staring at Ashley. When Chris spoke again, his voice was firm. "She'll be okay." He looked at Sam and smiled. "Hell, she's tougher than any of us. She just needs time to heal."

Sam chuckled and rubbed his neck where the collar had

burned him. "I think we all do," he said. "How long do you think we'll be safe here?"

"Not long enough," Chris mused. "They'll be looking in all the obvious places first, but sooner or later someone will think to check here. Hopefully we'll have tomorrow. It wouldn't be a good idea to go out during daylight. Tomorrow night we should move."

Sam suppressed a groan. "Any thoughts on where..." He trailed off as Chris suddenly raised a hand.

Clamping his mouth shut, Sam turned to stare at the door. For a moment, he thought Chris was being paranoid. Then he heard it—the distant echo of footsteps, coming closer.

As one, Chris and Sam rose to their feet.

It could be anyone, Sam reassured himself. *Just someone returning home late at night.*

The footsteps continued closer. There were four apartments on each floor, with a short corridor and landing shared between them. From what Sam could deduce from the echoes, the footsteps were coming from the stairwell. They slowed as they reached their floor—then picked up pace again as they approached down the corridor outside.

Go past, go past, Sam silently willed the walker.

Abruptly the footsteps ceased.

Right outside their door.

☙ 41 ❧

Susan Faulks shivered as a gust from the air conditioner blew across her neck. Picking up the pace, she strode down the starch-white corridors of the facility, eager to reach the laboratory. She was scheduled for the night shift, and while they were still short on personnel, operations had only grown busier over the past few weeks. The facility was now in full production mode, working to prepare commercial quantities of the PERV-A viral strain. With the mounting *Chead* attacks, the government was advancing its production cycle—imperfections or no.

The remaining geneticists were using blood samples from the failed candidates to refine the virus between reproduction cycles. They hoped to reduce the immunoresponse in hosts by identifying and removing DNA strands in the virus that the human immune system identified as foreign. Susan and the other doctors hoped it would reduce the need for immunosuppressants with future hosts, though they had yet to trial the changes on fresh candidates.

She guessed the government remained hesitant to waste valuable resources on a product with such a low success rate. They certainly would not be risking the lives of WAS soldiers when mortality was so likely. Their only hope was that the next batch of candidates would arrive shortly.

Susan shivered at the thought. She'd arrived at the facility during their last round of testing, and had struggled with the ethics behind the framework. She knew the candidates were already sentenced to death, but she couldn't help but empathize with them. When the viral administration had finally come, it had almost been too much. For weeks, the corridors had stunk of death, as the doctors tried and failed to keep the hosts alive.

Yet in the end, the sacrifice had proven a success. Susan had watched in awe with the other doctors as the two hosts faced off against the *Chead*, and matched the monster blow for blow. Caught up in the excitement, Susan had been honored to administer the final injection to the survivors after their fight. She'd experienced a moment of guilt, when the boy had looked at her with eyes that told her he knew she'd lied, but the results…

She smiled, remembering the sight of wings sprouting from human backs. It was a miracle—a breakthrough beyond anything that had been achieved before. When the virus was perfected, the *Chead* would be resigned to the pages of history.

At the thought of the creatures, Susan shivered. Memories of Fallow's betrayal twisted in her stomach. She still had nightmares about that day, about what the woman she'd thought of as a friend had done to them. Releasing the candidates was one thing—but the *Chead?*

Susan had already retired to her room when the alarms sounded. It was probably the only thing that had saved her. Safe behind the bolted steel door, she had listened to the shriek of the alarm, wondering what disaster it signaled. For a while, she'd thought about going outside, in case a fire was creeping slowly towards her. But the facility protocols were clear: in the event of an alarm, doctors were to return to their quarters and await further instruction.

Those procedures had saved her life.

It hadn't been long before the sirens were replaced by screams. Beyond the safety of her room, the guards had fought bravely, the chirps of their machine guns echoing loudly in the long corridors outside her room. They had managed to kill two of the creatures, before the rest finally fled. But their victory had come at a cost, and by the time they gathered to chase after the escaped experiments, there were few men left standing.

Susan shook herself free of the images she'd seen in the aftermath. Bodies had lain strewn in the corridors, and floors and walls had been stained red with blood. Few of the victims remained in one piece. Even now, the memories made her sick.

Turning down another corridor, Susan silently cursed the size of the facility and the distance between the laboratory and her sleeping quarters. Thankfully, more guards had been brought in now, enough to patrol the outer walls as well as the hallways. She was finally beginning to feel safe again.

She could hear a guard approaching. The light thud of his boots carried around the next corner, drawing closer. Fixing a smile on her face, Susan picked up the pace, wondering who else had drawn the night shift. Knowing the difficulty she'd had when she first arrived, Susan had done her best to befriend the burly newcomers. Though their roles were vastly different, they were all working towards a common cause, and she already knew most of the guards by name.

Turning the corner, Susan opened her mouth in greeting, but the words caught in her throat. She gaped, her heart lurching in her chest as she tried to scream. No sound came out, and clutching a hand to her breast, Susan staggered, unable to tear her gaze from the grey eyes of the boy standing in front of her.

He still wore the orange jumpsuit, but now the fabric was torn and stained brown with mud. His greasy black hair shone in the fluorescent lights. Fresh blood covered his arms and face, congealing beneath his filthy fingernails. A smile twisted his lips as he watched her, unblinking. Sleek muscles rippled along his arms as he took a step.

Susan stood frozen in place, unable to move for her terror as the *Chead* approached. Only as it reached out an arm towards her did she finally snap from the trance. Turning, she tried to flee. She made it three steps before the *Chead* caught her.

42

Chris stared at the doorknob, breath held, waiting for it to turn. Sam crouched beside him, his eyes wide, his lips pressed tight. His ears twitched, catching the distant rattle of a keychain. Chris frowned, glancing again at Sam, and saw the same question in his friend's eyes.

Who would be coming home at this time of night?

The clatter of keys hitting the floor was unbelievably loud in the silence of the apartment, even through the propped-up remnants of their door. Before they could react, the person outside was moving again, the thuds of their boots retreating down the corridor.

Cursing, Chris leapt at the door and hurled it aside. A shout echoed down the corridor as he bounded outside and turned toward the footsteps. Halfway down the hallway a man glanced back, his face pale in the darkness. The stranger's eyes widened, and he tripped over his own legs and fell in his desperation to flee.

Chris sprinted down the corridor as the man struggled back to his feet. He kept his wings tight against his back, his powerful legs closing the distance in seconds. Bounding into the air, he crashed into the man's back and drove him to the ground.

"No, let me go!" The man writhed, struggling to break free.

A fist flashed for Chris's face, but he caught it with ease. Twisting the man's arm behind his back, he cursed as another scream echoed down the corridor. He glanced at the doors to the other apartments, but no sound came from within. Grimacing, Chris rapped his fist on the back of his prisoner's skull. Though he held back, the man slumped to the ground without another sound.

Panting softly, Chris stood and stared down at his victim. The man was still breathing, though he wasn't sure whether that was a good thing or not. He shook his head and dragged the unconscious man back into their apartment. On the way inside, he scooped up the keys his victim had dropped. The number on the tag matched the one beside their broken door. This was his apartment.

Sam waited inside, and as Chris dragged his victim through the doorway, he quickly put the broken door back in place. Little good it had done them—the man had clearly noticed something was wrong. It was only a matter of time before the neighbors realized it, too. Perhaps they already had, and simply didn't care.

Dumping his victim beside the coffee table, Chris looked around the room. The commotion had woken the others, and they now stood around the apartment in various states of shock and fear. Ashley hadn't moved from where she'd been sleeping, but her amber eyes were wide as she stared at the man on the floor. Liz hovered near the doorway, her head tilted as she listened for signs of movement.

Only Jasmine seemed capable of action. Shrugging off Mira's embrace, she strode across the living room and glared down at the intruder.

"Who the hell is this?" she growled.

Without waiting for Chris to answer, she crouched down and began rummaging through the man's pockets.

"He lives here," Chris said warily, holding up the keys to the apartment. "It must be Danny's husband. Didn't she mention something about him being away?"

Sam only shook his head, but Liz nodded. "I forgot. How could we have been so careless?"

Jasmine snorted, then held up a wallet in triumph. She wandered around the room, flicking through the contents. Then she stilled and turned back towards them, a white identification card in her hand.

"He's from the government," she hissed.

"*What?*" Chris and Liz asked as one. Chris glanced at Liz, but she only shook her head and looked away.

Crossing the room, Chris took the card from Jasmine. The face of the man he'd tackled in the hallway stared back at him. His brown hair had been combed flat and he looked a few years younger, but there was no mistaking him. The government ID named him as forty-two-year-old Jonathan Baker.

Chris shivered and handed the card back to Jasmine. "Danny said he was a translator…" he murmured.

"A translator for *them*," Jasmine snapped.

She crouched beside the man again and grabbed a handful of his hair. Tugging back his head, she looked up at them, her lips twisted in a scowl. There was a fire burning in her eyes, and Chris had to steel himself not to look away.

"Let's throw him out the window," Jasmine suggested.

"No," Chris answered. "He's done nothing to us."

"*Yet*," Jasmine snapped. "You want to wait until he does?"

"We can't kill him, not in cold blood." Chris swallowed. "That would only make us as bad as them."

Jasmine gave a dry, rasping laugh. Releasing Jonathan's hair, her hand moved to his throat. "You wouldn't have to get your hands dirty, Chris," she said. "I'll gladly rip out his throat."

"*No*." Chris took a step closer.

"Are you going to stop me, Chris?" Jasmine's eyes flashed. "Are you really defending him? *He works for the government*—the same people who tortured us, who killed Richard."

"So did my parents." Chris looked around as a faint voice came from the pile of blankets. On the floor, Ashley straightened. "They didn't have a choice. They did what they had to, to protect me and my sister." Her voice shook as she finished, but she did not look away.

For a moment, Jasmine didn't move. The veins stood out on her arms, though her hand was still loose around Jonathan's throat. Chris swallowed, knowing she could kill the man long before he reached her.

Finally, she shook her head and sneered. "*He* may not have betrayed us, but remember what *they* did," she said, nodding in the direction of the bedroom. "His wife turned us in." Releasing Jonathan, she stood.

"She didn't know any better," Liz offered. She crossed the room to join them, squaring off against the taller girl. "They thought we were criminals, fugitives. And they paid for what they did with their lives."

Jasmine snorted, but Chris could see some of the rage had gone from her eyes. Liz stretched out a hand and placed it on Jasmine's shoulder, over her t-shirt.

"It's not his fault either, Jas," Liz whispered.

Jasmine's eyes shimmered and she quickly looked away. "What do we do with him then?"

"Let's start by tying him up," Sam offered. He walked to the closet and began rummaging inside. A few minutes later, he emerged holding a spool of thick wool. "Guess this will have to do."

Chris helped Sam secure their prisoner. The girls didn't speak as they worked, and Chris hoped they were thinking of a more long-term plan.

"That should hold him," Sam said, clapping his hands as they finished.

They had bound Jonathan's hands tightly behind his back with the wool, and then jammed a ball of the stuff into his mouth to keep him from crying out. Chris hoped he wouldn't suffocate, although he guessed that would at least solve the problem of his presence.

"The sun will be up soon," Jasmine commented. "If we're not killing him, what are we doing?"

Chris knuckled his forehead, his mind sluggish from lack of sleep. He looked around the room, searching for inspiration, but the plain white walls offered no answers.

"They're all against us now, you know." He looked up as Jasmine spoke again.

"What do you mean?" Chris asked.

"Humanity—the whole damn lot of them." Jasmine looked around. "Hecate was right. After what we saw on the news, they'll *all* be hunting us now."

Chris shivered, but he couldn't find the words to refute her. Shaking his head, he stared at Jonathan, watching his chest slowly rise and fall.

"If he was getting home at this hour, I doubt anyone will be expecting to see him today," Liz said finally. "That means we should be safe here until tonight at least. We won't have to leave during daylight hours."

"So we leave after dark?" Sam asked.

"Maybe…" Liz mused.

Chris looked up at her tone. Liz's eyes were distant as she stared down at the intruder, and Chris waited before pressing her further.

"Liz…" he said finally, "what are you thinking?"

Liz blinked and looked around, her bright blue eyes finding Chris's. For once she did not look away. "We all know what it's like to lose a loved one. He's just lost his whole world—the least we can do is tell him the truth."

"Why would he believe us?" Sam asked.

Chris nodded. Halt's team had cleared the apartment of any evidence of government's presence. The tranquilizer darts had been removed, along with most of the valuables, making it look like a regular break in. He shivered as he realized the same government this man worked for had let him return here, knowing what waited for him. Silently, he wondered how many others had perished like this, murdered to protect the government's dark secrets.

"We have to tell him," Liz continued, "have to make him

believe us. He needs to know what happened, has to know why his wife and daughter are dead."

"Good luck with that one, Liz." Sam gave a halfhearted laugh.

A smile tugged at Liz's lips. "Actually, Sam, I was hoping you would be the one to do it."

43

Sam sighed as he swiveled the wooden chair and sat down. Propping his arms up against its back, Sam watched the man sleep. He still had no idea what he was going to say. Mira leaned against the wall on the other side of the room, her green eye on him, the blue on their guest. Sam carefully kept his gaze averted from the strange girl. Her presence made him uncomfortable, but she had invited herself in, and he wasn't game to throw her out.

On the bed, the man gave a long, drawn-out groan. Sam's heart started to race, and he straightened in the chair. He glanced at Mira, wondering whether he should order her to leave, after all. She only smiled at him and nodded at the bed. Sam saw the prisoner's eyes were open.

The man wriggled slowly backwards on the bed. The task was made difficult with his hands tied behind his back, but reaching the headboard, he managed to sit up. Spitting out the ball of wool, he tried to get to his feet.

Mira gave a low-pitched growl and leapt onto the foot of the bed. Her back arched and her wings snapped open, their grey feathers seeming to fill the room. Sam flinched, but their guest gave a strangled scream, and promptly tumbled off the side of the bed.

"Please!" Jonathan gasped, as Mira towered over him. "We're on the same side!"

Sam raised an eyebrow as he stood. He waved Mira down, struggling to keep the smile from his face. He had to admit, the girl had style.

"And whose side would that be, Jonathan Baker?" Sam asked, moving around the bed to stand over the prisoner.

"The government!" Jonathan gasped. He lay helpless on the floor, his hands still tied behind his back.

"And why would you think we work for the government?" Sam asked.

On the floor, Jonathan blinked. His eyes were wide, and he slowly shook his head. "The…the wings?" he wheezed. "She's got wings…" He frowned. "And you, you're the boy from the press conference, aren't you?"

Sam sighed. He was already regretting letting Liz talk him into this. That was why she'd wanted him to be the one to break the news, of course—because by now, everyone in the Western Allied States knew his face. And they all thought he worked for the government.

"Yes, that was me," he muttered. "I hate to break it to you, but I wasn't there by choice."

Jonathan swallowed. "What do you mean?"

Giving his best attempt at a menacing smile, Sam took a step closer to the translator. "I was a prisoner," he growled, "but I escaped. Question is, now that I'm free, *why should I spare your life?*"

A shiver went through Jonathan then, and he shrank back against the wall. For a second, Sam thought he would beg. Instead, he let out a long breath, and nodded. "So be it." He closed his eyes. "Just don't hurt my girls."

Sam's stomach wrenched and he took an involuntary step back. Silently he slumped into the chair. It took a moment for Jonathan to look back up. When he did, his shoulders drooped, and there was a tremor to his voice when he spoke again. "Where are they, my family? *Where are Danny and Daniella?*"

Sam nodded at the bed. "Why don't you make yourself comfortable."

For a second, Jonathan didn't move. He lay staring up at Sam, his face twisted with hate and pain, before finally clambering to his feet. A low growl came from Mira's throat as he stepped towards Sam, and he stilled again.

"I wouldn't," Sam said softly, nodding to Mira, "she used to be *Chead*."

The man's eyes widened, and he glanced quickly at Mira, as though to reassure himself her eyes weren't actually grey. Sam could see him weighing his options, deciding whether to make a break for it or not.

"We're not going to hurt you," Sam murmured. "Just sit down and listen to what I have to say."

Jonathan gave one last glare, then sat down on the bed.

"Where are they?" he repeated.

Sam sighed. "First, tell me what you do for the government."

The man's eyes hardened, but he gave a grim nod. "I'm a translator," he grated. "I've been away on business, helping with our ambassador in Mexico. *Now, tell me where my wife and daughter are!*"

Mira growled and spread her wings as he raised his voice, but Sam waved her down. His heart ached, and he could barely bring himself to say the words.

"They're dead," he croaked. "I'm sorry."

At Sam's words, the fight seemed to drain from Jonathan. He went limp against the mattress and turned his face away, but not before Sam glimpsed the tears in his eyes. His heart ached for the man.

"How?" Jonathan whispered.

Silently, Sam returned to his chair. He closed his eyes and took a breath, before recounting the story, the one the others had told him. How they had met his daughter, Daniella, when she'd been waylaid in an alleyway by policemen, how she had brought them back to the apartment as thanks for their help, how Danny had cleaned Chris's gunshot wound. And how Danny had finally recognized them, and called the police.

"So you killed her?" There was anger in Jonathan's voice again.

"No," Sam whispered. He caught the fury in Jonathan's eyes, but he didn't look away. "When the SWAT team came, they were led by a man named Doctor Halt. You know him—he stood beside me during the President's speech. After they captured my friends, he ordered your wife and daughter to be killed, so there would be no witnesses to the escape of his precious experiments."

"No," Jonathan whispered. "That's not possible. We have laws—"

"They don't apply to people like Halt," Sam cut in. "They don't apply to the powerful, not anymore."

Jonathan stared at him for a long moment, and then bowed his head. Silence fell, and Sam wondered if he and Mira should leave the man to his grief. He was just preparing to stand when Jonathan spoke again.

"Where are they now?" he asked.

Sam paused. "They're…they're in Daniella's room."

"Can I see them?" Jonathan looked up at him, his eyes wet with tears.

"I'm not sure that's a good idea…" Sam said.

"Please," Jonathan begged.

Sam let out a long breath and closed his eyes. He didn't want to see what waited in that room. One glance had been enough. But who was he to deny a father, a husband, one last chance to say goodbye to his family?

He nodded. "Let's go."

44

Liz let out a long sigh as she sank onto the couch. Closing her eyes, she leaned back against the cushions. Her heart was only just beginning to slow. The sound of the front door crashing open had torn her from her sleep, and springing up, she'd raced into the living room, expecting to see soldiers charging into the apartment.

Instead, she'd found Sam standing defensively in the lounge, watching as Chris dragged an unconscious man through the front door.

Now the dull ache of her body was worse than when she'd gone to bed, and she wanted nothing more than to curl up and return to the land of dreams. Her conversation with Jasmine had left her drained, and she hadn't even begun to recover from the fight in the courthouse. But Jasmine and Ashley were still sitting at the propped-up kitchen table, and no one else seemed to want to sleep.

The cushions shifted beneath her as someone else sat on the couch. Liz cracked open her eyes to find Chris next to her, his hazel eyes watching her. Suppressing a groan, she rolled onto her side, turning her back to him. Exhausted as she was, she didn't have the energy to face him just then.

"Liz..." Chris whispered.

Feeling his hand on her shoulder, she shrugged it off and glanced back at him.

"What?" she snapped with more force than intended.

Chris flinched, and she saw the hurt in his eyes. At that moment, she didn't care. All she wanted was to curl up in his arms and fall asleep—but she couldn't. Fueled by that knowledge, her anger caught light.

"What do you want, Chris?" she pressed when he didn't answer her question.

His eyes hardened then, and he stood suddenly. "Nothing." He moved away.

Liz's rage died in her chest as Chris walked across the apartment to stand at the broken window. She wanted to call him back, to apologize and tell him how much she was hurting. But the words caught in her throat, and finally she slumped back on the couch and buried her head in the cushions.

A few minutes later she heard the door to the hallway click open. She carefully wiped away her tears before looking up at Sam. His face was grim, and he did not meet her eyes. Ashley stood and went to him, her white wings stretching out to embrace him. Running a hand through his hair, she stood on her toes and kissed him on the cheek.

"How did it go?" Ashley whispered.

"Did he believe you?" Liz added.

Sam looked from Ashley to Liz, then shook his head. "I don't know," he said, his tone unusually sober. "He was in shock, I think."

Liz shivered. "Who wouldn't be?" She glanced at Jasmine, wondering if the girl would press her case again. Sitting at the table, Jasmine caught Liz's gaze, but she only snorted and shook her head.

"Mira's watching him?" Chris asked as he moved away from the window.

Outside, the sun had just begun to stain the skyline. It was overcast, and the buildings she could see looked dull and lifeless.

Sam crossed to the table and sank into one of the chairs.

Ashley sat beside him as he nodded. "She's keeping him company. He's…with his family. I couldn't…" His voice trailed off, but Liz didn't need to ask him what he meant.

Glancing at the door to the hall, she swallowed. Former *Chead* or not, she didn't envy Mira's position. She saw again the eyes of the dead women staring up at her, the broken body of the girl Chris had saved, and shuddered.

"So, where are we going?" Chris asked.

Liz shook her head. She was out of ideas. In truth, there were only a few options. They could escape to the countryside, where they might avoid detection for months, or even years. The countryside was her home, and it would not be difficult to scavenge enough food to feed them. But if they retreated to the wilderness, they would be surrendering, giving in to the government's corruption.

After Richard's sacrifice, that was no longer an option. His death hung over them like a lead cloak, demanding justice, requiring retribution. They could not leave everything behind, could not pretend the fight in the courthouse had never happened.

"I don't know," she said finally. "I don't even know how we're going to navigate in the dark."

Sam was resting his head against the table, but he stirred at her words. "I can help with that," he said, smiling. "I might be a bit of an urbanite, but my father taught me a few things. Once we get beyond the city lights, I can use the stars to point us in the right direction. If that's where we decide to go, anyway."

"Well that's something," Jasmine murmured. She was leaning back in her chair, but her eyes had taken on a strange intensity. "I've been thinking…if no one has any better ideas, what if we went back to the facility?"

Liz lurched upright on the couch. "You can't be serious?"

Climbing to her feet, Jasmine shrugged. "Why not?" she asked, making her way across the room. "There's nothing for us here in San Francisco—not with the whole city out to get us. But even with Halt gone, someone is bound to pick up where he left off. They certainly won't have any lack of funding after your little display, Sam."

Sam cursed and climbed to his feet. Hands on the table, he glowered at Jasmine. "What did you say?"

Jasmine sneered as she faced off against him. Liz struggled up from the couch, remembering now the bad blood between the two. Her muscles screamed in protest as she stood.

"You heard me, Sam," Jasmine said slowly. "How could you do it? How could you support him? How many other kids like us have you sentenced to death?"

Liz quickly stepped between them as Sam stalked around the table, his face dark with fury.

"Stop that," Liz snapped, "both of you. Don't we have enough problems without fighting amongst ourselves?"

When neither of them answered, she turned to face Jasmine. "We've all done things we regret, Jasmine," she whispered. "Things we had no choice about."

"I didn't want to do it, Jasmine," came Sam's voice from behind her. She glanced back and saw the fight had gone from his eyes. "If it had just been me, I would have died before I helped him…"

Beside him, Ashley went rigid. A wave passed across her face and her lip trembled. Her eyes glimmered, but whatever she was feeling, she swallowed it down. Liz's heart went out for her—for the pain she must have felt, being helpless against Halt while he used her to get to Sam.

"Am I interrupting something?" a voice called.

Liz jumped, and the five of them turned as one towards the voice. They stared as Mira wandered into the room. The stranger Chris had knocked out was now standing behind her in the doorway to the corridor. His eyes travelled over the room, taking in each of them in turn, lingering on their half-folded wings. Safe in their own company, they hadn't bothered to cover them. Though his eyes were red, there was no sign of tears on his face now.

Swallowing visibly, the man looked back at Sam. "So…it's true. You all have wings…"

Sam shrugged and the rest of them nodded reluctantly. The newcomer shivered and lowered his eyes. "So the rest must be true as well," he said grimly. "What he said about where you came from, what they did to you…and my family?"

Chris slumped onto the arm of the sofa. "I'm sorry about Danny and Daniella."

Jonathan closed his eyes as Chris spoke their names, and Liz could see the effort it took him to maintain his composure. Sucking in a breath, he looked at them again, his lips drawn tight.

"I knew what they were capable of." His voice shook. "I just never…I never thought it would happen here, to my own family, on our own soil."

Liz frowned. "What do you mean?"

"During my travels with our ambassadors, I've…seen things, heard things. Even our traditional allies now question our methods. I've just returned from Mexico. Their president is concerned with the recent arrests carried out by the Department of Domestic Affairs."

"Some pretty legitimate concerns, it turns out," Sam muttered.

Liz nodded. They had all been victims of that program, along with the countless others who hadn't survived the project. Abducted in the night, their parents accused of treason, there had been no trial, no jury, just judgement. They'd been spirited away to a facility deep in the Californian mountains, never to be seen again—if not for the conscience of Doctor Fallow. Liz still woke screaming most nights, remembering the horrors they'd been subjected to.

"Yes, well, during my last trip, the Mexican government all but accused our ambassadors of using the war against terror as a cover to remove those who opposed our government."

"And you did nothing with that information?" Jasmine growled, stepping towards him.

Jonathan's eyes widened and he raised his hands. "What was I meant to do with it?" he asked. "Believe me, I've heard worse accusations brought against us over the years. Hell, I've seen things that would have people rioting in the streets. But who was I going to tell?"

"The media?" Liz suggested, without conviction.

Jonathan snorted. "The media are bought and paid for by the rich—who go hand-in-hand with the government. They have a very…narrow agenda."

Liz and the others nodded. That was no surprise. While not officially controlled by the government, like most assets in the country, the media had been consolidated and bought out decades ago. And the once popular social media was no longer an option. After ceding from the United States, the WAS had been determined to avoid the decay that had consumed their former nation. Fake news dispersed over social media had been identified as a key contributor. Taking a page from China's book, the government had erected a nationwide firewall to block the platforms. And these days…well, it was rare to have even an old desktop, let alone the internet.

"So what will you do now?" Chris asked. "Will you still go on as though nothing has happened?"

Jonathan shivered, and Liz caught a glimmer in his eyes as he looked away. He stared at the wall, as though he could see straight through it, to where his wife and child lay in an endless sleep.

"Now…" Jonathan croaked, "now it's too late, isn't it? I thought if I behaved, if I did what they asked and turned a blind eye, that my family would be safe."

He faced them again, jaw clenched, his red-stained eyes sweeping across the room. "I want to hurt them," he grated. "I want to make the ones who did this pay."

Liz's heart hammered against her ribcage as she looked into his eyes and saw the rage there, the untapped hatred.

"How?" she asked.

Jonathan sucked in a breath, and the tension left him. A smile touched his lips. "That's the thing, isn't it?" He shook his head. "How do you bring down a government?"

"We've been wondering the same thing," Chris answered. "It's not an easy task, with the world against you."

"You need allies," Jonathan replied. "You need a movement, need people who will stand with you against your enemies."

Jasmine snorted. "Let us know when you find them."

Jonathan's smile widened. "It just so happens, I already have."

45

Susan gasped as the *Chead* shoved her backwards into the laboratory. Her feet tripped on the slick floor and she went crashing down onto the linoleum. The impact drove the breath from her lungs, and choking, she scrambled away, trying to put as much space between herself and the *Chead* as possible.

Cold laughter chased her across the room. Finding herself in a corner, Susan looked back at the creatures, the cold fingers of terror clutching at her throat. They stood in the doorway watching her but made no effort to give chase.

Swallowing a scream, she struggled to get a grip on her fear. Her heart was racing, and panic had set in long ago, robbing her of reason. She sucked in a long, shuddering breath, and felt a little better.

Where did they come from? How did they get in?

Crouched in the corner, she stared up at them, struggling to make sense of the nightmare. Two more *Chead* had joined the first. They stood barring the only exit, their clothes stained with mud and blood. They whispered amongst themselves, but Susan couldn't make out the words over the pounding in her ears.

They went silent as she started to stand, their grey eyes turning to watch her. She stilled, but when they made no move towards her, she straightened the rest of the way. A quick glance around the lab confirmed her fear. There was only one panic button in this room—the one on the wall beside the doorway, right behind the *Chead.*

"Hecate..." Susan jumped as a fourth *Chead* appeared in the doorway. "The others are...secure."

The *Chead* that had abducted her turned towards the newcomer. "Good." A smile touched the creature's lips. "Bring them here...and send word...to Talisa. It is safe...for her."

The other creatures nodded and disappeared back into the corridor, leaving Susan alone with three again. Standing in the corner, she shivered as a memory tugged at her.

Hecate.

The name was familiar. It stuck in her mind, ringing through the vaults in her memory. And all of a sudden she knew where she'd seen the creature before, where it had come from.

It had been on her first day in the facility, when Angela Fallow had shown her the *Chead* they kept imprisoned. The doctor had explained how before her time, Halt's earliest viral strains had failed. Their minds overwhelmed by the physiological changes, the subjects had gone insane, mimicking the same phenotypes as those infected with the *Chead* virus. Hecate had been the name of one of the creatures, from before the change. But how...how did it remember?

And why had they returned?

A low groan came from Susan's throat, and the creature's eyes flicked in her direction. She sank back to her knees as it padded towards her. It looked down at her for a moment, before crouching beside her.

She wrapped her arms around her chest and looked away, but iron fingers grabbed her by the chin, forcing her to look into its stony eyes.

"Such fearful creatures." Hecate's words were mocking. "There is such...terror within you."

Tears burned Susan's eyes. "Please," she croaked, "don't hurt me."

A dry, rasping laughter came from the *Chead.* Its nostrils

flared as it studied her. "You are…new." Its grin spread. "Perhaps you will…help me?"

Susan nodded, grasping for the lifeline. "Yes! Whatever you want! Just…don't hurt me."

The laughter came again. They were in one of the laboratories, where the benches were crowded with various machines and tubes. Some were still whirring gently on the benchtop as they finished their cycles. Susan wondered where the doctor in charge was, before noticing the pool of blood seeping out from behind one of the benches.

"Where is our…" The creature frowned, pausing as if in thought. "Where is our…creator?"

"Creator?" Susan asked, her voice cracking with her terror. "I don't…I don't understand."

The *Chead* growled. Before she could react, it caught her by the throat. With its immense strength, the *Chead* hauled her up, and slammed her back against the wall. She gasped, struggling to inhale as it began to squeeze.

"Please…" she managed to whisper. Darkness swirled at the edges of her vision.

Without warning, Hecate released her. She crumpled to the ground. Eyes watering, Susan coughed, gasping as life-giving oxygen flooded her lungs.

"Tell me…" Hecate growled. "Where…is that which… created us?"

On her hands and knees, Susan looked up at the creature, her oxygen-starved mind struggling to process its demand. Slowly the cogs turned, and she shuddered, realizing there was only one thing the *Chead* could mean.

"The virus?" she whispered. "You want the virus…that made you?"

The creature's smile returned. "Yes…"

Susan nodded. "We…we have some…we have some in storage, I think," she stammered.

"Take me."

"Okay." Using the wall for support, Susan carefully climbed

to her feet. She looked at the creature and took another breath, then nodded to the doorway. "It's that way."

Laughter rasped from the creature's throat as it stepped aside to let her pass.

The virus storage facility wasn't far. Her legs trembling, Susan moved quickly past the other *Chead* and out into the corridor. Hecate followed close on her heels, and they made their way down the long corridors without incident.

A few minutes later, Susan drew to a stop outside a heavy metal door. She glanced at the *Chead*, wondering whether to say she didn't have the key, but one look in its grey eyes was enough to drop the thought. Reaching into her pocket, she retrieved her key card and unlocked the door. Air hissed as the lock released, and she stepped inside. The *Chead* followed her before she could slam it shut behind her.

Within, they found themselves in a small airlock facing a second door. There was a basin on the wall that was used for scrubbing down after trips inside, and shower heads in the ceiling were used in the case of accidental exposure. Fortunately, the viral samples they worked with were not airborne, and could only be transmitted through ingestion. That was how they believed the *Chead* virus had been spread through the nation—by deliberate contamination of food supplies. Texas was the lead suspect, although the Western Allied States were not short of enemies.

Susan moved to the second airlock and pushed the door open. Beyond, the air was cold, carrying with it the strong scent of bleach. The walls were lined with freezer drawers where they stored the various strains of the virus. Each drawer was color-coded for the generation of virus and labeled with the individual strain. Most drawers were filled with the PERV-A strain they had been replicating for the last few weeks, but in the corner, she could see the red label that marked the earlier, failed version of Fallow's virus.

"*Where?*" Susan jumped as the creature whispered in her ear.

Swallowing, she crossed to the freezer and pulled open the drawer. Inside, tray upon tray of little glass vials shone in the overhead lights. Each contained a single dose of the virus. They had been frozen in liquid nitrogen before storage and would remain viable so long as they remained that way.

She looked up as Hecate joined her. "This is the virus that created you," she croaked. "It needs to be kept frozen."

"How…is it moved?"

Susan swallowed, her eyes drawn to the portable refrigerators in the corner of the room. She nodded at them. "We…we send shipments sometimes…to other laboratories. Those…steel boxes are portable freezers. Their batteries will last twenty-four hours..." She trailed off as Hecate leaned down to study the vials in the drawer.

"PERV-ALPHA," it growled. "What is that?"

"It's…it's…the name for the virus you were given." Susan stammered. "They…it's infectious when ingested, or injected into the blood supply," she rambled on, eager to fend off more questions.

She fell silent as the grey eyes shifted back to her. A shiver ran through her and she took a quick step back, suddenly realizing how close she was to the creature. It caught her wrist, holding her in place. She tried to squirm free, but it pressed forward, pinning her against the freezer.

"You said…you said you'd let me go!" Tears blurred Susan's vision as a scream built in her throat.

"Did I?" The *Chead's* eyes bored into hers.

It leaned towards her, its nostrils flaring. She fought harder to break free, but its weight crushed her against the cold steel, leaving her with nowhere to go. The creature began to laugh, its eyes dancing with amusement at her feeble struggles. The sound wrapped around her, and Susan could contain her panic no longer.

She tried to scream, but a hand clamped down over her mouth, cutting off her cries. Staring up into the dark eyes, Susan fought to breathe, but its hand had blocked her nose as well. She gave another muffled shriek, but it was hopeless. The strength slowly fled her body, until her legs gave way, and the darkness came welling up to claim her.

46

Chris's eyelids were drooping by the time he finally staggered down the corridor towards the bedroom. The conversation in the living room had gone on for hours, until in their exhaustion they began to repeat themselves. By then, the morning had crept into the afternoon, and Chris was well beyond the point of caring. He had hardly slept in forty-eight hours, and now he could barely keep his feet.

The problem with which they were all struggling was whether they could trust Jonathan. They had already been betrayed once —by his wife—and while they'd torn the phone out of the kitchen wall, Chris still couldn't quite bring himself to believe that this wasn't all some elaborate trap.

The second problem was the nature of the allies he had proposed they approach.

The Madwomen.

He shook his head, wondering if they were mad themselves to even consider the idea. How could a group of old women—however great their courage—help Chris and the others bring down the entire government? If Jonathan was right, they had managed to avoid retribution so far, but Chris doubted that could last. Especially if word got out that the fugitives had contacted them.

In the end, they had decided to visit the Madwomen's protest the next morning. Chris had agreed more out of exhaustion than anything. With that finally settled, they had drifted off to bed, one by one. He'd caught Jasmine's announcement that she and Mira would keep an eye on the "prisoner," but by then he was too tired to care. Hopefully Jonathan could survive a few hours in their tender care.

Pushing open the door to the spare bedroom, he moved to the bed and threw himself down on the soft mattress. Breathing in, he caught a whiff of Liz's scent from the pillows and suppressed a groan. The look she'd given him earlier had been one of pure venom, and had left him regretting ever opening his mouth. He should have let her rest.

The door creaked and looking up, he was surprised to see her slip into the room. She stilled when she saw him, her mouth opening, one hand still on the door handle. An awkward silence followed, and Liz shifted on her feet, clearly anxious.

"I'm sorry." The words tumbled from her mouth in a rush.

Chris tilted his head to the side. "For what?" He forced a smile.

Liz shook her head and closed the door the rest of the way. "For snapping at you," she said, sitting on the corner of the bed. Her tone was flat. "For pushing you away."

Chris's heart pounded hard against his chest. Liz sat looking away from him, her black wings hanging loosely to either side of her. He could sense the distance separating them, the gulf that had opened up in the corridors beneath the courthouse. He knew she was suffering, though Liz had said nothing about what had happened to her since their escape. She hadn't even mentioned Halt, or how her very touch had burned his life away.

"Liz…" he whispered. Reaching out a hand, he stroked the small of her back where it was covered between her wings. "Liz, you haven't pushed me away. I'm right here…"

She flinched at his touch, but after a moment she relaxed, and he trailed his fingers up and down, taking care not to touch her skin. Shivering, she looked back at him, her blue eyes wide, and he saw the walls come tumbling down. Tears filled her eyes as she bit back a sob.

"Chris..." she gasped, "I'm sorry. I'm sorry. I miss you..."

"I'm right here, Liz," he repeated.

She only shook her head and looked away again. She was still trembling beneath his fingers, and he could sense the tension in her body, as though she might flee at any moment.

"I'm scared," she whispered after a few minutes had passed. When she looked back at him, her cheeks were streaked with tears, and Chris had to fight the urge to reach out and wipe them away. "I'm afraid I'll hurt you."

Somehow, Chris found himself smiling. Perched on the corner of the bed, her curly black hair in tangles, her broad wings wrapped around her shoulders and her knees tucked underneath her, Liz was a mess. But in that moment, he realized how much he loved her. He loved her fierce nature, her fire and courage and determination, even when all seemed lost. Seeing her like this, vulnerable and afraid, finally shook him from his own fear.

Taking a breath, he reached out and wiped the tears from Liz's cheek. Her eyes widened, but he did not take his hand away. Instead, he trailed his fingers across her skin and up through her hair, until he cradled her head in his hand. Staring into her eyes, he waited.

It started as a slight tingling in the tips of his fingers, but it did not take long to spread. Pinpricks danced along his arm, as though tiny needles were stabbing him. The sensation grew hotter as it reached his chest. He gritted his teeth as the flames swept through him, determined to hold on as long as he could. Finally, he could take it no longer, and he carefully removed his hand and closed his eyes.

Gulping in another breath, Chris struggled to control himself as the venom spread through his system. His body started to shake, and despite the fire dancing in his chest, he felt cold. The pain swept through him like the incoming tide, washing away his resistance, until he was panting hard just to keep himself from screaming.

Then Liz's hand was on his shoulder, squeezing gently through his t-shirt. Opening his eyes, he saw her beside him, her eyes shining. He forced a smile, trying to reassure her, to let her know he was okay.

A few minutes later, the pain began to recede, and he managed a more convincing grin. Liz offered a tentative smile back, and slowly shook her head.

"Chris..." she said. "Why did you do that?"

"To show you I could." He looked her in the eye, fighting the urge to kiss her. "Because I love you."

Liz's eyes watered and she closed them. Though she didn't say anything, he could feel the distance between them shrink, could sense the change in her.

"Think there's room for one more on that bed?" she asked finally.

Chris smiled and nodded. He wriggled over as far as he could as she slid beneath the blankets. With the remnants of the venom still sweeping through his system, he no longer felt the cold, so he stayed above the covers, where there was less risk of receiving a second, accidental dose. Rolling on his side, he allowed his wings to unfold as he looked at Liz.

"What?" she asked when she saw him watching her. Laughter bubbled up from his chest. Liz had tucked the duvet up to her chin, leaving only her head exposed and no covers for him. Her hair tumbled out across the pillow, and her big eyes stared up at him innocently. "You didn't want any, did you?"

"No," he replied with a grin. "Just...it's good to have you back."

A smile passed across her lips, and a gentle silence stretched out. This time there was no tension between them, and Chris's mind drifted. He thought again about their plan, but he still couldn't feel any enthusiasm for it. The Madwomen might be goodhearted and well-meaning, but what good was that against their enemies? Halt might be gone, but the Director was no less terrifying. If anything, he was afraid she might prove even more ruthless than the despicable doctor.

"What are you thinking about?" Liz whispered.

Chris jumped and looked at her, but her eyes were still closed. He sighed.

"I was thinking we're as insane as these so-called Madwomen."

Her eyes fluttered open. "Maybe," she said, "maybe not. Only time will tell. But at least we know one thing."

"Oh? And what's that?"

"I was right," she murmured, her smile spreading, "about telling Jonathan the truth. You should listen to me more often."

Shaking his head, Chris raised his hands in mock surrender. "Alright Liz, you were right. You can be the leader from now on."

"Good." Liz nodded solemnly. "My first order of business is to make you stop hogging the blankets."

So saying, she yanked the blankets out from underneath Chris, sending him tumbling from the bed in a pile of limbs and tangled feathers.

❧ VI ❧

SALVATION

47

Sam glanced left and right before he crossed the street, then pulled his hood tighter around his face. His wings tingled beneath the heavy folds of his jacket, and a tremor ran up his spine at the thought of unseen eyes watching him. The others pressed in close around him, their faces down, hidden beneath matching hoods. Together they struggled to make headway along the crowded San Francisco sidewalks.

Ahead, Chris walked with Jonathan. They were keeping a close eye on the translator. Despite the man's talk of fighting back, the others still didn't trust him. Sam could hardly blame them after what they'd been through. But they had not seen the man's face when Sam had shown him the bodies of his wife and daughter.

He shivered, remembering the sound Jonathan had made, a shrill, primal moan that seemed to rumble up from his very soul. The man had dropped to his knees beside the bed where his family lay and reached for his daughter's cold grey hand. After witnessing his grief, Sam could not believe the man would betray them now.

A gust of wind caught Sam's hood and almost tore it off. Snapping himself back to the present, he quickly pulled it down and then looked sidelong at the other pedestrians to make sure no one had noticed. A woman strode past without breaking stride, her eyes on her watch as she struggled through the crowd. No one else was looking in their direction, and he breathed a sigh of relief.

Returning his attention to the pavement, he chased after the others. They were close now, and looking up he caught a glimpse of the marble and granite obelisk rising from the top of the hill.

Independence Square.

He had only visited the memorial once, when his father had brought him to San Francisco as a child. They had sat beneath the towering obelisk and read some of the names inscribed in the stone. They were the names of those who had fought for the Western Allied States in the American War, the soldiers who had won them their freedom. The inscriptions stretched from the base of the obelisk all the way to the top, some seven hundred feet above.

They numbered in the hundreds of thousands.

None of his immediate family had fought in the war, but his father had still insisted on bringing Sam there. He had wanted Sam to know the price their young nation had paid to survive, wanted him to understand the weight of sacrifice that had bought their freedom.

Now Sam found himself wondering how many more names needed to be added to the obelisk.

How many did you murder, Halt, in your quest for perfection?

By the time they reached the top of the hill, Jonathan was puffing hard, and Sam couldn't help but grin. He'd found the forty-minute walk through San Francisco invigorating, but he guessed the rolling hills were not so easy for those without their genetic adaptations.

Keeping his hood low, he took a moment to study their surroundings while Jonathan caught his breath. The towering buildings had opened out, giving way to the wide park square that marked the spiritual center of San Francisco. The pale stone obelisk stretched up into the sky, towering over the dense trees and shrubbery ringing the park. There were no signs of disturbance, but the wall of greenery hid the open courtyard at the base of the obelisk.

"Bit out of shape are you, Jonathan?" Sam laughed when their guide finally straightened.

Jonathan only shook his head and nodded at the obelisk. "The Madwomen gather in the courtyard every morning, from what I've heard. The government has been trying to keep their presence under the radar, but word is slowly spreading."

"The news hasn't been covering their protests?" Ashley asked, frowning.

Jonathan shrugged. "Once or twice. That's where they came up with 'The Madwomen.' I guess someone was trying to make a joke out of them."

"Well, let's go see what we're dealing with." Liz walked out onto the road as the pedestrian light turned green.

Sam and the others followed her, and together they made their way into the square. Stepping onto the narrow path leading through the trees, Sam paused, thinking again of his father and the time they had visited San Francisco. The memory felt like someone else's, like a glimpse into some other life.

How long had it been since he'd been taken? Since his father had been arrested for treason, and Sam had found himself locked away in a cage beneath the mountains? What would his father think of him now if he still lived, after everything he'd done?

I did what I had to.

The thought did nothing to fill the emptiness in his chest.

Within a few minutes, the trees opened out again, revealing the full expanse of Independence Square. Stone tiles covered the ground in a five-hundred-foot circle around the obelisk. The colors varied from blue to black to red, and when viewed from above, they created a giant mosaic of a blood red sunrise. But just then, only a small collection of tiles was visible beneath the crowd that had gathered.

The Madwomen.

Sam shook his head, not sure whether to laugh or cry. Jonathan had told the truth—that much was certain. The women had gathered in the center of the square, their faces lined with age, their bodies withered by the cruel passage of time. They held no placards or megaphones, and they were silent as they made their way around the base of the obelisk. Many wore the faded army uniforms and shining medals of their fallen husbands.

A tremor went through Sam as he watched their slow progression. Though they made no sound, their message was clear to all who watched. And people were watching. They stood around the edges of the park, hundreds of wide-eyed onlookers, drawn here by the whispers spreading through the city. They had come to see the spectacle, to watch the women who dared stand in defiance of the government.

Despite his despair, Sam couldn't help but admire the women's courage. They might not have the power or influence to bring down the President or the Director, but here they were anyway. Here they stood, in open defiance of the powers that ruled them, with only the honor of their fallen loved ones to protect them.

Watching them, Sam could almost bring himself to hope things might change, that they might have a chance after all.

Almost.

He looked up as a shout carried across the square. Beyond the Madwomen, the crowd was drawing back, retreating before the thud of marching boots. A cold fist wrapped around Sam's chest as he glanced at the others. Before anyone could move, Jasmine leapt forward and caught Jonathan by the front of his shirt.

"You betrayed us!" she hissed.

"No!" Jonathan gasped as her fingers reached for his throat. "This wasn't me!"

Jasmine looked at them, her eyes alight with fury, and even Sam was loath to interfere. He glanced at the oncoming soldiers and then back the way they'd come. But the trees were empty, and he shook his head at Jasmine.

"They're not here for us," he said softly, "or we'd already be surrounded."

For a moment, he thought Jasmine would ignore him. Jonathan was standing on his toes to keep her grip around his collar from strangling him.

"Jasmine," Chris said, "put him down, before someone notices."

Chris's warning seemed to cut through Jasmine's rage, and snorting, she released the translator without any further argument. Jonathan coughed and bent in two, and Sam moved across and patted him on the back.

"Sorry, she's a bit jumpy," he offered.

Jonathan straightened. "They're probably here for the Madwomen." He glanced at them as he spoke. "After the attack on the courthouse, public gatherings have been banned."

"What will they do?" Ashley asked.

Hearing the tremor in her voice, Sam reached out and took her hand. His heart twisted as she glanced at him and he saw the fear in her eyes. The thudding of boots echoed loudly in the square now, seeming to come from all around. Beneath the obelisk, the Madwomen had drawn to a stop and stood watching the approaching soldiers. They made no move to flee as men in tidy green uniforms pushed through the onlookers and drew to a halt in front of them.

A woman in a suit strode forward through the ranks of soldiers. She moved with purpose, possessed of an unwavering confidence. The men parted before her like the red sea before Moses, eager to avoid the hard look in her eyes. Her thin lips twisted into a frown as she stopped at the head of the soldiers and studied the old women around the obelisk. The look on her face suggested she thought it beneath her just to stand in their presence.

Which probably wasn't far from the truth. There was no mistaking the Director of Domestic Affairs, and Sam nervously pulled his hood tighter around his face. This was the woman who had called them terrorists—the person tasked with bringing them to justice.

The Director placed her hands on her hips and slowly shook her head.

"What would your husbands think?" she spoke in a soft voice, but Sam heard her easily from across the square. "To see the lot of you standing here, undermining the nation they gave their lives to defend? And while we are in the middle of a crisis?" She shook her head again.

A soft whisper went through the Madwomen, but for a long moment, it looked like they would not respond. Then a woman stepped from the group. She wore a faded green uniform, and on her chest a silver cross gleamed. She stood with her shoulders held high and stared down the Director. From beside him, Sam heard someone gasp, but the old woman was already speaking.

"Who are *you* to talk of our husbands' sacrifices?" she asked, her voice firm. "Who are you to ask what they would think of us?"

For a second, the Director's mask slipped, and Sam saw the fury in her eyes. "I am the Director of Domestic Affairs, second only to—"

"You are a liar and a murderer," the woman said, interrupting the Director's words. She spread her arms to indicate the women behind her. "*We* are the Western Allied States. *We* are what our husbands fought for, what they gave their lives for."

The Director was shaking her head again. "This cannot continue," she said, pursing her lips. "Disperse, now. Or you will force me to act."

A smile flickered across the old woman's face as she crossed her arms. "We aren't going anywhere. Touch us if you dare."

"So be it," the Director snapped. "Men, take these women into custody."

"*No!*" Sam spun as Chris shouted out behind him.

Before anyone could react, Chris charged. Sam lunged after him, trying to drag him back, but Chris was already tearing off his jacket. His tawny brown wings snapped open, and in a single bound he was airborne. The *thump* of his wings echoed across the square as he raced towards the Madwomen.

"*Chris!*" Sam swore as Liz leapt past and raced after Chris.

"About time," Jasmine said, following him, a wild grin on her face.

Sam watched, helpless as the two girls took flight after Chris. His mouth hanging open, Sam turned to look at the others. Jonathan, Ashley and Mira stared back at him, each wearing a mixture of shock, fear and amusement on their faces.

Eyebrows raised, Sam shook his head and looked at Mira. "Is this just something we do now?"

Grinning, Mira walked past him, her grey wings already starting to beat the air.

"Let's make them hurt."

48

"Goddammit, Chris!" Liz shrieked as she rose from the courtyard.

Chris didn't look back. His wings glinted as they beat down, lifting him out of reach. The *thump* of feathers striking the air was barely audible over the thud of marching boots. The soldiers spread out across the square below, moving to surround the Madwomen. But as they looked up and saw Chris, they stumbled to a stop again.

Even from two hundred feet away, Liz could see their confusion. The onlookers gasped and the Madwomen shrank back as Chris's shadow fell across them. They retreated towards the obelisk, their composure broken by the appearance of the government's new weapons.

Liz smiled as her black-feathered wings carried her higher. In their eagerness to unveil the success of their experiment, the government had unwittingly given them an advantage. Those below only had eyes for their wings—not even the soldiers seemed to have realized their identities. In that moment, they didn't see them terrorists, but as allies of the government, come to bring peace to the Western Allied States.

Only the Director knew the truth. She was already retreating through the ranks of soldiers, waving frantically at the sky and screaming as she went. But her orders only added to the confusion of the men around her. The front ranks had already reached the Madwomen, while those in the rear were looking from the Director to Chris in bewilderment.

Before the woman could restore order, Chris folded his wings and plummeted towards the soldiers.

Finally seeing the danger, the men around the Director fumbled at their rifles. But they had obviously not been expecting the old women to put up a fight, and most still had their weapons slung over their shoulders. Before they could ready them, Chris slammed into their ranks like a wrecking ball.

The wind shrieked in Liz's ears as she beat her wings harder. Half a dozen men had fallen in Chris's initial attack, dropped by flailing wings and fists. But they'd only been glancing blows, and most were already regaining their feet. Behind Chris, the old women were trying to retreat, but they were hemmed in by the obelisk and the crowd of onlookers, who were pressing closer, eager for a glimpse of the winged teenagers.

Liz heard the *crack* of another pair of wings and glanced across the sky as Jasmine drew level with her. Below, Chris was a blur of movement. He seemed to be keeping half the soldiers preoccupied, but beyond him, the men around the Director had dropped to their knees and were lifting their rifles.

"Dive!" Liz screamed as a bullet screeched past her ear.

As one, the two girls tucked in their wings. Chris and the soldiers were still too far away, but the sky was no longer safe, and Liz shouted a warning to those below as she shot towards the ground. At the last second, she snapped open her wings, lurching painfully in the air, and then slammed down hard.

Cracks spread through the granite tiles as Jasmine landed beside her. The Madwomen scrambled back as Liz and Jasmine straightened. Their eyes were wide with fear, but Liz resisted the urge to reassure them. There was no time.

Turning, she searched for Chris, but he had disappeared behind the crowd. Cursing under her breath, she pulled her wings tight against her back and started in the direction of the soldiers. The crowd parted before her, all too eager to get out of Liz's way.

A soldier appeared ahead, and heart pounding in her chest, Liz charged. The man was standing over the body of an old woman, a pair of handcuffs in one hand. He looked up as Liz closed on him, but he had no time to react before her fist slammed into his chest. Pain shot through her knuckles as they connected with the body armor beneath his uniform, but it did little to soften her blow. The man's face went white as he collapsed.

"Nice work." Jasmine grinned as she leapt past, already aiming for another soldier standing nearby.

They had reached the center of the conflict now, where the soldiers were clashing with the Madwomen. Glimpsing more prone bodies, anger flared in Liz's chest. Whatever Chris's reasons were for charging in so recklessly, he was right about one thing: they couldn't stand by and let the government crush the helpless women.

She jumped as a second soldier came at her, then twisted to slam the heel of her boot into his face. The man's head whipped back with a sickening *crack* and he toppled over without a sound. Liz strode over his body without hesitation, still scanning the ranks of soldiers for Chris.

Ahead, Jasmine bore down on another soldier. The man saw her coming and wisely tried to flee, but Jasmine caught him by the arm and hauled him back. Screeching like a harpy, she spun, and hurled the soldier face-first into one of his comrades. Jasmine didn't wait to see whether either recovered. Wings still unfurled, she spun in search of another victim.

The soldiers were struggling to bring their rifles to bear in such close quarters. Without them, the men were practically helpless against the teenagers' altered physiology. Liz and Jasmine moved faster than thought, able to see danger and react before the soldiers could even lift their rifles. It also didn't hurt that some of the enemy still seemed confused about whose side the winged teenagers were on.

A soldier with a steel baton leapt at Liz, but as she turned to meet him, he hesitated, looking from her wings to her face. Then his eyes widened with recognition, and roaring, he continued his charge.

She batted away his attack with a casual swing of her arm, and then slammed the palm of her hand into his abdomen. He staggered and fell to one knee. As he tried to regain his feet, she drove her elbow down on the back of his head, sending him crashing to the pavement.

Spinning, she looked for Chris again, and caught a glimpse of his tawny wings through the press of soldiers. Before she could move towards him, Sam and Mira crashed down beside her. They nodded at her, and she pointed to Chris.

Before they could start after him, gunshots erupted from their right. Fire sliced Liz's arm as something grazed her skin. Swearing, she dove sideways. She struck the pavement hard and rolled as the rifle roared again. Stone chips sliced her face as the bullets thumped into the ground around her, then she was up and leaping into the air. Her wings beat down, carrying her over a body. Then the men who had been shooting were right in front of her. She slammed into their midst with uncontrolled fury.

One went down, his neck shattered by a swift blow from her boot. Wearing a savage scowl, Jasmine appeared beside her. She tore the gun from the hands of a soldier and swung it like a club at the man's head. Blood sprayed across Jasmine's face as the man went down screaming.

Cries came from behind them as the last gunman fell. Glancing back, Liz glimpsed blood on the granite tiles. Her stomach wrenched. The soldiers had fired indiscriminately into the crowd, and several of the Madwomen had been caught in the crossfire. They lay deathly still in the shadow of the obelisk.

Sam stumbled towards them, moving between the bodies littering the ground. Mira lay limp in his arms, her grey wings wrapped around her body. His own face was pale as a ghost's. Liz's eyes traveled down to the blood soaking through his trousers. Her heart lurched and she stepped forward and caught him as his leg gave way.

"Exciting life you guys live," he grunted as she held him up.

"Is she okay?" Liz asked, glancing at Mira. The girl's eyes were closed, but her wings hid any sign of injury. She looked around, her chest constricting in sudden panic. "Where's Ashley?"

Sam's forehead creased. "I thought she was right behind us." He bit his lip and looked at Mira. "Mira's okay, I think. She's still breathing."

Nodding, Liz spun, scanning the crowd for Ashley, but there was no sign of the redheaded girl. Chris had also disappeared into the stampeding crowd. The square had turned to pure chaos now. Bystanders stumbled through the throng of Madwomen, some attempting to flee while others sought the supposed safety of the soldiers. The chatter of gunfire echoed off the surrounding trees, sending people diving to the ground.

The Madwomen themselves were trying to regroup around their fallen members. They stood together, arms locked to protect those who had been injured by the soldier's bullets. Liz's heart swelled at the sight, but beyond, she could see the soldiers regrouping too. The Director was waving her arms, giving new orders. Already the men were turning in their direction. There were still too many to fight—especially with Sam and Mira injured, and Ashley missing.

"Ah…is that normal?" Sam asked, pointing behind her.

Liz followed the direction of Sam's gaze. A group of soldiers had surrounded Jasmine, but she didn't seem to care. Her wings snapped out as the soldiers pointed their rifles, and faster than thought, she was amongst them. A scream erupted as she caught one by the throat, then ended abruptly as his blood sprayed the air. Another went down as Jasmine drove her foot into his knee, snapping the bone like plywood.

Even Liz struggled to track Jasmine's movements as she tore through the soldiers like a hot knife through butter. They staggered back before her, some even turning to flee, but none escaped. A low growl rumbled from Jasmine's throat as she felled the last man and spun in search of her next victim. Her eyes settled on a nearby woman, and she started towards her.

"Jasmine!" Liz shrieked.

Jasmine didn't respond, but she paused mid-stride and turned towards them. Liz's heart lurched in her chest as she found herself staring into grey eyes. A deep, guttural growl came from Jasmine's throat as her lips drew back in a snarl. The hackles on the back of Liz's neck stood on end. Feathers bristling, she placed herself between Jasmine and Sam.

"Jasmine, stop!" Liz screamed as the girl stepped towards them. "Don't do this!"

49

A dull grin spread across Jasmine's lips as she cocked her head. Liz swallowed another scream. The *Chead* studied her with detached curiosity. Glancing back at Sam, Liz met his eyes. He nodded, and climbing to his feet, started to move away.

Liz turned back just in time to catch Jasmine's fist in the cheek. She reeled backwards, stars flashing across her vision, and only the instinctive beat of her wings kept her upright. Snarling, Jasmine came at her again, and Liz groaned as a boot slammed into her chest. Air exploded between her teeth and she bent in two, struggling to breathe.

She dove to the side as Jasmine attacked again. The girl stumbled past her, and Liz's wing flashed out to strike her in the face. The blow threw Jasmine off-balance, giving Liz time to recover. Straightening, the taller girl began to circle. A cold fury lit in Liz's chest, but she pressed it down, fearful of what might happen if she unleashed it. The last thing they needed was two *Chead* on the loose.

She leapt as Jasmine came at her again, her boot lashing out for the other girl's hip. Jasmine was quicker still. Spinning, she swept up an arm to catch Liz by the leg.

Liz screamed as Jasmine lifted her up and hurled her bodily into the crowd. She crashed into the Madwomen and went down in a pile of tangled bodies. Fear prickled her neck as she struggled to stand, while trying not to let her skin touch the civilians. Before she could free herself, a hand reached down and grasped her by the shirt.

Her stomach lurched as Jasmine dragged her up. Raising her arms in front of her face, Liz managed to block the first punch, before the second caught her square in the forehead. Her head snapped back, her neck jarring from the force of the blow. Before Jasmine could land a third, Liz twisted in her grip, and bunching up her legs, drove them straight into the taller girl's chest.

The kick broke Jasmine's grip and propelled Liz backwards through the air. Beating down hard with her wings, Liz steadied herself and dropped lightly back to the ground.

She straightened as Jasmine gave a high-pitched screech. The other girl hurtled at her, her fingers clenched like claws, teeth glinting in the morning sun. Liz leapt to meet her, and they came together in a crash of fists and feathers. For a second, Liz managed to fend her off. But Jasmine was no longer herself. The rage behind her grey eyes fed her strength, and Liz could not match it. A blow caught her in the chest, then the head, and suddenly she found herself on her knees.

Gasping, Liz rolled as Jasmine slammed her foot into the tiles where she'd been kneeling a moment before. A shriek of frustration chased after her. Liz struggled to regain her feet, but her vision swam and energy fled her tired limbs. She slumped against the cold stone.

Jasmine stepped towards her, a grin spreading across her face. Liz looked up as the other girl raised her fist. Without thinking, she reached out to catch the blow in her hand. The force of the punch rocked Liz backwards, but she wrapped her hands around Jasmine's fist and held on tight.

Baring her teeth, Jasmine struggled to free herself. Silently, Liz began to count as Jasmine raised her other arm, praying for the stinging nematocytes in her skin to take effect. How long had it taken for Chris to feel the pain from her touch?

Sparks flew across Liz's sight as Jasmine's fist slammed into her unprotected face. Still Liz did not relent, not until the second blow struck, and a second later, all her strength seemed to fade away. Jasmine roared as she tore herself free.

Liz slumped against the cold stone, darkness swirling at the edges of her vision. Jasmine towered over her. Snarling, she lifted her boot. Then she paused, a shadow passing across her face. Her eyes widened, and for a second, the grey flickered. Suddenly she was screaming and staggering back, tearing desperately at the arm Liz had held.

Appearing from nowhere, Chris stepped up behind Jasmine and drove his clenched fists down on the back of her head. She crumpled without a sound, but Chris caught her beneath one arm and hauled her onto his shoulder.

"You okay?" he asked, looking down at Liz.

Her vision still swirling, Liz shook her head. The movement made her stomach wrench, and rolling onto her side, she threw up the measly remnants of her breakfast. She sensed Chris beside her and felt his hand on her back. Still on her knees, Liz looked up and found the Director marching towards them, the remaining soldiers escorting her.

Groaning, Liz forced herself to her feet. She staggered slightly, and Chris struggled to help her with Jasmine still slumped over his shoulder.

"Where are the others?" she croaked.

Chris nodded behind her. Turning, she found Sam standing with the remaining Madwomen. Ashley had reappeared beside him, and now carried the unconscious Mira in her arms. There was no sign of Jonathan; he had probably fled when the chaos broke out. Together, Liz and Chris stumbled across to join the others.

"That's everyone," Sam commented, his voice strained. He nodded at the approaching Director. "Now what?"

Liz swallowed as she watched the soldiers converging on them. Some were already lifting their rifles; from this distance they couldn't miss. They glanced at the Director, awaiting her orders. Liz gritted her teeth and closed her eyes as the woman raised an arm.

Instead of the roar of gunfire, the patter of shoes on stone followed. Opening her eyes, Liz gaped as the Madwomen moved between them and the soldiers. Unbent, undaunted by the burly men and their dark weapons, they stood in the line of fire, shielding Liz and the others with their bodies.

A shout carried through the crowd as the Director demanded they stand aside, but the Madwomen didn't move. A moment later a woman screamed as the soldiers started to force their way through, but to Liz's relief, no more shots were fired.

"Come, they can't hold them for long," an elderly voice spoke.

Liz turned and found the old woman who had defied the Director earlier standing beside them. How she had evaded the first wave of soldiers, Liz couldn't guess, but all she could do was nod as the woman shepherded them around the obelisk. They sprinted across the square and ducked into the shelter of the trees.

"What about them?" Chris cried as the Madwomen's screams chased after them.

The old woman was struggling to keep up, but she shook her head without breaking stride. Together they burst from the park out onto the streets. The towering spire of the obelisk disappeared as they turned a corner. Ahead, tires screeched as a van pulled off the road and drove up onto the sidewalk. The sliding door rattled open and a man gestured frantically at them. Without hesitating, they threw themselves inside, while the woman climbed into the passenger seat.

Then the van was racing away, disappearing into the winding streets of San Francisco, and all Liz could do was stare at the others in shock. They looked back at her, eyes wide, feathers ruffled, and clothes bloodied. They looked just as lost as her. Sucking in a breath, Liz tried to make sense of the scenes in the square and failed.

What the hell is going on?

50

When the darkness finally retreated and Susan woke, she was surprised to find herself alive. Upon opening her eyes, she immediately wished she could return to the darkness.

She was lying on the floor in the laboratory again, but she was no longer the *Chead's* only prisoner. Around her, the other doctors stood in various states of dress. Some wore only nightgowns, while others had managed to pull on at least lab coats before the *Chead* had come for them. There was no sign of any guards. Susan shuddered to think what had become of them.

Blinking in the harsh overhead lights, she turned towards the doorway. Her heart sank. There were now half a dozen *Chead* gathered around the door. Their whispers carried across the room, but Susan could only make out the occasional word. The *Chead* seemed to be ignoring their prisoners for now, but with them standing in the only exit, there was no chance of escape.

Susan gritted her teeth as she sat up, her muscles screaming their protests. The other doctors stared at her, but no one moved to help. She cursed under her breath and slowly struggled to her feet. Glancing at the others, she wondered why they were all still alive. What were the *Chead* planning to do with them?

She looked around as the creatures suddenly fell silent. The group of *Chead* had straightened, and their eyes were alert now.

An expectant silence hung in the air. Susan craned her neck, trying to get a glimpse of the doorway. The other doctors began to whisper as a woman stepped into the laboratory.

"Silence!" one of the *Chead* roared, and the whispers died.

The doctors in front of Susan shrank back, and she managed to get a proper look at the newcomer—but the sight only added to her confusion. An old woman stood in the doorway, her eyes glazed white, her long black hair streaming down around her face. Her cheeks were creased with age, and her shoulders were hunched and shrunken. Despite her advanced years, there was no mistaking the power she held over the creatures around her. They made way before her, watching on in silence as she approached the terrified doctors.

As the woman advanced, one of the doctors stumbled forward. She reached out an arm towards the old woman. "Please, help us, the *Chead*—"

Her words were cut short as the old woman caught her by the throat. Lifting the doctor with a strength that belied her age, the old woman studied the doctor with cold white eyes.

Only then did Susan realize the truth. The wizened woman wasn't human at all—she was *Chead*, her eyes turned white with the premature aging caused by the virus. But how was that possible? The woman hadn't been one of the *Chead* imprisoned at the facility. So where had she come from?

The doctor in the old *Chead's* grip gave a strangled cry, her eyes bulging as she kicked feebly. An awful grin spread across the *Chead's* face, revealing perfect white teeth, and again the doctor cried out. With shocking finality, something went *crack*, and the doctor went still.

Susan screamed and stumbled backwards. Slapping a hand across her mouth, she struggled to contain her horror. Her stomach roiled, and suddenly she was on her knees, throwing up the half-digested remains of her last meal.

The doctor's body gave a wet *thud* as it struck the ground. Susan gasped as she found her dying colleague's eyes open and staring at her. A horrible gurgling came from the woman's mouth as blood gushed from her throat.

Susan quickly looked away, her stomach still churning. A moan rattled up from her chest.

"This is all of them?" the old *Chead* asked in a dry, rasping voice.

"All the ones…still alive," the one she recognized as Hecate answered. He nodded towards Susan and she scrambled backwards. "That one…led us to…what we sought."

"Did she, now?" The old *Chead* grinned and strode towards Susan.

Susan cried out and tried to back away, but the doctors behind her shoved her forward, eager to avoid becoming the next victim. She begged for their help, but they retreated together into the corner, leaving her alone in the middle of the room.

Still on the ground, Susan looked up at the old *Chead*. She trembled as the pale white eyes found hers. It took every last drop of her courage not to turn away. It felt as though she was being inspected for some unknown purpose, until finally she could take it no more.

The old *Chead* laughed. "Hecate, what do you know…of this woman?"

"Nothing, Talisa," Hecate replied. "She is…new. She was not one of…them."

Opening her eyes, Susan saw the direction of Hecate's gaze. The *Chead* was staring at the group of doctors. A dark rage danced behind its eyes, and suddenly she was glad they hadn't let her hide amongst them.

The doctors, if possible, shrank even more beneath the old *Chead's* gaze. A smile curled across her ancient lips. "Very well then," it laughed. "She is yours…if she accepts."

Hecate bowed, and a smile touched the creature's lips. "As you wish…Talisa."

"We shall offer her the choice," Talisa replied. "You have it?"

"Yes, though we have not…tested it."

"All the better." Susan shrank as the white eyes returned to her. "What is your name, girl?"

Susan pressed herself flat against the floor. Eventually, the question seeped into her consciousness, and she managed to stammer out an answer. "Su…Susan."

The old *Chead* leaned down, until its face was less than an inch from Susan's. She tried to shrink away, but firm hands caught her by the chin.

"Do you wish to live, Susan?" the aged voice rasped in her ear.

Susan's heart lurched, and she glanced at Hecate, then back to the old *Chead*. "Ye…yes."

The *Chead* nodded. "Excellent." It held out its hand, and Hecate placed something in it. "Then you have a choice. Join us, or join them," it said, nodding to the other doctors.

With its words, the old *Chead* revealed the vial in its palm. Even without reading the label, Susan knew what it was. PERV-ALPHA—the virus she had found for Hecate. Her stomach twisted and she struggled to breathe. Choking, she tried to break free of the *Chead's* grasp, to turn and flee and never look back.

But the old *Chead* only watched her, its eyes devoid of emotion.

"Choose," Talisa hissed.

Susan stilled at the command. She looked around the room, taking in the fear in the eyes of the other doctors, the blood pooling on the floor, her colleague's dead stare. She shuddered as she looked back at the *Chead*.

I don't want to die.

Closing her eyes, Susan nodded, and held out her hand. Ice tingled in her veins as the tube and a syringe were placed in her palm.

"Do it," Talisa ordered. "Now."

With trembling hands, Susan prepared the syringe, sliding the needle into the rubber top of the tube. She watched as the clear liquid disappeared into the syringe. The shaking spread as she held it up to the light, checking for bubbles. Desperately she tried not to think, not to contemplate what she was about to do.

Looking up, she found the *Chead* watching her, and almost dropped the syringe.

Do it, don't think, she ordered herself.

Silently, Susan studied the pale flesh of her arm. What would it be like, to change? She realized they had never bothered asking the survivors. The government had only ever hunted them, slaughtering them wherever they were found. Those they had created in experiments here were either executed or imprisoned like Hecate, to be the subject of further trials.

Susan took another breath, and her trembling stilled. Silently, she slid the needle into her flesh, and pressed down the plunger. When it had depressed the entire way, she pulled out the needle, and hurled the syringe away.

The breath caught in her throat as she felt the pressure building in her arm. There was an alien strangeness to the sensation, and she gasped as the first tingles of pain began. It spread quickly, moving to her shoulder, then her chest, then heart.

Groaning, Susan bent in two as agony wrapped around her body. Her skull prickled with a thousand needles, and she tore at her hair, unable to bear the pain. Fire seared its way down her spine, and she felt herself falling away. The darkness called, and she longed to embrace it. But the fire was all around her now, absolute, consuming, and she realized with horror the release of unconsciousness would not come.

A scream tore from her throat, and went on and on, until she tasted blood. A red light spread through her mind, consuming her, and slowly her sanity slipped away.

From the distance came an old woman's voice. "Watch her, Hecate," the voice said, "until the change is complete."

51

Chris still couldn't believe his eyes. Two hours had passed since the fight in Independence Square, and they were finally safe, but he was still shaking. During the fight, and their wild escape in the rickety van, there had been no time to think. Now, as he stood at the head of the table and looked around at the others, he should have been calm. Instead, his heart was racing like a runaway train.

Ashley and Liz sat to either side of him, their eyes shadowed with exhaustion. Each of them bore the cuts and bruises of their desperate battle. Their anger at him hung over the kitchen like a blanket, silencing all conversation. The others were resting in a makeshift infirmary in another room, where one of the Madwomen was examining their injuries.

Chris's chest tightened as he thought of them. Apparently, all three would recover, but he knew that his actions had put them at risk, that he had let them all down. Even so, he couldn't bring himself to regret his recklessness—not this time. Not when he was standing here, looking across the table at a woman he had never thought he'd see again.

She was the same woman who had stood in open defiance of the Director, the one who had raced forward to protect them, the one who had led them all to safety.

Maria Sanders.

"Nana." He gasped the word like a drowning man.

At the other end of the table, a smile spread across his grandmother's face. The wrinkles around her cheeks deepened and her eyes glistened.

"Chris," she whispered, "it really is you…"

Chris nodded. His mouth opened and closed, but no words came out. There were none to describe what he was feeling. He found himself moving around the table, his eyes fixed on the woman he hadn't seen in months, the woman he had long since given up for dead.

Then her arms were wrapping him in a warm embrace, and he was crying big, heaving sobs into her shoulder. All the pain, all the grief and anger and horror came pouring out as he held onto his grandmother for dear life. He could feel her shaking too, her own sorrow, her own loss a mirror of his own.

Finally, Chris managed to regain some of his composure. Pulling away from her, he wiped his tears. His grandmother smiled up at him, and then leaned forward and planted a kiss on his cheek.

"Nana…" Chris hiccupped. "She's…she's really gone?"

His grandmother's face pinched and her hands tightened on his shoulders. "Yes." She closed her eyes for half a second. "I tried to find you both…but no one would help. They called me mad, called us all mad." She laughed, the sound harsh and angry. "So we became the Madwomen."

Chris nodded, struggling to swallow another wave of grief. Taking a breath, he turned back to the others.

"This is…this is my nana, Maria Sanders," he croaked.

Ashley and Liz's eyes were wide, confusion adding to their rage and exhaustion. Beside him, his grandmother gestured to the seat at the head of the table, and Chris moved back to his chair. Ashley and Liz watched him, their eyes still hard, but his announcement seemed to have taken the edge from their anger.

His grandmother sat at the other end of the table and looked at them each in turn. "Welcome, all of you," she said with a smile, "and thank you for coming to my rescue."

"Thank Chris," Liz said, shooting him a glance. "We followed his lead."

"Even so, thank you." Maria stared at Liz until she looked away. "I've often wondered who you were, all of you so called 'terrorists' who have been keeping my grandson company on the evening news. Although you gave us quite a fright when you appeared today. I thought the winged people were meant to be fighting for the other side..."

A strained silence greeted her words. Maria looked from Ashley to Liz, waiting for a response. Chris let out a breath, knowing he had to face what he'd done.

"I'm sorry," he said, staring down at the table. "I should never have put you at risk like that. It was stupid and reckless, and I could have gotten us all killed. But when I saw them advancing on her, I didn't even think."

He jumped as Ashley placed her hand on his wrist. "Chris, it's okay," she whispered, her eyes suddenly soft. "I know if it had been anyone from my family...I just wish I'd..." Her voice cracked and she looked away.

Before Chris could ask her what was wrong, Liz cut in. "You should have told us. You should have waited for us, but...Ashley's right. If it had been my father, my mother..." She shook her head and looked at Maria. "It's nice to meet you too, Maria. My name is Liz, and this is Ashley. Thank you for bringing us here, and thank you for helping our friends."

"You're welcome, my dear," Maria said. "I'm just glad we could return the favor. Thanks to the chaos you inspired, most of us escaped. The soldiers you didn't...disable were too busy looking for you to pay attention to the Madwomen."

"What were you doing there?" Chris asked suddenly. He shivered as he remembered the soldiers marching towards her. "You could have been killed."

"I could have." Maria's eyes travelled around the table. "But I did it for you, Chris. I did it for all the people who have disappeared, the children who have vanished. I'm old, I've lived my life. I don't mind giving it away, if it makes a difference."

"But..." Chris croaked, his eyes beginning to water again.

He looked up as Liz placed her hand on his shoulder. Her eyes were wide, glistening with unspilt tears. She nodded to his grandmother, and Chris saw the sorrow in the tightness of her aged face.

"I've outlived my own daughter, Chris." She sounded defeated, but there was steel in her eyes as she continued. "I do not intend to outlive my grandson as well. So when I heard about the Madwomen, and realized I might be able to make a difference, I knew I had to stand with them."

Chris's heart gave a painful twist. "But I never asked you to, Nana," he whispered. "I was trying to protect you, by staying away. I didn't know what had happened to you, but I thought you'd be safe if I didn't go near you."

"Chris, it's not your job to look after me," she said, laughing. "Your grandfather gave his life so you could grow up in a world that was safe. I am only continuing his fight."

"Wrong." Chris looked up as a voice came from the doorway. Jasmine stood there, arms crossed, her lips twisted in a scowl. To his relief, her eyes had returned to their usual brown, though her fury looked undiminished. "This is our fight now—even more than yours. You're right, you've lived your life. And while you were busy living it, you allowed this to happen. Where were you when they started taking away our rights? When people started disappearing? Where were you while the *Chead* ravaged the countryside?"

Maria did not blink in the face of Jasmine's rage. "I was sleeping," she said softly. "Resting on my laurels. I thought the battle was won when the war ended. You're right—I let this happen."

Jasmine hesitated, clearly caught off-guard by Maria's admission. Liz gestured to an empty chair, and after a moment's pause, Jasmine crossed the room and sat down. She shared a long look with Liz, and then gave a quick nod. Liz smiled back.

"But I'm fighting now," Maria went on, "and not just protesting with the Madwomen." She looked around the table, and Chris noticed her eyes lingering on their wings. "There is a movement beginning. It's still young, but the Madwomen are the rallying point. We're the only ones who are safe to openly defy the government."

"Until today," Ashley whispered.

"Until today," Maria agreed with a sad smile, "but we always knew the risks. We knew the day would come, and we knew there might be losses. Thanks to you, most of us escaped. Now we must wait and see how the public reacts."

Chris glanced at the others. His grandmother was right—the Director would have a hard time spinning the attack in the square. The public wasn't likely to take kindly to the use of force against old women, especially not the widows of veterans. But then, the government had managed to spin their escape from the courthouse. Who knew what else they were capable of?

"What is this place?" Jasmine asked. "And what exactly is this 'movement' of yours doing?"

"This is a safe house for people the government are hunting," Maria replied. "There are a few in the city now. You should be safe here, so long as we weren't followed. Mike's making sure of that right now—he should be back soon."

"Mike?" Chris asked.

"Our driver," Maria replied. "As for what we're doing...for now, we've mostly been gathering information. There are several foreign nations concerned about what our government has been up to. So far they have been afraid to act, but the tide is turning. The President is losing control. Much of the countryside is close to open rebellion, and some of the cities aren't far from following. The growing poverty, the *Chead*, the military crackdowns, the curfews, they're all taking a toll. The people are losing faith in the government."

"In other words, the movement is doing absolutely nothing," Jasmine muttered. Chris waved a hand to quiet her.

"It's a start," he said softly.

"Yes," Maria replied, "but we need more. We need something to light the match, to start a fire in people's hearts. What just happened in the square, it is only the beginning. If we wait too long, the government will crush us all like flies."

"Sure hope not." Chris started as someone spoke behind them. Leaping to his feet, he spun to face the unfamiliar voice.

A figure stood in the doorway, watching them from beneath a broad-rimmed hat. He wore tight-fitting jeans and a buttoned shirt with long sleeves. His leather boots thudded on the wooden floor as he strode across the room and took a seat. A grin stretched across his bronzed face as he lifted his feet and rested them on the table.

"Y'all make yourselves comfortable?"

52

Liz stood staring at the newcomer. He had seated himself beside Maria and was now looking up at them from beneath his broad-rimmed hat. Her wings had snapped open as she stood, but his grin did not falter at the sight. Jasmine stood beside her, teeth bared, her whole body shaking with a rage only Liz's could match. Ashley had half-risen from the table, but her eyes remained downcast, and she seemed loath to take action.

"No one followed us?" Maria asked, apparently unaware of Liz and Jasmine's anger.

"Nope, we're in the clear," the man said, laughing. "Y'all caused quite the scene."

"*What is he doing here?*" Liz's words came out as a scream.

There was no mistaking his accent, the southern twang of a Texan. Fury burned in her chest, bubbling up to fill every inch of her body, until it was all she could do not to reach out and throttle the man. She was surprised Jasmine hadn't already.

Everyone knew Texas was responsible for unleashing the *Chead* virus on the WAS, for the decades of fear and suffering that had consumed the countryside, for the plague that had claimed her mother and so many others. The Lone Star State was the one entity everyone in her family, every rural citizen, hated more than the government.

Now one of them sat smiling in front of her, as though she didn't have every right to leap on him and tear out his throat.

At her scream, everyone at the table had turned to stare at her. A crown creased Chris's forehead as he half-rose from his seat. "Liz, are you okay?" he asked.

"No." She jabbed a finger at the Texan. "He's…his country…they're responsible…" Liz trailed off, her words choked.

"He's responsible for the *Chead*," Jasmine hissed.

Chris blinked, and Liz knew he'd been so engrossed by his grandmother's reappearance, he hadn't made the connection. He looked from his grandmother to the Texan. Realization dawned in his eyes and he rose to join them.

"What's going on here, Nana?" he whispered.

His grandmother raised her eyebrows. "Perhaps the three of you should sit and listen, before leaping to conclusions."

"I'll not sit at the same table as that…that monster," Jasmine spat. She slammed a fist into the table, splintering the surface. A smile tugged at her lips as the Texan showed the first signs of discomfort. "At least not while he's breathing."

"Easy now." The Texan straightened, lifting his hands. "Let's talk about this…"

"I don't think so," Liz growled, starting towards him.

His eyes widened and he twisted, his arm disappearing behind his back. A revolver appeared in his hand as he stood.

"Why don't we all just—"

Before he could finish, Jasmine lunged. Clearing the table in a single bound, she slammed into him with the force of a runaway tram and sent him tumbling. The revolver went scattering across the wooden floor to land at Chris's feet. He bent down and retrieved it as the two girls advanced.

"*Enough!*" The room froze as Maria Sanders climbed to her feet. Anger wrinkled her face as she looked at each of them in turn. "Sit. Down."

The three teenagers and the Texan exchanged glances. A moment passed, but one more look at Maria was all it took to convince them. With an effort of will, Liz retreated from the prone man and resumed her seat, the others a step behind. Ashley sank back down, her eyes downcast, avoiding Liz's gaze.

The Texan wore a sheepish look on his face as he regained his feet. "Sorry, Maria," he grunted. "Shouldn'ta reacted, old habits, ya know?"

Maria said nothing, only waved him back to his seat. She waited until he'd sat before addressing them again. "As I was saying, why don't we all take a breath before attacking one another?" Her eyes shifted to their wings. "After all, as far as the media is concerned, your kind works for the government."

A shiver went through Liz at Maria's words, though less from guilt at their reaction, and more from the casual way the old woman had dehumanized them. She might still think of Chris as her grandson, but suddenly Liz was less convinced about her benevolence towards the rest of them.

"This is Mike," Maria continued. "He came to me a few months ago, not long after I joined the Madwomen. This is his safe house, so before you resume your little fight, you might want to thank him for the rescue."

A stony silence answered Maria's words. A burst of laughter erupted from the Texan as he waved a hand. "Don't stress it, Maria," he said. "Can't blame 'em the hate." His eyes turned to them. "Y'all think I'm responsible for the *Chead*."

Jaw clamped, Liz forced herself to nod.

"What are you doing here?" Chris asked, his voice far calmer than Liz could have managed. But then, she supposed that coming from the city, he had never experienced the same terror she had from the *Chead*.

"Isn't it obvious?" Jasmine hissed. "He's a spy, come to spread more of the cursed things." Her eyes flashed. "I hope the WAS rains fire down on your damned state."

"We'd best pray they don't," Mike replied, "considering we seem to be the only ones on your side."

"On our side?" Liz snapped. "How can you say—"

"Cause it's a lie."

Silence answered the man's words. "What?" Chris asked finally.

Mike leaned towards them from across the table. "Texas did not create the *Chead*," he said. "No more than we created the six of you."

"Why should we believe you?" Liz rumbled.

"The same reason I trust you don't really work for the Western Allied States," he replied with a shrug. Leaning back in his chair, he placed his boots back on the table. It gave a loud groan, and Liz found herself wondering how much damage Jasmine had done to the heavy wood. "You saved my friends, I saved you. I'd say that's reason enough for a bit of flexibility on either side, don't you?"

Liz swallowed, looking from Chris to Maria to Jasmine, then back at the Texan. Just the thought of cooperating with one of them left a bitter taste in her mouth, and she was loath to agree. But the man's words made sense, and they needed allies.

"If you weren't behind the *Chead*, who was?" Jasmine muttered. She still looked ready for a fight, though so far was holding back.

"That's the million-dollar question, ain't it?" Mike replied. "To be honest, I was hoping y'all might have some answers."

Liz shook her head. "The doctors who created us are dead. They didn't spend too much time on history lessons."

"Shame," Mike replied. His voice changed as he continued, taking on a more western twang. "It gets exhausting, putting on an accent. I would have liked to clear up that little piece of misinformation while I'm here."

"Why *are* you here?" Jasmine cut in.

Mike glanced at Chris, who still held his revolver. "So long as you've got my gun, how about you fill me in a little more about yourselves?" he replied, one eyebrow raised. "After all, last I checked you belonged to the government."

A growl rumbled up from Jasmine's throat. Liz quickly reached out and placed a hand on the girl's shoulder. Jasmine turned her scowl on Liz, and for half a second, Liz thought she glimpsed specks of grey in the brown of her friend's eyes. She squeezed Jasmine's shoulder, part in reassurance, part in warning.

Jasmine's eyebrows lifted and her chest swelled, a shudder going through her. She closed her eyes for a moment. When they opened again, Liz saw the fear lurking behind the rage.

"It's okay," she said softly, aware the others were staring.

Liz waited until she was sure it was true before turning to the others. "You want answers, Mike?" she asked. When the Texan nodded, she went on: "Our parents weren't traitors; we were taken because the government needed fresh bodies for their experiments. We have no idea how many generations came before us, because they're all dead. We were just unlucky enough to be the first to survive."

"But why?" Mike mused, seemingly more to himself than them.

"Fallow told us we were created to fight the *Chead*," Chris offered.

"No," Ashley said suddenly. Liz looked at her friend, surprised by her outburst. The other girl swallowed, and it was a moment before she went on. "Halt…he visited me sometimes, when I was alone," she started.

Liz's stomach twisted, and she was about to grasp her friend's hand, when she remembered the nematocysts. Resting a hand on Ashley's back instead, she nodded for the girl to go on.

"He was obsessed," she whispered. "Some in the government wanted a weapon against the *Chead*, others a weapon against everyone else. But Halt…Halt, he wanted to create a whole new species, to evolve beyond humanity, become something else entirely."

"That's why he used the virus on himself," Chris muttered.

Ashley shrugged but remained silent. It seemed she had said everything she was going to say.

"Can it be reversed?" Maria asked. Liz did not miss the look she gave Chris. A tremor went through her wings, and she found herself wondering if she'd be willing to give them up for a chance to be normal again.

"We don't know," Chris replied. "There wasn't meant to be a cure for the *Chead* virus, but Mira was one of them, before she became one of us."

Liz remained silent at that, recalling her and Jasmine's own brief transformation, and the stinger cells embedded in her skin. Perhaps she *would* take the cure, if one existed.

"What if we found another doctor?" Liz asked suddenly. "One who knows about the *Chead*, and whatever we might be?"

Mike sighed. "Unfortunately, there's not many who exist. Everything about the *Chead* is top secret. We only know what your government tells us, and as I already mentioned, that information is more than questionable."

"A geneticist then, someone who could study the virus we were given, and tell us if it's reversible."

"There's a professor at the University of San Francisco," Ashley said, her words coming out in a rush. "I think he used to work for the government; specializes in genetic engineering. I'm…not sure how receptive he'd be to a bunch of fugitives on his doorstep, though."

"How do you know about professors at a university?" Liz asked, surprised by her outburst.

"I studied there for a few months, before…" Ashley trailed off.

Liz blinked. "You what?"

Ashley turned beetred. "I never mentioned that? I graduated high school six months early…"

Beside Liz, Chris started to laugh. "Well, maybe you can show us around when we visit this professor—"

"No," Mike and Maria said together.

"Out of the question," Maria continued.

Chris fell silent, his mouth hanging open as he stared at the two adults.

"It's too much of a risk," Mike added. "Between the wings and your photos in the papers, you're too recognizable."

"So what, we do nothing?"

"For now," Mike answered, his voice steady. Liz opened her mouth to protest, but he spoke over her. "But we don't all have to stay here. I'll go instead."

"Absolutely not!" Liz hissed, rising so quickly her chair tipped over backwards.

"You expect us to just sit here and trust you?" Jasmine was on her feet as well.

"Yes." Mike's smile returned. "Since regardless of what you believe about history, we have a common enemy. I guess it's time I told you why I'm here."

Liz glanced at the others, uncertain, and Mike took the opportunity to continue.

"I was sent by the Lone Star State. We've been watching the WAS for years—ever since they began accusing us of espionage. I've been here over a year, collecting information, sending updates back to my supervisors. It won't be the first risk I've taken, opposing your government. Trust me, I'm on your side."

"So you're a spy?" Jasmine asked bluntly.

Mike shrugged. "I'm whatever I need to be," he replied, "and right now, I'm the best chance you'll have of finding that cure."

Liz clenched her fists as she struggled to process his words. Looking around the table, she saw the same doubt in Chris's and Ashley's eyes, and the burning rage in Jasmine's. She drew in a long breath and returned her gaze to the Texan, wondering whether she'd completely lost her mind. But Mike was right: Texas and the six of them had a common enemy. And if they wanted to survive, they needed to trust *someone.*

"Why would you help us, though?" she asked quietly.

"To prove my people aren't evil," he replied quickly. "To prove we're on your side."

"Fine," Liz said. "Chris, you'd better give him back his gun. I have a feeling he's going to need it."

53

Sam groaned as he woke to find himself lying alone on a single bed. He started to sit up, then gasped as pain shot through his leg. Memories came rushing back, and he looked down to see the bandages wrapped around his calf.

Swearing under his breath, he pulled himself into a sitting position and looked around the infirmary. There were several other beds crammed into the little room, but there was only one other occupant. Mira lay in the bed beside his, her face pale and hair slick with sweat. A sheet had been tucked up to her neck, concealing any sign of her injuries.

Carefully, Sam lifted himself from his bed and hobbled over to Mira. His wings hung heavy behind him and his leg refused to take his weight, but he made it without falling. Cursing Chris and the soldiers, he sat on the edge of Mira's bed, and pulled back the covers. Mira shifted slightly with the movement, and he let out a sigh of relief to see she was alive.

Mira still wore her plain blue shirt, but her left shoulder had been swathed in white bandages. Her chest rose and fell in a gentle rhythm, and even to his inexperienced eye, Sam could see Mira was in far better condition than Ashley had been when she'd been shot.

"The doctor says she'll be okay." Sam turned as Chris's voice came from the doorway.

"Doctor?" he asked, raising an eyebrow.

Nodding, Chris crossed the room. "Luxury service here. One of the Madwomen was a medic during the war. Retired a long time ago, but she seems to know her stuff. Apparently, the bullet passed right through Mira's shoulder."

"That's good, I guess. How about my leg?" Sam asked sourly.

Chris flinched. "I told you I wasn't a leader, Sam."

"You're right about that," Sam groaned as he stumbled back to his bed. He lay down and tried to find a position where his calf didn't ache. "So, who is she?"

"What?" Chris blinked back.

Sam laughed. "The old woman who stood up to the Director. You know her—I saw it in your eyes."

A smile tugged at Chris's lips. "She's my nana."

Despite himself, Sam found himself grinning back. "I'm happy for you." He shook his head. "It's about time one of us had some good news."

"You aren't angry?" Chris asked.

"Furious," Sam said, winking, "but I'm sure the girls have already put you through the wringer. How is Jasmine, by the way?"

"Awake, and human," Chris replied. "The change didn't do anything for her temper, though."

Sam laughed. "Between you and her, I'll never understand how any you of survived long enough to rescue us."

"Believe me, it was a close thing," Liz said, appearing in the doorway. "Did you get the feather, Chris?"

"Not yet." Chris walked across to Mira's bed and then hesitated, glancing back at them. "Ah, you sure we shouldn't just use ours?"

"We're all donating, remember?" Liz replied, glancing at Sam.

Sam raised an eyebrow as Chris replied, "Don't suppose you want to do it?"

Liz crossed her arms. "Oh no, she's all yours. I'll get Sam's." Striding forward, she plucked a feather from Sam before he could object.

"Hey!"

"It's for research," Liz replied, grinning.

Chris rolled his eyes. His shoulders rose as he looked at Mira, then he reached down and plucked a feather from her half-exposed wing. A growl rumbled up from Mira's throat and she shifted beneath her covers. Her eyes remained closed, but Chris still made a hasty retreat.

"What's this all about?" Sam asked.

"Plan B," Liz answered. "Now, do you mind if I borrow Chris? I'm not quite finished telling him off."

Chris's cheeks turned red as Sam waved his permission. Lying back on his bed, he watched the two of them disappear into the hallway, then smiled as Ashley took their place. The grin fell from his lips when he saw her face. Her eyes were watering, and she stepped hesitantly into the room, as though afraid of what he might do.

"Sam…" she whispered.

"Looks like we've traded places, Ash," he joked, patting the bed beside him.

Ashley gave a half-choked laugh. Tears spilled down her cheeks, but her head bounced in what might have been a nod. As she sat where Chris had been, he reached up and brushed the hair from her face.

"What's wrong, Ash?" he asked.

A tremor went through her as she tensed. For a second, he thought she would flee, before the tautness left her in a rush and she slumped to the bed beside him.

"I'm sorry, Sam," Ashley whispered. "I don't know what happened, I just froze."

"What are you talking about?" Leaning over, Sam pulled her into his arms. "There's nothing for you to be sorry for."

She shook her head and pulled away from him. "You needed me, and I wasn't there," she croaked. "I just stood there with Jonathan and watched while the soldiers surrounded you!"

In the depths of her eyes, Sam could see her terror. He gripped her by the wrists as she tried to rise, drawing her back. "Ash, don't be silly, we all reacted differently! Heck, I wish Jasmine had held back, after what happened." Sam sighed. "Besides, you were there when we needed you the most."

"When *you* needed me." A faint smile crossed Ashley's face, but it did not touch her eyes. She brushed a hand across his cheek. "I was so afraid, Sam," she said, her voice wavering.

"It was your first fight." Sam took her hand and pressed it to his lips. "Next time it will be easier."

Ashley closed her eyes. "I was *terrified*." She stood suddenly, pulling herself free of Sam's arms. He tried to stop her, but she stepped back, and his hands caught only empty air. She shook her head, her eyes wide. "When the soldiers came, all I could see was Halt, standing over me again, using me..." She broke off, choking on her grief. "I'm as helpless now as I was chained to that hospital bed."

"No." Sam pushed himself up, though with his injured leg he couldn't move after her. "You came back, you helped us. Mira and I would never have escaped without you."

Ashley's shoulders sagged. "I don't want to go back, Sam." Her voice shook and his heart went out to her. "I can't…I *won't* be used like that again."

"You won't," Sam insisted. "I won't let them. I'll keep you safe."

Ashley's amber eyes met his, and a shadow passed across her face. "My parents told us that, once," she whispered. "My sister and I, they said they'd protect us…said they'd keep the dark things away."

"Ash…" He tried to stand, to reach her.

"Now they're all dead: my mom, my dad, my sister. I'm all there is left. Sometimes I wish I could join them. When I think of all those kids…the ones they're going to take, because of us." Her voice broke and she turned away. "I'm a coward. I should have made him kill me before I let you help him."

"No, Ash!" Sam stumbled after her, but she was already

halfway across the room. "It was my decision, my fault, not yours!"

"Their blood is on our hands, Sam," Ashley whispered.

Then she was gone, leaving Sam to stare at the empty doorway where she had stood.

54

Liz sighed as she lowered herself into the armchair beside Chris. They had just given their collection of feathers to the Texan, who had promptly left on his mission. Unfortunately, his absence had done nothing to cool Liz's angst about the man.

Chris's grandmother had retired to her room to rest. Liz could hardly blame her. After the morning's events, even she was exhausted, and Maria Sanders did not have her advantage of youth or genetically enhanced stamina.

Chris still stood beside her, staring at the plain walls of the lounge with nervous eyes. The room was empty except for another couch opposite her own, and a single painting of the Golden Gate Bridge on the far wall. Threadbare carpet covered the floor, and the couch was sagging badly. Feeling the tip of a spring prodding her backside, Liz shifted into a more comfortable position.

"You were quiet before," she said when Chris finally looked at her.

Shrugging, Chris sat down on the opposite couch. "After what happened at the square…I just thought…" He trailed off. "I've screwed up so many times…maybe it's time we let the adults handle things. Even if one is from Texas."

Liz snorted, doing her best to ignore his last remark. "As

angry as she is, Jasmine has a point. Maria and the other so called 'adults' had their chance to 'handle things'. That's what got us into this mess in the first place."

Chris sighed, and she saw the doubt in his eyes. The rush from the reunion with his grandmother was finally fading, and he could no longer hide from the consequences of his actions. They had almost lost everything because of him.

"What Mike said made sense," Chris said finally. "We'd be recognized if we went to the university."

"So what do we do in the meantime?" Liz pressed.

"We wait." Chris pursed his lips and stared at the worn carpet. "What do you think happened to Jonathan?"

Liz started. In the rush of battle, she had completely forgotten about the translator. "I don't know," she answered eventually. "We left him at the edge of the square. He shouldn't have been caught in the fight."

"Unless he tried to help as well," Chris murmured.

"I'm sure he's okay, Chris," Liz offered. "He wanted justice, but he wasn't an idiot. He wouldn't have gone charging into a squad of soldiers like a madman."

Chris winced, but Liz laughed to take the sting from her words. Their eyes met. She fell silent, searching for the boy she knew, but Chris blinked and looked away. She stood and crossed to the other couch.

"I'm sorry," he said as she sat beside him. "You were right, I should have waited..."

Liz laughed. "Yes, well, as I said earlier—I'm not quite finished with your punishment."

"Oh?" Chris raised an eyebrow.

Heart hammering in her chest, Liz crawled across the sofa until she was crouched over Chris. He lay still beneath her, his eyes wide. A tremor of desire swept through Liz as she watched him. She desperately wanted to relax, to collapse into Chris and feel him beneath her, to run her hand through his hair and feel his mouth on her neck.

Liz resisted. Instead, she leaned down and gently touched her lips to his.

Chris stilled at her touch, his fear revealed in the trembling in his body, and she almost changed her mind. Then Chris's lips were pressing back against hers, and his hands were in her hair, pulling her deeper into the kiss. Her lips parted, and his tongue darted out to meet hers. A groan rumbled up from her throat, warming her chest. Her arms shook, though from desire or the effort of holding herself up, she couldn't tell.

Carefully, Liz lowered herself down, until her breasts were resting against Chris's chest. Even through the fabric of her t-shirt, she could feel his heat. She dug her fingers into the cloth of his shirt, feeling his hips moving beneath her.

A moan tore from Chris's lips as they broke apart. Liz's heart pounded in her ears as need overtook her, and she leaned down to kiss him harder. His groan deepened, but his hands paused, and now he was no longer kissing her.

Then Chris began to scream.

Liz scrambled back as Chris thrashed on the couch. The words died in her throat as she saw the purple lines radiating out from Chris's mouth. He cried again, the sound like a dagger in her stomach, though this time he managed to clamp his mouth shut mid-scream. He clenched his jaw, his breath hissing between his teeth.

Kneeling beside the sofa, all Liz could do was watch as the seizures racked Chris's body. His back arched, his fingers clawing at the foam cushions, and his mouth opened again, though this time no sound came out. Tears poured from Liz's eyes as the frail hope she'd held for their relationship died in her chest.

Slowly the convulsions faded, and Chris grew still. His eyes fluttered open, but it was obvious that each inhalation was still a strain. Their eyes met, and Liz saw the pain he was struggling to conceal. A smile tugged at his lips as he tried to sit up.

"Don't," she whispered, holding out her hand. "You'll hurt yourself."

Chris only gritted his teeth and pulled himself up. "I'm okay, Liz—" He broke off as a coughing fit shook him.

Liz stood, but he waved a hand for her to stay. "That was

some kiss." He licked his lips and fixed the grin to his face again. "You took my breath away."

A shudder shook Liz. She tried to speak, but the words caught in her throat. Swallowing, she tried again, but it was no use. Her hands were trembling, and she wrapped them around her chest before they gave her away.

Chris's brow creased. "Sorry, bad joke."

"No, Chris," she managed finally. Her eyes stung but now she did not cry. "We can't…I can't keep doing this. I thought…but I was wrong, it's not going to work. I can't…"

Grief welled in her chest as she backed away. Chris tried to rise and come after her, but the venom had robbed him of his strength, and he failed to escape the sofa.

"Liz!" he called after her.

She was already gone. Spinning, Liz sprinted through the doorway and out into the hall. She longed to turn back, to sit beside Chris and let him hold her, but that was impossible. A lonely grief filled her, but she knew it was for the best. Her love could only bring pain and suffering now.

Only when she found an empty room did Liz let her tears fall.

55

The *Chead* woke to the whisper of voices, to the scent of fear and a red haze that wrapped around her mind. Opening her eyes, she screamed as a harsh white light flooded her vision. Pain split her head, and the red swirled. The *Chead* growled, rage curling through her veins and feeding her strength. A pang of hunger came from her stomach as she staggered to her feet.

Looking around, she found the grey eyes of another *Chead* watching her. He made no effort to move as she stumbled, her feet unwieldy beneath her. Her hand caught a bench and she steadied herself. She gritted her teeth and clenched her fingers, feeling the steel bench crumple before her power.

Laughter whispered up from her chest as she straightened. Joy swept through the *Chead* as she balled her hands into fists, rejoicing in her newfound strength.

Her ears twitched as something in the room whimpered. The *Chead* stilled, and she felt again the ache in her stomach, the rage in her chest. She looked around, taking in the plain steel benches and strange contraptions that filled the room. A voice whispered to her from somewhere in the back of her mind.

Laboratory.

Then the *Chead* found the pitiful creatures huddling in the corner. They watched her with wide eyes, scrambling over one another in their desperation to escape her gaze. Their fear was thick in the air, a rich, savory scent that made her stomach rumble.

Grinning, the *Chead* stepped towards them, and watched as they flinched. She laughed then, feasting on their terror. But it was not enough—not nearly enough. In two steps, she closed the distance between them.

The one unlucky enough to be standing at the front tried to dash past her. But the creature moved with slow, ungainly steps, and she reached out and caught it with ease. Her fist closed on its wrist, and with a wrench of her arm, she hauled it back. The creature's feet gave way and it fell to its knees.

"Susan, please no!" Its voice grated on her ears and she grabbed it by the throat.

The creature gave a strangled cry as the *Chead* lifted it into the air and hurled it at the wall. A sharp *crack* echoed through the room as it struck. She grinned as the creature slumped to the floor unmoving. Laughter whispered from her lips as she turned toward the remaining creatures.

The laughter went on and on as she leapt into their ranks. Some tried to flee, racing across the room in a desperate attempt to escape. But her brother *Chead* barred their path, flinging them back into the room with laughter of his own. He did nothing else to interfere, only stood and watched as she had her fun.

Others begged like the first, but their cries died on their lips as she tore them apart. Some called her Susan, others Doctor, but the words were unfamiliar, and their pitiful screams only fueled her rage. She drank in the sound of their terror, feasting on the tang of blood, and roared, drunk with her newfound power.

When it was over, and even the dying moans of the pitiful creatures had fallen silent, the *Chead* finally grew still. Licking her lips, she savored the metallic tang of their lifeblood. It covered her clothes, her face, her hair, covered everything in the room. Her nostrils flared as she breathed in its scent.

Her bloodlust sated, the red faded, and images rose from the depths of her mind. Memories of the creatures strewn around her rose from her past, their lips twisted in smiles, their eyes filled with laughter. She remembered the man who had died first, offering his hand, welcoming her, and others leading her down long white corridors, showing her to a room and a bed.

Susan stumbled backwards, her feet slipping in the slick blood covering the linoleum floor. The breath caught in her throat, and she grabbed at the bench, desperate to keep her feet. Looking down, she saw the blood on her clothes. Her stomach wrenched and she tasted bile in the back of her throat.

Choking, Susan struggled to hold down the contents of her stomach. But there was no escaping the blood. It filled the room, lingering in her nostrils, on her tongue.

"*No!*" The word tore from her lips.

She gasped, a scream building in her throat as she struggled to breathe. Her eyes swept the room and found the cold grey eyes of the *Chead* watching her.

"What did you do?" she screamed.

But she knew this had not been his doing. Hecate had never left his post, had only watched with the same quiet satisfaction he displayed now. This had been her doing, her slaughter. She had torn through her fellow doctors like death itself, rejoicing in their fear, their agony…

"No…" she whispered, shaking her head. Tears welled in her eyes as she looked at Hecate. "What have you done to me?"

A smile spread across the creature's face as it stepped towards her. It placed a hand on her shoulder.

"Now, you are one of us," Hecate whispered.

Before Susan could reply, the red haze rose again to claim her.

VII

RECOVERY

56

Liz paced down the corridor, her long strides eating up the distance in half a dozen steps. Reaching the end, she spun and set off back down the hall. Her wings stretched out to either side of her, as far as the narrow walls would allow. A spasm rippled down her back, the muscles stiff from the long days of disuse. Up and down she walked, stretching and folding her wings, working the knots free.

It wasn't enough, of course, and though she'd only had the strange limbs a few weeks, she longed to take to the sky. There was a recklessness within her, a need to escape the safe house and soar amongst the skyscrapers and hills of San Francisco.

Instead, she and the others had found themselves locked away, under strict orders to remain indoors and out of sight. That meant no midnight flights, not even an afternoon stroll through the suburbs. After their freedom in the mountains and plains of California, the restrictions were quickly driving her insane.

It didn't help that she had spent the past week dodging Chris. She could see the hurt in his eyes each time she spurned him. It mirrored her own pain, but she couldn't bring herself to wound him further.

Then there was Ashley, who had apparently decided to shun

them all. Liz had tried to console Sam, who was mostly confined to his bed while his leg healed. Mira was finally awake, and despite their best efforts to make her rest, the girl had taken to wandering the house at strange hours. Several of the men who guarded the house had already complained about her scaring them half to death in the middle of the night.

And Jasmine, well...she at least had calmed down since Independence Square. But she was going as mad as Liz was, locked away in the house.

Worst of all, there hadn't been any word from the cursed Texan. Over a week had passed since he'd left with their feathers. Maria and the other Madwomen had expected him back by now, though they still insisted everything was okay. Apparently, it wasn't unusual for the man to drop off the radar, but Liz was far from convinced. She should have trusted her gut and killed him on the spot—but between Chris's reservations and Maria's reassurances, she'd allowed herself to be convinced.

And so they waited, trapped in the house, at the mercy of a man whose nation had wreaked havoc on everything she'd ever known.

Her parents would be rolling in their graves.

During the day, they took turns watching television, waiting for news of the attack in Independence Square to surface. The government had been tight-lipped so far, suppressing all details while they 'investigated.' But with so many people involved, even the government-controlled news agencies had started asking questions. Unfortunately, the days when everyone had a smartphone in their pockets had ended when stocks of gallium and other rare earth metals ran dry. Thirty years ago, a dozen videos of the attack would have surfaced by now, but so far there had been nothing.

Liz froze as a door opened into the hallway. Ashley appeared, arms crossed and a scowl on her face.

"Do you have to do that?" Ashley asked, her voice sharp.

Leaning against the wall, Liz folded her wings behind her back and eyed the taller girl. The silence stretched out as she tried to pierce the veil Ashley had cast over herself. The girl standing in front of her was so different from the Ashley she'd known back in the facility. That Ashley had always seemed so perfect, as though the darkness could not touch her. Even in the mountains, with bullets flying all around them, Ashley had kept her cool.

But back in Independence Square, Ashley had frozen.

"Sorry, were you sleeping?" Liz finally replied.

Ashley's wings snapped out behind her, the feathers standing on end. "Of course I was sleeping!" she snapped. "It's 3 a.m.!"

"Oh!" Liz glanced at the clock on the wall, surprised she'd lost track of time. "Sorry, I didn't realize."

"Of course not," Ashley snorted, her eyes flashing. "Why would you?"

Liz raised her hands in surrender, unwilling to say anything that might provoke her friend further. Still scowling, Ashley turned and stalked back towards her room.

"What happened to you, Ashley?" Liz asked without thinking.

Ashley paused in her doorway, one hand on the wooden frame. With her back turned, Liz couldn't see her face, but a shiver went through her feathers. Her shoulders started to shake, and Liz realized Ashley was crying.

Liz was at her side in an instant. She gently rubbed the small of her friend's back. She had taken to wearing long sleeves and thin woolen gloves, but Liz was still careful not to touch Ashley's skin. Ashley looked back at her, her eyes red.

"I don't know, Liz," Ashley's voice shook. "I'm terrified…of everything. I feel so helpless, so useless, like every bad thing that happens is my fault."

"That's not true." Liz gripped her by the shoulder and forced Ashley to look at her. "You know that."

Ashley only shook her head. Breaking free of Liz, she leaned against the wall and slid to the ground. Hugging her knees to herself, she went on.

"You don't know what it was like, after you escaped. Halt had me so drugged up, I couldn't do anything to stop him. My…my mind was so muddled…the things he did, they're still coming back to me, even now. Every night I go to sleep, and I remember something new, some fresh, horrible thing he did while I was helpless in that hospital bed. It's like he's still waiting for me, every night…" Her voice cracked. "And then there's what Sam did…for me. I can't bear it."

Staring down at Ashley, Liz could only begin to imagine what vile things Halt might have done to her in retaliation for their escape. She crouched beside Ashley and hugged her as best she could.

"Come on," she said finally, nodding down the corridor. "We need some fresh air."

"But…" Ashley trailed off, and Liz saw the fear in her eyes.

"No." Liz gripped Ashley under the arm and hauled her to her feet. "Don't think it, don't say it. It's dark. There's no one looking for us out there, not at this time of night. We'll be fine. Sitting around stewing isn't doing you any good."

With that, Liz set off down the hallway, half-dragging the other girl with her.

Taking care to avoid the man on watch, they slipped out the back window into the garden, where a scattering of trees offered shelter from anyone who might have been watching. The last traces of Ashley's injury had faded days ago, and while she'd had less practice than the rest of them, she still managed to take flight after only a short run across the grass. Her white wings clipped the treetops as she rose from the yard, then she was free.

Liz laughed as she saw the grin on Ashley's face. Stretching her wings, she drifted sideways, allowing her friend to catch up. As they drew side by side, their wings stretched out to brush against one another, black on white. The lights of the houses fell away as they rose higher, the strong San Francisco winds sending them soaring.

High in the sky, it seemed to Liz as though the whole world was beneath them. The lights of the city shone like stars below, stretching north and east and south as far as the eye could see. In the distance, the lights merged with the sky, so that there was no horizon, only an endless tapestry of stars all around.

"How do you feel?" she called to Ashley over the howling wind.

Ashley grinned, her face more alive than Liz had seen it in weeks. Her amber eyes shone like twin beams in the darkness.

"Like I'm home!" she shouted back.

They fell silent then, drifting in the peaceful calm of the night sky. Liz studied Ashley as they flew, remembering again the girl she'd first met in their prison cell. Ashley had said something profound then—something that had given them all hope in those dark days. She'd told them that Halt and their captors were only human, that they would make mistakes.

Thinking about the past few weeks, the things they had endured, Liz found herself wondering if there was more to those words than any of them could have imagined. Because despite everything that had been done to them, the torture and experimentation, they were still only human. With all the loss and horror and guilt they had endured, it was a miracle one of them hadn't crumbled long ago.

And of them all, Ashley had endured the most. While the bullet wound had healed, the aftermath of Ashley's fall had left far deeper scars. Liz just hoped her friend could claw her way back from the brink.

"You know what I always dreamed of doing?" Ashley asked suddenly, a grin splitting her face.

Liz shook her head, and Ashley laughed. Without offering any further explanation, she folded her wings and dove towards the distant city. Liz's heart lurched in her chest. Tucking in in her wings, she gave chase.

"What are you doing?" Liz screamed, but the howling wind tore her words away.

Below, Ashley plummeted through open air, her wings still drawn tight against her back. Skyscrapers loomed as they drew level with their rooftops. Only then did Ashley pull out of her dive. White wings struck the air, sending her racing through the maze of buildings, until ahead, they gave way to the waters of the San Francisco harbor.

Liz adjusted her course, surprised by Ashley's speed. She

heard the soft crash of waves from below as the winds raged on the harbor, and away to their right she saw the lights of Alcatraz. The prison had been reopened during the American War, and had since been used to hold those convicted of treason while they awaited execution. Or so Liz had thought, until a few months ago.

But it wasn't the prison Ashley was making for. Her wings shifted, lifting her higher again, as lights loomed above. Blinking, Liz couldn't help but grin as they flew up through the twisting suspension. Red paint glimmered in the fluorescent lights, while below the odd car made its way across the harbor, unaware of the two fugitives soaring overhead.

Liz laughed as Ashley reached the top of the steel suspension and dropped onto one of the crossbeams. With the wind swirling around them, it was no easy feat, and Liz took care not to knock the other girl off as she followed suit. Landing lightly, she shivered as her bare feet touched the cold steel. She shook her head, a grin on her lips.

The Golden Gate Bridge.

The bridge of dreams, the symbol of their capital and the young nation that had been born from the ashes of the United States. It had survived the passing of the empire that had built it, and might yet live to see the fall of another.

Ashley lowered herself down, so that she sat with her feet hanging out over open space. With her white wings dangling behind her, she looked like some guardian angel, sitting in watch over the Golden City.

But Liz could see the fear in the whites of Ashley's eyes. Her face was pale and whatever courage had brought her this far, it was quickly fading.

Liz sat beside Ashley and wrapped an arm around her shoulders. "Are you okay?"

Ashley shivered in her arms. "This was a mistake," she whispered. "They'll see us."

She didn't move, and Liz pulled her closer. "No, they won't," she laughed, "and if they do, just let them try and catch us up here."

When Ashley didn't reply, Liz went on. "They're not going to find us, Ashley. I'm not going back to that laboratory, and neither are you. We'll never wear those collars again."

"Words," Ashley said, looking at her. "They're just words—from you, from Sam, from my parents. They *will* come for us, just like they did my sister. They have to. We're a loose end they can't afford to leave free. We barely survived the square."

"Then we'll go for them first," Liz growled. She gave Ashley's shoulder a squeeze. "The Director, the President, heck, Halt's ghost for all I care. We'll take them all down if we have to. That's what we're doing now, isn't it? When Mike comes back..."

"He's not coming back," Ashley whispered.

Liz shivered, her own doubts rising to the surface. She pressed them down. "Maybe, maybe not. If he doesn't, we'll go instead. We can't give up." She paused and stared out over the city. Finally, she went on. "I don't know what Halt did to you, Ash..."

"He broke me." There were tears in Ashley's eyes as she looked out at the city.

"Did he?" Liz asked softly, giving Ashley's arm a squeeze.

Ashley took a great, shuddering break. "No," she whispered. "I can't, I won't, let his cruelty define me. But in the square...I was so afraid, I couldn't move..."

"We're all afraid," Liz said, "and that's okay—but we don't have the luxury of giving up. Too many people have sacrificed their lives for us to go hide under a rock. Richard and Fallow, our parents, those women in the square. We can't run away now. We have to fight."

Ashley closed her eyes, but after a long moment, she nodded. Smiling, Liz let her go, and turned back to the city. Sitting up there, high above it all, it was easy to picture San Francisco as she had once imagined it. As a child, it had always been so distant, a mythical place she could only ever dream of visiting. Those dreams had soured her first day of boarding school. Her time there had taught her only hatred and cruelty, and within days she had longed to escape.

Now though, she felt a touch of that old magic return. Up

here, it was easy to forget the corruption that plagued the city, the vile cruelty of the men and women who ruled it. Up here, she could almost imagine the San Francisco of old, the city that had stood against the corruption of the United States, that had led the Western Allied States to freedom.

"I don't know how to face him," Ashley whispered suddenly.

"Who?"

"Sam," Ashley breathed. "I know he did it for me, but…I wish he hadn't. There is already so much blood on my hands, I can't take being responsible for the deaths of all those kids as well."

"It doesn't have to be that way," Liz said. "Help us stop them, before they have the chance to murder any more children. Whether the Texan returns or not, we need your help, Ash."

Ashley's chest swelled as she sucked in a breath and forced a smile. "You're right," she said, nodding. "We'll stop them, before it's too late."

"Good," Liz said.

"We should be getting back," Ashley replied as the distant screech of sirens carried to them. "The sun will be up soon."

Liz smiled. "Are you okay?"

Ashley shrugged. "It is what it is." Their eyes met, and for a second Liz caught a flash of the old fire in her friend's eyes. "But thank you, Liz. You were right, I needed this."

"We both did." Liz laughed, standing. "Let's go home."

57

Chris looked up from the sofa as the lounge window squeaked, then jumped as a head appeared beyond the glass. He relaxed when he saw it was only Liz. She scrambled inside before turning back to offer a gloved hand to someone behind her.

Anger flared in Chris's chest as Ashley clambered inside. Keeping their eyes carefully averted, the two girls slipped off into the corridor. Chris bit back his questions and rose from the couch to follow them. He'd woken an hour ago in darkness, and unable to sleep, had risen and taken over watch from the Madwoman sitting in the living room.

In the corridor, Liz bid Ashley goodnight and closed the door behind her. Her eyes widened as she turned and saw him, and for a moment they stood staring at each other in silence. Finally, she nodded and moved towards him. Chris let out a long sigh as they returned to the living room and took seats on opposite couches.

"What was that about?" Chris asked, trying to keep the anger from his voice.

"She's been struggling…with what Halt did to her. And what Sam did *for* her," Liz replied. "I think she'll be okay, but…" She trailed off as their eyes met.

Chris could feel the barrier stretching between them. Since

the agonizing kiss they'd shared, Liz had distanced herself, pushing him away until Chris found himself questioning everything they'd ever felt for each other.

Watching her now, Chris knew he had a choice to make: let whatever bond they shared between them shrivel and die, or push through the walls Liz had created around herself. Taking a breath, he stood and crossed to her couch. His heart pounded hard in his chest, and an icy tingle wrapped around his stomach as he sat. Remembered pain laced through his veins, but he bit his tongue and forced it away.

Liz watched him quietly, her eyes distant. "Chris..." She started to speak, but Chris pressed his lips to hers before she could continue.

She stiffened beneath him, and he paused, his lips lingering as he waited for her reaction. When she made no move to push him away, he kissed her again. A moan rattled up from her throat, but he felt her hand against his chest, as though she were gathering the will to push him away.

Stilling, he pulled back. Looking into her eyes, he waited for Liz to speak.

"Chris..." she whispered, her eyes watering. "What if..."

Chris shook his head. "What if we die tomorrow?"

Then his lips were hard against hers again, and now she was responding. Desire throbbed in Chris's chest as her arms encircled him. He threaded his fingers through her hair and kissed her harder. All thought of venom and pain fell away as they lost themselves in one another.

When the agony finally came, Chris did not resist. He embraced it, opening himself to its fiery touch. He didn't release Liz, only kissed her harder. His hands trailed down her back, stroking her jet-black feathers, even as lines of fire wrapped around his mind. Somehow, it made no difference. He clung to Liz beneath him, feeling the warmth of her body wash over him, mingling with the fire of her touch, until he could no longer distinguish between the two.

He shivered as her hands slid beneath his shirt. She had lost her gloves, and her touch sent tendrils of pleasure rippling through him. The fire was quick to follow, burning its way down his spine, though it was cooler now, softer.

Emboldened, Chris trailed his fingers up Liz's jeans and slipped them under her top. Pressed tightly together, there was little room for them to maneuver, but he felt the tremor sweep through her as he stroked her belly. Their lips broke apart as she gasped, then he was kissing her neck, her throat, and her arms were wrapped around his neck, pulling him hard against her.

When they finally broke apart, Liz was bright red and gasping for breath. They lay side by side on the couch, wrapped in one another's arms, basking in the heat of their bodies. Chris still felt the tingling of her venom seeping through his skin, a foreign heat in his veins, but it had been reduced to a dull ache now.

Smiling, he leaned across and kissed Liz on the forehead. There were tears in her eyes when he pulled away.

"Chris." She reached up and stroked his cheek. "I never thought…I'm sorry, I was only trying to protect you."

"Liz." He ran a hand through her curly black hair, lost in her big blue eyes. "I don't need you to protect me. I know I don't always make the best decisions, but they're still mine to make. I told you I could take it—you should have trusted me."

Liz closed her eyes, and he felt her shaking in his arms. "I know…I was afraid, though. Afraid of hurting you…or worse."

Chris laughed. "Let me worry about that."

He grinned as Liz wriggled closer. With her hand on his cheek, her fire still touched him, but their clothes protected the rest of his body.

"Does it hurt?" she whispered. He could see the anxiety in her eyes.

"A little," he replied with a smile, his hands trailing over her body. "It's getting better, though. You're just going to have to be patient..."

Liz tilted back her head and arched an eyebrow. "Oh, I'm going to have to be patient, am I?" she asked, a smile on her lips now. "So none of that was you?"

"Okay, maybe we both have to be patient," he chuckled. His

mind turned back to what he'd seen earlier, Liz and Ashley sneaking into the house. "So, what were you two doing out there anyway?"

Twisting, Liz sat up on the couch. Chris did the same, his eyebrows raised in expectation.

"We needed some fresh air," Liz said softly.

"Where did you go?" Chris asked.

Liz's cheeks turned beet-red, and there was a long pause before she answered: "The Golden Gate Bridge!"

Chris blinked, and then started to laugh. "Wow, so much for lying low!"

Liz leaned back on the couch and turned on her side. "You don't feel frustrated, sitting here, trapped like this, not knowing what's happening, whether the damned Texan betrayed us?"

"A little," Chris admitted, his stomach clenching, "but it's for the best. When Mike gets back, we'll know what our next move should be. Until then, we don't have anything to gain by going out there."

"I don't know how you can trust him," Liz replied. Her voice was strained, and Chris could hear the anger behind her words. "How you can trust *them.* I know Maria is your grandmother, but Jasmine's right, this isn't their fight anymore; it's ours. We need to be doing *something*, not sitting here, waiting like chickens for the slaughter."

Chris sighed, his eyes falling to the threadbare carpet. After everything he'd been through since the day they'd woken in their steel cages, he wanted nothing more than to rest, to have a few days or weeks without the weight of the world hanging over him. Let someone else to make the decisions for once—after all the mistakes he'd made, he was the last one Liz and the others should be turning to. At night he still found himself replaying the fight in the courthouse, wondering what he could have done differently.

Then, of course, there was massacre in Independence Square, and the bullets Sam and Mira had taken for his recklessness.

No.

Let the Texan and the Madwomen make the decisions.

He was done.

Chris could see in Liz's eyes what she wanted him to say, though. Liz wanted him to admit she was right, that they should go out and do *something*, anything to help undermine the government's power.

But he couldn't do it.

Because what if he was wrong, and someone else died?

Unable to meet her gaze any longer, he turned away. "Mike will know what to do. He's the professional."

"If he's telling the truth," Liz snapped. "And what if he doesn't come back?" Her strong hands gripped him by the shoulder, forcing him to look at her. "Chris, even if he does return, that man isn't one of us. He doesn't know what we've been through, hasn't seen what these people are capable of. *You* have. *We* have. We need to stick together, make our own decisions. All of us…including you."

Chris swallowed, trapped by the fire in her eyes.

"I don't know what's happening with you, Chris," she said softly, "but I need you to snap out of it."

With that, Liz rose and disappeared into the corridor, leaving Chris alone in the growing daylight. He sat staring at the worn carpet for a long time, wondering at her words, at whether she was right.

Yet even if she was, what could they do?

58

Susan groaned, the sharp pounding of a headache tearing her from sleep. Opening her eyes, she squinted into the dim light, struggling to take in her surroundings. Slowly, they came into focus, lit by a single lightbulb dangling from the ceiling.

She was in some kind of wooden hut, its single room furnished by two sets of bunk beds and a steel counter that served as a kitchen. The mattresses on the beds were half-rotten, and stains marked the ceiling where rain had seeped through the iron roof. Outside, the wind howled, and Susan shivered as a breath of cold air swept across her neck. The place stank of mildew and age, but another, sweeter scent lingered, too.

The only other sound was a dim whirring, and turning, Susan found one of her portable refrigerator units plugged into a wall socket. Her stomach twisted as everything came rushing back. She looked at her hands and saw the dried blood covering her skin. A scream built in her throat.

What have I become?

"Susan." She jumped as a voice spoke behind her.

Spinning, Susan stumbled backwards as she found the old *Chead* woman watching her. Aged beyond belief, she sat on a worn-out sofa, her murky white eyes aglow. A smile twitched her lips as she stood.

"Welcome, Susan," the old *Chead* said, spreading her arms.

Susan backed away as the woman approached. "Where am I? What...*what did I do*?"

The old *Chead* laughed. "We are someplace on the way to where we need to be." The wrinkled face tilted to the side. "Would you like to eat?" She ignored Susan's other question.

A lump lodged in Susan's throat as images from the laboratory flashed through her mind. Bending in two, she gagged, struggling to breathe through her twisted stomach. Over the sounds of her distress, she could hear the *Chead* laughing.

Managing to swallow her nausea, Susan straightened. The old *Chead* only grinned, then crossed to the kitchen bench. A pan sat on an old gas burner. Removing the lid, the *Chead* revealed the contents—a haunch of white meat that might have come from a turkey.

"We only consume...raw meat...when the rage is upon us," she said, answering Susan's unspoken question. Lifting the pan, she offered it to Susan. "Most times, cooked is preferable. We are not the animals humans believe us to be."

Susan stared at the turkey leg, her stomach rumbling. She glanced one last time at the old *Chead*, then snatched up the leg. The *Chead* cackled as she tore into the meat. Stepping around Susan, she returned to her seat on the couch.

Susan paused for breath, before taking another bite. As she ate, she studied the *Chead*. Back in the facility, the ancient creature had been terrifying. Susan had watched those wrinkled hands crush the life from a woman as easily as she would swat a fly. Yet now, the *Chead* seemed calm, almost kind. And sniffing, Susan realized the old *Chead* was the source of the sweet scent filling the cabin.

"Who..." She frowned, struggling to form the words. "Who...are...you?"

"Your speech will return, eventually." A smile spread across the wrinkled face. "And I am Talisa."

Susan shivered, her thoughts whirring. Frowning, she tried to find the words for her next question. It took several minutes.

"Where...did you...come from?"

"The wild," the *Chead* replied.

That's impossible, Susan thought, but the words would not form on her lips. Seeing the look on Susan's face, her companion continued.

"The humans hunt us, when we change," she whispered, "but they are slow and weak, and many of us escape. Our scent draws us together, and over the years we have gathered. When I first woke, I wandered alone for a time—until I found others of my kind. We are stronger together."

Susan finished her haunch of turkey and tossed the bone to the floor. She still stood in the middle of the room. The sweet scent lingered in her nostrils, seeming to call to her, and without thinking she crossed to the couch and sat beside the old woman.

"How…long?" she croaked.

The wrinkles around the woman's eyes crinkled with sadness. "I was a woman grown…when I changed. But time passes differently for our kind." She looked at her wrinkled arms. "I have only lived a few years with my new children. Already my time draws near."

"No…" Susan whispered, her heart twisting with an indescribable sadness.

The woman smiled. "I will not pass before my task is done."

Susan found her eyes drawn back to the storage container, and the stocks of virus frozen inside. The cabin must've had a generator—she could hear it whirring somewhere outside. She opened her mouth, but words failed her, and she jerked her head in frustration.

"Hecate was a blessing, when he came to us," the old *Chead* continued. "He must be rewarded for leading us to your home."

Remembering the hunger in Hecate's eyes, Susan shivered. "How…how could he…have found you?"

The old woman reached out and stroked her cheek. "He followed our scent, as so many others have before him. My pack and I found a haven. Over the years our numbers have swelled, as others were drawn to our home."

Fear turned the blood in Susan's veins to ice. "How…many?"

Soft laughter came from the old woman's throat. Standing, she offered her hand. "Come, let me show you."

Somewhere in Susan's mind, a voice screamed for her to run, but her body acted with a will of its own and she took the woman's hand. Rising, she allowed the *Chead* to lead her to the door. The hinges squealed as they stepped out into the darkness.

Above, not a star shone in the sky, and Susan blinked, expecting to be blind. But as she stared into the gloom, the world came into perfect focus. Open plains stretched around the cottage, while in the distance the silhouettes of mountains bordered the sky.

Movement drew Susan's eyes back to the fields. Shadows shifted in the grass, coming closer, and again the voice shouted for her to flee. With the iron grip on her hand, there was no escape, and she stood and watched as the *Chead* gathered.

There were dozens and dozens.

She shuddered as Talisa turned to face her.

"Welcome home."

59

"What are you doing out of bed, young man?"

Sam tried not to roll his eyes at the woman standing in the doorway. Eve had shown him nothing but kindness—stitching up his leg and changing his bandages every day—but her motherly care was beginning to grate on him.

It was understandable, of course. Eve was over seventy years old and had seen more than her fair share of wounds. According to her encyclopedic memory, his should have taken months to heal, and Mira's even longer. But she had never treated anyone with wings before. Ashley had only taken weeks to recover from the bullet that had almost killed her, and neither Sam nor Mira were anywhere near the state she'd been in.

"I'm fine, Doc." Standing on one foot, he waved his wounded leg in the air. "See?"

Eve tisked and strode across the room to grab him by the ankle. He squawked as she lifted his leg and touched a finger to his bandages. "Oh really?" She raised an eyebrow. "Doesn't look fine to me. You've ripped another stitch."

"Sorry, Doc," Sam said sheepishly.

The woman rolled her eyes. "You need bedrest, young man. So does that girl, come to mention it. Where's she gotten to this time?"

Sam shrugged, but he couldn't keep the smile from his face. If he was a difficult patient, Mira was an impossible one. Despite Eve's best efforts, the girl came and went as she pleased. Even posting a guard in the hallway hadn't helped. Mira could be as quiet as a mouse when she wanted to be—and seemed to take great joy in scaring those around her half to death.

"She's in the living room with Jasmine," said Ashley, stepping into the little infirmary. Sam's heart lurched.

The breath caught in Sam's throat as their eyes met. Ashley stared at him, her expression unreadable, before turning to Eve.

"I'll make sure he gets back in bed, Eve," she said. "Promise."

Eve nodded and flashed him another look. "Yes, maybe he'll listen to his girlfriend."

"We're not—" Ashley and Sam said together, but the woman was already gone.

Sam's cheeks flushed as he found himself suddenly alone with Ashley. He hadn't seen her in over a week, not since she'd fled the infirmary talking about blood and guilt.

"It's good to see you," he offered cautiously.

For a long moment Ashley said nothing. Then she was crossing the room, her wings and arms outstretched to embrace him. Sam gasped as she kissed him, taken aback by her sudden change. He staggered, groaning as his injured leg took his weight.

He fell heavily against the bed and held Ashley back, still struggling with the pain. Her face paled and she pressed a hand to her lips. "Sorry, I didn't mean—"

Sam forced a smile. "It's okay," he said, before a frown crossed his face. "Not that I'm complaining…but what's gotten into you, Ash?"

A smile tugged at Ashley's lips. She lay down beside him and pulled him into her arms.

"I've been so afraid, Sam. Afraid of letting everyone down, of being captured, of dying. Afraid of loving you." She kissed him again, softly now. "I don't want to be afraid anymore."

Her fingers stroked his cheek, banishing his last reservations. He drew her closer, their lips meeting once more. In his arms, she felt so small, so fragile—yet as she pressed herself against him, Sam could feel her strength. She had been through the flames, but here she was, alive and ready to face her fears.

His hands slid down her back, exploring the curves of her wings, feeling the feathers trembling at his touch. Slowly his fingers ventured further, raising goosebumps along the small of her back. Her lips parted, then she was kissing his neck, and her hands were sliding beneath his shirt, lighting fires with each soft caress.

Sam moaned as she climbed on top of him. His leg ached, but then she was tugging off her top, and the pain was forgotten. Sitting up, Sam kissed the small of her throat before moving to her breasts, savoring the softness of her skin beneath his lips. Her hands pulled at his shirt, then tore it from his shoulders. He jumped as her teeth nipped his neck, but he only pulled her tighter. His heart raced as her breasts pressed against his naked chest.

A gasp tore from Ashley's throat, and then she was pushing him down. He lay back on his pillow and stared up at her, feasting on the sight of her naked body. Her pale skin glowed in the incandescent light, a stark contrast to his own, while her white wings extended out to either side of her. The pink circles of her nipples lit a fire in his chest. He reached for her again.

Smiling, Ashley caught him by the wrists and pinned him to the bed. She arched an eyebrow and kissed him on the nose. A tremor went through him, but as Ashley pulled back, he caught a strange look in her eyes.

"What is it?" he whispered.

The smile fell from Ashley's lips as she released him. She looked down, one finger playing with the hairs on his chest. "Sam…I have to go away for a while."

Sam frowned. "What?"

Ashley sighed. "No one here wants to admit it, Sam, but the Texan is gone. I can see it in their faces. He should have made contact by now, but he hasn't. If we're going to find out more about this thing they did to us, if there's a cure, if we can fix what we did, we're going to have to see the professor ourselves."

"What we did?"

She looked away, but he could feel her starting to shake. "Halt used me, Sam. He used me to get to you. If any other kids die in their vile experiments, it will be my fault as much as yours. We have to stop them, before they hurt anyone else."

Sam reached out and brushed the scarlet curls from Ashley's face. "It doesn't have to be you, Ash."

Ashley leaned down and kissed him again. "Well, it can't be you. Someone went and got himself shot." Her smile faded and she grew serious again. "They need me, Sam. I'm the only one who knows the university. And I need to fix things."

Tendrils of fire wrapped their way around Sam's heart as he felt a terrible fear—not for himself, but for the girl he had come to love, who he had sacrificed everything to protect. But now it was her turn to put her life on the line, and there was nothing he could do to stop her.

Silently, he hugged Ashley to him. Closing his eyes, he tried to keep the tears from flowing. They lay like that for a long time, wrapped in each other's embrace, until Sam was sure Ashley must have fallen asleep. But when he kissed her forehead, she stirred. She lifted her head, and her golden eyes blinked down at him. A smile spread across her face, and leaning forward, she kissed him back.

"Let's not waste the time we have," she whispered in his ear.

❧ 60 ☙

Another day passed before Chris allowed himself to admit that Liz was right. It had been a week since the Texan had departed, and they couldn't sit waiting any longer to see whether he would return. Besides, whatever his grandmother and the Madwomen said, it was obvious something had gone wrong. It was clear in the faces of the men and women who guarded the house, in the hardening of their brows and the falseness to their smiles.

It could mean only one of two things. Either the Texan had been taken, or he'd betrayed them.

"He's gone, isn't he?" Chris said as he entered the dining room.

His grandmother looked up from the kitchen table. Their eyes met, and he watched a wave of weariness sweep across her face. His shoulders fell and he sank into a chair beside her. Until that moment, he'd still clung to the hope he was missing something, that there was some explanation for the Texan's continued absence.

A paltry lunch had been set on the table, and taking a slice of bread, he made himself a peanut butter jelly sandwich. As he buttered the bread, he struggled to hide the trembling of his hands.

"We can't know," Maria whispered as he finished.

Taking a bite of his sandwich, Chris considered her words. The food tasted like dust, and his stomach recoiled, but he knew he needed the sustenance. He had hardly slept or eaten since his conversation with Liz.

"He was meant to be back by now," Chris said finally. "We can't stay here. If he's betrayed us…"

"He hasn't."

"Then he's been taken, and it's only a matter of time before they make him talk," Chris countered.

His grandmother bowed her head, and Chris knew he was right. A dozen thoughts raced through his mind as he considered what their next move should be. A part of him longed to flee, to take his grandmother and the others and vanish. They could find a place in the countryside, somewhere deep in the mountain forests, and never be seen again.

Then Richard's face appeared in his mind, and Chris knew they couldn't do it. They had to fight, to make Richard's sacrifice worth something.

That meant taking the fight to the government.

The night before, he had toyed with the idea of revealing themselves. He had even discussed it with Sam. They'd both liked the thought of throwing a spanner in the government's plan. The Director would struggle to explain how the three teenagers she'd called terrorists had grown wings. But Chris feared it would never get that far. They had already revealed themselves in Independence Square, and while rumors continued to be reported, the truth was unlikely to emerge.

He feared the Madwomen who had died in the square had given their lives for nothing.

That only left their original idea—to go to the university themselves and speak with the professor Ashley had mentioned. He was the only one who could help them learn more about themselves: about what afflicted Liz and Jasmine, and whether their transformation could be reversed. It was a frail hope, but they had nothing else.

"So what now, Chris?" Liz asked, appearing in the doorway.

Chris sighed as the others followed behind her—Ashley and Jasmine and Sam and Mira. The later two were still recovering from their injuries, but he could see the fire burning in Jasmine's eyes. The edge seemed to have gone from her grief, but her anger burned on. He knew she wanted retribution—he just hoped it wouldn't consume her again.

There was still a wary look in Ashley's eyes, but they no longer held the terror he had seen there before. His gaze lingered on her face, wondering if she was ready for what would come next. They would need her help if they were going to reach the professor.

Feeling their eyes on him, Chris thought about Liz's question. He gripped the tabletop, feeling the weight of responsibility on his shoulders. Gritting his teeth, he glanced at his grandmother, seeking guidance. But he knew it wasn't up to her. What Jasmine had said all those days ago was true—this was their fight.

He sucked in a breath and nodded to himself. "I think it's time we paid the professor a visit of our own."

Silently, he watched the others for their reaction. They were blood now; he knew each of them better than even his closest friends from his old life.

Jasmine was the easiest to read. Grinning, she took her seat at the table. Liz joined her, the fire in her eyes almost as fierce as Jasmine's. Both had suffered the terror of losing control, of becoming *Chead*—the very creatures their communities feared more than anything else. Of all of them, it was Liz and Jasmine who wanted a cure more than anything else.

Not to mention a chance for revenge.

But it was Ashley they really needed. She stood staring out the kitchen window, her eyes distant. Chris could sense the war taking place within her—between the brave girl he had known back in the facility, and the one who had frozen in Independence Square. Holding his breath, he waited to see which would win.

Finally, Ashley nodded and sat. Sam and Mira followed suit, though a shadow hung over Sam's face. Neither he nor Mira would be able to come—not with their injuries. With the wound in her shoulder, Mira still couldn't fly, and both would be worse than useless if it came to a fight.

Sam reached across the table and gripped Ashley by the wrist. "You don't have to go, Ash," he said quietly.

Ashley returned a sad smile. "I do, Sam." She looked at Chris. "If I stay, it'll just be three."

"We don't even know there will be a fight," Chris replied, though he didn't believe the words, "and if there is, we've faced worse odds."

"And lost more than a few times," Ashley countered. She shrugged off Sam's hand and smiled, and Chris caught a glimpse of the girl he'd known before their escape. "No, you need me. Otherwise, who will keep you from getting distracted by all those college girls, Chris?"

Chris raised an eyebrow, and Liz chuckled. "He'd better not."

Ashley smiled. "If Mike really has been caught, they'll be watching the professor. But on the campus, we'll just be like any other students."

"You think we can sneak into one of his classes?" Liz asked.

"We won't even have to sneak." Ashley grinned. "Once we're on campus, they don't check student IDs for individual lectures. And the classes are usually big enough that no one will notice a few extras. We can walk right in and talk to him at the end of the lecture."

Silence fell around the table. Chris studied his hands, turning the plan over in his head, searching for holes. He bit his lip. Surely there had to be a less risky way of approaching the professor. If they were spotted, they would end up trapped in the lecture hall. But as the silence stretched out, nothing else came to him.

"It's a terrible risk." He looked up as his grandmother finally spoke.

Her eyes were cautious as she looked around the table, but she attempted a smile. "Your grandfather would be proud, Chris."

Letting out a long sigh, Chris nodded. "Okay, so we go with Plan C."

61

The *Chead* ran all the next day, their endless stamina carrying them over the long plains and raging rivers and rolling hills. Susan went with them—though each time she glimpsed the grey eyes of the creatures, she shook with fear. At times her mind wandered, and it seemed another presence took her place. Hours later she would wake and find the landscape had changed while she dreamed.

By the time the creatures stopped to rest, Susan's legs were burning and her whole body ached. The relentless sun had turned her pale skin red. She struggled to think through the pain, her mind unruly, her senses dulled by the scent of the *Chead*. It was a constant presence now, a sweetness that hung in the air, stirring dark desires in the pit of her stomach.

Susan slumped to the ground, wanting only to curl up into a ball and sleep. But as she closed her eyes, she felt that other presence in the back of her mind, a red haze swelling in the darkness, threatening to drown her. Her eyes snapped open again. Digging her fingers into the dirt, she fought the fog back.

They had stopped beside an old farmhouse, though it looked to be in far better condition than the last. A faint trace of smoke came from the chimney, and a long dried-up riverbed threaded its way past the house. She glimpsed several *Chead* wandering along the gravel. Movement came from nearby, and Susan was surprised when she found Talisa approaching.

"Susan," the old *Chead* said.

Susan shuddered. Something about the woman's voice called to her. Looking into Talisa's eyes, she could feel her will crumbling, swept away by a yearning to obey.

"Yes, Talisa," she whispered, still crouched on her knees.

Talisa offered her hand. "Come."

Susan followed the old woman through the host of *Chead*. She tried to count them as they passed, but her mind was foggy, sluggish, and she quickly lost track.

So many, she thought, but she couldn't know.

Ahead the ground dropped down to the riverbed. She followed Talisa out onto the gravel, and together they moved downhill, away from the other *Chead*. Susan watched the old woman, wondering where she was taking her, but Talisa did not look back, and all Susan could do was follow obediently in her wake.

Finally, Talisa drew to a stop in the shadow of the riverbank. Staring into the darkness, it was a moment before Susan realized there was more to the shadows. A cavern beckoned amidst the broken gravel, its mouth disappearing out of sight and knowledge.

"You will sleep within tonight." Talisa nodded towards the cave.

Susan's forehead creased, but as she started to object, her eyes met Talisa's. The sweet scent of the *Chead* wafted around her, and the words died in her throat. She swallowed and nodded demurely. Moving past Talisa, she stood in the mouth of the cave.

"What...do I...do?" she managed.

"Wait," Talisa replied.

Biting her lip, Susan lowered herself into the darkness before she could lose her nerve. Halfway down, a rock slipped beneath her foot, and before she could recover, she fell. Darkness rose to swallow her, and an instant later she struck the ground.

Groaning, Susan sat up on the hard rock, her scream still

echoing around her. In the pitch-black, even her newly-enhanced vision took time to adjust. Standing, she sucked in a breath to steady herself. The sweet scent had vanished, and her stomach twisted. A pain started in her chest as an awful emptiness crept through her. Wrapping her arms around herself, Susan spun, seeking something, anything, to distract herself.

She was in a narrow cavern, its stone walls worn smooth by the passage of water. Fine gravel covered the floor, while in the corner, a tiny pool of water had gathered. She crouched beside it and cupping her hands together, drank the cooling liquid. Afterwards, she tried to wash the dried blood from her skin. Unfortunately, there was nothing she could do for her clothes. She shuddered as her colleague's screams rang in her mind and straightened again.

Behind her, gravel crunched. Susan spun towards the sound. Heart racing, she scanned the gloom, and latched onto a figure moving towards her. A scream built in her throat and raising her hands, she stumbled backwards.

"Susan," a voice whispered.

Susan froze, staring into the shadows. The voice was familiar. She frowned as Hecate took shape from the darkness.

"Hecate…" Susan struggled to form the words. "What are… you doing…here?"

Hecate took another step towards her. His grey eyes glowed in the darkness, and Susan felt a sudden yearning for a mirror, though she knew what she would see in her own eyes—a monster.

She shrank as Hecate continued forward, his eyes never leaving hers. His scent drifted through the cavern, and Susan felt the emptiness recede. She moaned, struggling to control the sudden racing of her heart. Her breath quickened as she looked up at Hecate. Her teeth started to chatter, and she took a step back, fighting to keep her body from shaking.

"I was…sent," Hecate whispered.

"Why…are we…here?" Susan managed.

The *Chead* looked around at the rock walls. "For decades, the

Chead have hidden…in these places." He turned back to her. "I found Talisa…and her family…in a place like this."

"That doesn't—" Susan response turned to a yelp as Hecate took another step towards her. Raising her arms, she stammered a warning. "Stay…back!"

Her words sounded weak and feeble, and Hecate ignored them. She flinched as he raised his hand, but he did not strike her. Instead, the *Chead* lifted a finger to her cheek. "You are…home."

"Home?" Susan shook her head. "No…"

"Yes…" Hecate said. "You are mine…now."

Susan's whole body was shaking, and a voice was screaming in the back of her mind, but she stood frozen, her legs fixed to the ground. Looking up into the *Chead's* eyes, she saw something there. To her horror, she felt herself responding. Hunger swelled in her chest as the sweetness of the *Chead* wrapped around her.

Still she shook her head. Somehow, she found the will to move and staggered back. The gravel slipped beneath her feet and she tumbled to the ground.

"No, no, no," she whispered, scrambling away.

The *Chead* watched her with its strange, unblinking eyes. Susan stilled as she looked back and saw he had not moved. A long silence stretched out, the only sound the distant dripping of water. Susan hardly dared to breathe. Her heart was pounding in her ears. Fiery ripples spread across her skin, as though her entire body had come alive.

Still the *Chead* did not move, only watched her, waiting. Susan sucked in a breath, and the richness of his scent flooded her nostrils. She shuddered. The smell filled the cavern, drowning her, smothering her mind like a blanket.

What is happening to me?

She flinched as Hecate moved, but he only offered his arm. She stared at it for a moment, her terror fading. A strange peace took its place, sweeping away her worries. Looking into Hecate's eyes, she nodded, and took the offered hand.

With a yank of his arm, Susan was propelled to her feet. She gasped, her heart racing as the Hecate's strong arms wrapped around her. For a second, she felt herself again, and terror twisted in her stomach. She gasped, but her face was buried in his chest and his scent was so strong she could taste it. A yellow haze swirled around the edges of her vision.

"Hecate," she whispered.

The *Chead* nodded. For the first time Susan looked at him, and truly saw him. When she had encountered Hecate back in the facility, she had not stopped to think of him as a person. She had thought of the *Chead* as nothing more than monsters, creatures of the dark, come to kill them all.

Now Susan knew she had been wrong. As the yellow haze filled her mind, she realized the creatures had only wanted to free her, to break her from the shackles of her humanity. There was no terror or sadness now—only joy, only desire.

She shivered as Hecate's arms went around her waist. Another scream echoed in the back of her mind, but her entire body was aflame, and she ignored it. Her skin was alive; even the touch of her clothing made her scream with longing.

"You are mine," Hecate whispered, his grey eyes boring into hers.

His arms tightened around her, pulling her close, and she felt his power. Susan trembled in his arms, the strength fleeing her legs. She lifted her head, staring into those strange grey eyes, seeing their depth. Desire wrapped around her and she almost screamed for him to take her, to quench the longing in her stomach.

But Hecate only stared back at her, his eyes wide, his face expectant, and Susan realized his last words had not been a statement, but a question.

Shaking in his arms, Susan recalled a distant memory, one of disgust, of a voice screaming out in protest. Looking into Hecate's eyes, she could not think why. All memory was fading, falling away, until she could only remember this cave, this place, this moment.

"Yes," she breathed.

VIII
RETALIATION

62

Liz drew in a long breath as the elevator *dinged* and the steel doors clanged open. She cast a furtive glance outside before nodding for Ashley to take the lead. Her friend forced a grin, though her eyes betrayed her nerves. Pulling the raincoat tighter around her shoulders, Ashley stepped from the elevator. Liz, Chris, and Jasmine followed close on her heels.

They had landed on the roof of the ten-story library to avoid the guards checking IDs at the gates. According to Ashley, this was the only security measure the university took to stop interlopers, but Liz still couldn't help but hold her breath. The scent of old paper was strong in the air as they threaded their way between the rows of books and headed for the exit.

As they neared the sliding glass doors, Ashley slowed. Following the direction of her gaze, Liz saw the guard standing beside the exit. He wore a blue uniform and had a handgun at his side, but his eyes were bored, and he was practically leaning against the wall.

Laughing, Liz looped her arm through Ashley's and nodded towards the exit. "I know, Professor McKenzie's a bore, but just another hour and we're done for the day." She tugged on Ashley's arm and together they walked out, Chris and Jasmine a step behind them. The guard didn't give them a second glance.

A fine rain was falling outside, but they were all already soaked from their flight. None of them were complaining, though—the low-lying clouds had offered the perfect cover and there was no chance anyone had spotted their approach. Releasing Ashley's arm, Liz flashed her a smile.

"Easy!" she said. "So, where to now?"

"The engineering department, according to the schedule on the boards. His class starts in ten minutes."

Liz frowned. "Are you sure you got that right? I thought genetics was a biology class."

Ashley grinned. "Don't get me started. The schedules here don't make any sense. Now come on, we don't want to be late." She started off without waiting for an answer.

"Were you ever late in your life?" Liz called after her.

Ashley glared back at her. "Of course I was." She paused, her eyes growing distant for a second. "I just can't remember when."

Chris chuckled and Liz only shook her head. From the first moment they'd met, Ashley had appeared a model of perfection. While Halt's cruelty had shattered that image, Liz had still not been surprised to learn the girl had started university early. There was certainly more to her than looks.

A shiver ran down Liz's spine as the wind howled around them. Without prompting, Ashley picked up the pace. Liz could feel the water dripping from her feathers and down her back, but there was little she could do about it. The students around them were just as soaked. They joined the crowds, moving quickly through the open squares, heads down and shoulders hunched against the rain. That at least served their purpose—no one was paying attention to the four strangers in their midst.

When they finally moved back indoors, the four of them kept their hoods up, aware that even here they might be recognized. Many of the other students did the same, apparently in too much of a rush to adjust their clothing.

Studying their faces, Liz swallowed as memories from her boarding school days surfaced. That time was long behind her now, but it hurt all the same. Far from home, in an unfamiliar city, and the only student from the countryside, Liz had been desperately lonely.

It might have been different if she'd found friends. But with her rustic accent and olive skin, there was no hiding her background. The other children had looked down on her, thinking she was beneath them, and played cruel pranks on her when the teachers weren't watching. Some had even tried to ambush her while she was alone, though they'd soon learned she had been raised far rougher than them.

The students moving along the corridor with them looked much the same as the ones who had tormented her all those years ago. Their expensive clothes stank of privilege, and Liz's stomach roiled as she struggled with her old prejudice. She knew now the wealthy kids weren't all the same. Ashley had been one of these teenagers, and Chris had dreamed of joining them.

We're not all evil, Liz. Some of us want to fix things, want the government to be held accountable.

She smiled. Chris had said that, a long time ago, as they sat alone in their cell. She hoped he was right. They would need these young minds on their side if the government fell. Someone would need to put the pieces of their nation back together. The older generation had already failed miserably at that task.

Idly, Liz wondered if she might join these students one day. If things changed, maybe there would be a place for her here. What would it be like, to walk amongst these students as an equal? To attend lectures in science or engineering and expand her mind. For a moment she allowed her thoughts to drift, to imagine…

She shook her head, the cold hands of reality wrapping themselves around her heart. Even if they somehow won, and brought down the government, she could never study here. Not now. Not with the deadly nematocysts in her skin, and the wings and the *Chead* rages. Chris and the others might try to reassure her, to convince themselves this professor held the answers, but she didn't dare hope.

And if the students in her boarding school could not accept

her before, they would never accept the freak of nature she had become.

Pushing aside the depressing thoughts, she realized Ashley and the others were drawing to a stop. A crowd of students barred their path, gathering around a set of massive double doors. Ashley flashed Liz a nervous look, her hands deep in her pockets.

"This is it," Ashley shouted over the roar of a hundred voices.

The volume increased as the double doors cracked open, and a second group of students poured out of the lecture hall. Those outside pressed forward as well, creating a bottleneck where the two groups came together. Liz shook her head and wondered just what the university was teaching them.

When the students outside finally parted to let the departing students through, the crowd thinned, and it was soon their turn to enter. Sucking in a breath, Liz smiled at the others, and decided it was her turn to take the lead. She grabbed Ashley's hand again and together they followed the crowd through the double doors.

Liz blinked as the bright lights inside stung her eyes. When her vision finally cleared, she was surprised to find herself in a lecture hall far larger than she'd expected. Steps led down from the double doors to the carpeted stage, where a lonely lectern stood empty. Foldable seats and desks stretched out in rows to either side of them, filling every step, until they were on the same level as the stage. There had to be at least four hundred seats, though the students had already filled half of them.

Spying four empty seats halfway down the stairs, Liz started towards them, dragging Ashley with her. Moving along the row, she sat down and leaned back in her chair, trying to relax. With everyone facing the lectern, no one could see her face unless they turned around, so she reached up and pulled off her hood.

At that moment, the rumbling of voices started to trail off, and for a second Liz thought she'd made a terrible mistake. She shrank in her seat as the room fell silent, her wings twitching beneath her jacket. Then her eyes alighted on the lectern, where a grey-haired man was now standing. She blinked, wondering where he had come from, before noticing the door on the side of the stage with a glowing "EXIT" sign above it.

There was a small computer at the lectern, and the man tapped a few buttons, prompting the white wall behind him to light up. Liz's eyes widened—even in her boarding school, only a few classrooms had had computers. Looking above her, she found a long steel beam stretching overhead, and a pair of projectors pointed at the front wall.

Returning her gaze to the professor, she studied his face, searching for some hint of what had befallen the Texan. Even from halfway up the hall, she could make him out with crystal clarity. He had a strong face, though he had seen better days. Age had worn away the hard edges of his cheekbones, and his skin hung in bags from his face. His eyes were red, as though he hadn't been sleeping well, and while he wore an expensive suit, it was creased, as though he'd slept in it. There was a stain on his collar.

Licking his lips, the professor glanced up at his students, then back to his computer screen. He tapped a few more buttons, and the light on the wall flickered. The image of a chromosome appeared alongside a young man. It was a moment before Liz realized his eyes were the cold grey of the *Chead*.

She shivered and glanced at the others, the hairs on her neck standing on end. They stared back, their faces pale. She could see the question in their eyes—the same one running through her mind.

Is it a coincidence?

But they had nowhere to go now. They were stuck in the middle of the row, hemmed in by the students on either side of them. If they got up now, every eye on the room would be on them. Liz gave a quick shake of her head, and Chris nodded back.

Stay put, his eyes said. *Don't panic.*

Around the lecture hall, the other students had seen the

image as well. The low buzz of their voices returned, quickly growing louder. The image had obviously disturbed some of them. Just as it seemed the whole room would erupt, the overhead speakers crackled, and an old voice spoke over the din.

"Welcome back to Genetics 201."

63

Liz gripped her desk as the professor's voice echoed around the room. At his words, the students had fallen silent, and every face present now watched the man in expectation.

Professor McKenzie placed his hands on the lectern, as though just standing was an effort for him. An audible sigh whispered through the speakers. Liz did her best not to slide down in her chair, uncomfortably aware of how exposed they were. The only protection they had was numbers—with the theatre near capacity, the professor was looking at almost four hundred faces. Even so, Liz couldn't help but feel like he was staring straight at her.

"The *Chead*." She flinched as his voice crackled over the speakers again. "They need no introduction. They have been a plague on this country for decades, though the infection has only recently reached our sheltered cities."

He released the lectern and moved out into the center of the stage. Liz saw he wore a wireless microphone and shook her head. Either the equipment was decades old, or the university had an even larger budget than her boarding school had.

McKenzie held his hands behind his back and continued: "I have discussed them many times in this class, though always in a theoretical manner. The *Chead* virus, its genetic code, its makeup, everything about it, is highly classified. As it should be—such information is dangerous. Should it become public knowledge, who knows what terrorist organizations and foreign powers might do with it?"

He paused, turning to face the rows of watching students. "Or that is the story they tell the public."

The breath caught in Liz's throat. She bit her lip, wondering if the others read his words the same as she had. Did this mean the Texan had succeeded? If the professor had sequenced their DNA, who knew what he might have learned about them, about the *Chead?*

"As you will all recall, I have been critical of the government's response to this epidemic. Even recently, with their bizarre experiments, I have questioned their strategy. As far as we, the public, are aware, even the mechanism by which the virus is contracted remains a mystery."

Liz heart was pounding in her ears. She wanted to scream for the man to get to the point, to tell them what he had discovered. Despite herself, hope swelled in her chest. Had this geneticist discovered something that the government, with all its experts, had not? Had he found a cure?

"Despite my criticism, I have remained a patriot. I have supported our government through the good and the bad." He sighed and returned to his lectern. Perspiration dripped from his brow, and a vein was bulging in his neck. "Over the years I have decried the rebels and terrorists who sought to tear down our young nation. So when a…dissident…came to me a few days ago, I did what any patriot would do. I ensured he was brought to justice, before he could cause any more harm."

A vice closed around Liz's throat. She shivered, and this time it had nothing to do with the wet feathers dripping down her back. The professor was talking about Mike. Despite her dislike for the man…she shuddered to think might have been done to him.

"But there was something different about this dissident," the professor went on. "Something I couldn't help but wonder over. He gave me something, something my scientific curiosity couldn't resist pursuing further. It wasn't much: a couple of feathers. But he claimed they came from the government's experiments. From wings…grown on humans."

A collective gasp came from around the hall. Several students half-rose from their seats, but the professor raised a hand, and a reluctant silence resumed.

"It couldn't be true," McKenzie continued. "That's what I told myself. But a little doubt niggled at me—that his claim was so preposterous, so easily proven wrong by a geneticist…I decided I had to be sure. For my own peace of mind, I sequenced the DNA from each feather."

He pressed a button on the screen, and the image changed to six multicolored double helixes of DNA. Five were virtually identical: mostly grey, but in places banded by slivers of red. On the sixth, the red bands were still present, but green bands also shone amidst the grey.

"I thought the man was mad, but his samples proved me wrong. The feathers were undoubtedly human in origin. But while mapping their DNA, I found distinct anomalies in their chromosomes. Genes from species of avian, feline, canine, cnidaria and a dozen other animal families. I also found genetic markers associated with Porcine Endogenous Retrovirus, or PERV, for those of you who remember this from Genetics 101. I had no choice but to conclude the man had somehow managed to acquire his feathers from the government's experiments."

"He must have gotten them from Fisherman's Wharf!" a student at the back of the room shouted.

"That was my first thought," the professor answered, holding up his hands to fend off further questions, "until I examined the feather from the sixth subject."

Liz frowned, looking again at the feather on the end. She guessed it was Mira's, and that the green bands were the genes from the *Chead* virus she had been infected with. But what could that have told the professor?

"This sixth subject," McKenzie continued. At the tap of a button, the other helixes vanished and the sixth grew to fill the projection. "Has duplicated markers for most of the alien genes, and a few extra for good measure. This subject has been infected with a modified strain of the PERV virus, then re-infected with another, almost identical strain."

The whispers started again, but the professor made no effort to silence them. Several students were standing, while others only stared, but still Liz could not understand what it all meant.

"I didn't have time to map out every modification made between the two strains, but the source of the DNA—a human feather—is enough to establish that these samples came from our President's new creatures. I believe the virus that is present in all six was used to create them. The other strain…" He trailed off, closing his eyes for a second, before continuing: "It would appear, from the genes incorporated into its makeup, that the other strain is the *Chead* virus."

The whole class came to their feet in a roar. Voices echoed through the theatre, threatening to drown out the professor. Still he went on, though with each word he seemed to shrink, as though the very act of speaking was draining the life from him.

"As you can see, the two strains of the virus are almost identical. They are clearly related. One was created from the other. This would be inconceivable without a pure sample of the *Chead* virus, but as we can see from this sample, the *Chead* virus fully integrates with its host's genome. Its genetic mechanism to revert to an active form has been removed, making it non-infectious. There is no way to retrieve a sample of the complete virus from an infected host."

The professor took a breath. "Which means…whoever created our President's creatures, must have also had access to the *Chead* virus." His voice was barely audible now. "I fear it means our beloved government has been behind this plague, and has been using it to manipulate us all along."

64

"What's on TV, Mira?" Sam asked as he lowered himself onto the sofa beside the young girl.

The tiny CRT television sat on the coffee table in the corner of the room. A man on the screen was gesturing at a map of the west coast, pointing to the whirling weather system hovering over the city. Outside, rain lashed at the windows, and the wind had been growing stronger all morning. Sam hoped Ashley would be okay flying in the wild weather. She was less experienced than the others.

Mira said nothing, just snuggled closer to him on the couch. Grinning, Sam shook his head. Her wound was healing nicely—to the point Eve had finally let up with her nagging. In fact, the woman had taken to avoiding them altogether. When he'd asked Maria about her sudden absence, Chris's grandmother had only shrugged and said she'd gone out for the day.

But Sam had noticed the look in the old woman's eyes. It matched the frown Eve had given the night before, when she'd changed their dressings. They might not admit as much, but the adults were disturbed by their young charge's abilities.

Sam could hardly blame them. He'd noticed the stares of the men and women who had passed through the safe house over the last week. When they'd stretched their wings, it was enough to make grown men stop what they were doing and stare. The discovery that the six of them could heal from bullet wounds in a matter of weeks just added another level to their strangeness. Apparently enough to disturb even the kindly old doctor—and Chris's grandmother, for that matter.

A loud beep came from the television, drawing Sam's attention to the screen. It flickered red, the weather forecast vanishing, to be replaced by a picture of the President standing on a stage.

Sam sat bolt upright and snatched the remote from Mira. She growled, but ignoring her, he pointed the remote and turned up the volume.

"My fellow citizens of the Western Allied States." The President stood at a wooden stand, his hands resting on the smooth mahogany. His short, grey hair had been combed flat, and his hazel eyes stared into the camera as he addressed the nation: "I come to you today with grave news. As many of you will have heard, a week ago there was an incident in Independence Square. I apologize for our silence until today. We did not wish to incite panic with unfounded speculation."

"Maria!" Sam called, standing. As Chris's grandmother appeared from the dining room, he nodded at the television. "Something's happening."

"However, today I can finally come forward with the truth. The Director of Domestic Affairs and her department have been working tirelessly all week to uncover the truth about events in the square. Today I can confirm that last Monday, the Texan government launched a direct attack on persons of the Western Allied States."

"*No*," Maria hissed.

She staggered slightly, her face losing all color, before righting herself. Standing, Sam offered her his seat, and she sank onto the sofa with a grateful nod. She seemed to have aged ten years in the space of seconds. His heart beating hard in his chest, Sam returned his attention to the television.

"Not only can we verify the involvement of Texas, the nature of this attack confirms what we have always suspected: the Lone Star State is behind the infection and spread of the *Chead* virus."

"*Liar!*" Mira was suddenly on her feet, teeth bared, multicolored eyes flashing. Her wings snapped open, her every feather standing on end. A dangerous rumble came from her throat as she stepped towards the television.

"Easy, Mira!" Sam caught her by the waist and hauled her back. She struggled for half a second, then went limp in his hands. Frowning, he was still wondering what had gotten into the girl, when a gasp came from the sofa.

"Wha—?" he started to ask, before the image on the television caught his attention.

The camera had zoomed out, revealing the stage around the President. Mike stood nearby, his hands bound in heavy chains. His face had been beaten black and blue, and he looked to be favoring his left leg. A line of soldiers stood behind him, their sleek, black rifles held at the ready, their fingers hovering close to triggers.

"Nine days ago, this man…" The President waved a hand, pointing at Mike. "This *Texan spy* orchestrated an attack on the widows of our brave veterans in Independence Square. Working with the escaped fugitives, he infected several members in the crowd with the *Chead* virus, unleashing the creatures on our unsuspecting citizens."

"There's no way anyone will believe this," Sam whispered.

There had to be a video, had to be *something* to prove the President's words a lie.

"I know some of you may doubt my words," the President continued, as though reading Sam's mind. "So today I have invited a victim of this man's brutality to attest to what happened."

Gesturing to a curtain behind him, the President stepped away from the lectern, allowing a man to step into the light. Taking the President's place, the man looked around until he found the camera.

Sam gaped as Jonathan cleared his throat and addressed the reporters. "Thank you, Mr. President. My name is Jonathan Baker. It is my privilege to stand before you today—a privilege this traitor has denied my wife and daughter."

"Goddamnit, Jonathan," Sam whispered. "You said you wanted to get back at them."

"Who is he?" Maria asked, but Sam only shook his head.

On the stage, Jonathan bowed his head. "A week ago, I returned home to find my wife and daughter murdered. The fugitives had taken shelter in my apartment. Before I could escape, they knocked me out and dragged me inside. When I woke, I discovered they were being led by this man." He nodded at Mike.

Sam grabbed Mira as she tried to go for the television again. His own wings were trembling, his feathers lifting from his back with each inhalation. Teeth gritted, he looked at Maria, then back to the television.

"They forced me to take them to Independence Square. They didn't tell me what they had planned, or I never would have cooperated. There was group of older women gathered around the Independence obelisk, and many others. This man, along with the fugitives, grabbed several of the onlookers, and injected them with something. While they were preoccupied, I managed to escape, but it was too late. The *Chead* were already amongst the crowd."

The President stood beside Jonathan, his hands clasped at his front, his face solemn. He nodded as Jonathan finished. "And what happened next, Mr. Baker?"

Jonathan glanced at the President, and for a second Sam saw a flicker of something pass across his face. The two stood staring at each other for a long moment, before Jonathan finally looked away.

"The *Chead* were…amongst the crowd when the soldiers arrived. With them came…" Jonathan swallowed, his grip on the lectern tightening. "With them came…our saviors. The President's experiments, the ones he introduced two weeks ago. They took to the air, placed themselves between the crowd and the *Chead.* They matched the creatures blow for blow, forcing them back, until our heroic soldiers were able to put them down."

"Those…" Sam cursed. Spinning, he hurled the remote at

the wall. It shattered into a thousand pieces as he sank onto the sofa beside Maria.

"Mr. President!" a reporter called from below the stage. "How did you locate the spy?"

The President smiled. "As I said, the Director of Domestic Affairs has been working tirelessly to find the perpetrators of this attack. Mr. Baker here was found after the attack. He offered vital assistance in piecing together events in the square. And an esteemed member of our community also came forward, offering information about a dissident who had contacted him. This citizen led us directly to the Texan."

"Who was this citizen?"

"At this moment, we will not be disclosing his identity. However, I can assure you he is being watched around the clock, to ensure there is no retribution from those terrorists still at large."

The blood in Sam's veins turned to ice at the President's words. He gripped the arm of the couch and turned to stare at Maria. She looked back at him, her face pale, her eyes hollow.

"Ashley and the others have no idea what they're walking into," Sam whispered. And he had no way of contacting them.

65

"You disappoint me, professor." Chris's head whipped around as a sharp voice cut through the din of the other students.

His heart almost stopped beating when he saw the Director standing at the top of the stairwell. Two familiar faces flanked her on either side—Paul and Francesca, the other test subjects they'd been forced to leave behind in the courthouse. A host of men in plain clothes crowded the double doors behind them, each carrying a deadly looking rifle.

"How?" The professor's voice crackled over the speakers. The students had fallen silent now. Every eye in the lecture hall was fixed on the Director.

"Did you think we wouldn't check up on you?" the Director replied, spreading her hands. "After you handed over the spy, we thought your life might be in danger. We thought you might need protection. But now…I find you have turned traitor yourself?"

"No." Chris glanced back at the lectern. The professor made his best attempt to draw himself up to full height. "It doesn't matter now. You can't silence these kids. Their parents would ask too many questions. It's over—you'll never get away with what you've done."

"Silence them?" The Director started down the staircase. Paul and Francesca followed on her heels. The students sank back into their seats, doing their best to disappear. "Why would I want to silence them? They have been lied to—it is *you* who has committed the crime. How dare you taint their young minds with your filth?"

"It's the truth!" the professor shouted, his voice taking on a high-pitched tone. "*You* were behind the *Chead*. You're here to silence me—but you can't hide the truth any longer."

"Students." A collective shiver went through the lectern as the Director's eyes swept over them. "I assure you, there is no relation between our experiments and the vile *Chead*. Take a closer look—do they look like *Chead* to you?" Pausing on the stairs, she gestured at her two silent companions.

Paul and Francesca drew to a stop, then as one, their wings snapped open and they leapt into the air. Black wings swept down, almost striking the heads of the students below. They swooped towards the stage, where the professor yelped and ducked beneath the lectern. Laughter chased him as Paul and Francesca turned and rose to the steel beam overhead. Silently they settled themselves beside the projectors.

"See? If they were *Chead*, half of you would be dead by now." The Director flicked a curl of hair from her face. "No, they are *our* creatures. And I will answer all your questions, once we have taken the traitor into custody."

"*No!*" Chris's heart fell into his stomach as Liz's voice rang out across the hall. Spinning, he watched in horror as she stood. "He's telling the truth. We all saw it."

"My poor dear." The Director wore a sad smile on her lips. Apparently, they were too far away for her to have recognized Liz. "What lies has the traitor been feeding you?"

Growling, Liz tore off her jacket. The air cracked as her wings snapped open. Nearby, several students screamed and threw themselves on the floor as twenty feet of feathers and flesh stretched across the rows of seats.

After a moment's hesitation, Chris followed suit. Pulling off his jacket, he couldn't help but grin as his cramped wings unfurled. His feathers were still damp from the rain, and a fine mist appeared around him. Ashley and Jasmine did the same, their feathers seemingly aglow in the overhead lights. Together, they stood in defiance against the Director.

"He's no traitor," Liz growled. "You're the traitor. You're the ones who invaded our homes, who tore apart our families and murdered our friends. You're the ones who kidnapped us to use in your depraved experiments, who have killed God-only-knows how many people, all so you could perfect your awful virus."

The Director still had not moved, only stood staring down at them. The blood had drained from her face, and a slight whisper came from her throat as her lips parted. Chris could almost see the gears turning behind her eyes as she tried to process what she was seeing. The armed men shifted nervously on their feet.

Around the lecture hall, the students stared at them, their mouths agape. No doubt a few had already recognized them as the fugitives from the news—but that didn't explain how the four of them were standing there with wings sprouting from their backs. A few of those closest even reached up to touch their feathers, as though unable to believe what they were seeing could be real. Chris shivered at the sensation but didn't dare take his eyes from the Director.

Suddenly, he found himself smiling. Today was definitely not going the way she had intended.

"Take them," the Director said, finally regaining her senses. She glanced around when her men did not react, then pointed down at Liz and screamed, "*Take them!*"

The men exchanged glances and then finally began down the stairs. No doubt they knew what had happened to their colleagues back in Independence Square who'd dared challenge Chris and the others. Before they could make any progress, a young man slid from his seat to bar their path.

"No more," he said. He held out his arms, daring the soldiers to defy him.

His boldness gave the men pause, and they glanced back again at the Director for further orders. Her response was abrupt and to the point. The men started down again, using their bulk to push the student from their path.

But now others were jumping from their seats. A girl leapt

into the aisle, another boy following her—then suddenly the whole lecture theatre was jostling to join them. Students poured from the rows of seats and crowded into the stairwell. Linking arms, they stood together and barred the way against the Director's men.

Chris watched in silence, mouth hanging open, hardly able to believe what he was seeing. The students' actions echoed those of the Madwomen a week ago—except these young men and women had no grievance against the government. These were the children of the rich and privileged—those with every reason to take the government's side.

Yet here they were, defying the Director and her soldiers, putting their lives on the line for four fugitives they had never met.

"Go." Chris looked around as a girl spoke from the row above them. Her eyes caught his and she flashed him a smile. "Get out, quickly. Take the fire exit."

Swallowing a lump in his throat, Chris nodded. He turned and looked down at the stage. The professor still stood there, his face pale and arms trembling as he clutched the lectern like it was the only solid object left on earth. The stage was some thirty feet below them.

Chris flexed the muscles in his back. "Let's fly," he shouted to the others, and sprang into the air.

His wings beat down hard, lifting him over the front rows of seats. Gasps came from around the room as students ducked. The whisper of his friends' wings chased after him as he swept towards the stage.

All too quickly, he was landing beside the professor. Furling his wings, he checked on the Director, and grinned to see her still stuck at the top of the stairs. Her lips drew back in a snarl when she saw him watching, and he gave a little wave. She screamed again at her men, but there was no quick way of moving several hundred students from the cramped stairwell.

Chris turned to the professor as the others landed. "Time to go, I think, sir."

The man stared back at Chris, his mouth hanging open. But

they weren't safe yet, and there was no time to waste on the man's terror. Chris grabbed him by the shoulders and shook him.

"Get whatever information you have off that computer, professor. We've got to go!"

His words seemed to snap the man from his stupor. Blinking, the professor swallowed visibly and nodded. He pulled a thumb drive out of the side of the computer and handed it to Chris.

"That's everything!" he shouted over the din.

Chris's throat constricted as he took the drive—not with fear, but with sudden hope. They had come here for a cure, but if what the professor said was true, the thumb drive held all the proof they needed that the government was responsible for the *Chead.* He tucked it carefully into his jeans pocket.

"Let's go," he said, pushing the professor in the direction of the fire exit.

Liz and Jasmine took the lead, Ashley just a step behind. They raced across the stage, drawn towards the neon sign reading "EXIT." Chris sucked in a breath, hardly daring to believe they might escape the trap they'd unwittingly walked into.

He only heard the whisper of wings a second before the attack. He glimpsed a shadow on the ground, and a snarling face, then Paul plummeted from the air. The professor had time to glance up, for his mouth to fall open, before the boy's boot slammed into his neck.

An audible *snap* echoed through the theatre as the professor bounced across the carpeted floor. His body came to rest in a limp pile of arms and legs. Without checking, Chris knew he was dead. Turning from the lifeless body, he faced the boy now barring his way.

The *thump* of wings came from above as Francesca landed beside Paul. They faced Chris, wings spread, and hands clenched at their sides. Paul towered over them all, his dark skin and jet-black hair seeming to drown the overhead lights. He crossed his arms and smirked. Beside him, Francesca looked frail by comparison. With her pale skin and blonde hair, she looked more ghost than human in the bright lights.

"We haven't been formally introduced." Paul's lips drew back in a snarl. "I'm Paul. You must be Chris. Where's Sam? I wanted to say hello to the stinking traitor."

"Get out of the way," Chris snapped.

He made to step towards them and paused. He frowned, staring at them, then took a quick step back. Their faces were the same as the boy and girl he'd glimpsed back in the courthouse, but their eyes…whatever color they had been before, they were cold and grey now. They were the eyes of the *Chead*.

"Get on your knees, and maybe we'll let you live," Francesca said.

"You've changed," Chris whispered.

A rough growl clawed its way up from Paul's throat. "How could we not…when you and that bastard Sam…left us to die… in agony?" A ripple crossed his face, and his lips drew back, baring his teeth.

Chris clenched his fists. He stared at them, noticing now that neither wore the cruel shock collars they had all sported during their imprisonment. His heart lifted with sudden hope.

"You're free," he pressed. "We didn't want to leave you—we didn't have a choice. But you have a choice now—come with us."

Paul threw back his head and howled with laughter. "When they take you, I will watch you suffer as we did. I will watch you all turn, and the madness claim you."

Chris's heart sank as he slid into a fighting stance. "Not today."

66

"*Chris!*" Liz screamed, as he charged the pair standing between them and the exit.

Before she could intervene, Paul leapt forward to Chris. The two came together with a crash and rose into the air, their wings thumping hard as they darted apart.

Distracted by their battle, Liz gasped as Francesca's fist struck her in the chin. Rolling with the blow, she took a step back to right herself. Growling, Francesca came on, tackling her around the midriff and driving her back. Liz stumbled, but her wings beat down, steadying her.

Before Liz could recover, Francesca's hands closed around her throat like a vice. Gasping, she grabbed at Francesca's wrists with her gloved hands, struggling to pry away her fingers. Then Jasmine shot out of nowhere and slammed into the blonde girl. Her black wings flashed, adding to her momentum, and the hands around Liz's throat were torn away.

Coughing, Liz sucked in a lungful of air and straightened. Jasmine stood beside her now. Together they squared off against the other girl. Watching Francesca recover, Liz didn't miss the grey glint in her eyes. The girl had changed—that made her more dangerous than ever. If she lost control and went berserk, she would tear everyone in the lecture theater to pieces. What had the Director been thinking, bringing them here?

Jasmine snarled and started towards the girl. Liz swallowed as she remembered that Paul and Francesca were the ones who had attacked them in the courthouse. The fight had delayed their escape and had ended up getting Richard killed.

"Jasmine," Liz called as she joined her friend, "careful."

Jasmine flicked her a glance, her eyes shimmering, and for a moment Liz thought it was already too late. Then Jasmine let out a long breath, and the light faded from her eyes. She nodded and turned her attention back to Francesca.

With a roar, Francesca spread her wings and leapt into the air. Stretching her own wings, Liz was about to chase after her, until Jasmine grabbed her by the arm. Before she could object, Jasmine nodded in the direction of the soldiers.

The students were starting to fall back, as the soldiers used the butts of their rifles to muscle their way through. Enough still stood their ground to slow the soldiers' progress—and more importantly, hide Liz and the others from their line of vision. But if they took flight, the soldiers would have a clear shot.

Overhead, Francesca shrieked when she saw Jasmine and Liz weren't following. Folding her wings, she plummeted towards them. Her face darkened, her grey eyes growing hard, and Liz knew it was no longer Francesca staring out. Jasmine may have gotten a hold of her rage, but the other girl had succumbed.

Liz jumped back as the girl lashed at them, but Jasmine was too slow and a blow caught her square in the forehead. She staggered and dropped to one knee. Francesca landed on the stage with a thump and swung again, but Liz leapt in and deflected her blow before it struck Jasmine.

Growling, Francesca turned on Liz. Twisting, Liz leapt into the air, hoping to drop down on Francesca's back as she stumbled past—but the other girl was too quick. Before Liz could slam her heel into the girl's neck, Francesca was clear.

Liz hesitated. It was all the opening Francesca needed. Her hand shot out, her fingers closing around Liz's ankle like iron. Liz screamed, her wings beating hard as she struggled to break free, but with terrifying strength, Francesca hauled her back down.

Their eyes met, and Francesca laughed. Another hand wrapped around her ankle, and Liz's stomach lurched into her chest as Francesca swung her through the air. Liz shrieked as the ground came rushing up to meet her face.

A brilliant light flashed across Liz's vision as she struck. Wind hissed between her teeth, the impact driving the breath from her lungs. But Francesca had at least released her ankle, and gasping, Liz rolled before the other girl could stomp her into the ground. Struggling to regain her feet, she turned and saw Jasmine going toe to toe with the *Chead.* A fist flashed for her friend's face, but she ducked, and the blow caught only empty air. Then Jasmine charged, driving her shoulder into Francesca's stomach. Before the *Chead* could pull free, Jasmine wrapped both arms around Francesca's waist and lifted her into the air.

Seeing her opportunity, Liz launched herself forward, swinging at Francesca's face. At the last moment, the girl twisted in Jasmine's grip, and Liz's fist slammed into the base of Jasmine's skull. A low moan came from Jasmine as her eyes rolled back and she toppled to the carpeted floor.

Cackling, Francesca slipped free and spun. Her wing arched out and caught Liz square in the face. As she staggered, Francesca twisted again, her wing coming around for a second blow. Without thinking, Liz caught the bony limb in both hands.

Francesca screamed, her wing bucking as she tried to tear herself free. Liz stumbled several steps before she could dig in her heels. Grinning, she watched Francesca still. Their eyes met across the ten feet of feathers stretching between them. Then Liz wrapped both hands around the joint she'd caught, and wrenched.

The bones in Francesca's wings were no match for Liz's enhanced strength. They snapped like tissue paper, bending Francesca's wing at an awful angle. The color drained from Francesca's face as though sucked into a vacuum. An awful shriek escaped her throat as she thrashed, spinning across the stage, her eyes wild with pain and fury.

Liz leapt back, a few beats of her wings carrying her to safety. Francesca's grey eyes followed her, and in a blind rage she tried to give chase. But her broken wing could not carry her, and Francesca screamed and crashed back down.

Glimpsing her opening, Liz launched herself on top of the fallen girl. She gasped as Francesca surged against her, the girl's strength threatening to buck her off. Gritting her teeth, Liz clung on. Using her weight, she slammed the girl's head into the carpet, but the blow did nothing to diminish Francesca's strength. Catching a wing in the face, Liz almost lost her balance before she righted herself again.

Feeling her fury starting to build, Liz drove her fist into Francesca's kidney. They couldn't afford to sit here fighting. Though their fight had lasted less than a minute, the soldiers were drawing closer. She couldn't understand why Paul and Francesca were helping the Director of their own free will—not after everything that had been done to them. How could they support the government that had kidnapped and tortured them, that had taken *everything* from them?

Choking on her rage, Liz struggled to control herself. She could feel her strength building, and the bloodlust that came with the *Chead* rage. Her stomach roiled, and before she had a chance to stop it, her vision turned red.

Screaming, Liz grabbed Francesca by the hair and wrenched back her head. The girl was fighting her still, but Liz drove her knee hard into the small of Francesca's back, forcing her down. Then Liz gripped her by the hair and slammed her face into the ground, again and again, until the girl went limp beneath her.

Rage flickered in Liz's chest as she released her foe, but Francesca wasn't finished. She moved weakly beneath Liz, still trying to get back up. A growl built in Liz's chest as she removed her gloves. Gripping Francesca by the hair once more, she slammed her face into the ground one last time.

Then, slowly, almost gently, Liz slid her hands from Francesca's hair to the exposed nape of her neck. She felt the soft skin beneath her fingers, the fragile bones of Francesca's spine as she squeezed. From behind, she could not cut off the girl's air. But then, she didn't need to.

Francesca's flesh was warm to the touch. It felt good, to feel naked skin beneath her fingers again. It seemed an age since the night in the safe house with Chris. Her heart warmed at the memory, and its rapid thud slowed. Bit by bit, the red faded from her vision.

Only then did Liz realize Francesca was screaming. Pinned beneath Liz's weight, she writhed against the floor, her broken wing flailing uselessly at her side. Liz gaped, taking long seconds to comprehend what she'd been trying to do. In horror, she released Francesca and leapt back, praying she wasn't too late.

But Francesca's struggles were already weakening, and her wings had fallen still. She managed to roll onto her back, but now veins bulged on her forehead and a trail of blood ran from her mouth and nose. All around her neck, her skin had turned an awful shade of purple.

Liz pressed a hand to her mouth as Francesca staggered to her knees. Blood-red eyes stared at Liz, tight with agony, filled with hate. She almost made it to her feet, but finally her strength gave way. With a long, drawn out moan, she toppled face-first to the ground.

Liz stood staring at Francesca's lifeless body until a groan came from nearby. Struggling to shake off her horror, she saw Jasmine stirring and offered her friend a shoulder. They both took care not to let their skin touch.

"Good job," Jasmine gasped as she stood.

Liz nodded. "Sorry…about this," she offered lamely.

"Feels like you hit me in the head with a brick," Jasmine coughed. There were tears in her eyes. "Where's Chris and Ashley?"

☙ 67 ❧

Stars flashed across Chris's vision as Paul's fist collided with his chin. Raising his hands, he managed to deflect a second blow with a flick of his wrist, then spun on his heel and drove a back kick into the space where he hoped Paul was standing. He smiled with satisfaction as it connected and heard the *whoosh* of his foe's lungs emptying.

Chris took a step back as the force of his kick pushed him off-balance. The stars faded from his vision and he found Paul half-doubled over. Their eyes met, and Paul's lips drew back in a snarl. Black wings stretched wide to either side of him, dwarfing Chris's own. Paul's wingspan had to be close to thirty feet.

"It doesn't have to be this way, Paul," he shouted. "Come with us. Let Sam explain."

Paul laughed. "Oh don't worry…he'll get his chance—while I'm tearing those pretty wings…from his back."

Growling, Paul took a step towards Chris—then froze. His eyes widened, and a moan whispered up from his throat. Over the pounding of blood in his ears, Chris heard someone screaming, and shot a glance behind him.

His fight with Paul had carried him to the opposite side of the stage, but the others were still grouped near the fire exit. Liz was on her feet, while nearby Jasmine crouched on her hands and knees. Ashley still stood beside the lectern, her lips parted, staring back at Chris in terror.

And Francesca was lying face down on the floor, unmoving.

Chris started to turn back as Paul gave a strangled howl, but even his enhanced reactions were too slow to block the boot that slammed into his chest. Something went *crack*—then Chris was tumbling backwards across the floor. A gasp tore from his lips as he tried to sit up and felt a sharp pain stabbing into his lungs. The metallic tang of blood filled his mouth.

Across the stage, Paul leapt after him, and Chris quickly rolled onto his feet. Paul's grey eyes followed him, the last hints of sanity drained away. He was truly *Chead* now, consumed by anger, driven by a hatred that swept away all before it. Teeth bared, he stalked after Chris.

Bracing himself, Chris let him come. Every movement brought another jab from his chest, but he forced himself to ignore it. As the distance between them closed, Chris leapt. His foot flicked out and caught the larger boy square in the jaw. Paul's head whipped back, but to Chris's shock, he didn't fall.

As he straightened, a dark grin spread across the larger boy's face. Another blow slammed into Chris's chest before he could retreat.

Red flashed across Chris's vision as Paul's fist connected with whatever had broken inside him, and he felt something tear. Struggling to breathe, he doubled up and staggered away—but Paul wasn't about to let him recover. Fists raised, he stalked after Chris.

Gritting his teeth, Chris spread his wings and leapt into the air. He shrieked as the movement drove the broken rib deeper into his chest, but before he could lift off, something slammed into his wing and dragged him back down. The weight drove him face-first into the ground.

Before Chris could rise, Paul landed on his back.

"Going so soon?" Paul said, his grating voice almost metallic.

For a second the pressure on Chris's back relented—then Paul's boot came crashing down on his wing. Pain unlike anything Chris had experienced shot down the length of the new limb. He heard something go *crack* as Paul lifted his boot and stomped again. An awful scream tore from Chris's throat. Desperately he tried to roll away, but with his wing pinned beneath his foe's boot, there was no escape. An evil grin spread across the Paul's face as he ground Chris's wing into the floor.

A red mist circled Chris's vision, and he felt something dark stirring within him. His consciousness flickered. He bared his teeth, and a low growl rumbled up from his chest. Craning his neck, he met Paul's eyes—and the boy's grin widened.

"Go on…give in—"

Paul's words were cut off as, with a bloodcurdling scream, Ashley came barreling out of nowhere and sent him bouncing across the room. Her wings flared out as she landed, her tawny yellow eyes glowing like tiny moons. Red hair streaming down around her shoulders, she stood over Chris like an avenging angel.

Staggering across the stage, Paul's stony eyes flashed with rage. Blood trickled from his mouth, but reaching up, he wiped it away.

"Run away, little girl," he hissed. "Maybe I will let you live."

Ashley laughed in his face. "Go on, then."

His face darkening, Paul charged. At five-foot-one, Ashley looked like a child beside him, but she stood her ground. The fear had gone from her eyes, replaced by a cool determination, an unyielding will in the face of the boy's fury.

At the last second before he struck, Ashley leapt, her wings beating down, lifting her tiny frame over Paul's head. As he staggered past, her wings folded, and her heel slammed down into his neck.

Off-balance, the blow sent Paul to his knees. Grinning, Ashley landed gracefully behind him. She crossed her arms and watched him stumble back to his feet, a soft smile on her lips. Her amber eyes were aflame as she waited for his next move.

Chris looked around as Liz crouched beside him, her brow creased with concern. Jasmine had one arm draped over Liz's shoulder and her eyes were slightly glazed, but Chris was relieved to see she was okay.

"Are you alright?" Liz asked.

His chest tightened. Inhaling, he felt the broken rib digging deeper into his flesh. His left wing hung limp beside him, twisted at an awful angle. A glance up the stairwell told him their time was almost out. Only a few dozen students still stood against the soldiers.

Reaching into his pocket, Chris retrieved the thumb drive and pressed it into Liz's palm. "Take it. Get out of here."

"What?" Liz's eyes widened as she saw the thumb drive. "No, we're not leaving you, Chris. Come on, get up, there's still time."

Chris staggered to his knees. Pain radiated through his body, robbing him of strength, but he reached out and gripped Liz by the shoulder. "I can't fly, Liz," he croaked. "He broke my wing. If I come with you, they'll catch us all."

"Then they catch us all," Liz snapped, her eyes hardening.

She started to stand, but Chris caught her by the wrist and pulled her back down.

"No, Liz," he said, blinking back tears. "You need to live. You need to show the world what's on that drive, tell them what they did to us. Make all this mean something."

"But what about you?" Liz's voice cracked, and he could see the tears she was struggling to hold back. "I can't leave you like this. I…I love you, Chris.

Chris squeezed her wrist. Pulling her forward, he kissed her, hard and fast. His heartbeat quickened, and for a second his pain lessened—but when they broke apart, it returned two-fold. Biting back a scream, he gathered his feet beneath him and stood.

"I love you, too," he murmured, stroking her cheek, "but you still have to go."

For a long moment, he thought she would not reply. "I'll come back for you," she said finally, her voice breaking.

"No, Liz," Chris croaked. "I won't let them take me, not again." He forced himself to turn away. If he looked into her eyes any longer, he would never be able to do what was needed.

"Chris…"

"Go, Liz," he said again, swallowing his grief. "I'll distract him, so Ashley can follow you. *Go!*"

Across the stage, Ashley was running loops around Paul. Every time he attacked, she would dance clear, and he would stagger from another well-placed blow. Even as Chris watched, Paul leapt again, and earned a fist to the face and a knee to the groin for his efforts. Wheezing, he fell to the ground.

Steeling himself, Chris walked away from Liz and Jasmine. As he neared Ashley, Chris searched for an opening. He only needed to distract Paul for a second, but he had to act now. The last few students were crumbling, almost giving the soldiers a clear shot. A quick glance around reassured him Liz and Jasmine were almost to the exit.

Leaping to his feet, Paul began to circle Ashley. His face was bleeding from a dozen cuts and his chest was heaving, but he showed no signs of backing down.

Before Paul could attack again, Chris leapt forward, placing himself squarely between the two fighters. Paul's eyes widened and for a second, he hesitated. Chris took his opportunity.

"*Go!*" he screamed back at Ashley.

Then he faced Paul, and charged.

Paul's surprise turned to amusement as he watched Chris approach, but there was no turning back now. Fire lanced Chris's chest as he bounded forward. Twisting, he swung a punch at Paul's face.

Paul only grinned as he caught Chris by the wrist. Chris's heart fell into his stomach as the larger boy yanked him forward into a headbutt. White light flashed across his eyes as he fell to the ground.

Blinking, Chris tried to regain his feet, but the strength had fled his limbs, and when his vision cleared, he was still lying on his back staring up at the ceiling. A dull ringing sounded in his ears and he could hear distant voices. Then Paul's face appeared overhead, and Chris saw his own death reflected in the empty grey eyes. Letting out a pained breath, he waited for it to come.

Instead, there was a soft *thud* as Ashley came barreling into Paul. The larger boy stumbled back from the force of her attack, but Ashley was half his weight, and her attack had only stunned him. Snarling, Ashley chased after him and slammed a kick into his chest.

Paul was still recovering, and this time the blow put him flat on his back. Racing in, Ashley stamped her boot down on his face. There was a sickening crunch as his nose broke. Grinning, Ashley glanced at Chris. Before he could warn her, Paul's hand shot out and caught her by the ankle.

Ashley screamed as Paul surged to his feet, taking her foot with him. Thrown off-balance, Ashley was lifted high into the air—then slammed face-first into the ground. Paul released her ankle and dove at her, attempting to pin Ashley beneath his bulk. But Ashley had already recovered. Her wings contracting, she rolled to the side, and Paul slammed into the carpet.

Coming to her feet, Ashley fixed Paul in her sights and charged. Her eyes remained the same tawny yellow as always, but there was a glow to them that reminded Chris of the rage he'd seen when Liz and Jasmine had turned. Yet this was different somehow, controlled—as though Ashley had taken all her pain and fear and insecurity and turn them into strength.

Paul managed to stagger to his feet—then Ashley was on him. Raising a fist, he attempted to deflect her blow. A sharp *crack* rang through the lecture theatre as her knuckles caught his elbow. Paul screamed, his hand going to his arm as he tried to retreat. Ashley came after him, her eyes simmering. Her next blow caught him square in the forehead.

Chris flinched at the *crunch* that marked the impact. He watched, mouth hanging open, as the light in Paul's eyes faded to nothing, and he slowly toppled backwards. The dark-winged boy made no effort to break his fall, and with a sense of horror, Chris realized he was dead. His gaze was drawn back to Ashley. She stood over her fallen foe, chest heaving, white wings trembling with each inhalation. Fists clenched, she stared at Paul, as though waiting for him to get back up. But he lay unmoving, eyes blank, unseeing.

Coming to his feet, Chris crossed the stage to Ashley. She looked up as he approached. As their eyes met, the tension seemed to rush from Ashley's body. She staggered where she stood, and Chris barely made it in time to catch her before she fell. Agony sliced his chest, but he held her close and looked around.

To his relief, there was no sign of Liz or Jasmine, but while the fight had only lasted a few minutes, their time was up. On the staircase, the last of the students were on the ground. Many of them sported injuries, but there was no more time to consider their fate. The soldiers poured onto the stage, their guns held ready as they formed a semicircle around Chris and Ashley.

Chris pulled Ashley tight against him. He couldn't understand why she hadn't fled with Liz and Jasmine, but he was suddenly glad to have her there. Together they faced the black barrels of the soldiers' guns, and waited for death to come.

"On your knees." The Director's voice carried to them from the top of the hall.

Slowly, she descended to the stage. Chris's eyes were drawn to two silver bands she held in each hand. His heart clenched as he recognized the shock collars. Ashley's grip tightened around his waist. He felt her beginning to shake.

"Kill us," he croaked. "We're not going back."

The Director's face didn't change. The soldiers still on the stairwell gave way before her. As she reached the stage, she held up the collars. "They weren't meant for you." She nodded to the limp bodies of Paul and Francesca. "I removed them as a show of trust. But I kept them handy, just in case."

"Get it over with," Ashley whispered beside him. "You can't make us go back, so you might as well end this farce."

"But who will replace my faithful servants?" The Director raised an eyebrow. "You've made such a mess of them, the least you can do is take their place."

"Go to hell." Chris stepped towards her.

Two dozen rifles lifted half an inch and pointed in his direction. The soldiers glanced at the Director, waiting for her order. Despite himself, Chris hesitated. Now that the end had come, he found himself wanting to draw out this moment, to savor every last breath.

The Director pursed her lips. Turning her back on Chris and

Ashley, she looked up at the students. "They're all traitors, you know." She laughed, the sound cold and hollow. "You know the punishment for traitors."

As though following an unspoken command, the soldiers still stationed at the top of the lecture theatre swung the heavy double doors closed. The men on the stairwell pointed their rifles into the rows where the students huddled. Several cried out as the Director returned her attention to Chris.

"Don't," he whispered.

"Why not?" The Director raised an eyebrow.

"Please," Ashley begged, and a smile spread across the Director's face.

Lifting the collars, she tossed them down at their feet. "Put them on, and I will spare them."

"No," Ashley said, but even as the word left her lips, she was slumping to her knees.

Chris crouched beside her. They looked at each other, and he could see her terror. Then Ashley closed her eyes and swallowed. When they opened again, her fear had fled. She gripped Chris by the shoulder. Neither spoke, but Chris nodded. Together, they picked up the collars.

"Put them on," the Director repeated.

Nodding, Chris steeled himself, and lifted the collar to his throat. He shivered as the cold steel touched his flesh, fighting the urge to hurl the thing from him. Closing his eyes, he fumbled at the clasps, and pressed them together. The collar gave an audible *click* as it settled into place.

A pit opened in Chris's stomach. Another *click* came from Ashley's collar, sealing their fate. Together, they met the Director's gaze, now helpless slaves before her wrath. She smirked and lifted her wrist, showing them the controller she wore as a watch.

"You remember this?" She waited until they both nodded. "Good. Behave, and I won't have to use it."

Chris bit his lip and stared at the carpet, too afraid to do anything else. Despair welled in his chest, robbing him of strength.

"Excellent, you may yet prove useful." The Director laughed

and Chris flinched, the sound grating in his ears. "Okay, men, let's finish this mess. Kill them all."

Chris's heart lurched as he saw the soldiers lifting their rifles. A scream clawed its way up from his chest, and he started to his feet. The soldiers opened fire, and a deafening roar filled the lecture hall. Screaming again, he leapt at the Director, determined to tear her limb from limb.

Before he could take two steps, white fire wrapped around his neck and his feet went out from under him. Then he was on his back, his muscles spasming, his whole body convulsing as the boom of gunfire echoed around him. He opened his mouth, but no sound came out. Unable to breathe, to think, to do anything, Chris listened as three hundred students were murdered where they knelt.

Only when silence returned did the darkness finally rise to claim him.

68

Drenched from the rain, the earth sank beneath Liz's feet as she touched down in the garden of the safe house. Her legs crumpled beneath her and she fell into the mud. Raising a fist, she drove it into the ground, an awful scream echoing through the night.

Movement came from inside the house as a light switched on. A shadow appeared in the window, a face looking out. Then Jasmine was at Liz's side, grabbing her by the shoulders, shaking her and hissing for her to be quiet.

Liz didn't care. Her whole body ached from the fight with Francesca, but that pain was nothing to what she felt in her soul. It wasn't just Chris's death; her every loss, every hurt was resurfacing, bubbling up within until she felt she would explode from the agony of it all.

Another scream echoed through the night as she fought to break Jasmine's hold, to give action to her pain, to pound the earth until it broke, or she did. She wanted to rage, to scream, to—

"What happened?"

Liz froze as a familiar voice spoke from the darkness. She opened her mouth, but the words died in her throat. Sam stood over her, face gaunt, his jaw clenched hard, and she realized he already knew. But he had to ask the question anyway, she could see it in his eyes.

"Where's Ashley and Chris?"

"Dead." The word slipped from Liz like a prayer, as though if she put enough of herself into it, it might not be true.

The pronouncement struck Sam like a bullet. He staggered, his hand clenched hard against his chest. Jasmine's grip on Liz loosened, and tearing herself free, she went to him in a rush. Their sobs whispered through the trees as they clung to one another.

When they finally broke apart, Liz was surprised to find a crowd had gathered. She swallowed as she scanned the faces of the Madwomen, knowing Maria would be there, but unsure whether she had the strength to face her.

Tears shone on Chris's grandmother's cheeks as she stepped from the crowd. The rain had stopped long ago, and moonlight shone down from a clear sky, illuminating the age lines of her face.

"I'm sorry," Liz found herself saying, "he gave his life to help us escape. He gave his life so we could give you this."

Her hand slid into her pocket, producing the thumb drive Chris had given to her before she fled. Holding it up to the light, she offered it to Maria.

"Our government created the *Chead*. All the proof we need is on this drive."

A collective gasp came from the other women at her words. Sam's head whipped around, his eyes widening, but barely a flicker crossed Maria's face. She looked from Liz to the drive, and back again, then reached out and closed Liz's hand. Without saying a word, the old woman turned and stumbled back into the house.

"What…?" Liz whispered. She stood there in shock, staring after Chris's grandmother.

"Liz…" Sam murmured, shaking his head.

"What is it?" she hissed, her rage resurfacing. Chris had died so they could bring this drive to safety, so they could show it to the world. Now his own grandmother was rejecting that sacrifice, and she wanted to know why.

"We're at war," Sam replied. "The country is in lockdown. They've already taken the media. If what you're saying is true, if the government really did create the *Chead*, we have no way of telling the people."

"No," Liz whispered. A gulf opened inside her, threatening to swallow her whole. The only reason she'd left Chris was to share their discovery, to ensure his sacrifice brought down the ones that had done this to them. Cracks spread through her consciousness as she shook her head. "No, it can't all have been for nothing."

She swayed on her feet and would have fallen if Sam and Jasmine hadn't caught her. They held her tight, the three of them clinging to one another like they were the last people on earth.

"It won't be," Sam said finally. There were tears on his cheeks as he pulled back. "We won't let it."

Liz clung to his words like a lifeline. Gritting her teeth, she summoned every ounce of her rage. She drew strength from its fire, purpose from the hate that fueled it. Drawing in a breath, she nodded at Sam.

"Let's make them pay."

EPILOGUE

The breath caught in Susan's throat as she looked at the lights of the town. For endless days and nights, the *Chead* had raced across the open countryside. She had run with them, reveling in her newfound strength. Light bled into dark, but it no longer made any difference whether she traveled by the moon or the sun. At times, the red haze would sweep over her, but she embraced it now, thrilling in the power it gave her.

When they stopped for rest, she would find herself in Hecate's arms, his lips beneath hers, and all memory of her past life would fall away. The voice in her mind grew weaker with each passing day, until it seemed only a distant memory. She had become a creature of instinct, driven by need, by desire.

Now, darkness stretched out in all directions, except where the humans had built their homes. The ring of lights stood in defiance of the night, like a cocoon, protecting its occupants from peril.

That was how the humans were, she knew. Scurrying away in the dirt, always hiding from the power of Mother Nature, from the wrath she might bring. But it was not Mother Nature they need fear. Not tonight.

Tonight, it was their own folly that came for them.

Susan saw the truth now, saw the cruelty of the human

species, the lives they destroyed in their endless quest for power. How she longed to undo her past, to take back the evils she had wrought. Recalling of those strange memories, she found herself confused, unable to understand what had driven her in that time before the red haze.

There was only hunger now, the thirst for slaughter, the lust for her mate.

Hecate stood beside her, his scent lingering in her nostrils. It was intoxicating, like a drug she could not live without. Together they watched the little town, contemplating its distant glow. Movement came from around them. The full moon lit the hill-side, revealing the gathered *Chead*. They spread across the grassy slopes, preparing themselves.

Returning her gaze to the town, Susan thought of what was to come. From deep in her mind, she felt a tug, a remembered pang from another life. She shook her head and it faded. The red haze rose to replace it.

A call went out across the hilltop. It was followed by slow, silent movement as the *Chead* slid down the hill towards the unsuspecting town. Their faces took on a new light in the glow of the moon, so they seemed almost ghosts, spirits of the things they had once been.

Humans.

The word rang in her mind, and for a moment Susan paused. The red haze flickered, and the breath caught in her throat. Unbidden, an image appeared in her mind. She saw a dimly lit room. A fire crackled in the hearth, and there was a man and a woman in each other's arms, a child nestled up against their legs.

Pain seeped into Susan's chest as she stilled. The image grew, then shrank, as though struggling to exist in the darkness of her mind. She wondered where it had come from, what it meant, who they were.

"Are you…ready?" Hecate's lips brushed against her ear.

Susan sucked in a breath, the sweet scent of her mate filling her nostrils. She shivered as the haze returned, consuming the image in flames of rage.

I am yours.

Smiling, Susan looked up at Hecate. Today marked the beginning of a new age. Once, lions had roamed the earth from Africa to Europe to the Americas. Then had come *Homo erectus*, and the time of the lion had ended. Humanity had followed, creeping across the planet, extinguishing all that threatened it.

Now their time was ending.

Another species had come to take their place.

The age of the *Chead* had begun.

"I'm ready."

THE EVOLUTION GENE
BOOK THREE

THE WAY THE WORLD ENDS

NEW YORK TIMES BESTSELLING AUTHOR

AARON HODGES

Good versus evil is not a war.
It is a battle,
Fought within each of us,
Every day.

I
WAR

PROLOGUE

Liz sat on the edge of the rooftop, her feet dangling over empty air. Her body tensed as she looked out at the city, her gloved hands gripping tight to the concrete lip. Skyscrapers rose up around her, dwarfing the nondescript apartment building on which she sat. The first glow of the rising sun lit the horizon, but San Francisco remained in shadow, all color leached away. With strict power rations in place, there was hardly a streetlight left to cast back the gloom.

It made the night perfect for hunting.

Four weeks had passed since their time at the university. Hardly a day had gone that she did not curse herself for fleeing, for running away and leaving Chris to die. Never mind that there had been nothing she could have done to save him; she blamed herself anyway.

After all, Ashley had found the courage to stay and fight. Poor, broken Ashley, who just days before had frozen at the merest sign of danger. She had been through more than any of them, had suffered alone at the hands of Doctor Halt; yet when their backs had been against the wall, it was Ashley who'd stepped up. Alone, she had fought off the *Chead*, and given Liz and Jasmine the chance to escape.

Liz almost hated her for it.

It should have been me!

She stood suddenly, her boots balancing precariously on the thin ledge. Fists clenched, she stared down at the hundred-foot drop, her stomach swirling.

Again she saw Chris's face—tight with pain, his lips drawn back in a snarl, his broken wing hanging limp. Injured and outmatched, he had thrown himself between the *Chead* and Ashley, determined to sacrifice himself for his friend. But Ashley had remained, and the two of them had perished in the massacre that followed.

Liz's only comfort was that they'd died believing their sacrifice had meant something—that their deaths had allowed their friends to expose the truth about the *Chead*, that the government was behind the creation and spread of the deadly virus.

Battling through their grief, Liz and Jasmine had carried the thumb drive the professor had given them back to the safe house. Tears streaming down her face, Liz had told the old woman about her grandson's fate, and offered her the thumb drive.

But Maria had turned away, rejecting her grandson's sacrifice. At the time, Liz couldn't begin to understand her reaction. Between the thumb drive and students who'd witnessed Professor McKenzie's discovery, not even the Director of Domestic Affairs could silence the truth this time.

Or so she had thought.

Lost and confused, Liz had looked to her friends for an explanation. Only then had Sam told her what had happened.

The story had hit the news before they'd even reached the safe house. "Texas" had launched a counter-attack—supposedly in retaliation for the capture of their operative—and had slaughtered hundreds of students at the University of San Francisco.

In response, the Western Allied States had declared war on the rogue state, allowing it to enact emergency wartime legislation. The media had been censored, a nationwide curfew set between the hours of 7p.m. and 7a.m., strict rations placed over the nation's resources, and soldiers now patrolled the streets of San Francisco.

Worst of all, they had resumed the draft, requiring all able-bodied men and women to report to their nearest military recruitment office. One in five were to be conscripted and trained for the coming war. The process was supposed to be random, but in reality, it was rural youth they were taking.

Or so the rumors went.

Liz winced as pain flared in the palms of her hands. Fingers shaking, she saw the blood staining her white gloves. Her nails had cut straight through the fine material and pierced her skin. Sucking in a breath, she forced herself to relax. Rage bubbled in her chest, but she refused to set it free. A cold breeze blew across the rooftop, but her long black hoody and pants kept her warm. Spring was well underway, but this was San Francisco, and the wind rarely let up.

The massacre at the university had at least taught Liz one lesson—the President, the Director, the government, they would stop at nothing to win this war. No deed was too low for them, no act too foul. If the resistance wanted victory, they needed to be just as ruthless.

Watching the alleyway, Liz bent her head, listening to the telltale crunch of gravel beneath boots. The soldiers were growing closer, just a few minutes away now. Liz quickly tucked her curly black hair behind her ears, readying herself. From the noise they were making, she guessed there were no more than six.

She smiled. They didn't stand a chance.

Spreading her wings, Liz watched as the patrol turned the corner and started down her alleyway. The wind caught in her feathers, trying to pull her from the roof, but she crouched slightly, resisting its call. Her heart pounded in her ears as the soldiers drew closer. Dressed all in black, her wings the color of night, she was all but invisible to those below.

Without a sound, Liz stepped out into open space. Air whistled in her ears as she fell. She only had eyes for the soldiers. She could see them clearly now. Their youthful faces scanned the shadows, their eyes nervous, movements jumpy. It was obvious most were fresh recruits. Their sun-kissed skin proved the rumors were true—that her rural countrymen were being plucked from their beds to fight the government's war.

The two marching at the back were different, though. They moved with confidence, their backs straight and eyes hawkish. Their rifles were held with the casual indifference of professionals, and their pale skin betrayed their urban upbringing.

These were the men she wanted to speak with.

By now Liz was almost on them. Ten feet above the ground, her wings snapped open. They gave a sharp *crack*, slowing her descent abruptly, giving her time to adjust course. The men below looked up at the sound, alerted to her presence, but it was far too late.

As her boots struck the asphalt, Liz spun, her wings lashing out to catch the two leading recruits in the head. They dropped without a sound as those behind them screamed and lifted their rifles, but Liz was already moving. She leapt through the air and landed on the back of her next victim. Her weight drove him to his knees, and a single blow sent him face-first into the ground.

Standing, she searched for the fourth recruit, and found her further down the alley. She couldn't have been older than Liz's own seventeen years. Snarling, Liz stepped towards her, and the girl dropped her gun and fled.

Ignoring her, Liz leapt skyward as the rattle of gunfire came from behind. Bullets flashed past, tearing chips from the stone walls. Tumbling head over heels, she watched as the two soldiers tried to track her flight, but they were far too slow to catch her. Grinning, she landed between them. Her hands flashed out, catching both by their collars. She lifted them as though they weighed no more than pillows, and tossed them backwards into either wall of the alley.

One collapsed to the ground, unconscious, but the other staggered to his feet and tried to flee. Liz was on him in an instant. Catching him again, she drove him back into the wall. Teeth bared, she pressed her face close to his.

"Where do you think you're going?" she growled. "I thought you were looking for me?"

The man continued to struggle, trying to break free, until she lifted him and slammed him into the wall again. Air hissed between his teeth as his lungs emptied, and he gasped like a fish out of water. When he finally caught his breath, he slumped in her grasp, apparently accepting his fate.

"Where's the Director?" Liz leaned forward, whispering the question in his ear.

When she pulled back, the man cleared his throat, then spat in her face.

Liz's brow hardened, and without thinking, she tossed him across the alley. He flew several feet before slamming down into a pile of garbage. A can rattled along the concrete as Liz strode after him, struggling to lock her rage back in its cage. Silently, she wiped the spit from her face, then watched in amusement as the soldier tried to pull himself clear of the trash.

When he finally staggered out, she leapt forward and grabbed him by the throat. Forcing him to his knees, she towered over him.

"They didn't tell you much about me, did they?" she hissed. "Now, *where is she?*"

Since the massacre, neither the Director nor the President had been seen in public. Instead, they hid within the television, broadcasting their propaganda to the nation from behind locked doors. No one knew where they were hiding, only that they were well-protected. Liz didn't care. She had only one desire now, one objective.

To kill the woman who had taken Chris from her.

The soldier's mouth opened and closed, but no words came out. Rolling her eyes, Liz loosened her grip around his throat, and waited for him to speak. He gave a muted choking sound and started to cough.

"Go…to hell—"

Whatever else he might have said was cut off as Liz slammed her boot into his unprotected crotch. He crumpled without a sound, his sudden convulsion tearing his throat from her grasp. Not that it mattered—he wasn't going anywhere now. Lying on the ground, the man gave a low, almost inhuman moan as he clutched his groin.

Liz knelt beside him. Her anger was raging again, begging to be released, and she felt a desperate need to indulge it. How satisfying would it be, to watch this man die, to feel his life slowly drain away, smothered by her touch?

Her glove was off before she realized what she was doing. Only as she reached for his unprotected throat did she stop herself.

"Tell me where she is," Liz said, her voice husky, "or die in agony."

On his back, the man stilled. His eyes flickered up at her, then down to her naked hand. He swallowed, visibly afraid. Apparently word had spread about the awful pain and death her touch brought.

"I don't…" He shook his head, his voice little more than a squeak. "I don't know."

Liz sighed. "That's too bad." She reached for his throat.

The man flinched, raising his hands to fend her off. "Please! I'm telling the truth," he stammered.

Smiling, Liz nodded. "I know."

Before he could respond, she caught him by the throat again. His eyes bulged and he managed a strangled cry that faded to a squeak. He batted weakly at her arms, struggling to break her iron hold, but it was already too late.

Liz watched dispassionately as purple lines spread up the man's neck. He gaped at her as a low gurgling started in his chest. His feet beat helplessly at the concrete and his hands gripped her wrist, as though even now he might break her death grip. A wild ecstasy swept through her as she watched him, as she felt his life slowly drain away. She could almost taste his fear, his panic, as death took him.

When he finally stilled, Liz released him and stood. There was still one soldier left to interrogate, but as she turned towards him, she heard the click of steel on concrete. She froze, catching sight of the rifle in the man's hands, pointed straight at her chest. For a second, time seemed to stand still. She was too far away to reach him. In the narrow alleyway, he couldn't miss.

The soldier grinned as he pressed a finger to the trigger.

Before he could fire, a whisper of feathers came from overhead—then an emerald-winged banshee dropped from the sky and landed on the man's neck.

The audible *crack* of the soldier's spine breaking was still echoing through the alleyway as Jasmine settled down beside her victim. Her wings thumped one last time, scattering garbage across the alleyway, before tucking neatly behind her back. Folding her arms, she raised an eyebrow.

"You missed one," Jasmine commented.

Liz eyed the other girl. At five foot five, Jasmine was taller and more muscular than her, despite Liz being one year older. Jasmine was wearing her black hair in a ponytail, giving her a more youthful, innocent look. Of course, these days none of them were anything close to innocent.

"I was getting to him," Liz said, a little too sharply.

"Looks like he almost got you," Jasmine replied with a smirk.

Liz let out a long breath she hadn't realized she'd been holding. "How long were you watching?"

"Long enough."

Liz glanced around at the five soldiers scattered amidst the garbage. There was no sign of the one who'd fled. The three recruits she'd dropped still seemed to be breathing. Finally, she looked back at Jasmine. "You could have given me a hand."

"And deny you the chance to let off some steam?" Jasmine laughed. "I don't think so. We don't need that kind of anger bottled up in our little prison."

Liz scowled. "You weren't so different…not long ago."

Jasmine stilled. "Yes…" She glanced away, the mocking smile slipping from her lips. "And look where that got us."

A strained silence hung over the alleyway, until Liz kicked a can, sending it rattling across the concrete. With a sigh, she let the subject drop. "Well, what do you want?"

The only time Liz saw Jasmine or the others on her nightly forays was when they needed something. Unfortunately, their heightened sense of smell meant these days tracking each other down was becoming easier and easier.

"What? Can't a girl enjoy an early flight to stretch her wings?"

Now it was Liz's turn to raise an eyebrow. "What is it, Jasmine?" she pressed. "What's happened?"

Jasmine shrugged and spread her wings. They filled the alley, her emerald feathers catching in the first rays of daylight. "I'll explain on the way." She grinned. "You're not going to like it."

She lifted off before anything more could be said, and all Liz could do was follow.

I

Sam's wings creaked as he settled on the smooth granite surface. The stone was slick beneath his feet, still wet from the night's dew, and he took a moment to balance himself. The top of the obelisk on which he stood formed a half pyramid, with the tip sliced flat rather than the usual point. He supposed someone had suggested the change to differentiate Independence Monument from the Washington Monument—although by then that old relic would have been long gone, burned away by the nuclear blast that had engulfed the American capital two decades ago.

Skyscrapers towered around the obelisk, their silent glass walls staring down at Sam's solitary perch. Absently, he wondered if today would be the day someone finally noticed him, but he doubted it. He had been coming here for weeks now, winging his way through the skies before the dawn's light broke over the city. It was a good place to think, to watch and listen to the activity taking place below. With his enhanced senses, he had little trouble see those below, while it would be all but impossible for his audience to spot him perched seven hundred feet above them.

Now he scanned the crowds, wondering how the world had spiraled so far out of control. Thousands of refugees packed the square, camping out on the cold tiles, beneath the trees surrounding the obelisk, on the sidewalks and benches—wherever they could find even a hint of shelter. They had come from all across California, from small rural towns and villages, fleeing the scourge of the *Chead*. Rumors abounded of great packs of the creatures roaming the countryside, driving people from their homes, slaughtering them with wanton abandon. Desperate and afraid, those who survived had abandoned their homes and fled to the one place they believed safe.

San Francisco.

But their plight had made them easy targets for the government's draft. Thousands of their youth had already been conscripted into the army. Many even went willingly, believing the official line that Texas was behind the spread of the *Chead* virus.

Those below were the ones who had escaped selection—people too old or young to be of use. Yet after their long journey in search of shelter, they now found themselves shunned by a city and a people unmoved by their plight. Ruled by fear, the urbanites had slammed their doors in the faces of their fellow citizens. No one dared risk inviting a soon-to-be *Chead* into their home.

So, homeless and alone, the refugees gathered in the streets and parks, making homes for themselves wherever they could.

Watching the first of them stir, Sam couldn't help but think they might be the lucky ones. It was the fate of their children that worried him, that kept him up at night, haunting his dreams.

Because he knew all too well what the government was capable of, what they would do with all those young bodies. Halt might be dead, but his project lived on. Sam had seen to that. Somewhere out there, in the mountains, beneath the earth, somewhere, the experiments continued.

How many of the conscripted youth would find themselves in cages instead of battlefields?

He closed his eyes, shivering as Ashley's words echoed in his mind.

Halt used me, Sam. He used me to get to you. If any other kids die in their vile experiments, it will be my fault as much as yours. We have to stop them, before they hurt anyone else.

Gritting his teeth, Sam carefully lowered himself onto the cold granite and dangled his legs over the side. He tried and failed to ignore the awful pain of Ashley's loss. How long had it been now, since that fateful day? Three weeks? Four?

He pushed his hands deep into the pockets of his jeans, trying to keep the tears from his eyes. Hard as it was, he had to move on, had to focus on living. It was the only way he would find the strength he needed to fulfill Ashley's final wish—to put an end to the government's vile experiments. Spreading the truth about what the others had discovered at the university had been his sole purpose since recovering from his bullet wound.

For decades, the people of the Western Allied States had suffered the scourge of the *Chead*. For decades they had suffered, battling an enemy they could not see. Texas had been blamed, but the Lone Star State had never had any hand in the virus.

It had been their own government all along. The leaders of the WAS had needed a distraction from their own malicious deeds, and a patsy on which to blame all the ills that befell their young nation. Texas and the *Chead* had served their purpose well, giving the President and his Director the pretext to increase their powers time and again.

Broadcasting that truth to the nation had become an obsession for Sam, but it mattered little. Apart from the Madwomen and their limited allies, he was pretty sure everyone else in the world thought he was insane.

I miss you, Ash.

He cast the thought into the void, wondering if somewhere, she was thinking the same thing—though he knew it was impossible. He had held out hope for days after the university massacre. After everything they had been through—the trials and the torture, the bullet wounds and imprisonment, how could she possibly be alive?

Days had turned to weeks, and the only story to emerge was that two fugitives had been involved in the attack on the university and had been killed by government operatives. They'd plastered Ashley and Chris's faces all over the television, as the Director crowed of their demise.

Beside her always was the translator Jonathan, with his trustworthy face and easy smile. He would nod along to everything the woman said, before stepping up to play his role in their little act. With teary eyes he would explain how hard the government was working to bring his family's murderers to justice, how much it meant for him to see their deaths avenged.

It made Sam sick to his stomach that he'd ever trusted the man.

In the end, he'd been forced to admit the truth. If Ashley or Chris had been captured, the Director would have happily staged an execution for the whole world to see.

No, Ashley was gone, her life snuffed out, as if it had never been.

If only I had been there…

He forced the thought back down. Wallowing in regret would not help him now. With the bullet wound in his leg, he had been in no state to go with the others to the university. He would have only been a liability. If he'd joined them, no one would have gotten out alive.

Sam sat up as the tone of the whispers below changed. Leaning out over the ledge, he watched a group of old women make their way through the crowd. His heart lifted as the Madwomen returned to their station around the base of the obelisk. In silence, they began their solemn march, eyes fixed straight ahead, ignoring the soldiers stirring around the square. The green-uniformed men readjusted their rifles, but they made no move to intercept the protesters.

Since the official story about the attack on the monument had painted the Madwomen as innocent victims, the group had returned to their march in force. With hundreds of refugees now packing the park as witnesses, there was little the government could do to stop them. Only the women still on the wanted list stayed away—such as Chris's grandmother, Maria.

Their courage gave Sam hope that things might still change, but their defiance hadn't come without cost. With the prospect of open war on the horizon, few citizens were willing to stand with them. Even the refugees below, persecuted as they were, directed their hatred at the Texans, for the plague the Lone Star State had supposedly unleashed on their lives. It was a narrative the President and his people had used successfully in the past, and without a way to prove their involvement with the *Chead*, there was little way to counter it.

Still, Sam wasn't about to give up without a fight. Swinging his backpack from his shoulders, he unpacked the shortwave radio and placed it on the granite surface. He quickly looked over the steel box, ensuring everything was still in one piece, then picked up the transmitter. It wasn't much, but it was a start. Each morning he had been broadcasting to anyone who would listen, although he had no way of knowing how many that might be. He might be talking to ghosts for all he knew.

Clearing his throat, Sam lifted the transmitter and spoke: "Good morning, America! Testing, testing, one…two…three. Is anybody out there? Hey, isn't that from some song about a war? Someone with the internet look that up for me would ya…" He paused and then laughed. "Yeah, that's what I thought, phone lines are dead. Guess you're all in bed still or something. Come on, it's only…oh my god it's 6a.m., maybe I should go back to bed myself."

Standing, Sam moved to the edge of the platform. He still held the transmitter, its long cord stretching out behind him. "On second thought, it's a beautiful morning here in San Fran. Why don't you make a start to the day instead? There's a lot of people here in Independence Square who've had a hard night's sleep—come down and see for yourself! Or are you still listening to our noble dictator's wild tales of covert operatives and foreign spies?"

Sam sighed audibly into the microphone. "Yeah, thought so. Sad to think we've all become such suspicious creatures. Time was a madman could claim he'd build a 2000-mile-long wall and we'd believe him. Maybe I should ask the President for an interview…think he'd let me talk this time? Haven't you wondered why I never said anything, standing there beside him with my wings out, like some pet chimp?"

He paused, remembering that day on the stage, the crowds thronging the streets around Fisherman's Wharf. What if he'd said something then? If he'd stepped forward and told them all it was all a scam?

Don't look back. He took a breath and forged on.

"I was in Independence Square too, when the attack went down. But I wasn't fighting for the government. I took a bullet fighting off their soldiers, protecting the widows of our veterans. Just come down and ask the Madwomen, they'll tell you the truth."

Releasing the transmit button, he chuckled to himself. No doubt he was coming off as stark raving mad to anyone listening. "Still not convinced? How about if I told you the government was behind the *Chead?* That they created them twenty years ago, and have been using them to control us ever since? What's that? You think I'm crazy? That I should be locked up in a mental asylum?"

He paused to take a breath before continuing: "Too bad, budget cuts got rid of 'em all. Guess a shift in Alcatraz will have to do. Maybe I'll fly over and hand myself in. That's right, I have wings remember?"

Taking a break, Sam leaned out over the edge. A touch of vertigo swept through him, despite the wings sprouting from his back. His lips tightened as the Madwomen continued their march. Sadness touched him as he counted their numbers and noted several more absentees. He shook his head, wondering where they got their courage.

The fact that the Director couldn't act openly against them had only slowed her crusade. Over the past four weeks, dozens of the Madwomen had gone missing. At first they'd thought the women had merely given up. But when their houses were found empty, it became clear something more sinister was behind their disappearances.

Still the marches continued. Some had taken refuge in safe houses dotted throughout the city, but most refused to be driven from their homes. They stood in open defiance against the threat of violence—and paid for it with their lives.

Sam bit his lip as he lifted the microphone again, taking on a more serious tone. "Look, I know you have no reason to believe a disembodied voice on the radio. Heck, a few months ago I would have been at the head of the queue baying for my blood. But I'm telling you, every word I've said is true. I know you don't want to believe it, that you want to stay safe in your own little world, ignoring the voices outside screaming for help. But it won't work. They're coming for us, for all of us, and whether you stay in your bubble or not, one day it'll be your turn. So come down to Independence Square, look at what's happening here. Speak to the Madwomen, listen to their stories. And decide for yourself what the truth is."

Sam sucked in a long breath and switched off the shortwave. Exhausted by his outburst, he sat down too quickly and almost slid off the side of the pyramid. Recovering, he leaned forward and placed his head in his hands, feeling the oil in his long brown hair. He needed a haircut, but there had been no time to keep up with things like personal grooming. His palms brushed the soft fuzz of his beard, and he wondered what Ashley would have thought of it.

Lying on his back, he rested his head against the cold stone and closed his eyes. Despite his weariness, he fought the pull of sleep. It wasn't safe to stay here—not in daylight. He had to leave, had to return to the safe house before it got any brighter. Even so, he was loath to desert his friends below.

His ears twitched, catching the faint whisper of wings from overhead. Opening his eyes, he watched as Mira's small form settled down beside him. Her mismatched blue and green eyes watched him closely as she folded her slate-grey wings behind her back. The wind gusted around her, lashing at her grey hair until she reached up and pushed it to the side.

"What are you doing here, Mira?" Sam asked, sitting up. "You could have been spotted."

Mira stood on the edge of the obelisk and looked down at the crowd. "They don't see good," she commented. "What are you doing…up here?"

Sam sighed. "Thinking. Watching." He forced a smile. "What about you, Mira? To what do I owe the honor?"

"Honor?" Mira's brow creased as she returned and seated herself beside him. "What do you mean, honor?"

Sam sighed. "Never mind. I just meant, what brings you up here? My captivating radio show?"

Mira wrinkled her nose. "Liz is more fun."

Sam rolled his eyes. "Just because she spends her nights beating up soldiers…" He trailed off as he saw the glimmer in Mira's eyes. He scowled as a mischievous smile spread across the girl's face. "Okay, troublemaker, what's the news?"

"Not supposed to say." Smiling, she lay back and looked at the sky. "Secret."

"So what are you doing here?" he sighed. Talking with the strange girl was like conversing with a brick wall.

Mira had lifted her legs until they were perpendicular to her hips, but now they flicked back down, her wings extending at the same time, propelling her to her feet. Sam raised his eyebrows, waiting for a response.

Instead, she wandered back to the edge of the obelisk. "You have to promise…not to get mad," she said, glancing back at him, "that's what Jasmine said."

Groaning, Sam lifted himself to his feet. "I promise."

"Good." Mira smiled, her face lighting up like Christmas. "Let's go."

She stretched her wings and crouched at the edge of the obelisk, but before she could take off something below caught her attention. "Oh," she murmured, casting a sheepish glance over her shoulder. "I think…they've seen us now."

Sam muttered a choice curse under his breath as the first shout carried up to them. Stepping up beside Mira, he shook his head. The soldiers at the edge of the square were gesturing up at them. Several began pushing their way through the crowd towards the obelisk, as though that would somehow bring them closer to the winged fugitives seven hundred feet above them.

Scowling, Sam glanced at Mira. "Brat," he muttered.

She only grinned back at him. "Shall we go?

2

Mike's head whipped back with an audible *thud* as the guard's fist slammed into his forehead. He slumped forward in the chair, blood dripping from his cracked lips, a faint moan escaping his emaciated chest. Before he could recover, the guard swung again, a left hook that sent the imprisoned Texan reeling sideways. Only the steel shackles strapping Mike to his chair kept him from falling.

Chris watched on, a silent spectator to the Texan's torture. A steel helmet with a full-faced visor concealed Chris's features, and the skintight polyester uniform he wore made him a clone to the other guards standing around the room. Only the wings sprouting from his back gave him away. Those, and the steel collar strapped tight around his neck.

On the other side of the room, Ashley stood in a matching outfit. The sleek black material clung to her figure, leaving little to the imagination. Red hair tumbled down from the back of her helmet, and her wings were half-spread, the slightest of tremors running through her white feathers. Around her neck, the collar shone in the harsh glow of the overhead lights.

Mike coughed blood as the guard drove a punch into his stomach. Chris's heart went out to the man. In the four weeks since their capture, he had watched Mike wilt before his eyes. His bronzed Texan skin had faded to grey, and it seemed now that a man in his sixties sat in the chair. There was little left of the man who had bounded around the safe house back in San Francisco.

Chris made no move to aid him as the beating continued. He had learned during his first week it was every man for himself here. Even while his wing and ribs were still healing, the Director had brooked no disobedience. No transgression, however small, went unpunished. And while she lacked Doctor Halt's deranged taste for violence, she was well-versed in the art of breaking men—mind and body.

She stood beside Chris now, arms folded, watching the Texan with a disinterested frown. As the guard stepped up to continue his assault, she lifted a hand to stop him, then strode forward to stand in front of the Texan. Her thin frame moved with overt confidence, her authority over the room unquestionable. Her hazel eyes stared down at Mike, her short blond hair carefully dyed and styled to mask her age. Crouching beside the chair, she took a handkerchief from her pocket and gently dabbed at the blood dribbling down the Texan's bearded chin.

Groaning, Mike lifted his head. Uncertainty flickered through his eyes when he saw her. "What do…you want?" he croaked.

The Director smiled. She dropped the handkerchief in his lap and stroked his cheek.

"We only want the truth, Mike…" she said softly. "Where have they gone, these renegades of yours? We know you're hiding them."

"Please…" Mike sobbed, his eyes rolling around in his skull as though searching for a way out, "I already told you…where they are."

Chris shivered. He had—after a week of enhanced interrogation had left Mike a broken man. The Director had ordered the house raided and everyone inside killed. Chris had tried to stop her. It had been the last time he tested the Director's patience. Thankfully, the house had been empty when the soldiers arrived.

Yet the Texan's interrogation continued. Once he had been left in this windowless cell for almost a week. They'd given him a bottle of water, and one meal a day, but otherwise he'd been alone in the darkness. Chris still shuddered at the thought of the blubbering creature who'd emerged at the end.

By now, Mike had nothing left. No lingering secrets, no hidden safe houses. Nothing, that is, but the pride of his nation.

"That's right," the Director murmured, her hand still caressing the Texan's cheek. "How could I have forgotten? Such a good boy. But you were too slow, Mike. *You betrayed us!*" Her voice turned hard as she gripped Mike by the hair and pulled back his head.

She moved behind the chair, still holding Mike by his long hair, forcing him to stare into the bright fluorescent lights.

"No, no, please," Mike croaked, his voice half-mad with terror.

The Director leaned down until her lips were an inch from Mike's ear. "You must confess, Mike," she whispered. "It's the only way to redeem yourself, to save yourself."

Tears ran down Mike's face. "No…"

Abruptly, the Director released her captive's hair and stepped away, nodding to the guard as she did so. The man's face revealed no emotion as he drew a baton from his belt.

"No, no, no, please!" Mike screamed, but still strapped to the chair, he had nowhere to go.

The baton descended again and again, smashing into his shin, his elbow, his jaw. Chris closed his eyes, unable to watch any longer, but there was no hiding from the sounds. A sharp *crack* marked each blow, followed by the Texan's shrieks.

When the guard finally ceased, all Mike could do was slump in his chair and sob. Across the room, Ashley stood as tense as an iron rod, fists clenched at her sides. She looked on the brink of mutiny, though they both knew there was nothing they could do for the Texan. One step out of line would see them crumple to the floor in agony—and that would only be the beginning.

"Come now, Mike," the Director was speaking again, "be reasonable. We know you were behind the attack in Independence Square. We know you're here as a spy, infecting our food supplies with your vile virus."

Mike lifted his head to look at her.

"Do you really think my confession will make a difference?" His eyes were bloodshot and his jaw swollen, but there was a surprising clarity to his voice. "You think it will save you? That it'll stop the vultures from circling?"

The Director slammed her fist into his face. His head whipped back in the chair, but she retreated, cursing under her breath as she cradled her hand. Thin as her arms were, it was likely she'd hurt her wrist. Chris smiled beneath his visor.

When she'd finally finished swearing, the Director swung toward the nearest guard. "Give him a good workover," she said through clenched teeth, "then throw him in the hole again for a couple of days."

"No!" Mike strained against his bindings, his eyes wide with panic. "No, please, not again!"

But the Director was already walking away. A guard opened the door, and Chris quickly stepped after her. Ashley was a second behind him, her head still half-turned to watch the Texan. Chris nudged her, nodding at the retreating back of the Director. They hurried to catch up, all too aware what would happen if she saw them hesitating.

The Director was halfway through the door when Mike screamed again.

"I did it!"

She froze in the doorway, before slowly turning to look at the hapless prisoner. "Keep going."

Mike gasped great lungfuls of air, as though with those three words he'd scaled a mountain. Finally, he lifted his head. Chris saw the darkness of self-loathing in his eyes as he spat out the words.

"I did it. I conspired with Texas. I brought the *Chead* here. I killed the Madwomen."

A grin spread across the Director's face as she stepped back into the room. "Very good, Mike. You've earned a reprieve." She looked at the guards. "Skip the beating. Throw him straight in the hole. He can spend some time in the dark while we get things ready," she said, before addressing Mike again: "Wouldn't want you having second thoughts before your big debut."

The Texan seemed to wilt at the Director's words. He shook his head, face ashen, but his pleas were ignored.

Chris's legs trembled as he followed the Director outside. Ashley fell into step beside him, and silently he reached out and took her hand. He squeezed her fingers, the only reassurance he could offer, then released her again.

Together they followed the Director down the long corridors of the facility.

3

The *Chead* roared as another man leapt at her. He held a baseball bat in one hand, but from her perspective, it seemed to move in slow motion. She skipped back as the bat swung in a lazy arc, then lunged forward and tore it from his grasp. The man was still standing there gaping when she slammed the bat into the side of his head. The wood gave a loud *crack* as it shattered against his skull. He toppled without a sound, and she strode on, already seeking out fresh prey.

Her nostrils flared at the scent of blood. It mingled with the acrid tang of smoke, masking the revolting stench of humanity permeating the town. The *Chead's* keen eyes scanned the shadows as she continued down the dusty street. Firelight flickered in the windows of a nearby building, but otherwise the town was dark. Her brethren had cut the power before their assault. Without light, the humans were stranded, like helpless sheep waiting for the slaughter.

She glanced around as the thundering of hooves came from behind her. A horse and empty carriage raced down the street, eyes wild as it fled the strange smells of the massacre. The other *Chead* moving through the streets ignored it—they were not here to slaughter humanity's mindless creatures.

Then the *Chead* saw a man leap from an alleyway. Running

forward, he tried to catch the wagon, but cried out as the horse outpaced him. His mouth fell open when he turned and saw her in the street.

Fire stirred in the *Chead's* stomach. She started forward, the red haze spreading across her vision, washing away all thought but the need for blood. The man watched her approach, seemingly unable to move, even to save himself. Only at the last second did he come alive and turn to run.

The *Chead* bounded into the air and crashed onto his back before he could take two steps. Her weight bore him down, slamming him face-first into the ground. Now he found the will to fight, and twisting, he swung at her face. With casual ease, she caught his fist in her dainty hands.

She grinned down at the helpless man. "Trying to leave…the party?"

The *Chead* tore out his throat before he could respond. Sitting on his chest, she watched in ecstasy as the blood bubbled from his mouth. He started to thrash, but she held him down, waiting until the last drop of life had drained from him.

Standing, she surveyed the chaos, savoring the taste of victory. The *Chead* were everywhere, slipping silently through the narrow streets, moving from building to building, seeking out the humans wherever they hid. The signs leading into the town had called it Sutter Creek, but when they were done it would be like all the others—a ghost town, empty, abandoned by all but the corpses they left behind. It was the fifth they'd struck in as many weeks, and the largest.

A smile spread across her lips as one of her brethren forced a family from a nearby house. The man died choking on his own blood, while the woman and son were dragged away.

Feeble creatures.

She shook her head. Humanity, in its arrogance, had grown weak. Watching the woman meekly being led away, the *Chead* felt only contempt for her own past. The memories that still flickered in her mind showed a weak and cowardly woman, a timid doctor who had bowed to lesser creatures.

But that woman was gone, burned away by the fury of the *Chead*, and she was free.

The rage rose again as she watched the human woman. She longed to embrace the anger, but fought the urge. Her body shook and pinpricks trailed along her skin, raising the hairs on her arms. Gritting her teeth, she turned away, seeking a fresh victim to spend her rage on. Talisa had been clear—the women were hers, and hers alone.

Susan's nose twitched as a fresh scent drifted across the street. She raised her head, scanning the neighboring buildings, and caught the slightest shift in the curtains of a house. She moved towards it, heart racing.

The door crumpled like paper beneath her boot, exploding into the hallway with the shriek of splintered wood. She stalked inside as someone screamed. Tasting the air, she savored the scent of her quarry's fear. Her fingers bent like claws, ready to rend and tear as movement came from the room ahead. She started towards it.

The occupant fled into an adjoining room as Susan stepped through the doorway. Laughter hissed from her lips and she leapt over the sofa in pursuit, the *Chead* rage already taking hold.

Bounding into the next room, the *Chead* ducked as a vase flew at her head and shattered on the wall. Teeth bared, she clenched her fists and advanced on her prey. Her heart pounded in her ears, flooding her veins with rage, the red haze rising, washing away all reason.

In the corner, the woman she had chased through the house sank to her knees and buried her head in her hands. She sobbed softly as the *Chead* approached. Pausing above the woman, the *Chead* drank in the woman's fear. The room reeked of it. Curled up in a ball, crying into her hands, a human had never seemed so pitiful. Raising a fist, the *Chead* readied herself for the kill.

Before the blow could land, an iron hand caught her by the wrist and dragged her back.

"Susan…" a voice whispered. "Stop…"

She spun and swung at her attacker. Hecate caught the blow with the same ease she had caught the human's earlier. She screamed with a desperate rage and tried to break free, but her mate only embraced her, smothering her in his arms.

As the scent of him filled her nostrils, the fury fell from Susan as quickly as it had come. She stilled, the tension fleeing her in a rush. Taking another breath, her mind swam with the sweetness of her mate. Her eyes were caught in Hecate's cool gaze.

A smile tugged at his lips. Lifting his finger to her chin, he leaned towards her. This time she did not resist. She shivered as their lips met. The last traces of the red haze fell away, though her racing heart did not slow. A fresh yearning burned in her stomach as she wrapped her arms around him, pulling him close.

Chuckling, Hecate broke away. He growled, the sound familiar, holding a promise for later.

Susan stepped back from Hecate, her mind returning. She reached out to stroke her mate's chest, her breath slowing. Then, together, they looked down at the woman she had cornered.

"Talisa…wants you," Hecate said softly.

Susan nodded. "We had better…join her."

Idly, she twisted her fingers through the woman's auburn hair. A scream echoed through the room as she hauled the prisoner to its feet, but *Chead* rage or no, Susan felt no compassion for her prey's pain. Pain was weakness. Pain was human. And she had no patience for either.

Talisa was waiting.

⁂ 4 ⁂

The sun was still low in the sky as Liz followed Jasmine down into the backyard. The flight had only taken twenty minutes, but after a long night hunting the streets for stray soldiers, Liz was nearing exhaustion. There was no sign of movement below, but even so they came in low and fast, wings retracted as they swept between the towering pines lining the property of the safe house.

Liz let out a long breath as she settled on the damp grass. They were onto their third safe house now. The first they'd left after Mike's capture, and the second had been abandoned as a precaution when a strange van was spotted several times parked in the street. With soldiers marching through the city and the public on high alert, they couldn't be too careful. Especially after word had reached them that their first location had been raided.

Their current house was well outside the city center, almost in Daly City, but at least the heavy tree-coverage offered good protection from eyes on the ground. Not that Liz had exhausted much time in the safe house lately. With her nights spent prowling the city, she often couldn't make it back before daylight, in which case she would find an abandoned building to spend the day in. And when she did return, she preferred to sleep in the treehouse out back.

Turning towards the house, Liz found Jasmine still standing where she'd landed, watching Liz with folded arms.

"What is it, Jasmine?" she sighed. "Whatever you're not saying, spit it out."

Jasmine blinked as though leaving a trance, then smiled. "But there's so much to choose from, where would I begin?" When Liz only raised an eyebrow, Jasmine's smile faded and she went on, "Well, for starters, you look like crap, Liz."

Liz scowled. "You're not looking so hot yourself. A ponytail? Really?"

Ignoring the taunt, Jasmine stepped in close. "That's not what I meant and you know it." Her eyes softened. "We're worried about you, Liz. You're out all hours of the night, disappearing for days. Most of the time we don't know if you're alive or dead. Not unless we risk ourselves looking for you. I'm getting tired of tracking you down."

"Then stop looking," Liz snapped. She made to step past, but Jasmine held out a hand and caught her.

"You're the one who said we're a family, Liz," Jasmine remarked softly.

"And you're the one who said it was everyone for themselves," Liz retorted. She threw off Jasmine's hand and stalked towards the house.

"Liz, wait!"

Something in Jasmine's tone gave Liz pause. She glanced back at her friend. "What now?"

Jasmine started after her. "There's something you should know before we go inside." She walked past Liz, waving her on.

"And what's that?" Liz asked, matching her stride for stride.

"We have a…visitor," Jasmine offered cautiously. "A doctor."

"A doctor?" Goosebumps tingled on Liz's arms. She paused mid-stride and looked at Jasmine. "You don't mean…?"

"Not one from our…facility." Jasmine's eyes flicked down, then back to Liz. "He's from another place, but…yes, I mean one of the doctors involved with our experiments."

Liz's mouth opened and shut again, unable to voice her disbelief. Spinning on her heel, she hauled open the back door, then slammed it behind her. She was halfway down the corridor before Jasmine could follow her inside. Blood pounding in her temples, she stepped into the dining room and looked around, seeking the monster someone had invited into their house.

Her fellow rebels sat around the dining table, their own eyes wide as they stared back. Maria occupied the head of the table, her hands clasped in front of her. Chris's grandmother looked as exhausted as Liz felt. The wrinkles on her face had deepened in the last few weeks, and there was a sorrow in the way she carried herself, as though she were simply going through the motions of life.

To the side of Maria sat Harry, an army veteran who had recently joined their fledgling resistance. He was close to Maria's age, a man who, by luck or skill, had survived the ravages of the American War. His kind was a rarity these days—most men of his generation hadn't lived past sixty—but he'd appeared not long after the government's condemnation of the attack in Independence Square.

Together with Maria, they were coordinating the resistance. Looking at the two of them now, Liz could not help but think that had been a mistake. Both were old and tired, well past their prime. They didn't have the energy to fight this war, or the resolve to do what was needed to win. The proof of that was sitting at the table beside them, staring at her with unconcealed awe.

Jasmine had been right about one thing—she didn't recognize him. He hadn't been there, hadn't been amongst the doctors who had imprisoned them, who had systematically gone about culling hundreds of innocent children. It hadn't been him who'd held her down, who'd injected her with the awful serum that had changed her life forever. It had not been this doctor who'd thrown her, still weak from a coma, into a room with a *Chead*, to watch and see whether she would survive.

But he had done it to others.

Ignoring Maria and Harry, Liz strode around the table. Her whole body was shaking, and without even thinking her wings had opened, stretching out to fill the room. The wonder had fallen from the doctor's face now, and he shrank down in his chair as she approached. Coming to a stop in front of him, Liz leaned forward, until their faces were only an inch apart.

"So, you're the doctor?" she hissed.

The man swallowed visibly, and nodded.

"How many children have you killed?" Liz growled. Her hands shot out and caught him by the shoulders, shoving him. He yelped as his chair tilted backwards, but she held him still. He hadn't answered, and with a snarl that rumbled up from the depths of her soul, Liz lifted him into the air.

"How. Many?" she shrieked.

The color drained from the doctor's face. "I…I…" He closed his eyes. "I don't know. Too many to count."

Liz released him so suddenly he crumpled to the floor beside his fallen chair. Clenching her fists, she struggled to control herself. Flames burned her stomach and she fought the urge to tear the man limb from limb. Obviously, the Madwomen wanted him for something, though she couldn't think what.

"Why is he here?" she grated.

"I…I…I want to help," the doctor stammered from the floor.

"Did I ask you?" Liz snapped, glaring at him. He promptly shut his mouth.

"He has information we need," Maria said, drawing Liz's eyes back to the table.

Liz stared at Chris's grandmother for a long moment. Her words came out in a shriek, "You can't trust anything these people tell you!" Taking a breath to calm herself, she cast a disgusted glance at the trembling doctor. "They're scum. We should kill him now, before he betrays us."

The doctor whimpered and scrambled away. Grabbing the chair, he jumped to his feet and thrust it in front of him like a shield.

Liz sneered. "You really think that will stop me?"

"Liz…" Jasmine's voice came from behind her. She crossed the room, until she stood between the doctor and Liz. "Hear him out."

"You're protecting him?" Liz asked softly.

Jasmine didn't back down. "If that's what it takes to get the Director."

Liz paused at that. "The Director?"

Nodding, Jasmine turned to the doctor. "Speak, now. Do it quickly, before I change my mind." Despite her interference, there was no mistaking Jasmine's hostility.

Still shaking, the doctor lowered himself back into the chair. He closed his eyes, as though summoning the courage to face them, before looking at Liz.

"My name is Edwin Reid," he began, "until a few months ago, I was working in a top-secret laboratory near Seattle."

"How many of these foul places are there?" Liz spat.

The doctor shook his head. "I have no idea. For a long time, I thought we were the only one. I guess they keep it all separated–"

"Just get on with it." Jasmine said, advancing a step.

The doctor yelped and almost fell off his chair. Liz waited impatiently for him to right himself, her foot tapping against the porcelain tiles.

Finally, Edwin took a long breath and went on: "Like I was saying, a few months back, the Seattle operation was closed down..."

"What a shame for my hometown economy." Liz spun as a new voice came from the entranceway. Sam stepped into the room, Mira shadowing him. A broad grin split his face. "Someone start the party without me?"

"You kids really can't keep a secret, can you?" Maria said wearily, scowling in Mira's direction.

Smiling, the girl wandered across the room, past the doctor and Harry, to Maria. Pulling up a chair beside Chris's grandmother, she took a seat, placed her arms on the table, and leaned her chin on her arms. At just four feet in height, her head barely reached the tabletop.

Maria stared at her for a second, then shook her head and laughed. Leaning back in her chair, she waved a hand at Sam. "Come in, Sam. Sit down. The good doctor here was just about to tell us why he's come."

"Doctor, ay?" Sam said as he took the last seat at the table.

He looked at Liz—where she still stood with Jasmine—then at the doctor. "You're either really desperate or really stupid, buddy. You know how many of your colleagues we've killed?"

The doctor frowned at Sam. "You…you're the one from the–"

"Don't say it." Groaning, Sam threw his arms in the air. "I thought it was meant to be thirty seconds of fame. How long is that damn joke of a press conference going to haunt me?"

Doctor Reid coughed. "I was actually going to say the radio. There's a receiver in the staff quarters at the new facility I was transferred too. You're quite popular."

Liz raised an eyebrow as Sam burst into laughter. "You're kidding me?" he managed finally, wiping tears from his eyes.

The doctor's gaze switched to Sam's wings and then back to his face. "Most of us thought you were a nutcase. Guess we were wrong."

Sam stilled. "Wrong about a lot of things." He turned to Harry. "How did he get here?"

Until then, Harry had watched the exchange in silence, his dark eyes giving away nothing. Now, he leaned forward in his chair, his hands clenched in front of him as he studied the doctor.

"He contacted the Madwomen in Independence Square yesterday afternoon. Said he could give us the Director of Domestic Affairs if we helped him. We spent the night transferring him from location to location, making sure he wasn't being followed or monitored. He still hasn't told us exactly how he can lead us to the woman, though."

Edwin cleared his throat. "Yes, well, the interruptions..."

Tired of his excuses, Liz snarled and started towards him. Still standing between them, Jasmine held out an arm, barring Liz's path. Their eyes met. For a moment Liz contemplated batting her aside, but decided it wasn't worth it.

"Get on with it."

"I'm trying!" the doctor said. "Where was I? Yes, the Seattle facility. I was recruited there after university, worked my way up through the ranks before they transferred me to the Evolution

Gene project. My predecessor had failed to reduce the psychological stress caused by the virus's integration with its host's DNA. Sadly, I wasn't any more successful. It wasn't much of a surprise when they shut us down."

"Out of a perverted curiosity, what do you mean by psychological stress?" Sam asked, his voice dangerous.

The doctor let out a long sigh. "It means the subjects who survived the physiological alterations...suffered the same fate as the *Chead*. They were driven mad by the strain on their nervous system, succumbing to fits of rages that–"

"They became *Chead*," Jasmine cut in. "Tell me, *Doctor*, I'm curious too. What exactly brought you here? When were you finally convinced the government had crossed a line?" She snorted. "Obviously not murdering kids."

"It's amazing, the things you'll do, when your back is against the wall." He looked around, though his eyes didn't seem to register them. "So many came and went, all their faces have blurred into one. It was easy to justify, when it came down to it. Why not? It was their parents who had sentenced them to death, not me. There was nothing I could do to save them—only offer a purpose to their passing."

"They died in agony!" Jasmine said, choking on the words.

"They died for a cure," the doctor shot back, then bowed his head. "At least, at first. That's how we all started. I learned that later, when I arrived at my new laboratory a few weeks ago. They've brought doctors there from all over the country. Each of us began our careers studying the *Chead* virus in search of a cure, but after years of research, sooner or later we all realized it's impossible. That's when they would switch us to their so-called Evolution Gene, their plan to 'fight back'."

"You seem bitter, Doctor Reid," Harry spoke before anyone could respond. His cool blue eyes watched the doctor with detached curiosity. "I take it you no longer buy the company line, as they say?"

The doctor's eyes returned to Jasmine. "You asked me what my line was? When it all became too much? It was the day I arrived at the new facility, right here in San Francisco, and realized we were no longer working on the 'children of traitors.' It was the day I first walked along those underground corridors and realized who my new candidates were. It was the day the government started conscripting young men and women to use as their guinea pigs."

"Some line," Sam muttered as Liz's heart sank.

She closed her eyes, despair for her fellow countrymen welling in her chest. Her suspicions were true: the government was using the draft as an excuse to find fresh candidates for their experiment. Chris had died to stop exactly this—the continued abduction and slaughter of the nation's youth.

Quick as thought, she side-stepped Jasmine and leapt at the doctor. He yelped and tried to escape, but she had him before he could leave his chair. Shoving him back down, she towered over him.

"So, where are they?" she snapped. "These children who so damaged your pathetic conscience?"

The doctor swallowed. "I'll tell you, gladly," he paused, eyes traveling around the room, directed anywhere but at Liz, "but first…I need your help."

Liz's hand flashed out and caught him by the throat. Jasmine stepped towards her, but froze when Liz fixed her with a glare. Returning her attention to the doctor, she leaned in close. "*Where?*"

"I…please…" the doctor choked, and she momentarily loosened her grip. "Please, you can do whatever you want with me. But you have to help my family!"

Liz paused. "Your family?"

The doctor nodded desperately. "Yes! My wife and sons. I'm not supposed to be here—not even supposed to leave the facility. They'll know I'm missing by now. Please, I've already been gone a day. I don't know how long before they…" He shook his head. "Just…protect my family, and I'll tell you anything you want to know."

Liz studied the man. It had to be a setup, a trap to lure them out of hiding. He seemed sincere, but she knew better than to trust appearances. They had been betrayed far too many times for that. She knew one way of getting the truth from him. Tugging off her gloves, she tossed them aside and reached for him again.

"Liz, stop!" Jasmine caught her around the waist and hauled her back.

Hissing, Liz spun, extending her wings to thrust the other girl back. Jasmine staggered away before straightening. "Don't do this, Liz."

Liz scowled. "You of all people should know he can't be trusted!"

"Maybe, but this isn't the way. Chris wouldn't want this," Jasmine countered.

"Chris is dead," Liz said flatly. "I don't think he cares–"

"*Enough!*" Maria's voice cut through their argument.

Liz turned, and quickly looked away again, shocked at the rage on Maria's face. Her hands dropped to her sides as she clenched her fists.

"Harry," Maria went on, her voice calm now, "choose some men to observe the family, see if there's anything suspicious. If nothing is amiss, we'll grab them tonight. So long as you've told us the truth, doctor, your family should be safe within twelve hours."

Her eyes swept the room, daring any of them to object, before returning to the doctor. "But if you're lying, I'll drive the knife through your heart myself."

5

Sam groaned as he leaned against the wall of the treehouse. Rays of sunlight bathed his face, streaming down through the cracks in the poorly-constructed roof. His eyelids drooped, the pull of sleep irresistible. With only the cover of night offering them a chance to stretch their wings, they had all taken on a nocturnal lifestyle, and it was now well past his bedtime. Still, he was glad Mira had dragged him to the meeting. Too often, the Madwomen and their handful of allies made decisions while Sam and the others slept.

Despite his exhaustion, he found sleep would not come. His mind kept returning to Maria's rescue plan, going over the details, over everything that might go wrong. According to the doctor, his wife and two sons lived in a condo in Sea Cliff, one of the most expensive suburbs in the city. Apparently working for the government came with a few perks.

Unfortunately, it made surveillance difficult, and the prospect of removing them without being spotted became all but impossible. Thinking of the task ahead, he found himself wondering whether Liz had been right after all. The cold, logical solution to their problem was to force the doctor to tell them what he knew.

That was what the Director would do.

Sam pushed the thought from his mind. Whatever happened,

they had to be better than their enemy. If they allowed themselves to sink to the government's level—to be corrupted by the very forces they fought—what was the point? Ultimately, they would only succeed in replacing one evil with another.

Maybe that was why he'd volunteered to go with the team to bring back the family. He needed to remind himself they were fighting for more than just themselves, that there was more at stake than their own pitiful lives. After all, wasn't that what the students at the university had sacrificed themselves for? Wasn't that what Ashley and Chris had died believing?

However, there was a more compelling reason to take Liz's option. The government was continuing its crackdown against dissenters, and just last night another safe house had been burnt to the ground. Its owner, a kindly woman who'd recently joined the cause, and everyone else inside had been killed. The news this morning had shown their bodies as they were carried out one by one, labeling each an enemy of the WAS.

The traitor Jonathan had been there, explaining how joyful he was at the government's progress against the rebels, and Sam had switched the television off in disgust. Jonathan was all over the news now, adding weight to the Director's crusade against the rebels, reminding everyone just what they stood to lose.

But it hadn't been Sam and the others who'd killed Jonathan's family. Doctor Halt had murdered his wife and daughter to ensure their silence. Now the man stood beside Halt's successor, spouting her accolades like a pet chimp.

Hearing the thump of wings, Sam sighed and sat up, surrendering all pretense of sleep. Wind swirled as Mira landed on the wooden deck, followed a second later by Jasmine. Mira wandered across the half-finished treehouse and settled herself beside him. Her soft grey wings stretched out, warming in the sun.

Sam grinned. It had taken two bedridden weeks for them both to fully recover from being shot. Now that they were fighting fit, there was no fighting to attend too. Well, not unless they wanted to spend their nights ambushing soldiers with Liz.

Sighing, he turned to Jasmine, aware of the uneasy tension that still lay between them. She wandered across the wooden boards and leaned her arms against the makeshift windowsill. Her wings hung limp behind her, emerald-green feathers trailing along the ground.

Watching her, Sam struggled to recall the girl he'd first met back in the facility. She had been easygoing then, lighthearted despite the cruelty of their imprisonment. But that was before they'd been forced to choose their own lives over those of their friends. Jasmine and Chelsea had gone into a room together, but only Jasmine had walked out.

Except the girl he'd known had never really come back.

Jasmine looked at him now, eyes hard, as though reading his thoughts. Sam only smiled back. Whatever bitterness still lay between them, he was done with it. They needed each other, now more than ever. Richard and Chris and Ashley were all gone, and Liz was falling into a pit she might never climb out of.

Pushing himself to his feet, he joined her at the window. A sharp pain came from his palm as he placed his hands on the raw wood. Cursing, held up his hand and saw the splinter. The flesh was already starting to swell around it.

"That looks nasty," Jasmine murmured.

Sam shook his head. "Think I should sue?"

Smiling, Jasmine took his hand. Sam said nothing as she inspected the damage. Before he had a chance to object, she pinched his palm with her long nails. Sam swore and jerked his hand away.

Jasmine arched an eyebrow. "Really? You took a bullet just a few weeks ago..."

Sam gave a sheepish grin and extended his hand again. Jasmine bent to the task again, her brows knitted together in concentration.

"Mira seems to have taken a liking to you," Sam offered, distracting himself from the pain in his palm.

"Yes, well, with Liz going all psycho-soldier and you busy with your gadgets, I seem to be the only one with the time." She paused, looking up from beneath a fringe of black hair. "Although she seems quite fond of you as well."

Sam shrugged. "I'm a likeable kinda guy." He glanced at

Mira. Her breathing had already softened and she appeared to be asleep. "She's a curious creature, actually seems to love the radio. But I'm still getting used to her."

As he spoke, Jasmine gave an exclamation of triumph and held up a finger. At its tip was a tiny black splinter of wood.

"Thanks, doctor," Sam chuckled. "Think I'll live?"

Jasmine waved a hand. Leaving the window, she wandered across the treehouse, the boards creaking beneath her feet, her black hair dangling down around her shoulders. She leaned against the wall where Mira was sleeping and sat beside her. Running a hand through the girl's grey hair, she looked up at Sam.

"She's a little odd, I'll admit. But she's family," she said.

"What does that make us?" Sam joined her in the sun, leaning his head against the wall. "Her mom and dad?"

Jasmine snorted. "At this rate, we might be the only sane ones left."

"Wasn't so long ago *you* were the one going mad," Sam replied carefully.

A strained silence followed his comment. Biting her lip, Jasmine shook her head and looked across at him.

"Yes," she said, then took a deep breath and continued in a strained voice, "and in Independence Square, I almost killed those people, almost lost control of who I was. If Liz hadn't stopped me..."

"Hey, that's what family's for, right?" He gave her shoulder a squeeze.

She nodded, looking miserable. Sam could sense there was more.

"I'm worried Liz is going down the same path," she said, eyes to the floor. "She's already changed once, when the soldiers tried to...take her. Now she's on a one-woman crusade, and I don't think she sees the line anymore. She's becoming like that doctor—willing to do whatever it takes to get what she wants."

"To be honest, I wasn't far from agreeing with her." Sam shrugged. "Can't say I feel much sympathy for the doctor."

"Maybe not." Jasmine pursed her lips. "But they weren't all

bad, remember? If it wasn't for Angela Fallow, we'd still be prisoners. Or worse—dead."

Sam nodded, remembering the kindly doctor who had freed them from the facility in the mountains. "You think he's the same?"

"Maybe not…but maybe we should give him a chance to put things right, to balance the scales. When this is all over, he can face justice. But we can't be judge, jury and executioner."

"Look who's gone soft," Sam teased.

"I've seen the alternative," Jasmine replied. "This morning… I found Liz choking the life out of a man with her bare hands. He died in agony. And her eyes…I could swear they were beginning to turn."

Ice spread through Sam's stomach. "She changed?"

Jasmine shrugged. "No. Or at least, I don't think so. But she's losing control. She's taking too many risks, running around like Rambo."

Sam chuckled. "You've been watching those movies, too?" On the days they couldn't sleep, there was little else to do but watch reruns of old movies on the CRT television.

"I'm serious, Sam," Jasmine replied. "I don't want to lose her as well."

Sam squeezed her shoulder again. "I know." He smiled, trying to reassure her. "I'm glad we don't have you both going off the rails, though."

The hint of a smile tugged at Jasmine's lips. She looked down at Mira. "No time for that, between babysitting the two of them," she whispered, before her eyes turned serious. "What about you, Sam? How have you kept it together? Ashley was everything to you."

Sam's chest tightened at the mention of Ashley's name, and he sucked in a deep breath before answering. "You're right." He paused, fighting back tears. "That's why…that's the only thing I've got left to hold onto. She might be gone, but she still needs me."

"Sam…" Jasmine's face betrayed her concern. "You can't think she's still alive?"

His heart lurched again, but he forced himself to look Jasmine in the eye. "No…" he croaked, swallowing his grief. "That's not what I meant."

"Then what?"

He sighed, wondering how to explain himself. "What the doctor said downstairs, about the project being restarted, about the conscripted kids—it's all my fault. You know that." He looked at her, daring her to argue, but she remained silent. Not long ago, Jasmine had accused him of that very crime. Releasing his breath, Sam forced himself to go on, "If I hadn't stood with Halt and the President, hadn't let them use me to strengthen their hold over the people, this might have all been over by now. Instead, things are worse than ever. Ashley…she couldn't stand the role she played, that Halt used her to get to me."

"So you're keeping it together for her?" Jasmine murmured.

Sam nodded, his vision blurring. "When the time comes, when I'm finally face-to-face with the Director, with the President, they'll see my anger. Until then, we have to be smart, have to outthink them, have to play their game and win. If we don't, we've already lost."

He looked at Jasmine for a response, but for once, she did not speak. Shadows ringed her eyes, her lips were pulled tight, but finally, she shrugged.

"We still need to do something about Liz," she said. "She's hurting."

"I know." Sam's heart ached for his friend, but since the university, Liz had steadily pushed everyone else away. "She's frustrated. It's been four weeks, and we've gotten nowhere. But if Doctor Reid is telling the truth, this might be our chance."

"Or maybe Liz is just unstable enough to get us all killed," Jasmine shot back.

Sam looked away at that, unable to argue with her reasoning. What Jasmine said was true—she was living proof of how unstable they could be, after what had happened in Independence Square. But then, they all might just be bombs waiting to go off. That same rage lurked inside each of them. He had felt it himself, when he was imprisoned. He was sure of that now.

And while Liz might be the most at risk, they had no chance in hell of convincing her to stay behind if they went after the Director. After all, no force on earth would stop *him* from going on that mission.

Finally, he sighed. "I'll talk to Liz."

6

"Knock, knock." Liz looked up as the door to the bedroom creaked open and Sam's face appeared.

Sitting up on her bed, she raised an eyebrow. "It's your room too, Sam. You don't have to knock."

The narrow space held two sets of bunk beds. Sam and Mira had claimed the bottom bunks. Liz still wasn't sure how she'd ended up with top bunk again, but she wasn't too bothered. Most days she didn't even step foot inside the house, and the sparse plaster walls and rickety bunks reminded her too much of the prison cell they'd shared in the facility. But the safe house was a refuge for more than just the four of them—there were almost twenty people crammed into the little villa—and there was no room for luxury.

"I thought you might need some time to yourself," Sam offered as he sat on his bed.

Liz shrugged, although that was exactly why she'd retreated to their dormitory. "Not from you, Sam."

"Well, that's good to hear." Pulling off his shoulder bag, he removed his radio and set it on the table between the bunks. Plugging it in to charge, he looked up at her. "You lost control back there."

A strand of hair drifted across Liz's face. She blew it away with an angry exhalation. "I didn't lose control." She gestured in the direction of the dining room. "That man has information we need. Instead of dragging it out of him like they would us, we're risking our lives for a family that may or may not even exist."

"So you'd leave them to die, and torture the information out of him?" Sam asked softly.

Liz swung her legs over the side of her bed and dropped to the floor. Lowering herself onto Mira's bed, she scooted back until she could lean against the wall. She stared at Sam, wondering how he could stay so calm.

"Whatever it takes," she replied finally. "I'm going to kill her for what she did to Chris and Ashley, for what she did to those students. If that means going through that monster, so be it."

"He's just a pawn, Liz," Sam argued, his eyes boring into hers. "And that performance back there was about more than just getting information out of him."

Liz's cheeks warmed. "Maybe it was," she said, pursing her lips, "but you of all people know what they did to us."

Leaning his head back against the plasterboard wall, Sam closed his eyes. "I do. But killing him won't change what happened, and it won't help save all those other kids who are suffering."

Liz's stomach twisted. "If they've started the project…then it's already too late for them."

"You don't believe that…"

"I do!" Liz interrupted. Her lips drew back in a snarl. "Don't you see? It's too late for everyone. The Madwomen are slowly being picked apart. Jonathan is spreading propaganda all over the airwaves. Chris and Ashley and Richard are dead. We've already lost, Sam. We just don't know it yet."

"Then what are you still fighting for, Liz?" Sam stared at her, his lips turned down, sadness in his dark eyes.

Liz's shoulders slumped and she struggled to keep the tears from her eyes. "Revenge," she murmured. "That's all there is left. She's already stolen whatever life Chris and I might have had. I intend to take hers before they come for me."

"And to hell with everyone else?" Sam asked.

"Maybe," Liz replied.

Climbing out of bed, Liz moved to the window. Outside, the sky was a dark grey, the wind blowing through the treetops. She could feel the cold air seeping through the thin glass. There was a storm brewing, and who knew if any of them would survive it? Swallowing, she thought of Ashley and Chris, and the awful hole in her chest.

She shivered as a hand settled on her shoulder. Liz found Sam standing behind her, his lips drawn tight, his jaw clenched. She embraced him, burying her face in his broad chest. A tremor ran through him too, fed by his silent sorrow, a mirror of her own. They stood like that for a long time, drawing what comfort they could from each other's presence. But in the end, all it did was make Liz lonesome. His arms around her were just another reminder of what she'd lost; that without Chris, she would never feel the true warmth of human touch again.

When they finally separated, Liz forced a smile. Sam returned it, tears on his cheeks. "I know what Chris would do," he said.

"Me too," Liz said, wiping away her tears. "He's not here now though, is he?"

"No, but he believed we could be better than them."

"Maybe." Liz slumped onto her bed. "But at what cost? How many more of us have to die doing the right thing?"

"I don't know," Sam replied, "but I know they didn't die so we could become the monsters we're fighting, Liz."

"Then what do you propose we do?" she asked, her heart pounding. She felt at once drowsy and energized, exhausted from her night's activities, but stressed by the confrontation in the living room. And now the conversation with Sam.

"What Maria said," he replied. "We think things through, take our time, do this the right way. Tonight, if it's safe, we'll bring his family here, make sure they're protected. Then we'll find out where the Director is holed up and make a plan. We'll save the kids she's taken, and find the base of operations she broadcasts from."

Liz looked up at that. "What do you mean?"

Sam smiled. "You didn't stick around long enough for that part. Apparently the Director has hardly left the doctors' facility over the past four weeks. She's managing everything from there. Which means those broadcasts she gives each day, they're coming from the same place."

"So that means..." Liz breathed.

Reaching into her pocket, Liz pulled out the thumb drive Chris had handed her back at the university. Without a computer, they hadn't been able to access the information, but if what Professor McKenzie had said was true, it contained everything they needed to prove the government's responsibility for the *Chead* epidemic. But after the university massacre, regular news broadcasts had been shut down. A constant stream of reruns and the government-mandated news was all that remained.

Sam saw the thumb drive and nodded. "That's right. Not only do we have a shot at her, we'll have a chance to put things right, to give meaning to Chris and Ashley's sacrifice."

Liz carefully put the drive back in her pocket. "You really think he can lead us to her?"

Sam shrugged. "We'll soon find out. I'm going with them tonight, to bring back his family."

"Why?" Liz asked with a frown.

Sam grinned. "Thought it was my turn for a midnight escapade."

Despite herself, Liz flushed. "I had to do something..." she murmured.

"Maybe," Sam said, "but was beating up helpless conscripts really the best way of fighting back?"

"I only hurt the ones who put up a fight."

"I don't doubt it," Sam replied, "but can you say the same thing for your other half?"

Liz shivered. She didn't bother denying Sam's words. It was a constant presence now, a force bubbling just below the surface of her consciousness. All it would take was one slip, one moment of weakness for it to break free, for the *Chead* to take over.

Clenching her fists, she took a deep, shuddering breath. "It's under control."

Sam eyed her a moment. “Good,” he said finally. “Save it for the Director. I know I am.”

Silence fell between them then as Liz drifted into her own thoughts, daydreaming about what was to come. Whether the doctor was telling the truth or not, Sam and whoever went with him tonight were likely to be in danger. If the doctor had truly slipped away, they would be watching his family by now, waiting for him to return. No one just walked away from the government, not once it got its claws in.

She thought, too, about Sam’s plan to use the Director’s own broadcast and tell the world the truth. Despite her words, she could find little hope there. It would take all their resources just to infiltrate a government facility. Other than them, there were maybe ten fighters in their safe house—disenfranchised men and women from across the city who were prepared to put their lives on the line to set things right. Harry had given them some training, and there was plenty of weaponry left over from Mike’s stash, but his people were untested. They would never be able to hold the broadcast room for long enough.

No, whatever Sam said, she would be going for one thing, and one thing only.

Revenge.

7

Chris kept his gaze fixed straight ahead as they followed the Director down the brightly lit corridor. From beneath his visor, he counted the rows of iron bars, glimpsed the pale, desperate faces of those trapped inside the cells. They called out as the Director and her silent protectors passed, begging for help, pleading their innocence. Their cries fell on deaf ears. The Director had no interest in her prisoners—only what they would become.

A group of doctors waited at the end of the corridor. The four of them stood with their hands in the pockets of their lab coats, watching the Director's approach. Beside them, a familiar steel trolley gleamed in the overhead lights. On its surface, an array of scalpels, syringes and vials lay waiting to be used.

"There's still no sign of Doctor Reid?" the Director asked as she joined the waiting men and women.

The doctors exchanged nervous glances before shaking their heads. Chris caught the glint of anger in the Director's eyes, but she only waved a hand. "No matter. If he thinks he can leave so easily, the man's a fool. He will be found." She looked at the collection of instruments on the trolley and then back at the doctors. "Are we ready to proceed?"

Chris shivered. Glancing at Ashley, he tried to read her reaction. She no doubt knew as well as Chris did what was coming, but the reflective visor revealed nothing of her expression.

The doctors around the trolley took up their instruments and stepped towards the first cell. Chris caught the glint of perspiration on the leader's forehead as he addressed the Director.

"Yes, ma'am," he hesitated, "but…I feel it's imperative you know we're still not convinced this is the best way forward. The framework followed by Doctor Halt and Fallow…we believe it was integral to their success."

"The framework was used to filter out weak candidates, correct?" the Director asked blankly.

The doctor nodded. "That is correct, ma'am."

"What do you think will happen if an inferior candidate receives the virus?"

"Fallow's notes…mention only those with the strongest mental and physical constitutions will survive the change…intact."

"The rest will die?" the Director pressed.

"That or…change."

"No matter. The tests would kill them anyway. And what about the immuno…the immunoresponse?" Her tongue tripped over the last word, but the doctor wisely ignored it.

"From their notes, we believe Halt and his team were able to correct the flaw in the virus, before…before they were attacked. This is the last strain they were working on. From what we can tell of its genetic structure, it should be undetectable to the host's immune system."

"Excellent." The Director clapped and nodded to the first cell. "Shall we proceed then?"

Still the doctor hesitated. "Will your guards be assisting us?" he asked. Other than the Director and her personal guards, they were alone.

The Director laughed. "They're too well-paid for that." She looked at Chris and Ashley. "My dears, would you be so good as to help the doctors prepare your soon-to-be brethren?"

Ice spread through Chris's veins. The four occupants of the first cell stood watching him. Three sported the sun-kissed tans of the rural population, while the fourth had the pale complexion of an urbanite. Each wore a steel collar clasped tightly around their neck.

Looking at them, Chris remembered being the one locked up, waiting with Sam and Ashley and Liz as the doctors made their inexorable way through the prison block. He recalled the screams, the agony as a syringe injected the fateful virus and changed his life forever.

Ashley still hadn't moved. He could hear her breathing growing shallow, could see the trembling in her fists as she looked at the Director. She was just seconds away from doing something reckless, something that would see them both punished.

Swallowing his memories, Chris approached the cell. Behind the bars, the children retreated from his masked figure. They stumbled over one another in their haste to get away, until they stood between the two sets of bunk beds.

There was nowhere for them to go from there, no escaping their fate.

He glanced at the Director, and she reached down to touch her watch. A buzzer sounded somewhere above the door as the steel bars rattled open. Inside, the four teenagers flinched.

"Chris, don't," Ashley called as he made to step inside.

The pain in her voice froze Chris in place. Bowing his head, he weighed his options. He could still choose to fight, to turn and throw himself at the Director and her doctors. But he knew where that choice led. The collar would drop him before he could take two steps. Then he would spend the night writhing in agony, unable to sleep, to rest, to think. The pain had almost driven him mad the last time.

He shook his head. "I'm sorry, Ash," he whispered, his voice barely audible.

There was no saving these teenagers—just like there had been no saving the students back at the university. Unbidden, the scene played out again in his mind. He heard again the click of the collar as it fastened around his neck, saw the smile that spread across the Director's face. The roar of machine guns had followed as the soldiers turned on the helpless students.

Shuddering, Chris tore himself from the waking nightmare and again cursed his foolishness. He should have stood his ground, should have died before allowing the woman to trap him. Instead, he had sacrificed his freedom, his body, and for what?

The students had died anyway.

He had learned his lesson now. There was no helping anyone in this awful world, no protecting the weak, no saving them from the cruelty of the powerful. Every time he tried, every time he interfered, he only made things worse, only added to his own suffering.

So why should he try anymore?

He looked at each of the prisoners in turn. "Lie down. Resisting will only make this worse."

"There's only one of him," the boy at the front said sharply. "We can take him!"

Chris gave a sad smile beneath his visor. He remembered his own last stand, when he—along with Ashley, Liz and Sam—had tried to fight off a pack of guards. They'd almost managed it, but numbers had overwhelmed them in the end. If there'd been just one, he would have liked his odds as well.

Unfortunately for these four, he was no ordinary human.

Arms crossed, Chris let the first teenager slide towards him. The boy had his hands raised like a boxer, but from his stance, Chris could see he was no fighter. His feet were so close together a weak breeze would knock him over.

Chris let the boy throw a punch anyway, though he hardly had to move to avoid it. Then, faster than thought, his hand swept out and tapped the boy on the side of the head. The blow sent his opponent reeling. Stumbling back, the boy tried to recover, but his legs no longer seemed to obey him, and finally he slumped down against one of the beds. Cradling his head in his hands, he began to sob.

"I'm sorry," Chris said as he faced the others. "I don't want to hurt you, but I can't let you go. *They* have plans for you." He nodded at the doctors waiting outside.

The only girl in the cell swallowed. "Please…" she said, her head down, her big brown eyes reminding him inexplicably of Liz. "Help us. You could stop them..."

Chris waved at the collar around his throat. "We both know better. Trust me, it'll go...easier, if you don't fight it."

The girl shivered, her eyes darting past Chris to the doctors. "What...what is it?"

Chris followed her gaze, his keen eyes lingering on the syringe a doctor was preparing. "The future."

The girl bit her lip and retreated to where her remaining cell-mates waited. Chris stood in the space between the bunks to hem them in. Then he gestured to the boy.

"He won't put up a fight now," he said to the doctors.

The boy sat with his back against the wall, still moaning softly, one hand clutching his head where Chris had hit him.

Wary, the doctors held back, until a look from the Director sent them scuttling into action. Three of them entered the cell, one holding a syringe, the others holding the boy in place. Only one remained outside, preparing the next syringe.

Chris's eyes drifted to Ashley. She stood with her arms crossed, and he quickly looked away again. He couldn't understand where she found the courage to resist. Since their capture, the terror-stricken girl they had rescued from Halt had vanished. In her place was the Ashley Chris remembered from their imprisonment, the girl whose will never wavered, who had never given up despite the odds stacked against them.

And while he was glad to have her back, seeing her only reminded Chris of his own failed courage.

He watched the three prisoners in silence as the doctors finished their work. Fists clenched, he waited for what came next.

It took thirty seconds, but the boy's first scream was as sharp as he remembered. Despite himself, Chris flinched. Something inside him recoiled from the agony contained in that cry. He closed his eyes, resisting the urge to slap his hands over his ears. It was happening all over again—the torment, the death. Only he was no longer the prisoner, but the perpetrator.

"The next subject, Christopher," the Director called from outside the cell.

A tremor went through him as he looked back. The boy's screams echoed off the concrete walls, deafening, especially to his sensitive ears. He stared at the Director, teeth clenched, rage building in his chest.

Then his gaze caught the woman's eyes, and he knew it was hopeless. Whatever he did, she was always a step ahead, waiting to catch him out, to punish his transgressions. Even were he to somehow succeed, if he managed to break her little neck, the torment wouldn't cease. She had taught them that their first day, when she had taken off her watch. Instantly, their collars had given a harsh *beep*, and sent them crashing to the ground.

She had left them there for ten minutes, writhing in helpless agony, before finally strapping the device back to her wrist.

"If my heart stops, those collars will choke the life out of you. That should be motivation enough for you to keep me alive."

And with that, she'd made them her guards. She seemed to take a perverted enjoyment in having them around, though Chris suspected it was more than that. She had deliberately worn him down to the point he would do anything to avoid more pain.

Even if it meant subduing innocent teenagers for the government's experiments.

Facing the huddle of prisoners, Chris caught another boy by the hand. The kid yelled and tried to pull away, but there was no resisting Chris's strength. He dragged the next candidate out as though he weighed no more than a sack of potatoes.

When the doctors had finished with him, Chris went back and took the third. His eyes caught the girl's as he dragged her last friend away. She had retreated to the back of the cell, her cheeks wet with tears. Her curly black hair hung around her face, and again Chris was reminded of Liz. He watched the girl as the doctors finished their work on the last boy, wondering absently where Liz was, what she was doing.

He knew by now their gambit had failed. They'd had no contact with the outside world since their capture, but surely they would have heard if the truth about the *Chead* had reached the public. Not even the President could survive if the entire country rose against him.

The third boy's voice joined the chorus of screams. Knowing the order was coming, Chris started towards the girl.

"Your turn," he said, offering his hand.

She shook her head, her eyes wide, pleading for his mercy. He had to grab her by the waist and haul her out, kicking and screaming. As he cleared the bunk beds, her elbow caught him in the face. Off-balance, he staggered past the doctors, out into the corridor. They crashed into the trolley, sending equipment flying as the doctors and the Director retreated out of range.

Still struggling to get a firm grip on the girl's twisting body, Chris cursed as her knee came dangerously close to his groin. Finally losing patience, he lifted her up and hurled her down on the concrete. The impact drove the breath from the girl's lungs, and she lay back, mouth wide and gasping.

Turning, Chris found the Director, flanked on either side by her guards. The other doctors had left the remaining candidates in the cell and followed him into the corridor. The first boy had finally passed out, though the occasional convulsion still raked his body. The second's screams were beginning to fade, while the third still writhed on the floor.

The Director smiled as she approached. "You've done well, Christopher. I—"

A scream cut her off. Spinning, Chris saw the girl spring to her feet. She'd managed to grab a scalpel from the fallen trolley, and now she leapt, eyes fixed on the unarmed Director. With her guards behind her, there was no one left between the Director and the girl.

Chris acted without thinking. Stepping in front of the Director, his fist flashed out to catch the girl square in the chest. A sharp *crack* echoed down the corridor as the blow brought the girl to a sudden halt, then hurled her backwards. She struck the ground with a thud. Her eyes flickered closed, and a long sigh hissed between her lips.

For a moment, no one moved. They all stared down at the fallen girl. Then, as if on cue, the doctors and guards rushed forward, one picking up the discarded scalpel while the others gathered around the girl. One of the doctors put a finger to her throat, checking for a pulse, but a few seconds later she shook her head.

Chris choked and stumbled back. Tearing his eyes from the girl, he looked at his trembling fist. There was no trace of blood, no hint of the life he had just taken. Desperately, he shook his head, as though that might somehow take back what he'd done.

He flinched as a hand brushed his hair. "Very good, Christopher," the Director whispered, her breath hot in his ear. "Very good."

The doctors quickly gathered up the instruments that had fallen from their trolley. Two took the girl between them and dragged her from the prison block. Another pressed a finger to her watch, and the cell door slid closed.

Standing amidst them, all Chris could do was stare at the pale concrete. He didn't need to look to know that Ashley's eyes were on him, that beneath her visor she was watching him, hating him.

When the doctors were done cleaning up, the Director strode forward. Placing a finger beneath his chin, she forced him to look up. Grinning, she nodded at the next cell.

"Shall we continue?"

8

Susan shoved the woman through the barn door and followed her inside, Hecate one step behind. Within, the heady scent of the *Chead* swept over them like a blanket. Its cloying sweetness calmed her racing heart, and she drew in another breath, savoring its ecstasy. Then she pulled the roller door shut, the metal wheels squealing.

The few dozen women and teenagers kneeling on the concrete floor flinched at the sound. Their soft sobs echoed from the tin walls, interspersed by the rumbling of the generator outside. A ring of *Chead* surrounded the prisoners, while in the corner the cylindrical refrigerator unit gleamed in the faint light. The *Chead* had carried it faithfully across the countryside, from farmhouse to town, ensuring its precious contents remained viable. Now it was all but empty. If things went well, this would be its final stop.

Turning, Susan found her captive standing nearby. Her eyes wide, she had stumbled to a stop. Seeing Talisa waiting, Susan grabbed the woman by the hair and dragged her to where the other prisoners knelt. The women and teenagers scrambled back from her until the barn wall brought them up short. Soft laughter came from the other *Chead*. Smiling, Susan strode to where Hecate waited with Talisa, and bowed her head.

"You are late, my child," Talisa whispered in admonishment.

Susan shivered as the elder *Chead's* milky white eyes bored into her. "I'm sorry…Talisa," she stammered. The change had robbed her of speech, and she was still struggling to regain her words. "The rage was…on me. Hecate…brought me back."

The lines on Talisa's aging face deepened as she smiled. "You must learn control, child." She gripped Susan by the arm. "Come, you are needed."

Talisa led Susan past the kneeling women. Her eyes drifted over the faces of their captives. They were all young, in their late teens or early twenties. Most kept their eyes fixed to the ground, but a few had the courage to stare back, defiant, the dried tears on their cheeks the only sign of their fear. The few males present had been herded into one corner. They would face the choice last —if there were any vials left.

She counted thirty prisoners in all—too many. But no doubt some would refuse; they always did.

The refrigerator unit waited for her in the corner. The steel casing had seen better days; its sides were streaked with mud, and several dings now marked the metal where its minders had been less than careful.

Talisa nodded for Susan to proceed. She knelt beside the unit, her hands trembling, eager to do the ancient *Chead's* bidding. There was an aura about Talisa, a power that demanded obedience. Taking a deep breath, Susan waited until her hands stilled before opening the lid.

Licking her lips, Susan counted the remaining vials. Once there had been hundreds inside—now there were only a few dozen left. Quickly, she checked the power level on the side, then waved at the two *Chead* who guarded the contraption. Each took one handle and followed her to the waiting prisoners. Several whimpered as the *Chead* set the unit down in front of them.

Susan smiled, tasting the bitter tang of their fear. Outside, distant screams could still be heard, as her brethren continued their wanton slaughter. Watching the pitiful creatures huddle on the ground, Susan wondered how she had ever been so weak. Memories drifted through her mind, of a woman lost and alone, scared to live. Those emotions now seemed as foreign to her as the moon.

Hecate crossed the barn to stand beside her, his arm curling around her waist. Her own hand drifted to her stomach, to the life growing there. It was already beginning to swell, the accelerated growth of the *Chead* taking hold. She recalled their reproductive cycle from her other life, though her small mind had never contemplated experiencing it herself.

Almost always in heat, the *Chead* could have anything from one to eight eggs attach to the uterus at one time. And once fertilized, gestation took only six weeks before birth. Her children would then continue growing at an accelerated rate, reaching the size of teenagers within two years.

Detaching herself from Hecate, Susan smiled up at him. It had been four weeks since their night in the cave. The birth would not be long now, and she was glad this would be their last stop. Shortly, they would set out for the underground labyrinth Talisa had made home for the wild *Chead*. There her children would be safe. Warmth filled her stomach at the thought of holding them in her arms.

But for now, there were new souls to welcome into the ranks of the *Chead*.

Susan delved into the cylinder and retrieved a syringe and the first vial. The captives watched as she prepared the needle, silent now. The process only took a few seconds. Holding it up to the light, she checked for bubbles, before nodding at Talisa to proceed.

Striding forward, the elder *Chead* grasped the nearest prisoner by the shirt and hauled her to her feet. The woman tried to resist, but she was only human, her strength like a mouse before the cat for the *Chead*. Talisa slapped her hard across the face. The blow whipped the woman's head to the side, and she sagged in the elder *Chead's* arms. Scowling, Talisa tossed her at Susan's feet.

"Stand," Susan growled.

Sobbing, the woman scrambled to her hands and knees. Blood ran from her lip, but when she saw Susan's cold grey eyes, she quickly nodded. Her legs trembled beneath her weight, but somehow she managed to stand.

"What is…your name?" Susan whispered, moving forward until her face was just an inch from the prisoner's.

The woman swallowed, her eyes darting around the room before returning to Susan.

"My name…my name is Lucia." The woman barely managed to get out the words. "How…?"

"Lucia…" Talisa murmured, ignoring the question. "Do you wish to live?"

The woman moaned, looking from Talisa to Susan. For a moment it seemed she would bolt, but finally her shoulders sagged and she shook her head.

"I don't want to die," she said, the words barely audible.

The soft laughter of the *Chead* whispered around the barn. Holding out the syringe, Susan offered it to the woman. "Then join us."

The color drained from Lucia's face as comprehension came. The liquid inside the syringe gleamed in the moonlight streaming through the slits in the ceiling. The other *Chead* stood in silence, watching with their cold grey eyes, waiting.

Lucia started to back away, but Susan's hand whipped out to catch her by the shirt, bringing her up short. Lucia shook her head, her mouth gaping, still trying to break free, but no words came out.

"Is that your final…answer?" Susan asked.

A tremor passed across Lucia's face as a single tear slid down her cheek. "Please…" she whispered.

"There is only…one answer," Susan replied.

She tightened her grip around the woman's shirt, pulling her closer. A growl rose from Susan's chest as she bared her teeth. She could sense the woman's terror; she was on the brink of panic. If she cracked, if she succumbed to it, she was worthless to them. The *Chead* needed to be strong, to cast off the weakness of humanity, not continue its follies.

"Don't do it, Lucia!" one of the captives shouted, leaping to her feet. "They're m—"

Whatever she'd been about to say ended abruptly as Hecate sprang. Catching the woman by the throat, he lifted her into the air and hurled her at the wall. She managed a brief, bloodcurdling scream before slamming headfirst into a steel beam. A sickening *crack* came from her skull as she slumped to the ground.

The prisoners screamed and scrambled away from Hecate, but there was nowhere for them to go.

"*Silence!*" Talisa's voice cut through the high-pitched cries.

As one, the voices died away. The prisoners turned to stare at Talisa, their eyes wide, mouths open. Not one of them moved as the old *Chead's* gaze passed over them. A long moment stretched out before Talisa nodded for Susan to resume.

Susan smiled at Lucia. "What is…your choice?"

The woman swallowed visibly. Her eyes were red from crying, but she didn't hesitate now. With a trembling hand, she took the syringe and stabbed it into her arm. Susan waited until she pressed the plunger, sending the virus whirling into her bloodstream, before releasing her. The woman shivered as Susan brushed the hair from her face.

"Welcome, Lucia."

A *Chead* stepped up and gently led Lucia across the concrete floor. They only made it a few steps before Lucia crumpled to the ground and started to scream. Lifting Lucia in his arms, the *Chead* carried her the rest of the way, even as the woman thrashed in his grip. Her gut-wrenching shrieks were loud enough to rattle the walls, but Susan ignored them.

She turned to the remaining prisoners. "Who…is next?"

9

"So, just the girls tonight?"

Liz looked up from the sofa at Jasmine's voice. The other girl stood leaning against the doorway, a smile on her face as she surveyed the room. Liz was sitting on the couch with Mira, a worn book cradled in one hand. The title read "1984," which hardly seemed relevant in 2052. She had been trying to read it for half an hour, but with Sam out on his mission, her mind was elsewhere, and she'd hardly managed a couple of pages.

"I guess so," Liz replied, forcing a smile.

Jasmine wandered into the lounge and took a seat on the couch across from Liz. "You still don't think it's a good idea, do you?"

Liz shrugged. "No, but there's not much I can do about it." She eyed Jasmine before going on. "What about you? I'm surprised you haven't torn his head from his shoulders yet, after what they did to Richard." She felt a sense of satisfaction when Jasmine looked away, but shame quickly rose to swamp it. "Sorry," she murmured, biting her lip. "I didn't need to bring him into it."

"It's amazing how much they still affect us," Jasmine murmured, pulling her knees up to her chest. "I can still hear his voice sometimes, whispering to me."

"What does he say?" They both looked around as Mira spoke. She sat up on the couch, her dual-colored eyes looking at each of them in turn.

"Mostly the opposite of what I've been doing," Jasmine laughed. The smile fell from her face. "I think he'd want me to run, to take you and anyone else who'll come and leave the city, before it's too late." she shrugged. "Or maybe that's just my subconscious talking."

Silently, Mira left Liz's couch and went to Jasmine. Snuggling in beneath her arm, she murmured, "But I like it here."

Liz hardly heard the girl. She sat staring at a hole in the plasterboard, remembering Richard. He had said more than once that they should do just as Jasmine said. But at the end, he'd done the opposite. Instead of running from danger, he'd charged straight into it, sacrificing his life for theirs.

Shifting on the couch, Liz stretched her wings, feeling the pain beginning in her back. She would need to go for a midnight flight soon, or her muscles would start to cramp and spasm.

"I don't know what Chris would want anymore," Liz said finally. "Not really. I don't hear him, don't see him. It's like he was never here."

"Maybe that's just your mind's way of protecting you," Jasmine offered.

"He wouldn't want you to die," Mira said quietly.

Liz opened her mouth, then closed it again as a lump caught in her throat. Swallowing hard, she tried to keep them from seeing her tears.

"She's right, you know," Jasmine said. "He wouldn't agree with you going off alone like you're some one-woman army."

Liz scowled. "You're one to talk."

"I know I sound like a hypocrite," Jasmine replied, "but that was before we met the Madwomen. Before I saw just how far they're willing to go to make things right. Before their courage gave me hope." There was fire in her eyes as she spoke. "They don't have wings or super strength. They can't heal from bullet wounds in a matter of weeks. They aren't strong enough to fight back when the soldiers come for them.

But they're out there anyway, marching, fighting for a better future."

"And they're losing, dying by the dozens, because of it," Liz shot back.

"Yes," Jasmine said, her eyes shining, "but unlike us, they have a choice. They could stay at home and live out the rest of their lives in peace if they wanted. But they're not, and that gives me hope that others might do the same. Then maybe, just maybe, we might have a future."

"It's too little, too late though, isn't it?" Liz asked sadly. "The government is all but untouchable." She leaned back in the sofa and eyed the other girl.

"Maybe, but better late than never," Jasmine replied half-heartedly.

Liz snorted. "I suppose you feel the same way about the doctor?"

Jasmine looked away. "He'll face justice, eventually."

"Not if Sam's caught. Not if we're all killed. He'll be praised as a hero," Liz snapped.

Jasmine shivered at that. A tear rolled down her cheek, quickly wiped away, but not before Liz had noticed. She frowned and bit her lip, wondering what she'd said to upset her usually staunch friend.

"What's wrong, Jas?"

Standing, she crossed to the other couch and sat beside Jasmine. Mira seemed to have drifted off to sleep, apparently bored by all their talk of rebellion and the government. Reaching out a gloved hand, Liz squeezed her friend's shoulder.

Jasmine's eyes were brimming with tears now. "I don't want to lose anyone else, Liz," she croaked. "I know you loved Chris, I know Sam loved Ash…but they were my friends too, and now you three are all I have left."

"Jas…" Liz said, struggling to speak through her own tears.

Shaking her head, Jasmine hiccupped and forced a smile. "Why do girls' nights always end in tears?" she laughed, but the grief remained in her voice as she continued, "Just, swear to me you'll be careful, Liz. I don't want to lose you, one way or another."

"I swear," Liz whispered back, though she wasn't sure she could keep the promise. If tomorrow she had the Director in her sights, if she had the chance to end the woman once and for all, she would take it—even if it meant giving up her life.

"Knock, knock."

Liz and Jasmine looked up as Maria appeared in the doorway. Liz swallowed as the old woman's eyes took in the sleeping Mira and Jasmine's tear-streaked face, before settling on her. The two of them had hardly spoken over the past few weeks—not since Liz had told her about Chris's death. It was as though the pain of their shared loss was too much, as though the combined weight would crush them.

Or, if Liz was honest with herself, it was because she was afraid to face the woman. Strong as Maria was, Chris's death had almost broken her. And however much Liz told herself otherwise, she felt responsible. She was the one who'd left him behind, who'd turned her back and fled while Chris and Ashley fought to the death.

"Liz," Maria said, pulling the girl from her inward spiral, "a word?"

Holding her breath, Liz glanced at Jasmine, then nodded. She stood and followed Maria out into the corridor.

II
BETRAYAL

10

Sam sighed as he reversed a chair and sat down. Leaning his arms against the backrest, he looked at the terrified family huddled together on the white leather sofa. The doctor's wife sat in the middle, her two young children clutched tightly against her sides. The boys were sobbing, but only quietly. The presence of men with guns and a boy with wings had terrified them half out of their minds, and they seemed to have lost their voices.

We should have brought the doctor, Sam thought to himself.

But Maria had immediately vetoed that option when he'd suggested it. If the man was telling the truth, he was too valuable to risk. Especially with the government no doubt aware by now that he was missing. The men Harry had sent to scout out the condominium hadn't seen any suspicious activity, but even so, they had to assume someone was watching. That meant quietly breaking into the parking garage after dark to allow them access to the elevators, while Sam surveyed the building from above.

They had made it inside without trouble, but their first misstep had come when Sam's fellows broke down the front door to the woman's apartment. They had charged inside before Sam could object, rifles at the ready, as though they were storming a terrorist hideout.

Too much television. Even now, Sam couldn't help but shake his head.

It had taken precious minutes just to calm the woman down enough so she would sit quietly on the couch. He just hoped the neighbors hadn't heard her earsplitting shrieks.

Now, Sam couldn't help but glance out the fourteenth story window. Anxiety gnawed at his stomach, and he half expected a helicopter to appear, machine gun at the ready. But the night sky remained empty, and turning back to the family, he cleared his throat.

"Look, I'm sorry about the door. My friends here were just a bit overeager." He scowled at the four men. "But as we've already said, your husband sent us."

The woman's eyes flicked in the direction of the men with guns, lingering on his half-folded wings before returning to his face. She swallowed. "I…I know you. You…you work for the government."

Sam bit back a curse. It seemed his involuntary media appearance would never cease to haunt him. He'd become a household face—synonymous with the government and their war on the *Chead*. A symbol of hope, of the strength and bravery of their hallowed President.

Never mind that Sam had only been there to save Ashley, or that the government had actually created the *Chead*.

"Yes…no…look, it's a long story, all right? Here, your husband wrote you a note, see?" He handed over a piece of paper. "You recognize his handwriting?"

The woman stared at the piece of paper as though it might bite her. Finally, she reached out and took it, scanned over the words, then folded it up and put it in her pocket.

"How do I know he wasn't forced to write this?" she asked softly.

"You don't," Sam replied. Concentrating on his back, Sam spread his copper wings. They stretched across the room, brushing the kitchen counter and almost knocking a lamp from a table. "But he must have told you what he does? Some of what he's seen? You know the truth, or parts of it.

The question now is, will you choose what's right, or what's easy?"

"I haven't seen my husband in weeks..." the woman murmured. "Not since we moved here, and he started work in his new...laboratory."

Sam narrowed his eyes, catching the pause. "He hasn't been back here?"

"No." The woman pursed her lips, glancing at her children. "My boys...what happens if we go with you?"

"They will be protected," Sam reassured her. "Trust me, enough children have suffered at the government's hands. I'll die before I let anything happen to them."

The woman studied him for a long while before nodding. She stood, lifting the children with her, though they still held desperately to her skirts. One looked to be around twelve, the other a few years younger. Their scared brown eyes watched him cautiously from beneath mops of blonde hair.

"How much time do we have?" the woman asked.

"None," said Leo, the man Harry had selected to lead the team. He crossed the room, rifle held at the ready. "We've already wasted—"

"Enough, Leo," Sam spoke over him. Getting to his feet, he barred the man's path, a smile tugging at his lips. Leo was just five-foot-eight and Sam towered over him. "Call the van, have them drive up to the parking garage. By the time they're in place, we'll be heading down in the elevator. Trust me."

Leo scowled, clearly upset at being overruled, but he finally nodded and turned away. Drawing the radio from his belt, he began speaking into the transmitter.

Smiling, Sam turned his attention back to the woman and her children. Despite his calm words, he was aware of the time ticking away. He glanced out the window again, wondering where the watchers were. Surely they wouldn't have left the doctor's family unguarded?

"Grab your things, quickly," he said finally. Across the room, Leo held up five fingers. "You've got five minutes," Sam added.

The kids looked from him to their mother, eyes uncertain

until she nodded her permission. Not needing to be told twice, they fled into their bedroom. One of the men made to follow, until a look from Sam stopped him in his tracks.

"Leave the gun," Sam said. The man was right about keeping an eye on them, but even Sam didn't feel safe with all the guns being waved around.

"They won't be long." The woman straightened and started towards the second bedroom. "My name's Jocelyn, by the way. I'd better pack a few things for myself."

Sam followed close on her heels. He didn't trust the kids alone, and he certainly wasn't going to leave the woman to her own devices. One phone call was all it would take to bring the government's wrath down on them. Liz and the others had already made that mistake once, and he wasn't about to repeat their errors.

"He talks about you, you know." Jocelyn's voice carried across the room. She had pulled a duffel bag from the closet and was busy stuffing clothes inside. "After we saw you on the TV. He couldn't believe someone had actually succeeded. He's been trying for ten years…" She trailed off with a shrug.

Sam frowned. "Do you know where he worked?"

Jocelyn laughed. "As I said, I haven't heard from him since he started the new job." She pulled out a jacket. Sam thought he detected a strained note in her voice.

"There wasn't even a hint of where they were taking him?" he pressed.

Her lips stretched in a wide smile. "Not a word." She bent her head back to the task of shoving the jacket into the duffel bag. "What about you? Where are the Madwomen planning on hiding us?"

Sam started to answer, before breaking off with a frown. "How do you know about the Madwomen?" he asked sharply.

Jocelyn stilled, then gave a nervous laugh. "You mentioned them out in the living room, remember?"

"I don't think so…" Sam took a step towards her.

The woman's eyes moved around the room as though searching for an escape route. The master bed took up most of the space, coupled with a heavy wooden dresser. A wide inset window took up most of one wall, revealing the pitch black of the night's sky. There were no stars out tonight, and the city was dark. Curfew had started hours ago. Only the richest neighborhoods were allowed to use electricity at this hour.

Neighborhoods like Jocelyn's.

Sam advanced across the room, fists clenched as she backed away. "You've…what have you done?"

"No, we never, please I swear, he told you the truth."

"How do you know what he told us?" Sam growled.

Suddenly, strength seemed to abandon the woman. She sagged against the bed with a heavy exhalation. "I lied," she whispered. "He came by yesterday, told me what he was going to do, about the Madwomen. He told me to stay put, in case things went wrong. He said someone would come and collect us."

Sam shook his head, the tension slowly leaving him. Her words had a ring of truth about them. He let out a long breath, his mind going over the new information, considering the implications. It might not be so bad. Obviously, the apartment hadn't been under surveillance then, or they would have arrested the doctor immediately. They couldn't have a traitor running around the city, blabbing to whoever would listen…

"Oh no," Sam breathed.

He started towards the door before reconsidering, grabbing Jocelyn, and hauling her out with him. The other men looked up as he emerged, the doctor's wife limp in his grip.

"Get the kids," Sam ordered, already moving towards the door.

The two boys were just appearing from the bedroom, little backpacks hung over their shoulders, blonde hair dangling across their faces. When they saw Sam, his wings half extended, they darted into their mother's arms.

"What's the sudden rush?" Leo asked, his voice raised. "The van should be just pulling in."

Ignoring him, Sam pushed Jocelyn towards the door. "Come on, *get moving*! Do you want your family to live? It's only a matter of time before they come back!"

"Come back?" Leo called after him. "Sam, what's going on?"

Sam shoved the terrified family into the elevator and faced the men, his arm holding the door open. "Get them to the van, there's no time to explain." He took the radio from his belt and waved it in their faces. "I'll be in touch. Keep them safe, Leo. Especially the kids."

Then he was running back into the apartment, past the perfect white sofa and sleek tiled floors, to the sliding door leading out onto the balcony. It was a tiny thing, big enough for a hammock and little else. Tall railings ensured the children couldn't climb over, but they were no barrier to Sam. Without hesitating, he leapt over the side, his copper wings snapping open.

The muscles along his back strained and his wings beat down, lifting him higher. Below, treetops flashed past as he raced over the suburbs. Condos dotted the neighborhood, towering alongside vast mansions and individual houses. Trees lined the roads, their fresh green leaves providing shelter against anyone who might be breaking curfew. Not that Sam was concerned about being spotted.

It had taken him fifteen minutes to fly from the safe house to the condominium.

He made it back in ten.

He was still too late.

❦ 11 ❦

Liz wandered along the corridor after Maria, still wondering what the old woman wanted. She peered into each room as they moved passed, taking in the safe house's occupants as they prepared for their mission. Half were members of the Madwomen, driven from their homes by the threat of government persecution. Despite their advanced years, they did not seem daunted by the coming fight. They worked alongside the rural refugees and other disillusioned citizens—young and old in concert, united by their desire for change.

The whole house was a hive of activity. In one room, Liz glimpsed a frightening array of weapons that were being lifted from a heavy case brought from Mike's safe house. Rifles were handed to those preparing the ammunition, then placed on a rack, ready for use. There were also several handguns on a table, and to Liz's horror, what looked like a belt of grenades.

In other rooms, people were packing clothing and supplies. Those who weren't joining the mission were moving to a new house, where they would be safe if anyone was captured and tortured for their location.

Finally, Maria led Liz into the dining room and waved towards the table. Liz eyed Maria before taking her place, still uncomfortable in the woman's presence. Putting her hands in the pockets of her jacket, she waited as Chris's grandmother sat across from her.

"You loved him," Maria said abruptly.

Liz jumped at the pronouncement, her mouth falling open, then snapping closed again. She shivered, seeing the sadness in the crinkles around the old woman's face, the downward turn of her lips.

Slowly, Liz nodded. "I did."

"I'm glad he had someone, before…" Maria's voice cracked.

Liz licked her lips, lost for words, but the old woman only smiled. Her eyes shimmered, but no tears fell.

"It seems my family is destined for heartbreak," Maria murmured. "First my husband, then Chris's father, now Chris. Anyone would think we were cursed."

"I don't think that, Maria," Liz murmured. "If Chris… dying…is anyone's fault, it's mine."

"*No*." Liz looked up at the sharpness to Maria's tone. The old woman's tears had vanished and her eyes were hard now. "You cannot blame yourself, Liz. It was that spiteful woman who took my grandson from us, not you. Your only crime was loving him."

Despite herself, Liz grinned at the old woman's fierceness. "Crime?"

Maria waved a hand. "An old expression, my dear." She sighed. "I just mean, I can see the truth. You feel you need to be punished for losing him. It's not true. You're a brave girl, but that's not your burden to bear, Liz."

Liz's own vision blurred. "We should never have gone there," she murmured, staring at the striped grain of the wooden table.

"I am as much to blame for that as anyone," Maria replied. "I was afraid of what Chris had become, of what you all had become. I should have accepted you, rather than set off, searching for a cure."

"I wanted it as much as you," Liz whispered. "I goaded Chris to act…"

"And you were right. We couldn't just keep standing around with our hands in our pockets. Someone had to shock us out of our reverie. The longer this fight goes on, the more time they have to crush us."

Liz toyed with the thumb drive in her pocket before looking up at Maria. "Then why are we delaying now? Why not force the doctor to tell us where she's hiding?"

Maria leaned back in her chair. "If that's what you truly want to do, Liz, I won't stop you."

Liz looked away, unable to meet Maria's gaze. She remembered the soldier in the alleyway, the one who had died screaming in her hands, and bit her lip. "What I want doesn't matter," she answered. "It's what's necessary."

"And what about Chris?" Maria countered. "Would *he* want you to do this?"

"Doesn't really matter now, does it?" Liz said, standing suddenly, her lips pulled back in a snarl. "He's gone."

"Maybe, but..."

Liz raised a hand before Maria could finish, her eyes drawn to something outside the window. The old woman trailed off as Liz stared out into the darkness. The girl held her breath, waiting. Her ears twitched at an unfamiliar sound. She frowned. Was Sam back already?

"What is it?" Maria asked.

Outside, a sudden flash lit the front yard. Liz spun on her heel as the first bullet shattered the window and went shrieking through the room. Diving, she tackled Maria from her chair and they slammed into the kitchen table. It splintered like paper and they went crashing to the linoleum floor.

Then the whole world turned to thunder.

The outside wall exploded into pieces as bullets sliced their way through, hammering into the kitchen furniture. The hiss of their passage was deafening, amplified by the crash of breaking glass and splintering wood. On the other side of the room, the high caliber rounds made short work of the drywall, tearing their way into the hallway beyond.

Liz caught a glimpse of a man standing in the entrance to the hall. His body jerked as blood blossomed from his chest. Eyes wide, he lifted a hand to the wound, before two more bullets sent him tumbling back.

Clenching her eyes shut, Liz pressed Maria flat against the floorboards and spread her wings to shield them from the flying splinters and glass. There was nothing she could do about the bullets, but most seemed to be aimed at chest height. Helpless, she waited for a break in the fire.

When it came, Liz leapt to her feet, dragging Maria with her. They stumbled across the room, Liz cursing as broken glass cut her bare feet.

Half-carrying Maria down the hallway, she staggered towards the back door. They stumbled over a bullet-ridden body, then another. Dust drifted in the air as the only remaining lightbulb dangled from its cord, sending light scattering across the hallway. Liz had counted five bodies by the time they reached the corner of the corridor. There was no sign of Mira or Jasmine. She prayed they were in the treehouse.

Reaching the corner, Liz glanced back, her ears picking up the slightest rustle of clothing. She squinted through the dust, wondering if someone had survived. The crunch of breaking glass followed. This time she recognized the familiar tread of combat boots. Cursing, she gathered Maria over her shoulder.

"Wait!" Maria gasped, struggling in her grasp. "The doctor!"

Liz paused with sudden indecision. The back door was just around the corner. It was their only way out now, although what was waiting on the other side, she couldn't say. Glancing back the way they'd come, she listened for the approaching boots. They had a few seconds yet, but she'd already passed the doctor's room.

She swore and bounded back down the corridor. Ducking into the doctor's room, she hunched her shoulders, expecting to be met with gunfire, but the strained silence continued.

Unfortunately, the doctor's room hadn't been spared. Holes riddled the walls and dust choked her lungs. Through the broken window, Liz could see flashlights in the garden.

Ducking low, she set Maria down. Her keen eyes swept the gloom and found the body propped up against a set of bunks.

His chest had been torn open, but a streak on the floor showed where he had dragged himself from the middle of the room. He wasn't moving now, though.

"He's dead, let's go," Liz said quickly, but Maria was already up and moving towards the ruined man.

As she knelt beside his body, the doctor coughed. Blood gushed from his chest as something rattled at the back of his throat.

Leaning over, Maria gripped him by the shirt. "Listen to me, Reid." To Liz's surprise, her voice was devoid of compassion. "Tell me where she's hiding."

The doctor coughed again, his head lolling on his shoulders as Maria shook him. Liz watched, lips pursed, shocked the man was alive at all. With the hole in his chest, that wouldn't be the case for long. Maria dragged him up, and a half-muffled shriek tore from the man's throat.

"Where is she?" Maria growled.

The doctor groaned, a long, drawn-out hiss whistling from his throat. For a moment Liz thought he had spoken, but the exhalation went on and on, until it died away to nothing. As the last whisper of breath faded, his eyes rolled back in his head, and he slumped sideways in Maria's hands.

Maria released him and made her way back to Liz in a half-crouch. Liz raised an eyebrow at the old woman, but Maria shook her head and continued into the hall. She moved confidently now, recovered from the initial shock of the attack, although she kept her eyes carefully averted from the bodies of her friends. Before they reached the corner, she diverted into another room.

"*Maria*," Liz hissed, glancing back at the dining room, where the crunch of breaking glass was growing nearer. There was no doubt now—the soldiers were in the house. In seconds they would reach the doorway at the end of the hallway and see them.

A moment later, Maria re-emerged, a handgun in one hand and a spare clip in the other. More shocking still, she had slung the belt of grenades over her shoulder.

Liz raised an eyebrow. "Ah…" Her words deserted her as Maria strode past, the hint of a smile on her lips.

"Let's go, Liz," the old woman whispered.

Moving quickly, they turned the corner in the corridor, taking them out of view from the dining room. The back door loomed, but as Liz reached for the handle, Maria pulled her back.

"Wait," she said. She took a grenade from the belt and studied it, before handing it to Liz.

Liz hesitated for half a second before accepting the weapon with cautious hands. She swallowed, looking from the grenade to Maria. It looked different from the ones she'd seen in the movies —more like a steel cylinder than the typical ball-shaped grenades. The pin at the top was familiar, though.

"If memory serves, that's a flash grenade," Maria said, casting a nervous glance behind them. "If there's anyone out there watching, they're probably using night vision goggles. That should blind them long enough for us to get away."

"And how do we get *you* away?" Liz asked. If it came to it, she thought she could fly with the old woman, but it would take a long time to get airborne. They would be easy targets.

"There's a getaway car, one block over," Maria replied. "We just have to get through the back fence and across the neighboring property. The keys are in the sun visor."

"Okay." Liz gripped the grenade tightly in her hand, before nodding to the door. "You open it, I'll throw."

"Don't forget the pin," Maria whispered as she grasped the door handle.

Liz tore the pin from the grenade as Maria hauled the door open. A shout came from outside, but Liz had already hurled the grenade. Maria dropped to the ground beside Liz as gunshots rang out.

Then a flash of light erupted through the backyard.

Liz had already covered her eyes, but even so, the light burned through her eyelids. Stars danced across her vision when she looked up again, but they quickly faded to shadows.

Outside, someone was screaming, and she grinned at their small victory. There was no time to enjoy it, though. She picked up Maria and slung the old woman over her shoulder. Breath held, half-expecting a dozen bullets to riddle her body, Liz leapt outside.

Silence greeted her.

Struggling to contain her relief, Liz raced across the dewy grass. Maria barely weighed a hundred and twenty pounds—nothing for her enhanced strength, and she was across the backyard in a heartbeat. The tall wooden fence loomed, but Liz didn't even bother stretching her wings. She bounded forward and sprang, her powerful quads sending her soaring over the seven-foot barrier.

They crashed down on the other side with a squelching *thud.* Her feet sank slightly into the soft earth, but she pulled herself out and ran on, hardly breaking stride. She felt Maria struggling on her back and heard a half-muffled curse—something about putting her down—but they weren't clear yet. Liz could carry Maria far faster than the old woman could run.

The lights were off in the neighbor's house, but Liz recalled from earlier flights that it was occupied. She kept her head low as she raced past the windows, though she doubted anyone would be venturing outside. They could not have missed the gunshots. They'd probably switched off the lights and were huddling somewhere inside, praying that whoever was shooting left them alone.

Too bad they had us for neighbors, Liz thought wryly.

Ducking beneath a low-lying tree, she moved into the bricked courtyard that was the front yard. Free of weeds and moss, the owners obviously took great care to maintain their property. A row of tall oaks trees marked their boundary with the road. Liz rushed towards them, glimpsing the dim sheen of a car beyond their wide trunks.

As she reached the center of the courtyard, the trees seemed to shift, and two soldiers stepped from the shadows. Liz froze, praying they hadn't seen her. The click of their safeties being released shattered her thin hope. Neither said a word, but both raised their rifles. Weighed down by Maria, trapped out in the open, Liz was too far away to reach them. Gritting her teeth, she closed her eyes and thought of Chris.

A *thud* and a *thwack* followed. Liz's eyes snapped back open, and she stood gaping as Jasmine and Mira strode towards her, the soldiers now lying slumped on the cobbles. Jasmine grinned and raised an eyebrow.

"You really are getting slack, Liz," she smirked.

Liz let out a long sigh and smiled back. "Thank you, Jasmin—"

Boom.

The words died in her throat as the gunshot rang through the night. Jasmine's eyes widened, her mouth falling open. She swayed, her gaze dropping to the blood that blossomed from her chest. Her emerald wings, still extended, trembled as she looked back up at Liz with fear on her face.

Screaming, Mira threw herself at the man on the ground. Barely conscious, he had somehow managed to swing his rifle around and aim it at Jasmine's back. Mira tore it from his hands before he could fire again and embedded it in his face.

Then Jasmine's legs gave way, and she was falling, her eyes rolling up into the back of her head.

And Liz was stepping forward to catch her, a single word screaming on repeat in her mind.

No, no, no!

12

Chris shivered as the frigid blast of the air conditioner struck his naked body. Extending his wings, he wrapped himself in their soft embrace. On the other side of the room, Ashley was already doing the same. The white feathers hid her nudity, though he noticed now there were patches on her wings where she had begun to molt. It had been weeks since they'd seen sunlight, since they'd been able to stretch their wings and soar. Their captivity was beginning to take its toll.

The whine of the air conditioner changed, and Chris braced himself for the return of the icy blast. The chain attached to his collar rattled as he moved. Ashley sported an identical chain, a steel leash that ran from her collar to a solid bolt in the floor.

This was how they had slept for weeks—stripped naked and chained like dogs at the foot of the Director's bed. He could hear the shower now, could see the steam billowing from the ensuite bathroom. It drifted across the room, forming a light fog over the massive king-sized bed. At the sight of the cotton sheets and silk duvet, Chris's stomach twisted with yearning. He longed for a hot shower and a proper bed, to escape the hard tiles and freezing air conditioner—if only for a night.

The two walls against which he and Ashley leaned were plain white concrete, their surfaces unadorned, but the far wall was taken up by a massive LED screen. There was not a single window in the facility, but the screen almost made up for it. At the moment, it showed the towering trunks and tangled branches of a forest. Brilliant green leaves swayed in the breeze, so detailed that even Chris's hypersensitive vision could barely tell the difference from reality. As he watched, a brown squirrel darted across the leaf-strewn ground and raced up a tree trunk.

He quickly looked away, wishing he could join the furry forest creature. His gaze settled on Ashley, and he swallowed as her eyes found his. She shifted position and her wings fell away a moment, giving Chris a clear view of her body. The weeks of sparse food and sleepless nights had lessened her, but there was still no denying Ashley's beauty.

"How could you do it, Chris?" Ashley asked softly.

"I didn't mean to—" Chris began.

"Not the girl," Ashley interrupted. "If anything, you did *her* a favor."

Chris pulled his knees up to his chest and leaned his head against them. He knew what Ashley was asking. "What else could I have done, Ash?"

"You could have *not helped them*," she hissed.

Chris spread his hands. "They were doomed either way."

Ashley clenched her fists into little balls. "But you know what happens next. How many kids did you just sentence to death, Chris?"

Swallowing, Chris tried to keep the pain from his face. He managed to suck in a breath, trying to stall, but when he looked up, Ashley was still waiting.

"What else could I have done, Ash?" he repeated. "She's broken me. I can't fight her anymore. I don't know where you get the courage."

Ashley turned away at that, and for a minute there was silence. Chris leaned back, listening to the roar of the shower, wondering how much time they had left. Five minutes? Ten? He dreaded what would come next—though he wasn't the one who would suffer tonight.

"When they caught us, when they had us cornered in that

lecture hall, I'd never been so frightened." Ashley's whisper carried across the room. "It was Independence Square all over again. I froze on that stage, Chris. All I could think was that my worst fear had come true, that I was going to be caught and thrown back in a cage." She drew in a breath before continuing: "Then you screamed for my help, and I saw you all fighting for your lives, and I realized it didn't matter. That I'd already faced the worst they could throw at me and survived."

"But why did you stay, Ash?" Chris asked, eyes fixed to the floor. His voice broke. "Why didn't you run? You could have saved yourself."

"I know," Ashley replied, "but I couldn't let him kill you, Chris. As foolish, as hopeless as it was, I couldn't leave you to fight him alone."

"And now you're trapped here with me, suffering your worst nightmare, and somehow you're the one with the courage to resist her." Chris's voice was bitter, filled with self-loathing.

"It's not courage if you're not afraid," Ashley replied. Chris's brow creased at that but she continued, "I realized something else in that lecture hall. As awful and cruel and tormented as Halt was, it wasn't those things that terrified me. It was that feeling of being powerless, of being used. So she can torture me all she likes, it won't make a difference. I will never let them use me like that again, Chris. Never."

Staring into Ashley's eyes, Chris frowned. Despite the dim light, they seemed to glow with a light of their own. For a moment, she seemed something else, *someone* else. Then she blinked, and it was just Ashley again.

"Well, well, well." The lights brightened as the Director stepped out from the bathroom. "Do I hear my pets talking?"

Pressing his lips firmly closed, Chris shook his head.

The Director smiled, her naked body still dripping water. Her short blonde hair clung to her neck, but otherwise there was not a hair on her body. She patted herself dry in front of them, taking no care to hide the tight mounds of her breasts. Finally she tied the towel around her hair. Putting her hands on her hips, she looked from Chris to Ashley.

"No?" She smiled. "Very good."

She crossed to the bed and threw herself down on her stomach, then turned to face them. She leaned her chin on her hands and studied them with a curious smile.

"Such interesting creatures," she murmured. "You have no idea."

"What do you mean, ma'am?" Chris whispered.

The Director laughed. "I've been reading Halt's writings. I'm no scientist, but it's fascinating stuff." Her voice was light, almost friendly. "The things that he and Doctor Fallow did, the genes they managed to recombine into your genetic makeup. Those reflexes you showed today—you saw the girl, reacted, moved, killed, all before even my best guard could blink. According to Halt's notes, those traits—your speed, agility, reflexes—they come from the genes of *Bassariscus astutus* and *Suricata suricatta.*"

"And what the hell are those?" Ashley asked flatly.

The Director turned to look at her. Her brow hardened, and there was a distinct warning in her tone as she replied, "The ring-tailed cat and the mongoose." Slowly, she stood from the bed and walked over to Ashley. "Which certainly explains your stubborn tendencies."

Ashley glared back. Eyes locked, the two faced each other for a long moment, neither willing to retreat.

Then Ashley suddenly laughed. "Go ahead, do your worst." She spread her wings, though crouched on the floor, she wasn't particularly imposing. "You couldn't hold a candle to Halt when it comes to torture."

Chris flinched, cursing Ashley's recklessness. Her punishment would be bad enough without provoking the woman.

The Director only shook her head. "Whatever am I going to do with you, my pet?" She tapped her watch and moved away. Chris shared a glance with her friend as lights flashed on her collar. Despite her brave words, Chris saw the shadow pass across Ashley's face.

"You've been bad." There was pity in the Director's voice now. "You know I don't enjoy this, but you leave me no choice." She pressed her watch again.

Ashley shrieked and collapsed, the chain rattling as she convulsed. Her wings beat against the floor, dislodging white feathers that drifted through the air. Her legs kicked out blindly and her back arched, her fingers clawing the tiles.

Seconds later it was over, leaving Ashley gasping. Blood dripped down her chin where she'd split her lip hitting the ground face-first, and it was a long time before she managed to sit upright again. Her wings hung limp behind her now, her feathers still trembling. She glared at the Director, her teeth clenched with the aftershock of pain.

"As usual, the timer has been set," the Director said, ignoring Ashley's hate-filled stare. "The collar will remind you of your transgressions every thirty minutes. Enjoy your night, my pet."

Chris shuddered. He watched Ashley pull her knees up to her chest and lean back against the wall. Her wings wrapped around her again as their eyes met. Chris's heart went out to her, but he kept his mouth shut. He had no wish to share her fate.

How many nights had he lasted, before succumbing? He could hardly remember now, though he had resisted through several nights of sleepless agony. It was not just the pain, but the anticipation, the creeping dread of it that broke him. By the end, his eyes had been red from lack of sleep, his mouth filled with ulcers where he'd bitten himself, and he could resist no longer. The next command the Director gave, Chris had obeyed. And the next, and the next, until today he had killed an innocent girl.

Looking down, Chris sucked in a breath. His ears twitched, listening to the soft tread of the Director's feet as she crossed the room. He tried not to flinch as she knelt beside him, unable to avoid her hazel gaze. The hardness in her eyes was gone, the anger replaced by warmth. She reached out with a slender hand and stroked Chris's cheek. He shuddered at her icy touch but did not pull away.

"Such a good boy." She stroked his hair, as an owner would her dog. "You did well today. Very well. Perhaps you're finally ready."

"Ready?" Chris croaked.

Her hand trailed down past his ear and under his chin. He

swallowed, feeling the cold bite of the collar around his neck. Her scent filled his nostrils, a rich, perfumed aroma of flowers. But it was artificial, sickly, overwhelming. She forced his chin up, so that their eyes met.

They were close now, her naked body almost pressing against him. Despite himself, Chris felt a stirring of desire. Her breasts rose with each breath and her pupils had narrowed to slits.

Chris swallowed, thinking, *One blow, that's all it would take.*

One punch, and the world would be free of her.

But Chris and Ashley would not be released. When her heart stopped, the collars around their necks would trigger, and they would suffer a long, agonizing death. Not quickly—she liked to remind them of that. The collars would switch on and no one would be able to deactivate them. The current wouldn't kill them, at least not immediately. They might even change, might succumb to the mindless rage of the *Chead*, before the end came.

Despite the consequences, Chris still felt tempted. He clenched his fist, willing himself to do it, to summon the courage to act. She was so bold, so confident that she had crushed his will, that she had him wrapped around her little finger.

If only it weren't true.

Chris unclenched his fists, the tension flooding from him like water down a drain. A flicker of a smile tugged at the Director's lips as she wiped the unspilt tear from his eye.

"My dear Chris," she breathed, her face close to his. "Would you like to sleep in a bed tonight?"

Shuddering, Chris felt again the cold tiles seeping through his skin, chilling his bones. He clenched his jaw shut, willing himself to ignore her.

"Say the word, and you can join me," she continued, then laughed gently. "I promise I don't bite."

There was a suggestion in the woman's eyes now. He jumped as her hands slid down his back, trailing across his skin, exploring the joints where his wings met his spine. They continued along the limbs, sending electric jolts up his neck.

With an awful yearning, Chris looked at the bed. For weeks he had slept on this floor, freezing and exposed to the relentless air conditioner. Each morning he woke to numb legs and cramping muscles. To be warm, to sleep in comfort…

His eyes drifted past the Director to where Ashley sat in misery. She would spend the night screaming, in endless anticipation of the collar's bite. The Director would not hear her—she wore special steel earplugs, ensuring her sleep did not suffer along with her pets. Chris's stomach twisted with shame at even considering the idea, and slowly he shook his head, hardly daring to look at her.

Her eyes narrowed as she stood. "I'm disappointed." She towered over him for a moment, as though weighing his fate. Finally, she crossed to the desk beside her bed and rummaged inside, returning a moment later. Chris flinched as she tossed a set of earplugs in his lap.

"Loyalty must be rewarded," she said, her face expressionless.

At that, the Director retreated to her bed and crawled beneath the covers. A tap to her watch plunged the room into absolute darkness. Shivering, Chris lay down on the cold floor. He kept one wing beneath him, protecting against the cold tiles, while the other covered him like a blanket. He was already beginning to regret his decision.

In the darkness, he could hear Ashley making the same preparations for sleep, though her efforts would be in vain. They did not speak. There was no need. They both knew their lot.

Curling up, Chris clutched the earplugs in his hand, but refused to use them. He may have given in, may have surrendered to the Director's will, but that didn't mean abandoning his friend. If he wore them, he would be leaving her alone in the darkness, alone with her torment. No, he would rather suffer a sleepless night with Ashley than desert her now.

He closed his eyes.

Ashley's first scream came twenty minutes later. He listened to the sounds of her thrashing, his enhanced vision unable to pierce the absolute black. After thirty seconds, Ashley stilled, though her desperate gasps were audible in the silence.

"Are you okay?" Chris whispered. With her earplugs, the

Director would not hear them now, but he had no wish to tempt fate.

Ashley gave a low whimper, but didn't reply. Sighing, Chris closed his eyes and sought sleep once more. He was just beginning to drift off when Ashley's scream came again. This time he didn't bother to speak.

He pressed the earplugs into place.

And slept.

13

The dark slope stretched out ahead of them, the long grass overgrown from years of neglect. It crunched beneath Susan's feet as she jogged, parched from drought. This was rugged country, abandoned by humanity as the climate shifted, driving them down towards the coast. Only the stubborn remained now, their numbers dwindling with each passing year.

Her brethren intended to quicken that process.

So far, the *Chead* had kept to these far-out pastures, close to the shelter of the mountains and the network of tunnels criss-crossing the plains. They were safe here, confident in their power, untouchable by the foolish humans.

Yet it was not enough. There was little food in this country. As their numbers grew, they would need to spread into the lowlands, where humanity numbered in the thousands rather than hundreds. When that time came, they would need a plan.

Susan looked around as she jogged. The night was alive with the movement of the *Chead*. They had travelled long miles since their last raid, and Susan was beginning to flag. Her belly weighed her down, the new life within draining her strength, though she refused to give in to her weakness.

Hecate ran beside her, his sweet scent feeding energy to her failing legs. Despite his years in captivity, he was tireless, his long strides carrying him effortlessly across the rolling hills. Somewhere behind them, Talisa and her guardian *Chead* brought up the rear. Ahead, the latest batch candidates who had chosen life lurched along. Some ran with the mindless strength of the *Chead* rage, while others stumbled, their consciousnesses still at war with the change.

Watching them, Susan wondered how long it would take for the last to succumb, to release the final treacherous emotions of humanity and embrace the *Chead*. How long had it taken her? Her memories of that time were blurred, like trying to glimpse a familiar face through water. But as she sucked in a fresh breath, the images crystallized, and she saw a woman's face staring back at her, blue eyes wide with fear.

She staggered midstride and started to fall. Before she could strike the ground, Hecate's arm shot out and steadied her. Glimpsing him in the moonlight, she felt a moment of remembered terror, before the scent of her mate blanketed her, and it all fell away.

"Come. We are almost…there," Hecate said.

Susan smiled back. Using Hecate's arm, she regained her feet. Most of the *Chead* were past them now, their passage flattening the grass around them. Untouched by the lights of humanity, the moon was bright in the sky and a thousand stars stretched from the mountains to the distant horizon. A breeze blew past where they stood at the top of the hill and down towards their brethren.

Warmth wrapped its way around Susan's chest as she turned back to Hecate. Her hand was still in his, she pulled him close. His arms went around her as she pressed herself against him. She tilted back her head and felt a tingle of electricity as their lips met.

Boom.

Hecate stiffened as an explosion rocked the night. Springing apart, they turned to stare down the slope. At the bottom of the hill, orange flames had erupted from the earth, flinging *Chead* in all directions. Their remaining brethren scattered in every direction, blinded by the flames. But the curve of the valley hemmed them in, slowing their flight.

Movement appeared on the opposite hill, followed by the flash of gunfire.

"Humans," Susan whispered.

A guttural howl came from Hecate. Then he was racing away around the hillside, screaming unintelligible words to the fleeing *Chead* fleeing. Still high on the hill, the flames shielded him from view of the soldiers, but the *Chead* in the valley were sitting ducks. An orange ball erupted from the soldiers' vantage point, racing downwards. Another explosion shook the ground.

Susan shuddered as the screams of her brethren traveled up to her. Rage flooded her chest and she ran after Hecate, bounding through the long grass, a demon in the night.

The soldiers were positioned on the opposite hillslope, looking down into the narrow gulley the *Chead* had been traversing. With the men downwind, the *Chead* had been unable to scent them and had stumbled straight into the trap. But the humans had not been as successful as Susan had first thought. The *Chead* were resilient, and nothing short of a bullet to the brain or heart would stop them. Already her people were regrouping, their eyes adjusting to the firelight, picking out the flash of gunfire above. They melted into the long grass and raced uphill towards the enemy.

The soldiers saw the danger and started to pull back, but Hecate and the *Chead* who had joined him were quicker still. While those below had charged up the slope, Hecate had followed the curve of the valley, circumnavigating the flames in the gulley. Reaching the crest of the slope, they moved onto the flat ground beyond, cutting off the soldiers' retreat.

Susan chased after them, just a few steps behind now. The soldiers were nearing the top of the hill now. Glimpsing the dark gleam of their vehicles, a growl rumbled from her chest.

Bounding forward, she narrowed the gap between herself and Hecate, as the *Chead* below caught up with the slowest of the soldiers. She grinned as screams carried across the valley, but the fastest men were already closing on the vehicles. They had thrown away their weapons in their haste to escape, thinking only of the danger behind.

Hecate reached the Jeeps as the first soldier leapt into the driver's seat. The engine roared to life, but before the man's comrades could throw themselves inside, Hecate smashed a fist through the plate glass window and tore the soldier from his seat.

Then the other *Chead* were there, those above and below converging on the fleeing soldiers, cutting off their only escape route. Susan joined them, driving a man from his feet to land on his chest. The coward had already discarded his weapon, and died screaming as she tore him to pieces.

Her vision stained red, Susan searched for a fresh victim. A soldier nearby still carried a rifle. As she watched, the gun flashed, and somewhere behind her a *Chead* howled. Screaming, Susan leapt forward and tore the weapon from the soldier's hands. Raising it like a bat, she readied herself for the kill, then froze.

The soldier's helmet had been knocked loose, revealing a mop of long curly hair. A woman. Stumbling back, the woman tripped on a patch of grass and crumpled to the ground. Susan kicked the woman in the stomach, winding her and pinning her down.

Silently, Susan waited as her brethren finished off the last of their enemy. Cornered, the soldiers put up little fight. The loss of the vehicles had broken them, and they fled in all directions, only to be brought down by the chasing *Chead*.

When silence finally returned to the night, Susan crouched beside her captive. The woman had caught her breath now, but said nothing—only lay staring up at Susan with hate-filled eyes. Susan smiled back. Many of the prisoners back in Stutter Creek had declined life, and there were still a few doses left. Perhaps this creature would prove smarter than those in the town.

As the *Chead* gathered on the top of the hill, Susan allowed her gaze to drift back to the flames. The scent of blood and ash was thick in her nostrils, though the flames were already beginning to die. The bodies of soldiers dotted the hillslope, their camouflaged uniforms blending in with the long grass. But it was to the bottom of the valley that her eyes were drawn.

Dozens of *Chead* lay dead amidst the embers, many riddled with bullets, others burnt and torn by the explosive rockets used by the humans. In the center of the carnage were the women they had taken from the last town, their bodies broken, their new lives cut short. They had been among the first to fall, their lingering humanity hampering their instincts, slowing them enough for the soldiers to pick them off. Only a few had survived the slaughter.

Susan's eyes turned to the woman at her feet, and she felt the rage threatening, begging to be released.

It could have been me!

Gritting her teeth, she forced the rage back down. Now was not the time. She needed Hecate, needed Talisa, needed to protect her children. Silently, she picked the woman off the ground and dragged her through the *Chead.*

She found Talisa and Hecate at the edge of the hillside, looking down at the slaughter below. Talisa's white eyes glowed in the moonlight as Susan approached.

"My child," she murmured, her eyes flicking to the soldier. "What have you brought me?"

Susan forced the woman to her knees at Talisa's feet.

"A gift," she whispered.

14

The car screeched around the corner and straightened out. With the headlights off and the streetlights out, the only light came from the full moon. In the back, Liz held on for dear life as Maria took another corner. Mira sat in the front seat looking back at them, a low moan coming from the back of her throat. But Liz had no time to worry about the girl now.

Jasmine's head lay in Liz's lap, long black hair dangling across her face. Her breathing was shallow, coming in desperate gasps, and her eyelashes fluttered as she struggled to remain conscious. There was blood on Jasmine's lips. She stared up at Liz with unmasked terror.

"Hang in there, Jas," Liz whispered, pressing the ruined bundle of her shirt to the gaping wound in her friend's chest. Blood was already seeping through, and Liz knew more would be dripping from the smaller entry wound in her back.

"Doing…my best…" Jasmine coughed. A flicker of pain passed across her face as Maria spun the wheel again. She was going far too fast for the suburban streets, but it wouldn't take long for their enemies to realize someone had escaped. They needed to get as far away as possible, before the soldiers could close a net around them.

Fortunately, the broad oak trees lining the streets in this part of the city provided shelter from eyes above. Liz searched for the lights of a chopper, but there was nothing yet. They had to get off the streets before backup was called in.

But none of that mattered if Jasmine bled out in the back seat of the car. Twin Peaks Hospital was close. Going there would mean giving Jasmine over to the authorities, but Liz couldn't face watching another friend die. It had taken a few dire threats, but Maria was heading there now. They would have to leave Jasmine with the first doctor they saw, but it was better than the alternative.

As if reading her mind, Jasmine's eyes flickered open. "Where are we…going…Liz?"

Liz stroked the hair from her friend's eyes. "It's okay, we're taking you to a hospital. You'll be alr—"

"*No.*" Jasmine's hand shot out and caught Liz by the wrist. Despite her injuries, she was still shockingly strong.

"Jasmine…" Liz began.

"No," Jasmine repeated, her eyes wide. "I'm not going… back…Liz. No hospital."

Tears shimmered in Liz's eyes, but there was no give in Jasmine's voice. "Maria," she croaked finally.

"I heard her," Maria replied softly. "There's a park nearby. We'll hide out there for the night."

Liz's stomach tied itself in knots as the old woman did a U-turn. Jasmine was worse than Ashley had been after being shot out of the sky. Only Doctor Halt and the resources at the facility had saved Ashley from death then. What chance did Jasmine have of even surviving the night?

It took them another ten minutes to reach the park. By then Maria had slowed down to avoid unwanted attention, though just being outside so late meant they were breaking curfew. The sign at the entrance named the place Lake Merced Park.

They parked the car beneath a grove of peppermint willow trees to hide it from circling helicopters and bailed out. A toilet block hid the vehicle from the road. Liz hoped that would be enough to conceal it from any search parties. Otherwise, it wouldn't take long for the soldiers to realize that the back seat was stained with blood. Then the whole weight of the government would come crashing down on them.

Lifting Jasmine into her arms, Liz carried her through the park after Maria. They walked for ten minutes before coming to a grove of pine trees. Ducking beneath the low hanging branches, they entered the shelter of the trees.

Dry pine needles crunched as Mira set about making a bed, and then Liz carefully lowered Jasmine down. Her emerald wings fell limply against the ground as Liz released her. The bleeding seemed to have slowed, but the bullet had left a gaping inch-wide hole in Jasmine's chest.

A harsh cough tore from Jasmine. Blood bubbled between her lips, and it was several minutes before she recovered. Maria offered a pocket handkerchief as Jasmine's breathing turned to a strained wheeze. Liz used it to wipe the blood from her friend's face, feeling an awful helplessness in the pit of her stomach. Jasmine's eyes were closed now, though her body was still taut, her fingers clenched in claws. The harsh lines of a scowl marked her forehead.

We should have taken her to the hospital.

It was too late for second thoughts now. Liz doubted Jasmine would survive another wild ride in the car. Sweat beaded Jasmine's forehead and goosebumps stood up on her skin. Liz used the other side of the handkerchief to wipe her friend's face, then stretched her wings to cover Jasmine like a blanket.

"I don't want to die, Liz," Jasmine whispered in the darkness.

Her eyes were open again. A tear ran down her cheek. Seeing her friend's terror, Liz entwined a gloved hand around Jasmine's fingers.

"Not going to happen," Liz said with as much conviction as she could muster. "You're going to be fine, Jas. You're strong. A little bullet won't stop you."

Jasmine smiled, but the movement triggered another fit of coughing, and it was several minutes before she had the strength to speak again.

"It hurts so much," she said at last, breathless. "Do you think it hurt…for him…at the end?"

Liz shivered. She didn't need to ask who Jasmine was talking about. Richard's last stand played itself out in her mind, and she saw again the dozen bullets strike his body. "I don't know."

"I guess…no one does," Jasmine said, her voice barely a whisper, "at the end..."

"Jasmine…"

"Promise me," Jasmine said, cutting her off. Liz blinked, not understanding, until Jasmine's head turned and her eyes found Liz's. "Don't…lose yourself…Liz. We need…your heart."

A smile touched Liz's lips. "I won't," she insisted, "but you're not going anywhere, Jas. Just…save your strength."

Nodding, Jasmine closed her eyes. Her breath softened, and for a while Liz thought she slept. She sat in the darkness, Jasmine's hand wrapped in her own, watching the slow rise and fall of her friend's chest. The bleeding had stopped now—at least outwardly—but her usually tanned skin had lost all its color.

"I didn't hesitate…you know." Liz jumped as Jasmine spoke again.

She glanced down, but Jasmine's eyes were still closed. Before she could ask what Jasmine meant, her friend went on.

"It was me…or Chelsea. She was my friend…but I didn't even hesitate."

"We all chose ourselves, Jas," Liz said softly. "That's why we're here."

"Not…Richard." She sighed then, a long, harsh exhalation that seemed to go on and on.

Liz couldn't find the words to argue. What more could she say? Tears burned her eyes and she squeezed Jasmine's hand. But something had changed in their little grove. A heavy silence hung over the trees. She looked around, searching for the difference.

Heart pounding, she turned back to Jasmine.

"Jas?" She leaned closer, waiting for a response. Only then did Liz realize why it was so quiet.

"*Jasmine!*" she shrieked.

Liz grasped Jasmine by the shoulders and shook her. Jasmine's head lolled to the side, but her eyes remained closed. A thin trail of blood ran from her mouth. Her chest was still, her breath silent.

"Jasmine!" Liz screamed again.

But Jasmine did not reply.

She was already gone.

15

Sam sat and held his hands out to the tiny flame burning on the concrete floor. It was all they could manage in the abandoned basement, and soon even that would be gone. The little collection of old magazines and newspapers they'd found in the corner wouldn't last long.

Looking at Jocelyn and her children, he cursed under his breath. He shouldn't blame her, but there was no helping it. It was her husband's fault. If he hadn't met with her, the government would never have found him, never been able to follow him back to the safe house. But he had already suffered for his stupidity. Yet here Jocelyn sat, the one thing the man had cared about, while Sam's friends were dead, their hopes of striking back at the government in ruins.

At least the children were safe. He could not hold the crimes of their father against them. How exactly the government agents had tracked the doctor—despite Harry's precautions—he might never know. Unlike their fledgling resistance, the Director was not limited to twentieth century technology. Satellites or street cameras or GPS tracking; any one of them could have done it. All Sam knew was, they'd been found.

He'd arrived at the safe house well before the van. Lights and vehicles had been everywhere. From his vantage point high in the sky, Sam had taken in the destruction wrought on the house. The walls looked more like a cheese grater than solid wood. He hadn't lingered; there'd been no point.

Turning in the air, Sam had returned to the van and diverted them away from the house. They'd found an abandoned building nearby and hidden the van around back. It was the best they'd been able to do by that point. They wouldn't have gotten far with the soldiers crawling over the neighborhood.

Now morning was fast approaching, and Sam was no closer to knowing what had happened. He could hear the choppers circling outside and hoped that meant at least someone had gotten away. There was another safe house they could have retreated to—though only those not involved with the next attack knew its location. Sam cursed as he realized none of the rebels with him knew where it was.

"It's all over," Leo was saying, his voice low, though the children would have no problem hearing him. "They've won."

"Looks that way," another of the men replied.

"Maybe the girl was right," Leo muttered, looking at the family, "maybe the doctor betrayed us."

"Not deliberately." Sam's feathers bristled as he spoke over their muttering,

"How do you know?" Leo snapped.

"Because we're alive. If it'd been a setup, we would have all been dead the moment we stepped into the apartment," Sam growled. He nodded at the doctor's wife. "They were watching her, waiting for her husband to show up. They probably listened to their conversation about the Madwomen and followed him. Whatever precautions you took bringing him to the safe house weren't enough—he led them straight to us."

Leo snorted. "So what now?"

"Any of you know the location of the next safehouse?" Sam asked.

None of them answered. "Thought so. We have to—"

"We don't have to do anything," Leo said, standing. "You may not see it, but I do. We've already lost. There's nowhere left to run. May as well give ourselves up now."

"Rubbish," Sam hissed.

He stood and stared at the man until Leo looked away. Grabbing the last stack of newspaper, Sam tore it to pieces and slowly fed them to the flames.

"They're on the defensive," Sam mused. "Can't you see that? Refugees filling the streets, protesters at their doors. Dissent is spreading. We can't let them quash it now, not when it's just beginning."

"Why does it have to be us?" Leo asked miserably.

Looking at the man, Sam realized for the first time Leo wasn't much older than his own eighteen years. Sam had grown so used to the constant danger, he'd forgotten it hadn't been the same for others. Leo was little more than a boy, and Sam felt a moment of empathy for him.

"Because we're here, Leo," he said. "Because no one else will. Because we're the ones fate chose to make a stand. It doesn't matter why—just that we do it. This is important, this fight. You all know that, otherwise you wouldn't be here. We have to stop them, now, while they can still *be* stopped."

"But they've already won," another man whispered.

"No," Sam replied firmly, "they can't win, not while we're still here, not so long as someone continues fighting."

"Do you truly believe that?"

They all looked around at Jocelyn's voice. She sat with her back against the concrete wall, her legs stretched out towards the flames, a boy asleep under each arm. Her eyes pierced the shadows of the basement, watching them by the light of the fire.

"I do," Sam replied

Jocelyn nodded, her lips tight. "Maybe if more of us believed the same, we wouldn't be in this mess." Her eyes drifted to her children. She ran a hand through the youngest's mop of hair. "It's so easy to ignore the suffering of others, when it means protecting the ones you love. My husband never spoke much about his work, but I know it changed him. Even from the little I learned in the last few years, I knew something wasn't right, that something was rotten."

Sam didn't respond. He'd heard the same story over and

over, of people trapped by fear, disturbed by what they'd heard, what they'd seen, but too afraid to act. Without an independent media, without an open internet, there was little people could do to organize themselves. Every five years they could vote, but even that was a farce. Each state chose an Elector from two candidates, but it didn't matter which one you chose. Both inevitably elected the same President.

Now though, the Madwomen's protest in Independence Square had provided a rallying point. And bit by bit, a resistance was growing around them. So long as this setback hadn't destroyed the emerging movement.

"He tried to quit once, you know." Jocelyn gave a little laugh, though it held no humor. "Only once, mind you. I'm sure the thugs would have done worse to me if he'd tried again. Not that they ever admitted who'd sent them." There was steel in her eyes as she looked up. "But maybe now's the time we do something."

"That was our plan," Sam murmured. "Your husband…he told us the Director runs the new facility he was working at. He wouldn't tell us where it was though, not until you were safe."

A wry smile twisted Jocelyn's lips. "Some job you're doing," she said. "He told me where it was…his lab…when we met. Just in case."

Sam's jaw dropped. "Where?"

Jocelyn was staring down at her boys, her eyes sad. "Whatever crimes my husband has committed, whatever crimes I've been a party to, they're innocent." She looked up at Sam, eyes wide. "Will you still protect them, even now?"

Sam pursed his lips. He could offer Jocelyn the world, but what position was he in to fulfill those promises? Who knew if the resistance even existed still, after last night's attack?

"I honestly don't know, Jocelyn. We might be all that's left now. If the worst has happened and our friends are dead, I don't know if there's anything I can do to protect you…"

"I'll do it," Leo said from his place in the corner.

Sam raised an eyebrow. Leo smiled back as the other men nodded.

"You will?" Jocelyn whispered.

"You have my word, ma'am," Leo replied. "They're just kids, after all. If we're not fighting for them, what's the point?"

"Thank you," Jocelyn said, choking on the words.

Sam could hardly breathe. "Then you'll tell us where he worked?"

Jocelyn nodded. "I will, but you're not going to like it."

16

Liz sat high in the treetops and watched as the sun slowly climbed into the sky. Its light stained the horizon red, so that it seemed San Francisco's towering skyscrapers wore a coat of blood. Shivering, Liz looked at her hands. Dried blood stained her gloves and clothing. She fought back her tears.

For half the night she had sat by Jasmine's side, talking into the darkness. She had begged her friend to come back, to not leave her alone, but her cries had fallen on deaf ears. Her friend was gone, her soul had fled. All that remained was an empty shell, a lifeless husk. Jasmine's fight was finally over.

Now, as Liz watched the sun rising, she wondered about the promise she'd made to Jasmine.

Don't lose yourself.

Liz swallowed her grief and stood. The branch swayed beneath her as she watched the helicopter buzzing in the distance. Fire flickered in her chest. Liz longed to tear it from the sky, but she had made a promise.

Stepping from the branch, Liz's wings caught the air, and she drifted lightly to the ground. She stumbled slightly as she alighted on the dewy grass, but recovered in a few steps. When she looked around, she found her two comrades standing in the shelter of the trees.

Mira walked forward, her grey wings trailing behind her. As she approached, tears spilled from her multicolored eyes. Liz opened her arms and the girl threw herself into the waiting embrace.

"Liz," she sobbed.

Liz held her tight against her chest. "I know, Mira. I know."

She could feel the tremors running through the girl, the silent sobs of her grief. Gently, Liz stroked Mira's silver-grey hair, whispering soft consolations, even as her own grief spilled. She could feel the dampness of Mira's tears on her shirt but made no effort to pull away. The two of them stood like that for a long time, united in their loss.

Finally, Mira released her with a sniff. "Where's Sam?"

Liz bit her lip. "I don't know," she replied, looking at Maria. "Will they go to the next safe house?"

"They don't know where it is," Maria said. She gestured towards the trees. "Come into the shelter. There are still helicopters out looking for us."

Staring at the dark shadows beneath of the grove, Liz hesitated. Somewhere beyond the leafy branches, Jasmine's lifeless body waited. Ice wrapped around her throat and she squeezed her eyes shut, barely able to breathe.

A new set of arms gripped Liz—gentle, but firm—then she was burying her face in Maria's cardigan, and all her grief and pain and fear came pouring out. It had been so long since she'd been held, since she'd allowed anyone to comfort her. Even with the long sleeves and gloves, she was terrified of the harm she might cause. Yet she needed the comfort now, more than she could have ever imagined.

First it was Richard, then Ashley and Chris, now Jasmine. Maybe even Sam. She couldn't take it, couldn't bear the thought she might be all alone in the world. That she and Mira might be the only survivors left—from the hundreds who'd once graced the corridors of Doctor Halt's facility.

When they finally separated, Liz took a deep breath. Maria gripped her by the shoulder, a smile wrinkling the skin around her eyes.

"You're not alone, Liz," she whispered, as though she'd read Liz's thoughts. Taking Liz's hand, she gestured to the trees once more. "Come on, she's waiting for you."

Liz shook her head but didn't resist the old woman's gentle tug. Breath held, she allowed herself to be led meekly back into the grove.

Jasmine lay where Liz had left her, eyes closed, black hair merging with the shadows. She seemed to have shrunk in the past few hours, as though that last memory of life had left her body. Her skin had turned a pallid grey, and the sheen had gone from her emerald feathers.

An involuntary sob tore from Liz's throat. Hot tears stung her eyes. Angrily, she wiped them away and knelt beside Jasmine's body. Mira sat cross-legged on the ground nearby, staring at Jasmine, as though still waiting for her to wake.

Removing her gloves, Liz took Jasmine's hand in hers. She shivered, surprised at how quickly the warmth had fled her friend. Closing her eyes, she remembered Jasmine as she'd been —passionate and strong, unyielding, unrelenting, never willing to back down.

"Goodbye, Jas," she said.

Liz stood then, her eyes still closed. She didn't open them until she'd turned away. Maria sat waiting on a nearby log, and Liz strode across to join her.

"I'm sorry for your friend, Liz," Maria offered in a low voice.

Liz took a seat beside the old woman. "Thank you, Maria." She sighed and looked away. "Curfew's over now. I should take you to the next safe house."

"That could be difficult," Maria replied. "Given I don't know its whereabouts."

"What?" Liz's head jerked up.

Maria offered a sad smile. "You didn't think I was going to let you go after my grandson's killer without me, did you?"

"You were planning on coming with us?" Liz asked incredulously. When Maria only shrugged, she swore. "I guess it doesn't matter now, anyway. I'll take you to Independence Square, then.

You can wave down some of the Madwomen when they're leaving."

"No." Liz raised an eyebrow at the tone in Maria's voice. The old woman sat staring off into the distance, to some unseen place beyond the tree branches. "I'm not going back," she continued.

Liz shifted nervously on the leaf-strewn ground. "I don't understand. Where will you go?"

Taking the handgun from the log, Maria drew back the rack and released it, chambering a round. "I had it in mind to kill the woman who murdered my grandson."

Liz blinked. "And how do you intend to do that?"

Maria grinned. "So you didn't hear the last thing Doctor Reid said, before he died?"

"What?" Liz's heart began to hammer.

Laughing, Maria set aside the gun and lifted the grenade belt. There were still five grenades left. "I know where the Director is hiding."

Liz's chest tightened. "Where?"

"It won't be easy, getting to her," Maria said, her face turning serious. "You and Mira will have to carry me."

"Carry you?" Liz asked, confused. "But...you can't come."

It was Maria's turn to raise an eyebrow. "And why not?"

Liz blanked. Her mouth opened and closed like a fish out of water. Finally, she managed to stammer, "You're...you're too old!"

To Liz's surprise, Maria threw back her head and laughed. Liz winced, but after a few seconds the laughter died away. Maria wiped tears from her eyes. "Oh, my dear," she said, "you don't pull your punches, do you?"

Not having an answer, Liz decided it was best to keep her mouth shut this time.

Maria chuckled. "You're right, of course." She still held the grenades in her hand. "But then, you would have never made it out of the house without me."

"Yes, but—"

"They trained us all to be soldiers, you know," Maria said over her objection. "Back in the war. The men all went off to battle, but we never knew what would happen next, if the US would send troops behind the front lines to invade our cities. So even we regular citizens had to train, to ready ourselves, in case the fight ever came to us."

"You'll only hold me back, Maria," Liz argued. "Even the men back at the safe house, they would only slow me down."

"Perhaps," Maria replied, "but then, this fight won't be won by brawn alone. The Director is cunning, ruthless. Do you really intend to take her on all by yourself?"

"I won't be alone." Liz gestured at Mira. "You think she'd let me go without her?"

At that, Mira looked up. She wandered across to them and sat in Liz's lap. After a few seconds of wriggling, she leaned against Liz's chest and closed her eyes.

"We'll make them pay, Liz," she murmured sleepily.

Liz stroked the soft down of Mira's wings. "We will, kid."

"I think you'll find I'm just as stubborn as that one," Maria announced into the silence that followed.

A long moment stretched out as Liz and Maria held each other's gaze, testing one another's resolve. Finally, Liz sighed. In truth, she didn't *want* to go alone. She prayed Sam was still out there somewhere, but she had no idea how to find him. Trying would take precious time—time they didn't have. Every day they waited was another chance they gave the government to wipe them out.

Even so, bringing Maria wasn't an option. Chris would have her head if she let his grandmother walk into the middle of a government stronghold.

"Maria, I can't…Chris…"

"Is gone." Maria reached out and gripped Liz by the arm. "Don't you see, Liz? I have to do this. I've lost *everything* because of that woman—my home, my daughter, my grandson. I have nothing left to lose. So let me do this. Let me do *something* to put things right. If I have to die, let my death have meaning." She smiled then. "Besides, you might need someone with a cool head if you're going to break into The Rock."

It took several seconds for the old woman's words to sink in.

Liz stared at Maria, her mouth hanging open, a chill spreading through her chest. Her fingers dug into the cold dirt as she struggled to steady herself.

"You're saying…you're saying the Director is in Alcatraz?"

Maria grinned. "Aren't you glad you'll have company?"

✥ 17 ✥

Chris staggered to a stop as a wave of putrid air struck him like a blow. Bending in two, he breathed through his mouth as a keen wailing carried through the open door. Ahead, even the Director had halted, overwhelmed by the sight that greeted her. Only the man beside her seemed unaffected.

Striding past the massive steel door, the President surveyed the rows of cells before turning to stare at the Director. His jaw clenched and there was anger in his hazel eyes. Despite his greying hair, his skin was unmarked by age, and there was no mistaking the power he carried in his massive shoulders. This was a man who ruled with an iron fist, who for over twenty years as President had faced challenges from friend and foe alike, and left them all for dead.

He was not a man one crossed lightly.

Watching him now, Chris couldn't help but suspect the Director's position was teetering on the brink of oblivion.

"Seventy five percent mortality, you said?" the President asked.

The Director's face was pale. Chris had never seen her so rattled, but at the President's words she straightened. Pushing the hair back from her face, she nodded. "Yes."

"Halt's mortality rate was forty percent," he murmured, his

voice so low even Chris had to strain to hear him. "What happened?"

Swallowing, the Director glanced around as though searching for someone to blame. "The doctors in his facility...they modified the virus before the *Chead* came. They thought they'd managed to prevent host immune systems from rejecting the virus. But the modifications, they..." Grimacing, she gestured at the cellblock, apparently lost for words.

The President started down the hallway without saying another word. The Director trotted after him, Chris and Ashley following close behind.

"They were correct—the virus was undetectable to their immune systems," the Director was saying now, her voice emotionless. "Accelerated viral reproduction rates meant it spread through their bodies in a matter of hours. The problems started post integration..." She trailed off, her eyes flicking into the nearest cell.

Within, the fit, healthy teenagers they'd seen just yesterday lay dead. Some had collapsed against the bars, their hands stretched out in desperate beseechment. Others had never moved from where they'd fallen after receiving the injection. A few had managed to drag themselves to the toilet in the back of their cells, where they'd thrown up bile and blood, before surrendering to the inevitable.

Among the dead, the few living still writhed in helpless agony, their foreheads beaded by sweat, their moans whispering through the cellblock like the voices of ghosts. They lay in their beds, on the concrete, in each other's arms, each just barely clinging to life.

The doctors were already present, masks covering their faces as they went from survivor to survivor. Guards went with them, lending their strength to the grim task of removing the dead.

"Once the virus was integrated, their immune systems could no longer recognize their own cells," the Director was saying. "Fallow's strain of the virus apparently reprogrammed the host's immune system, so the altered cells wouldn't be rejected. However, the process takes time to establish, until which time their immune systems continue to attack the altered cells. Inadvertently, the immunosuppressants Fallow's candidates were given prevented this from happening."

"And the candidates are still alive?" the President snapped.

"It appears…it appears only those with ineffective or compromised immune systems survived the change."

"This is unacceptable, Director," the President said, continuing his march along the corridor. "I expected more from you. We need these creatures. The public was buoyed by our initial presentation, but perceptions are changing. We need a symbol of hope, before the *Chead* become any more disruptive."

"Why the rush?" the Director countered. "This could have been avoided if we'd been given time. The Madwomen are certainly no longer a threat. The idiot doctor that snuck out on the shipping barge led us to another safe house last night. Their numbers are dwindling." She hesitated. "Or is it the *Chead* that concern you? Surely you cannot believe the rumors?"

The President snorted. "No, I have sent our best recruits to deal with that overblown gossip. They've tracked a group on our infrared satellites. They'll make short work of them."

"Best recruits?" the Director questioned.

"Yes. Did you think I had entrusted you with *all* the conscripts?" he asked. "And no, it's not the *Chead* that concern me—it's Mexico. They've stayed neutral until now, but they're calling for an investigation into our claims concerning the *Chead* and Texas. There are some who claim they have proof *we* are behind the plague."

"I told you, that was taken care of at the university," the Director replied demurely. She leaned her head to the side and smiled. "As for proof of *Texas's* involvement, I have made headway in that matter."

"Tell me."

The Director strode on, seeming to regain confidence with every step. "The spy is ready to talk. I have scheduled a conference for tomorrow morning. He'll confirm the Lone Star State created the *Chead*, and that he played a role seeding it into our food chain."

"It won't be enough," the President interjected.

"Perhaps not, but it should buy us time." The Director gestured into one of the cells. Inside, a girl was being attended to by one of the doctors. "We still have forty-odd candidates left. In a few days they'll be ready for the homeotic activator injection. You'll have your symbol."

"It's an army I need, Director," the President pressed.

The Director leaned against the bars of the cell and looked up at the towering man. "Bring me more candidates, and you'll have it."

At that, she started down the corridor towards the exit. Shaking his head, the President followed her, his anger apparently mollified. Chris went with them, until he realized Ashley had stopped outside the open door to the girl's cell. He continued a few more steps before coming to a stop. Cursing under his breath, he darted back towards Ashley.

"Ash, what are you doing?" he hissed.

Ashley disappeared into the cell before he could reach her. Glancing back, Chris found the Director watching him, her brow hard, arms crossed, and he staggered to a stop. Beside her, the President's face remained expressionless.

Swallowing, Chris moved to the door of the cell. Inside, Ashley had shoved the doctor back and was kneeling beside the bed. The girl's eyes were open, but there was a faraway look to them. She was mumbling under her breath, a string of nonsensical words interspersed with occasional curses.

"Please...don't want to...where am I...are my parents...the *Chead!*" She shuddered and her eyes suddenly focused on Ashley's face. "Who are you?" she croaked.

Ashley stroked her hair. "It's okay." Her voice cracked as she spoke. "You're going to be okay."

A shudder went through the girl. Her eyes rolled back into her skull and she began to convulse. The doctor quickly returned to her side as Ashley stepped back, her face a mask of horror. Chris looked away as a needle was pressed into the girl's neck. When he looked back again she'd stilled, though her teeth were still clenched and her chest rattled with each breath.

"Get out of there." Chris jumped as the Director's voice came from behind him.

Ashley looked up from where she still knelt on the concrete. Her eyes shone as she stood and stepped towards the Director. Seeing the strange glow to her eyes, Chris retreated from her path. He had seen that look on her face before—back in the university, when she'd beaten Paul into submission without breaking a sweat.

"This is my fault," Ashley said as she emerged from the cell.

Chris stood on the far side of the corridor as Ashley faced the President and the Director. The two had taken a step back at her appearance. Apparently, he wasn't the only one who'd noticed the change. Her eyes might not have turned grey, but there was clearly *something* different about her.

"I should never have let Sam do it," Ashley continued, starting towards the Director. A tear spilled down her cheek. "I should have died."

"Stay back." There was fear in the Director's voice.

When Ashley didn't stop, the woman pressed a finger to her watch. Ashley flinched as her collar lit up, but to Chris's shock, she didn't collapse. Baring her teeth, Ashley took another step, a low growl rasping up from her throat.

"I. Won't. Let. You. Do. This," Ashley panted, each step slow now, as though she were wading through a swamp.

The color drained from the Director's face as she tapped her watch again. The President started backing towards the door, but the Director stood her ground, scowling as she played with the settings on her controller watch.

Fists clenched so tight her knuckles had turned white, Ashley continued to advance. The tendons in her neck stood up like iron cables as the collar around her throat flashed red. It made no sound, and Chris could only guess how much electricity was flowing through Ashley's tiny body.

Finally, the Director retreated a pace, but she was so focused on her watch that her feet tripped. She cried out, crashing to the floor. Ashley's eyes glowed and redoubling her efforts, she reached for the Director's throat.

On the floor, the Director screamed and slammed her palm down on her watch. Chris's collar gave a shrill beep. He had a split second to realize she'd activated a panic button, before a ripple of electricity coursed through his body, worse than any he'd felt before. His jaw locked in place, silencing the scream in his throat, and he dropped to the floor, paralyzed. From the corner of his eye he saw Ashley fall, finally overwhelmed by the collar's power.

The collar's bite ceased within a few seconds, but it took a long moment for Chris's senses to return. He lay on his back, dark spots dancing across his vision, the brilliance of the fluorescent lights drilling into his skull like sharp screws. Finally, he groaned and forced himself to sit up, though it only made the pounding in his head worse. Fire wrapped around his throat as he swallowed.

His eyes settled on Ashley. She lay on the ground nearby, her wings splayed out around her, her scarlet hair tangled in the white feathers. Her breath came in short gasps and every few seconds her body spasmed, her back arching against the concrete. A light still flashed on her collar, but as the Director walked up and tapped her watch, it clicked off. Ashley's body relaxed with a sigh.

"I'm disappointed, Director." The President had almost reached the exit to the prison block, but he approached again now, one cautious eye on Ashley. "I had expected your pets to be under control by now."

The Director scowled, obviously trying to cover her fear, though her hands were still shaking. "They're not my pets," she snapped, still staring at Ashley. "They're Halt's. His methods made them feral."

"Yes, well, you had best improve with the next batch—or I might begin to question whether you're truly the best candidate for this position." He strode out the open door, leaving Chris alone in the corridor with the Director and the unconscious Ashley.

Fear twisted around Chris's heart. Holding his breath, he

forced himself to look at the Director, steeling himself for what was to come.

The woman still stood over Ashley. "You disappoint me," she said, her eyes catching his. "I expected more of you. After yesterday, I thought you were ready. Now, I wonder if you ever will be."

She stared at him until Chris lowered his gaze, unable to match the power in her eyes. Huddled on the ground, he tried to find his voice, and failed. The sound of marching boots came from the entrance to the prison block as guards raced towards them, having apparently been summoned back from body disposal duty.

"Take her to my room," the Director snapped, waving at Ashley. Turning, she looked down at Chris. "I'm done with you for the day. The guards will escort you. I will deal with you both tonight."

Chris glanced at Ashley, then back at the Director, hesitating.

"*Go!*" she snapped.

Chris went.

18

Susan fell back against the gravel, Hecate's weight pressing down on her. His mouth met hers, their tongues entwining. Wrapping her arms around his powerful shoulders, she pulled him closer, digging her nails into his back like claws. Their lips separated and she gasped, sucking in a fresh lungful of air. The tang of blood lingered in her nostrils, fueling her lust.

She shuddered as Hecate's lips moved to her neck. His long black hair hung across her face, and she could feel his power, sense his desperate desire—though it was tempered with caution now, by the need to shelter her swollen belly.

But the life growing within Susan had not stemmed her lust, and she gripped Hecate by the waist and toppled him. Straddling him before he could sit up, she leaned down and nipped at the soft flesh of his neck. He shivered and pulled her to him. She went gladly, sliding down, burning with heat, with desire.

Susan gasped as he entered her, her hips thrusting down to draw him deeper inside. A wild howling filled the cavern as their bodies moved in concert, driving each other to greater and greater heights. Her hands tangled in Hecate's long hair, Susan threw back her head and screamed her ecstasy.

Pressure built in her stomach as Hecate grabbed her by the hips. Before she could react, he lifted Susan and pushed her to her hands and knees. Crouching there, Susan trembled, waiting for him to claim her.

His arms went around her from behind, stroking her flesh, circling the sensitive points of her nipples. A rumble came from her chest, a warning for her mate to be quick, to sate her growing need. Hecate's laughter whispered in her ear as he slid between her lips. She cried out as he began to thrust, edging him to higher passions, and they both gave way to the desires of the *Chead* within…

Afterwards, they lay in each other's arms, the rush of their passion slowly draining away. Susan lay with her head on Hecate's chest, listening to the quick pounding of his heart. Her hands drifted to her stomach, and she shivered as her children kicked. She took Hecate's hand and placed it on her naked belly.

A protective growl came from his chest. Smiling, Susan wriggled closer to her mate.

Safe.

They had travelled through the rest of the night to reach the home caverns. It had been a long journey, and for the first time since her rebirth, Susan had felt the cold touch of fear. Not for herself, but the children growing inside her.

But they had found no more soldiers waiting for them, no more explosions or bullets to tear away their lives. They had slipped into the outer tunnels as the first light of morning lit the sky, traveling the final miles in the darkness, relying on scent and sound and touch rather than sight. Talisa and her people knew the way, but even Susan could have followed the scent home. The cloying sweetness of the *Chead* had grown stronger with every passing mile, until the tunnels finally opened out to reveal the great expanse of a limestone cavern.

It was there that Talisa's *Chead* had made their nest. Those who'd remained behind gathered around their returning brethren, offering food and water, while Hecate led Susan to where a crack in the cavern led to the antechamber that he had made his home.

Lying in his arms, Susan finally allowed herself to take it in. The *Chead* must have been raiding nearby settlements for some time, as Hecate had lit several candles when they'd first entered. The chamber was maybe ten feet wide, with smooth limestone walls and a gravel floor. Water trickled down the rock in a far corner, before disappearing beneath the stones. A pile of rags served as a bed, although in their haste it lay forgotten.

Home.

Susan frowned at the thought, her hand drifting again to her stomach. It would not be long now before her children took their first steps into the world. Would they truly be safe here, deep beneath the earth, while humanity roamed above? Could they truly prosper in a world where they were despised, where they would be hunted and killed on sight?

"My children..." Susan flinched as a voice spoke from the entrance to their chamber. She sat up as Talisa entered, the gravel crunching beneath her bare feet.

"Talisa," Hecate said, standing. "What brings you...here?"

Silently, Talisa took a seat on an outcropping of rock. It was the only place in the cavern to sit. Uncomfortably aware she was still naked, Susan's cheeks flushed as the woman's milky eyes settled on her. Though the ancient *Chead* appeared blind, Susan was sure by now she wasn't. But Hecate seemed unconcerned by her inspection of their bare bodies.

As though reading her thoughts, Talisa chuckled. "You forget, my child." Her voice whispered through the cave. "You are *Chead*. Your body holds no shame for us. Especially not with the precious gift you carry." She held out a wrinkled arm towards Susan.

Susan hesitated before taking it. Talisa pulled her to her feet, the old woman's strength belying her age. A shiver ran up Susan's spine as the *Chead* placed a cold hand on her swelling stomach.

"You are progressing well." A smile cracked her ancient face. "Soon your children will join with mine."

Susan grinned, joy washing away her fears.

Removing her hand, Talisa returned to her seat. She swayed as she sat, and for a second it seemed she might fall.

"Talisa." Hecate placed a steadying hand on her shoulder. "What is…wrong?"

"I am old, my child," Talisa said. "My time approaches. Soon I will be gone. It is the price we pay for our existence."

Susan's heart quickened and she wondered suddenly how long it would be before she faced the same fate. Talisa had said she'd been nearing fifty when the change came on her, but just a couple of years living as *Chead* had aged her decades. Susan was only thirty. Her best years should have been ahead of her. Now, she might be lucky to live another decade. Her stomach clenched at the thought.

Sensing her distress, Hecate returned to her. Bending down, he stroked her cheek. "My mate…" he breathed.

Her closed eyes at his touch, his scent stilling her racing heart. Drawing in a breath, Susan resolved to embrace her fate. At least as *Chead*, she could truly live. She might only have ten years, but they would be spent free of the shackles of humanity. Gone were her days locked in grey-walled rooms, far from the thrill of life.

"There is still time," Talisa continued, her voice strengthening. "Before I go, I intend to see my purpose fulfilled."

"Your purpose?" Susan pressed.

Talisa nodded. "Humanity has proven time and again they will not tolerate us. They will hunt us to extinction, stop at nothing to destroy us. I will not die while my children still face that threat."

"But how, Talisa?" Susan asked. "How can we defeat them? Our numbers have grown, but humanity is legion. In just one battle we lost a tenth of our fighters."

Beside her, Hecate hissed. Standing, Susan took his hand, feeling the tension radiating from him, the wild heat of his anger. All his life he had been imprisoned, tormented by the creatures she had once worked alongside.

"We must destroy…them all," he rumbled.

She shivered as the grey in Hecate's eyes darkened. Still fresh from the passion of battle, he was teetering on the brink. She stood on her toes and kissed him on his beard. Her hands went around his waist as she pressed her body against him. He blinked, looking down at her. Smiling demurely, she watched the darkness fade, to be replaced with hunger.

On her makeshift chair, Talisa laughed. "You are right, my child." She stood and wandered around the cave, her fingers trailing over the smooth rock. In the corner, a candle flickered as a slight breeze passed through the cave, its flame burning low.

"But we must not be reckless," Talisa went on. "As you say, our enemy is legion. Our people must have a chance to grow, before we face them in open battle."

"We will not…fight them?" Hecate hissed.

Turning, Talisa stared him down, her eyes aglow in the darkness. After a long moment, Hecate lowered his head in deference, and she went on, "Until now, they have been ignorant to our presence, but that is changing. If they come for us in strength, our people will be wiped away."

"What can…we do?" Susan asked softly.

Talisa watched her, a smile on her lips. "You did well, my child, capturing the woman."

"The woman?" Hecate's head whipped up. "She has… accepted the change?"

"No…" Talisa replied, "she has refused."

"Then she has joined her fellow humans?" Hecate questioned.

Talisa had finished her loop around the cavern and now stood before them again. "Patience, my child," she said. "The woman may yet prove…valuable. She is the first of their warriors we have captured."

"All the more…dangerous," Hecate growled. "You do not know…the things they are…capable of."

Talisa stilled. Face impassive, she stepped towards Hecate. She caught him by the throat before he could react and lifted him into the air. Stumbling back, Susan watched as Hecate's legs kicked uselessly at empty air.

"Do not question me," Talisa snapped.

With a flick of her wrist, she sent Hecate tumbling across the cave. He landed with a crunch of gravel near the entrance. Talisa didn't move as he climbed to his feet, a snarl on his lips. His eyes darkened, but before he could speak, Susan stepped between them again. She placed a hand on her mate's naked chest.

"Enough," she said, her eyes drilling into his.

Hecate stared back at her, and she saw the madness flickering there. Silently she held him in place, waiting for the rage to die. When he finally sighed and nodded, Susan stepped aside.

Bowing his head, Hecate approached Talisa. "Forgive me, Talisa," he murmured. "This is your…domain. You are…master here."

"Yes…" Talisa murmured, her eyes turning distant. "When I first came here, we were nothing. Only my strength has brought us together, has saved us from the hunters." She stared at the stone walls, as though seeking out each of the *Chead* she had gathered here beneath the earth. "Soon I shall die, and the fate of my children will pass to another." Her voice turned hard. "But not before I have carved them a nation from the bones of this earth."

"How?" Susan asked.

"With fire and fury," Talisa replied.

19

Slumped against the wall, Chris watched as the guards marched outside, leaving Ashley and him alone in the Director's apartment. On the other side of the room, Ashley's chest slowly rose and fell. Her face had softened, losing the tightness of pain, and she seemed to be sleeping now. Chris was relieved that she lived, though he could not help but curse his friend for her recklessness.

What were you thinking, Ash?

Shivering, Chris recalled the look in Ashley's eyes as she stalked towards the Director. In that moment, she had seemed unstoppable, as though no force on earth could prevent her from tearing out the woman's throat. He wondered what it had taken, how much electricity had coursed through Ashley's body to finally bring her down.

He had already tried and failed to understand what had happened. Her eyes had not turned grey, and when she'd spoken, it had still been Ashley. Yet there was no denying that a change *had* come over her, a shift that had allowed Ashley to resist the collar's bite like none of them ever had before.

A moan pulled Chris from his thoughts as Ashley rolled onto her side and sat up. The thick chain rattled, pulling her up short as she tried to stand. Blinking, she looked around, taking stock of their surroundings.

"What? Were we grounded?" she croaked, her throat sounding raw.

Chris scowled. "Hardly the time for jokes."

Ignoring him, Ashley crossed her legs and lay back against the wall. Her forehead creased and she closed her eyes, a grimace on her lips. "Ahhh…but that hurts." She reached up and touched her throat. The skin beneath her collar was inflamed, and she flinched as her fingers made contact.

"Are you okay?" Chris asked, his voice softening.

Ashley shrugged. "Better than those kids."

Chris bit his lip and quickly looked away, unable to face the accusation behind her words.

"I'm glad you're alive," he replied.

"For now." He looked back up, alarmed by her words, and she continued, "I doubt she'll want me around after that."

Chris started to argue, but she spoke over him. "I'm glad, really," she murmured, glancing at the door, as if expecting death to come marching through at any moment. "I don't know how much longer I could have lasted, screaming in the darkness, alone. Days, weeks, it doesn't matter, she would have broken me in the end." Ashley looked at him as she finished, her eyes sad.

"It doesn't have to end like this, Ash," Chris choked out.

"It does, Chris." Tears shimmered in Ashley's eyes as she smiled. "Don't you see? Death is my only way out now."

"But it's not," Chris cried, his voice growing loud. He gestured at the door. "Aren't you tired of putting everyone else first, Ash? Of sacrificing *everything* for others?"

He waited for a reply, but Ashley's eyes remained fixed on the ground, her scarlet hair hanging in greasy tangles across her face.

Baring his teeth, he continued, "What does defying her achieve, Ash? When has anything we've ever done changed things, for that matter? Every sacrifice we've made, everything we've given up, it's all been for nothing. Those students still died, the President is still in control, our parents, our families, they're still gone. Yet here we sit, in chains, suffering every night, not even allowed a bed to sleep in."

As he spoke, Chris felt a weight lifting from his shoulders, his guilt and regret falling away. Seeing Ashley, at her haggard face and sallow skin, her red-stained eyes and molting feathers, he shook his head.

"Look at what you've done to yourself, Ash, and for what?" he whispered.

There was pity in Ashley's eyes. "The Chris I used to know would understand."

"That Chris died with the kids at the university," Chris retorted.

She closed her eyes at that, and a tear dripped down her cheek. Regret twisted in Chris's stomach, but he could not take back the angry words. After all, they were the truth. Ever since they'd escaped, he'd been punished again and again for helping others. He couldn't do it any longer.

A long silence stretched out as they both sat staring into space, each stewing in their own private misery.

"You know what comes next, don't you, Chris?" Ashley asked softly.

Before he could respond, the door clicked and swung open. The Director strode inside, her face a carefully blank mask. Her eyes travelled around the room, lingering on Chris, then Ashley, before she let the door swing closed behind her. Her long legs carried her across to where Ashley crouched. Arms folded, she slowly shook her head.

"I cannot forgive this, my pet," she murmured.

Lips pursed, eyes defiant, Ashley didn't budge an inch. Chris waited, heart pounding, as the Director uncrossed her arms.

"That's it then? No excuses?" she whispered, then paused, as though waiting for a response. When none came, the Director nodded. "Very well. You have written your own fate. *Guards!*"

Chris flinched as her shout echoed around him. The door slid open and two men stepped inside and joined the Director.

"I've made my decision." She waved at the doorway. "Take her back to the cells. I'm tired of looking at her. She can spend the night with the other experiments she deemed so precious. In the morning I'll oversee her euthanization."

"*No!*" The scream tore from Chris's throat before he could stop himself. He lunged forward, but the chain brought him up short, and he cried out as the collar cut into his neck.

Ignoring him, the guards busied themselves detaching Ashley's chain from the ground, but the Director turned and walked towards him. Behind her, Ashley had slumped against the wall, her eyelids half-closed, her wings limp against her back. There was no mistaking her terror, but in her weakened state she made no effort to fight back.

One of the guards lifted the chain and gave it a tug. The chain went taut, pulling Ashley off-balance. She placed a hand down to steady herself, but the guard pulled again, half-dragging her across the floor. Coughing, she gripped the makeshift leash and yanked back. The guard stumbled, her strength taking him by surprise, but held on. Before she could try again, the other guard drove his steel-capped boot into the side of Ashley's head.

Still kneeling on the floor, Ashley couldn't avoid the blow, and the kick sent her reeling back into the wall. She made to sit up, but the guard delivered another kick to her stomach before she could recover. The breath hissed between Ashley's teeth and, gasping, she collapsed face-first to the ground. When she tried to crawl away, another boot caught her on the side of the head.

All semblance of resistance left Ashley then, as she slumped to the floor, unconscious. Taking up the chain, the guard dragged her towards the door. Half-starved and sleep deprived, Ashley couldn't have weighed more than a hundred pounds, and the man had no trouble lifting her. The second guard followed close behind.

Chris watched from his knees, the collar tight around his throat as he strained to intervene. Now, as he caught his last glimpse of Ashley before she disappeared into the corridor, he felt hot tears on his cheeks.

Why, Ashley? he screamed in his mind. *Why?*

"Christopher." He shuddered as the Director's voice came

from overhead. Swallowing his grief, Chris looked up and found her cold eyes on him.

"What?"

"You disappointed me today." His stomach swirled at the tone in her voice. "Perhaps you are less evolved than I thought. I'm of half a mind to send you after your friend."

A shiver ran down Chris's spine. Gone was the warmth she'd shown him yesterday—the Director meant what she said. He was teetering on the edge of a precipice: one wrong step, and he would tumble down into the abyss after his friend.

He lowered his eyes. "I'm sorry, ma'am," he breathed, "I…"

"Yes?" the Director pressed. "Tell me, what excuse do you have for your failure?"

Chris closed his eyes. "I have no excuse," he said, blinking back tears. "I should have…I should have protected you…" He trailed off, his voice fading to nothing, and bowed, exposing his neck as though awaiting execution.

Strong fingers gripped him by the chin and forced his head back up. The Director's lips were drawn tight, her brow hard. He flinched as her fingers dug into his flesh.

"Please," he gasped, unable to keep the fear from his voice, "I don't want to die."

The Director raised an eyebrow. "No?"

He shook his head, though his movement was restricted by her hold on his chin.

"Then perhaps you can redeem yourself." She tapped a finger to her control watch. It beeped and the chain fell away, though the cold embrace of his collar remained.

Standing, she offered him her hand. "Rise, Christopher."

Chris shivered as he looked up at her. A lead weight settled in his stomach. He knew what she was asking, what it would mean if he took her hand. It was a line that, once crossed, he could not return from. There would be no redemption.

He would be hers—body and soul.

But what choice did he have? To refuse was to join Ashley, to wait in a cell for the sun to rise, and the end to come. Even as he considered the idea, a gulf opened in his chest. With Ashley gone, he was truly alone now. Isolated from his friends, from his family, what darkness would he fall into?

Yet he would be alive. He would be safe, free of the torments Ashley had suffered. In that moment, he made his decision.

Chris took her hand, and rose.

❦ III ❦

VENGEANCE

20

Sam squinted into the darkness, his wings creaking as the San Francisco winds battered him. He was flying higher than he ever had before, and even his powerful muscles were struggling to keep his wings straight in the howling wind. They pushed him around like a ragdoll, but he only gritted his teeth and pressed on. He was almost there.

He had wanted to set out earlier, when there'd still been light in the sky. But the government had proven relentless—continuing its hunt for the fugitives all through the next day. So instead, he'd been forced to remain in the basement with Jocelyn and the other resistance fighters, listening to the buzzing of helicopters outside, his nerves growing more frayed by the hour.

Only when darkness fell once more did the hunters relent. Patrols still swept the streets, but the roaming helicopters had returned to their nests for the night. Sam had seen Jocelyn and the others safely out of the search grid, and then wished them luck. The fighters had waved him goodbye with grim faces—they all knew this would probably be the last time they saw each other.

One simply did not break into Alcatraz and expect to survive.

Despite the odds, Sam knew he had to try. They'd had no word from the Madwomen, no news about what had happened at the safe house. He didn't want to think about what that meant. He still clung to the hope that Liz, Jasmine and Mira had made it out, but he couldn't wait around to find out. The government was closing its net around the resistance, and if he delayed any longer, there might not be anyone left to fight for.

Unfortunately, a storm had broken with nightfall and now he was beginning to doubt he could even make it to the island. Another gust buffeted him. Tensing the muscles along his back, he trimmed his wings and drifted lower. Through the clouds, the dark waters of the harbor appeared. White-capped waves churned the surface as salt spray drifted upwards. Thunder clapped and a patch of rain swept past, soaking him to the skin.

Cursing, Sam searched the waters and finally found the orange glow of a lighthouse. As he flew closer, other shapes appeared from the darkness. Buildings rose from the steep cliffs of The Rock. The lighthouse was the tallest, and shifting direction, he headed towards it.

When he was still some twenty feet out, Sam glimpsed a guard on the observation deck atop the lighthouse. The man was leaning against the rails, squinting out through the pouring rain with a sour look on his face. He carried a rifle slung over one shoulder, but Sam had no intention of giving him a chance to use it.

Approaching from above, Sam ensured he was outside the guard's line of sight. When he was still several feet above the tower, he folded his wings and dropped from the sky. A gust of wind almost threw him off-course, but with a twist of his wings he recovered, and crashed down on the man's back. The impact of Sam's two hundred pounds drove the guard face-first into the railing.

Sam landed lightly and delivered another blow to the back of his victim's head for good measure. Then taking hold of the man's legs, he dragged him into the lighthouse tower and shoved him into the nearest closet.

Returning to the observation deck, Sam took a moment to assess his surroundings. His vantage point on the lighthouse gave him a view over half the island. Lightning flashed, illuminating the stark concrete walls and barred windows of the prison block. A dark shadow was all he could see of the entrance, but as the lightning died away, he saw the dim glint of solid steel doors.

His heart sank. Even with his considerable strength, he couldn't break through that. Shivering in the rain, he continued his examination of the island. To his right, the ground dropped away in a sheer cliff, but beyond he could just see the rooftop of another building below. From its open windows and plain walls, he guessed it was the residential quarter for staff.

Sam returned his attention to the main prison building. In the darkness, he could see no way to force his way inside. The grounds of the island were empty, without so much as a guard standing outside the main entrance. There might be others patrolling the island, but he guessed the majority were stationed within at night, where the real threat resided.

After all, Alcatraz had been reopened to contain the most dangerous criminals of the Western Allied States, the traitors and terrorists who posed a threat to their very way of life. Or so it was said. Now, of course, Sam knew better. The prisoners inside were likely no different from his parents—falsely accused, locked away without trial, sentenced to death for the crime of questioning the government.

His hands tightened on the railings as he studied the barred windows, wondering if he might force his way inside. But the bars were also solid steel, at least half an inch in diameter. He doubted he could do much more than dent them.

No, he would have to wait until someone came or went. When the doors were unlocked, he would make his move.

Retreating under the eaves of the lighthouse, he lowered himself to the steel deck and leaned against the wall behind him. Silently, he crossed his legs and settled in to wait out the night…

Sam snapped awake to the crash of thunder. Cursing, he sat up, the harsh light of dawn burning at his eyes. In the distance, waves crashed. As he stood, a gust of wind pushed him sideways and almost tore him from the deck. Above, the storm had built itself up into a fury.

A clang came from somewhere in the lighthouse and a voice

carried up. "Jerry! You fall asleep again?"

His heart pounding, Sam slid back inside the building. Cut off from the wind, he could hear the steady pounding of boots on the staircase now, approaching rapidly. He slipped across the room and peered over the rail into the stairwell. Below, a man was climbing the winding stairs.

Crouching in the shadows, Sam waited for the guard to come to him.

"Jerry, where you hiding, man?" the guard wheezed as he reached the top.

Sam didn't bother to reply. Leaping forward, he punched the man square in the chest, driving the air from his lungs and stealing his voice. A second blow to the head dropped the guard without a sound. Dragging his victim across to the closet, he tossed him in with his friend. The first man was beginning to stir, but another knock to the head returned him to sleep.

Stepping outside again, Sam crouched on the observation deck and looked back out over the island. Despite the storm, the sky was quickly brightening, and he cursed himself for falling asleep. He was more exhausted than he'd realized, but it was too late to reconsider his plans. It was now or never.

Movement near the residential block drew his attention. Squinting through the rain, he watched a group of three figures run from the building to a waiting golf cart. The three had barely scrambled into the vehicle before the driver took off. They went lurching along a muddy path before disappearing behind the lip of the cliff.

A few minutes later, the cart reappeared at the top of the cliffs, having wound its way up the road from below. Sam caught the distant whir of an electric engine as it settled back onto flat ground. His heart surged as he realized it was headed towards the prison. A clang came from somewhere below. Leaning out over the edge of the platform, Sam saw the prison doors swing open. Two men in blue uniforms matching the ones in his closet stepped out into the rain. Both carried rifles, but they appeared at ease. They walked a few steps through the mud and waved at the cart.

As the golf cart approached, Sam climbed onto the rails of the observation deck. He moved slowly so as not to draw the guards' attention, but they were too preoccupied with the vehicle to notice the winged boy atop the tower. Stretching his wings, Sam waited until the cart pulled to a stop in front of the prison, and then hurled himself from the lighthouse.

The passengers in the golf cart were just stepping off when he landed among them. He dropped the driver first, a blow to the man's neck sending him sprawling against the steering wheel. Spinning, he took in the empty hands of the three passengers and then leapt at the guards by the door.

They were still frozen in shock as he landed between them. One tried to lift his rifle, but Sam was already too close and a blow to his chest dropped him like a rock. The other turned and tried to make it through the steel doors. He managed two steps before Sam caught him by the collar and hauled him back. After finishing the man off with a cuff to the head, he turned his attention to the passengers.

There were two men and a woman. As he'd hoped, they were civilians, unarmed and clearly terrified by his sudden appearance. They flinched as he stepped towards them. Before any of them thought to shout for help, Sam darted forward and caught one by the shirt.

"Not a word, or you won't live to see tomorrow," he growled.

The man struggled to break free, until Sam lifted him into the air and shook him. His head lolled like a bobblehead doll's, and when Sam dropped him to the muddy ground, he didn't make a sound. Scrambling back towards his colleagues, he stared up at Sam, lips clamped shut.

Sam grinned. "Atta boy." He glared at the others, inviting them to try their luck, before continuing. "Good, you're quick learners. Do what I say, and you might just make it off this rock alive."

Eyes wide, the three of them stared back at him. After a moment's hesitation, each of them nodded.

"Great." Sam waved at the doorway. "Shall we get out of this rain, then?"

21

Stepping through the giant steel door, Sam found himself in a grim, bleach-white room. Steel beams reinforced the walls and ceilings above, while a series of unidentifiable grey stains marked the linoleum floor. A metal detector like those used in airports stood waiting, and beyond it, a steel bench stretched down the middle of what looked like a waiting room. To the right, a window looked into a guard booth. It was empty now, but behind the glass a computer screen displayed camera feeds from around the facility. One showed the ground outside where the unconscious guards still lay, another the room in which he was standing.

There was no one else in sight, but Sam doubted he'd seen the last of Alcatraz's guards. The cameras needed to go. One was on the ceiling, in the corner. He leapt up and tore it from the wall, then moved outside and did the same to the one outside. He hoped this would buy him a few extra minutes.

A new pair of double doors stood on the other side of the waiting room, but there was no obvious lock or handle on the steel panels.

"How do they open?" he asked his guides.

The woman swallowed and held up her arm. A familiar watch shone on her wrist.

"What's on the other side?" Sam pressed.

The woman hesitated, but any thought she had of lying evaporated as Sam stepped towards her. "The control room," she stammered. "There'll be more guards."

"How many?"

She only shook her head, her mouth hanging open, eyes wide. She'd obviously run out of words.

"It varies," the man Sam had attacked earlier answered in her stead. "Five, ten, depends who's on duty, what's happening with the prisoners and…" He trailed off, clearly realizing he'd said too much.

"And the experiments, right?" Sam snapped. His eyes narrowed and he stepped towards the group, wings trembling. "What exactly do you three do here?"

"We're…we're no one," the man stammered quickly.

Sam snorted. "I doubt that." He gestured to the watches they all wore. "I recognize those. Pack quite a punch with the right prisoners, don't they? Must be terrifying for you, having one of us free."

The three exchanged glances but wisely kept their mouths shut.

Scowling, Sam held out his hand. "Hand them over, all of you. *Now!*"

They obeyed, and Sam pocketed two of the watches, before nodding to the woman. "You, unlock the door for me." He held out the third watch.

The woman didn't move, and Sam stepped forward and grabbed her by the wrist. She yelped and tried to pull away, but he didn't budge. Shoving the watch into her trembling hands, he bared his teeth.

"Do it," he snapped.

Sobbing, the woman tapped a few buttons on the screen. With a groan, the doors started to open. Sam took back the watch and released the woman.

Sam started towards the double doors. "You might want to lock yourselves in the guard booth," he called over his shoulder.

"I'd say things are about to get ugly." Then he darted through the gap that had appeared between the doors.

"Problem with the camera, Je—"

A guard was speaking behind the opening doors, but his words were cut off as Sam leapt inside and drove his foot into the man's knee.

Screaming, the guard went down, but Sam was already moving past him. The room he found himself in was cluttered with desks and chairs. Old CRT monitors sat on the desks, and filing cabinets had been pushed up against the far wall. It looked more like a downtown office in San Francisco than a prison. Except for the men with guns.

They obviously hadn't been paying attention to the cameras before he'd disabled them, but their shock was already evaporating as Sam stepped around the fallen man. They scrambled backwards, putting tables and chairs between themselves and the intruder.

Darting forward, Sam glimpsed a window in the far wall. Behind the glass was a kind of visitor's room, with rows of steel tables and chairs—although Alcatraz hadn't allowed visitors in decades. Beyond the tables, thick steel bars separated the room from the prison proper.

But he was getting ahead of himself.

There were still half a dozen guards to deal with. Unlike those outside, these men only carried handguns, but the weapons would be no less deadly in the tight space.

Sam ducked behind a desk as the first guard opened fire. It was a thick wooden thing, probably weighing forty pounds, and offered plenty of shelter. But Sam wasn't about to let them pin him down. Gripping it in both hands, he gritted his teeth and sent it flying across the room.

It slammed down among the guards, crushing one and scattering the rest. The momentary panic was all Sam needed to reach them. Even without his special gifts, he was larger than most men. Add two extra limbs, enhanced strength and reaction times, and the men were hopelessly outmatched.

As one raised his gun, Sam's wingtip flashed out and sent it flying. At the same time, he kicked out at another guard, hurling him into the window. To Sam's surprise, the glass didn't so much as crack, and the man slumped to the floor with a moan.

A gunshot rang out and Sam ducked as a bullet whizzed past. Hurling himself sideways, he tackled another guard, knowing if he stood still they would have him. He used his momentum to pick up the man and charge the gunman. The guard in his arms screamed before the three of them crashed together and they went down in a pile of thrashing arms and legs.

On the ground, Sam was hidden from the last gunman. He finished the two men with a few solid blows, catching a fist to the jaw in the process. Then he rolled to his knees and sprang, his wings beating down to carry him across the room, seeking out the final guard. A flash of movement came from Sam's left as the man rushed for a red panel in the corner, but when he glanced back and saw Sam bearing down on him, he stumbled and fell.

Sam was on him before he had a chance to recover, dragging him away from what must be the alarm. The man groaned and tried to fight him off until Sam punched him squarely in the stomach. Gasping, the man's face turned white as he strained to suck in a winded breath.

Crossing his arms, Sam took a moment to survey the room. None of the other men were moving, and satisfied, he turned his attention back to his new captive.

"Listen very closely," he whispered, leaning in. "I'm not going to kill you—even if you probably deserve it. Well, not so long as you cooperate."

The man had finally managed to catch his breath. Jaw clenched, he shook his head.

Sam sighed and caught the guard by the wrist. Grasping one of his fingers, he began to bend it backwards.

"A colleague of yours taught me this," he said conversationally. The guard tried to bat him away with his free hand, but Sam was implacable. "Doctor Halt. I don't suppose you know him."

The guard screamed as his finger snapped with a sickening *crack*. He tried to break away, but Sam caught him by the throat and pulled him forward.

"Listen up," he snapped, his face less than an inch from his prisoner's, "I don't have time to mess around. Next thing I break will be your arm. Now, tell me, how do I release all the prisoners up here?"

The guard stared back at him, mouth open. "What?" he croaked, aghast.

"You heard me," Sam said dangerously. "I've seen those prison movies. There's far too many cells in Alcatraz to open them all manually. You must have electronic locks. So where's the button?"

The guard swallowed. "You're insane. Don't you know... who's in there?"

"Traitors? Terrorists? The worst of the worst? Or so I'm told," Sam replied. "Seems like a fun bunch. So, how do I let them out?"

It looked like the man would refuse, but he quickly gave in when Sam gripped him by the elbow and started to twist. Sam dragged him across the room to a computer, and watched as the man navigated through the menus, ensuring he didn't set off any alarms. Sam had never used a computer before, and he was quickly lost in the complexity of the system, but his captive didn't know that. Finally, the option to "open prison cells" popped up on the screen. With a last fearful look at Sam, the man pressed the "okay" button.

The distant rattling of steel wheels came from the window to the prison. Sam gave the man a tap on the head, knocking him face-first into the computer. Leaving him unconscious at the desk, Sam strode into the visitor's room and onwards through the chain-wire gate into the prison block.

Striding across the concrete floor, Sam watched as the first prisoners stepped hesitantly from their cells. They looked around at each other, eyes wide and shoulders hunched, as though anticipating a trap. Sam rubbed his jaw where the guard had struck him and waited for them to notice him.

Each wore an orange jumpsuit, although many were worn with age. The inmates were in poor shape, their eyes sunken pits in starvation-ravaged faces, more skin and bone than human.

"Welcome to the greatest prison break in history," Sam boomed when he thought enough prisoners had emerged from their iron shells.

As one, the men and women looked around. Their confusion turned to open fear as he spread his copper wings. A few darted back into their cells, while the others sank to their knees.

When no one spoke, Sam went on. "I mean all of you, in case that wasn't clear." He gestured at the open door behind him. "The guards are unconscious. You'll want to take their guns before you go overrunning the rest of the island. Don't kill too many people. Or do, I don't care, they probably deserve it."

The prisoners still didn't move. Rolling his eyes, Sam started forward. There were two levels to the prison, with cells on the ground floor as well as a second level of cells attached to a boardwalk above. He strode down the narrow lane between the two blocks. The men and women shrank back as he approached, but he ignored them now. The prisoners were just a distraction—though he was glad he'd helped them. Conditions obviously weren't exactly humane in Alcatraz, and he doubted many were the criminals the government claimed them to be.

No, these people were like his own parents, arrested for unfounded suspicions of treason—or for merely being related to someone accused. They were all older, at least in their thirties, and he supposed that in a way, they were the lucky ones. It was their children, rather than themselves, who would be tortured and experimented on, forced to fight and suffer and kill just to survive.

Children like himself.

He shuddered at the memories and focused on the task at hand. Ahead, an old elevator with iron grating for doors loomed in the wall. It was a far cry from modern, but he guessed the government had wanted it to blend in with the dated architecture of Alcatraz. If one didn't know the prison's history, one could easily believe it had always been there.

Pulling open the iron grate, Sam stepped inside. There were only two buttons. He pressed the bottom and yanked the iron grate shut again. Somewhere above, a motor ground into gear.

The elevator lurched and began to descend. Turning, Sam looked through the iron grating at the dimly-lit prison.

Several hundred faces stared back.

Grinning, he gave two thumbs up as he slowly dropped from view.

Then he was alone in the darkness.

22

Liz shivered as she dropped through the clouds. The rain had long ago seeped through her clothes, soaking her to the skin. The flight had been a rough one, but at least it had been short. They'd spent the day building a pyre for Jasmine—placing her body inside the battered car and filling it with dried branches. With the fall of night, Liz, Mira and Maria had said their final farewells, and then set the car alight. They had fled the park as the first downpour broke over the city.

But they had not anticipated the storm. Liz had only managed to fly a few blocks with Maria on her back before the powerful winds forced her down. And so they had traversed the winding hills of San Francisco by foot. Fortunately, Chris's grandmother was fit for her age, and it wasn't until they reached the harbor that Liz had to carry her again.

Now, Liz's wings creaked as she drifted down through the storm. The wind tore at her feathers, forcing her to retract her wings as close to her body as possible or have them torn off. On her back, Maria clung to her shoulders, further hampering her maneuverability. The old woman might only weigh a hundred and twenty pounds, but Liz was already counting the minutes, trying to estimate how much of the one mile between the mainland and the island remained.

At least the storm hid them from prying eyes. With a thick fog hanging over the harbor, Liz could not make out the distant beacon of the lighthouse. Even Mira, swooping through the clouds somewhere to her right, was barely visible. Maria had given the girl the handgun and grenades to carry, but while Liz was glad to be relieved of the extra weight, the thought of Mira with explosives made her more than a little nervous.

Finally, Liz decided they had to be close. Tucking in her wings, she drifted down through the clouds. Slowly the fog cleared, and she saw the waves crashing against stony cliffs.

Bingo.

She frowned as her keen eyes made out figures moving across the open ground. Hundreds of people were pouring from the main building in the middle of the island. Their orange jumpsuits stood out against the muddy ground as they swarmed across Alcatraz.

What the hell is going on down here?

With the howling wind, there was no time to ask Maria her opinion, and angling down, Liz searched for a place to land. She settled on the lighthouse. Standing several stories aboveground with only one entrance, it would be easily defensible if those below proved dangerous.

Although it looked for all the world like the prisoners had somehow broken free of their cells.

She scanned the walkway at the top of the lighthouse as she swooped down, but there was no sign of movement and she landed quickly, Mira just a wingbeat behind her.

"Who were those people?" Maria shouted over the wind as she staggered down off Liz's back.

"They looked like inmates," Liz yelled back.

The old woman nodded, then smiled at Mira, who promptly tossed her the grenade belt. Liz's heart lurched in her chest as the explosives tumbled through the air, but Maria caught them calmly. Looping the belt over her shoulder, she raised an eyebrow at Mira.

"Cheeky."

Before Mira could reply, the distant whine of a siren carried across the island. Liz looked down as lights flashed above the entrance to the prison.

"What now?" Maria asked.

"You tell me," Liz shot back. "You're meant to be the brains, remember?"

The old women pursed her lips but did not reply. Liz sighed. All they had to go on was one word—Alcatraz. That was all the doctor had managed before life fled his broken body. Which meant from this point on, they were going in blind.

"Let's take a closer look at those prisoners," Maria said finally.

The same thought had occurred to Liz, though she still couldn't make heads or tails of what was going on. If the people they'd seen were really The Rock's inmates, how had they escaped their cells? It couldn't be a coincidence.

They took the stairs two at a time and rushed across the muddy field towards the prison. Liz scanned the rooftops as they went, alert for prowling guards. Ahead, the open doors to the prison beckoned.

Halfway across the muddy ground, a barrage of gunshots rang out, bringing them to a panicked halt. Ducking, Liz swung around, seeking out the shooter. The last of the orange-garbed figures were disappearing around the corner of the prison building, but otherwise there was no sign of movement. Whoever was shooting, they weren't aiming at the three of them.

They started out again, crossing the last few yards to the entrance. Liz took the lead, stepping inside and scanning the room, still expecting bullets to come hissing out of the shadows. Instead, she found half a dozen guards piled against the far wall, their hands cuffed behind their backs and mouths stuffed with rags.

What the hell is going on?

Liz glanced at Maria and raised an eyebrow, but Chris's grandmother had already crossed the room and was staring through a window into what seemed like a tiny guard booth.

Two men and a woman stood on the other side of the glass. It was obvious that the group of prisoners who'd just left had tried unsuccessfully to get to them. The steel door had taken a beating and cracks crisscrossed the window. Only the wire reinforcing had held it together.

Joining Maria, Liz contemplated the door, before giving it a solid kick near the handle. It slammed open with the shriek of tearing metal. The three inside screamed and tried to climb over each other to get away. Stepping in, Liz grabbed the first one and hauled him out.

Tossing him to the floor, she pinned him beneath her foot. "What happened here?"

The man blanked, looking too terrified to speak.

Liz crouched beside him. "I suggest you tell me." She nodded in the direction the prisoners had taken. "Unless you want me to go fetch your friends out there."

"No…no," he stuttered. Blinking, he looked at Liz as though seeing her for the first time. His eyes settled on her wings. "Your…friend, he's already gone below."

"My friend?"

"Yes, the boy, with the copper wings…the one from the television. I assume—"

Liz hit him in the head before he could finish, knocking him unconscious. She'd heard enough.

So, this was Sam's doing. He was alive and already well ahead of them. But unlike her, Sam was alone. She shook her head at his hypocrisy for telling her to be careful and then doing this.

So much for not going off like Rambo, Sam.

More red lights were flashing as they made their way into the prison block. Marching past empty cells, Liz clenched her fists, the sight of the bunk beds inside summoning all-too-vivid memories of her own time behind bars. Taking a breath, she tried to banish the feelings of helplessness. She was strong now, strong enough for whatever waited within.

Ahead, she could see the steel grating of an elevator and guessed that was where Sam had gone. The government seemed to enjoy hiding things underground. Bracketed by Mira and Maria, she pressed the call button. An engine whirred and the cable beyond the grating began to move, raising the cart back to their level. It took long minutes, and Liz didn't waste any time pulling open the iron grate when it arrived. She stabbed the down button.

"Sam's here. How is Sam here?" she muttered as they lurched downward, more to herself than the others.

Maria shook her head. "Had to have been the doctor's wife. Somehow, she must have found out where her husband worked. I wonder if Sam brought the men he went with. We could use the extra firepower."

"I don't think so." Liz eyed the concrete scrolling past. "A boat wouldn't have made it in that storm, and he can't have carried them all. Either way, it looks like the Director might be the one who's outgunned."

Maria pursed her lips. "We'll see."

The elevator *dinged*. Gathering herself, Liz yanked open the steel grate and leapt into the corridor outside.

And froze.

The corridor might have been a replica of their facility back in the mountains, or the one below San Francisco, for that matter. A stark white hallway stretched away from them, lined on either side by steel doors.

Only this corridor was littered with broken bodies. Blood and bullet holes splattered the white walls, and a distant chorus of moans and shrieks came from the fallen. Some were slumped against the walls, while others lay face down, their limbs bent at awkward angles. Most seemed to be alive, although a few lay deathly still, their faces drained of color. None of them looked like they'd be getting up any time soon.

Liz swallowed hard. Her heart pounded against her ribcage and she took a deep breath, trying to calm herself. A cool breeze filtered down the corridor as the air ducts sucked up the humid air from the elevator shaft. It carried with it a strangely familiar aroma. She frowned, lifting her head, trying to recall the scent.

Finally, she shook her head and started down the corridor after Sam.

"Save some for me, Rambo."

23

Chris stood in silence as the guards wheeled Mike into the room. He had lost more weight in the last few days, and now his eyes were little more than dark pits in the purple and blue mess that was his face. He made no effort to look around while the guards parked his wheelchair in front of the cameras. Not that he had any chance of escaping. His arms and legs had been cuffed to his chair.

Watching the Texan, Chris tried and failed to feel pity for the spy. After all, hadn't it been Mike's own carelessness that had gotten him—and ultimately Chris—caught? Wasn't it his fault that Chris now found himself standing there with the Director, used and broken, all alone in the world?

No, let the man make his confession and pay the price for his treachery. At least *his* torment was almost over. For Chris, there was no such hope.

Chris looked dispassionately around the room. The Director sat on a stool beside him, allowing a young woman to apply fresh makeup to her polished face. On her other side, a familiar face was going over notes with her. Chris had glimpsed Jonathan several times while in the facility, but the two had never made contact.

When he'd first discovered the man's betrayal, Chris had

been enraged. Now though, he could only stare in silence at Jonathan, unable to summon the will to care. For his own part, Jonathan treated Chris with studied indifference—though it would be difficult to recognize Chris behind his steel helmet and visor.

Nearby, the film crew was busy setting up. Large cameras and an entire wall of computer equipment were needed to make the broadcast. The Director intended to send a signal to the whole world this time.

The soldiers were busy making sure the brakes on Mike's wheelchair were properly secured. Beside the man, two vials of clear liquid and a jet-injector waited on a steel tray. A memory flashed before Chris's eyes—of a boy, writhing on the floor, dying in agony.

In his chair, Mike's eyes fluttered as he lifted his head. Squinting against the bright lights, he looked around, as though seeking out a friendly face among those who had gathered to watch him die.

"Christopher."

Chris swung around as the Director called him. His heart started to race as she waved away the makeup girl. Stepping from her chair, she tugged at Chris's helmet. It came away with a click. She placed it on a nearby bench, then leaned in and kissed him.

A moan whispered from Chris's mouth as the void in his stomach widened. But despite his shame, he kissed her back, struggling to blot out the memories of the night before.

When the Director finally withdrew, there was a smile on her lips. "Good boy," she said softly, stroking his cheek. "Keep an eye on our guest. We're almost ready for the show."

She moved away, and Chris crossed the room to stand in front of Mike.

"What has she done to you, Chris?" the Texan mumbled.

Chris looked down. He had no answer to that. His tension grew as the door clicked and swung open, but it was only one of the doctors arriving for duty. The woman crossed the room and began inspecting the equipment on the tray.

"Is everything in order, Doctor?" the Director asked.

The woman nodded nervously. "Before we begin…there's been a new development with the subjects—"

The Director waved a hand before she could finish. "Whatever it is, I'm sure your people are on top of it, Doctor. Or did I place the wrong person in charge?"

The doctor swallowed and opened her mouth as though to object, before apparently thinking better of it. "Yes, ma'am." She nodded. "I've left…instructions for the day staff. They should be arriving shortly."

Silently, Chris wondered what the problem was. For half a second his thoughts turned to Ashley, locked in the cells with the other subjects, before his mind shut down the thought.

She's gone. He repeated the words in his head. *Gone.*

"Excellent." The Director clapped her hands and faced the film crew. "Shall we begin?"

The men with the cameras quickly moved into position. Chris retreated to the far wall, putting himself out of sight. There he folded his arms and watched in silence, happy for once to be no more than a spectator to the coming horror. The cameraman held up five fingers and quickly counted down to zero.

"My fellow citizens of the Western Allied States," the Director began, as a red bulb lit up on the equipment. "It saddens me to come to you in such grave times, when the very future of our great nation is under threat. Beyond our borders, enemies conspire against us, working their vile plots to sow dissent and terror."

"And yet, their efforts have only brought us closer together. Their hatred has made us stronger. Long may we continue to see the WAS as one country, one nation united against the chaos of the independent states. Let the cowards of the Lone Star State conspire. Let them send their monsters, their spies, their soldiers. Together, we will send them all screaming back into the holes they crawled out of."

She paused, then crossed the room until she stood beside Mike. The camera panned, revealing the broken man to the nation, and the world. Sagging in his chair, the Texan looked up with red-stained eyes. His lips parted, as though to speak, but after a long moment he only bowed his head again.

The Director smiled. "As you know, this man is responsible for the attack on Independence Square. He appears before you today to give his final confession, before he faces justice." At her words, she nodded to the guards behind the Texan.

The men sprang into action, uncuffing Mike and lifting him to his feet. He swayed between them, eyes lowered to the ground. For a moment, Chris thought he would resist, that his honor would shine through and he would refuse to read the confession the Director had given him. He held his breath, cradling the spark of hope in his chest.

"I did it." The words were so soft, Chris thought he had imagined them. Slowly the Texan lifted his head until he was looking into the camera. "I did it. I infected them, all those innocent people, I turned them into *Chead.* I used them to attack the noble widows of your veterans."

He closed his eyes as he finished, sagging in the arms of the guards. They lowered him back into the chair and refastened the handcuffs as the Director stepped forward again.

"Thank you, Michael." She placed a hand on his shoulders and stared into the camera. "Your honesty has earned you mercy."

She nodded to the doctor. Stepping up beside her, the woman took one of the vials from the tray and inserted it into the jet-injector. She moved behind Mike and looked at the Director, awaiting her command.

The Director shook her head. "Not you." Her eyes settled on Chris. "Christopher, come here."

Chris's heart fell into his stomach. A shudder swept through him, and somewhere in his mind a voice screamed, but his legs were already moving him. Crossing to where the others stood, he reached for the jet-injector. The doctor handed it over without argument and retreated, relief showing in her eyes.

His heart pounding, Chris looked at the camera and realized for the first time that he was exposed. As far as the world knew, he was a renegade, an escaped prisoner from a maximum-security facility, hellbent on destroying the government. Beside him, the Director smiled and placed a hand on his shoulder.

"Christopher Sanders, who worked with this man to attack Independence Square, will carry out the sentence today. For the past few weeks, he has been working tirelessly with me to put an end to his former comrades. This will be his final act of redemption."

Chris shuddered. He could hardly breathe, hardly think. The jet-injector in his hand shook as he stared down at Mike. The Texan's head was bowed, his neck exposed, waiting for the end. A hiss issued from Chris's throat as he stood taut. In his hand, the injector gun gleamed in the overhead lights, the clear vial of liquid waiting to be released.

Finally, he let out a long breath and lowered the jet-injector until the steel tip pressed against Mike's neck. The Texan flinched as the cold metal touched his skin. Then he seemed to relax, his shoulders slumping as he embraced his fate.

"Do it, Chris," Mike whispered.

Closing his eyes, Chris squeezed the trigger.

Then an alarm began to sound.

24

Sam slumped against the wall as the last guard screamed and fell back, clutching his shattered kneecap. Gasping, Sam struggled to keep his feet, and failed. He slid slowly down the wall, leaving a trail of blood and copper feathers on the white-washed concrete. Stifling a groan, he closed his eyes and decided to take a moment and regather his strength. His wings hung heavy on either side of him, and it took an effort of will to re-tuck them behind his back.

There had been more guards than he'd expected—definitely more than he could reasonably handle. Only the facility's corridors had saved him. Their narrow width meant only two guards could come at him at once, and those waiting behind couldn't get a clear shot at him.

Of course, the long corridor had also almost been his end when he'd first stepped from the elevator. A guard had been stationed some twenty feet from the elevator doors. With only open space between them, Sam had had to employ some creative flying, but unfortunately the guard had been smarter than the others upstairs. He'd managed to activate an alarm panel before Sam could reach him.

Things had only gone downhill from there.

But Sam hadn't been joking about saving his anger for the

Director. Ever since Liz and Jasmine had returned from the university alone, it had been bubbling beneath the surface. So, as the corridor flashed with red lights and the alarm started to shriek, Sam gave his rage free rein.

Reinforcements had been quick to arrive, tumbling from a door halfway down the corridor like lemmings, racing to their deaths. Some wore identical uniforms to the guards upstairs, others the green camouflage of the national army. Despite their awkward emergence, they formed up in seconds, lifting rifles to take aim.

But Sam was already a step ahead. Picking up their fallen colleague, he charged. Gunshots cracked loudly in the narrow space and he felt the hard *thwack* of bullets as they struck the body he carried, tearing through his body armor and into flesh. A few whizzed overhead, and one found its mark, slicing Sam's forearm like a hot knife through butter.

Then he was among them. Driven by an instinctive fury, he moved without thought, little more than a blur to the soldiers. He had held nothing back, and body armor or no, the men he struck did not get back up.

Two had managed to deal lucky blows—a knife to Sam's hip and another bullet to his shoulder—but in the end, Sam was the only one left standing.

Now, the facility was still but for the low moans of those he'd left conscious. A guard whose leg he had just snapped was trying to crawl away, his pitiful cries echoing off the concrete walls.

"Oh, shut up," Sam barked. He dragged the man back and knocked his head into the ground.

Lying down again, Sam sucked in another breath. He could barely comprehend the wreckage of broken bodies he'd left behind. There were almost two dozen guards and soldiers lying around him. Most sported shattered legs or broken arms. The few still conscious were in no condition to continue fighting—and he'd broken their guns anyway. More lay comatose, dark bruises already swelling on their faces where he'd struck them.

And a few lay dead, their lifeblood pooling beneath them on the concrete floor.

Sam's stomach swirled at the sight and he quickly looked away. He shook his head. They had chosen their side. Working in a place like this, they could hardly claim ignorance.

As he breathed, he caught the whiff of a familiar scent. Turning, he frowned, sniffing the air again, sorting through the smell of blood and chlorine, seeking out the one he recognized. It was just the faintest trace, but somewhere in the back of his mind he could feel something respond to it.

Gathering himself, Sam struggled back to his feet. Was it the scent of the latest subjects? Of a new batch of winged humans like himself and the others? Had they already completed their transformation?

The thought of conscripted teenagers locked in cells rekindled his anger, and he quickly set off down the corridor. He'd caught glimpses of white-coated doctors fleeing as he fought the guards, but there was no sign of them now. The corridors had been abandoned, leaving him to explore the secrets of Alcatraz in peace.

Coming to a crossroads, he tasted the air, seeking out the direction of the scent, and took the turn to his right. He made his way through the twisting corridors in silence. The shriek of the alarm had stopped now, but emergency lights still blinked at short intervals, staining the walls red. Each step sent fire burning through the gash in his hip, and he could feel the blood seeping from his other wounds. His left bicep throbbed and his arm hung limp at his side now.

Thankfully, he didn't encounter any more guards as he continued through the maze. Whoever had been guarding the deeper sections of the facility, they were obviously gathering elsewhere. No doubt the Director was making sure she had plenty of guns around to protect herself from the intruder.

Finally, Sam found himself confronted by a heavy steel door inlaid with reinforcing bars, and knew he had the right place. He had expected guards to be stationed at the entrance to the cells, but if there'd been any, they had already abandoned their post.

The door was closed, but he was starting to get the hang of the doctor's watch, and after a few minutes of fiddling, the panel beside the door gave a loud beep. The door swung open, its well-oiled hinges shifting without so much as a squeak.

Sam started forward, then staggered to a stop as a wave of putrid air struck him. He gagged and quickly covered his mouth with his shirt, though it did little to keep out the stench. Breathing through his mouth, he continued, already dreading what he would find within. It certainly smelled nothing like the pleasant scent he'd followed to get there.

Beyond the doors, a smaller model of the prison block awaited. Rows of cells stretched out to either side of the corridor, only single story here, and only about twenty cells long. Inside, he glimpsed the same four-bunk-bed arrangement they'd had back in the Californian mountains.

Which meant the prison block could hold up to one hundred and sixty tortured souls.

Sam choked as he looked through the bars of the first cell. The two occupants had once been human, but no longer. Strange lumps had erupted from their backs, a cruel imitation of his own wings. Their skin was red and scaled in places, while long claws had sprouted from their fingertips. The familiar steel collars shone around their necks, but they were no longer needed. Both were dead. At the end, they hadn't even been able to make it to the toilet in the back of their cage. The cell was a stinking mess of bodily fluids.

His stomach rebelling, Sam slowly backed away. A dull cry left his throat, but there were no words to articulate the horror in his heart. He stumbled further down the corridor, looking from cell to cell, seeking out someone—anyone—who had survived. Most held only one or two occupants, though the unmade sheets on the bunks suggested there had once been four in each. It didn't take much to guess the missing occupants hadn't survived this far into the project.

When Sam was halfway along the corridor, he noticed a boy lying in one of the cells who showed no sign of mutation. Frowning, he moved closer. The occupant lay on the bottom bunk, eyes closed and unmoving. Yet Sam could see no obvious sign of injury or deformation.

Leaning his head against the bar, Sam closed his eyes. What had killed this one?

Suddenly the hairs on his neck stood up. His eyes snapped open as in the cell, the boy sat up. Before Sam could react, the boy leapt, his hand shooting between the bars to catch Sam by the shirt. With terrifying strength, he dragged Sam forward, a wild snarl on his lips.

Looking at his eyes, Sam recoiled as he saw the harsh grey of the *Chead*. He clasped his hands together and brought them down on the boy's elbows. There was a sharp *crack* as the joint snapped. The *Chead* screamed and stumbled back from the bars. Staggering away from the cell, Sam listened in horror as the prison block came to life around him.

Most died during the change, he thought, watching as the grey-eyed occupants threw themselves at the bars, *and the others—the others succumbed to the madness.*

His shoulders slumped as he thought of Ashley, of her quest to put right the wrong he had committed. He had sworn he would do everything he could to save these kids for her, to make up for what he'd done at the President's press conference, but he had failed. Guilt swirled in his chest, and falling to his knees, he vomited the last remnants of his stomach onto the concrete floor.

"Sam?"

Sam was so preoccupied, he didn't hear the voice call his name at first. Only when it came again did he pause and look around.

Ashley stood at the bars of a nearby cell, her amber eyes wide, one hand over her mouth. Her familiar white wings stretched out to either side of her, glowing in the fluorescent lights, and her fiery red hair tumbled down around her shoulders.

"Sam," Ashley repeated. Her voice was filled with disbelief.

"Ash?" Sam whispered, his heart pounding like a runaway train.

He stared at the ghost in the cell, unable to believe what he was seeing. How could it be true? Chris had sworn he would die before he was captured—Liz had told him so. And for Ashley, returning to captivity, to be used and abused again, would have been worse than death.

Yet there she stood, her pale skin aglow with life, the murderous collar locked around her elegant neck.

"You came," Ashley breathed.

25

Liz ducked back around the corner as bullets tore into the concrete wall where she'd just stood. Her two companions in espionage waited behind her, eyebrows raised. Maria clutched her gun in both hands. She'd given the grenade belt to Mira again, much to Liz's chagrin.

"I'm pretty sure Sam's behind the door at the end," Liz said. When Maria's doubtful look didn't change, she went on. "I'm not nuts. I can smell him, I swear."

Despite her words, Liz wasn't as confident as she'd been when they'd started out. She'd followed the familiar scent through the winding corridors, keeping an eye out for guards and the facility's other occupants, but until now, they had encountered no one.

Apparently that was because they'd all been here. At the other end of the corridor were a dozen men, and unlike the ones outside the elevator, these were more than capable of fighting back. Several wore the blue uniforms of guards, but the rest sported sleek, tight-fitting black uniforms with helmets that concealed their faces.

Unfortunately, if her sense of smell was correct, they had captured Sam and were holding him behind the door at the end of the corridor.

Silently, she cursed her friend for rushing in without backup—never mind that she hadn't been much better. If not for Maria's insistence, she would have come alone as well. Glancing at the old woman now, she wondered again whether bringing her had been the right decision. Much as Liz was enjoying the old woman's company, the real fighting was about to begin, and she couldn't help but think of Chris again. He would be horrified to know she'd let his grandmother go storming into battle.

"You should wait here, Maria," she said, making one last attempt to protect the old woman. "This is going to get ugly."

Maria only smiled. Turning, she took the belt from Mira and unclipped a grenade. "Use this one, my dear," she said, offering it to Liz and passing the belt back to Mira. "Then we'll see who's left."

Liz swallowed as she took the heavy steel ball. This grenade had the more traditional shape, with a cross-pattern of grooves striping its circular surface. After a moment's hesitation, she held down the safety lever and pulled the pin. Then she darted into the corridor and hurled it with all her strength.

A good sixty feet away, the guards managed to get off a couple of shots before Liz could retreat to safety. She cursed as hot lead tore through her right wing, but took some satisfaction from the sight of a soldier's head whipping back as the grenade struck him in the jaw.

Panicked shouting carried down the corridor, followed by an earsplitting *boom*. She closed her eyes as the ground shook and a wave of heat swept around the corner.

When the warmth dissipated, Liz stood and peered cautiously at her handiwork. She shuddered at the destruction left by the explosion. The men had been wearing body armor, but it had been no match for grenade's power. The leading guards had been cut to pieces by flying shrapnel, and even those near the back of the group had been knocked from their feet.

But several were already recovering. With sixty feet of open space to traverse, Liz didn't waste another second. Leaping from cover, she sprinted down the corridor towards them.

The surviving soldiers were shaking their heads, dazed, but

several saw her coming. In their shock they hesitated, and Liz managed to close the gap to thirty feet.

Then they raised their rifles.

Cursing, Liz sprinted on. It was too late to retreat now. All she could do was pray they were terrible shots.

She flinched as gunshots echoed loudly in the corridor, and waited for the pain to follow. Instead, one guard went down, then another, as bullets tore into their massed ranks.

Gaping, Liz risked a glance back and took in the sight of Maria standing at the end of the corridor. Both hands clenched around her handgun, she emptied the clip into the soldiers. Pressed against the wall, she had an easy shot over Liz's shoulder into the grouped men.

As her gun clicked empty, Maria vanished back into cover, but she had given Liz the seconds she needed.

Returning her attention to the soldiers, Liz counted four still standing. Less than fifteen feet separated them now, and she was upon them before they could fire a shot.

She slammed into the first, hurtling him backwards into his comrades. In the chaos that ensued, Liz made short work of the others. The guards in their fancy uniforms were no more of a match for her than the others had been.

Puffing lightly, Liz waved for her friends to join her. She grinned sheepishly as Maria walked up, Mira a step behind.

"Thanks for your help," she mumbled.

Maria smiled. "Only one clip left. Let's make it count. You think he's behind there?"

Liz sighed. "I honestly don't know. I hope so."

They studied the door for a moment, wondering what was on the other side. Whoever hid within remained silent, leaving them no clue as to what waited. Beside Liz, Mira said nothing, her multicolored eyes staring into empty space.

Liz's heart contracted as she looked at the girl. Mira had seen far too much death for someone so young. Crouching, Liz squeezed the girl's shoulder.

"Hey, I want you to stay here and look after Maria, okay?" she whispered.

Mira's eyes flickered back into focus. Silently, she hugged Liz, who smiled and returned the gesture, gently stroking the girl's hair. Then she pulled away and looked at Maria.

"I'll go in first. If anything goes wrong, the two of you can bail me out."

Maria snorted. The old woman's eyes told Liz she wasn't buying it, but even so she nodded her consent.

Liz let out a long breath and she faced the door. It was paneled steel, but as long as there were no reinforcing bars on the other side, it didn't look thick enough to keep her out. Taking a step back, she sprang forward and slammed her foot into the door near the latch.

Just like upstairs, it gave way with a harsh shriek. She smiled as it swung inwards, and leapt through, wings flared.

26

"Cut the cameras."

A red emergency light flashed in the corner of the room. The Director strode across to the computer and picked up a radio, but Chris couldn't tear his eyes away from the Texan.

Mike sat in the wheelchair, arms straining against his bindings. Teeth clenched, tendons taught against his neck, he started to convulse. A low keening came from the back of his throat as the first traces of poison reached his vital organs.

Chris still held the jet-injector in one hand. In horror, he tossed it aside. Glass tinkled as the empty vial shattered on the concrete floor. Looking at his hands, he retreated across the room until the wall brought him up short. He shook his head, as though that would somehow take back what he'd done.

The alarm suddenly ceased, plunging the room into silence. Silence, except for Mike's increasingly loud cries. Raised voices broke out as the camera crew began asking questions, but a scream from the Director cut them off.

Opening his eyes, Chris watched the film crew flee through the door. He wished he could go with them. Opposite him, Jonathan had backed up against the camera equipment and now stood staring at the exit as though expecting a monster to come charging through. With a wave from the Director, guards took up positions around the door.

"I want every gun we have at the transmission room, *now!*" the Director screamed into the radio and then slammed down the receiver. Her eyes settled on her guards. "Get out there and guard the door. Shoot anyone who comes down the corridor."

Her guards marched outside, the door swinging shut behind them with a harsh *bang*. The Director quickly swung the latch down to lock it. Then she faced the room.

Mike was still moving, but his cries were fading now. His head slumped forward in the chair and he barely moved as the Director grabbed him by the hair. Tilting his head, she looked at his face, before nodding to herself and releasing him once more.

"You did well, my pet," she murmured, crossing to where Chris stood.

Chris forced himself not to look away as she placed a hand on his chest. "What's happening?" he whispered.

"Terrorists have infiltrated the facility," she said. Her hand stroked his cheek. "Will you protect me?"

Looking from her to Mike, a moan built in Chris's throat. The Texan's eyes were drooping, his breath growing shallow as he swayed in the chair. The Director's hand trailed through Chris's hair, drawing his gaze back to her. His will crumbled. Eyes shimmering, he nodded.

The Director pushed him towards the door. "Kill whoever comes through."

With that, she returned to the radio and began speaking into the receiver again. She tapped at a keyboard and the screen flickered. Out of the corner of his eye, Chris glimpsed what appeared to be a live camera feed of outside, but from his position by the door he couldn't make out any details.

Taking a breath, Chris steadied himself and looked at the steel-paneled door. Silently, he wondered who had the resources to attack them here. He still had no idea where here *was*—he and Ashley had been knocked unconscious after their capture—but this was the base of operations for the Director of Domestic Affairs, a well-guarded, top-secret facility. It would surely take a small army to storm the place. He wondered if Texas had sent troops to rescue Mike. If so, they were already too late.

Half an hour passed before shouts erupted outside the door, the rattle of gunfire quickly following. Then a *boom* shook the floor beneath Chris's feet. He staggered back as hot air swept beneath the door. More gunfire ensued, and he took a step closer to the entrance. Whoever had come obviously meant business.

Chris cast a quick glance back at the Director as silence returned to the corridor outside. She still stood at the computer, her fists clenched and face pale as she watched the screen. Jonathan hid behind the camera equipment, eyes wide, making Chris wonder why he hadn't fled with the others. It was too late now—not that Chris would mind throwing the man to the wolves outside. If only he could do the same with the Director.

As he turned back, the metal door suddenly exploded inwards. He leapt sideways as the steel panels slammed into the concrete wall. Recovering, he spread his wings and hurled himself forward…

…and froze as Liz's bright blue eyes appeared from the darkness.

Her name left him in a rush, "*Liz!*"

Liz looked back at him, her curly black hair in wild tangles, eyes wide, mouth hanging open. She had frozen in the doorway, same as he. They stood staring at each other as though they'd both seen a ghost.

"Chris," she whispered. Tears brimmed in her eyes.

The breath hissed between Chris's lips as he stepped towards her and stretched out a hand. Then he paused, the awful bite of reality striking him. Shaking his head, he retreated from her, bitter bile rising in his throat. Liz watched him go, the light in her eyes turning to confusion. With his wings spread, she could not see what waited behind him.

She could not see the man he had murdered.

Or the woman he had betrayed her to.

"Don't move." The Director's voice cut through the silence like a knife.

Chris froze at her voice, even as Liz tensed and started forward again.

"I said, *don't move!*" the Director shrieked.

This time Liz stopped. Glancing back, Chris saw the Director standing beside Mike's chair, a handgun pointed at Liz's chest.

"Good girl." A smile twitched on her lips as she stepped beside Chris. "Elizabeth Flores. So you're the one who's been causing all the excitement."

"Not just her." Chris staggered as his grandmother entered the room, gun outstretched. She calmly pointed it at the Director's head. "Put it down, *witch*."

"You first, old woman," the Director laughed. "I'm sure you don't want to kill your grandson."

"What?" Maria scowled, her arm wavering.

Lowering her gun, the Director tapped her watch. "If I die, the collar around Chris's neck will kill him." She looked from Maria to Liz. "I don't think any of us want that, do we?"

The two of them exchanged a glance, before Maria bowed her head. Smiling, the Director took the weapon from his grandmother's limp fingers. Maria's shoulders fell as she released the weapon, as though her will had gone with the gun.

"There, isn't that better?" A gun in each hand, the Director crossed to where Mike still lay slumped in his wheelchair. Turning, she waved to the newcomers. "Come in, come in, you remember Mike, don't you? I'm afraid he's not feeling too talkative today."

Chris lowered his gaze as Liz and Maria edged forward cautiously. Mike was no longer moving. His face had turned a pallid grey, and his lips were a sickly blue. There was no doubt now—he was dead.

"Oh, Mike," Chris heard his grandmother whisper.

"*You!*" Liz growled, stepping towards Jonathan. She froze as the Director aimed a gun at her face, but her gaze never left the man. "How could you let her do this?" she demanded.

Jonathan didn't move from where he hid behind the camera equipment. "Let *her?*" He looked from Liz to Chris. "Why don't you ask *him* how the Texan died?"

Liz's eyes found his. "Chris?" she whispered, starting towards him.

Unable to meet her accusing stare, Chris backed away. "You shouldn't have come here, Liz," he murmured.

"I thought you were dead," Liz murmured. "What happened to you?"

Chris swallowed as his chest grew tight. He felt a desperate yearning to go to her, to kiss her, to hold her in his arms. Never in his direst dreams had he thought he would see her again. Yet here she was, and he had nothing left to offer her.

Laughing, the Director strode across to join him. He shuddered as she pulled him to her, her lips meeting his, unable to resist. When she pulled away, he lowered his eyes to avoid looking at Liz.

"He's mine now," the Director mocked.

"No," Liz spoke in no more than a whisper. "Chris, look at me. Whatever she's done to you, it's over. We're getting you out of here."

Chris wanted more than anything to believe her. But as he moved, the collar seemed to tighten, reminding him of his fate. His life was bound to the Director's. There was nothing they could do to help him.

And there was nothing he could do to help Liz.

The Director was laughing again. "It seems we have a second renegade to execute."

"Vile witch," Chris's grandmother said sharply. "You think you've won? You think you can just get away with murdering innocent people, with torturing children?" She started towards the Director but froze as the woman pointed a gun at her. Shaking her head, Maria went on, "They'll find out the truth—you can't keep it from them forever."

"And what would this truth of yours be, old woman?" the Director asked with a grin.

"That you created the *Chead.* That you murdered widows and innocent students to hide it," Maria growled.

"I did," the Director cackled, "but you have no proof."

For half a second, Maria's eyes flicked to Liz before she

looked away again. "It's out there. It's only a matter of time before it comes out. When it does, your regime will crumble. Sooner or later, justice will find you."

The Director did not reply. She stood staring down the barrel of her gun at Maria, her eyebrows knitted in a frown. Slowly she turned the gun on Liz. "Ms. Flores, please turn out your pockets."

Liz's face paled and she retreated a step. The Director advanced on her. "Jonathan, if you'd be so kind as to search the girl?" she snapped. Her eyes never left Liz.

With the wall behind her, Liz had nowhere left to go. She glared at Jonathan as he stepped up beside her, but did nothing to resist as he rummaged through her pockets. It only took him a couple of seconds to find the thumb drive. Chris's head spun as Jonathan lifted it up for the Director to see.

"I'll take that," the Director said, holding out her hand.

Jonathan handed it over, and she dropped it on the ground and smashed it beneath her boot.

"*No!*" Liz breathed, tears appearing in her eyes.

"Glad we got that loose thread taken care of. I take it you didn't have the resources to make a copy of Professor McKenzie's work? No? Excellent!"

"It doesn't matter," Maria replied, though her voice was thick with despair. Her eyes shone. "How could you create such monsters…"

The Director laughed. "The *Chead* were only ever a happy by-product of the war. We had been working on a virus, one that would make our troops unstoppable, but the war ended before we could perfect it. The *Chead* were as close as we got to success – until now."

"But *why?*" Liz asked. "My family, my people, we suffered for *decades*. How could you do that to us?"

"After the losses rural communities took during war, they asked too many questions of us." The Director shrugged. "We needed a new enemy, something to strike fear into the nation and silence our detractors. The *Chead* provided the perfect tool."

"You're monsters."

The Director sneered. "No more than you, my dear."

"The truth will come out," Maria repeated.

"One day, maybe," the Director replied. "By then it'll be far too late. Soon we will have an army of creatures just like your grandson, ready and willing to obey our every command. Then it won't matter what the sheep think. You'll all do as you're told, or die."

"Witch," Maria said again. Before she could say anything else, the Director slammed the butt of the pistol into her cheek. Maria crumpled to the ground with a cry.

"I've heard enough," the Director sighed, pointing the handgun at Maria's head. "For obvious reasons, you're going to have to die off-camera, Maria."

Chris's heart froze in his chest. His grandmother had gone completely still now. She crouched on the ground, staring up at the gun, her eyes sad. The rest of the room looked on, helpless to intervene.

"Go on then," Maria said softly. "Do it. Show everyone here how powerful you are, how you'll murder a defenseless old woman in cold blood."

A twisted smile crossed the Director's face. "Gladly."

"*No!*" Chris screamed as a gunshot echoed through the transmission room.

27

Reaching through the bars, Sam pulled Ashley into an awkward hug. He couldn't believe his eyes, could hardly trust the feeling of her thin frame beneath his fingers. She had lost a lot of weight since he'd seen her last. Her ribs stood out through the thin cotton shirt she was wearing, and her face was pale and drawn. A dozen white feathers were scattered around the floor of her cell, and there were patches of skin showing on her wings.

But none of that mattered just then. Despite everything he'd believed, everything he'd convinced himself of, Ashley was alive. He kissed her through the bars, the cold steel pressing against his cheeks as their lips met. He breathed in the scent of her, savoring the familiar taste of her tongue.

They were both panting for breath when they finally broke apart. The screams of the *Chead* still echoed around them, but Sam only saw Ashley. He held her arms, staring into her amber eyes, seeing the pain there but also recognizing hope. Hope that her torment was almost at an end.

"You're alive," he whispered.

He cupped her cheek and pulled her in for another kiss. She trembled beneath his fingers, and Sam shivered as her hands went around his waist. Their tongues danced as they pressed hard against one another.

There were tears in Ashley's eyes as they separated. She angrily brushed them away. Hiccupping, she shook her head. "What…what's that thing on your face?"

Sam grinned and rubbed his beard. "You don't like it?" Then he sighed and closed his eyes. "I thought you were gone, Ash."

He fought back tears as her hand stroked his cheek. "I'm here, Sam. I'm safe."

A sob tore from Sam's throat. For the past four weeks he had mourned her loss, had cursed and berated himself for not going with her to the university, for not being there to save her.

"What happened here, Ash?" he asked when he finally regained his composure.

A tremor swept through Ashley. Her eyes drifted past him, to where the *Chead* still raged in their cages.

"They messed with the virus," she said. "It killed half of them in the first few hours. Then today…" She trailed off, her voice breaking.

Sam cupped her cheek, offering his silent comfort, knowing she would go on in her own time.

Finally, Ashley sucked in a breath. "The Director was impatient. She didn't test them like Halt did with us, just ordered the doctors to administer the virus to everyone. Those who survived the first few hours…" She swallowed. "They weren't strong enough, Sam. In the night they started going mad, throwing themselves around their cells, screaming about voices in their heads. I tried to help them, but one by one they either succumbed to the *Chead*, or…or mutated."

Sam nodded grimly. Images of the deformed bodies had been burned into the back of his eyes. Another thought occurred to him. "Where's Chris?" He looked around, half-expecting to see his friend in another cell.

"He's…in trouble, Sam." Ashley's voice drew his gaze back to her. "She's broken him. I don't know what she's going to make him do."

Sam frowned. Chris had always been so strong, Sam couldn't imagine him giving in to the vile woman. "What do you mean?"

"You'll see." Ashley looked around her cell, searching for a way out. "I don't know how to open these things. I think they're controlled remotely."

Sam held up the watch he'd taken from the doctor and started tapping through the menus. His spare hand dangled between the bars, and Ashley took it in hers. She kissed it, eyes fixed on the control watch.

"So, they missed you at the safe house, Samuel." Sam jumped as a crackling voice spoke from above.

Releasing Ashley's hand, he spun, seeking out the owner, but he was still alone in the corridor. On the ceiling, a camera swiveled in his direction. He glanced at Ashley. They both recognized the voice.

"Honestly, I thought you'd be dead by now," the President continued, the speakers clearer this time. "Especially with those dreadful radio broadcasts. The Director has a lot of explaining to do."

Sam smiled. He'd chosen to broadcast from the top of the monument for just that reason. Sure, they might track him to Independence Square. But with thousands of people cramming the grounds below, he had been like a needle in a haystack.

"Still, I'm glad," the President continued. "I never had the chance to thank you for helping me win back the public."

"I didn't do it for you." Sam's anger flared and he spun, half-expecting the man to pop out of some hidden corner. "Come out and face me!"

Laughter crackled over the speakers. "Oh, Samuel, if only I could *properly* thank you for everything you've done. Alas, I'm presently engaged elsewhere."

Sam paused. "You're not even here?" A cold chill spread up his spine.

"Of course not. I have a country to govern. I can't spend all my time hiding under some old rock."

"Well, wherever you are, I hope your guards are better than

the bozos you employed here." He pointed at the ceiling. "Because I'm coming for you next."

Ashley pressed herself up against the bars to get a better look at the camera. "Aww, did the big bad President get cold feet?" she called mockingly. "Did I scare you away?"

Silence met her taunts, and Sam flashed her a glance. *Don't piss him off*, he mouthed, but she only shrugged.

"I'm disappointed the Director did not deal with you as promised, Ashley," the President said after a long pause. "I suppose it's up to me to ensure you are adequately disciplined."

Ice spread to Sam's stomach, but Ashley was undeterred. "Do your worst," she laughed. "Wherever you're hiding."

This time there was no answer, but before either of them could think of another taunt, a buzzer sounded, and all along the corridor the prison cells rattled open. Ashley blinked, staring at the open door to her cell for a moment, before stepping outside.

"Some punishment," she muttered.

Sam didn't respond. He was watching the other inmates emerge silently from their cells. He swallowed as the grey eyes of the *Chead* turned and found them standing nearby. Mad laughter carried down the corridor as their lips drew back into snarls. Growling, the *Chead* started towards them.

Ashley stilled as she saw them coming. Her wings trembling, she turned and watched the *Chead* advance. There were maybe twelve of them in all, enough to tear both Ashley and Sam to pieces if they wanted. And from the dark glint in their eyes, he guessed there would be no reasoning with them.

Taking a deep breath, Ashley stood on her tiptoes and kissed Sam on the cheek. "Stay here. You look like you could use a rest." She wrinkled her nose. "And you're shaving when we're done here."

Ashley drew in another breath. A calmness settled over her face, an almost imperceptible change. Her jaw tightened as she looked at the *Chead*. And her eyes…staring into them, Sam wanted to run away, and pull her to him, all at the same time.

She stepped towards the *Chead* without a backwards glance.

Her wings spread to fill the corridor, giving even the *Chead* pause. Sam watched on, frozen with indecision.

Overcoming their hesitation, the *Chead* started forward once more. They moved on ungainly legs, still struggling to control their altered bodies. Their inexperience was Ashley's only advantage, but she was still badly outmatched by twelve of the creatures. Sheer weight of numbers would overwhelm her.

Shaking free of his fear, Sam started after Ashley. His boot scuffed the concrete, and she shot a warning glance over her shoulder. The glow of her eyes brought him to an abrupt stop, and suddenly all he could do was hold his breath and watch as Ashley closed on the *Chead.*

Roaring, the leading *Chead* bounded towards her. Its wild howl echoed down the corridor, and Sam yearned to leap to Ashley's aid. Together, they just might have stood a chance. Instead, he remained frozen in place, unable to break whatever impossible spell Ashley had placed over him.

Fortunately, Ashley had no need of his help.

She twisted as the *Chead* leapt, leaving it stumbling through empty space. Before it could recover, she caught the creature by the back of its shirt and catapulted it back into its comrades. The other *Chead* leapt aside as it crashed onto the concrete with a hard *thump*.

The *Chead* stared at their downed brother for a second, then turned to look back at Ashley. Folding her arms, she glared at them. Wings still spread, she contemplated each of the remaining *Chead* in turn.

"You're young," she said suddenly. Her voice echoed loudly in the corridor. "I will forgive you your insolence."

A shiver went through the creatures as she took a step towards them. As one, they shrank back from her. She laughed, and for an instant Sam was reminded of the cold, grating laughter of the *Chead.*

"Get back in your cages," Ashley snapped. "I will deal with you later."

The *Chead* didn't hesitate. Retreating down the corridor, they disappeared into their cells without looking back. The doors remained open, but none of the twisted inmates so much as poked out a head to check on them.

As Ashley turned back towards Sam, he caught a last glimpse of the glow in her eyes. Then she blinked, and it was only Ashley looking out at him. She slumped suddenly, and he caught her as she fell.

"What the hell was that?" he asked as she draped an arm over his shoulder.

Ashley gave a dry laugh. "I'll tell you when I figure that out."

"You do that." He smiled and started towards the exit, doing his best to ignore the grey eyes watching as they stumbled past. "What are you, Lord Commander of the *Chead* now?"

"Really, I have no idea." Ashley wrinkled her nose. "I just… acted on instinct."

"Good instincts," Sam snorted. Ahead, the exit loomed. "Guess we'll figure it out later. Let's just get out of here, before our luck runs out."

As they moved into the narrow hallways of the facility, Ashley seemed to recover enough to stand on her own. Taking back her arm, she paused. "We can't leave yet. Chris needs us."

Grimacing, Sam glanced at her. Despite her show of strength against the *Chead*, she was clearly exhausted. Whatever they'd done to Ashley over the past four weeks had drained her strength. And if anything, Sam was in even worse shape.

But however desperate they were, she was right. They couldn't leave Chris behind.

He nodded and gestured towards the corridor. "Lead the way."

28

"No, no, no." Chris crouched over his grandmother, shaking her in desperation. "Nana, no…"

Liz could only stand and stare in horror at the body of her friend. She couldn't look away, couldn't move, couldn't do anything other than watch, helpless. The Director towered over Chris and Maria, a triumphant grin on her face. Slowly she turned the gun on Liz.

"I guess you're next," she said softly.

Looking down the barrel of the gun, Liz didn't move. She was still reeling, struggling to comprehend everything she'd seen.

Chris, alive, waiting on the other side of the door. Chris, kissing the Director.

Jonathan, taking the precious thumb drive from her pocket. The Director, crushing it beneath her boot.

And Maria, reeling backwards as the bullet tore away her life.

Liz shook her head as a tear streaked her cheek. "You're… vile," she grated, "you're sick, twisted. You're worse than Halt."

"Halt was an animal." The Director smiled, the expression cold, devoid of emotion. "This? This was all just necessary."

"Necessary?" Jonathan spoke from across the room. Liz clenched her teeth as he walked towards them. "How was any of this necessary?"

Frown lines crisscrossed the Director's forehead. "Jonathan?" She raised an eyebrow. "What are you doing?" She still held the handgun pointed at Liz, its tip unwavering.

"What is necessary," Jonathan replied.

"What?" The Director blinked. "What are you talking about?"

His lips drew back in a sneer. "You finally made a mistake. All this time, I've been waiting for my chance. All I needed was an opening, a single chink in your armor. And you've finally given it to me." He smiled, though the expression did not reach his eyes. "My family will have their justice."

"Justice?" The Director shook her head and turned the gun on Jonathan. "Justice? We already gave them justice, Jonathan."

"False justice." Jonathan stared her down, unflinching.

The Director curled her finger around the trigger. "So you wish to betray me? You have a poor choice of timing, Jonathan. What brought about this sudden death wish?"

"You still don't get it, do you?" Jonathan asked. "Six weeks ago I held the lifeless bodies of my wife and daughter in my arms, and swore I would do whatever it took to avenge them. At Independence Square, I saw my chance, realized you were my gateway to the truth. Now you've admitted that truth to the entire world."

Liz stared at the man, unable to understand what he was saying. The Director took a step closer to Jonathan.

"*What are you talking about?*" she grated.

But Jonathan was no longer looking at her. His eyes had travelled to where Chris lay crouched over his grandmother's body.

"I wasn't quick enough to stop you," he murmured sadly. "Or maybe I didn't want to. There'll be no coming back for you, not after murdering an innocent old woman." He looked up at the Director then, eyes hardening. "The camera has been broadcasting this whole time, *Director*. I switched it back on when you were distracted by the explosion. Everything you've said, everything you've done, the whole world has been watching."

For a moment there was silence. Liz stared at Jonathan, her heart hammering in her chest. She hardly dared to breathe.

Could it be true? Looking past Jonathan, she saw the tiny red light flashing on the camera. Easy to miss, when you weren't looking for it.

"No…" the Director croaked. Her arm wavered, the gun shaking in her hand. "You're lying."

"See for yourself." Jonathan nodded at the camera.

But the Director didn't move. The evidence was clear for all to see. Her lips drew back in a mad grin as she strode across the room and pressed the gun to Jonathan's forehead.

"You'll die for this," she hissed.

There was sadness in Jonathan's eyes as he shrugged. "Do it, I'm ready to join my family. It won't change anything, though. It's over. You've lost."

"*It's not over!*" the Director screamed. Suddenly she was behind Jonathan. Her arm wrapped around his throat as she put the gun to his temple. "*Christopher! Help me!*"

Chris looked up from his grandmother's body. Tears streaked his cheeks and there was no missing the hatred in his eyes. He stared at the Director for a moment before turning to Liz.

"Kill her," he gasped to Liz. "Let me die. I don't care anymore."

Then he bent back over Maria, leaving Liz to face the Director alone. Balling her fists, Liz stepped towards the woman.

"If you kill me, Chris dies!" The gun left Jonathan's head and Liz ducked as she fired, but the shot was wild and went well clear. The gun returned to Jonathan's temple. He jerked as the hot barrel burned his flesh, but her grip around his neck held him in place. "The moment my heart stops, the signal goes out. He'll die in agony!"

Swallowing, Liz came to a stop. A tense moment stretched out as they eyed one another, locked in a desperate stalemate. Finally the Director sneered.

"Good," she hissed, "we understand one another." She started to back towards the open door, dragging Jonathan with her.

Liz clenched her jaw tight. Blood thumped in her ears, but she made no move to stop the woman. Silently, she cursed herself for a coward. This was the moment she had been waiting for, her chance to end the woman's tyranny—whatever the cost.

Yet Jasmine's final plea echoed in her ears, and Liz knew she couldn't do it. Not if it meant losing Chris again, not after she'd just found him. Her shoulders sagged as she realized the evil woman was going to escape.

Movement came from the door, drawing Liz's attention. With her eyes on her enemies, the Director didn't notice as Mira stepped into the doorway. The girl's multicolored gaze surveyed the scene, taking in Chris and Maria, before settling finally on Liz.

Liz's racing heart froze as Mira smiled. It was a small, hesitant thing, as though the girl wasn't quite sure of what she'd done, as if she was still wondering whether she could take it back.

Across the room, Liz started to cry out, but Mira was already stepping forward, opening her arms to embrace the Director. And the Director was turning, her eyes widening as she saw the grey-winged girl for the first time. The chime of steel pins striking the concrete seemed unbelievably loud in the silence.

Then an explosion rocked the room, swallowing them all in its fiery embrace.

29

The young soldier was on all fours, lapping water from a stream as they entered, but when she saw them, she quickly darted back into the corner of the cave. Talisa strode after her, catching the girl by the foot and dragging her kicking and screaming across the sharp stones. She still wore her green and brown uniform, but it was filthy now, the badges and insignia streaked with mud.

She gasped as Talisa threw her at Susan's feet, her green eyes casting wildly around in the darkness. Her auburn hair clung to her face, wet with sweat.

"Have you reconsidered, human?" Talisa asked.

Susan glanced back at the two *Chead* who guarded the cave's only entrance. They stood nearby, watching the girl closely, alert for any sign she might threaten the elder. But this girl was too terrified to even stand.

Leaning closer, Susan wondered at the soldier's fear. Earlier too, the girl and her comrades had fled when the *Chead* had charged. Such bad discipline was unusual among the soldiers of the WAS. Even the guards who'd protected her facility had been better trained.

This girl reminded Susan more of her former self, of the fearful woman she'd been before the change. She had her arms wrapped around her own chest, as though that could somehow protect her from the *Chead*. Yet despite her fear, the girl still shook her head at Talisa's question, even as she bit her lower lip to keep from crying.

"You disappoint me," Talisa rumbled.

Leaning down, she gripped the captive by the hair and hauled her to her feet, then shoved her at Hecate. The human screamed as he caught her in his powerful arms, struggling to break free, but he gripped her around the waist and hurled her to the ground. Even then she tried to crawl away, but she was nowhere near fast enough to escape. Hecate's foot slammed down on her ankle, and a harsh *crack* echoed through the cavern. Susan flinched as the girl's scream followed.

"You have chosen death," Talisa said in a calm voice, as though nothing had happened, "but it will not be quick. First, we will have all you know."

Beside Talisa, Hecate slowly ground the girl's ankle beneath his foot. Pinned to the floor, the girl gave a pitiful cry and started sobbing into the gravel.

Susan watched the girl suffering, heart torn between pity and disgust. After a moment, she raised an eyebrow at Talisa. Normally the woman was quick to put her prisoners to death. Susan had never seen one tortured.

"We have never captured a soldier," Talisa said, answering her unspoken question. "I wish to know more of our enemy."

She waved to Hecate as she finished. He retreated to Susan's side.

"Where are you from, soldier?" Talisa asked as she crouched beside the girl. When the prisoner only whimpered, the elder *Chead* grasped a handful of hair and forced the girl to look at her. "Would you like him to start again?"

The soldier bit her lip again and shook her head.

"Then speak," Talisa commanded.

The girl's eyes switched from Talisa to Hecate and back again. She nodded quickly. "I'm from…Oakdale," she whispered, then her jaw hardened. "Or was…before you destroyed it."

Talisa chuckled and released her hair. Standing, she crossed her arms. "So why did we find you with that pitiful army, soldier?"

The girl sat back and looked up at them. "I didn't want to be there," she spat, "but I'm glad we took some of you with us."

Hecate started towards the human, but Susan put out her hand to stop him. She nodded to Talisa. This was her interrogation.

"You did not want to be there?" Talisa asked softly.

"I was drafted," she murmured. Her eyes flashed and she seemed to regain some of her fight. "After you drove us from our home, my family fled to the city. But my brother and I were taken by the army, to be trained for the war."

"The war?" Talisa pressed. "Against the *Chead?*"

The girl snorted. "Against Texas. We know who your masters are."

Talisa raised an eyebrow. "Texas? What do they have to do with my *Chead*?"

"They created you, didn't they?" the girl snapped. "Sent you to kill us, to weaken the WAS so they can take our land."

Talisa began to laugh. "Such imaginative creatures. Who told you such a tale?"

The girl bared her teeth. "The President himself," she hissed.

"The President?" Susan stepped up. "He sent you?"

The girl blanked. "Well, no...we...we were just the ones he selected for special training at his base."

"And where was that?" Talisa pressed.

But the girl had realized she'd said too much. Clamping her lips shut, she glared at them in defiance. Hecate stepped towards her, a dark grin spreading across his face, but Susan was quicker still. Placing herself between the *Chead* and their prisoner, she raised her hands.

"Let me speak with her," she asked softly. "Perhaps I can convince her to join us." Her eyes moved towards Talisa.

Talisa eyed her closely. "Cut off their leadership, and the humans will be too busy fighting amongst themselves to come for us."

Susan nodded. "Trust me."

After another moment's hesitation, Talisa nodded back. Taking Hecate by the shoulder, she led him across to the entrance of the cavern, giving Susan and the girl space to speak.

Susan let out a long sigh and faced the young soldier. The girl still knelt on the ground, her broken foot stretched out in front of her, twisted at an awkward angle. Susan sat down beside her.

"What's your…name?" Susan asked.

The girl swallowed. She looked at Susan, then back at the doorway where the others waited. Apparently deciding it was better to talk with Susan than face Hecate, she answered: "Lisa."

"My name is…Susan. Nice…to meet you…Lisa," she said, offering her hand.

Lisa turned away with a snort of disgust. Susan sighed. "Defiance will…get you nothing," she murmured, "but a long… and painful…death."

"What would you know, *Susan?*" Lisa snapped, her eyes flashing, "What does a monster like you feel anyway?"

Susan's anger flared and she fought the urge to strangle the life from the girl. Scarlet stained her vision as she took a long breath, her stomach straining against her shirt, and then exhaled.

"I was…like you…not long ago," she replied at last. "I too… was offered a…choice."

That got the girl's attention. She looked from Susan's face to her swollen belly. "You…you were *human?*"

Susan's lips twitched in amusement. "I was…a miserable creature," she said. "The *Chead*…freed me."

Lisa snorted. "Looks like they did more than that." Shaking her head, she went on, her voice incredulous. "You *bred* with these monsters?"

Susan bared her teeth at the insult and wrapped a hand around the girl's slim throat. It felt good beneath her fingers, and smiling, she started to squeeze. "Hecate is…my mate." The words were softly spoken, but no less feral.

The girl's mouth opened and closed as she batted at Susan's hand, but her human muscles were nothing to the strength of the *Chead*. The panic grew in the girl's eyes as she choked. When

Susan finally released her, Lisa bent in two, gasping in great lungfuls of air. Susan watched on, impassive, waiting for the girl to recover. She didn't speak again until Lisa fell silent.

"I was once like you…weak…miserable…alone," she said. "Now you have…a choice. End your suffering…join us."

Tears streaked Lisa's cheeks as she met Susan's gaze. For a long moment she was silent, her lips pressed tightly together, her green eyes shimmering in the light of the nearby candles. Susan could see her fear, her desire to live, but there was something else too, something she did not recognize until Lisa's lips drew back in a sneer.

"Thanks," she spat, "but I'm no coward. I'd rather die than become a whore for these monsters."

Faster than thought, Susan's fist lashed out and caught Lisa on the side of the face. She heard a *crack* as the blow shattered the girl's cheekbone and sent her reeling. Screaming, Lisa tried to scramble away, but Susan was on her in a second, fist raised to deliver the final blow. Before it could fall, Hecate caught her by the wrist.

"Enough," he said as she tried to pull away.

Rage rumbled through Susan's chest, but she was no match for Hecate's strength. He dragged her back from the prisoner as Susan screamed at him. "She needs to die!"

Silently, Talisa crossed the cave to stand beside the prisoner. "She will." Her voice carried back to Susan. "But not before she tells us everything."

Lisa's screams echoed from the stone walls as the elder *Chead* leaned down and twisted her broken foot. Watching from Hecate's arms, Susan's reason slowly returned. She sagged against her mate, and after a few more minutes, he released her. They stood in silence as Talisa went to work.

Susan licked her lips, savoring the taste of blood in the air. Each time Talisa released her victim, the girl would try to crawl away, crying pitifully as the stones shifted beneath her broken bones. Her loyalty was impressive, her fortitude to be admired. Yet the girl had insulted the *Chead*, had called Hecate a monster, and Susan felt no pity for her now. She watched on, taking pleasure from each agonized scream.

In the end, the girl's resistance made no difference. Talisa would have what she desired. There was no resisting her iron will. When Lisa finally broke, she shouted the words so loudly they must have echoed through half the cave system.

Lisa sobbed as Talisa released her. One last time she tried to crawl away. Talisa waved Susan forward. Her mouth watering, Susan obeyed. Talisa handed her a rock and nodded towards the girl. Crouching beside her, Susan brought the rock down on the back of Lisa's head. There was a sickening *crack* as her skull shattered, and the pitiful sobs abruptly died away.

Smiling, Susan stood and looked at Talisa, the girl's final words still ringing in her ears. They sounded oddly familiar, like a place she should know, though the memory seemed half a lifetime ago now.

Kirtland Air Force Base, Albuquerque.

30

Sam and Ashley heard the explosion a few minutes before they reached the transmission room. By then, the fight was already over.

Turning the final corner, Sam stumbled to a stop. Bodies lay strewn across the corridor, their blood staining the walls and floor. Beyond, the air was thick with dust, and a gaping hole waited where a door had once stood.

"Quickly," Ashley said. She started down the corridor without waiting for an answer. Sam followed her, his exhausted legs barely able to keep up.

The dust was clearing as they neared, revealing the full extent of the damage. A burn mark amongst the bodies showed how the first soldiers had died. Others they encountered sported bullet wounds and broken bones. None of them were moving.

Ashley and Sam shared a glance. Reaching the ruined doorway, they waved away the last of the dust. There was little left of the transmission room. Part of the ceiling had collapsed, leaving rubble strewn across the little room. Ruined computer equipment and cameras lay scattered around the far wall.

Sam glimpsed another scorch mark near the door, before his eyes were drawn to a body in the corner. He started towards it, and then stopped when he recognized her face.

"Oh, Maria." Ashley's voice broke as she stepped past him and knelt beside Chris's grandmother. She put a hand to her throat, but after a moment's pause she met Sam's gaze and shook her head.

Hot pain stabbed Sam's chest. Staggering forward, he dropped to his knees and took up Maria's hand. Her skin was still warm. "What was she doing here?" he whispered.

Before Ashley could answer, a piece of rubble shifted, sending a block of concrete crashing to the floor. Instantly, Sam and Ashley were on their feet. They stepped cautiously towards the pile, eyes alert for danger. But there was no more sign of movement, and after moment, Sam knelt and began lifting concrete from the pile.

After a few minutes, he lifted a chunk of concrete and found a patch of pitch-black feathers beneath. The breath caught in his throat, and tossing the block aside, he redoubled his efforts. With Ashley's help, they quickly removed the rest of the rubble covering Liz.

She coughed as Sam lifted her out, a dim groan rasping from the back of her throat. Her wings had taken the brunt of the damage, and from the unnatural way they hung from her back, he guessed that she had broken several bones. A trickle of blood trailed from her mouth and her face was a mess of purple and black. But she was alive, and that was all that mattered.

Ashley called out as Sam lowered Liz to the ground. Turning back, he watched as Ashley shifted another block of rubble, revealing Chris's face. They dragged him out, and then Ashley lifted him over one shoulder. She stumbled as a jagged edge of concrete caught her boot, but quickly recovered. Silently, she set Chris down beside Liz. He didn't move, but Sam let out a long sigh as he saw his friend's chest lift.

"What happened here?" Ashley asked softly.

On the ground, Liz stirred, her eyelids fluttering. She whimpered as her wings shifted and Sam quickly placed a hand on her shoulder. Her clothes had been torn in the explosion and he had to take care not to touch her flesh.

"Don't move, Liz," he said quietly. "You've been hurt, but

we're here, Ashley and me. It's going to be okay. We're going to get you out."

Liz's eyes flickered open. "Sam?" she murmured.

Sam nodded and squeezed her shoulder. "Where are the others, Liz?" he asked. "We found Chris. And Maria…she's gone, I'm so sorry. But what about Jasmine, and Mira? Were they here?"

A tear streaked Liz's cheek, carving its way through the dust. Her blue eyes stared up at him, the whites stained red.

"Gone," she mumbled, even as her eyes slid closed again, "they're all gone."

IV

REBELLION

31

Sam groaned as he lowered himself into the chair beside the hospital bed. His body creaked, his bones grating as the pillows took his weight. The injuries he'd taken in Alcatraz were healing quickly, but even his genetically modified body couldn't recover from half a dozen bullet wounds in a week. At least he could still fly though. The girls had just taken off to test Liz's freshly healed wings—her first flight since she'd been crushed by falling concrete.

As for Chris…well, it was anyone's guess whether he would ever fly again.

Sam's face sagged as he looked at his friend. Chris's chest rose and fell in smooth succession, his eyelids fluttering gently. He had yet to open his eyes. The bruises had almost faded from his face, but the deeper wounds still lingered. Even now, a week since their prison break, Chris remained in a coma.

Liz had done her best to protect him. In the video that had streamed across the globe, she had turned as the grenade exploded and hurled herself across his body. It hadn't been enough. As the rubble came crashing down, a chunk of concrete had slammed into Chris's head so hard it cracked his skull, only missing Liz by inches.

It was a miracle any of them had survived. Even Ashley, freed from her cell, would have been killed had it not been for Mira. The grenades had engulfed the Director in a ball of flames, incinerating her control watch before it detected her death. Only that had spared Ashley and Chris an agonizing death from the collars fastened around their necks. Whether Mira had realized that or not, they would never know.

A tear trickled down Sam's cheek. Angrily, he wiped it away. Not for the first time, he cursed Liz for bringing the girl and Maria along. Alcatraz had been no place for either—and both had paid for the mistake with their lives. Yet, he knew Liz hadn't had a choice. There had been no refusing either of them when they set their minds to something. And without poor, brave Jasmine, there'd been no one else for Liz to turn to.

Sam took a deep, shuddering breath. Richard, Jasmine, Mira. They had lost so many friends, their families, their lives. When would it all end?

Letting out his breath again, Sam stood and crossed to the window. They were in a stone building that had once been the embassy for Portugal. Parting the curtains, he peered out into the street. A crowd of protesters thronged the sidewalk, spilling out onto the road in places. A manicured hedge and tall cast-iron fence held them back for now, but it would do little to stop the protesters if they realized who was in the building.

Chris was a wanted man after what he'd done.

All hell had broken loose following the Director's accidental confession. For decades the threat of the *Chead* had hovered over the people of the Western Allied States, uniting them in fear of a common enemy. With the revelation that their own government had been behind the epidemic…order had collapsed overnight. Haunted by two decades of suffering at the hands of the *Chead,* rural refugees had unleashed their pent-up rage against the capital.

The foundations of their nation undermined, officials had tried gathering the remnants of the police and military, but their best efforts had been in vain. It hadn't taken long for open war to break out on the streets of San Francisco.

Urban citizens, terrified for their safety, locked themselves away in their apartments. But day by day, more refugees poured into the city, dislodged by the hordes of *Chead* ravaging the countryside. When the last emergency services collapsed, the rioters had turned on their urban neighbors. After suffering so long under the terror of the *Chead*, it was impossible to believe the urbanites in their sparkling cities hadn't been involved in the conspiracy.

So had begun the bloodiest week in the history of the Western Allied States.

Outside, a few of the protesters were stirring, and Sam quickly drew back from the window. Despite his efforts in Alcatraz, Sam was quite sure he remained at the top of the public hit list. After all, he had stood beside the President all those weeks ago, offering his silent endorsement.

The President himself had been the first to flee. The man was no idiot—he'd been long gone by the time the rioters reached Congress. Where, no one knew, but it wouldn't be long before they tracked him down. With civilization itself on the brink of collapse, there weren't many places left to hide.

A hinge creaked, and Sam turned in time to see Harry step through the door. His crutches tapped on the linoleum floor as he shuffled across the room. A bandage covered his right leg from ankle to knee. Unbeknownst to Sam, the old veteran had survived the massacre at the safe house and been shipped off to a medical cell in Alcatraz.

Luckily, Sam's prison break had freed Harry before he could be interrogated.

"Sam." The old man smiled as he waddled around the bed and took Sam's seat. "How is he?"

"Still no change," Sam replied, adjusting the radio on his belt and looking down at Chris. "The doctor says the swelling has gone down, but she's not sure how much lasting damage the impact might have caused."

"Perhaps he won't wake up," Harry said with a sigh. "It might be for the best. It would make my job easier."

Sam grimaced, but he was too exhausted to argue. Harry might have fought in the American War, but he'd never experienced the trials that Sam and the others had been through. Harry couldn't understand the power Doctor Halt and the Director had wielded over those in their thrall.

Although, even Sam was still struggling to reconcile what Chris had done.

Out loud, he said, "Your little council still hasn't decided what to do with him?"

Since being freed from Alcatraz, Harry had reconnected with the survivors of the Madwomen. Along with several other political prisoners he'd met among the inmates at Alcatraz, he had established a shadow government of sorts here in the embassy. Though his council held no official power, they'd been talking with the refugee leaders, along with some of the city's more influential residents. And they'd gathered the remnants of the police force, restoring order to at least a few city blocks.

Harry shook his head. "There are larger issues at hand. We will deal with him when he wakes."

"No doubt," Sam mused. "What about the President? Any word on his location?"

Leaning back in his chair, Harry eyed him closely. "We've narrowed it down to a few possibilities. He could be in San Diego, at the Naval Base there. Or Oregon. Or Albuquerque. Don't worry, he can't hide from us forever."

"And the reinforcements? Has there been any progress with Texas and Mexico?" Sam pressed. He knew Harry had reached out to a few of Mike's old contacts in Texas, at least.

"Those are details I cannot go sharing with just anyone, Samuel," Harry replied wearily.

Sam smiled. "But you'll tell me, won't you?"

Harry laughed. "Your assistance at Alcatraz will only get you so far, my friend."

"Assistance?" Sam raised an eyebrow. "I'd call that a little bit more than just 'assistance.'"

The old veteran rolled his eyes. "You are persistent, aren't you?" A pained look crossed his face as he stretched his injured leg. "Very well. Texas and Mexico are mobilizing their forces, but these things take time. The first peacekeepers will reach San Diego and Albuquerque in a few days."

"You think we can trust them?" Sam asked.

Harry spread his hands. "There's not much else we can do." His gaze travelled to the window. The protesters were beginning their first chants of the morning. "Our police are outnumbered. The army is in tatters, divided between three wayward generals. We're doing our best, but water, electricity, gas, they're all just one bad day from shutting off. We need their help. If they decide not to leave…well, we'll deal with that if it comes to it."

Sam nodded, but before he could reply, movement in the bed drew his attention. Chris still lay motionless beneath the white sheets, and the hospital machines continued their rhythmic beeping, unchanged. Perhaps he had imagined it. He was about to look away when Chris's toe twitched. Then a finger. A sharp beep followed as his heartbeat spiked.

Sam shared a glance with Harry. Then he reached for his radio.

32

Liz closed her eyes as the ground fell away, the powerful beat of her wings sending her soaring. Relief swept through her as the winds pushed her higher. Spreading her wings to their full extent, she drank in the freedom of flight, the release of gravity's relentless pull. Gliding through the sky, far above the chaos below, she almost felt free, as though she could leave behind her awful past, and soar into a new future.

If only it were so easy. But somewhere below, reality lurked, a truth that would not be denied. The radio weighed heavily on her belt, a constant reminder of the darkness waiting for her back at the embassy.

Wind tugged at her hair and rustled in her feathers, racing around her, cutting off all sound of the city, stealing away the harsh scent of gasoline and humanity. She shivered as it sliced through her thin black top, but with the summer sun beating down on her back, it was almost a relief. Her long-sleeved blouse and jeans were insufferable in the Californian heat, and the gloves only made things worse.

Liz watched the skyscrapers flash past. Green trees dotted the streets, their branches swaying in the breeze. There were only a few cars about. They crept through the rolling hills like mice eager to avoid a predator's detection. The day was clear, and across the harbor, Liz could see Alcatraz rearing up from the white-capped waters.

She shuddered and quickly averted her gaze. In the week since their final confrontation with the Director, Liz had barely left her bed. For the first few days, even the slightest movement would bring sharp pain to her wings. They had taken the brunt of the explosion as she'd spun and thrown herself over Chris. She couldn't remember anything after that—at least not until Sam and Ashley had dug her out of the rubble that had crashed down on them.

The others had tried to keep her company while she healed, but Chris also needed watching, and for long hours she'd been left alone to stew in her thoughts. In her grief, and pain.

Chris…

The air racing past her face whipped away Liz's tears. She still felt the shock of stepping through the broken door and finding him standing there. For weeks she'd thought him dead—then suddenly he'd been there, alive, whole. In that one moment, all her hopes and dreams had come rushing back.

Only to be torn to pieces an instant later.

Liz shivered as she recalled watching the video of Mike's execution, in the days after the prison break. A chill had spread down her spine as Chris stepped up and pressed the deadly jet-injector to the Texan's neck.

A moan built in Liz's throat and she was filled by a desperate yearning—to twist in the air and race back to Chris's bed, to grab him by the shirt and shake him until he roused.

She needed an explanation, a reason for all of it. It was as though some part of her was still waiting for Chris to wake, to tell her none of it had been real, that he hadn't really done the things she'd seen.

That he loved her.

Wings cracked next to Liz as Ashley drifted into formation. She smiled as her friend's broad white wings struck the air, sending her spiraling ahead, red hair whirling.

Ashley had recovered well in the last week. With proper food and sleep, she'd put some weight back on her skeletal frame.

Fresh down was sprouting where her wings had molted, and life had returned to her amber eyes. There was a joy to her now, a freedom in the way she moved. But there was also grief, long silences during which she would stare off into the distance, remembering some moment lost in time.

Ahead, the Golden Gate bridge loomed, its red pillars rising up from the harbor. Angling her wings, Liz aimed for the pillar furthest from the city. As she dropped, her wings beat faster, slowing her descent. She eyed the red beam cautiously as she approached, but clear skies and warm nights meant its surface was dry, and she landed easily. Folding her wings, she watched as Ashley followed her down.

Turning, Liz sat on the edge of the beam and hung her feet over the seven-hundred-foot drop. A car rumbled across the bridge as Ashley took a seat alongside her. Then without warning, Ashley embraced her. So taken by surprise, Liz almost toppled from the ledge—only her firm grip on the girder kept her in place.

When she recovered, Liz managed half a laugh and hugged Ashley back. Disentangling themselves, Liz eyed her friend. "What was that for?"

Ashley smiled. "Because you're here." She sighed, her eyes creeping inexorably out towards Alcatraz, "Because for the first time since they took me, I feel like I'm really free."

Liz's heart clenched and she gave Ashley's shoulder a squeeze. "I'm glad, Ash."

Her friend wiped away an unspilt tear. "I just wish the others were here to enjoy it with us." The howling wind seemed to steal away her words.

Liz swallowed the sudden lump in her throat. Images flashed through her mind—Richard, collapsing beneath a hail of gunfire…Jasmine, the light slowly fading from her eyes…and poor, sweet Mira, engulfed by the blossoming flames. Her grip on the girder tightened until her arms shook.

It was a long time before she found the strength to speak again. "Jasmine…she missed you. She told me…she hated how she never put things right with you."

Ashley's eyes were distant. "I miss her too. We never should have let them drive us apart. We were all forced to do despicable things, but they don't define us."

Knowing Ashley was talking about more than just Jasmine, Liz bit her lip. An image of Mike flickered through her mind, of the Texan convulsing in the chair, strapped down, dying in agony as Chris watched on.

Ashley might be right—they had all done despicable things. But what Chris had done, that hadn't been a fight to the death. His life might have been on the line, but it had still been cold-blooded murder.

And then...then there was the kiss he'd shared with the Director.

Her gut clenched as she forced the image from her mind. It shouldn't matter—not beside his other crimes—but it did. At least to her. Her insides turned to liquid every time she thought of him. The passion, the love of just a few short weeks ago, was gone. In its place was an empty abyss that threatened to drown her.

In her heart, she knew that whatever he said, whatever explanation he offered, it wouldn't be enough. There was no coming back from what he'd done—not for them.

"Did you ever think it would end like this?" Liz asked suddenly, still staring out over the harbor. "The last time we were up here...did you think this was how things would be? That we'd...that we'd lose Mira and Jasmine and Maria? That Chris would..." She swallowed, barely able to get the words out. "That Chris would betray us?"

The wind shrieked again as it passed between the wire supports of the bridge. For a long time Ashley did not speak, did not move. She sat looking off into the distance, hair curled around her elegantly shaped ears, her soft white wings resting on the scarlet pillar.

"Don't give up on him, Liz," she said finally. "You don't know what it was like for him, locked down there with her, without any hope. You don't know what it was like to be her prisoner, to have her slowly crush the life from you."

"But she didn't crush you," Liz replied.

Ashley pursed her lips. "I had already been broken," she said, then shook her head. "No, not broken. But I had survived the worst Halt could throw at me, and walked out the other side. Thanks to you, Liz."

"Me?" Liz asked, frowning.

"When we last sat up here, you reminded me who I was, helped me find the courage to pull myself back together." She looked away, her voice growing sad. "Maybe you can do the same for Chris."

Liz swallowed. The past week, she had felt as though a vice were closing around her heart, crushing the love from her. She didn't have much left to give. "I don't know if I can, Ash," she murmured into the breeze. "I'm not sure he can come back from this. I'm not sure if…if I can forgive him."

Ashley's hand settled on her shoulder. Looking up, Liz found herself trapped by her friend's amber gaze. "Maybe you can, maybe you can't." Ashley's voice was soft. "But at least give him a chance. Let him explain. And give yourself time to heal."

A sigh escaped Liz's lips. She wanted more than anything to follow Ashley's advice, but she wasn't sure if it was possible, if she could find the strength. Watching the replay of the news broadcast, it had been as though *her* Chris had been in that chair with Mike, as though the boy she loved had died with the Texan.

Liz didn't know what kind of man remained now, but she didn't think she wanted to find out.

Before she could put her thoughts into words, the radio on her belt crackled. They both looked down as it started to squeal, then Sam's voice whispered from the old speaker.

"Hey girls, you there?"

Liz's heart lurched. There was only one reason Sam would be calling them. Hands trembling, she unclipped the radio and lifted it to her mouth. "Yes, Sam…we're here," she said, pressing the button on the side.

"Great!" His voice came again, stronger now. "Well, wherever you are, I suggest you get back here pronto. It looks like sleeping beauty is waking up."

The radio went silent. Liz sat staring at Ashley. Her friend's eyes were wide, shining with the light of the noonday sun. For a long moment they sat there, frozen by the news, by what it meant.

Suddenly Liz felt as though she were suffocating. She gasped, sucking in great lungfuls of air. A fire lit in her stomach and every hair on her body stood on end. Her mind raced, searching for some way to escape the coming confrontation, to cling to the illusion of the past week, if only for a moment longer.

"Liz," came Ashley's voice, calling her back. A firm hand gripped her by the shoulder. "Liz, it's going to be okay."

Liz blinked and looked at her friend. She nodded slowly, though the movement felt detached from her mind. A passenger in her own body, she stood as Ashley took her hand and drew her up.

"Come on, Liz," Ashley whispered, holding her on the edge of the girder. "Let's go see what he has to say."

33

Chris's wings beat harder, hurling him through the sky. The dense clouds churned, enfolding him in their cold embrace, until he could see nothing but the whirling black. His heart raced as he fled the unseen creature behind him. Its howls whispered in the darkness, chasing after him. Its stench filled the air, putrid, decaying, death.

A shadow flashed at him, dark claws extended towards his throat. His wings twisted instinctively, sending Chris spiraling sideways. Pain seared down his back as something struck him. Screaming, he slammed his wings down, rising higher.

"Chris!" *a voice screamed.*

Choking, Chris spun, seeking the source. His wings beat the swirling clouds as he hovered, spinning, searching. The voice was filled with warmth, with love—but also a desperate fear. It was a voice Chris had never thought he'd hear again.

"Mom!" *he called as the clouds closed in.*

His throat contracted as a figure took shape. She strode towards him, her bare feet seeming to float on open air, green eyes aglow. Her curly auburn hair swirled in the breeze, though where Chris hovered, the air was still. She drew to a stop in front of him, a ghost from the nightmare of his past.

"Son," Margaret Sanders whispered.

"Mom," Chris choked. Hot tears streamed down his face.

He drifted towards her, arms outstretched, desperate to hold her again, to be held. She smiled as he approached, a gentle warmth that reminded him of cold winter nights, of dinners by the fireplace, of the safety of childhood.

Yet as he reached out to take her hand, her smile faded. Her face seemed to change, her lips turning hard, her eyes flickering to hazel, her hair growing straight, fading to blonde. And suddenly it was no longer his mother standing there, but the Director. Rage glinted in her eyes as she caught him by the wrist.

"Christopher," she growled. "You failed me!"

Then Chris was falling, his stomach rising into his chest as he plummeted through empty air. Screaming, gasping, he tried to stretch his wings, only to find them gone. Helpless, he fell. All his old fears came rushing back, and Chris found he could do nothing but scream and scream and scream…

"No!" Chris shouted as he sat bolt upright.

Chains rattled as he thrashed, trying desperately to cling to some impossible ledge. Eyes shut tight, he fought the darkness that still held him, pulling him back down, drawing him into the abyss. He opened his mouth to scream again.

"Chris!" a voice called, only this one was a man's. A hand grasped him by the shoulder.

A trace of sanity trickled into Chris's consciousness. He realized he was no longer falling. Panting, he cracked open his eyes and was met by the harsh glint of fluorescent lights. Pain lanced through his skull and his vision flashed red. The strength went from him in a rush. He collapsed back on the bed.

An ache began in his back as he landed on his wings, followed by relief that they were still there. Taking another breath, he tried opening his eyes again. This time it was almost bearable, though the light made his head pound like a drum. The room slowly came into focus, and he saw a familiar face staring down at him.

"Sam?" he croaked.

For a moment he was confused. His thoughts were a mess of splintered memories. He looked around, surprised to find himself in a hospital bed. Chains rattled again as he found his hands cuffed to the steel rails along the side of the bed. A trail of wires and tubes led from his arm to a host of machines behind him.

He frowned, trying to piece together the memories. They

returned slowly, as though trickling back through a sieve. He saw again his hellish captivity with Ashley, felt the slow dwindling of hope, the ghoulish deaths of the Director's experiments. He remembered Ashley raging down the corridor, feral, unstoppable —then Ashley on the ground, helpless, being dragged to her death. And the Director, offering him her hand, pulling him to his feet, stripping the buttons from his shirt…

He choked, trying to resist the flow now, but the memories continued to come. He saw the night he'd betrayed his heart, and the morning after, as he took the jet-injector and placed it to the Texan's neck. He watched as Mike thrashed in his chair, saw his last agonized throes of death.

Then Liz was there, and his grandmother—only for her to be stolen away forever. And Jonathan was speaking, revealing how he'd tricked them all, had exposed the truth to the world. And the Director was fleeing, escaping…until little Mira stepped up behind her, a grenade clenched in her tiny fist.

Squeezing his eyes shut, Chris felt the tears streak his cheeks.

"You remember?" he heard Sam ask.

Shame welled in Chris's chest, and for a moment he wanted to deny it, to pretend he couldn't remember, that it had all been someone else. He couldn't bear to look in his friend's eyes, to face Sam's judgement, not after what he'd done. He wanted to flee, to run and hide and escape the truth.

Instead, Chris nodded. "I remember."

Sam exhaled loudly.

Chris looked up at his friend. "Where are we? How am I alive?" His hand drifted towards his neck, to feel for the collar he had worn for weeks, but the handcuffs brought him up short.

Sam's eyes shimmered as he sat in the chair beside the bed. "Mira…" He swallowed. "The grenades…they incinerated everything. The Director's watch was destroyed before it could activate either of your collars."

"Either?" Chris whispered. "Ashley…?"

"She survived," Sam said, though he didn't smile. "And Liz. Jasmine didn't."

"How?"

"She was shot, when soldiers raided our safe house," Sam replied. "It's just the four of us left now."

"I shouldn't be alive." He looked up at Sam. "You know what I did."

It was not a question. Sam nodded.

"The whole world saw," Sam said. "You really messed up this time, buddy."

"I know..."

"But I'm glad you're okay."

Sam gripped Chris's wrist. Their eyes met and Chris quickly looked away again. His vision started to blur. He didn't deserve kindness, didn't deserve anything but a bullet in the head. His stomach churned, and a dark gulf filled him, a sickly guilt that threatened to engulf him. He jerked his hand back from Sam.

"I shouldn't be *alive*," he repeated, tears in his eyes. "I told Liz to end it, to kill the Director and *end it*," he choked.

A strained silence filled the room as Chris started to sob. He had killed a man in cold blood, had given himself to the woman who'd tormented them, then watched as that same woman killed his grandmother. In that instant, Chris had truly been lost, had lost his will to live. After everything he'd suffered, he could go no further.

"Liz didn't want to lose you, Chris," Sam said finally, his voice soft, sad.

Chris blinked the tears from his eyes. "Lose me?" His heart gave a little flutter, before the yawning gulf consumed it. "She already lost me, Sam."

Before Sam could respond, the door clicked and swung open. Chris shrank in his bed as Ashley stepped into the room, followed a second later by Liz. Their wings were still half extended, but they tucked them neatly behind their backs as their eyes found him in the bed.

"Chris..." Liz's voice was strained, her hands trembling at her side.

Sam stood abruptly, looking from Chris to Liz to Ashley. "Why don't we get some fresh air, Ash?"

Without waiting for a response, Sam took Ashley by the hand

and fled. Chris watched as they departed, begging silently for them to stay. Then they were gone, leaving him alone with Liz.

Chris forced himself to look at her. "Liz…" he whispered.

34

The moment Liz saw Chris sitting up in bed, whatever doubts she'd had about her feelings for him vanished. Stepping across the threshold into the room, it was as though some veil had been lifted, and the fog impeding her judgement was swept away.

She saw Maria again, Chris's own grandmother, defying the Director to the death.

And Mira, sacrificing her short life to end the woman's evil.

Then she saw the video of Chris, meekly following the Director's commands, submitting to her power, murdering his own friend to survive.

And Liz knew she could never love him again.

"Liz…" he started after the others had left.

"*Don't,*" Liz spoke over him, her voice sharp as a knife. "Don't speak. Don't talk. Don't try to explain, Chris."

She stalked across the room, her knee-length boots thumping loudly on the linoleum. Chris's gaze dropped to the floor as she stopped beside his bed. He couldn't even look at her. It only enraged her further.

"*Look at me!*" Suddenly she found herself screaming, unable to contain her fury.

Until this moment, Liz had clung to the hope Chris could

somehow explain everything away. But now the thought of him even speaking made her tremble. She knew anything he said would only add gasoline to the flames of her rage.

He had murdered Mike, had given himself to that vile woman, and done God only knew what with her. Whatever Ashley might have hoped, Liz could never forgive him for it.

Still chained to the bed, attached to the whirring machines pumping him full of drugs, Chris slowly lifted his face to look at her. Tears brimmed in his hazel eyes. His face had grown thin and haggard in captivity, but it was still the face Liz knew, the one she had kissed, had loved. Now, it only made her sick to her stomach. They might share the same face, but the Chris she had known was gone, betrayed by the coward now lying before her.

"Liz…" he tried again.

"*I said don't speak!*" she shrieked. Her vision blurred and instinctively her wings snapped open, beating down to send air swirling. A magazine someone had left on the coffee table shot across the room.

Chris shrank down in his sheets, though with the cuffs chaining his wrists to the bed, there was nowhere he could go. She leaned over the bed, her wings casting him in shadow, until there was nothing but him and her and her rage.

"How could you do it?" Her voice had dropped to a whisper. Their faces were only inches apart now. Slowly her anger slipped away, leaving only the empty abyss where her love for him had once been. "How?"

Liz shuddered, biting back tears. Her whole body was trembling, her wings shivering as they fluttered. Something caught in her throat, and unable to look at him a moment longer, she turned away.

Behind her, Chris wisely remained silent.

"I thought you were dead," she mumbled to the wall, hardly knowing what she was saying now. "You said you'd rather die than be caught. You made me leave. It broke my heart, but I did it." She spun back, her anger returning. "You *coward!* Why couldn't you just have *died* like you said? *Like you promised*!"

She stood over him, fists clenched, teeth bared. Chris lay still in his bed, eyes wide. Words had apparently abandoned him.

"Your nana would be ashamed of you," Liz spat. "She would have despised you. She died for you. *Mira* died for you. And Richard. And Jasmine. They all died, *but you're still here*, and for what? So you could kill their friend? So you could screw that vile woman?" The words tumbled from her mouth, an unstoppable stream of pent-up emotion. "They all threw away their lives, thinking they knew who you were, that you were good, believing *you* would make a difference. All those students, all those widows, they're dead, and in their place, all we get is *you!*" Liz was screaming now, her words rattling the windows.

Raging, she gripped the chair beside Chris's bed in both hands. It was a heavy thing, all wood and cushion, but she hurled it across the room as though it weighed nothing. It smashed into the stone wall and shattered into a thousand pieces. Chest heaving, Liz turned on Chris.

Red stained her vision and a desperate yearning rose within her, a desire to throttle the life from him. She felt as though that was the only way to end her pain, to quench her rage. Only with his death would she find peace, could she escape the sight of him.

A growl rumbled from Liz's chest as she towered over Chris. She half-expected him to try to flee, but he didn't move. Reaching down, she took his throat in her hands. Her gloves had somehow been lost during her outburst, and she shivered at the warmth of his skin beneath her fingers. Through pain and bloody-minded determination, he had developed an immunity to her touch weeks ago, but that wouldn't save him now. Slowly Liz began to squeeze.

Chris didn't try to fight back, although with his arms cuffed to the bed and the machines pumping him full of morphine, there wasn't anything he could have done to stop her. His eyes stared up at her, sad and unblinking, almost begging her to do what he could not. A single tear crept its way down his cheek.

As she took a deep, shuddering breath, the red faded from Liz's vision. Shivering, she released him and stepped back, though their eyes never left one another. A long silence stretched out until finally, Liz could take it no longer.

"Why, Chris?"

Chris shook his head. "You should have let me die, Liz," he croaked. "You're right, I shouldn't be here. It should have been me that died with the Director."

To that, Liz had no answer.

Spinning on her heel, she fled the room.

35

In the darkness, all Susan knew was pain. It was her entire world now, her whole being. She could feel herself tearing up, her insides ripping apart. Her mind rebelled, wanting to flee, to depart her mortal shell and escape the red-hot coils of her agony.

Instead, she gritted her teeth and clung on.

"Breathe, Susan," Talisa's voice whispered in the darkness, drawing her back.

Susan looked around, but the candles had burnt out long ago and none of the *Chead* had bothered to get more. She sucked in a breath, savoring the sweet scent of her brethren, and sighed as the pain receded for a second. A hand gripped her by the shoulder. She shifted on the stones to look for its owner.

"You are almost there…my mate," Hecate's stilted words whispered in her ear.

Susan nodded, though in the pitch-black, she knew he could not see her.

"Light, please!" she gasped. Talisa would not be pleased—the *Chead* did not need sight—but in that instant, Susan hardly cared.

A hand stroked her hair. Somewhere in the darkness she heard the faint whisper of a candle being lit. A flame appeared, its glow casting back the pitch-black. Talisa and Hecate sat on either side of her, their scent enveloping her, while a third *Chead* held the candle near her feet.

She sensed the pressure building again. Clenching her teeth, Susan struggled to control her breathing. A wave of pain swept out from her abdomen. Her legs spasmed. A sharp cramp had begun in the small of her back hours ago, and it flared again now. Arching against the cold ground, she cried out as the contraction ripped through her.

Suddenly she found herself in another place, another body, another time.

Susan laughed as she wandered through the museum, her mom just two steps behind. The crowds pressed in around her, but she didn't mind. This was her special day, her time in the sun, and she was going to make the most of it.

After all, it wasn't every day you turned ten.

The day passed in a blur, as she led her mom through the countless exhibits detailing the history of the Western Allied States. How they had departed from the United States and set off to forge their own path. How the United States had attempted to undermine them. How for a decade, war had raged across the North American continent.

And how the detonation of a nuclear warhead in Washington, DC had finally brought the devastating conflict to a close.

At the end, Susan and her mother found themselves in the museum's feature exhibit—an expose on the WAS's nuclear independence. Newspaper articles had been blown up and plastered over one wall, featuring articles declaring "VICTORY" alongside images of a mushroom cloud rising from the wreckage of DC.

Walking through the exhibit, Susan wondered at the life-sized rockets littering the room. For a ten-year-old, the sleek steel contraptions seemed the epitome of man's accomplishments. How these strange devices could be sent hurtling thousands of miles through the sky was beyond her comprehension. Television screens around the room showed videos of glowing reactors and rockets soaring across vast oceans. In that moment, it seemed to Susan that her nation must be capable of anything.

Slowly the vision faded, the edges turning to black. Feeling the pull of pain, Susan clung to the memory, desperate to remain. From a distance, she watched her ten-year-old self studiously reading her way through the exhibit, learning of the process of nuclear fission, the development of the triad, the map of the Western Allied States and their known nuclear bases.

As the last traces of the memory vanished, Susan glimpsed the words inscribed beside "Albuquerque."

Kirtland Air Force Base.

Susan screamed as the pain came rushing back. Thrashing, she caught Hecate by the shoulder and hauled him towards her. He yelped as her nails dug into his flesh, but for once he lacked the strength to tear himself free. Panting, Susan shrieked again, her cries echoing through the cavern.

"Almost there, Susan." Talisa's voice was disgustingly calm. Susan wanted to hurl a rock at the elder *Chead.*

"Breathe, my mate," Hecate whispered.

With an effort of will, Susan lay back against the stones. Her chest constricted, reducing each inhalation to a desperate gasp. She clung to Hecate until she felt blood beneath her fingers, but now her mate did not pull away. Warmth flooded Susan as their eyes met, and she screamed one last time.

A sudden rushing sensation came from between her legs. The pressure wrapping around her abdomen lessened, and Susan collapsed back against the stones, crying and panting, coughing as her chest relaxed. Finally, she managed to take a proper breath.

For a second, there was silence in the cavern. Then a piercing cry split the darkness, and the *Chead* at her feet lifted something from the stones. Susan's heart fluttered as she saw her baby in the *Chead's* arms. She scrambled to sit up, though fire still burned in her stomach. Reaching out her arms, she cried wordlessly for her child.

But the *Chead* only turned away. Before she could stop him, he disappeared into a side cavern, stealing her child from view. A strangled cry built in Susan's throat as the warmth turned to rage. It cast aside the agony and fed strength to her limbs. Arms trembling, she started to stand.

An iron hand gripped her shoulder and forced her back down. Snarling, Susan lashed out at Talisa, but the elder *Chead* caught her fist and shoved her back.

"*Down, child,*" she commanded.

With a pitiful moan, Susan slumped against the stones. Tears sprang to her eyes as her baby's cry echoed through the caves. She twisted around, trying hopelessly to find him.

"*Enough!*"

Talisa's weathered hand slapped Susan hard across the face. She started to cry. The pain was returning now, the pressure building once more.

"Please," she moaned.

"No," Talisa growled, murky white eyes flashing in the light of the candle. "Your child will wait. The others cannot."

Susan looked up at the elder *Chead*, uncomprehending. Seconds ticked past before it struck her. Agony had driven the knowledge from her mind, but now it came rushing back. The *Chead* did not have single child births. Like rabbits and cats, they had litters, multiple births. Except unlike their furry relatives, birthing was not easy.

It was agony.

Sobbing, Susan collapsed back against the cold stones.

36

Sam sighed as he fell back on the double bed. Placing his arms behind his head, he grinned up at Ashley.

"A little early for bed, isn't it?" she asked, eyebrow raised. "It's three in the afternoon."

"Perfect time for a siesta." Sam laughed, patting the empty space beside him. Even now, he couldn't stop smiling, couldn't stop looking at her.

Ashley had been skin and bone when she'd escaped, her hair matted and eyes lined by shadows. She had slept for two days straight—and upon waking had wolfed down enough food to feed a lion. Even now, she became like a fox in a henhouse at the merest mention of food. But the extra sustenance had done its work, returning muscle to her lithe frame, the subtle curves to her hips.

Taking a step towards the bed, a playful smile tugged at Ashley's lips. To show his appreciation for his rescue, Harry had given them a room to themselves, and they were both still savoring the novelty of privacy. For months they'd lived in prison cells and cages or camped in tiny hideouts. To suddenly have a master bedroom and ensuite bathroom all to themselves was something of a shock.

Of course, they had taken full advantage.

Still on her feet, Ashley brushed the scarlet hair from her face and fluttered her eyelashes. "You want me to join you?"

Impatient, Sam sat up and grabbed her around the waist. Ashley yelped as he threw her down on the bed, but she was too quick to be pinned. Twisting to the side, she laughed as he landed beside her. Then she wriggled closer and wrapped her arms around his waist. Leaning in, she planted a kiss on his lips.

Sam kissed her back, tasting the sweetness of her tongue, the closeness of her body, but Ashley pulled away again before things could progress. He eyed her closely, seeing her mind wasn't completely with him. He tucked a strand of hair behind her ear, to which she scowled and dislodged it again.

"Don't do that." She tapped him on the nose like he was a bad puppy.

"Where are you?" he asked softly, stroking her cheek.

Ashley sighed. "What do you think…they're going to do?"

Sam exhaled. He didn't need to ask who Ashley meant by "they."

"I don't know," he offered. "What Chris did…"

"I tried to make her understand," Ashley replied, absently stroking his chest. "What it was like for us…"

"I think she knows…" Sam said with a shudder. He wished he could forget his time locked alone in Halt's cell, powerless to resist the beatings by the guards. And Ashley's terror as Halt had snapped her fingers, one by one. "But I'm not sure it matters."

"We've all done terrible, awful things though," Ashley murmured, rolling onto her back to stare at the ceiling. Her chest rose as she sucked in a breath, drawing Sam's eyes to the soft curves of her breasts.

"In the heat of the moment, when it was them or us," he muttered.

Closing her eyes, Ashley nodded, and Sam knew she was seeing Chris on the screen, ending Mike's life. He watched her face, wondering again how she had found the strength to resist, to defy the Director while Chris—always so strong, so determined—had crumbled.

But then, Ashley herself was stronger than most. Even when

she'd been struggling to overcome her own demons, Ashley had placed the wellbeing of her friends above her own life. When they'd needed her at the university, she hadn't hesitated to help, despite her terror.

"Chris…he lost himself in there," Ashley was saying. "It wasn't the torture that broke him, or the sleepless nights, or the cold or starvation or pain. It was the absence of hope." Her voice cracked as she turned her head towards him. "All those kids, Sam, all those students. They stood up for us. And there was nothing we could do to save them. Chris couldn't take that, couldn't take knowing he'd given up his freedom to protect them, and they'd died anyway."

Sam nodded. Even after learning the government had been behind the *Chead* epidemic, the scenes of the university massacre had shocked him. Chris and Ashley had sacrificed their freedom to try to stop it—he could understand how that might have broken his friend.

He could, but could Liz? Could Harry and his council?

Shivering, he stroked Ashley's hair again. Her eyelids slid closed at his touch. Leaning in, she nuzzled his neck. Tingles of fire ignited where her lips met his skin, and the heat of desire clutched him. Opening his arms, he drew Ashley into his embrace.

She came willingly, her arms slipping beneath his shirt, touching lightly, taunting. He groaned as their lips locked together. Her tongue darted out, the taste of her filling him, fueling his desire. The heat in his chest spread, becoming a desperate yearning, an insatiable need.

Her fingers were tugging at his shirt now, and he lifted his arms eagerly, allowing her to draw the thin material up over his broad shoulders. Then her hands returned to his naked chest, hungry, eager, even as he still struggled to pull the shirt over his head. As always, the slits at the back caught on his wings, and in a sudden fit of impatience he yanked at it. Fabric tore, and he hurled the ruined shirt across the room.

Watching him, Ashley lay back on the bed, her white tank top hugging her body. A teasing smile crossed her lips as she spread her wings. With them extended, there was no way to remove her top intact. But the glimmer in her eyes told him what she wanted.

Growling, he leaned over her, tongue tasting, teeth nibbling at the soft flesh of her neck, her shoulders. His fingers danced across her stomach, floating over the mounds of her breasts, coming to the thin strap at her shoulders. He took it between his fingers and tore it before moving on to the other side. Ashley gasped mockingly as the second ripped. Grinning, he gripped the fabric where it curved down to cover her breasts, and tore it clean in two.

Sitting back, he took a moment to admire his work. Ashley still lay on the bed, wings still spread, her ruined top exposing the glorious curves of her body. Sam held himself on all fours, their naked chests just inches from touching. Face to face, they stared into one another's eyes, their breath mingling.

In a rush Sam kissed her, feeling Ashley's lips melt beneath his, her body rising up to meet him. Her soft breasts pressed against his chest, igniting a primal moan deep in his throat. Her fingers were in his hair, pulling him down, holding him tight, desperate to ensure he wouldn't escape. But he wasn't going anywhere. Her scent was in his nostrils, her taste in his mouth. He wanted nothing more than to stay in this place with her forever, and let the world outside do what it would.

She fumbled at his pants, and then they were gone. Hers quickly followed. Sam gasped as her hands gripped him by the waist. Grinning, she pushed him, and suddenly he was tumbling sideways. She laughed as she straddled him, her sleek breasts glittering in the fluorescent lights. Her amber eyes were aglow, shining with that light he'd seen in the corridors beneath Alcatraz. Leaning forward, she whispered in his ear.

"Take me, Sam." Her breath was hot against his flesh.

He had no choice but to obey, his hips rising to meet hers. A gasp tore from his lips as he found her. Ashley's lips parted, her breath quickening as she pressed her lips to his neck. Wrapping his arms around her waist, Sam moved slowly, feeling her respond, her hot gasps on his flesh.

Ashley's hands slid through his hair, her moans in his ear. He could feel her all around him, moving faster, every thrust of her hips encouraging him to greater heights. His own hands moved with a will of their own, trailing through her wings, down the small of her back, gripping her ass, her hair, her feathers.

A ferocity built within him, a burning desire for more, a feral need to take control. Moving one arm behind her waist, he lifted her and spun. Ashley gasped, her eyes widening as she found herself beneath him once more. Her eyes narrowed, but he kissed her hard and felt her relent. Sliding his hand behind her neck, his other beneath her waist, he pressed close against her.

Tearing her lips from his, Ashley groaned, her nails digging into the flesh of Sam's back. He kissed her neck, breathing in the sweetness of her, and increased the pace again. All thought, all reason left them as they moved against each other, joined as one, ignorant to the troubles that had driven them to the room.

When they finally collapsed back to the sheets, Sam was gasping. Ashley was still trembling as he drew her tight against him, her head resting against his chest. Suddenly heavy, his eyelids slid closed. Embracing the warmth of his mate, he heard the call of sleep, and welcomed it before the chaos without could intrude.

✤ 37 ✤

Chris lay in bed staring at the ceiling. His mind was adrift, set loose by the confrontation with Liz. His thoughts swirled, drowning in the cocktail of drugs being pumped into his arm. A deep sense of lethargy clung to him, a hopeless resignation to his fate. Thinking back, he could hardly believe what he'd done, the atrocities he'd committed. It seemed almost a dream to him now, an awful nightmare he could not wake from.

But there was no escaping the truth. Mike was dead—his blood was on Chris's hands. There was no changing that, no denying it. The whole world had seen him execute the helpless Texan. One way or another, he would have to pay the price for his actions.

What form that price would take had yet to be determined. In the corner, the television buzzed as images flickered across the screen. They showed the riots engulfing San Francisco, the buildings burning and protesters marching in the streets. People were screaming for justice, for the fall of the government and all those involved with the spread of the *Chead.*

Chris watched the rioting without emotion. After all this time, after everything he'd suffered at the hands of the government, he felt strangely disconnected from the outside world.

Thinking back to the boy he'd been, to the teenager looking forward to finishing school and graduating with his friends was like looking into another life, another world.

His grandmother had been his last connection to that life, to a time before Doctor Halt's insane experiments. But now she was gone, and he felt more alone than ever. It was as though each new loss pushed him farther and farther from humanity.

Without Liz, without Ashley and Sam, what would he become?

He shuddered, recalling the raw hate in Liz's eyes. Was that the price his crimes demanded? That he be left completely and utterly alone?

Gritting his teeth, Chris forced aside his self-pity. If that was the case, if his friends and the world no longer wanted anything to do with him, so be it. He deserved no better.

A harsh beep from the corner drew Chris's attention to the television. He frowned as the screen flashed red. With a sigh, he reached for the remote. But flicking through the few available channels, he saw they were all the same. He was about to switch the television off when the screen returned to life. An image of a broad mahogany desk appeared.

Chris's blood chilled as a man stepped into sight and sat down. The President wore a broad smile as he straightened his tie and looked into the camera.

"My fellow citizens of the Western Allied States," he began. "It is with regret that I come to you today from hiding. Terrorists and political traitors have undermined our great nation, driving your elected representatives from government and inciting violence across the country. I have been forced to take leave from my office in fear for my own life."

He paused, eying the camera, and Chris swallowed. The glint in the President's eyes was not one of a defeated man. If anything, he looked invigorated, as though this week of chaos had revitalized him.

"It grieves me that our great nation has come to this. But fear not. I will not let chaos stand. I will not allow treacherous generals and foreign devils to overthrow our nation. This will not be the end of democracy in the Western Allied States."

Chris scowled, cursing the man's hypocrisy. The President himself had been the first to undermine the country's democracy. Who else could have been behind the spate of disappearances, the bribery scandals and treason charges brought against opposition leaders? By the first postwar election, the opposition party had plummeted to record lows in the polls. Eventually they had crumbled to infighting, fracturing into half a dozen minor parties who could never truly challenge the President's party.

"Myself and a few loyal souls have already begun preparations to restore order. While our armies are fractured, we will soon have the force needed to bring peace to New Mexico. We expect Arizona, California, Oregon and Washington to quickly follow.

"In the meantime, I ask those of you who believe in this great nation to have patience. Have faith that this is not the end, that our union will win through. The chaos of today is not our fate—peace will be restored. Though our foes surround us now, their greed will be their downfall. We will prevail."

A shiver went through Chris. Gripping the rails of his bed, he tried to sit up. The steel cuffs cut into his wrists as he strained against them, teeth clenched with rage. Hands trembling, he searched for the remote to hurl it at the television, but somehow he'd lost it in the folds of the sheets. The speakers screeched as the President continued his address.

"And to those who would oppose us, to the traitors marching in our streets, and those powers threatening our borders, I say this: defy us at your peril. Foreign acts of aggression will not be ignored. Any movement of troops across our borders will be met with swift and fatal recourse."

Leaning forward in his chair, the President stared through the screen, eyes alight. "I have taken refuge with loyal soldiers at the Kirtland Air Force Base. In doing so, I now have sole command of our nuclear defense system. Should foreign powers seek entrance into the Western Allied States, I will have no choice but to unleash these powers. Mexico City, Houston, Austin—every major urban center you possess will be wiped from the map."

At that the President leaned back and smiled. "And to those domestic traitors who desire my position, well, you know where I am." He spread his hands. "I'm waiting."

38

The setting sun stained the skyline red as Liz drifted down towards the city. For once, the San Francisco winds had died away, and she glided easily through the open air, her feathers making miniscule adjustments in the shifting air currents. Banking left, she slid between the skyscrapers, watching the hills rolling up towards the peak of Independence Square, then back down towards the suburbs.

Breathing in the fresh salt air, high above the chaos, Liz struggled to relax, to forget for a few minutes about Chris and Mike, about Mira and Maria, about Jasmine dying in her arms. But it was hopeless. The ghosts of the past chased her wherever she went.

The skyscrapers fell away as Liz soared over the suburbs. The hills flattened, the buildings changing to a miss-match of single-story villas and dense townhouses packed into the narrow San Francisco streets. Trees lined the sidewalks, their branches flourishing with the green of summer. A few cars dotted the roads, but most residents had retreated to their homes to wait out the night.

Liz hadn't left the embassy with a purpose or destination in mind, only in the knowledge she had to get out, had to escape the narrow hallways and rooms and put as much distance between herself and Chris as possible.

Now though, she began to recognize the landscape below, the trees and twisting streets. With a jolt, she realized where she was going.

It didn't take her long to reach the park. Tucking her wings in close, Liz dropped from the sky, watching as the pine trees grew in her vision. When she was some thirty feet above the ground, her wings snapped back open, and she lurched to an abrupt, mid-air stop. The muscles along her back clenched, tying themselves up in knots, but in a way the pain was welcome. At least it was real.

She drifted down to the ground, scanning the familiar parking lot, taking in the seedy public bathroom and the distant row of pines. The faintest whiff of ash drifted on the air. Steeling herself, Liz walked around the corner of the toilet block.

The breath caught in her throat as the burnt-out car came into view, her chest swelling with anticipation. It was as though she expected to find Jasmine waiting there for her, eyebrow raised, foot tapping impatiently against the concrete.

Instead, Liz found herself alone. Her gut clenched. Tears streaming down her face, she crossed to the car. A sob wrenched its way up from her stomach as she placed a hand on the blackened roof and looked through the shattered window.

The flames had licked the old sedan clean, melting the paint from the exterior and leaving the steel frame a twisted wreck. The back seat where she'd laid Jasmine down and said her goodbyes was bare. There was nothing more than a pile of ash where her friend had been. It was as if Jasmine had never existed.

A wave of nausea struck Liz. Staggering sideways, she dropped to one knee. Panting, her vision blurring with tears, she grabbed at the car to steady herself. Her stomach cramped, and she groaned as her legs turned to jelly. She sat down hard, pulled her knees to her chest and leaned back against the car.

"You were right, Jas," she whispered, her eyes fixed on the empty asphalt. "We should have listened to Richard, back in the mountains. We should have just disappeared, run away and never looked back."

A soft breeze blew through the parking lot, rustling the leaves of a nearby tree. She waited as the breeze died away, as though somehow her words might reach through the veil and draw back a response. The last glow of the setting sun had fallen beneath the treetops. Darkness pressed in around her. But there was no response, only the calm silence of night.

Liz shook her head. "It's all been for nothing. Everything we've sacrificed, everything we've done, it's only made things worse."

Who could have imagined the truth would have such disastrous consequences? That it would turn rural on urban, and send the nation to the brink of another civil war? In the last week, she had witnessed the true depths of humanity's evil, had watched as society unraveled and her country reverted to mob rule.

Not that Liz could blame the refugees for their rage. After all, they were her countrymen. She had grown up alongside them, had suffered the same poverty and rampant depredation that had come after the American War. The postwar depression had crippled the rural economy, bankrupting farmers across the country. With their land lost to wealthy investors from the cities, rural communities had spent the last two decades scraping a living from the pennies left to them.

Now, that brooding resentment had been set aflame by the Director's confession.

Slowly the pains in Liz's stomach faded away. She sucked in fresh air as her grief relaxed its iron grip. Staring into open space, Liz remembered again her fiery friend, remembered the tears they'd shed together after Richard's sacrifice, after they'd thought Chris and Ashley lost. Despite their rocky beginning, Jasmine had become like a sister to her. More than anything, Liz regretted pushing her away in those final weeks.

She would have given anything to have her there, to talk with her about Chris. No doubt she would have ended up crying into Jasmine's shoulder. Liz smiled at the thought. Closing her eyes, she bid a final farewell to her friend. Then she placed her hands against the asphalt and pushed herself back to her feet. Brushing the stones from her gloves, she gave the burnt-out car a final glance, and turned away.

Wandering through the park, Liz found her thoughts drifting to the future. She wondered whether she was destined for the same fate as Jasmine. They had won the battle, had defeated the Director and driven the President from the western seaboard, but the war was far from over. So long as the madman lived, he remained a threat. The President had proven in his two decades of rule to be a man without rival. If he said he would return, Liz had no doubt he meant it.

But with the President's finger on the button of a nuclear arsenal, there was little anyone could do to act against him. Anyone that is, but Liz and her friends. They were the only ones who stood a chance of getting close, the only ones powerful enough to take on whatever forces the man had gathered around himself. Yet if they did, any one of them could be next on the funeral pyre.

Shuddering, Liz gathered herself and leapt skyward. Her wings beat down, sending dust swirling around the empty parking lot. Airborne, she raced across the treetops, her wingtips barely missing the tallest branches. Her heart hammered in her chest, and an icy fear crept through her veins. Her wings moved faster, hurling her through the sky. The park flashed past below, then gave way to the dark waters of the harbor.

Taking a breath, Liz forced all thought of the future from her mind. Her heart slowed as her fear fell away. Banking, she turned back towards the coast. The houses here had once been the pick of the city, golden mansions that looked out across the harbor to the scarlet expanse of the Golden Gate Bridge. Now they stood empty, great stone and metal monuments to the arrogance of man.

Concrete seawalls had protected them from the incremental sea level rise of the last thirty years. But it had only been a matter of time before the warming oceans brought the devastating hurricanes of the tropics to San Francisco. Hurricane Huerta had spared most of the city, but its low-pressure eye and howling winds had driven waves up above the high tide mark, smashing seawalls to pieces and sweeping through the mansions below.

With the storms only forecast to worsen, the owners had

finally abandoned their properties to the ocean. For ten years they had stood empty, their lower floors inundated, their walls crumbling to neglect and decay.

Looking at them, Liz realized a new group had taken up residence. The refugees who'd streamed into the city were quick to occupy any available space, and the upper levels of the mansions were still untouched by the rising waters. A shantytown now packed the spaces between the buildings, as desperate souls threw up makeshift walls and corrugated iron roofs to protect themselves from the elements.

There, finally, Liz spied people. Unlike their urban cousins, the people below had no fear of the darkness. They stood in the open, gathered around flaming barrels and spreading out into the streets beyond the shantytown. Most looked harmless, wandering the maze of crude alleyways with empty hands, eager just to go about their lives safe from the hordes of *Chead* roaming the countryside.

Then, as Liz drifted over the maze of crude alleyways, a scream pierced the night.

39

Susan settled back on the rags and closed her eyes. The weight of five tiny bodies lay across her stomach and breasts. Their fiery heat radiated through her, reassuring her that they lived, that her babies had survived. She could hardly believe she'd survived the ordeal herself. Yet here she was, alive and whole, basking in the warmth of her future.

Three girls and two boys.

Stones rattled, and Susan watched as Hecate entered their cavern. He slid through the shadows until he stood over her. His grey eyes glowed in the light of the candles, staring down at them.

Smiling, Susan gestured to the empty rags. A smile appeared on Hecate's face and he quickly settled himself beside her. She shivered as he embraced her, embraced them all. Closing her eyes, her worries faded away, a soft blanket of contentment wrapping around her.

Resting her head against Hecate's chest, she breathed in the scent of him, of their family, their life. Settled there, she could almost forget the trauma of the past hours, almost ignore the hot cramps still wrapping around her abdomen.

"My congratulations, Susan, Hecate," Talisa whispered in the flickering light.

Susan's eyes snapped open, her heartbeat quickening. Hecate stirred, and one of the boys on her stomach started to wriggle. She stroked his head as the elder *Chead* approached them. A flicker of red drifted across her vision. There was a bitter taste in Susan's mouth as Talisa took a seat on the outcropping of rock beside their makeshift bed.

Finally remembering herself, Susan nodded. "Thank you, Talisa."

A smile spread across Talisa's aging face. "You have done well, ensuring our people's survival. The *Chead* could not have asked more of you."

Lying flat on her back, staring up at the ancient *Chead*, Susan felt small. With the tiny bodies wrapped in her arms, she was vulnerable, trapped by their presence. She didn't dare move for fear of waking them.

"It's not over," Susan whispered, glancing at the sleeping faces of her children. "This world will never…be safe for them, not while…humanity hunt us."

Talisa's bleached white eyes studied Susan closely. "That is a worry for others now, my child." Her voice was dry, rasping as it echoed from the cold rocks. "Your children need you."

Susan frowned and she tried to sit up. A sharp cry came from one of the girls, and cursing under her breath, Susan stilled. But she wasn't about to give in so easily. "I will not stand idle…while the humans plot against us. I cannot rest…until the world is safe for them."

"My child, we have warriors who will carry the fight to the humans," Talisa replied, her voice hardening. "Tomorrow they will leave these caves and travel through the mountains. Hecate and I will lead them. We will kill this President and leave the humans leaderless. But you must remain." She grinned. "We cannot risk such a fertile female beyond our safe haven."

Anger lit in Susan's chest. She sat up, taking care to place her babies gently on the rags beside her. One of the girls started to shriek, but Susan only handed her to a surprised Hecate. Standing, she faced Talisa. "You think killing their leader will stop them?" she asked, the words coming easily for once. "You think they'll leave us alone, now that you've revealed our strength?"

Susan suppressed a shudder as Talisa stepped in close. The elder *Chead's* eyes seemed to glow in the dim light, but Susan refused to bow down.

"You would defy me, child?"

The edge to Talisa's voice raised the hairs on Susan's neck. There was a warning there, a threat. Swallowing hard, she lowered her gaze, suddenly unable to meet the elder's eyes.

"No, Talisa," she murmured demurely, "but…I have another idea…something I remembered."

A long silence stretched over the cavern, broken only by the soft murmuring of Susan's upset children. Her heart wrenched as she looked back and saw Hecate cradling two of the girls to his chest. For a moment she was filled with a yearning to obey Talisa's command. The desire to wrap her children in her arms, to give her life to them, was all but irresistible. It would be so easy to remain here, to forget the dangers of the outside world, the cruelty of humanity, and dedicate herself to the *Chead.*

Yet even surrounded by the sweet scent of her brethren, a part of her still resisted. A voice deep inside her called out, demanding her to act. Because if she did nothing, Talisa would lead them all to destruction.

"Explain yourself, child," Talisa said finally, her voice laced with anger.

Susan glanced from Hecate to Talisa. "There's something I remembered…" she repeated, slowly regathering her confidence. "A final piece to the puzzle of our survival."

"And what would that be?"

"A way to defeat them," Susan whispered. "A way to wipe humanity from existence."

40

"No! Stop! Leave me alone!"

The scream echoed from an alleyway running between two of the rotting mansions. Scanning the shadows, Liz found the silhouettes of two men and a woman advancing on a fourth figure. As the scream came again, she folded her wings and dropped from the sky.

Stones crunched as Liz slammed into the ground, her jet-black wings flaring out to fill the alleyway. The three assailants flung themselves away from her, eyes wide. Shouts echoed off the narrow walls as they tripped and went down in a heap. A low growl rose in Liz's throat as she stepped towards them.

The three scrambled to their feet, but now that the initial shock of her appearance had worn off, they stood their ground. The tall walls of the alley cut off the last glow of the setting sun, but Liz had no trouble making them out in the gloom. Her eyes swept over the three, taking in their tanned skin and angry eyes. The woman with them held a pistol gripped tightly in one hand, while one of the men cradled a sawed-off shotgun. The last towered over the other two, a crowbar in hand.

"It's one of them freaks!" the woman with the pistol shouted. "You know, the old President's lackeys?"

"Yeah, we're not blind, Sally," the man with the shotgun

replied. His eyes glinted in the darkness as he pointed his weapon at Liz. "What do you want, freak?"

Liz could hear their victim whimpering behind her. Glancing back, she saw a girl on her knees huddled up against the wall. Cursing, she swung back to the assailants. Only a few feet separated them—she could cross that distance in the blink of an eye. Making up her mind, she gave a dark smile and folded her arms.

"Leave now, and I won't break your legs," she said, flashing her most menacing grin.

The three shared a glance and edged back a step, eyes wary. The public hadn't seen what they could do, but these three came from the countryside; they would be all too familiar with the *Chead*. To her surprise though, they stood their ground, seeming to take confidence from their numbers and weapons. The two in the lead hefted their guns and pointed them at her chest.

"What's the girl to you, freak?" The man with the shotgun smiled and gestured at the terrified girl. "Pretty urban thing like that needs a lesson on how the world works now."

Fists clenched, Liz took a slow step forward. Stones crunched as the three took a matching step back, the guns wavering in their hands. Fury lit in Liz's chest as she watched them, the bitter taste of disgust on her tongue.

"You make me sick," she spat. "What has she ever done to you? You think just because the government set the *Chead* on us, it gives you some right to take that injustice out on her? You think this is *her* fault, just because she's from the city?"

"What would you know, freak?" the woman with the pistol snapped. Anger seemed to give the woman courage. "Why don't you go scampering back to your maker? I'm sure you've got things all nice and comfy, being his pet guinea pig and all."

"Is that what you think?" Liz growled. Her wings beat down, sending dust swirling through the alleyway. "You think I've had it good, do you?"

The woman's face paled as Liz approached, the handgun wavering. The man with the shotgun stepped in front of her. "Hey, stay back!"

Liz ignored him. "You think it's *fun*, being locked away for months? You want to try it? Maybe we should throw you in a cage and spend a few weeks prodding and poking you, tormenting you like some animal. Maybe then we'll see who's the *freak!*" Her voice rose to a scream as she lunged forward and tore the shotgun from the man's hands.

He stumbled back as she slammed the gun down on her knee. It snapped in two with a shriek of twisting metal. Hurling the pieces aside, Liz leapt as the woman pointed her pistol. The gunshots roared in the narrow space, but Liz was already airborne, her black wings merging with the night.

Then she was among them, her wings flashing out, sending them reeling. Spinning on her heel, she jumped at the woman with the gun, driving her boot down into the woman's knee. There was a satisfying *crack* as it gave way. A high-pitched scream filled the alleyway as she dropped her gun and staggered back.

Recovering from his shock, the first man shouted and lunged at Liz. Pressed against the wall, she had no space to avoid him, but it hardly mattered. His fist flashed for her face, but she only reached up and caught it with a gloved hand. The color drained from the man as she grinned. Before he could pull away, she dragged him forward into a headbutt.

He staggered back as she released him, hands on his head. When he didn't go down, she leapt, wings beating to add to her momentum, and kicked him square in the chest. The blow hurled him back into the concrete wall. Groaning, he slid to the ground and did not get back up.

Liz nodded with satisfaction and searched for the last man. He was already fleeing down the alleyway, his broad back disappearing into the shadows. Anger lit in her stomach. Baring her teeth she started after him, before a soft sob drew her attention back to the girl. Pausing, Liz sucked in a long breath, and dismissed the fleeing man as a coward.

The woman with the broken knee was still cursing under her breath, trying to drag herself away from Liz. The pistol lay nearby and Liz quickly kicked it out of reach, before aiming a solid blow at the woman's head for good measure. Only then did she approach the girl.

Her blonde hair was a tangled mess, and when she looked up at Liz, there was naked fear in her eyes. Dirt streaked her pale face and covered her clothes. She couldn't have been older than Liz's own seventeen years of age.

Liz offered a friendly smile as she crouched beside the girl. "Hey, it's okay, they're gone now."

Wide-eyed, the girl stared. "Please, no," she stammered, shaking her head. "Please, just leave me alone."

Liz blinked, her brow creasing in a frown. "It's okay, I'm not going to hurt you. Here, let me help you up." She offered a hand.

Screaming, the girl scrambled back. "Stay away from me, *freak!*"

Liz flinched as the shout echoed through the alleyway. Slowly she straightened, the smile falling from her face. Where the men's insults had slid from her like oil on water, this one cut straight to her soul. She opened her mouth, then closed it again, struggling to find the words to reassure the girl.

"I…I'm only trying to help," she stammered finally.

"I know what you are," the girl spat as she scrambled to her feet. She jabbed a finger at Liz like a knife. "You're one of *them*, one of the *Chead*!"

"What? No! I'm not *Chead*." Liz gave a hesitant smile and nodded at her wings. They lifted gently from her back, though in the darkness her black feathers were almost invisible. "See?"

The girl's face only paled further at the sight of Liz's wings. She backed away, her feet stumbling over the garbage littering the ground. "No, you *are!* I heard on the radio…you and that boy, you're just the *Chead* in disguise, come to take us away, to make us all into freaks like you!" She was screaming at the top of her lungs now, gesturing wildly with her hands, her high-pitched voice drilling into Liz's skull.

Liz fought for calm. "What? That's ridiculous, I don't want to hurt you. I just want to make sure you're okay." She gestured at the unconscious man and woman behind her. Trying to keep her voice light, she continued, "Look, it's not safe out here. Why don't you tell me where you live, and I can take you home?"

Smiling, she held out her hand again, but one look at the

girl's face told Liz she wasn't buying it. Eyes wide and shining, the girl shook her head. "I'm not going anywhere with you." Drawing herself up, she spat at Liz's feet. "I'd rather die than become one of you."

All Liz could do was stand and stare. Hate and fear warred on the youthful face. Shivering, Liz glanced at the two she'd downed. With the chaos gripping the city, there was a good chance more like them were lurking in the streets. Could this girl really hate her so much? Was she really so afraid she'd rather risk being mugged, or worse, than accept Liz's help?

Blinking back tears, Liz shook her head. "I only want to help you," she tried one last time.

"I'm sure that works on rural tramps like you," the girl sneered, "but us city girls aren't so gullible."

The girl glared at Liz, as though waiting for a response, but Liz couldn't find the words. She stood there in silence, eyes downcast, the wings hanging from her back like lead weights. Finally, the girl snorted and spat again, then spun on her heel and marched off down the alleyway.

Liz watched as the girl disappeared into the shadows, leaving her alone in the alleyway. The rush of the fight had left Liz, and now she felt lost and empty. Loneliness clung to her like a dark shadow. She yearned for someone to hold her, for the warmth of love to fill her. Instead, there was nothing but a vacant hollow in her chest.

She stood there for a long time, listening to the sounds of the night, the distant echoes, the whisper of voices. She tried to pick out the girl's footsteps, but either she was too far away, or she had already made it home. Despite the pain in her heart, Liz hoped it was the latter.

Finally, as the dim glow of the half-moon lit the alleyway, Liz faced the sky. A sudden yearning filled her, a need to see the man she had once loved, to go to Chris and listen to his story. Every day her hope for the future faded and the hole in her heart grew, the walls hardening. She didn't want to be that person anymore, that girl who shut out the world.

No, she needed to talk to Chris, to hear him out. She might

never love him again, but maybe if she could just understand *why* he had betrayed them—why he had betrayed *her*—she could at least move on. Maybe then the jagged hole in her heart would start to heal.

Taking a breath, Liz wiped the unspilt tears from her eyes.

Then she spread her wings and hurled herself into the sky.

41

"So, I understand you want my help?"

Sam sat quietly at the boardroom table, watching as the speaker paced the length of the room. The man wore a dark green military jacket sprinkled with an impressive array of medals and ribbons, which no doubt meant he held a position of some prestige. Not that military rank meant much these days. The thousand loyal troops the man commanded were an entirely different matter.

"That's right." Though he spoke softly, Harry's voice carried easily across the room. The veteran sat in a simple wooden chair at the head of the table, fingers folded in front of him.

Reaching the end of the room, the commander turned and made his way back to the table. He stopped beside Harry and looked down at the old man. "And who are you to request my help?" There was no mistaking the disdain in his voice.

Towering over the table, the man made an imposing sight, but Harry met his steely gaze with a calm smile. "Why, I'm just an old man, Commander. I am no one. I only hope to serve my country one last time. I believe I have earned at least a little trust in the community since the government's collapse. Perhaps if we work together, your men can help me restore some peace to San Francisco."

The Commander eyed Harry, then gave a snort. He pulled out the chair beside the old veteran, then sat and looked around the table. Sam shrank in his chair, but the man's eyes traveled past him without seeming to note his attendance. Most of the others present, Sam didn't recognize, but he smiled as he met Jocelyn's gaze. Hers at least was a friendly face—the rest regarded his appearance with either cold indifference or outright hate.

The eight men and women at the table made up the "council" that Harry had brought together to help him restore order. They included a captain from the small group of police who'd fallen in with Harry, the new leader of the Madwomen, a doctor and several former politicians, Jocelyn, and a couple of self-appointed leaders from the rural refugees. It was they who had given Sam the darkest looks as he sat down. No doubt they recognized him from his press conference with the President.

"And I suppose you'd like me and my men to fall under your command, Harry? Can I call you Harry?" The commander laughed and patted the old veteran on the shoulder so hard it almost knocked him from the chair. "I'm not sure that'll work for me, Harry. You see, you're just a civilian. My men, they don't respect civilians, not with the way your lot have let things go to hell. I hear a general up in Portland has declared martial law, taken control of the city himself. Not a bad idea, if you ask me."

A strained silence fell over the room. The members of Harry's council shifted uncomfortably in their seats. Harry said nothing, but took a moment to straighten his tie. Finally, a smile spread across his wrinkled cheeks and he nodded at the commander.

"I suppose that's fair," he said in his soft voice. "I know how they feel, these men of yours. My comrades and I, we used to talk about the injustice of it all ourselves, back in the war. How we had to take orders that might very well get us killed, while those giving them sat back in the safety of San Francisco."

The commander's eyebrows knitted together. "You fought in the war?"

Harry's smile spread. "Oh, yes. Lieutenant Harry McCrae,

Third Division, Artillery, at your service. Well, that was my position for most of the war, anyway." Placing his hands on the table, Harry pushed himself to his feet. Wandering around the room, he continued, "Not at the end, mind. You see, those politicians back in San Francisco were devious creatures. They came up with a plan, one that would have saved thousands, maybe millions of lives."

He had circumnavigated the table by now. Stopping behind his chair, he leaned against its back and stared down at the commander. "Only thing was, they needed a few brave soldiers to see it through. They needed a few men to face almost certain death, and light the fuse of the new world."

Sam's heart hammered in his chest. All eyes were on the old veteran now. Slowly Harry pulled back his chair, its wooden legs scraping loudly against the tiles, and resumed his seat. Clasping his fingers together, he smiled grimly at the commander.

"My friends and I, we were those men. I was the only one who made it out of DC, the one who drew the short straw. I got to live on, and see the world that my friends died for become corrupted. To watch as the rich and powerful turned it into their plaything." His eyes drilled into the commander, unblinking. "So when you say your men won't respect a civilian, after the mess the President and his Director have created, I understand." Harry leaned forward in his chair, his voice turning hard. "Now you understand this, *Commander.* I will not let the Western Allied States fall."

Sam almost smiled as the commander's throat contracted. The man's eyes were wide, becoming great globes in his pale face. The silence stretched out as he stared at the old veteran, lost for words. It seemed to take an effort of will for him to finally tear his gaze away.

"Yes, well, with certain conditions, perhaps we could come to an arrangement, *sir*," the commander mumbled.

Harry's face brightened and the tension in the room melted away. "I'm glad to hear it." He gestured around the table. "I'm sure my friends and I can oblige."

The commander nodded. After taking a moment, he continued, "I see you have one of *them* with you." His eyes flicked to Sam. "Mind explaining to me why?"

"Samuel is here at my invitation," Harry replied. "He was instrumental in the Director's fall. We are all in his debt for breaking open Alcatraz. I thought it appropriate he join us."

The commander said nothing, but a man sitting at the other end of the table had apparently had enough. "Rubbish," he growled, pulling himself to his feet. Sam tensed as he looked at the refugee leader. "I'll not sit here and discuss the future of our country while one of *them* sits listening."

Anger lit in Sam's chest as a rumble of agreement carried around the table, but Harry cut across the whispers before he could respond. "We would not be sitting here at all, if not for him, Diego."

"We only have your word for that," the woman beside Diego replied.

"And in the brief time we've known each other, Margery, has my word ever been false?" Harry replied.

Margery pursed her lips. "No, but these days that's hardly much reassurance."

"Then let *me* reassure you," Jocelyn cut in. "I can vouch for Samuel as well. He rescued me and my children, when the government would have executed us as traitors. I would, and have, trusted him with my life."

Still standing, Diego snorted. "You might trust him, but I don't. Not after what I saw his friend do. His kind, what they can do, they're not even human."

"My kind?" Sam asked, climbing to his feet.

The man sneered. "Would you prefer 'abomination'?"

"Why don't you come over here and say that," Sam said dangerously. A tremor ran through his wings, and they rose slightly from his back.

"*Enough!*" Harry hardly lifted his voice, but his command cut through the tension like a knife.

Blinking, Sam glanced at the veteran, before running his eyes over the rest of the room. He realized with a start that his wings were almost fully extended now, their copper feathers throwing a shadow over the table. The other members of the council stared at him, eyes wide and faces pale. With his teeth bared and fists clenched, he must have looked a demon, ready to tear them all to pieces.

Letting out a long breath, Sam quickly furled his wings and sat. On the other side of the table, Diego hesitated half a moment before resuming his seat. "I only want justice for my people," he muttered.

"Then we want the same thing," Sam replied. Their eyes met across the table as Sam continued. "Do you think we had any choice in this? That *I* had a choice when I stood on that stage beside the President? They murdered my parents, kidnapped me, and threw me in a cage to be their guinea pig. There were hundreds of us, hundreds of kids just like me, who weren't lucky enough to make it this far."

He fell silent then. Diego stared at him for a long moment before looking away. Sam doubted the man had heard a word of what he'd said.

"You will have your justice, the both of you," Harry said quietly. "The President will not escape the laws he swore to uphold. The Texan army is poised at the border, ready to strike when we give the green light. They can be at the Kirtland Air Force base in a matter of hours."

"That's too long," Jocelyn replied. "He'll have eyes on them—they won't make it a mile before he launches his arsenal. Unless you think he's bluffing?"

"He's not bluffing." Harry's eyes took on a haunted look. Remembering Harry's tale, Sam bit his lip as the veteran continued, "He was the one in charge, when we burned DC. He had no qualms then—he won't now. He'll wipe us all out in a heartbeat if he thinks he's threatened."

"Then it's a stalemate," the commander replied. "We can't act against him, and with my men, he doesn't have the numbers to act against us. I say we leave him there to rot."

"Didn't you hear what he said?" Sam cut in. "He already has the numbers to control New Mexico. If we leave him alone, he'll only grow stronger. He'll come for us, sooner or later. It's what the man does."

The commander snorted. "No one in their right mind would follow him after the Director's confession. He may not be bluffing about the nuclear codes, but he is about this so-called army of his. I doubt he has more than a handful of supporters left by now."

Sam gritted his teeth. "You're wrong," he grated out. "There were plenty who knew about what he was doing to us, but they still followed him. So long as he lives, so long as he holds an ounce of power, others will flock to it. It's what you—what we—do."

Looking around the table, he searched for an ally, but the eyes of the others were downcast, avoiding his gaze. Even Jocelyn looked uncertain, but she nodded. "Sam's right. We can't forget how ruthless this man is. So long as he's at large, the WAS will never be safe."

"We're not safe right now!" a woman cut in. Her sleek black suit and manicured nails marked her as one of the elite—one of the few who hadn't fled when the riots broke out. "Hooligans are marching in our streets, burning our property, threatening our lives. My husband was *killed* because he ran into the wrong people."

"Your people have been killing mine for decades," Diego snapped.

"How dare you—"

"Enough," Harry spoke over the top of them. His eyes swept the table, ensuring silence before he continued. "We will find a way to deal with the President in due course. But as you say, Grace, we must also restore order at home. Commander, we return to the reason I asked you here. Your men are the only organized force left who can help bring peace to San Francisco. Will you do your duty, and help us?"

A smile flickered across the commander's face. "I will, sir. But as I said, there are conditions." His gaze wandered to where the refugees sat at the other end of the table. "Peace must also mean restoring law and order. How can that happen, when I am told you have a known traitor in your custody, *sir?*"

Harry shook his head. "According to our illustrious government, *I* am a traitor, Commander. You might have to be more specific."

"The boy, *his* friend," the commander said, nodding at Sam, "the one who killed the Texan on live television."

For a long moment, Harry said nothing. Sam held his breath, heart racing as he waited for the veteran to deny the accusation.

"It's true," Harry said, finally breaking the silence. "We have Christopher in custody."

"*I knew it!*" Diego was on his feet again, his teeth bared. He looked ready to throw himself at Harry. "I knew you couldn't be trusted, old man!"

Harry raised his hands in a gesture of peace. "As I said, he is in *custody,* Diego. He's not going anywhere. When the time comes, he will face justice for his actions."

"I want him to see justice now," the commander cut in. "I want to see whether you really mean to uphold our laws, or if you intend to let the injustices of the old government continue."

Sam's chair clattered to the ground as he leapt to his feet. "You can't be serious!"

Across the table, Diego sneered. "Guess we know where your boy's true loyalty lies, Harry," he snarled. "What about yours?"

Sam started to reply, but Harry spoke over him. "Samuel, sit," he said, even as he stood.

"You cannot be considering this?" Sam snapped, refusing to back down.

Harry met his gaze. "I'm sorry, Samuel. You saw the footage, the same as the rest of us. Do you deny Christopher murdered the Texan?"

"None of you were there," Sam replied. "None of you have gone through what we had to, just to survive."

"Maybe not," Harry replied, "but this is real life, Samuel. The decisions we make have consequences. Like it or not, Christopher killed an innocent man. That cannot go unpunished."

Sam swallowed, his gut churning. “So what, suddenly it’s okay to punish people without a trial?”

Harry’s eyes lowered half an inch. “Maybe,” he murmured, his voice suddenly weary.

“I won’t stand by and let you do this,” Sam all but roared.

“I know, Samuel,” Harry answered sadly, “but I suspected it would come to this. Which is why I took measures before this meeting to have Christopher moved.”

Sam stared at the old man, breath held, unable to believe what he was hearing. “You betrayed us?” he whispered.

Closing his eyes, Harry nodded.

V

COMPROMISE

42

The creak of hinges drew Chris's attention to the door, but he quickly looked away again as Ashley stepped inside. Hours had passed since Liz had stormed out, and now darkness hung over the city beyond his window. With nothing but the television to keep him company, Chris had been drifting towards sleep. Now his heart raced as the patter of Ashley's footsteps crossed the room.

"Hello, Chris," Ashley said as she came to a stop beside his bed.

Chris steeled himself. "Ashley..." he began, then trailed off as he looked up.

She was staring at the broken chair, but her amber eyes moved back to him as he spoke her name.

"I see things went well with Liz," she said, eyebrow arched.

A lump rose in Chris's throat. Swallowing hard, he managed to find his voice. "I'm sorry," he croaked, fixing his eyes on the far wall. "I'm so sorry, Ash."

"Oh, Chris," Ashley whispered, her voice cracking.

Chris's mouth fell open as he realized she was crying. Before he could react, she threw herself at him, drawing him into a hug. For a second he stiffened, shocked by her reaction. Then he was hugging her back, clutching awkwardly at her with chained hands, her warmth against his chest. Burying his head in her shoulder he started to sob. He clung to her as though she were his last grip on reality, as though if he let go, he would fall away into the darkness, would lose himself forever.

"What have I done, Ash?" he gasped, eyes clenched closed.

"It's okay, Chris," she cooed, stroking his hair. Drawing back, she pressed her forehead against his. "It's okay. I'm here, I'm alive. We're safe, we survived."

Chris nodded, still choking on his grief. With his hands fixed to the rails, he couldn't reach his face to wipe away the tears, but in that moment, it didn't matter. All that mattered was they were safe, free of their tormentor.

When they finally broke apart, Ashley sat on the edge of the bed, her eyes shimmering. A soft smile touched her lips as she wiped the tears from Chris's cheeks. Hiccupping, Chris nodded his thanks. A wave of nausea swept through him at the movement. Beside his bed, a machine continued to beep, delivering morphine through a plastic tube into Chris's arm.

"How do you feel?" Ashley asked finally, placing a hand on his shoulder.

Chris shrugged. "Drunk, sluggish. At least it numbs the pounding in my head."

"Head wounds take the longest to recover from, apparently," she replied, "but your last x-ray showed the fractures in your skull have all but healed."

"Well, that's something," he mumbled, then swallowed. "I don't deserve your kindness, Ash. I don't deserve your friendship."

"Nonsense," Ashley replied tartly. She hit his leg, drawing his attention back to her. "We've all done despicable things, remember? Should be our motto."

"But Mike was...different," Chris said, fixing his eyes to the floor. "He was a friend."

"So was Liam...but I still killed him."

Chris looked up, startled. Ashley never talked about her own fight back in the facility, about the boy she'd killed.

After a moment's hesitation, Ashley continued. "At least you and Liz weren't friends with them. Liam…he was…he had become almost like a brother to me." As she spoke, her eyes turned distant. "Whenever I fell in those first few weeks, he would be there beside me, lifting me back up, urging me on. Without him and Sam, I never would have survived."

"You always seemed so strong, when we were locked in our cell…" Chris said, remembering the girl he'd first met in the prison deep in the Californian mountains, the girl who'd told him they were all in this together.

"I had to be, didn't I?" Ashley was staring out the window now. "He told me I had to go on, to be strong without him."

"He refused to fight?" Chris breathed. "Like Jeremy?" Jeremy was the boy who'd sacrificed himself rather than fight with Richard.

Ashley pursed his lips. "No," she murmured, looking back at Chris. "Liam…made me kill him. He threw me around that room like a ragdoll, screaming for me to fight back, to attack him. Until…I did. At the end, when he lay there dying, he smiled…and told me to be strong." Ashley's voice cracked as she finished.

"I never knew," Chris breathed, squeezing her arm.

"Not even Sam does." She clenched her eyes shut. Her chest swelled as she inhaled. "I'm only telling you because you need to hear it, Chris."

Chris's gut clenched. "It's not the same. Even if it was, I still abandoned you, Ash. I left you to die alone."

"It was what I wanted, Chris." Her eyes glinted. "If she hadn't…if things had continued, she would have broken me—same as you."

Chris hung his head, unable to find the words to reply. He saw again Ashley being dragged into the corridor, felt again the last spark of hope dying in his chest. In that moment he had broken, had found himself truly, completely alone.

"So what happens now?" he asked finally.

"They're going to execute you, Chris," Ashley replied.

Chris's head jerked up, his eyes widening, but there was no

trace of humor in Ashley's face. Taking a breath, he bit his lip and nodded.

"So be it," he said. Turning, he stared out the window.

Beyond the glass, the orange lights of distant skyscrapers lit the darkness, but overhead the sky was black, the stars hidden behind a blanket of clouds. Sadness weighed on Chris as he realized he would never soar through those skies again, never feel the wind in his feathers, or watch as the ground fell away beneath him. No, his end would be here, trapped in this concrete room, chained and helpless.

"No," Ashley growled. Chris turned at the anger in her voice, and flinched when he saw the fire in her eyes. "No, you don't just get to give up, Chris."

"What are you saying, Ash?" He frowned. "I know what I did. I have to accept the consequences."

"So you're just going to check out?" Suddenly Ashley was on her feet. She stood over Chris's bed, wings spread, eyes aglow. "You're just going to abandon us? Leave the world to wallow in the mess you created?"

Chris blinked, shook his head. Opening his hands, he rattled the handcuffs. "What do you want me to say, Ashley?" he cried. "What do you want me to do? Fight my way out when they come for me? What good will that do, other than hurt more innocent people?"

"I expect you to do *something!*" Ashley gestured wildly. "Your grandmother *died* for you. She stood up to the Director, gave away her life to show you the way, to remind you who you are, what you're capable of. Now we finally have a chance to make this world a better place, to *finally* have peace, and you're just going to give up?"

"I deserve to die for what I did, Ashley!" Chris shouted, sitting up in bed. His heart was racing. Fists clenched, he strained against his cuffs. "Don't you see, it's the only way I can make up for it? The only way I can make things right!"

"Coward!" Ashley shot back. "Your death won't change anything. It's the easy way out, to escape your own guilt. Why don't you do something decent with your life for once, instead of running away from everything?"

Metal rattled as Ashley tossed something at his chest. Chris looked down at the keychain lying on the sheets, then back at Ashley.

"You'd better get moving," Ashley said softly, her anger gone as quickly as it had come. "They'll come for you soon. Sam just left for a meeting with Harry's council. They're going to take you while he's distracted."

Chris stared for a moment longer at Ashley, then grasped at the key. Awkwardly he began to unlock his cuffs. While he worked, Ashley pulled the stent from his arm and then went to the wardrobe in the corner. Rummaging inside, she came back with a pile of clothes. Unlocking the second handcuff, Chris rolled out of the bed and tore off his hospital gown. After their time as the Director's pets, he didn't worry about Ashley looking. By now, they knew every intimate inch of each other's bodies.

When he was dressed, he stood before Ashley, still unsure. He'd followed her directions this far without thinking, his drugged-up mind hardly able to resist his friend's urgent commands. But now he hesitated, looking from her to the window, wondering whether running away was the right thing to do.

"What if…"

"No," Ashley cut him off. Stepping past him she pulled open the window. A cold breeze whistled inside, tugging at their feathers. "No more arguments, Chris. You want to make up for abandoning me? Then *live!* Get out there and do *something*, anything, to help. Don't stay here and die for nothing."

Chris stepped up to the window. The muscles down his back twitched as he spread his wings. He shivered as his dream returned, and he wondered if he even had the strength to fly. If not, this argument would hardly matter in a few minutes. It was debatable whether he would survive the fall from five stories.

His stomach twisted as he looked at the distant lights, old fears rising up from the past.

Gritting his teeth, he pressed them back down. Silently, he

reminded himself that if this was the end, if his strength failed him and he plummeted to his death, it was what he deserved. It was only right he pay for Mike's death, for the deaths of the teenagers he'd helped the scientists murder. For betraying Liz.

At the thought of the blue-eyed girl, Chris glanced back from the window.

"Liz..." he murmured.

Ashley stared back, eyes sad. "Fly away, Chris," she said softly. "There's nothing left for you here."

Hearing the message behind Ashley's words, Chris nodded. Liz would never accept him now, never find it in her to love him again. Their future had died the night he'd accepted the Director's offer of life. Nothing could change that now.

"Goodbye, Ashley," he murmured.

Without another word, he stepped out into open air.

And flew.

43

Flying back towards the embassy, Liz quickly realized her fight with the thugs had left her with more than just bruises. An itch started in the small of her back, and spread until it felt as though her skin was alive. By the time she landed on the rooftop, she was ready to tear off her clothes and hurl them into a furnace. Obviously, in addition to being idiots, the thugs didn't know how to bathe, and now her clothes were infested with fleas or lice or some other awful insect.

Muttering under her breath, Liz stalked through the rooftop door and raced down the stairs four at a time. It took her less than a minute to reach the fourth floor, where she slipped quickly into her room.

There she tore off her infested clothes and hurled them at the waste bin in the corner. Without pausing for breath, she headed for the bathroom. Marching across the tiled floor, she stepped into the glass box and flicked on the shower. She cursed as a stream of cold water engulfed her, and fiddled with the knob until it warmed.

Letting out a long sigh, Liz lifted her head and let the water pour down over her hair and feathers. The heat brought immediate relief to her itching skin, and closing her eyes, she allowed her mind to drift. A shiver went through her as the girl's words whispered in her ears.

Freak!

Impulsively, Liz lashed out at the wall. Pain seared her knuckles as they struck the tiles. Biting her lip to keep from crying out, she looked down and saw the sliver of broken tile embedded in her flesh. Teeth clenched, she pulled it out, and then ran her hand under the water. The floor of the shower turned red as her blood swirled into the drain.

When the bleeding finally stopped, Liz grabbed a bottle of shampoo and emptied it into her hair. She scrubbed herself down, praying the soap would kill whatever bugs still clung to her. Then she leaned forward and let the water run over her wings, sighing as the heat seeped through her feathers. They would take hours to dry, but the relief was instant.

Afterwards, she wandered out of the bathroom with her wings extended, still drying her naked body, only to find Ashley waiting for her.

"Did you have a good flight?" her friend asked, lips twitching.

Rolling her eyes, Liz finished patting herself down and wrapped the towel around herself. They were both well used to seeing each other naked, but there was no point in being overly familiar. She seated herself on the couch beside her friend, taking care not to sit too close. Without her long sleeves and gloves, she didn't want to risk poisoning Ashley with her touch.

"They hate us," Liz said softly.

Ashley shrugged. "Harry said we shouldn't go into the city."

"He was right." Liz sat staring at the coffee table. "But I had to get away, had to clear my thoughts so I could think…"

"About Chris?" Ashley asked.

Liz shrugged. "Chris, Maria, Jasmine, Mira." She shook her head. "It's all too much."

Ashley pursed her lips. "Chris is gone."

For a moment, Liz wasn't sure she'd heard her friend right. Slowly, the significance of Ashley's words seeped through. Her fingers dug into the sofa.

"What do you mean?" Liz croaked, her mind racing. Had the

doctors missed something? Her chest clenched, her skin crawling at the thought her conversation with Chris might have been their last.

Beside her, Ashley flinched and slapped her arm. "Ow!" she muttered, her eyebrows knitting in a frown. "Was that a flea?"

Liz blinked, momentarily confused by the change of subject. She stared at her friend, and then angrily shook her head. "Never mind that! What do you mean, Chris is gone? He hasn't..." She swallowed, unable to finish the question.

Ashley's eyes widened. "No, no, he's fine. Or he was when he left," she replied, then looked away. "But I told him to go. He couldn't stay here any longer, not after what he did."

"What?" Liz spluttered. "But...I thought...?"

Ashley stood and wandered around the room. Her eyes were distant, her steps hesitant as she circled the couch. Liz watched her, wondering what was going on in her friend's head. Hadn't Ashley been the one telling her all week to give Chris a chance?

Making a loop around Liz's room, Ashley returned to the sofa. Her hands trailed along the back of the cushions. Liz shivered as they touched her wings. Alarm prickled Liz's neck as Ashley sat down beside her, their bare legs touching.

"I can forgive Chris, but..." Ashley paused. "But not yet."

"Ashley..." Liz began, but words failed her as she saw Ashley's amber eyes aglow.

"He can't be here, not now. They were going to come for him, Harry and his people. And...we need time. He needs to earn back our trust, but he can't do that here. He would have been executed if I hadn't set him free."

Liz hardly heard what Ashley was saying. She sat staring at their legs pressed together, unable to pull away. "Ashley," she gasped. "Your leg, it's touching me."

Ashley blinked. A frown creased her forehead as she looked at Liz. Finally, she seemed to realize what Liz was saying, and jerked away. Together they looked at where Liz's leg had met hers, waiting.

Several minutes passed before Ashley shook her head. "I

don't feel anything." She looked askance at Liz. "Can you control it now?"

"No," Liz croaked. She was still watching Ashley's leg. "I don't…I…" She broke off as Ashley hugged her.

Liz sat frozen in Ashley's embrace. Unable to pull away, she went rigid, too terrified to breathe, to believe she might finally be able to hold someone again. Closing her eyes, she waited for Ashley to scream, for the deadly nematocysts in her skin to trigger, sending venomous barbs deep into Ashley's flesh.

The minutes trickled by and still nothing happened, until finally Liz started to relax. Hot tears gathered in her eyes, and sobbing, she threw her arms around Ashley. She clung desperately to her friend, feeling her skin beneath her hands, hardly caring that she was half-naked, that her wings might still be infested with fleas, or that the boy she was supposed to love had run away.

Chris.

The thought of him pulled her back. Sucking in a breath, Liz detached herself and watched Ashley through shimmering eyes. "I don't know how this is possible."

Ashley's lips twitched. "Neither do I. Sometimes it just feels like this is all too much, all the sadness and anger and pain, I feel like I'm about to burst. Then I take a breath, and all that stuff slips away. Everything becomes so clear, like I'm seeing the world through a whole new set of eyes. And I feel like I can do anything."

Liz laughed softly. "I'm starting to think that might be true." Her smile faded. "Where has Chris gone?"

"I don't know," Ashley replied. "I told him…I told him there was nothing left for him here."

Liz's throat constricted and she closed her eyes, remembering Chris lying in the hospital bed, staring up at her, unable to speak. He had taken everything she'd said, all her accusations and insults, without objection. He hadn't offered any arguments, any excuses, only his regret.

She realized then how much she hadn't said, how much more she needed to tell him. How she'd missed him every day, when she'd thought he was dead. How her heart had soared when she'd leapt through that door beneath Alcatraz and found him standing there. How she'd decided to do anything it took to kill the Director—and then spared the woman's life to save him.

How despite everything, a part of her still loved him.

Suddenly she was standing.

"What are you doing?" Ashley asked as Liz stalked into her bedroom.

The room was plain and undecorated, with only a bed and dresser for furniture. She began extracting clothes from the drawers. Pulling on a top, she searched for a clean pair of underwear. Following her into the room, Ashley watched on in silence.

"I don't care what he did," Liz muttered as she slid into a pair of jeans. "I'm not losing him again. He doesn't just get to run away."

"He's already gone, Liz. He can't come back. They'll kill him."

"Then I'm going after him." Liz cursed as she tried to spread her wings and realized the top she'd pulled on was one of the new ones the council had provided them. She hadn't had a chance to cut slits in the back.

Rummaging in the drawer, she came up with a knife and offered it to Ashley. Her friend took it after a second's hesitation, and Liz turned around to expose her back.

"I thought you couldn't forgive him," Ashley said as she started to cut.

Liz shrugged. Eyeing the clothes in the dresser, she wondered if she should pack a bag. She quickly dismissed the idea. Every minute she delayed, Chris only got further away. Sensing Ashley was done, Liz turned around again and spread her wings. A few feathers caught in the fabric before pulling free, allowing her wings to spread across the room. A tremor ran through them, spraying water through the air.

"Hey!" Ashley shouted, holding up her hands.

"Sorry," Liz grinned wryly. Stepping past Ashley, she returned to the living room. "It's going to be a long flight with wet feathers."

"You're really going after him?" Ashley asked.

"I think I have to," Liz replied. Crossing the room, she pushed the window open and looked out into the night.

"What will you say when you find him?"

Liz sighed. Then she laughed. "I'll probably yell at him some more."

At that, she turned and stepped out into open air.

44

"Chris is gone." said Sam, adding several expletives to the statement as he stepped into his room and found Ashley waiting.

Ashley sat up on the bed. "I know."

Sam paused in the doorway. "You do?"

"Yes, well, I'm the one who let him go," she said with a wink.

Sam stared at her a moment, then pulled her quickly into a hug. She went willingly, her slim frame folding into his chest. The honeyed scent of her hair wafted in his nostrils as he kissed the top of her head.

"You must have been just in time," he said as they separated. "Harry betrayed us. He sent someone to move him while I was in his meeting."

"Did he?" Ashley smiled wanly. "I guess the other council members are going to be upset."

"Furious." Sam grinned, though it quickly faded. "I guess we can't really blame them. So many have spent their whole lives suffering from the *Chead*. All they know is conflict."

"You sound like Liz," Ashley replied as he sat beside her and wrapped an arm around her waist. "She left, too."

Sam frowned. "With Chris?"

"No…" Ashley sighed, "but she went after him, when I told her. It's just the two of us now."

"Well that's not entirely true." Sam looked up as Harry's voice came from the doorway.

Clenching his fists, he stood and moved in front of Ashley. "What do you want, Harry?"

The old man chuckled and swung the door shut behind him. "I came to make sure that Christopher got away safely."

"What?" Sam croaked.

Ashley pushed off the bed and stepped around Sam. "Thanks to you, Harry." Grinning, she patted Sam on the shoulder. "He warned me how the meeting would go. I made sure Chris wasn't there when they came looking for him."

Sam blinked, looking from his mate to the old veteran. "You…you…"

"I am sorry for the deception, Samuel," Harry said quietly, "but I needed your anger to be convincing. They won't be happy Christopher escaped, but with luck your display will have them convinced I was not involved."

"You used me?" Sam managed to stutter.

"Sorry I didn't tell you, Sam." Ashley squeezed his arm. "Harry came to me just before the meeting. There wasn't any time to warn you."

Sam let out a long breath. "They're not going to be happy."

"I know." Harry smiled. "But life is full of disappointments. I just hope Chris is smart enough to get out of the city. We'll have to send out search parties. They'll insist on it."

Ashley frowned. "Liz is out there too. That could be dangerous."

"I will make sure they have instructions to capture only," Harry responded.

"I meant for *them*." She snorted, before her face turned serious. "What about us?"

Harry sighed. "I think it's best if you continue to lie low," he said. "It's not just the refugees who are angry. The public has been deceived for so long, and like it or not, your kind have become the face of that deceit. It'll be bad enough with just Elizabeth and Christopher out there."

"And what are you going to do about the President?" Ashley asked.

"Unfortunately," Harry replied, "nothing. We cannot act against him just now. Hopefully he'll stay where he is until we can restore order."

"In that case, we're going to have to decline your invitation, Harry," Ashley said. Sam raised his eyebrows, but she pressed on without answering his silent question. "Sam and I have a job to do."

Crossing to the sofa, Harry sat down with a weary groan. Gripping his cane in both hands, he looked up at them, dark eyes peering out from his wrinkled face.

"You're thinking about going after him alone," he stated matter-of-factly.

"Yes." Ashley nodded. Sam looked at her sharply and opened his mouth to speak, but a glance from beneath her long lashes shut him back up. Her eyes were aglow again. There was no arguing with Ashley when she was like that.

"This won't be like Alcatraz," Harry murmured. "The Director underestimated you—the President won't make the same mistake. The Kirtland Air Force base can host up to 10,000 active troops. If he's managed to staff it to even a tenth of its capacity…"

"I wasn't the one who broke into Alcatraz." Ashley flashed Sam a grin. "We'll try to be a little more subtle this time."

"Even so…you can't honestly think you'll succeed?" Harry pressed.

"We have to," Ashley said, turning the golden glow of her eyes on the old man.

To Sam's surprise, Harry didn't so much as blink. "Why?" he questioned. "Why not leave it to us? Haven't you and your friends done enough? You revealed the truth, stopped the Director. Why not sit this one out?"

Ashley stared at him for a moment, as though weighing up the idea, before shaking her head. "Because we've seen what he's capable of, Harry. Because I don't believe we'll ever be safe while he's alive. You think he's sitting there twiddling his thumbs? You think he'll stop because you have him surrounded?" She blew a strand of hair from her face and went on, "You think he isn't working on a plan to take back what he's lost? That he won't try and create more of us? No, even now he's probably experimenting on more innocent people, doing anything he can to give himself an edge. We have to end this before it's too late. And if you can't act, it'll have to be us."

A faint smile crossed Harry's face. "You know, if I were a gambling man, I might just put money on you pulling it off." He shook his head. "But you can't seriously think the two of you can take on a thousand trained soldiers?"

Sam laughed at that. Stepping up beside Ashley, he placed a hand on her shoulder. "Let's just say I wouldn't want to be one of those soldiers."

Lifting her head, Ashley stood on her toes and kissed Sam on the cheek, before turning back to Harry. "Wish us well?"

Smiling, Harry leaned on his cane and used it to push himself to his feet. He shuffled across the room and placed a hand on Ashley's shoulder.

"Always," he said.

45

Chris sat on the ledge, his legs hanging over the narrow canyon. His mind was lost in a rush of memories. Beside him, the stream roared along its stony bed before plunging over the edge into empty space. There it was caught by the swirling winds and torn to pieces. Mist swirled down into the canyon, settling on the broken scree and trickling over rocks to reform the stream below.

Staring into the canyon, Chris remembered again their desperate race up the riverbed. Their escape seemed a thousand years ago now, another life. Back then they'd all been so innocent, had still believed in things like mercy and right and wrong. Back then, Liz had begged him to spare Doctor Halt's life, despite everything the vile man had done to them.

Chris doubted anyone would have stopped him now.

Not that there was anyone left to offer their opinion.

His gaze travelled up the winding valley, to where the jagged hill of rocks leaned against the canyon wall. He remembered their desperate climb up its side, gripping at thorny bushes and wriggling between boulders, only to reach the top and find a sheer rock-face barring their escape.

And he remembered standing on the edge of the cliff with Liz, looking out over the valley, at the guards approaching with their high-powered rifles. Together they had taken a leap of faith, had stepped out into the void and plummeted towards the valley floor. And together they had flown, their new-grown wings halting their fall, propelling them upwards.

One by one the others had followed, and together Ashley and Sam, Jasmine and Richard and Mira had soared up to join Liz and Chris in the heavens.

Then Ashley had fallen, shot from the sky, and her blood had stained the pure-white snow of the mountains. They'd thought her lost then, but Ashley was a survivor. Now Chris knew that if any of them was going to survive this bloody war, it would be her.

If only the others had been so lucky. Sitting on the ledge, he could almost see the ghosts of his fallen friends, darting through the whirling clouds, dancing in the air, free of the horrors of life. A part of him yearned to join them, to fold his wings and hurl himself from the ledge. It would be so easy to end it all, to escape the pain and suffering.

Angrily, he shook his head. Tears streaked his face as he stood. Despite the summer sun, the cold mountain winds bit into his flesh. Ashley had been right. His death would change nothing—it was the coward's way out. No, he had to go on, had to be strong, endure and make things right.

He sucked in a breath through his nose, tasting the air, searching for the lingering sweetness of the *Chead*. They were lurking somewhere in these mountains. It wouldn't be long now before he found them.

He had spent the last few days tracking them across the Californian plains. While their passage seemed to leave no physical trace, the sickly sweetness of their aroma hung thick over the countryside. At first, he had struggled to make sense of it—the scent seemed to come from all directions. He soon realized his senses were not deceiving him. The deadly creatures were everywhere now, stalking through the forests, hiding beneath the earth, spreading through the hills. Yet those he'd encountered in his first few days were alone, nothing like the roaming packs described by the refugees flooding into San Francisco.

Alone, an individual *Chead* was no threat to humanity. But someone—something—had clearly begun organizing them. It wasn't until Chris scented a distant, familiar tang that he guessed the truth.

Hecate.

He still remembered the *Chead's* words, back in Liz's house. Somehow, Hecate had known what lurked out on the Californian plains, about the hordes of *Chead* waiting to be brought together. Wherever they'd been hiding, Hecate had obviously found them, molded them to his purpose. The torture he'd suffered at the hands of humanity had lit an awful hatred in Hecate's heart. The boy would stop at nothing to have his revenge.

At the top of the cliff, Chris spread his wings and hurled himself off the ledge. He smiled as the crisp mountain air caught in his feathers, propelling him upwards. Unlike his first flight, his wings and body were in tune now, their adaptation complete. His powerful, high-density muscles tensed and his wings beat down, hurling him upwards. Before, he had struggled just to make the short flight to the clifftops.

Within minutes, the valley was left far behind. Chris glimpsed the shining walls of the facility as he flew past but did not stop. He had no wish to revisit those dark corridors, no desire to see the cell he and his friends had shared for so many weeks and months.

The scent of the *Chead* drew him on. Lifting higher, he glided between the mountain peaks. He hardly felt the cold now. With the sun high overhead and the muscles all along his body working in concert, he was almost overheating. But it didn't matter. His quarry was close, his hunt almost at an end.

Below, bright red rocks glowed in the heat of the sun. Spindly scrub clung to the flats of the valley floors, while overhead the white-capped peaks glinted in the noonday sun, so bright Chris had to avert his gaze. The roar of a river echoed from the cliffs, its banks packed to bursting with the summer melt.

Not for the first time, Chris found himself wishing they'd never left this towering mountain range. Here, divided as they'd been, at least the five of them had been free. He could still see

Mira's youthful joy as she had danced through the clouds, diving down to inspect the frozen streams, quiet but happy. And Richard, as he'd smashed through the ice to catch a trout. Liz, doing her best to forage in the barren country. He could even see Jasmine, always so stoic and withdrawn, smiling at some secret joke Richard had whispered in her ear.

But instead they had left, had returned to civilization, and died for it.

Or lost themselves.

Tears blurred Chris's vision, but he quickly blinked them away. There was no point dwelling on the past. Ashley had challenged him to do something with his miserable life, and he didn't intend to disappoint her. Not again.

His eyes scanned the earth, taking in the folds of the mountain slopes. They were starting to fall away now, as the mountains dropped towards Arizona. The snow-capped peaks were behind him, giving way to mountains that seemed to wind together like some ancient tapestry. Chris squinted, studying the shadows cast across the rocky valleys. The scent was strong now. He was almost on them.

Movement shifted in the shadows. Angling his wings, Chris headed towards it.

46

Susan lay in the shadows staring up at the mountain peak. Her head rested on Hecate's shoulder, but her mate was fast asleep, his soft snores whispering through the night, merging with the rumblings of the other *Chead*. Talisa had brought a hundred of her best warriors with them—a small army that would tear through whatever resistance humanity might offer.

It had taken every inch of Susan's will to convince Talisa to bring her along. Even after Susan's revelation, the elder *Chead* had been adamant she remain behind. Her children needed her, Talisa had argued with cold eyes, even as she sought to steal away their father.

But in the end, the prize Susan had promised was too tempting, and Talisa had yielded.

Now though, in the cold, unforgiving mountains, Susan found herself plagued by doubt. Her heart ached, the absence of her children like a physical blow. She had left them in the caverns, in the care of another *Chead*—one with her own litter. They would be safe with the other newborns, protected by the maze of tunnels, and the *Chead* who had remained behind.

Still, Susan could not dismiss the uneasiness in her stomach, the fear she had made a terrible mistake. What if the humans came for them, if they unleashed their deadly weapons on the

Chead's hidden tunnels? Her children would be helpless, would die in agony, knowing their mother had abandoned them.

Shivering, Susan rolled on her side and stared at Hecate's sleeping face. The movement disturbed him, and his eyelids fluttered open, revealing the grey sheen of his eyes.

"My mate," he breathed, "why do you…not sleep? Night will come…soon."

Susan nodded, but the sorrow still lodged in her throat, and she struggled to find the words to respond. "I…am…worried," she murmured, "about our…future."

A rumble came from Hecate's chest as he stroked her cheek. A shiver ran through Susan as his scent caught in her nostrils. The fiery tendrils of desire wrapped around her throat, but for once she fought them back, desperate to cling to the remnants of her sanity.

"No…" she whispered as Hecate's fingers drifted down her throat.

Her mate stilled, his hand lingering on the small of her chest. A frown creased his forehead. "No?" he asked, his voice soft.

Susan shook her head, struggling to keep a grip on the train of her thoughts. Hunger slivered through her mind, distracting her, but she forged on.

"Humanity…is cruel...without mercy…what if…they come for them?" she pressed.

Laughter whispered from Hecate's lips. "Then we shall avenge them…a thousand-fold." Susan's eyes widened at the power in her mate's voice. His arms wrapped around her, pulling her on top of him. This time she lacked the will to resist. A smile spread across his lips. "The fire you shall light…will burn them all away."

A moan built in Susan's throat as Hecate's fingers danced along her back. She found herself nodding to his words, her worries assuaged, her path determined. Feeling him beneath her, flames filled her chest, and leaning down, she pressed her lips hard against his. She gasped as his taste washed away the last of her fear.

Suddenly Hecate stiffened beneath her. His hands gripped

her hard and tossed her to the side. She gasped as the cold mountain stones cut at her. Hecate clambered quickly to his feet.

"What are you doing?" she hissed, her lust turning to rage.

Her mate shook his head. He looked out over the other *Chead*, to where the mouth of the canyon opened out. There, the light of day shone brightly on the hillside.

"We have...a visitor," Hecate said finally.

He set off through the sleeping *Chead*, his bare feet making no noise on the sharp stones. Susan stared after him, anger churning in her chest. Without waiting for an invitation, she rose and followed him.

It only took them a few minutes to traverse the *Chead*. A hundred sleeping bodies dotted the ground between the towering cliffs, tucked into crevices and between boulders, wherever they could avoid the howling mountain winds. In the shadow, they were all but invisible.

Susan's heart raced as they made their way out into the sunlight. What did Hecate mean by a visitor? The *Chead* had hidden their tracks well, only traversing the wide Californian plains by night, hiding during the day, ensuring the humans remained unaware of their passage. Yet now Hecate was saying someone had found them, had managed to slip through their scouts and come within yards of their nest.

On the gravel slope, Hecate lifted his head and stared up at the mountains. Susan stood behind him, her eyes following his gaze. The sky was empty, but Hecate clearly knew something she didn't. Yet he did not seem concerned—in fact, there was the slightest of smiles on his face. Gritting her teeth, Susan settled beside him.

They did not have to wait long.

Within minutes, a speck appeared in the sky. Susan held her breath as it grew, waiting for the roar of an engine. She glanced at Hecate, expecting him to act, but still he did not move.

Slowly the speck grew larger, and Susan realized the visitor was not one of humanity's deadly aircrafts, but something else entirely.

The strange boy with tawny brown wings drifted towards

them, finally settling on the slope below. The stones gave way beneath his boots as he landed, almost sending him face-first into the ground.

Hecate snorted as the boy's curses carried up to them. "Welcome, cousin," he barked in greeting. "I thought…you were dead."

Scowling, the boy folded his wings behind his back and straightened. A tingle of recognition shot through Susan as his hazel eyes met hers, but after a moment he turned his gaze back to Hecate. Frowning, she tried to place him. The memories rose like shadows from her mind, blurry and indistinct, but she could not find his face among them.

"No thanks to you," the boy said, "and you're no relative of mine, Hecate."

Her mate grinned. "My apologies…Chris, yes?" He trailed off, and then shrugged. "We did not mean…to lead the humans…to you. They proved…persistent. Have you finally come…to join us?"

"No, I've come to stop you," Chris shot back.

Hecate chuckled. The sound echoed off the surrounding cliffs as he spread his arms. "You think…you stand a chance?"

The boy bared his teeth, his wings lifting slightly from his back. Susan eyed him, her lips pursed, but did not move. This was Hecate's fight to enjoy; her mate had no need of her help.

The boy twisted so he was standing side-on to Hecate, fists outstretched. "Why don't we find out?" he growled. "I've been dying for a rematch."

"Gladly," Hecate sneered.

At that her mate charged, his powerful legs sending up a shower of stones behind him. The boy Chris had only a split-second to react before Hecate was on him. Her mate's meaty fist swung at his face. Susan grinned as the blow sent the boy reeling.

But unlike so many humans before him, the boy did not go down. His feet shifted deftly in the loose gravel, steadying him. He tried to straighten, only to catch a foot square in his face. This time the impact flung Chris backwards across the rocky ground. He bounced several times before a boulder brought him to a stop. Blood trickled down his chin as he staggered back to his feet.

"Had enough?" Hecate asked lightly.

Chris didn't answer. Spreading his wings, he leapt into the air. Her mate crouched as the boy's shadow raced across the slope towards him. Eyes narrowed, he watched the tawny wings fold, sending Chris into a dive. At the last second, Hecate hurled himself to the side.

The boy cursed, but his wings were already shifting, redirecting his course. Hecate had no time to recover before Chris's boot struck him in the chest. This time it was Susan's mate who was sent hurtling backwards. But Hecate twisted as he fell, landing easily on his feet. A savage growl rumbled from his throat as he rubbed his chest and glared at Chris.

Rage lit in Susan's stomach as she sensed her mate's pain. She glared at the boy, though she did not move. This was still Hecate's battle—she would not intervene unless asked. No matter how much she longed to tear the hideous wings from the boy's back.

Raising a hand, Chris beckoned Hecate forward. "Come on, show me what you've got, *Chead.*"

A sharp hiss came from Hecate, but this time he did not rush the stranger. The two circled one another, grey and hazel eyes unblinking, never leaving their opponent for even a second.

Finally, Chris broke the stalemate. Lurching forward, his fist flashed for Hecate's face. Hecate reached up to catch the blow, but at the last second Chris dropped his shoulder. Instead of a fist, the boy's body slammed into Hecate's chest, sending him stumbling back. Using his momentum, Chris spun, and his wing snapped out to catch Hecate clean in the face. The force of the blow whipped her mate's head back with a sickening *thud.* Tumbling backwards, Hecate lost his footing and fell—just in time to avoid a second blow from Chris's boot.

On the ground, Hecate rolled as the winged boy gave chase. Gravel rattled down the slope as Chris leapt. His fist caught Hecate again as he regained his feet, but recovering, Hecate managed to catch the next wild kick. Digging in his fingers, Hecate locked the boy's leg in an iron grip.

Hecate grinned at his helpless opponent, but Chris only smiled back. Leaping off his other leg, he twisted mid-air, his free foot coming round to catch Hecate in the side of the head. Susan's mate staggered, his feet suddenly unsteady, his eyes whirling.

Chris landed lightly, his wings beating slightly to keep him upright. Folding his arms, he shook his head. "Not so fun when it's a fair fight, is it?"

Susan caught the steely glint in her mate's eyes as he straightened. She smiled to herself. Hecate was beyond reason now, caught in the red-hot insanity of the *Chead* rage. The imposter didn't stand a chance.

Roaring, Hecate charged. Chris fell into a crouch, wings outstretched, fists raised to guard his face. Even so, the ferocity of Hecate's attack drove him back. Chris gasped as the *Chead* batted away his feeble blows and grasped him by the waist. A cry echoed off the cliffs as Hecate lifted the boy above his head, preparing to slam him into the gravel.

Before Hecate could strike, Chris's wings beat down, sending dust swirling across the mountainside. The power of his wings yanked them both off their feet, allowing Chris to twist around and punch Hecate in the face.

Losing his grip, Hecate fell. He grasped at Chris's wing, and the boy shrieked as a handful of feathers tore free. The great wings beat down again, but off-balance now, Chris went spinning sideways and slammed into the loose gravel.

Hecate stalked after the fallen boy. Cursing, Chris rolled, narrowly avoiding being stomped into the side of the mountain. Coming to his feet, the boy narrowed his eyes as Hecate came after him.

Susan watched on from the slope above, the blood thumping hard in her skull. She could almost taste her mate's triumph now, could almost see the boy's face as his life trickled away, as he died alone in these merciless mountains. Breathing in, she savored the tang of blood in the air. Lust rose in her throat as she watched Hecate beat his way through the foolish boy's defenses.

Blood streamed down both their faces now, and half a dozen cuts marked their flesh. But Chris was slowing, his strength worn down by the fight, while Hecate seemed to find fresh stores of energy. The *Chead* rage was unquenchable, unstoppable. The pathetic creature would not prevail.

The two closed on each other again. Sensing his opponent's weakness, Hecate launched a flurry of blows. Chris staggered back, his reflexes barely able to keep stock of the *Chead's* fury. Dark bruises appeared on his arms and his shirt was in pieces. It would not be long now.

Then, as Hecate readied himself for another blow, the boy's foot slipped on the loose stones. He struggled to regain his balance, but Susan's mate was on him in an instant. Hecate clenched his fists together and swung at the boy's head.

Except Chris was no longer there. Spinning on his heel, he dodged Hecate's double-handed blow, allowing the *Chead's* momentum to carry him past. Suddenly the boy was behind Susan's mate. Before Hecate could react, Chris's arm was around his throat, hauling him back, tightening until the veins on both their necks were bulging.

Choking, Hecate struggled to break the boy's hold, but his phenomenal strength was rendered useless with his center of mass pulled off balance. His hands slapped at Chris's arms, his iron fingers digging into flesh, but the boy did not flinch. Teeth bared, he held on for dear life.

On the slope above, Susan shook herself free of her shock. Fists clenched, she started forward, the flickering of the *Chead* rage beginning in her stomach. The familiar red haze settled over her vision as she closed on the boy. His attention elsewhere, he did not notice her approach.

But as Susan closed on him, a sharp *crack* came from overhead, and a black-winged girl fell from the sky to land between them.

47

For three days, Liz had tracked Chris across the Californian plains, winging her way from abandoned farmhouse to rundown shack to open pasture. His distant scent drew her on, close, yet always just out of reach. However fast she flew, somehow he managed to remain one step ahead of her.

Only when she followed him into the mountains did Liz sense she was closing on him. Unfortunately, another scent was also growing, a sickly sweetness that tainted the crisp mountain air and set her stomach on edge.

The *Chead.*

Now, as she stood between the creature and Chris, she wondered what insanity had brought him here. Why had he come all this way to confront the *Chead*? What had he hoped to achieve out here, all by himself? She could smell the sweetness billowing from the dark canyon above—the stench of a hundred *Chead*, all gathered in one place.

On the slope above Liz, the female *Chead* had frozen, but now her lips drew back in a snarl and she started forward again.

"Enough!" said a gruff voice from behind Liz.

Risking a glance back, she realized her appearance had given the other *Chead* a chance to break free of Chris's hold. Liz blinked as she recognized him. It was the same creature they'd fought in the facility, who had escaped into the mountains and saved them from the soldiers.

The one who had led the government to her childhood home.

Hecate took a step back from Chris, his eyes gleaming in the dying sunlight. His gaze flickered up past Liz, to where the other *Chead* lurked. "Enough, Susan," he repeated.

Stones rattled as Susan came to a stop. A low growl came from the woman's throat and Liz saw the hunger lurking behind the grey eyes, the desire to tear her limb from limb. A long minute stretched out before the woman gave a curt nod.

Smirking, Liz turned her back and started down the slope towards Chris and Hecate. They watched her come, Chris with wide eyes, Hecate wearing a slightly bemused grin. Both were looking worse for wear. The fight had left their clothes in tatters, and dark bruises were swelling on their arms and faces. Approaching them, all Liz could do was shake her head. It seemed boys, whatever their species, would be boys.

Hecate's grey eyes looked her up and down as she reached him, and his grin spread. He opened his mouth to speak, but Liz was faster still. Stepping in close, she slammed her knee into his crotch, and the youthful *Chead* crumpled to the ground with a pained squeak.

"That's for my house," Liz snapped.

Stones rattled, and she turned in time to see the second *Chead* leap. Hands bare—she'd left her gloves in the embassy—Liz reached up and caught the woman by the fist. The *Chead* swung at her again, but she was obviously not accustomed to fighting someone with matching abilities, and Liz easily sidestepped her. She quickly drove a blow into the woman's stomach, forcing her backwards.

"You might scare humans," Liz laughed, "but you're no fighter."

Growling, the *Chead* started climbing to her feet. She made it to her knees before a convulsion shook her, bending her in two. A sharp scream echoed from the surrounding cliffs as the *Chead* collapsed on her side, clutching a swollen hand to her chest.

So I'm still venomous, Liz thought wryly. It was good to know—although it didn't explain why Ashley had been unaffected.

Hecate remained crouched on the ground, but now he slowly pulled himself to his feet. Concern marked his forehead as he looked at the woman.

"What…is happening to her?" he rumbled.

"She'll be fine," Liz replied. "Just give her a few minutes for the poison to wear off."

"Poison?" Hecate repeated.

"Yeah, it packs a real bite," Chris muttered as he joined them. Her stomach twisted as his hazel eyes found hers. "Liz… what are you doing here?"

"Looking for you," she replied.

Chris swallowed visibly. Wisely though, he chose not to respond.

"Humanity must be…desperate…if they have sent you," Hecate commented in a mocking tone.

Liz raised an eyebrow. "What makes you think we were sent?"

Laughing, Hecate only shook his head. He crouched beside the moaning Susan and lifted her into his arms. Leaning down, he kissed the red and purple mark left by Liz's touch. The woman's cries faded slightly, and she seemed to regain some of her composure.

"I know her…" Chris said as he stepped up beside Liz, "but she wasn't one of the *Chead* who escaped with you."

"No…" Hecate smiled. "We took her…from the facility. She chose…to join us."

Liz blinked at the creature's words as Chris paled, his eyes widening. "I do know her!" His jaw hardened and he pointed a trembling finger at the woman. "You're the one who gave us the second injection! You told me it was antibiotics!"

Susan wriggled in Hecate's arms, and the *Chead* hesitantly placed her back on her feet. A smirk twisted her pained face. "You are…truly gullible creatures." She laughed. "At least I… have left that misery…behind."

Liz looked from Hecate to Susan, struggling to catch up. She didn't recognize the woman, but then, she had been unconscious at the time. Chris had mentioned the doctor who'd come to their cell after their fight with Hecate, though Liz had never seen her. But if Chris was right, this woman was the one responsible for giving them their wings. Even after all this time, Liz still wasn't sure if that was a gift or a curse. Growing them had been the most painful thing she'd ever experienced. And now…now they marked them as outcasts, abominations, *freaks*.

Beside her, Chris was glaring at the woman, apparently lost for words. Smiling, Hecate stepped carefully between them. "It seems we have…much to discuss. Perhaps our kinds can…come to a resolution." His eyes lingered on Liz as he spoke, and she found herself shivering.

"A resolution?" she asked quietly. "What kind of resolution?"

Hecate shrugged. "That is not…my decision to make."

Chris frowned. "You aren't in control here?"

Hecate's laughter came again, its soft rasp slithering across the mountainside. He started towards the shadow of the canyon. His voice carried down to them as he glanced back. "Come… there is someone…you must meet."

48

Chris watched as the two *Chead* disappeared into the shadows, then, steeling himself, he started after them. His body ached from the fight with Hecate, but he did his best to keep the pain from showing. He didn't want the *Chead* to realize how much the fight had cost him. And, if he was honest with himself, he didn't want to seem weak in front of Liz.

The soft crunch of her footsteps came from behind him, but Chris didn't glance back. His mind was still reeling from her sudden appearance. He couldn't understand, couldn't comprehend why she'd followed him. The sight of her dropping from the sky had given him such a shock he'd released Hecate.

Thinking of the *Chead*, he wrenched his thoughts back to the present. Ahead the shadows loomed. He could see the dark-haired *Chead* waiting for them there, the former doctor close beside him. When they was still a few steps away, Liz moved up beside him, her footsteps matching his own. Chris shivered as her hand brushed his and he found her eyes on him.

"Liz…" he croaked. The words died in this throat, but he forced himself to continue. "What are you doing here? It's too dangerous."

For the briefest of seconds, a smile twitched on her lips. Her hand caught Chris's fingers and gave a soft squeeze. "Let's just see what they have to say." Her crystal eyes met Chris's. "We can talk later."

Before Chris could reply, her hand was gone and she was moving in front of him. Chris sucked in a breath and tried to still his racing heart. The gloom of the canyon swallowed them up.

Chris blinked, while ahead, Hecate continued over the hard ground. His vision slowly cleared, adjusting to the darkness. He clenched his jaw as, for the first time, he realized just what a mess he'd gotten them into.

Dozens of *Chead* lay sleeping around them, their soft snores echoing ominously from the towering cliffs. Swallowing, he edged his way between the sleeping bodies, following the retreating backs of Hecate, Liz and Susan.

Grey eyes flashed as Susan glanced back. He saw again the memory of her poised with a needle back in the facility. He could still recall the scene clear as day: Susan, young and nervous, eager to complete her task and flee their cell. Even at the time he'd been suspicious, but neither he nor Liz had been in any state to resist.

But it seemed that karma had found the young doctor in the end. Chris's gaze switched to Hecate, and he shivered, wondering at the relationship between the two. It was clear Hecate cared for the woman, but from the way they walked close together, the shared glances and closeness between them, he suspected it went much deeper than that. The thought made him nauseous.

"You don't remember giving us the injection?" Chris asked, momentarily forgetting where they were.

Liz flashed him an angry glance, nodding at the sleeping *Chead*, but Susan only shrugged.

"The *Chead*...has burned that foul creature away," she replied. Her hand drifted out to take Hecate's. "My mate...has shown me the way."

Hecate growled his agreement and stroked Susan's hair affectionately. Chris was suddenly reminded of the way the Director had treated him, as though he had been some pet to toy with. Even at the end, when she had taken him...

Bile rose in his throat and he pushed the memory back into the abyss.

Chris couldn't help but think about the fire burning in the woman's grey eyes. Remembering the demure woman from the facility, he wondered how her nature could have changed so unequivocally. The creature standing before him, draping herself over the towering figure of Hecate, could not have been more different from the terrified doctor she'd been.

Still, the transformation went some way to explaining the reports of the *Chead* taking villagers captive. Chris shuddered as he imagined the fate of those poor souls, to be stolen away by the *Chead*, forced to join them, to breed with the very creatures they'd spent their whole lives fearing.

Ahead, Chris's keen eyes made out a darker patch on the cliff-face. Hecate and Susan headed towards the cave, though they needed to half-climb, half-scramble up a steep slope to reach it. Shaking his head, Chris bounded into the air, his wings beating quietly in the darkness. Liz followed him, and together they settled down at the top of the slope. Smiling lazily, they watched Hecate and Susan finish their climb.

The two *Chead* said nothing as they pushed past, and chuckling to himself, Chris followed after them. Inside, the gloom deepened, but Hecate and Susan pressed on as though a thousand candles lit their way. Chris and Liz stumbled the first few feet, still waiting for their eyes to adjust. When things finally came into focus, they found themselves in a narrow tunnel, its ceiling and floor marked by the thin slivers of stalactites and stalagmites.

Weaving their way along the corridor, Chris wondered where Hecate was leading them, who they were supposed to be meeting.

Finally, the soft glow of candles appeared in the darkness ahead. Chris squinted at the flickering light. A *Chead* stepped forward to bar Hecate's path. Whispers, barely audible, passed between them, and the newcomer disappeared again.

"She comes," Hecate said, turning to face them. "The

journey has been long…and her strength is not…what it was. She is sleeping."

"Who's sleeping?" Liz asked.

Hecate only smiled and turned away. Across the cave, movement came from an adjoining tunnel as a woman stepped into the cavern. Striding past the candles, she took a seat on a small boulder.

Chris shuddered as the woman's milky white eyes traveled around the cave. Grey hair tumbled down her shoulders. Her face was wrinkled with age, the skin hanging in folds from her cheeks. Her shoulders were twisted and shrunken, her muscles shriveled. Yet there was a wordless strength in those white eyes, and Chris found himself unable to look away.

"Talisa…I have brought…guests," Hecate whispered.

"You have." The ancient *Chead's* voice echoed through the cave. Her milky eyes never left them. "Step into the light, my children."

Chris found his legs obeying without thought. "Who are you?"

The woman did not answer, only sat studying him, her cold eyes taking in his half-folded wings and muscular shoulders. Only when her gaze flicked to his side, and he saw at the empty space beside him, did Chris realize Liz had not moved.

"And you, my child?" the ancient *Chead* questioned.

Hesitantly, Liz stepped into the light. Her blue eyes were wide, her mouth hanging open as she stared at Talisa. Fists clenched, a shiver went through her, and the wings half-lifted from her back. Her face was pale, and she looked ready to flee, as though a terrible fear had gripped her. A low moan came from her throat. Her eyes never left the ancient *Chead.*

"Mom?" Liz whispered.

49

Sam groaned as he shifted on the rocky ground, cursing as a new stone dug into his backside. Across the fire, Ashley giggled. He shot her a scowl. Giving up on finding a comfortable spot, he stood and walked around the fire. Flashing Ashley a grin, he attempted to sit in her lap.

"Hey!" she squealed, scrambling out of the way.

Laughing, Sam quickly stole her spot.

"Oy!" Ashley shrieked, clambering to her feet. "I'd just finished brushing away the stones!"

Wriggling his bottom, Sam nodded appreciatively. "You did a good job." He laughed as her eyes flashed, and quickly opened his arms. "Come here, I'm more comfortable anyway."

She kept up her scowl for a moment longer, and then promptly folded her wings and settled in his lap. He wrapped his arms around her as she snuggled in close to his chest. Her hair dangled beneath his nose, the smell of dust and smoke mingling with the familiar scent of the girl he loved.

"How long did Chris and Liz say they'd been in the mountains for?" Ashley mumbled into his shirt.

Sam chuckled. "A week?"

"Don't know how they survived."

Feeling the rumble of Ashley's stomach against his chest,

Sam laughed again. He reached out and turned the stick they'd propped up over the fire. A skinny rabbit was slowly browning in the flames.

"It'll be ready soon," he murmured.

Like Ashley, Sam had never spent much time in the outdoors. Once upon a time, his father had liked to take him camping. But with the price of living in Seattle spiraling out of control, his parents had soon found themselves too busy working for weekends away. The only skill he remembered nowadays was how to navigate using Orion's Belt.

"Poor little *conejo*," Ashley whispered. "Hope he's tasty."

As Sam stroked her hair, he smiled. Ashley was the one who'd caught the poor thing. After two days without food, she'd spotted the rabbit mid-flight, and had been on it in seconds. The little critter had never stood a chance against the starving girl. "Since when do you speak Spanish?"

Ashley flashed him a youthful grin. Sam loved these quiet moments with her, away from the rush of the world, from the pressures of life. Only when they were alone did Ashley drop her guard, becoming the sweet-hearted girl that lurked beneath her tough façade. He liked the Ashley who could stop a *Chead* with nothing more than a glare, but this was the part of her he loved most.

"That was the name of my pet rabbit growing up," she mumbled. "We didn't eat him, but if he was here now, I would. We should have brought *food*."

"Probably, but who would have carried it?" Sam asked.

She nudged him in the ribs. "Thought that was why I brought you along."

"Is that so?" Grinning, he slid his hand up her hip and squeezed her side. Ashley yelped and tried to spring away, but with his arms encircling her, there was no escape. She burst into laughter as he tickled her, until a wild beat of her wings flung them both into the air. They landed together in a pile of tangled limbs and feathers.

"Never do that again!" Ashley panted as she picked herself up from the dirt.

Sam laughed. "Never."

Pointing her finger, Ashley took a step towards him. "I swear to God, Samuel."

Sam raised his hands in surrender. "Okay, okay." He grinned. "You win!"

"That's better." Turning on her heel, she marched back to the fire.

Crouching, she inspected the rabbit, then picked up the branch on which it was impaled. Returning to her spot on the dusty ground, she sat and started tearing at the meat with her teeth.

Sam raised an eyebrow. "Going to leave some for me?"

Ashley paused, looking him up and down before returning to her meal. A long strip of meat tore away and disappeared into her mouth. She chewed slowly, looking at him thoughtfully. "You'll be lucky," she muttered between bites.

"Oh yeah?" Quick as thought, Sam snatched the rabbit from her hands and sank his teeth into the hot flesh.

Yelping, Ashley leapt after him, and they went down in a heap again. Sam rolled, pinning her with his weight as he held the rabbit up out of reach.

"Truce?" he said.

Her amber eyes stared up at him, drawing him in. He shook his head, breaking the spell, and she pouted. "You know I could throw you off if I wanted," she muttered.

"Okay, Supergirl." Smiling, he released her and held out his empty hand. "Truce?" he repeated.

Rolling her eyes, Ashley took his hand, and they settled back down beside the fire. Sharing the skinny rabbit, they fell into a comfortable silence, lost in their own thoughts.

"Do you really think they'll change?" Ashley asked eventually, a piece of greasy meat held precariously between two fingers.

"Who?" Sam replied, staring into the fire.

"People," Ashley murmured. "With everything that's happened, do you think…they'll ever accept us?"

"I don't know…" Sam answered. "I think maybe they have different expectations than we do."

"Expectations?" Ashley put her head on his shoulder. "What do you mean?"

"I just mean...well, they think things will go back to normal, don't they? Back to the old days, before the *Chead* or people with wings ever existed."

Ashley fell silent at that. Finally, she shrugged. "I don't know about the *Chead*, but *I'm* not going anywhere."

Sam tightened his hand on her shoulder. "Neither am I."

"Then I guess they're stuck with us."

"Guess so..." Sam murmured. "Have you smelled them, the *Chead?*"

Ashley nodded. "Now that we're away from the city, I can. They're...everywhere."

"I don't think anyone realizes just how many are out here," Sam said, lips pursed. "Or that they're...sentient. Harry wants to kill them all, once he has things under control in San Francisco."

"Genocide," Ashley said softly. "That's what they want, isn't it? You're afraid we'll be caught up in it too."

"Maybe. Maybe I just don't like the idea of exterminating an entire species. It's not their fault, the deaths they've caused. The government was using them, just like they used us."

"They're dangerous, Sam. You know that as well as anyone."

"So are tigers, but we don't go around trying to murder all of them. At least, not anymore."

Ashley sat up. "You really think it's the same?" She frowned, uncertain. "Yes, they're sentient, but look what they've done with it! Driving people from their homes, slaughtering entire towns. We can't just let them keep doing it."

"Of course not," Sam replied. "You're right, they have to be stopped. But...I guess what I'm saying is, does that necessarily mean they have to be exterminated? What if that very fear is what's driving them? What if they're only attacking us because they're afraid we'll do the same?"

A long silence stretched out as Ashley rested her head against Sam's shoulder again. She picked at the bones of her rabbit, pulling the last tendrils of meat from the carcass. "I don't know…" she said, "but, I guess they're a worry for another day. It's the President we should be concentrating on."

"Of course." Sam smiled, pulling Ashley closer. The fire had died to embers now, but Ashley's eyes still gleamed in the light of the stars. "When we get that far."

He pressed his lips to hers. A soft "oh" whispered up from the back of Ashley's throat, and then she was kissing him back, her arms going around his waist, her body pressing against his. He gasped as her fingers twisted in his long hair, pushing him down.

Together they fell back on the hard ground, limbs entwined. Dust rose around them as they rolled, tongues dancing, hands tearing at each other's clothes. Ashley gasped as the buttons of her shirt popped open. Sam broke off their kiss, his mouth moving to her neck. She moaned as he nibbled at her flesh. His hands drifted across her naked skin, touching, tickling, feeling the heat in her skin, the racing of her heart.

Then she was sitting up, her hands tugging at his shirt, pulling it over his head. A second later it was gone, and now it was Ashley's hands on his naked chest. He shuddered as her cold fingers trailed along his body. Opening his wings, he wrapped them in a feathery embrace. Her head lifted as he leaned down. Their lips met again in a hard, desperate kiss.

Growling, Sam pressed Ashley down. She went willingly now, falling back on the dusty ground. Leaning in, he drank in the sight of her bare body, the glow of her skin in the starlight. Her lips parted, and he saw the invitation in her eyes, the naked lust.

Crouching on all fours, Sam poised his body over hers, until they were only inches apart. She stared up at him, eyes wide and expectant, but still he lingered. Pinned between his arms, there was no escape for Ashley now, and he wanted to savor this moment.

Finally, he lowered himself as Ashley lifted to meet him. He moaned as her breasts brushed against his chest. Her hand went around his waist, pulling him down, drawing him in, until he could feel her all around him. Burying his head in her shoulder, he gave himself to the rhythm of their bodies, his mind falling away in a rush of ecstasy.

VI
MANIPULATION

50

"Mom?"

The word seemed to come from nowhere. It echoed through the cave, lingering in the darkness long after Liz had spoken it.

No one moved, no one spoke. Every eye in the cave was fixed on her, but Liz hardly noticed. She couldn't tear her eyes from the old woman sitting on the boulder, couldn't bring herself to believe what she was seeing.

Because it was impossible, wasn't it? She had seen her mother change, becoming the bloodthirsty creature that had torn away her father's life. She had watched the soldiers disappear into the woods, rifles at the ready, prepared to shoot her mother on sight. Not once in the last two years had she considered the possibility that her mother had survived.

Yet here she was, aged far beyond her years, but still unmistakably her mother. The milky white eyes were frighteningly different, but the shape of her face, the curls of her hair, even the way she carried herself, all were unchanged. And her voice…her voice had transported Liz back in time, to quiet nights spent around the kitchen table and long days in the fields. It was a voice Liz had never thought she would hear again.

Slowly, the old woman climbed to her feet and started

forward. Watching her come, Liz found herself fixed in place, trapped in the gaze of the old *Chead*, by the eyes of her mother. The *Chead* came to a stop just a foot away. Long seconds stretched out as they stared at each other.

"Mom," Liz croaked again, barely able to get the word out.

After everything she'd been through since that day on the mountain, everything she had suffered, it was all too much. Her vision shone as the ancient *Chead* reached out and cupped her cheek. White eyes drank her in as her mother slowly shook her head.

"My Elizabeth," she whispered. "My daughter."

A shrill keening began in the back of Liz's throat. She didn't know whether to scream or cry. Emotion welled within her, the swirling memories of her grief, the rush of sudden hope. Love and despair crashed together, filling her until Liz thought she might drown in it.

She saw again her last memory of her mother—of a grey-eyed creature covered in blood, standing over the body of her father. It had been the moment Liz had lost both of her parents.

Yet now here she was, the woman who had raised her, who had loved her and held her tight on cold winter nights, who had cared for her when she was sick and had kissed her bruises better.

A tremor started in Liz's legs. It spread until her whole body was shaking. "How…how is this possible?" she managed.

A smile wrinkled her mother's cheeks. She stroked Liz's face before turning to Chris. Talisa circled him, her lips pursed in the same way she had once inspected livestock at the market. Catching Chris staring at her, Liz quickly looked away.

Completing her circuit, her mother returned to Liz. "This is your mate?"

"I…I…" Liz opened her mouth and closed it again, unable to answer. Her cheeks flushed, and she carefully avoided meeting Chris's eyes.

Chuckling, her mother returned to Liz's side, and reached out to stroke the jet-black feathers. "What have they done to you, my daughter?"

Liz swallowed as tears welled in her eyes. She fought the urge to throw herself into her mother's arms and sob the whole awful story to her.

It's not her. She grated the words in her mind. *It can't be her.*

And yet it was. She could see it in her eyes. Gone was the mad glint of the *Chead*, the ferocious hunger of the creature that had killed her father. In its place was a shining warmth, a softness that could only be the love of a mother for her child.

This was her mother, the one who'd been stolen from her, taken away by the government's heartless cruelty.

Liz clenched her fists, swallowing her pain, her grief. "It's..." She shook her head. "It's a long story...Mom."

The word tasted strange in her mouth, like she'd almost forgotten how to speak it.

A withered hand stroked her cheek again. Liz closed her eyes, shivering at the warmth of her mother's fingers. A soft, sweet scent danced in her nostrils, at once familiar and foreign. Breathing it in, Liz's heart slowed. She felt her body relaxing, the racing thud of adrenaline beginning to cool.

Then Liz's eyes snapped open as she realized her mother had touched her skin. Stumbling back a step, she gaped, staring, her heart tumbling into her stomach. "No..." she whispered, her hand going to her mouth. Her mother was so aged, the venom would surely kill her...

Her mother leaned her head to the side and frowned. "What is the matter, my daughter?"

The keening built in Liz's throat again. "You...you touched me," she gasped finally.

The pale eyes studied her for a moment. Then, smiling, her mother lifted her hand and inspected it. Liz stared at the wrinkled flesh, searching for the redness that marked her touch, the purple that followed. But her mother's skin remained a pale white, unmarked by sun or venom. She lowered her hand and looked at Liz again.

"You have the touch?" she asked.

Not knowing what to say, all Liz could do was nod. Her mother's eyes danced as she pulled Liz into an embrace. Liz tensed as the wrinkled arms wrapped around her. A tremor ran through her wings, her feathers standing on end. She held her breath, eyes squeezed shut, hardly daring to move. Breathing in, the sweet scent of her mother filled her nostrils. Memories flashed through her mind, of her mother kissing her goodnight, hugging her goodbye on her first day of school.

Finally, Liz could fight it no longer. Shuddering, she hugged her mother back. "Mom," she choked into Talisa's shoulder, "I missed you so much."

Strong hands stroked her back. "There, there, my daughter. I'm here now. You are home."

"Home?" Hiccupping, Liz managed to regain some of her composure. Pulling back slightly, she looked at her mother.

"Home," her mother repeated. "Is that not why you are here?"

Liz swallowed, not knowing what to say. She thought of Chris, of the compulsion that had drawn her after him, that had led her across the sprawling plains of San Francisco, back up into those icy mountains. But staring into her mother's face, into her strange-yet-familiar eyes, those thoughts drifted away, and finally she shook her head.

"I don't know," she whispered.

"Oh, my daughter," her mother murmured. "We must find your way."

Shivering, Liz closed her eyes again. Pressure grew in her chest as she struggled to breathe.

"We're here to stop you." Chris's voice echoed through the cavern.

The words cut through the haze blanketing Liz's mind, through the shock of her mother's resurrection. Blinking, she looked around. Chris still stood nearby, his face pale. He watched them with wide eyes.

Soft whispers spread around the cave as the *Chead* laughed. Her mother turned to look at Chris, her milky eyes hardening, though the smile never left her lips. "Stop us from doing what, child?"

Chris swallowed visibly. His wings started to tremble, but he lifted his head in defiance. "Stop you from slaughtering innocent people."

"I see." Talisa stepped towards Chris, her wrinkled legs carrying her slowly across the cavern.

Jaw clenched, Chris stood his ground. Liz watched on, feet fixed in place, unable to move or even speak. She found herself a silent observer to the conflict between her mother and Chris.

"Do you not want revenge, child?" Talisa whispered as she reached Chris. She brushed a hand through his feathers. "On the ones who did this to you? Who locked you in cages, who tortured you and so many others? Hecate has told me of humanity's experiments."

Chris frowned. "They're…already dead," he croaked. His eyes moved to the girl, Susan. "You killed them."

Talisa's laughter echoed through the cave as she left Chris where he stood. With slow steps, she returned to the boulder and sat. A sigh escaped her lips as she shook her head.

"Not all of them," she said, eyes moving from Chris to Liz. "Not the one responsible for my people's suffering."

"What do you mean?" Chris asked. "Hecate said you destroyed the facility up here in the mountains."

"We did," Talisa replied, "but those pathetic creatures were only pawns, child. Do you not wish to punish those truly responsible? To destroy the one who had you taken, who has hunted you all this time?"

Forehead creased, Chris took a step closer to Talisa. "What do you mean?"

"Are you truly so clueless?" Talisa chuckled. "Has your time with the humans taught you nothing? Their leader still lives. Only with his death will my people have their retribution."

"You mean the President?" Chris breathed. "How can you…"

"President, Master, Butcher, his name does not matter. He will die regardless, so that my people may have peace."

"Peace?" Liz spoke up, her mind finally beginning to work again.

"Yes, my daughter." The milky eyes switched to Liz. "My time is short, but I shall not rest until this world is safe for *all* my children." She gestured around the cave, encompassing the silent host of *Chead.*

A lump rose in Liz's throat. "What do you mean, your time is short?"

"It is the curse of the *Chead,* my daughter." Sadness touched her mother's words now. "We burn brightly, and then we die."

Liz blinked back tears as she tried to put her emotions into words. But they would not come, and finally she shook her head, grasping at the message behind her mother's words. "You want peace?"

"We do," her mother replied.

Liz nodded, steeling herself. She glanced briefly at Chris, then turned back to her mother. "Then we'll help you."

51

Susan's teeth grated as she watched the strangers leave the cave. Fists clenched, she struggled to control her anger. She could still see the boy attacking Hecate, humiliating her mate, though he had cheated with those cursed wings of his. And the girl…her arm still itched where Liz had touched her. Susan's lips drew back in a snarl as she imagined tearing the black feathers from those wings, one by one.

Only Hecate's presence kept her under control. Despite his encounter with the boy, he remained strangely calm, unperturbed by Talisa's welcoming of the two strangers. Even during the fight, he had not seemed to take the boy seriously—at least, not until the end, when the deceitful creature had almost killed him.

The girl's revelation about Talisa had shaken him, though. It had shaken Susan as well. An inexplicable rage had overtaken her as the elder *Chead* embraced the girl. Teeth clenched, she'd watched in silence as the two conversed, exchanging declarations of love and affection. The sudden emotion, the *humanity* in Talisa's expression made Susan sick to her stomach.

Even now, she could hardly bear to look at the elder *Chead*.

"Why, Talisa?" she growled as the two disappeared around the bend in the cave.

Talisa's milky eyes turned towards her. "What do you mean, my child?"

Susan shivered, her fingers turning to claws as she approached the old *Chead*. "How could you…tell the strangers our plans? How could you invite them into our ranks?"

Sitting on her outcropping of rock, Talisa did not respond. Her eyes had returned to their normal, unreadable hardness. "She is my daughter," she murmured. Standing, she stepped up to Susan.

Susan bared her teeth. "They cannot…be trusted—"

She broke off as Talisa lunged. Her feet scrambled on the loose stones, but the elder *Chead's* hand shot out and caught her by the wrist before she could retreat. Pain shot through Susan's arm as iron fingers dug into her flesh, dragging her forward until only an inch separated them.

"You would have me spurn my own child?" Talisa hissed in Susan's ear.

A lump lodged in Susan's throat as she locked eyes with Talisa. She tried to pull away, but her will fled, and suddenly she found herself on her knees. Talisa stood over her, eyes aglow in the darkness.

"You would have me kill her?" she growled.

Susan bowed her head. "No, Talisa."

The iron hold on her wrist did not relent. "You disappoint me, girl," Talisa murmured. "I should return you to your own children."

Tears stung Susan's eyes. Shivering, she looked up at the elder *Chead*. The ache in her chest told her what such a fate meant. She would lose her place at Talisa's side, would become little more than an incubator for a new generation of *Chead*. And she would be without Hecate, without her mate—the one thing holding her to sanity.

Somewhere deep inside, a flame lit the darkness of her despair. Suddenly she found herself able to meet Talisa's gaze. Gathering herself, Susan climbed back to her feet and faced the ancient *Chead*.

"No."

The word rang in the darkness, a declaration, a promise. Looking into the Talisa's eyes, Susan thought she saw something change, a sudden doubt, quickly gone.

The wrinkles deepened in Talisa's forehead. "Who are you to refuse *me*, child?"

With a jerk of her wrist, Susan tore her hand free. "I am *Chead!*" Her words echoed through the cave, gaining power, restoring her will.

Seconds turned into minutes as Talisa stood staring at her. Susan held her breath, fists opening and closing, clinging to the strength that had propelled her to her feet.

Finally, Talisa gave the slightest of nods. "Very well, child," she whispered. "You may remain."

Relief swept through Susan. Her shoulders sagged, her eyes fluttering closed in sudden exhaustion. "Thank you."

A smile twisted her elder's lips. "Perhaps you can help us deal with my daughter and her mate."

"What do you mean, Talisa?" Hecate asked, joining them.

"There is more of the *Chead* in them than they realize, child," Talisa replied. She returned to her seat on the rock. "My daughter will come to accept our world, given time."

"Then why…did you not tell them…everything?"

"They are not ready," Talisa murmured. "The boy may never be, but my daughter, I can sense the *Chead* within her. She must embrace her true nature, must accept the change and become one of us. Only then can she learn the truth."

"And until then?" Susan pressed.

"Our plans must remain secret," Talisa whispered. "You have done well to give us hope, child, but the stench of humanity still clings to my daughter and the boy. If they discover our true goal, they will rebel."

Hecate grunted. "They did not seem…concerned about their President's death."

"No," Talisa mused. "It is strange, but still, they may balk when faced with humanity's execution. They cannot yet see the true nature of their former species, that humanity will never tolerate an equal. Only their extinction can bring the peace we seek."

"Yes," Susan bowed her head. "We will do as you say, Talisa."

She turned away, her eyes drawn to the shadows around the cave's entrance. The strangers were long gone, but her lips pulled back in a snarl as she thought of them. An orange glow lit her mind as she imagined the flames that would soon engulf humanity. She smiled, thinking of the winged girl burning alongside them.

Yes, let them all perish, she thought. *And the freaks with them.*

52

Chris staggered sideways as a *Chead* pushed past him. His feet slipped on a loose rock and he almost fell. Only a slight flutter of his wings kept him upright. Straightening, he glared at the creature, but the perpetrator was already moving off, winding between the faded stone buildings of the abandoned settlement. It had hardly spared him a glance as it shouldered past.

Gritting his teeth, Chris headed in the other direction. The darkness was just beginning to give way to the light of day, and Talisa had finally called a stop. Though Chris would never admit it, the news had come as a relief. They had left behind the mountains a few days ago and were now somewhere out on what he guessed were the plains of Arizona. Dry, inhospitable land stretched out all around them, and he had no desire to spend another day exposed to the unforgiving summer sun.

It would have been easier if they could fly, but out of respect for their flightless cousins, Liz had decided they should run alongside them. Not wanting to argue, Chris had agreed, though by now he was long past caring if he insulted the *Chead.*

As Talisa's daughter, Liz had been welcomed by the deadly creatures as one of their own. Chris, however, was treated with cold indifference. Only Hecate seemed to enjoy his company, though Chris wasn't sure why. Perhaps he'd won the young

Chead's respect in their fight—or perhaps Hecate simply found it amusing to watch Chris struggle with the grueling pace set by his kind.

Shaking his head, Chris dismissed the dark-haired *Chead* from his thoughts and turned his attention to the buildings around him. Liz had headed this way a few moments ago, though she hadn't bothered telling him where she was going. Still weighed down by guilt, Chris hadn't said anything, but he was quickly becoming irritated by her behavior since joining the *Chead.*

When she'd appeared out of nowhere to save him, Chris had allowed himself to hope they might have a future after all. Her whispered promise that they would talk as they crept through the sleeping *Chead* had only reinforced that hope.

But the reappearance of Liz's mother had changed everything. She had taken to spending all her waking moments with the old *Chead*, though Chris had no idea what they discussed. He was rarely invited to join them. Instead, he was left to wander their campsites alone, surrounded by the hostile grey eyes of the *Chead.*

Ahead, he caught a glimpse of Liz through the old mud-brick buildings, and picked up his pace. The settlement must have been a mining village once upon a time—he couldn't think of anything else that could have drawn so many people out into this barren place. The buildings were probably a hundred years old, but in the dryness of the desert, they remained in good condition. A few had collapsed from the slow corrosion of time, but most still stood as they had been built. Inside, the floors were dirt, most of the furniture long removed, but they at least offered protection from the sun.

"Liz!" Chris called as he turned a corner and saw her in the doorway of one of the buildings.

Her blue eyes widened when she saw him. A frown marked her forehead as she turned away from the door. "Chris? What are you doing?"

Chris closed the remaining distance and came to a stop in front of her. Tucking his hands into his pockets, he stared at her boots, struggling to find the words he wanted to say. "I…" He bit his lip, then forced himself to look at her. "I'm not sure," he finished lamely.

Liz stared at him for a full second, before rolling her eyes and turning away.

"Wait!" Unbidden, Chris's hand shot out and caught her wrist. "Wait...Liz...can we talk?" As Liz spun to glare at him, he quickly added, "Please?"

"Talk?" Liz's lips twisted into a frown. "What is there to talk about, Chris?"

Chris swallowed, his nerve failing him. But gritting his teeth, he forced himself to say the words. He needed to know, one way or another. He couldn't stand this in-between, this being caught between hope and despair.

"About us," he mumbled. "About why you came after me."

A softness appeared in Liz's eyes, and for a moment his heart lifted. Then a steely hardness came over her face. Her jaw tightened, and she gave a curt shake of her head. "There is no *us*, Chris," she said. "Not anymore."

Throwing off his hand, she disappeared into the house. There was no door to keep him out, but Chris made no move to follow her. He stood staring into the shadows of the doorway, then turned away. His legs shook as he stumbled through the settlement, ignoring the stares of the *Chead* still out in the streets. Their sweet scent pressed in around him, and his stomach twisted with nausea. The need to escape rose in his chest, a desire to spread his wings and fly away, to flee the girl he loved, escape the truth of her rejection.

The *Chead* made no effort to stop him as he leapt into the air. His auburn wings beat down, hurling him skywards, and he raced up towards the harsh glow of the sun. As the stench of the *Chead* fell away he sucked in a breath, savoring the crisp, dusty scents of the desert. Angling his wings, he circled the settlement, watching as the last of the *Chead* disappeared into the buildings. Marking the spot in his mind, he turned away, wings beating hard.

Soaring out over the vast desert, Chris almost felt free.

He knew he'd lost Liz for good, that she could never forgive what he'd done in Alcatraz. He didn't blame her. Even now, among the clouds, Chris could not escape his own guilt, his own bitter self-loathing.

All that was left for him was Ashley's command—that he make his life worth *something.* He had thought by coming here, by stopping Hecate's slaughtering of innocent people, he might make a difference. But nothing had been as he'd expected. Hecate, the dark, powerful monster from his past, was only a pawn.

It was Liz's own mother who controlled the *Chead.*

Chris shuddered and dipped slightly as he remembered Liz's tale of how her mother had turned. Liz had found her mother standing over the body of her father, in the middle of her ruined house. Outside, all her childhood friends were already dead.

Yet even then, Talisa had spared her daughter.

And now the ancient *Chead* had welcomed Liz into a new family, a new life.

Tucking his wings, Chris dived. His stomach lurched into his chest as he plummeted towards the distant ground. Blood pounded in his ears and adrenaline flooded his veins. For just a second he felt alive, almost his old self again.

The ground raced up towards him, swelling until it filled his whole vision. Gritting his teeth, Chris snapped open his wings. Pain tore along his back as he lurched to a stop. His wings beat down, stabilizing him.

For a while he drifted close to the ground, his mind lost in thought. Moving into a thermal, he let the hot air gather beneath his feathers and send him soaring upwards. High above the desert, he looked around, a distant flicker of movement catching his attention. Turning towards it, he spotted the dark, glimmering streak of a highway. A van rumbled along the road, a cloud of smoke billowing up behind it. He guessed it must be heading towards Las Vegas.

More movement appeared on the road ahead of the truck. Chris stared as the roadside seemed to come alive. A dozen figures swarmed across the asphalt, barring the van's path. The squeal of brakes carried up to Chris as the vehicle slammed to a stop. His jaw dropped as he realized a group of *Chead* had intercepted the van.

Shouts rang below as the *Chead* tore open the doors of the van. Without hesitating, Chris folded his wings and raced towards the *Chead* and their prey.

By the time he reached them, the *Chead* had the occupants of the van surrounded. Kneeling on the scorching asphalt, they looked around at the bloodthirsty creatures, faces pale with fear. There were four of them in total—a middle-aged man and woman, plus two women in their twenties.

The *Chead* jumped as Chris slammed into the ground nearby. He swallowed as their cold grey eyes turned towards him, counting four of the creatures—until Hecate wandered out from behind the van to make it five.

"Chris." Hecate laughed. "What are you doing…so far from your babysitters?"

"What are you doing with these people?" Chris replied, ignoring the taunt.

On the road, the humans squirmed on their knees. Chris could feel the heat radiating from the asphalt. It was late in the morning and the temperature had already climbed well above a hundred degrees. The road would be hotter still. They looked at him, mouths clenched closed, probably trying to work out if he was there to help them or kill them.

"Making war," Hecate growled.

Chris's eyes returned to the *Chead*. "These people aren't any threat to you."

Hecate's lips twitched as he raised an eyebrow. "No? Well, let us see."

Before Chris could move, Hecate grabbed the kneeling man by the scruff of his shirt. Helpless, the man screamed as Hecate lifted him into the air. Chris moved to intervene, but Hecate only laughed and tossed the man at another of the *Chead*. Leaping, the creature caught the man mid-air.

Gasping, the man tried to break free, but he was no match for the *Chead's* strength. As Chris turned towards the creature, it laughed and passed their victim to a third *Chead*.

Chris staggered to a stop and looked around, realizing the *Chead* had encircled him. The man screamed as he was sent soaring again. His face had lost the last of its color and he looked close to throwing up. Standing his ground, Chris turned to face Hecate.

"You've had your fun," he grated through clenched teeth. "You've proved he's harmless. Now let him go."

Laughter whispered around the circle of *Chead* as the man was passed again. This time though, he twisted as the next *Chead* caught him, his foot sweeping up into the creature's groin. Roaring, the *Chead* hurled the man at the ground. He bounced once on the asphalt before coming to a stop. Groaning, he tried to crawl away, but the *Chead* he'd struck bounded forward and drove its foot down on his skull. A sickening *crunch* ended the man's cries.

As one, the remaining passengers screamed and scrambled back towards the van. Hecate leapt to intercept them, but Chris was faster still. He tacked Hecate to the ground and slammed his fist into the *Chead's* face. Before he could land a second blow, Hecate rolled, sending Chris toppling sideways.

Coming to their feet, they squared off against one another. Chris sneered. "You want to try your luck again?"

Hecate straightened and chuckled. "Perhaps." He shook his head and nodded at the cowering family. "But not today. What are these…humans to you? You know…what they did to us. To you."

"Not these humans," Chris replied.

"They are all the same. Such pitiful creatures…do not deserve our mercy."

"Leave them be," Chris pressed. "They have nothing to do with your war."

Hecate laughed. "They have *everything* to do with it." He licked his lips, eyes drinking in the sight of the three women. "But perhaps…you are right. The young ones…do not have to die."

Chris's stomach twisted at the look in Hecate's eyes. He edged slightly forward. "What do you mean?"

The cold grey eyes returned to him. "The *Chead* are still…too few. We need…mates…to prosper."

"They're human," Chris managed to stammer, mere words unable to express his horror.

Hecate chuckled. "Yes…and we have no more…virus," he mused, "but…the *Chead* are strong. If the offspring…are weak… they can be culled."

Bile rose in Chris's throat. The girls whimpered, clinging to the older woman that could only be their mother.

Standing in the middle of the road, Chris gathered himself. "I won't let you touch them. This is wrong."

"Wrong?" Hecate asked, starting towards the group.

Chris tried to intercept him, but two *Chead* leapt in and grabbed him by the arms, pinning them behind his back. He fought to break free as Hecate approached the huddled humans. Quick as lightning, he had one of the younger girls by the hair. He pushed her towards Chris.

"Your mate…has abandoned you," he said, head tilting to the side. "Would you not like…a fresh one?"

Chris growled, trying to throw off his assailants, but together they were more than his match. "Let me go!"

"Not to your liking?" Hecate smiled.

His arm shot out and caught the girl by the neck. The girl opened her mouth to scream, but his hand gave a sharp jerk. A sickening *crack* broke the desert's silence as the girl went limp. She toppled face-first to the asphalt when Hecate released her.

"*No!*" Chris screamed, but Hecate was already dragging the second girl towards him.

"What about…blonde?" the *Chead* cackled, shoving the screaming girl at Chris.

The girl fought to break Hecate's hold. Her hands lashed out, her fingernails digging into his arms, but the *Chead* didn't seem to notice. He pushed her forward until her tear-streaked face was an inch from Chris's own.

Her big brown eyes suddenly found his. "Please," she croaked.

"I…" Chris gaped, hardly able to breathe.

"No?"

Before Chris could reply, Hecate drove his fist into the girl's back. The sickening squelch of tearing flesh and breaking bones followed. The girl's mouth fell open in a silent scream. A shudder ran through her body as her eyes rolled back in her skull. As Hecate released her hair, her head lolled forward, but she remained on her feet, propped up by the fist embedded in her back. With a jerk of his hand, Hecate let her body fall.

Chris sobbed as he stared at the dead girls. He hung limp from his captives' arms now, but behind Hecate the woman screamed and charged the grey-eyed boy. Hecate batted away the woman's fists with casual ease, then downed her with a blow to the forehead. She collapsed without a sound, dead before she struck the ground. Wiping his bloody hand on his shirt, Hecate grinned at Chris.

"You're right, Chris," he said, stepping in close. "These creatures were…beneath us. I'm glad…you set us straight."

Laughing, Hecate nodded to the *Chead* holding him. Chris sagged to the ground as they released him. The hot asphalt burned his palms, but he hardly felt it. Unable to tear his eyes from the slaughtered family, he listened to the crunching of stones as the *Chead* moved away.

Only when silence returned did Chris climb to his feet. Swallowing his horror, he closed his eyes, then forced them back open. He looked at the dead women and man one last time.

"I'm sorry I couldn't save you," he whispered.

Then he was turning, spreading his wings, throwing himself into the sky. The wind caught in his feathers, hurtling him back towards the settlement. As the ground fell away, there was only one thought in his mind.

I have to warn Liz!

53

Liz smiled as her mother dismissed another group of *Chead*. She was still struggling to accept this new reality, this impossible dream come true. How many days had it been now? Three? Four? She'd already lost count, swept away in the wonder of it all. She was afraid to pause and take a breath, lest she wake and the dream end.

Crossing the room, her mother settled down on the crumbling couch alongside Liz. The foam cushions had rotted away long ago, but Liz had found some moth-eaten blankets in the cupboard. Folded up beneath them, they weren't exactly comfortable, but were still better than the dirt floor.

Liz shivered as Talisa pulled her into a gentle hug. A part of her still flinched at the touch, fearing the deadly nematocysts lacing her skin cells. But like Ashley back in San Francisco, her mother seemed immune, and closing her eyes, Liz returned the embrace. Breathing in, she drank in the familiar scent of her childhood. She hardly noticed the pungent sweetness of the *Chead* anymore.

"How can you touch me?" Liz croaked when they finally broke apart.

Her mother smiled, the wrinkles spreading across her face. "I am *Chead*, my daughter," she replied. "I have spent years wandering the wilderness, gathering our people, providing them shelter. In that time, I mastered our true nature, harnessed my potential. Your venom holds no bite for me."

"What do you mean, 'harnessed your potential'?" Liz asked, frowning.

Her mother sighed. "You have witnessed the rage, the uncontrollable madness of our kind?"

A tremor went through Liz. She remembered that anger all too well, the rage that had flooded her mind, burning away all thought and reason. In that moment, she'd felt all-powerful, as though no feat was beyond her strength—even as her control was stripped away, and she found herself in the grip of some inner beast. In that state, she had torn grown men apart, leaving them in bloody pieces on the laboratory floor.

"I have felt it," she whispered finally.

"You have?"

Liz looked up at the sharpness of her mother's voice. But the ancient face only offered another smile.

"My poor child," she murmured, stroking Liz's cheek.

Liz bowed her head, her eyes fluttering closed at her mother's touch.

"When unleashed, our rage is a terrible thing," her mother continued. "In its grip, our true potential is revealed. Our power, our strength is unrivaled. But the madness consumes us. Without our minds, we become mere beasts, unrestricted by the feeble limits of humanity, yet unable to think, to plan, to truly rival our makers."

Liz looked away. "It was terrifying. I never want to feel that way again."

Her mother chuckled. "But you must."

Liz's head snapped up. Her chest clenched and she found herself struggling to breathe. Her mother stared back, the smile still on her face.

"What do you mean?" Liz asked, her heart pounding. She glanced around, suddenly aware again of where she was. The windows of the abandoned building had been boarded up, but sunlight streamed through the empty doorway.

She shivered as Talisa's soft voice called her back. "Relax, my daughter, you are safe here."

Liz found herself caught in the cool white eyes of her mother. A warm blanket settled over her mind and the pounding in her ears slowed. Letting out a long breath, Liz nodded. She took her mother's hand, drawing reassurance from her touch.

"The rage is only one step on a great journey, my daughter," Talisa continued. "With time, the beast inside you can be controlled, mastered, tamed. Only then will you reach your true potential. Then there will be no fury, but a state of bliss, of mindfulness, that allows you to move beyond the limitations of humanity. It is a state of mind humans have sought for millennia—that their monks and pilgrims spend entire lives seeking. It can be yours, if only you have the courage to grasp it. With it, you can command the world."

Liz's fear cut through the warmth entrapping her mind. "It almost consumed me, Mom," she whispered.

"You are my daughter," Talisa pressed. "You will not succumb."

Pain sliced Liz's palm as her mother's fingers tightened. Gasping, she tried to pull away, but her mother's grip was like iron.

Then a shout came from outside. The pressure vanished as they both turned towards the door. Half a second later, Chris burst inside, several *Chead* hot on his heels.

"Liz!" he cried out, stumbling to a stop. Spinning to face the *Chead* behind him, he spread his wings. "Liz, we need to leave!"

Liz had sprung to her feet at Chris's appearance, but now she paused, looking from Chris to the *Chead* who had followed him inside. Relief swept through her as she recognized them as Talisa's guards. They stood in the doorway glaring at Chris, obviously annoyed at his unannounced entry, but otherwise made no move towards him.

Scowling, she shifted her attention to Chris. "What are you doing in here?"

Ignoring her, Chris turned on Talisa. "You're monsters!" He

jabbed a finger at Liz's mother. By the door, the *Chead* started to edge around the room, placing themselves closer to Talisa.

Talisa stood and waved the guards back. "Christopher, what is the meaning of this intrusion?" Her voice was quiet, but laced with iron.

"Don't give me that," Chris growled. His hands were shaking, and his eyes were dark with rage. "Hecate and some of your other so-called children just slaughtered an innocent family! You're telling me you don't know anything about that?"

Liz frowned, taking a step closer to her mother. "Mom, what's he talking about?"

Talisa sighed, looking from Chris to Liz. "What would you have us do, Christopher?" she asked. "Should the humans spot us, more will come. Soldiers with guns and other far more dangerous weapons. We are only a hundred—if the humans are forewarned, we could be wiped out."

"Then go around them!" Chris shouted back. "And they weren't just going to kill them…" He trailed off, swallowing, as if unable to get out the words.

Eyes narrowed, Talisa walked to where Chris stood. She studied his face for a moment, then turned her back on him. Rejoining Liz near the couch, she reached out and gripped her daughter by the shoulders.

"Do you trust me, my daughter?" Talisa asked softly.

Staring into her mother's ghostly eyes, Liz felt suddenly lost, her mind frozen.

"Liz, they're killing innocent people!" Chris said hotly. "You can't stay here!"

"My daughter," Talisa continued, lifting her hands to cradle Liz's head. "Do you not see, we only do what we must. The humans were a threat. They had seen us. If we let them go, more would have come to kill us. They had to die, so we could live."

Liz struggled to think, to reason, but her mind was trapped in the tangles of a hot blanket, and she could not put the pieces together. The harder she tried, the tighter the tangles became, the less anything made sense.

Then, unbidden, an image of the woman from the alleyway rose in her mind, and she heard again the spiteful words.

Freak.

Tramp.

Chead.

Liz's eyes watered as the final word rang in her mind. Humanity had rejected her, pushed her away when all she'd ever wanted was to help them. Yet here, amidst the monsters she had feared all her life, she had found acceptance. They had embraced her, welcomed her as family, despite their differences.

Now Chris was telling her she had to leave, that her mother was evil. A red-hot rage swept through her as she looked at him. She moved away from her mother. Images flashed through her mind, of Chris murdering the Texan, of him kissing the vile Director. Even now, he cowered away from the *Chead*, from her family.

A growl rose in Liz's throat as she stepped towards Chris. Red clouds obscured her vision as she closed on him, teeth bared. In the middle of the dusty room, Chris stood his ground and watched her come. Only when she spread her wings did he waver, his foot sliding back half an inch.

"Liz, what are you doing…?" he asked, jaw clenched. They were alone now. The other *Chead* had retreated to the walls and stood watching in silence.

Liz blinked as he spoke her name, a distant bell sounding in her mind. But the red clouds continued to swirl. Somewhere deep within she could hear a voice screaming, though the words were muffled by the pounding of blood in her ears. Sucking in a breath, she struggled to control herself, to master the rush of emotions.

Finally, she looked at Chris. "Go, Chris," she ground out the words, her voice taut with the effort it took not to tear him in two. "Get out. There's nothing for you here."

"Liz, please don't do this," Chris begged, his eyes wide. He reached out a hand for her.

Liz's lips drew back in a snarl. Hissing, she stepped towards him. Chris yanked back his hand as though she'd bitten him, but her advance continued. He lingered half a moment more, eyes shimmering as he watched her come. For a moment it seemed he would remain, offering himself up for the slaughter. Then his courage failed, and turning on his heel, Chris fled.

Watching him go, Liz fought the waves of anger washing over her, resisting the desire to chase after him, to tear the wings from his back and watch him plummet from the sky. In the end, it was only her mother's hand on her shoulder that stopped her.

Liz shivered as her elder's voice whispered in her ear. "Well done, my daughter." The words curled around Liz's consciousness, pushing her down, eating away at her. "You truly are *Chead.*"

54

Sam crouched beneath the scraggly bushes and peered out into the darkness. Headlights flickered in the distance as the convoy reached the top of the hill and started down the other side. The roar of engines carried through the night, growing louder as the trucks made their ponderous way along the metal road. Whoever was driving obviously felt no rush to reach the airbase. Either that, or they were rightfully wary of potholes in the poorly-maintained road.

Whatever the excuse, Sam was tired of waiting. On the other side of the road, he could just make out Ashley's shadow. To the ordinary eye, she would be no more than a smudge in the darkness. Only the slight glint of moonlight gave her away to Sam's enhanced eyesight.

Between them, the herd of cows was making its slow way along the side of the road. The soft crunch of dirt beneath their hooves mingled with the whisper of the engines. The beasts did not seem to have seen the approaching vehicles yet. Hopefully the soldiers would at least notice the cows.

Quickly, Sam checked the distant glow of the Kirtland Air Force Base. Lying some ten miles outside of Albuquerque, it was the only industry keeping the war-torn city afloat. The once prosperous city had formed the frontline of the American War, changing hands half a dozen times before finally coming under the umbrella of the Western Allied States. Unfortunately, by then there hadn't been much left of the city's 500,000 inhabitants. Today, Albuquerque housed maybe a tenth of that number.

Of course, the Kirtland Air Force Base was an entirely different matter.

Sam and Ashley had spent the last two days staking out the base from the nearby mountains. Their observations had quickly confirmed Harry's warning—there would be no winning in an all-out attack. A ten-foot chain-link fence surrounded the fifty-thousand-acre base. It would have been no barrier to a winged assault, but for the manned guard towers stationed every two hundred yards around the fence. Their mounted machine guns would pick them from the sky before they even got close.

Then, of course, there were the five hundred soldiers they'd counted on the parade ground yesterday. Admittedly, that was far less than Harry had predicted, but it was still beyond their ability to match. Unfortunately, even genetically engineered mutants had their limits.

Within the walls, buildings sprawled across the base, a massive maze of iron and concrete that would be almost impossible to navigate. Half of the place seemed to consist of giant aircraft hangers. Over the last two days, they had watched a steady stream of jet-fighters, helicopters and transport aircrafts come and go. Some buildings sported a bewildering array of radar dishes, while others simply appeared to be military barracks. In the very center of the base, a sleek steel and glass building rose several stories above the others. The guards manning its door at all hours suggested it was the base's headquarters. If they were going to find the President anywhere, it would be there.

They'd ruled out a frontal assault within a few hours, but it had taken another two days before a way in had finally revealed itself. During that time, their hunger had steadily grown, until no amount of scavenging could fill the holes in their stomachs. When the midnight convoy had rumbled through last night, Sam had barely dared opening his mouth around Ashley, lest he risk getting his head bitten off.

Not that Sam's temper was much better. He was looking forward to taking out his hunger pangs on a few of the President's unsuspecting guards.

Hoping another convoy would appear tonight, they'd managed to wrangle half a dozen cows from a nearby paddock out onto the road. Now, they just had to hope the convoy would stop long enough for them to sneak aboard one of the trucks.

Sam had to admit, it wasn't a great plan. But starving stomachs didn't tend to offer the best ideas, and they were growing desperate.

The rumble of engines grew to a roar as the first truck topped the rise above them. The gleam of headlights swept the road, catching on the wide eyes of the waiting cows. Brakes screeched as the leading truck slammed to a stop. More screeches followed, then a sharp *bang* as someone in the convoy reacted too slowly. Red lights lit up the road behind the convoy.

Sam cursed under his breath. The trucks were still a dozen yards away—they'd stopped too soon. If he and Ashley were to slip onboard, they would have to move, and hope the soldiers didn't spot them.

He was just lifting himself off the ground when the *crack* of a gunshot tore through the night. Sam threw himself flat against the earth, covering his head and folding his wings tight against the back. Heart pounding, he stared through the bushes, desperate to see if Ashley was okay.

On the road, a cow screamed, the harsh sound rending the darkness. Another gunshot followed, then the thunder of fleeing hooves. Lifting his head a fraction, Sam watched the cows stampede down the road away from the convoy. Two of the beasts lay on the ground. Stones crunched and Sam ducked back down as several soldiers stalked past, rifles pointed at the fallen beasts as though they might leap up and attack them. An awful cry came from one of the cows as it tried to stand.

A third gunshot rang out, and the beast's cries ceased.

Laughing, the soldiers fired a couple more shots after the

fleeing herd. Sam gritted his teeth. He'd thought the men would just chase them off the road—it would have been easy enough. Instead they'd decided to use the herd as target practice.

Out on the road, the soldiers swung their rifles over their backs and waved at the convoy. A moment later several more soldiers joined them. The group gathered in the middle of the road. Their whispers carried across to Sam.

"Food for a week…" one was saying.

"Can't risk the delay," another argued.

In the bushes, Sam could only hold his breath and wait. With the headlights illuminating the roadside, the soldiers would spot even the slightest of movements. He and Ashley needed to wait until they returned to the vehicles to make their move. Even then, the drivers might still see them.

Finally, the soldiers decided to leave the cows where they lay. Several grumbled as they started back towards the trucks, while one turned and fired several rounds into one of the bodies. When the last man finally turned away, Sam rose to his knees and crawled after them, expecting at any moment for gunshots to ring out and hot lead to tear through his body.

He kept his head down as he moved, and prayed Ashley was doing the same. Up ahead, the truck waited, its headlights shining like the eyes of some dragon in the darkness. He could feel its bulk looming over him, a deadly threat he could not fight. He watched from the wiry bushes as several soldiers piled into the truck's side door, while the rest continued around the vehicle. A steel door rattled, and the men disappeared into the back of the truck.

Sam's heart sank. Their only chance of catching a ride had just been ruined. They'd planned on breaking the latch and concealing themselves in the back of one of the trucks, but obviously whatever this convoy was transporting warranted additional security. Dropping to his stomach, Sam ground a fist into the dirt, cursing their luck.

The rumble of engines grew as the lead driver put his truck in gear. Sam watched as it started off. It was still a few feet up the road, but just as it passed them, Sam caught a glimpse of Ashley as she leapt from the bushes on the other side of the road. His heart lurched in his chest as she rolled across the gravel and disappeared beneath the truck.

Sam's jaw dropped, but there was no time to question Ashley's plan. Scrambling up, he dived onto the road. The engine roared again as the truck picked up speed. Looking up, he saw the wheels racing towards him. Rolling, he was plunged into shadow as the truck thundered over him. He scanned the underbody, then steeling himself, snatched at a metal bar as it passed by.

The sudden jerk as its momentum caught him almost pulled his arms from their sockets. Instantly, he went from lying still to being dragged over unrefined gravel by a ten-ton truck. Within seconds, the road cut his jeans to tatters, and he swore as stones sliced into the flesh of his calves.

Taking a better grip, Sam desperately clenched his abdomen and hauled his legs up off the ground. Hanging there, he scanned the underbody again, and managed to jam his feet into a narrow space above the wheels. Letting out a long breath, he made sure his wings were tucked securely against his back. Then he finally looked around.

Ashley's amber eyes glowed in the darkness as she looked back at him.

"Not exactly my ideal ride," Sam commented wryly.

Ashley's teeth flashed as she grinned. "I improvised."

55

Liz cursed as she slipped on the steep slope. They were in the mountains again—somewhere in eastern New Mexico, she guessed, from the little she recalled of her geography classes. Here the mountains were smaller, their red peaks free of snow, mere children to the great beasts they had left behind in California.

A steadying hand gripped her by the shoulder. She smiled as the *Chead* continued past, nodding her thanks. Somewhere in the lead, Liz knew her mother would be waiting. For just a moment, she felt a yearning to spread her wings and soar over the heads of the *Chead*. The thought made her tingle with excitement. Her wings lifted slightly, her feathers standing on end, before she caught herself.

Biting her lip, she tucked them neatly back into place. Talisa had ordered her to remain on the ground, where she wouldn't be spotted by prying eyes. In the sky she was vulnerable, isolated, alone. But down here, in the ranks of the *Chead,* with the sweetness of her family all around, she was safe.

She shivered as Chris's face flickered into her thoughts. Two days had passed since he'd left. Idly, Liz found herself wondering after him, how he would survive all alone. Had he fallen victim to the desert's heat, to starvation or dehydration? Out here, all it took was one mistake for death to find you.

Shaking her head, Liz forced the image of Chris dead in some ditch from her mind. Anger gave her strength, and picking up the pace, she overtook several of her brethren. Chris had made his choice, had sided with those who wished to harm them, to harm her mother. Liz could never forgive him for that.

Slowly the *Chead* wound their way down the slope towards the distant plains. On the horizon, the gleaming lights of a city could be seen. It could only be Albuquerque, and the Kirtland Air Force Base where the President was hiding.

A glow appeared at the ends of the earth as they entered the foothills. Liz watched as the plains took shape through the gloom. Great, blackened circles appeared, staining the red soils—remnants from the desperate battles of the American War. Thousands upon thousands had fought and died here for principles long forgotten by their descendants. Now the plains were all but empty, and even the once great Albuquerque was but a shadow of its past.

A shout carried up from below. As though acting by some pre-arranged plan, the *Chead* drifted across the slope towards the shadows of a valley. Slipping into the darkness, they settled in for the day. So close to their goal, they could not risk being seen by the enemy's spies.

Relief swept through Liz as she staggered to a stop, her wings hanging heavily from her back. She stood swaying on her feet, darkness swirling at the edges of her vision.

They had been running for twenty hours straight now, all through the day and night, and even her enhanced body was reaching its limits. It had been the same since the first day she'd joined the *Chead*. Liz was sure the endless journey would have driven her mad, if not for the strange passage of time as they ran. At times she would set out, watching as the sun lifted into the sky, only to blink and find the scarlet globe falling towards the other horizon.

Hands on her hips, Liz tried to focus her vision. Her stomach swirled, nauseous from the day's exertion, until she became afraid she might throw up. Sinking suddenly to her knees, she put her head in her hands.

"Liz," Talisa's voice whispered, cutting through the fog.

Liz blinked, shocked to now find herself standing in a cave before her mother. Talisa's white eyes shone as she waved for Liz to sit on the rocks beside her. "Rest, my daughter. Your body is still adjusting to our ways."

Looking around the cave, Liz struggled to focus her thoughts. Her mind was sluggish, but she could have sworn she'd just been watching the last stars fade from the sky…It was pitch-black inside the cave, with only the flicker of a candle for light, and she could not tell what time it was.

She looked again at her mother. The sharp ache in her legs reminded Liz of her exhaustion, and nodding, she took a seat beside the ancient *Chead.* Without thinking, she lay down and put her head in her mother's lap, the way she had as a child.

"My daughter," Talisa's voice whispered through the cavern. "How I missed you, all these years."

Liz shivered, tears springing to her eyes. Closing them, she allowed her mind to drift, safe in her mother's embrace. The familiar sweetness of the old woman wrapped around her, comforting her as soft fingers stroked her hair. Her mother's immunity remained beyond her understanding, but she had long since given up questioning it.

For a while, time seemed to stand still. A soft tranquility settled around Liz. Exhausted, she gave herself over to sleep. Darkness swirled and images flashed through her mind, bordering on dreams. Movement came from the shadows, a flickering light that threatened to tear the sweet blanket of sleep away. She tried to rise, to lift herself from her fatigue and concentrate on the shadows, but her body resisted. Chains wrapped around her spirit, and it wasn't until they finally fell away that she returned to the light.

Liz smiled. Her mother's warmth still lay beneath her head, the soft fingers in her hair.

"Elizabeth…" a voice whispered from above.

A tingle of alarm touched Liz. The voice had not been her

mother's. Breathing in, she tasted a new scent, a harsh, raw sweetness that set her heart racing. Her eyes flickered open, but shadows still clung to her vision. She struggled to think, her mind rebelling against the cobwebs clogging her thoughts.

"My daughter, wake." The words this time were her mother's, but they came from across the cave.

Throwing off the last shackles of sleep, Liz blinked the shadows from her eyes. She found her mother immediately, standing in the center of the cavern, watching Liz with her murky gaze. Frowning, Liz looked up as the hand stroked her hair again.

Hecate smiled down at her, his grey eyes glowing in the light of the candle.

Inwardly, Liz recoiled. A voice deep in her mind cried out, yet her body did not respond. To her horror, Liz realized she was no longer in control. With agonizing slowness, a hungry smile spread across her lips. Her head lifted from Hecate's lap. She felt him stir with the movement.

"What is this, Mother?" she croaked, her voice stiff as iron.

Talisa smiled back. "My time approaches, daughter," she whispered, moving slowly towards them. "You must take my place and lead our people against humanity. But first, you must truly become *Chead*."

Liz shivered. Hecate's fingers were trailing their way down her chest, plucking at the buttons of her jacket, igniting fire wherever they touched. Her mind swirled, struggling to think past the desire burning in her stomach. She looked from Hecate to her mother, mouth open, hardly able to breathe, suffocated by the scents filling the cave.

"How?" she murmured.

Hecate's hands were inside her jacket now, slipping beneath her shirt, sliding rough fingers across her skin. A groan rumbled up from her throat.

"Be my mate." Hecate's mouth was at her ear, his breath hot. "Join with me, and we will watch humanity burn."

Liz shuddered as his hand cupped her breast, and then she was gone. A haze swept across her vision, washing away all thought and reason. Suddenly her lips were locked with his. Her hands tore desperately at his clothes, ripping away his shirt and pants.

A savage growl came from her mate as he responded. In seconds her jacket vanished. Her shirt followed, and Hecate's lips were on her neck, and all she could do was dig her fingers into his muscular back. A moan tore from her throat as his kisses trailed down, drifting towards her breasts. She shuddered, her hands gripping at his hair, desperate to sate the fire burning inside her.

Then Hecate was withdrawing, his hands retreating. Anger flaring, she tangled her fingers in Hecate's hair, pulling him down, desperate now. Flames scorched her stomach, demanding she satisfy them..

Hecate shuddered beneath her fingers, but still he resisted her. She could hear his breath in the darkness, its rugged gasps. A growl rattled in Liz's throat as she realized he was taunting her. Her fingers dug into his scalp, insistent.

A scream echoed through the cave, horribly loud in the rocky confines, and suddenly Hecate was gone. Liz gasped as the heat of his touch vanished, leaving her alone. Sitting up, she bared her teeth and searched for the cowardly male.

He stood transfixed in the center of the cave, eyes wide, his whole body shaking. Purple lines streaked down his face and arms, and a strangled cry tore from his lips. His feet went out from under him, and he collapsed in a heap on the cavern floor.

Liz's lust turned to confusion. Her heart lurched as she noticed her half-naked state. With horror, she realized what she'd been about to do. Her mind swam and she staggered to her feet, then dropped immediately to her knees and threw up on the rocky ground.

Acid burned her throat as she gasped, but her stomach was not done. Another spasm rocked her. Tears stung her eyes, but for the first time in days, her thoughts were clear. The fog fell away, and with it she saw again Chris in the abandoned building, begging her to leave, to come with him. Her stomach lurched, and sobbing she bent in two, though only bile came up now.

When Liz had finally recovered enough to look around, she found Talisa still standing nearby. Her mother's brow was knitted in anger as she watched Hecate writhe, the stinging venom of Liz's nematocysts burning through him.

"I thought he was strong," Talisa muttered, turning back to Liz. "I will find a better mate for you, my daughter."

Mind rebelling, Liz leapt to her feet. Her stomach ached, and waves of revulsion set her body trembling. "I'm leaving," she gasped defiantly.

Laughter whispered through the cave as Talisa moved towards her. "Oh, my daughter, I am sorry I chose one so unworthy. But do not despair, the *Chead* are strong."

The cloying sweetness in the air grew stronger as she neared, blanketing Liz. Her thoughts swirled, beginning to calm, blunting the crisp horror of her memories. She shook her head violently, fighting the fog, and retreated a step.

"Stay away from me!" she shouted, more for her own benefit than anything. The words did nothing to halt her mother's approach. Slowly Liz retreated to the corner of the cave. She could feel the scent pulling at her, drawing her consciousness back down, feeding the *Chead* raging within. "Please," she croaked, desperate.

"Do not fight it, my daughter," Talisa whispered. "You are one of us now."

Talisa opened her arms to embrace Liz, and then froze. Her eyes widened, the eerie glow abruptly fading away. She swayed on her feet, a low moan coming from her lips. Without a word, she toppled to the ground, dead.

Behind her, fist red with the elder *Chead's* blood, stood Susan. Liz's heart lurched as she looked from her dead mother to the woman. A sneer spread across Susan's lips, her eyes now a murky white.

"You tried to steal my mate," Susan growled.

Bloody fist raised, she stepped towards Liz.

56

Susan smiled as she stepped towards the winged girl. Her heart was aching for her mate, sorrow for his pain mingling with rage at his betrayal—but those emotions quickly fell away, vanishing back into the abyss. A sense of calm gripped her as she stepped over Talisa's broken body and continued towards the treacherous girl.

Earlier, Susan had watched Liz collapse on the side of the mountain. Her heart had lifted at the sight, at the knowledge the imposter had finally revealed her weakness. She was no *Chead*, was not worthy of her place beside Talisa. Teeth bared, Susan had started towards her, eager to end the pathetic creature's life.

But Talisa had appeared first. Crouching beside her so-called daughter, the elder *Chead* had called Liz back, the power in her voice lifting the abomination to her feet. Together they had wandered across the slope, the winged girl staggering along in a listless stupor, following Talisa's lead.

It was then that Susan had recalled her first night with Hecate, her joining with the *Chead*. Talisa had led her away from the others, given Susan to Hecate. Filled by a sense of premonition, Susan had followed them, hiding in the boulders outside the cave when the two disappeared inside. There she had waited, knowing the male would come later, if that was what Talisa intended.

Only when Hecate appeared had Susan realized the depth of Talisa's betrayal. Wrapped in the grips of a terrible rage, Susan had silently followed Hecate into the cave. There, she'd watched in a helpless horror as her mate seduced the abomination.

Then Hecate had lurched away from the winged girl. His screams had torn Susan from her shock, bringing her back to herself. Yet still she'd hesitated, uncertain. The rage had built within her, threatening to tear her in two, but a desperate fear held her back. She could not go against Talisa. The elder *Chead's* power was unquestionable; if she wished, she could stop Susan with a glare.

Just as it seemed that Talisa's daughter would be trapped again, Susan's gaze had fallen on Hecate. His grey eyes had pierced her through the darkness, unblinking. His writhing had slowed by then, though his breath still came in ragged gasps. As their eyes met, a silent message had passed between them. Susan had seen the depth of his regret, his sorrow.

A strange calm had come over Susan then, her rage falling away. She had stepped up behind the old woman. Talisa had been so focused on her own daughter, she hadn't even sensed the blow coming. Susan had hardly blinked as she drove her fist through the elder *Chead's* spine, had hardly felt the soft flesh giving way, the bones snapping beneath her strength.

Now, watching the cowering girl, Susan still felt that strange calm. Deep within, her anger raged, demanding retribution for the girl's treachery, but outwardly she felt nothing. The freak would pay for seducing her mate, for trying to take Susan's place. She would die in agony for harming Hecate, for daring to believe she was worthy of the *Chead.*

"You tried to steal my mate," she said.

Elation washed through Susan as she saw the girl's fear. Black wings trembled in the darkness as Liz shook her head. "Please, no. I didn't want him."

Whatever fire, whatever courage the girl had once possessed had abandoned her now. Susan smiled. In the end, Talisa had been a fool. Blinded by her own blood, she could not see the girl's weakness, or Susan's strength. Not that it mattered now. The girl would not survive the night.

"I saw you," she hissed, moving closer. "You tried to take him."

"No, I was…lost. I never meant to. Just let me go, I don't want anything to do with you!" She finished the sentence with a shout.

Straightening, the girl spread her wings. It seemed her fire was not entirely extinguished.

Susan laughed. "Can't have you warning the humans."

"I won't warn them," Liz shot back, clinging to Susan's words. "I *want* the President dead."

"The President means nothing to me," Susan smirked. "His death was Talisa's design. I only wanted his help, so that I might burn humanity from this earth."

It was strange, with the peace that had settled over her, the words came easily to Susan now. For the first time since the change, her mind and mouth worked as one.

The girl held up her hands as she retreated. "Just let me go, Susan. We don't have to fight—" She broke off as her back touched the wall of the cave.

Her hands pressed at the cold stone, and the jacket Hecate had torn fell open. Liz quickly pulled it back into place, but the sight of the girl's breasts brought back images of her in Hecate's arms. Growling, Susan stalked forward until only an inch separated them.

"I'm sick of the sight of you."

Her foe blinked, then apparently decided the time for talk was over. Lurching sideways, she threw a punch at Susan's face. Susan grinned as she stepped back, allowing the blow to strike empty air. Off-balance, Liz staggered, and Susan caught her by the joints of her wings. Spinning, she hurled the girl at the wall.

Screaming, Liz held up her hands to break the impact. A harsh *crack* echoed through the cave as she slammed into the rock, and then slid listlessly to the ground. A low moan came from Liz as she regained her feet, clutching at her arm.

Susan stepped mercilessly after her.

Now the girl spread her wings. The cave's ceiling was only a few feet above their heads, and Susan quickly moved to block the exit. Black feathers struck the air, sending the girl streaking towards Susan.

A boot flashed towards Susan's face, but twisting, she calmly caught the abomination by the ankle. Liz shrieked as Susan slammed her into the rocky floor, before the breath whooshed from her chest, leaving her voiceless. Smiling, Susan released Liz and watched as she folded in two, gasping desperately.

Her gaze was drawn to the wings flapping uselessly against the ground. Susan sneered. Before the girl recovered, she stomped down on the nearest limb, and laughed as her enemy screamed. Bloodied and bruised, the girl tried to crawl away. Her sobs echoed through the cave as Susan followed her.

The slightest whisper was the only warning Susan had before the boy appeared. Whirling towards the sound, she tried to grasp the flickering shadow, but a fist caught her in the chin and sent her tumbling backwards. Wind swirled through the cavern as great wings beat down.

Susan gritted her teeth as she struck the wall. Catching herself, she landed lightly on her feet and looked around for her assailant.

The boy was already kneeling beside the girl, lifting her into his arms. Before she could leap at him, he hurled himself towards the exit. His wings beat hard, their tips brushing the narrow walls as he shot up the tunnel and disappeared around the bend.

Then he was gone, leaving Susan standing alone in the cave with Hecate.

57

Chris was panting hard by the time he settled on top of the narrow cliff. He had flown hard and fast from the cave, fleeing into the sky and out across the plains as far as his wings would carry them. Unfortunately, with Liz dangling from his arms, that wasn't half as far as he would have liked.

But he could go no further without rest. He had chosen the narrow escarpment in the hope the steep cliffs would slow the *Chead* if they gave chase. He had no doubt they would have tracked his flight across the cloudless sky, but there was nothing he could do about that. At least it would take the creatures a few hours to traverse the few dozen miles he'd placed between them.

Crouching, Chris lowered Liz gently to the ground, watching as her head rolled loosely to the side. Not long after their escape, he'd felt her go limp in his arms, overwhelmed by the pain of her injuries. Now, he shuddered at the sight of her wing, remembering the agony when his had been broken. It would take at least a week to heal.

Another shiver went through Chris as he watched the slow rise and fall of her chest. He moved to the edge of the escarpment and looked out over the plains. To his left he could see the bleak buildings of Albuquerque rising from the desert, bleached grey by the unending sun. His eyes were drawn westward, to the scarlet mountains rising from the plains. He watched them for a long time, seeking movement, searching out signs of pursuit.

But there was nothing, and giving up, he returned to Liz's side. Lying down beside her, he lifted his wings to shield them both from the sun. The stifling heat radiated up from the ground, but exposed as they were, it was the best he could do. Chris swallowed as he watched Liz sleep, his mind drifting to what she would say when she woke.

After their last encounter, he wasn't sure she'd be pleased to see him.

He was glad he'd stayed close though, shadowing the *Chead* from a distance. He still didn't know what had happened to Liz, how Talisa had corrupted her. When Liz had chased him from the abandoned settlement, she'd been hardly recognizable, more *Chead* than the girl he loved.

But Talisa was dead now. They had Susan to thank for that, though from what he'd seen, the girl may yet prove more dangerous than the elder *Chead*. Chris had caught a glimpse of her eyes as he raced into the cavern. They had shifted to a murky white, a color he'd only ever seen in Talisa's eyes.

What that meant though, Chris wasn't sure. But Susan had reacted far faster than he'd expected. Despite being taken by surprise, she'd still almost caught Chris when she'd spun on him. He didn't want to think about what might have happened then.

A moan called his attention. Chris watched as Liz's blue eyes blinked open.

"Hey there," he said, sitting up. "Don't move. Your wing is broken."

Liz lay still for a long moment, her eyes unblinking, fixed on Chris's face. Chris sat waiting, breath held, heart hammering in his chest.

"Chris…" Liz croaked finally, her voice filled with warmth. A tear streaked her cheek. "You came back."

Chris swallowed as he opened his mouth, then closed it again, the words dying in his throat. He wanted to tell her he had never left, that he couldn't bring himself to abandon her, couldn't stomach the thought of living the rest of his life alone without her. He wanted to say he'd been a coward, that he didn't deserve to sit there with her after everything he'd done.

But he was finished with the self-loathing, with clinging to his mistakes, with condemning himself to misery.

Instead, a smile touched his lips. He reached out and brushed the tear from her cheek. "I'll always come back for you, Liz."

Liz scrunched her eyes closed as a sob tore from her. "What have I done, Chris?"

Chris shifted closer, opening his arms to embrace her. She flinched at his touch, but when she nuzzled her face into his shoulder, he realized it was only from the pain of her injuries. He took her in his arms and rocked her gently against his chest. Hot tears seeped through his shirt, but he said nothing, only held her, only waited. Liz would speak when she was ready.

Finally, she pulled back and wiped the tears from her face. "I'm sorry, Chris," she said. "I'm sorry for chasing you away."

"There's nothing to be sorry for, Liz," Chris replied. "It wasn't you. I don't know what your mother did…"

"That *thing* wasn't my mother," Liz said, her voice cracking. She turned her head away. "I don't know *what* that was, but she wasn't my mother, not anymore."

Chris nodded. He reached down and squeezed her hand. Only then did he realize that Liz's left arm hung limp at her side. Dark bruises radiated up from her wrist.

"Are you okay?" he asked, nodding at her arm.

"I'm fine," Liz replied.

Her face tightened as she placed her good arm beneath her and pushed herself into a sitting position. The color fled her face as her wings shifted, and a moan grew in her throat. She managed to complete the maneuver without complaint, though she kept her injured arm clutched protectively against her stomach.

"I think it's broken," she said quietly, looking at her darkening wrist.

Chris nodded. "What happened down there, Liz?"

In the darkness, he had only caught glimpses of the cave's occupants. Earlier, he'd watched from a distance as Talisa led Liz into the cave. When Hecate entered sometime later, followed separately by Susan, he'd known something important was happening. Slipping closer, he'd heard Liz scream. The sound had sent him barreling into the cave without a second thought—though even then, he'd almost been too late.

Liz's eyes fell to the ground. "She wanted Hecate to take me as his mate," she whispered. "I…I couldn't stop myself. I wanted…no, I needed him." Her fists tightened into balls. "Only my touch saved me."

Chris's fingers dug into the dirt beneath his palms. A rumble came from his chest and his stomach clenched at the thought of Hecate with Liz, at the image of them naked, bodies pressed against one another, limbs entwined…

Gritting his teeth, he forced the thoughts from his mind. This was no time for jealousy—Liz had been attacked, almost taken, by the darkness of the *Chead*. He remembered Hecate's laughter as he slaughtered the innocent people from the van. Hecate was a vile, soulless creature that deserved only death. At least he'd suffered for trying to force his will on Liz.

He gripped Liz by the shoulder. "I'm glad you're okay."

A smile flickered across Liz's lips. "I'm glad he's not." She took Chris's hand in hers and pressed it to her lips.

Chris shivered at the gesture. Looking up, he found Liz's big blue eyes watching him. A lump swelled in his chest, and he savored the touch of her hand around his, her presence so close. There, high on the escarpment, in the quiet New Mexican wilderness, they were utterly alone. In that moment, it felt as though their past did not exist, as though everything that had come before was just a figment of their imagination.

Slowly Liz leaned towards him, her eyes unblinking. Chris found himself responding. A jolt of electricity rippled through him as their lips met. The kiss was soft, cautious and tender, neither of them quite sure of themselves, of what they were doing.

Shivering, Chris fought back tears. Even as the taste of Liz filled his mouth, he could hardly bring himself to believe they were kissing, that they'd found their way back to one another.

Her scent wafted to his nostrils, a rich, almond aroma he would never forget.

She shivered as he took her in his arms, but Chris was careful not to jolt her broken bones. Lips still locked, they fell gently to the ground, wrapped in each other's embrace. Chris swallowed as Liz's good hand drifted through his hair. He trailed his fingers across her neck, felt her trembling against him.

For a long time they lay like that, eyes closed, touching and tasting, breathing in the scent of one another. It was as though they hadn't seen each other for years, as though they were long-lost lovers, finally reunited. They made no effort to remove their clothing—high up on the escarpment, there was no urgency, no need to rush. They could lie like that forever, free from the outside world.

Eventually, sleep tugged at Chris, and he drifted into a dream. With the warmth of Liz's body beside him, the nightmares of the last few days fled, leaving him at peace. Eyes closed, he slept.

It was dark when he woke again, though it felt as though only minutes had passed. Liz was sitting up beside him, her face aglow in the moonlight. She glanced back as he rose from the ground, a smile crossing her lips.

"Hey there," she said.

"Hey there," Chris replied, wrapping an arm around her waist.

Some of the color had returned to her face now, though her arm and wings were still a mess. He would need to carry her closer to the city soon if they were to find food and water. His heart quickened as he remembered the *Chead* were still out there. The creatures could be creeping up the cliffs towards them at this very instant.

"They're not here," Liz said softly, as though she'd read his mind. "You looked so peaceful, I thought I'd let you sleep. But I've been keeping a lookout."

Chris leaned his head against her shoulder. "You should have woken me, but thank you."

Liz nodded. Her eyes returned to the dark plains. In the distance, Chris could just make out the lights of Albuquerque.

"There's something I've been wondering," Liz said suddenly. "Something about what Susan said to me at the end."

"What do you mean?" Chris asked, frowning.

"She said she was going to burn humanity from the earth."

Chris snorted. "Hecate said the same thing, back at your farmhouse, remember? The *Chead* are dangerous, but even now, they don't have the numbers to overthrow humanity."

"Maybe not." Liz pursed her lips. "But I don't think that's what Susan meant. She said killing the President was Talisa's plan—so what is *she* hoping to achieve out here?"

Chris frowned, distracted by the way the moonlight played over Liz's body. Her jacket had been torn in the…conflict with Hecate, and he could just make out the curves of her breasts beneath. Shaking his head, he tried to focus on what she'd said.

"What else could they want?" he asked.

"What if she knows about the President's threat? What if she wants to use his nuclear arsenal to cripple humanity?" Liz replied.

Ice tingled down Chris's spine at Liz's words. Their eyes met in the darkness. Said out loud, the idea didn't seem so outrageous. No, it seemed a certainty. After all, as Chris had just said, the *Chead* did not have the numbers to match humanity.

Unless something were to level the playing field.

The two of them came to their feet as one, turning to face the distant city. The glow of the Airforce Base remained unchanged, but as they watched, lights began to flash between the buildings.

Through the darkness came the far-off wail of an alarm.

58

"You think he's even here?" Ashley whispered, her voice echoing from the narrow walls.

Squinting, Sam could just make out her shadow in the darkness. He sucked in a breath, trying to focus his thoughts in the stifling heat.

"We'll soon find out, Ash," he offered, finally.

Closing his eyes, he sat back and tried to ignore the suffocating darkness. Every inhalation brought with it the stench of gasoline—an unwelcome reminder of the hour they'd spent latched onto the bottom of the truck. Ashley's improvisation had quickly turned into the most uncomfortable ride of Sam's life.

Pelted by rocks flung up by the tires, Sam's wings and back were now one giant bruise. Dust had clogged his lungs, making it difficult to breathe, and by the time the truck finally pulled to a stop, it was all Sam could do to keep from groaning out loud.

Instead, he'd held his breath, listening to the men whispering over the rumble of the engine. Boots had crunched on gravel as a pair of guards circled the truck. Hinges screeched, followed by laughter as the men inside conversed with the guards. The stench of cigarettes soiled the crisp night air.

Then a buzzer had sounded, and the clang of metal

announced the opening of gates. The engine picked up again as they moved off.

Ten minutes later, Ashley and Sam had found themselves alone in what Sam assumed was a vehicle hangar. They'd listened to the soft patter of retreating footsteps, the distant *bang* of a door opening and closing, then silence.

After a second's hesitation, they'd both dropped to the concrete. Sam groaned as he struck, the sound surprisingly loud in the darkness, but in that moment he hadn't cared. He clenched his fists, wincing as pins and needles shot down his arms. Stifling another groan, he rolled out from beneath the truck and slowly climbed to his feet.

He'd half-expected to find himself surrounded by soldiers, but instead there was only Ashley, still looking all-too-fresh for someone who'd just spent the better part of an hour being dragged along by a truck. Two-hundred-foot-tall iron walls stretched up around them, curving at their apexes to meet in a giant ceiling above their heads. The first light of dawn was just beginning to shine through the skylights, revealing all manner of vehicles.

Their convoy had parked in a line along the side of the hangar, probably to be unloaded in the morning, but the other vehicles in the hangar were not so mundane as their simple truck. From fighter jets to tanks, the President's base looked far too well-armed for Sam's liking.

With daylight rapidly approaching, there'd been no time to linger on what the madman's stockpile meant for the rest of humanity. Ashley and Sam had shared a glance, then headed for the nearest hiding place.

An M3A3 Bradley tank—according to the label on the exterior.

But after spending eight hours cooped up inside the thing, Sam was sure they'd picked some outdated model, long since retired from service. Even in the shade of the hangar, the air inside the tank had quickly risen to boiling point. Within a few hours they'd stripped down to their underwear, and for once Sam was too uncomfortable to be distracted by Ashley's body.

Now, silence had finally returned to the hangar outside their iron tomb. He prayed that meant night had fallen once more.

Sam shared a glance with Ashley. “Think it’s time?”

Ashley pursed her lips, her shoulders rising and falling as she took a breath. “Let’s go.”

She went first, pulling on her clothes and clambering up the ladder to crack open the lid. Sam followed her, his body aching from the long hours spent cramped in the tiny compartment. Fresh air wafted over him as they emerged from their cocoon. He took a moment to savor the sudden cool, before Ashley’s whispers drew him back.

Jumping down beside her, he raised an eyebrow. “Where’s the exit?” It was almost pitch-black inside the hangar now, but he could still pick out the dull shadows of the other vehicles.

He looked around for a door, but Ashley was already moving, grabbing him by the hand and dragging him along with her. Together they threaded their way across the concrete floor, taking care not to disturb anything that might make a noise. Sam kept his ears peeled, listening for the slightest hint of movement, but all was silent.

The exit Ashley had spotted turned out to be a regular door fashioned into the wall. Beside it, a staircase ran up the side of the building, leading to a catwalk that weaved its way between the larger planes. Ignoring the stairs, Sam pressed his ear to the door.

For a moment, all he could hear was the thudding of his own heart. Taking a breath, he tried again. Seconds ticked by and he could feel himself growing anxious. His fingers curled around the door handle, preparing to hurl it open.

Then he heard it—the soft crunch of footsteps.

Retreating from the door, he looked at Ashley and mouthed, “Guard.” Her lips tightened and spreading her wings, she readied herself. Moving back into position, Sam gripped the door handle, and with a last glance at Ashley, yanked it open.

Outside, there was a low gasp as the guard staggered back. He had half a second to fumble for his rifle before Ashley struck him like a sledgehammer. The sound of his body hitting the ground was loud in the night's quiet.

Darting after Ashley, Sam grabbed the unconscious man by the ankles and dragged him inside the hangar. Then he stepped back into the moonlight and closed the door behind them. Outside, the building didn't seem half as large. The smooth outer wall stretched up behind them, concealing its size—along with half the airbase.

Ashley was already scanning their surroundings, searching for the glass tower they'd decided was the President's headquarters. Joining her, Sam took up her hand. Her skin was like ice, but she flashed him a smile when he squeezed her fingers.

"No one in sight," she whispered. "Most of the guards should be stationed on the fences."

"Let's hope," Sam replied.

He scanned the nearby buildings, but there was no sign of the tower. Sam cursed as he realized it had to be on the other side of the hangar. They shared a glance, their gaze traveling skywards.

"Do we risk it?" Sam asked, staring at the distant watch towers.

Ashley was looking in the same direction. "They're focused on things happening outside—I think we'll be safe." Her wings snapped open and she leapt into the air.

Already second guessing himself, Sam cursed and leapt after. Ashley's white feathers all but glowed in the moonlight; there would be no missing her if those in the watchtowers happened to glance in their direction. But there was no turning back now.

Muscles working hard, Sam joined Ashley as she hovered above the roof of the hangar. His wings brushed hers as they turned, seeking out the elusive tower, and found it several rooftops over. Its sleek glass panels towered over the dull metal and concrete of the other buildings. Angling their wings, Ashley and Sam shot towards it.

They were halfway there when the first siren began to screech. Sam lurched in the air as red lights flashed across the base. He swore and drew his wings tight against his body. Diving towards the rooftop, he leveled out with barely a foot between himself and the hard steel. Ashley was faster still, her white wings flashing in the darkness.

Sam glanced around, expecting bullets to tear them to shreds at any moment. Instead, he caught the flash of gunfire from a distant watchtower. He frowned, staring as dark figures swarmed the fence. Screams echoed through the darkness and the gunfire ceased.

A few seconds later it started again—only now the shooter was targeting the neighboring towers. Sam gaped as guards fell tumbling through the darkness.

"Ashley, wait!" he called. His wings flattened out, bringing him to a mid-air stop.

"Sam! What are you doing?" Ashley screamed back to him. The crack of feathers on air announced her return. "What are you doing?" she repeated, her voice barely audible over the gunfire.

Sam nodded at the shadows now swarming into the compound. "Something's happening," he murmured. "I think it's the *Chead.*"

VII
RETRIBUTION

59

Susan squinted through the darkness, taking in the wire fences and looming guard towers. There was no sign of power lines or a power plant they might sabotage. Arriving beneath the cover of night, they had seen little of the base, but it was clearly larger than any of the towns they had slaughtered.

It did not matter. The humans would fall. At the first sign of trouble, they would turn tail and flee. It was their nature.

Beside her, Hecate was silent. Since the encounter in the cave, he had not dared raise a word against her. After the boy had fled with Talisa's daughter, Susan had taken Hecate there on the floor, as he still lay recovering from the venom lacing his body. He had submitted meekly, bowing to her newfound power. A day later, he still showed the cuts and bruises Susan had left, to remind him of his place.

The other *Chead* had fallen into line without quarrel. That Susan had killed Talisa did not matter—only that she had the power to command them. Now, Susan's hundred warriors were aligned behind her,.

From the moon's position in the sky, Susan guessed they were passing midnight. Time was marching on and she dared not wait another day. So close to the base, the *Chead* would not go undetected for long, and the element of surprise was their greatest weapon.

She would let her *Chead* overwhelm the guards and keep their reinforcements occupied while she and Hecate tracked down the President. Only he had the power to accomplish her plan, to unleash humanity's vile weapons on its own cities.

A smile flickered across Susan's face. In a matter of hours, humanity would be brought to its knees. She licked her lips, savoring the thought, then pointed at the closest guard tower.

Silently, the *Chead* started towards it.

The humans did not notice the impending horde until the *Chead* leapt onto the chain-link fence. Standing ten feet tall, with the guard tower stretching up another fifteen, it was an imposing feature. Razor wire curling along its top made the fence almost impossible for a human to scale; the *Chead* were over it in seconds. As the guards swung searchlights towards the rattling of steel, the first of Susan's warriors were already nearing the top of the tower.

Screams rent the night as the *Chead* swept over the railings and tore into the guards. A few gunshots followed, then silence. Searchlights from the neighboring towers swept towards them, as somewhere in the base an alarm started to screech.

Before the other guards realized what was happening, the *Chead* at the top of the tower leapt onto the machine gun turret and swung it around. White flashes lit the night as they opened fire. A deadly barrage of bullets ripped through the nearest guard tower.

Susan smiled, and with Hecate at her side, joined the stream of *Chead* scaling the fence. Those in the lead had already used their immense strength to tear the razor wire free, easing her passage. The *Chead* scattered through the base ahead of them. Screams drifted through the night, mingling with the roar of automatic gunfire. Unprepared, two towers had already fallen; the others were too far away to interfere.

Gunshots rang out from deeper inside the base as Susan reached the compound. Crates and vehicles littered the yard near the fence, and ducking down, she raced into cover. Most of the

Chead had already vanished. Silence fell as the humans lost track of their targets.

Susan crept through the stillness, eyes wary for movement. The thump of running boots on pavement announced the arrival of human reinforcements. Peering out from cover, Susan watched as two dozen soldiers edged their way through the junk-yard. Rifles held at the ready, flashlights cutting the gloom, they moved as one, taking each corner with painstaking care. Helmets and heavy body armor covered them, but it would do little good against the power of the *Chead.*

A howl sounded in the darkness.

Amidst the wreckage, the soldiers spun, seeking the source. Shadows came alive as their torches caught the grey eyes watching them. Gunfire roared and flashes lit the yard.

Screams followed, then silence.

Susan grinned as the *Chead* slipped back into the night, leaving the dead soldiers in a bloody pile. Several of her people had fallen, but they were only the weak, those too sluggish to avoid the humans' bullets. The *Chead* would only grow stronger without them.

She started from cover when a sharp *crack* came from over-head. Susan ducked as a shadow rushed at her. The rustle of feathers followed as the winged creature turned and came at her again. Rage built in Susan's chest. Teeth bared, she leapt to meet it.

A fist swung at her face, but she deflected the blow and caught the creature by the wrist, then hurled it into the ground. A male voice cried out. She leapt on his chest, eager to punish the boy who had stolen her prize.

A dark face stared back at her. It was not the boy who had fled with Talisa's daughter. He gave a choked cry and tried to push her off. She brushed off his blows and leaned in.

"Where is Elizabeth?" Susan growled.

The boy's mouth opened and closed. "Wh...what?"

Susan broke off her questioning as a scream came from nearby. She watched another winged shadow drop from the sky and land on one of her people, snapping the *Chead's* neck before it had a chance to react. More winged figures appeared as the creature leapt back into the air, darting down at the *Chead* as they dove for cover.

A hiss exited Susan's lips. The boy's eyes widened as she lifted her fist. He tried to raise his arms to defend himself, but she tore out his throat all the same. Leaving him choking in his own blood, Susan rose and rejoined Hecate.

"How many are there?" she asked.

The *Chead* had melted into the darkness, but wings still fluttered overhead, circling. Hecate shook his head. Scanning the sky, Susan tried to count the flitting shadows, but it was impossible to keep track. There might be a dozen, or half a hundred. But she was sure the *Chead* still outnumbered them.

With whispered instructions, she ordered her people to spread out and gather the humans' weapons. The *Chead* might not have wings, but they could adapt. The winged abominations would fall soon enough. She just hoped Talisa's daughter was not among them. Her life belonged to Susan.

Finally, she turned back to Hecate. The *Chead* would keep the winged creatures at bay, but she and her mate had another task. Another alarm sounded in the distance as she took his hand.

"Let's end this," she breathed.

60

The door on the rooftop gave way on Sam's second kick. He stumbled inside, dragging Ashley with him, then slammed the remnants of the door back into place behind them. From outside came the bloodcurdling howls of the *Chead* as they tore the soldiers to pieces.

After the first guard tower had fallen, they'd hovered in place long enough to count the creatures swarming over the fence. The darkness made the task difficult, and Sam had given up at eighty. The creatures had swept away a squadron of guards like ants before a flood. That was all the motivation Sam and Ashley had needed to get out of their way, and turning, they raced for the tower. Whatever the *Chead* were here for, Sam and Ashley wanted nothing to do with it.

Fortunately, the door on the tower's rooftop had offered little resistance. Now, as they moved deeper into the stairwell, Sam wondered what fresh horrors awaited. Outside, the *Chead* were tearing men to pieces, but somewhere in this building, the President lurked—or so they hoped. The man had commanded the devotion of both Doctor Halt and the Director. Who knew what fresh depravities they might find here?

Red flashes of emergency lights lit their way as they moved down the concrete stairwell. Within minutes, they found a fire door barring their way. They paused behind it and shared a glance. Sam caught the golden light in Ashley's eyes and smiled. So close to their objective, the sight gave him strength, gave him hope they might just both get out of this alive. With her eyes aglow, Ashley had done incredible, impossible things.

Grabbing her, he pulled her into a kiss. He shivered as her lips pressed against his, all fire and passion, and for just a second he forgot where they were. His arms wrapped around her, a moan echoing up from his throat as she responded, her body melting into his, trembling beneath his hands.

Then she was pulling away, turning towards the door, kicking it from its hinges, and they were charging together into the room beyond.

Sam blinked and stumbled to a stop, his eyes struggling to adjust to the sudden brightness of the fluorescent lights. Squinting, he struggled to comprehend the vast, elaborately decorated apartment they'd found themselves in. Soft red carpet covered the floor, spiraling out from the stone wall from which they'd emerged. Other than where they stood in its center, the apartment had no walls, only windows looking out over the dark expanse of the airbase. The room took up the entire floor of the tower, with the circular wall behind them holding the elevators, stairwell and bathrooms.

A smattering of furniture dotted the space, almost like an afterthought, except where the massive mahogany desk sat on the far side of the room. Its sleek wood gleamed in the overhead lights, dominating the room. A large man stood behind the desk, his shoulders square and arms clasped firmly in front of him. At their appearance, a look of pure panic had swept across his features—but an instant later it was gone, replaced by a smooth, contemplating smile.

Sam swallowed, unable to tear his eyes from the President. He was almost as shocked to see the man as he obviously was to see them. Flicking his eyes around the room, Sam checked for guards, but the President appeared to be alone. A smile tugged at Sam's lips as he gathered himself. They'd expected to spend half the night rummaging around dark rooms searching for the man, but it seemed they'd finally had a lucky break.

"Ashley, Samuel, you've come at a rather inconvenient time." Despite the smile, there was a slight quiver to the President's voice.

"I bet," Ashley hissed, starting towards him.

Sam caught the flicker of movement a second before the creature leapt from a nearby sofa. He lifted his fists to defend himself, but Ashley was faster still. She spun on her heel, a boot lashing out to strike their assailant in the chest. The blow caught the girl mid-leap and sent her tumbling across the room.

The girl scrambled to her feet. Silky auburn hair dangled across her face as hazel eyes locked on Sam and Ashley. Her face contorted into a snarl as she faced them.

And spread her wings.

Sam gaped as the golden feathers appeared, stretching until they seemed to fill the whole apartment. Teeth bared, the girl started towards them again. She moved with confidence, suggesting she was already well-adjusted to the weight of her wings. The President had obviously been busy with a few experiments of his own.

Ashley moved to meet the girl.

"Pascaline, that's enough," said the President, bringing both girls up short.

Sam shivered as he glanced at the President. The man had taken his seat and was now leaning back in his chair, watching them. For a man they supposedly had cornered, he looked awfully calm.

"I can take care of them, sir." The girl's voice rang with anger. "Then I'll find whichever of your guards let them inside."

"I think the *Chead* have already found them, my dear Pascaline," the President laughed before turning on Ashley. "And I'm not altogether sure you could take Ashley here—at least, not while she's worked up like this."

Ashley stepped towards the President. Alarm tingled in Sam's stomach. He quickly moved after her and caught her by the wrist. Something wasn't right.

"Smart boy, Samuel," the President murmured.

The President's words lit a fire in Sam's chest. Memories of his own time in captivity rose, the beatings, the terror of seeing Ashley chained to her hospital bed, the helplessness, the agony. Ignoring his own warning, he started forward. This time the girl, Pascaline, made no move to stop him, but the President leaned forward and placed his hand over something on his desk.

"San Francisco. Houston. Vancouver. Los Angeles," He boomed, his voice echoing from the windows. Outside, red lights still flashed across the base. "Mexico City. *London. Buenos Aires. Tokyo.*"

Sam slowed. Closer to the mahogany desk now, he could see a steel panel beneath the President's hand. Between his fingers was a silver key.

"What are you saying?" Ashley demanded, joining Sam. Pascaline retreated to the President's side and sat on the mahogany desk. It was so big she could spread her wings, and they still wouldn't touch the President.

"You hold a billion lives in your hands, my girl," the President replied coldly.

Ice trickled through Sam's veins. "That's not possible, there are safeguards—"

"You think I'd leave anything to chance?" The President broke off into laughter. "*This* is the only safeguard. This key here —and the one my dear, faithful Pascaline now holds. Two keys, two turns, and the world burns."

Sam threw a glance at the winged girl. Beside her on the desk, another panel reflected the glow of the overhead lights. Pascaline took a key from her pocket and inserted it into place, then offered them a wicked grin.

His heart sank as he realized the President's bluff. They'd had half a chance—just a moment where they might have reached him before the girl could use her key. That door of opportunity had just slammed closed in their faces. The man could still be lying, but judging by the dark glint in his eyes, Sam didn't think so.

Sam tried to reason with the madman. "You wouldn't kill all those people, *your* people…"

"The people who threw me away like yesterday's trash?" the President sneered. "Let them burn."

"Please, Pascaline…that's your name, right?" Beside him, Ashley turned to face the golden-feathered girl. She took a tentative step closer, but a warning growl from the girl brought her up short. "Please, Pascaline, you don't have to do this. Just take the key and walk away."

At Ashley's words, Sam realized with a start the girl wasn't wearing a collar. Hope surged in his chest as he added his voice to Ashley's. "He hasn't got anything over you, Pascaline. We can help you, protect you from him. All you have to do is walk away."

Pascaline looked from Ashley to Sam, then back again. A smile spread across her tanned face. Throwing back her head, she howled with laughter. "*You* can help *me?*" she gasped finally. "How, exactly, could a couple of failed experiments like you possibly help me?"

Feathers bristling, Ashley spread her wings. "Do we look like failures to you?"

The girl raised an eyebrow. "You look broken," she said, levering herself off the desk. "Like a thin breeze would push you over. You wouldn't even stand a chance against the *Chead!* Good thing you're not out there, with my brothers and sisters, or they'd tear you to pieces."

Sam risked a glance out the window. Darkness still hung over the base, lit only by the whirling red of the alarm and distant flashes of gunfire. Shadows rushed between the ground and sky. Squinting, Sam took a step closer to the window and shivered as the silent battle drew to a close. *Chead* rushed across the ground, wielding rifles taken from the fallen guards, while overhead, winged warriors darted at them.

Swallowing, he turned back to the President. "How many more of us did you create?" he whispered. "How many more did you *kill?*" Fists clenched, he would have leapt at the man if not for Ashley's sudden hand on his shoulder.

Behind his desk, the President waved a hand. "As you can see, my methods inspire a great deal more loyalty than those employed by my Director or the good Doctor Halt. I always did find honey more effective than the stick." He rose from his chair. "Of course, the stick *is* necessary at times, with uncooperative subjects such as yourselves."

Sam's heart beat frantically against his ribcage as the President walked out from behind his desk. Gathering himself, he waited for his chance. Only a dozen feet separated him from the President—he could cross that distance in a second. But the President and Pascaline were still close enough to turn their keys.

The President came to a stop in front of his desk. A baseball sat on a stand there, an autograph scribbled down its length in black marker pen. He picked it up. "The question is, who goes first?" Holding the bat aloft, he took a practice swing. Then he stepped away from the desk.

In that moment Sam sensed the trap, but it was already too late. Ashley's wings snapped open and she leapt before Sam could stop her. Wind swirled around the room as Ashley propelled herself forward. She only made it half a dozen feet before her wings folded, sending her crashing down into the floor.

Cursing, Sam started after her, but his vision swam with the movement. He staggered sideways, clenching his eyes closed and opening them again, but it did nothing to halt the swirling lights. His feet turned to lead as he took another step, then his legs collapsed beneath him. His head jarred as he struck the ground. Gasping, he found himself on his side, watching as the President wandered across to the fallen Ashley.

"What have you done…to us?" he managed to croak, his words slurring.

"Sarin gas," the President laughed as he stopped beside Ashley's prone body and tapped a finger to his watch. Somewhere in the room, something went *beep*. "There, the gas release is closed again. Pascaline and I have been inoculated, but even that won't last forever! Now, where was I? Ah yes, the gas. It's been specially altered to induce paralysis, without causing any other nasty side-effects. I had my office rigged weeks ago, in case of unexpected visitors. All I had to do was keep you busy until it took effect."

He nudged Ashley with his boot. A rasping noise came from her throat as she toppled onto her back, but she made no move to resist.

"You…bastard," Sam managed.

Smiling, the President hefted his bat. "It takes a few hours to wear off in a normal human. Even with such fine specimens as yourselves, we should at least have a few minutes." A dark glint shone in his eyes as he looked at Ashley. "I'm going to enjoy this."

61

"Leave her alone," Sam cried from where he lay.

Grinding his teeth, he tried to sit up, but his limbs were like lead, his muscles refusing to obey.

Ignoring him, a smile played across the President's lips.

"Not so strong now, are you, bitch?" he shouted.

At the words, he drew back his boot and slammed it into Ashley's stomach. Unable to defend herself, Ashley went tumbling across the carpet like a ragdoll, her wings lolling limply around her. She gasped, clutching at her stomach as the President strode after her.

"Thought you could kill me, did you?"

His boot caught Ashley again with an audible *crunch.* Her head whipped back as blood splattered from her nose. Groaning, she managed to roll onto her stomach. Fingers like claws, she tried to drag herself away, but before she could go half a foot, the President's foot slammed down on her back. The breath exploded from between Ashley's teeth as she collapsed.

Laughter slithered through the room as Pascaline joined the President. "They're more pathetic than you led me to believe," she said, shaking her head.

The President smirked, then grabbed Ashley by the foot and

dragged her across the room towards Sam. Watching them come, Sam managed to pull himself to his hands and knees. Panting with the effort, he looked at the President with what he hoped was disdain.

"You really are…pathetic," he managed, still slurring. "Harry…and the rest…will finish you in the end."

"Harry?" The President tossed Ashley down beside Sam. "You can't mean Lieutenant Harry McCrae, surely?"

Sam blinked, unsure whether to admit the truth or not, but the President had already seen it on his face. Throwing back his head, he howled with laughter.

"Oh, my dear Samuel, obviously you haven't seen the news. Here, allow me to crush your last pathetic remnants of hope." Returning to his desk, he picked up a remote and pointed it at one of the windows. The world beyond the glass vanished, replaced by the flickering image of a woman in a news chair. The picture distorted as the video rewound, then a woman's voice erupted into the room.

"Clashes between rural and urban populations continued to mount today. Rioting has now spread to LA, San Diego and Seattle. Tensions reignited several days ago when it was revealed that the fugitive Christopher Sanders had escaped custody with the help of the self-styled 'San Francisco Council'. The leader of the council, one Lieutenant Harry McCrae, was not available to comment. However, soon after learning the news, protesters stationed outside the council's center of operations stormed the building. It is thought no one inside survived.

"Meanwhile, General Thompson of Oregon has—"

The voice was interrupted as the screen flashed, turning back to a window. Sam sat staring out at the night, hardly able to believe what he'd heard. Harry and the others were dead. The protesters had torn them to pieces, and none of Harry's careful planning or quiet authority had been able to save them. And all because they'd helped Chris…

"I guess a free press has its uses," the President mused. Wandering back to Ashley's prone figure, he crouched, addressing Sam, "Do you finally see the truth now, Samuel?"

"What are you…talking about?" Sam murmured, struggling to meet the President's gaze.

"Are you truly so blind, that you cannot see it?" He gestured at the blank screen. "*That* is what you've all been fighting for, *that* is what your precious freedom means, Samuel. *Chaos!* Two hundred million people free to tear each other to pieces, to riot and rise up against their betters. Can you see *now* why they needed to be manipulated, why they needed an enemy to fear, to unite them?"

"You slaughtered thousands," Sam grated.

"And how many lives has your alternative already claimed, Samuel? How many of your friends have already died in this brave new world of yours? How many helpless mothers and children?" He shook his head. "Do you really think the people are happier now, living in the world your truth has given them?"

Sam closed his eyes, trying not to listen, to allow the man to manipulate him. The darkness in his mind's eye swirled and his stomach clenched. Wheezing, he bent in two, struggling not to bring up yesterday's dinner.

"The best part is, even this so-called freedom of yours won't last," the President continued. "My former generals, those who still command the loyalty of their men anyway, are already lining up to take my place. It won't be long before the nation dissolves into individual states, each ruled by a new dictator for you to fight."

Swaying on his knees, Sam could hardly make sense of the man's words. Even so, he looked up at the President and spat at his feet.

"Better them than you," he snapped. "You tortured…and mutilated children. Spread a plague…across the country, all so you could…control us."

"So I could *unite* us," the President boomed. "So I could bring strength to our fledgling nation. You think we would have survived this long if I hadn't? Even now, the remnants of the United States are circling. Texas, Florida, Ohio, they can't wait to take a piece out of us. They *hate* us for what we did to them, for destroying their precious union and casting them out into the wilderness, for razing their cities and obliterating their economies when they refused to bend. If we had not stood together, we would have fallen."

"I don't believe that." Somehow, Sam managed to climb to his feet. "It's your deception, your lies and manipulations that have torn us apart. But this is not the end. We'll find a way to continue, to unite. We don't need your fear to force us together."

"We?" The President smiled. He moved forward until they stood face-to-face. "Have you not heard what they've been calling *you*, Samuel? They may fear the *Chead*, but they *despise* the lot of you. You'll never be one of them, never be human. Not so long as those *things* hang from your back."

Sam's stomach curdled, but he stared back into the man's eyes, unflinching. A long silence stretched out as they glared at each other, each unwilling to back down, to give an inch.

Then Ashley, still lying in a pile on the floor, lurched forward and sank her teeth into the President's ankle.

A high-pitched scream rattled the windows as the President stumbled back. His foot lashed out, catching Ashley on the side of the head and sending her sprawling, but Sam saw his chance. Gathering his fading strength, he lunged, arms outstretched...

Only for the golden-winged girl to catch him by the throat, and slam him face-first into the carpet.

"Too slow, Samuel," she muttered, before turning to check on the President.

Sam groaned as delayed pain shot through his body. His wings lay like deadweights to either side of him, and he found he no longer had the strength to even sit up. Across from him, Ashley had curled up in a ball. A fresh bruise swelled on her forehead where the President's blow had caught her.

A roar came from the President as he grabbed a fistful of Ashley's hair. She cried out as he yanked back her head. Tears stung Sam's eyes as he met her gaze. There was no mistaking the fear shining from her amber irises.

"Stupid. Stubborn. Bitch."

With each word, the President slammed Ashley's face into the ground. Even with the carpet, Sam could feel the thud of each blow through the floor.

"Leave her alone!" he gasped, struggling to rise.

An awful moan rose from Ashley's throat. She tried to push the man away, but her strength had fled. Blood streamed from her nose, bubbling as she struggled to breathe. She gave a gurgling cry as the President hauled her to her feet, his fingers still tangled in her hair.

"Ashley…" Sam managed to croak.

"Sam…" she cried back, her voice laced with agony. Only the President's grip kept her upright.

Laughing, the President shoved Ashley at his desk. Her feet crumpled as he released her, and she toppled headfirst into the mahogany. A sharp *crack* rang through the room, and a bloody streak appeared on the wood as Ashley fell.

The President shook his head. "Do you think she's still breathing, Samuel?" He swung the baseball bat loosely in his left hand. "Probably, you freaks are tough to kill."

Heart in his throat, Sam managed to pull himself back to his hands and knees. Ignoring the President's taunts, he dragged himself across the carpet, eyes locked on Ashley. From his vantage point, he couldn't see if she was breathing or not—but he could see the dark smear of blood on her forehead.

The President kept track with him as he crawled. "I warned you," he said conversationally. "I was surprised when you survived the *Chead*, back in Alcatraz. You should have called it a win and left it at that. I would have spared you, you know. Now…now you'll have to pay."

Sam was almost at Ashley's side, but as he reached for her arm, the President knocked his hand away. Stepping past him, he loomed over Ashley, bat held aloft.

"I really am sorry about this, Samuel," the President said, glancing at him. "I know you were fond of her. But really, the girl is a danger to everyone around her. It's better this way."

He lifted the bat above his head. Ashley lay unmoving on the ground, her scarlet hair matted with blood, eyes closed, face pale.

Sam's heart dropped into the pit of his stomach as the President took aim.

"No!" he screamed as the bat descended. Desperately, he threw out an arm, as though by will alone he could move himself into the path of the blow.

The soft *thud* as the bat struck Ashley's head was horribly loud in the vastness of the apartment.

62

Susan paused in the stairwell as a shout echoed down from above. She glanced back at Hecate, eyebrows raised, then continued upwards. Above, light billowed from a partially open door, beckoning.

It hadn't been hard for them to skirt the battle between the *Chead* and the winged mutants. Threading through the junkyard, Hecate and Susan had disappeared into the maze of buildings. From there, they made their way towards the only destination that remained unaffected by the chaos unfolding across the base.

The glimmering tower of glass rising into the night.

Keeping to the shadows, they skirted the patrols racing towards the conflict, and made their way steadily towards the tower. Once there, it had been a simple matter of walking through the front door.

The dozen guards stationed in the entranceway had stared in shock at their sudden appearance. It was all the opportunity the two *Chead* had needed.

Now they were nearing the uppermost floors of the tower, and Susan had begun to worry they'd come to the wrong building. The lower floors had been empty, filled with an assortment of desks, computers, and laboratory equipment. The last level had been packed with beds. The familiar stench of the winged creatures had wafted out into the stairwell when she'd opened the door, but the room was empty.

At least now they knew where their assailants outside had come from.

Susan smiled as they reached the open door, taking a moment to sniff the air. She recognized the stench of humanity and their winged rivals. There was something else too, but it was faint, already fading. Hecate shifted beside her, teeth bared, eyes eager. They shared a glance, then Susan pushed the door open.

Three pairs of eyes swung around as they swept into the room.

"Well, well, well, what have we here?" Susan growled as she took in the scene.

The first thing she noted was the man standing in the middle of the room. Clutching a bloody baseball bat in one meaty fist, he exuded a power those around him could not match. Despite his obvious humanity, he was clearly in charge. At his feet, a girl with white wings lay still, blood matting her face, while another winged boy lay with an arm stretched towards his fallen companion. A third freak stood silently nearby, arms crossed.

Turning to the man, Susan grinned. There was no mistaking him. "Mr. President, it's so good to finally meet you."

Uncertainty flickered across the President's face as she started forward, Hecate just a step behind. Paling, he backed away, and stumbled over the fallen girl. The shock seemed to snap him back to reality, and straightening, he pointed his bat at Susan's chest.

"Pascaline, stop them!" he snapped.

Laughter came from the golden-winged girl as she stepped between Susan and the President. "That's far enough, *Chead*," she said, barring their path. "Allow me to introduce myself—I'm your replacement."

Susan stopped a few feet from the girl. Her eyes swept the arrogant creature up and down, taking it in, before looking into its dim hazel eyes.

"My replacement?" Susan questioned. "My dear girl, your kind are but children to the *Chead*."

"Children?" The girl bristled. Her wings snapped open, the feathers quivering. "I am superior to you in every way!"

"Oh yes?" Susan tilted her head to the side, an amused smile playing across her lips. "Then why don't you try me?"

Growling, the girl sprang, her wings sweeping down to propel her forward. The smile never left Susan's face as she watched her come. Feet fixed in place, she leaned back as a fist flashed at her, allowing the blow to sweep harmlessly past. Straightening, she savored the sudden surprise on her opponent's face. Overbalanced and within inches of Susan, Pascaline could not avoid what came next.

Susan drove her knee into the girl's stomach, crumpling her in two. Mouth wide, she clutched at her chest, desperate for breath. Still smiling, Susan locked her fists together and brought them down on the back of the girl's head. The blow drove her opponent face-first into the carpet.

Satisfied, Susan watched for a moment as the girl twitched listlessly on the ground, before turning back to the President.

The man had turned a ghostly white. He backed towards his desk, as though something there could possibly save him. Susan leapt after him, her powerful legs propelling her across the dozen feet in a single bound. Courage fled the man and he tried to flee, but she caught him by the collar and hauled him back. He gave a strangled scream as she lifted him off his feet.

"Mr. President, as I was saying, I am pleased to make your acquaintance." She grinned as the supposedly most powerful human on earth squirmed in her grasp. "The *Chead* send their regards."

"Please!" he cried, clawing at the fist clenched around his collar. "Let me go!"

"Very well."

With a flick of her wrist, Susan tossed him to the floor. He bounced once before coming to rest in a tangled heap against his desk. He tried to scramble up, but Susan was on him in an instant.

"My dear President, where do you think you're going?" she

asked pleasantly. "You wouldn't be so rude as to leave your guests unattended, would you? After all, we need to talk."

"Ta…talk?" he stuttered.

Susan sneered. Whoever this man had been, he was nothing now. Stripped of his power and authority, he had reverted to humanity's natural state—a pitiful, cowardly excuse for a creature. It took all her willpower not to snap his neck right there.

"Yes…" she breathed, pulling him close, until their eyes were only an inch apart. "About our place."

"Your place?" The President repeated her words like a trained parrot.

Susan laughed. "Yes. I come to negotiate a place for the *Chead* in this world you affect to rule."

The President stared at her, uncomprehending. "What…do you mean?"

An exasperated groan rattled up from Susan's throat. She risked a quick glance around, but only the winged boy was moving. He had almost managed to drag himself across to the red-haired girl. Whatever had happened to them, they were obviously no longer a threat. Hecate hovered behind her, his eyes alert.

Satisfied they were safe for the moment, Susan crouched beside the President. "We only wish to assure our survival, Mr. President," she said quietly. "We are not so numerous as humanity—if you wished, you could wipe us out within a year. I cannot allow that to happen."

The President swallowed. "So what do you want from me?" Despite his predicament, he seemed to be recovering some of his confidence. He took a moment to straighten his shirt and then lifted himself to his knees. "Some kind of peace treaty?"

Susan smiled. "I was one of you once. I know what peace treaties mean to you. No, I need a stronger guarantee."

"Anything," the President gasped.

"Well, aren't you cooperative?" Susan murmured. "Very well. I wish to know how to unleash your nuclear arsenal."

The President went deathly still. A strained silence fell suddenly across the room, as though her words had flicked a switch. Whatever color the President had left fled from his face. His mouth opened and closed as he struggled to find the words to reply.

"The nuclear…arsenal?" he managed, finally.

"Yes, Mr. President." Susan carefully lifted him back to his feet. "My memories are imperfect, but I recall the President is traditionally the one who commands your nuclear capabilities."

"Yes…yes that's…correct."

The smile faded from Susan's face, her voice taking on a dangerous tone. "Then you won't mind showing me how that works."

The President swayed on his feet, as though her words had rocked him to his very foundations. He blinked rapidly and seemed to come back to himself.

"I would need…assurances," he replied in a quiet voice.

"Assurances?" Susan growled, stepping in close.

This time the man did not flinch. The faintest hint of a smile crossed his lips. "My life, for one," he said.

Susan almost laughed. The man's sense of self-preservation was something to behold. Instead, she raised an eyebrow. "So you can continue to murder my people? To use us in your vile experiments?"

The President shook his head. "I will lead the survivors." he replied resolutely. "There will be peace between our peoples."

This time Susan allowed herself a smile. The man was naïve beyond all imagining. She knew humanity's nature. They were parasites, feeding off the world's life for their own selfish ends. If they were allowed to prosper after the destruction, war between their peoples would be inevitable.

No, far better the Chead *wipe your kind from the Earth*, she thought. Out loud she said, "Your conditions seem…reasonable." She offered her hand. "We have a deal."

Some of the color returned to the man's face as they shook hands. "Deal."

"Monsters!" a voice croaked from behind them.

Susan glanced back and saw the winged boy sitting up on the

floor. He stared at them, eyes shining with rage. Slowly, painstakingly, he climbed to his feet.

"Monsters!" he repeated. "You'll kill millions."

Heat swirled in Susan's stomach, her rage flaring at the boy's nerve. Glancing at Hecate, she made a gesture. Grinning, he started towards the boy.

Susan turned back to the President. "So, where do we begin?"

The President was still watching the boy, but her voice brought him back. "Oh, it's simple." He pointed at his desk, where Susan now noticed two silver panels inlaid on the wooden surface. A key had been inserted into each. "All the safeguards have been removed. We only have to turn those keys together, and...well...the targets are already set...That's...it..." He trailed off as the boy screamed.

"So it takes two," Susan mused. She glanced behind her, where Hecate had just tossed the boy halfway across the room. "Hecate, leave him. I need you."

"What do you need him for?" the President asked. "Let him finish off Samuel. We can end this together, my new friend," he said with a smile.

Susan looked up at the towering man, a smile of her own on her lips. "Thank you, Mr. President. But the *Chead* can take things from here."

She wrapped her fingers around the President's throat. His eyes widened, but before he could open his mouth to shout, Susan wrenched her hands violently sideways.

The *crack* his neck made as it shattered was music to her ears. It was still whispering through the room when the *ding* of the elevator came from behind them.

63

Liz shivered as the elevator dinged, announcing their arrival at the Presidential suite—or so the label above the buttons read. Beside her, Chris took her hand. She forced a smile, even as she tried to conceal her pain. Her left arm hung uselessly at her side, while her wings were a mess of red-hot agony.

He had tried to convince her to stay behind, but even injured, she couldn't let him face Susan and the *Chead* alone. The idea was suicide, and Liz couldn't stomach the idea of losing him again. Not after finally getting him back.

Yet even now, as the elevator doors slid silently open, she still had no idea how they were going to stop Susan. Below, a dozen guards had been torn to pieces, and outside a war was raging between the *Chead,* humanity, and a host of winged teenagers that appeared to be the President's private army. Their presence had made it easy for Chris to fly into the base's airspace unnoticed—even if his wings had finally given in when they were still a few hundred yards from the tower.

Stepping from the elevator, Liz braced herself for the carnage the *Chead* left wherever they walked. She wasn't disappointed. The breath caught in her throat as she took in Susan standing over the broken body of the President. Closer to them, Hecate stared back at her, his eyes dark with hatred. Movement came from beside his feet, and Liz gaped as Sam sat up.

"Liz?" Sam croaked.

Blood pounded in Liz's head as she found two more winged bodies lying nearby. One was unfamiliar, but the other she recognized immediately by the scarlet hair and white feathers. A moan built in Liz's throat as she started towards Ashley's prone body.

"Elizabeth." Susan's grating voice drew Liz's attention back to the *Chead*. "So good to see you again. I was disappointed our playtime was cut short." The *Chead's* eyes slid to Chris, her lips drawing back in a snarl.

Liz shuddered, remembering how easily the woman had batted aside her attacks in the cave. She had no desire to let Susan get that close again. Yet if the *Chead* had killed the President, she must already have what she needed. Despite her pain, Liz plucked up her courage and sneered.

"Why don't you try your luck again, then?" she hissed.

Susan laughed. "Have you recovered so quickly, my dear? I will have to make your injuries more permanent this time. Yes, I think it would give me great pleasure to tear those pretty wings from your back." The *Chead* stepped towards them, then caught herself and shook her head. "Alas, you will have to wait. First, there is the matter of humanity's extinction. Hecate, come."

Hecate turned and started towards Susan. Heart hammering in her chest, Liz looked from the *Chead* to the President's body. Obviously, whatever Susan had in mind required Hecate's help.

"What, are you still afraid I might steal him?" Liz asked mockingly. Hecate paused and looked back, his eyes darkening. Batting her eyes, Liz blew him a kiss. "Promise I won't bite this time, Hecate."

A growl rumbled across the room, but it didn't come from Hecate.

"*Stay away from him.*" Susan's voice was sharp enough to cut glass.

Eyes flashing, the *Chead* stepped away from the mahogany desk. Liz stood her ground, though it took all her will not to turn and flee. Even Hecate paled as his enraged mate stalked past him.

"Did you really have to piss her off?" Chris hissed as she closed on them.

Forcing the pain in her arm and wings from her mind, Liz braced herself. "Did you have a better plan?"

Susan was on them before Chris could respond. One second she was gathering speed, the next she was among them, fingers flashing like claws for Liz's throat. Liz leapt back, her wings flaring out instinctively, and the blow missed her by inches. Then the pain of her broken bones struck, tearing through her like wildfire. Her legs buckled. Hissing, Susan came for her again.

Brown feathers flashed as Chris collided with the rampaging *Chead*, driving her sideways. Susan snarled and turned on him. Her knee flicked up, catching him square in the stomach as he struggled to overpower her. Air hissed between Chris's teeth as he staggered back. Susan leapt, her foot swinging around to slam into his head.

Screaming with agony, Liz forced herself to her feet and back into the fray. Susan heard her coming and turned to meet her, a dark smile twisting her lips. Liz feinted with her good hand, then kicked out at the *Chead's* ankles. Susan cackled and leapt over the blow, then drove her boot into Liz's face.

Stars burst across Liz's vision. Crying out, she tried to recover. The room faded in and out of focus, and she didn't even see the next blow coming. It slammed into her chin, lifting her to her toes and sending her reeling. Coughing, Liz tasted blood in her mouth.

Somewhere, a voice roared. Squinting through the stars, Liz watched a dark shadow slam into Susan's back. Copper wings beat down as Sam lifted the *Chead* above his head and hurled her across the room. Laughing, Susan twisted in the air and landed easily on her feet.

Still struggling to see, Liz stumbled forward to join Sam. A second later Chris was at her side. The three of them exchanged a glance. Questions raced through Liz's mind, but try as she might, she couldn't make sense of her friends' presence. The answers would have to wait. Together they faced the white-eyed *Chead.*

A smile spread across Susan's face. "Three? Are you sure that's enough?"

Liz swallowed, in too much pain to answer. The *Chead* had already proven Chris and herself were no match for her in their current state. From the look of Sam, he wasn't much better off than them. But there was still one way they might subdue Susan's insanity.

Liz clenched her bare fists, readying herself.

Susan caught the movement and grinned. "You think your little trick will work a second time?"

"Let's find out."

Teeth bared, Liz lunged, desperate to lay a hand, a finger, even a kiss on the insane creature—anything that would allow her venom to work its magic. Susan made no move to avoid her, but stood fixed in place, eyebrows raised, and let Liz come. At the last second, her hands shot out and caught Liz by the wrists.

"*No!*" Liz shrieked, her heart plummeting into her stomach.

She fought desperately to break free, but Susan's fingers were like iron shackles around the cuffs of her jacket, protecting the *Chead* from her skin. The hairs on Liz's neck tingled as the white eyes fixed on her. Lips twitching with amusement, Susan studied her as the others watched on, helpless to intervene. Then, laughing, the *Chead* leaned in and licked Liz's cheek.

"Argh!" Liz choked, pulling away. To her surprise, the hands around her wrists vanished. Overbalanced, she toppled back and slammed into the ground.

Liz quickly scrambled back towards the others. With Chris's help, she managed to regain her feet. Together, they stared at the mad creature that had once been a doctor in their facility. Breath held, they waited to see whether Liz's venom would work.

Seconds turned quickly to minutes, and their hope withered and died.

"Are we done?" Susan asked finally, her eyes darkening. "I am the *Chead*, foolish children. Your tricks are nothing to me."

Before they could respond, she lunged. Liz had half a second to register the movement before Susan's hand closed around her throat. She gasped as the woman hoisted her off her feet. Iron fingers dug into her windpipe, choking off her air. With a strangled cry she kicked at the *Chead* and felt the blow connect, but Susan only sneered.

"Are you ready to die, daughter of Talisa?" she whispered, pulling Liz close.

Darkness obscured Liz's vision as she beat desperately at the *Chead*, but it made no difference. Blood pounded in her ears, all but deafening her. She could feel the power radiating off Susan, crushing the life from her, as though it were some physical force.

Through the dancing shadows, she watched Chris charge, Sam just a step behind. Her heart lurched as she realized with sick certainty that they didn't stand a chance. Susan would snuff the life from them as easily as Liz would blow out a candle.

Then she would do the same for the whole world.

One hand still locked around Liz's throat, Susan turned to meet Sam and Chris. Her mouth opened as she shouted a command. Liz barely heard what was said over the pounding in her ears, but the word rang in her mind, smothering her last thoughts of resistance.

"*Stop*."

Liz watched in horror as Sam and Chris staggered to a halt. A sly smile spread across Susan's lips, and her grip around Liz's throat loosened. Liz gasped, the darkness retreating for a second as fresh air flooded her lungs.

"Well, well, well. Your mother was right, Elizabeth," Susan mused. Liz moaned as the fingers clamped tight again. "Your kind are have more of the *Chead* in them than I thought. Now, kneel."

Eyes shining with unspilt tears, Chris and Sam fell to the floor, and Susan turned her attention back to Liz. The white eyes flashed, haunting, terrifying—yet now Liz found herself unable to even look away.

"You tried to take my place," Susan whispered as she choked the life from Liz. "You tried to steal my *mate!*"

Liz's head rolled violently on her shoulders as Susan shook

her. Her vision had shrunk to tiny pinpricks of light, until all she could see was the haunting glow of the *Chead's* eyes. Somehow, the glow inexplicably reminded her of Ashley.

"Don't worry, Elizabeth," Susan breathed, her face just inches from Liz's. "Your friends will join you soon."

"Wanna bet?" a voice came from behind Susan.

Susan's eyes widened. Releasing Liz, she spun to face the voice.

The baseball bat caught Susan in the side of the head before she could raise an arm to defend herself. Blood sprayed Liz's clothing as Susan reeled back, one hand clutching at her forehead. Snarling, the *Chead* swung around, seeking out her assailant.

Golden eyes glowing, Ashley strode after her. Blood covered her face, knotting her flaming hair, and her white wings flared out to fill the room. Before Susan could recover, Ashley swung the bat again. The wooden weapon became little more than a blur as it caught the *Chead* square in the face.

This time Susan went down, her strength fleeing in a rush. But she was far from done. Sagging to the ground, she snarled up at Ashley, white eyes wide, aglow with the power of the *Chead.*

"Stop, child! You are *mine!*" she screamed.

For a second, Ashley paused. The golden light in her eyes seemed to flicker. Liz's heart lurched in her chest, but Ashley only blinked and shook her head. The glow returned as she towered over the cowering *Chead.*

She shrugged. "Guess not."

The bat descended a final time.

64

I*t's finally over.* The thought swept through Sam like a whirlwind as he watched Susan fall.

His body sagged as whatever compulsion she'd placed on him vanished. Sucking in a breath, he stared at Ashley, unable to look away. Wings flared, blood still dripping from the gash in her forehead, she dropped the bat and turned towards him. The glow in her eyes flickered and went out. Suddenly she was falling.

Sam was on his feet in an instant. Rushing forward, he caught Ashley and pulled her into his arms. Panic constricted his ribs as he fell to his knees.

"No, no, no," he whispered, cradling her in his arms.

Her wings hung limply against the red carpet. Her skin seemed unbelievably white beneath the fluorescent lights. A trickle of blood ran from her forehead. He couldn't tell if she was breathing.

She couldn't be dead.

He'd just watched her beat a rampaging *Chead* to death with hardly a pause for breath.

She couldn't be dead.

Hugging Ashley to his chest, a sob rattled up from his throat. His eyes burned as he clenched them tightly shut.

"Hey, not so hard," a muffled voice came from the vicinity of his chest.

Blinking, Sam lifted his head. Ashley's amber eyes stared up at him, streaked with red. "That's better."

Choking with relief, Sam leaned down and kissed her on the forehead. "I thought you were gone," he whispered. "Twice."

Ashley gave a faint smile. "Not yet." Her eyes flickered closed again.

Movement came from across the room. Sam's throat constricted as he saw Hecate still standing, his grey eyes fixed on the body of his mate. In the rush of their fight with Susan, Sam had forgotten about the other *Chead*. Now he tensed, readying himself for one last battle. He wasn't about to let the creature avenge its fallen mate.

But Hecate did not seem to notice them. Shoulders slumped, the *Chead* staggered across to Susan and fell to his knees beside her. "I'm…sorry," he croaked, taking the woman's hand in his. "I should never…have betrayed you…my mate."

A lump lodged in Sam's throat. Swallowing, he blinked back tears of his own, a wave of compassion sweeping over him. Watching Hecate, Sam saw his own grief from a moment before reflected in the *Chead's* eyes. Only there would be no respite for Hecate, no reprieve from his loss.

Ashley had made sure of that.

Sobs racked Hecate and a low keening filled the apartment. Sam stared, mesmerized by the *Chead's* pain, by its humanity. Finally, he forced himself to look away, unable to watch any longer.

Liz still lay where Susan had dropped her, just a few feet from the grieving *Chead*. Climbing to her knees, she stared at Hecate, as though still not quite able to believe they'd won.

Beyond Hecate, Chris stood poised, ready to leap if the *Chead* moved, until it became obvious the creature had eyes only for its dead mate. His shoulders slumped, his wings sagging to either side of him as he looked away.

Sam let out a long sigh as looked back at Ashley. Her eyes were closed, but the soft whisper of her breath reassured him she lived. He just hoped the President's blow to her skull hadn't left any lasting damage.

"We did it," he said softly.

Eyes still closed, Ashley nodded. A smile played across her lips. "We did."

Sam's eyes travelled to where the President lay. "We have to tell the world," he said.

"Redemption," Ashley murmured back.

His stomach clenched at that. *Redemption.* The word rang in his mind. He glanced at Chris, nodding slowly to himself. Ashley was right—this news would bring redemption for both of them. Whatever crimes they'd committed would be wiped away when the world learned what they'd done, when the people heard that the so-called winged freaks had put an end to the tyrant.

They would no longer be demons, but heroes.

"Redemption," he repeated finally. "For all of us."

Movement came as Liz staggered to her feet. Stumbling slightly, she looked down at Hecate. "I'm sorry, Hecate."

The *Chead* looked up at her, grey eyes blank. "You..." He growled, blinking. Lines creased his forehead as he frowned. "This is...your fault. You...tempted me."

"No, that was Talisa," Liz whispered. "I never wanted any of this."

"*Liar!*"

Growling, Hecate climbed to his feet. Liz's eyes widened. She shuffled backwards, but her wing snagged beneath her boots, sending her staggering sideways. A shriek started in her throat, quickly cut off as Hecate charged, his arm wrapping around her neck.

"Stay back," he hissed, eyes wild. Holding Liz in front of him, he backed away.

Sam was already on his feet. He shared a glance with Chris and the two edged slowly apart, though Sam made sure to keep himself between Hecate and Ashley. Breath held, they shuffled after the retreating *Chead.*

Teeth bared, Liz stared back at them, her face a mask of agony. Her wings hung limply behind her, crushed against

Hecate's chest. From the way she'd moved earlier, Sam guessed they were broken. Her left arm, dangling uselessly at her side, definitely was, but her right was already clasped tight around Hecate's wrist. Her eyes flashed as she looked from Sam to Chris.

Sam gave the slightest nod. He understood. It was only a matter of time before her venom incapacitated Hecate. They just had to make sure he didn't do anything rash before it took effect.

"Let her go, Hecate," Chris said, his voice shaking. "Take Susan and go, we won't stop you. Just let Liz go."

Hecate's eyes switched between the two of them. Behind him, the mahogany desk brought him up short. Uncertainty flashed across the *Chead's* face, but his hold around Liz's neck did not relent.

Sam tried to judge the distance between them. His strength was growing by the second now, as the last traces of sarin gas left his system. All he needed was a second, a moment to close the gap and pull Liz to safety.

"Hecate!" he shouted, taking another step. "You heard what he said."

But now Hecate grinned. Pulling Liz tight against his chest, he snarled. "Stay back. Or I snap…her pretty little neck."

65

"Just let her go, Hecate," Chris whispered. His legs shook, and suddenly those were the only words that would come to him. A sick sense of helplessness wrapped around his stomach as he watched the vile creature hold Liz hostage.

Hecate stood in front of the President's desk, eyes wild, a dark smile on his twisted face. He didn't seem to care that Liz's fingers were wrapped tightly around his wrist. It only added to Chris's terror. The scene in the desert played itself out over and over in his mind, Hecate murdering the innocent family. His stomach swirled. It was all he could do not to fall to his knees and throw up.

This couldn't be happening.

"What do you want, Hecate?" Sam asked calmly.

Relief washed through Chris. He wasn't alone. Sam was with him—strong, reliable Sam, the one who had never let them down. Sam would find a way out of this.

He had to.

Because Chris's mind had come to a sudden, grinding halt.

"Please, Hecate, just let her go," he said again, his words a broken record now.

"No," Hecate laughed. The *Chead* was gaining confidence, his eyes filled with a sick sense of joy at their fear. "At least, not yet."

"Don't hurt her," Chris croaked.

Grinning, Hecate stroked a lock of Liz's black hair. She flinched from his touch, but his grip pulled her back.

"Oh, I won't," he said, turning on Chris, "at least, not if you give me what I want."

"And what do you want?"

"What *she* wanted," Hecate whispered, nodding at Susan. "What she…gave her life for."

Chris stared into the mad eyes of the *Chead*, then staggered as the full meaning of Hecate's words sank in. Nausea filled his stomach and he croaked out something unintelligible.

"The keys are…in their places," Hecate continued. In his arms, Liz had gone still. She stared at Chris, eyes shimmering. "All I need…is someone to help me."

The words shook Chris to his core. Tears stung his eyes. He could hardly breathe. Fists clenched, he watched, helpless, as Hecate dragged Liz around the desk until they stood in front of the silver panel. The keys still sat in their locks, the dull black metal gleaming with the promise of death.

"We don't have…much time," Hecate rasped, his voice slithering through the room. "I can already…feel her venom. Do not wait too long…Chris. Not like last time." His laughter echoed around the room, taunting him.

"Hecate, please," Chris gasped.

He saw again the murdered family, their blood staining the asphalt.

Beside him, Sam stood fixed in place, frozen by the creature's words. Somewhere behind them, Ashley lay on the floor, but she couldn't help them now. Chris had seen her after facing down Susan. His friend had used up everything she had.

It was just Chris and Hecate now.

"Come now…Chris," Hecate breathed. "What do they mean to you? What have they ever done but use you? But hurt you? Join me. Use the key. Save your mate. Help me end the tyranny of those who created us."

"I can't," Chris said in a shaking voice. He said the words, but he didn't know what they meant.

He couldn't help the *Chead* end the world. He had come here with Liz to stop them.

But he couldn't face a life without Liz. Not again.

The first traces of pain appeared on Hecate's face. His lips drew back in a snarl, revealing yellowed teeth. "Hurry, Chris. Time is running out!" The fingers of his spare hand trailed down Liz's cheek. This time she didn't flinch.

Instead, her crystal eyes found Chris's, soft, fearless. A sob tore from him as somewhere deep inside a part of him broke, torn asunder by the impossible choice before him.

His love.

Or the world.

"Time is wasting, Chris," Hecate whispered.

Chris looked at Liz one last time, taking in every inch of her, freezing her forever in his mind. The silky curls of her pitch-black hair, the sweet crinkle of skin at the corners of her mouth, the curves of her long neck. Her dark feathers hung behind her, limp and broken. She must have been in terrible pain, standing there with Hecate pressing against her broken bones. But when she looked at him, a smile touched her lips, a silent farewell.

Closing his eyes, Chris made his choice.

EPILOGUE

TWO YEARS LATER

Chris smiled as the wind caught beneath his wings and lifted him higher. Air rushed past his face, tugging at his long hair and cutting through his jacket. Sucking in a breath, he savored the crisp winter air. In his arms, the baby goat began to squirm, and he tightened his grip around its tiny legs. One thousand feet above the Californian plains, he didn't think it would survive the fall.

He'd found the goat wandering alone in a field as he scouted for food. Unable to resist such a golden opportunity, Chris had swooped down and plucked up the kid before it could realize what was happening.

Ahead, the towering peaks loomed, calling him home. His wings beat down as another gust swept around him, trying to pull him from the sky. He glanced back, checking the progress of the storm. The sky was dark, almost pitch-black, and gathering himself he picked up the pace. He wanted to be home and indoors long before it struck the mountains.

Feathers cracked alongside him and he smiled as Ashley drifted into view. Her white wings swept down, propelling her into the lead. Chris sighed as her voice called back.

"Told you a goat was too much."

Rolling his eyes, Chris picked up speed. The plains fell away behind them, turning to the rocky slopes of the foothills. Chris shivered as he saw the dark pines rising from the mountainside ahead. In his mind, he watched again their desperate flight through the trees, all those years ago. He recalled the fear in the eyes of Richard and Jasmine as the soldiers encircled them. It all seemed so long ago now.

Tearing his gaze from the forest, Chris focused on the white peaks stabbing up into the murky sky. Thunder rumbled, echoing from the cliffs. Screaming, the baby goat started to kick again. Cursing his own foolishness, Chris kept on. He wasn't about to abandon the thing now, not after carrying it all this way.

Below, the trees gave way to the stark grey stone of the mountains. Here the soil was thin, and only scraggly bushes were able to survive. He winced at the memory of their thorns. Scrambling up the side of the mountain, guards hot on his heels, he'd hardly noticed them at the time. But the things had ached for weeks afterwards.

Fortunately, the miracle of flight meant he no longer had to worry about such trivialities. He watched as a blanket of snow turned the barren rock to white. Light shone from all around them as they soared deeper into the mountains. Watching the snow, he remembered the day he'd seen Ashley fall, how her blood had stained the snow red.

But Ashley had survived, had endured torture and torment where so many others had crumbled, and emerged stronger for it. From the very start, she had been their strength, always the first to offer encouragement, the one with the words to keep them going, whatever the odds.

Yet it wasn't until that day in the Kirtland Air Force Base, when all had seemed lost, that Ashley had shown her true strength. When all of them had failed, when he and Sam and Liz had succumbed to the *Chead's* power, Ashley had stepped up. Even injured and broken, she'd prevailed where no one else could.

If only I'd had that strength. Chris's heart twisted. He forced the thought from his mind.

Chris squinted, trying to make out the way ahead. Even with

the darkening sky, the glare off the snow threatened to blind him. Ahead, Ashley's wings seemed to merge with their surroundings, almost disappearing into the storm. His strength flagging, Chris fixed his gaze on her scarlet hair and chased after her.

Hours passed as they raced between the jagged peaks, every wingbeat bringing them closer to the facility where they had been reborn, nearer to home. The thought still brought a smile to his face. Once the place had been a prison to them, a ghost that haunted their dreams, hovering over their lives like some invisible force.

After everything they'd been through in New Mexico, they'd needed a sanctuary, a place to escape from the chaos—if only for a while. It had been Ashley's idea to reclaim the facility, to take the nightmare and make it their own. They'd tried to dissuade her, but by then there'd been no arguing with Ashley. Not when her eyes were glowing, anyway.

Now though, Chris had to admit that she'd been right. The *Chead's* raid had left the facility silent and abandoned. With the Director running the laboratory beneath Alcatraz, Chris guessed the government had had no need for such a remote outpost. But it had served their purpose perfectly.

Together they'd made their slow way back across New Mexico and Arizona, following their instincts, retracing their steps back to the place where they'd been created. Thinking of that time now, Chris couldn't help but feel they'd been reborn within those cold walls. It was as though from the moment he'd woken in that steel cage, his old self had died, and a new Chris had emerged into the world.

He shivered at the idea and turned his thoughts back to those long days after Susan's death. Outside, they'd found the Kirtland Air Force Base in mid-evacuation, the *Chead* fled and the President's winged experiments in disarray. Sam had flown across to face them. A few short words had passed between him and the other experiments, and most had turned and fled to the skies. But a few had remained, joining Sam and the others as they took to the air.

Chris smiled as he thought of them now. Dalton, Angela,

Marcus, Rebecca, Abby, Josephine. Their new friends. Their new family. The six almost made up for everyone else they'd lost.

Almost.

The boom of thunder pulled Chris back to the present. He swore as rain swept past, drenching him to the skin. Ashley's white wings reflected the clash of lightning overhead. Beyond, Chris caught the faint glint of light on the mountainside.

His heart lifted and drawing on his last reserves of strength, Chris forced himself on. Pulling level with Ashley, the two shared a grim smile. Misery was etched across Ashley's soaking face. Chris felt a pang of guilt as he realized she probably would have beaten the rain if he hadn't slowed her down. Still, he consoled himself, she would thank him when they had fresh meat for dinner.

Finally, they found themselves above the bright glow of the facility. Angling their wings, they spiraled down through the darkness. Water dripped from Chris's feathers, dragging on his wings, but it didn't matter now. They were almost home.

The courtyard in the middle of the facility beckoned. Chris breathed a sigh of relief as they touched down. Quickly he lifted his wings above their heads, sheltering them from the pounding rain. Ashley shot him a glare, eyebrows raised, and a smile twitched on Chris's lips.

"Better than nothing?" He laughed over the crash of thunder.

In his arms, the goat began to bleat. Ashley gave a weary shake of her head. "Let's get inside."

Nodding, they started towards the door. Light spilled from the windows, and Chris glimpsed shadows moving within. His heart lifted at the thought of the others. He hoped someone had thought to save them dinner. They were more than a few hours late, but that wasn't unusual. Surely...

A hinge squealed as the door into the facility swung open. Lighting flashed, silhouetting the figure standing in the doorway.

"Is that a goat?" a voice called.

Laughing, Chris nodded and picked up his pace. He could sense the temperature dropping, the rain turning to ice around them. The storm was building, preparing to hurl all its might against the stony Californian peaks. It would be a long night.

But with the warmth of home beckoning, Chris didn't care.

In the doorway, the shadow shifted, the last of the lightning fading away. Smiling, the figure stepped into the rain to meet them. Her wings lifted, merging with the darkness of the storm, protecting her from the rain. His heart swelling, Chris moved to meet her.

They came together in a rush, as they always did, wings entwining, arms embracing, bodies uniting. It didn't matter that the poor goat was caught between them, that its terrified bleats were ringing from the courtyard walls and sleet was dripping down Chris's back. All that mattered was they were together, that Chris could feel her warmth in his arms, her breath against his skin, her lips beneath his.

The world be damned, nothing else mattered but this.

THE END

Or is it?

...

Discover a fallen world in...

Warbringer

NOTE FROM THE AUTHOR

What would you do? You might notice I left the ending there a little open for interpretation. I think after a thousand odd pages with Chris and his friends, you're qualified to guess what he might have decided. And if not…well read on and enjoy a free sample of my latest novel, which might give just a little hint as to what comes next in a fallen world. Warbringer is fantasy, but it too features And if you would like to find out more about myself and where in the world I am right now (and maybe find out what I'm working on next!), be sure Be sure to follow me on Facebook or by weekly newsletter.

FOLLOW AARON HODGES…

And receive TWO FREE novels and a short story!

www.aaronhodges.co.nz/newsletter-signup/

DESCENDANTS OF THE FALL

If you've enjoyed this book, you might want to check out another of my fantasy series!

Centuries ago, the world fell. From the ashes rose a terrible new species—the Tangata. Now they wage war against the kingdoms of man. And humanity is losing.

Recruited straight from his academy, twenty-year-old Lukys hopes the frontier will make a soldier out of him. But Tangata are massing in the south, and the allied armies are desperate. They will do anything to halt the enemy advance—including sending untrained men and women into battle. Determined to survive, Lukys seeks aid from the only man who seems to care: Romaine, the last warrior of an extinct kingdom.

THE SWORD OF LIGHT TRILOGY

If you've enjoyed this book, you might want to check out my very first fantasy series!

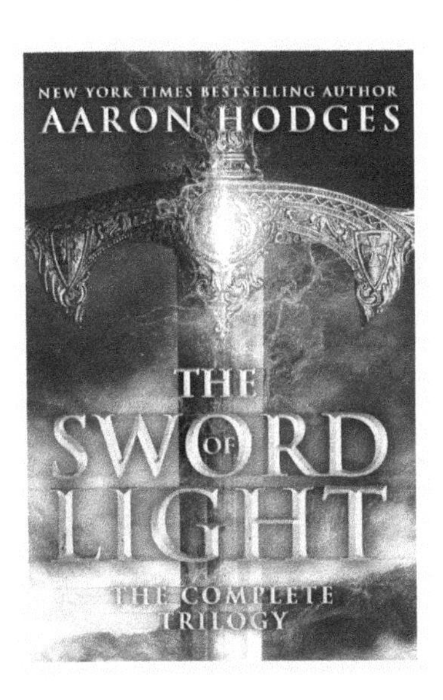

A town burns and flames light the night sky. Hunted and alone, seventeen year old Eric flees through the wreckage. The mob grows closer, baying for the blood of their tormentor. Guilt weighs on his soul, but he cannot stop, cannot turn back. **If he stops, they die.**

ALSO BY AARON HODGES

Descendants of the Fall

Book 1: Warbringer

Book 2: Wrath of the Forgotten

Book 3: Age of Gods

The Evolution Gene

Book 1: The Genome Project

Book 2: The Pursuit of Truth

Book 3: The Way the World Ends

The Sword of Light

Book 1: Stormwielder

Book 2: Firestorm

Book 3: Soul Blade

The Legend of the Gods

Book 1: Oathbreaker

Book 2: Shield of Winter

Book 3: Dawn of War

The Knights of Alana

Book 1: Daughter of Fate

Book 2: Queen of Vengeance

Book 3: Crown of Chaos

Lightning Source UK Ltd.
Milton Keynes UK
UKHW020742301120
374363UK00013B/740